I0749081

Dead Alone

J. LORIN

Presage Publishing * Ohio
2017 Presage Publishing Print Edition

Published in the United States by Presage Publishing

1236 Robins Run
Dayton, Ohio
45458-1492

Hard Cover: ISBN:-978-0-9852713-4-3
Electronic: ISBN: 978-0-9852713-6-7

Cover Design: Laurn Maloon, Pelican Technologies 1139 West 3rd Street, Dayton Ohio, 45402

Dedication

Susan McDermott: I never forgot what you said at our tenth year reunion. That is why I dusted off my hard drive and got back to writing.

Acknowledgments

Robert Laws: *Every writer needs a second set of eyes and another brain to shape and expand the vision. Your insights, comments, and provocations helped make this possible. Thanks, brother!*

Susan Strecker *and* Barb Lauger: *Thanks for your fiction craft advice and editorial work. Without a good polish a novel, no matter how long, is merely a dripping myopic mess.*

Lauren Maloon *and* Pelican Technologies: *Loved your creativity and the fact that you restored my faith in graphics designers. Creative people can keep their word and deliver on time! Who knew!*

And my Father: *I'm so glad you told me after the first draft to whack the first twelve chapters. Thanks for being my biggest fan.*

ACT 1

1

Global Infection: ≤ 29.9000%

The slide toward tribalism is almost irresistible in the face of danger. The tyranny of the tribe is perpetuated by the necessity of protection. Individuals are reduced to cogs in a wheel. Force is given to a few in the name of safety and never relinquished . . . unless lovers of liberty resist with all their might.

Ryan Sage, The Berkeley Riots

Pittsburgh, Pennsylvania

Like all disagreements about the proper role of government, this one started with gunfire and bullets and dead bodies.

At full dark looters dressed in green fatigues amassed outside the Renaissance Tower, in downtown Pittsburgh, Pennsylvania. They attached one end of a chain to the locked security doors and the other end to the hitch of a truck, started the engine and pressed on the gas. The magnetic locks held tight, the clear polymer windows bowed and the tires smoked, but the end was inevitable: twisted metal and ravaged Plexiglas and a gaping hole that exposed the lobby. The looters threw flash bang grenades inside that rolled and rattled like heavy marbles on stone. The world exploded into light and noise and confusion.

Ryan Sage thought he was going to die.

He was inside the Renaissance Tower because a few days ago it had become his new home. Ryan needed to defend his home, but he was hiding under the lobby security desk clutching a shotgun to his chest, head throbbing from the noise and light. He knew the looters were rushing the threshold now. He knew he should rise, aim and shoot. But he couldn't make his right leg stop moving up and down like a sewing machine. He rolled to all fours feeling the holstered Glock poking his muffin top, fixating his mind on the prodding like a nagging wife—dull, persistent, and annoying. He used the desk to pull himself to stand on wobbly legs and brought the shotgun to his shoulder. He blinked though the dancing spots looking for a target, a black silhouette outlined in the haze.

Ryan's mind stuttered and then clicked. He heard gunfire—a distant chatter on the edge of his brain, the high *crack crack crack* of 5.56 ammunition and then his brain registered a new sound, the low chugging thunder of another weapon, but he didn't know what it meant.

But Marco Paguero knew the sounds of a .50 caliber and grabbed Ryan's belt and drug him to the floor just before the lobby walls disintegrated in a storm of .50 caliber lead. Ryan curled into a ball, whimpering.

The .50 paused.

"We are not sick you, mother fucker. Stop the extermination," someone shouted in the street beyond the tower.

The Army Joint Light Tactical Vehicle spotlight swept toward the voice and the loud speaker squealed. A voice said: *"You are all in violation of the National Defense Resource Preparedness Executive Order. Surrender now or you will be destroyed."*

"Lieutenant? Lieutenant? God dammit, cut that shit out. You are not going to destroy us."

"Sergeant?" the Lieutenant's voice blared over the speaker, the JLTV spotlight stabbing a hole in the darkness, searching. *"Sergeant? Is that you?"*

"Yes, it's me, you little pin prick."

"That is Lieutenant, *and I ought to add insubordination to the charge of desertion. You abandoned your post, soldier, and you took thirty others with you."*

"Are you that much of a fucktard? Wake the fuck up, Lieutenant. There is no post. There is no chain of command. They fucking left us here to die when that last train pulled out of the station. Those rear echelon mother fuckers are halfway to Colorado. No matter what they said, they are not coming back. You know it. I know it. It's all gone to shit."

"I have my orders!"

"You ain't got shit! And you and that stupid bitch on the .50 cal just killed two of my men. I should kill you both, but all we want is the food in this building. You understand? And we want some payback."

"Payback?" the Lieutenant asked.

"The mother fuckers in this tower killed one of our own a couple days ago. Put a bullet in his head. That kid never hurt any fucking body. And one of these morons gunned him down."

"Shit," Marco said, rising his knee surveying the lobby and the street beyond the windows. "That is all we need. Hungry people motivated by revenge."

"There death is on you, sergeant," the Lieutenant said. *"If they had not abandoned their post, they would still be alive. The articles of the National Defense Resource Preparedness Executive Order places all resources under the jurisdiction of Homeland Security, which means you were caught*

breaking into government *property. The penalty is summary execution but if you put down your weapons. I will let you live and they will probably even reinstate you. We need everyone . . ."*

The voices on the street grew dim.

"What are they saying?" Ryan asked.

"I can't hear them," Marco said.

Ryan pulled out his phone and tapped through the Renaissance Tower security system app that fed audio/video surveillance into the phone. It took a minute to orient his mind to the cameras, to the drama unfolding on the streets outside and the four points of the compass.

The Renaissance Tower sat on the edge of the mighty Monongahela River. The tower lobby faced Smithfield Street and its north side ran along First Avenue. Ryan found the camera view that showed the intersection and framed the standoff between the Lieutenant and the Sergeant; they faced off 80 feet apart. The Sergeant's forces had the Lieutenant outnumbered four to one, but the Lieutenant had a Joint Light Tactical Vehicle with a .50 caliber machine gun on top.

Raphael Paguero appeared out of the darkness like a great white shark from the deep blue sea—smooth, quiet and deadly. He peered under the desk, his Kalashnikov gripped easily in his hands, his tactical vest filled with ammunition and weapons. He pulled Ryan by the collar to whisper directly into his ear. "I hear you from over there. If I hear you, they hear you. I see the light from your phone. It lights your face. You make a good target." He vanished into the blackness.

Ryan Sage hadn't been scolded like that since his mother passed. He felt the heat of shame as he crouched deeper under the desk, trying to make his bulk fit in a small space. He twisted, searching for a tolerable position that prevented the Glock holstered on his belt from stabbing into his muffin top; the weapon seemed to pluck at a nerve deep in his soul, prodding him to curse the Italians for making great-tasting sandwiches.

He tapped through the security app looking for security system sound settings: most tower cameras had audio capabilities.

"Did you not hear me? There is food in this tower," the sergeant shouted from behind a stone pillar holding up the portico just outside the large windows. *"If you help us get in that building, we will give you some. Aren't you tired of MREs?"*

"Sergeant, surrender now or be destroyed!" the Lieutenant said.

Movement . . .

Ryan saw something moving in the top edge of the camera but he couldn't tell what. The street lights blinked with power fluctuations, making the world look like a cheap Hollywood horror flick. Ryan pinched his eyes, trying to squeeze the fatigue out of his mind. The movement could be a trash bag blowing in the late April wind, or a biohazard banner that cast off its moorings, or the churning acrid fog from burning skyscrapers. The movement could be windblown detritus and low swirling smoke. The canvas of black disaster could be tricking him into seeing ghouls inside every shadow. He could be manufacturing visions of calamity and pending doom.

Faces!

"Oh shit. Oh shit. Infected," Ryan said.

They emerged from the murk—like fetid bodies floating to the surface of a lake—first one, then five, and then more than he could count: men in shredded business suits, nurses in scrubs, teenagers in hoodies and jeans, police officers in ragged uniforms. They all had dark patches around the mouth, as if they forgot to clean up after dinner. Some walked with slow single-minded purpose; others stumbled and twitched with each stride, but together they came, a juggernaut of homicidal menace.

Marco looked at the phone, the subtle sheen of fever glistening in the light. "Do not interrupt your enemy when he is about to make a mistake," he rasped, holding Ryan Sage's shoulder to keep him from moving.

"They don't see them," Ryan said, "I need to warn them."

"We don't *want* the bad guys to see the infected. If the looters win they kill us, if the military wins they take your tower as government property. Those 2091s just tipped the scales so that maybe we live."

"You are outgunned, Lieutenant. You have six men! I have thirty. You know what these men can do, and the only advantage you had was that .50 cal. But the second that bitch stopped shooting we put two snipers on her head. The only thing keeping you alive is me. I give the order we shoot the gunner first and then we slaught—"

"Jesus Christ!" someone shouted. *"Jesus Christ! They're here! They're here!"*

"Contact! Contact," the Lieutenant shouted, *"Three o'clock! Three o'clock!"*

The .50 cal gunner panicked. Her finger crushed the trigger as the weapon swung in an arc. Lead sawed a line through concrete and glass and metal as the muzzle swept west down First Avenue. Ryan curled into a ball under the desk until he felt hands pawing at his legs.

"Get up you knob! The 2091s are coming into the tower!"

2

Global Infection: ≤ 29.9001%

Simone Paguero exaggerated, as obnoxious teenage boys are in the habit of doing. The zombies were not coming into the tower . . . yet.

The scene beyond the lobby glass was pandemonium. The Lieutenant and his soldiers fought the 2091s coming from the west; a mob pouring from the east surrounded the looters.

"We gotta go," Simone said, his brown eyes afire, his pimply face glowing as he started to push through the wrecked lobby exit.

"Halt!" Raphael said to his young son, "You will follow my orders."

"But—"

"There *es* no but!"

"We should wait," Ryan said his palms sweating as he clutched the shotgun. "We can't fight the infected, the military and looters."

"We can no wait," Raphael said, "They will be overrun. And we have many of these devils to kill. You follow me. Then you go left," he said, pointing toward the infected surrounding the Joint Light Tactical Vehicle. "You stay left. Keep your weapon pointed that way. You shoot infected."

"I got it," Ryan said. "I go left and I shoot the infected." His eyes strayed to the chaos, the shouting, the gunfire, the blood and the violence. His hand shifted to the shotgun trigger.

Raphael grabbed the weapon and pushed the barrel straight up. "Keep your finger off the trigger."

Ryan looked at his hand like it was disconnected and made his index finger straighten. "Okay."

Raphael snapped his fingers in front of Ryan's face. "We need you to fight. You can no hide. We need you to kill. You can do this, yes?"

"Yes," Ryan said, his face pale. "I can fight."

Raphael pointed at Simone. "You! With me! Marco, you are overwatch."

"Copy that," Marco said, his fever sweat beading across his forehead.

Raphael gave a signal with his hand and Simone strode through the wrecked vestibule.

Ryan cleared the threshold. Acrid smoke, swirling through the Pittsburgh streets, slashed at his throat like a thousand razors. Gunfire pounded in his ears and human shrieks tore at his mind. He sprinted from one stone portico pillar to the next, jumped down a terrace level and ran toward the infected laying siege to the JLTV, spewing .50 caliber lead. The weapon vaporized glass, liquefied metal and turned bodies into puree filling the air with the taste of copper.

Ryan jumped to the bottom terrace and almost into the arms of a man in a Boston Celtics jacket. For three heartbeats they stood, each working through the calculus of violence. The mind infected with the RVJC 2091 virus solved the equation first. Madness surged in Celtics fan's brain and his body surged toward Ryan.

Ryan pulled the trigger . . .

Everything else was savagery and survival.

"It's over," Marco said. "You can get up."

"It is?" Ryan asked. He was on all fours behind the wheel of a truck, gasping.

"Yes," Marco said. "Here, use this on your face." He handed Ryan a ripped T-shirt.

"What is on my face?" Ryan asked, looking around as he absently wiped away gritty bits of white stones mixed with smears of red and gray. "Everything happened—"

"Fast?" Marco nodded. "Combat always happens fast."

"The infected? The looters?"

Marco pointed with his nose at the carnage. "It was a slaughter. Impossible to tell who is who now. I did see three looters running across the bridge carrying wounded—"

"Get off me!" The voice was muffled under an assaulting RVJC 2091. "Get the fuck off of me!"

Raphael got to the far side of the JLTV in four strides, kicked the infected away and shot it in the head.

Marco limped toward the soldier and knelt. He saw the bar stitched into the lapel. "Lieutenant, did it bite you? Are you hit?" he said. He yanked the battle kit away looking for the source of the blood. "Can you tell me your name?"

"I'll kill you! Get off me! I'll kill you!" the Lieutenant said, fighting Marco.

Marco grabbed his jaw and forced him to look. "Lieutenant! Focus! Can you tell me your name? Can you tell me what day it is?"

The Lieutenant said, "I don't know. Friday? I don't know. I've lost—" He looked down at his stomach "Oh God! Fuck me. Fuck me. I've been hit? Medic! Medic!"

Marco grabbed Ryan's arm and pulled him down. "Hold him!"

"There *es* nothing for you to do," Raphael said. "He *es* gut shot. His neck *es* bit. He *es* losing too much blood."

"We've got to try," Marco said as he opened the medical kit on the Lieutenant's hip.

The Lieutenant said, "How come I don't know you? Where's Katie? Is she dead? Did the crazies get her?"

"Marco," Raphael said. "If reinforcements come, we will no be able to *esplain* this. We must get off the streets."

"We don't need to explain trying to save a soldier's life," Marco said.

Raphael nodded. "Simone, collect weapons and ammunition and gear. Put them in the JLTV."

"I'm watching for zombies," Simone said, standing atop a van looking east and west down First Avenue. Then he jumped down, sprinted south and climbed up a panel van, looking east and west along Fort Pitt Boulevard.

"No, you get the weapons," Raphael said.

"What are *you* gonna do?" Simone asked, jumping down and running back to the van on First Avenue.

Raphael fixed Simone with a hard gaze.

Simone blinked. "Okay!" he said, and jumped from roof to hood, from hood to ground. "But if the zombies come and you get bit, I won't help."

"Ryan, turn that spotlight on me here," Marco ordered.

Ryan moved to the JLTV to shift the light.

Marco drew his combat knife from his tactical vest and cut the Lieutenants shirt open and then cut away his pants. He rocked back on his heels. "Shit!" he said. "Shit! Shit! Shit."

Ryan looked at the gaping wound from belly to hip and the chunks of white mixed into the pulpy red mash of flesh. "That can't be good."

Marco flashed Ryan a hard look but the Lieutenant already knew the diagnosis. The shock had worn off and his mind was sharp. He clasped Marco's hand like they were brothers. He looked into Marco's eyes. "You are Delta, aren't you?"

"What? How could you kn–"

The Lieutenant's knuckles grew white as if to transfer his pain through his hand. "It is crazy what you see in combat. It makes no sense sometimes . . . what you remember. I did a tour in Italy with the Tenth Mountain. We were deployed with 1st SFOD. I went into combat with Delta four times. The way they fight, the way the move . . . it's . . ." He groaned. "Fuck me. This hurts."

"Where's your Combat Medic? Where's your morphine?" Marco said. "They're not around your neck."

The Lieutenant shook his head. "I used them on Private Collier. You remember Collier, don't you? Little shitbird could not get himself squared away. The fucking crazies were coming by the hundreds. Collier ran the wrong way when we hit the claymores. Took his right leg off."

"Ryan, check those soldiers," Marco said, "Look around their necks for two Syrettes about the size of your little finger. One should be green and the other should be red. Move!"

"Don't hit me with the Combat Medic, Sergeant. I can't take any more pain."

"That is what the green is for sir," Marco said. "The green makes you feel good."

"Delta," the Lieutenant said, "I knew you were Delta. Saw you fight. Saw how you attacked that emplacement. Textbook, really. Goddamned genius. You saved my ass that day. And we beat back Jihad Johnny. We beat him good. Sent him to his 72 virgins. I hope they are all guys, those virgins. I hope they all have peckers and have to give blow jobs in paradise."

Ryan slid back beside Marco. "Is this what you are looking for?" he said, handing him a green and red Syrrette attached to dog tags.

The Lieutenant squeezed Marco's hand. "Don't forget me, Delta. Please don't forget me." His body deflated like a stretched out balloon.

Marco's chin dropped to his chest.

Raphael put a hand on Marco's shoulder. "We must move these bodies before reinforcements come."

Marco nodded, collected himself, and snapped off the Lieutenant's dog tags. He read: "His name was Bathgate, Drew J. Protestant." One tag went into his pocket; the second was fixed to the Lieutenant's boot.

Raphael saw Simone standing atop the van. "Did you get the weapons and ammunition?"

Simone shrugged. "I got it all."

"I see the weapons there and there," Raphael said, pointing with his nose.

"Fine!" Simone said, "I'll keep looking."

Ryan stood and for the first time looked at the Renaissance Tower. Its entrance was almost two hundred feet back from Smithville Street, with four levels of granite terracing lined with planters and trees. Each terrace had its own small covered pavilion, a place where people could meet for lunch or wait at leisure for a Port Authority bus. But now the planters were shattered and dirt sloshed across the stone, the pavilions were toppled and it looked like someone had drawn a dotted line with bullets through windows that spanned the tower front, creating spider web cracks and fist-sized holes.

"Now the infected can walk right in!" Ryan said.

"Worry about that later," Raphael said. "We must move these bodies and get back inside."

"What? Bodies? Why?" Ryan asked.

"Because I say this is what we will do." Raphael moved close.

Ryan took a step back. "No, I mean. I'm sorry, my brain is not working. There are a hundred bodies here and if we move them we will leave a mystery. You see all the shell casings?"

"I do no care about a mystery. I care that they will get— " Raphael shook his head. "No time to argue."

"Okay! Okay!" Ryan said, frustration rising, his body starting to shake. Suddenly, he was breaking down from the inside out, millimeter by millimeter.

Marco said. "Mr. Sage? Mr. Sage? Are you okay?"

"Yes, I'm fine! I just need—" Ryan bent to grab the legs of a dead solder, but stopped to rest his hands on his knees.

"Breathe," Marco said. "Your body is coming down off a combat rush.

"Combat," Simone snorted. "I don't think he hit a thing. The knob hid behind a truck."

"Shut up, Simone," Marco said. "He killed three and then beat two 2091s to death with the butt of his gun."

"That is because the knob forgot to draw his sidearm," Simone said.

"I forgot what?" Ryan said, his breath coming in shallow gasps. It was as if Simone's words reminded him of the Glock on his hip stabbing mercilessly into his belly.

"Damned thing," he muttered as groped for the weapon.

"Easy," Marco said, "Easy, Easy. You're feeling the adrenaline fade."

"I'm feeling this damned thing poking me," Ryan said as he snatched the gun out of its holster. He pulled the holster but it was snagged on a belt loop. Tugging became pulling and pulling became wrenching. "Move, you goddamned thin—"

"Mr. Sage. Take it easy," Marco said, taking a step forward.

His hands shook like he had the palsy and sweat dripped into his eyes. Ryan's left arm rose to wipe the sweat from his brow, his hand shaking as the gun traveled toward his head.

"Mr. Sage!" Marco said. "Freeze!"

The Glock's polymer frame felt oily and slithered through his fingers, coming alive like a serpent. Ryan's hand squeezed.

It was a reflex, the barest application of four pounds of trigger pressure. The serpent struck like it had been prodded with a stick. Its fangs bit into Ryan's forehead as the slide cycled. Then the serpent twisted harsh and violent, biting his cheek with a smoldering smoking shell.

Ryan saw stars. He couldn't hear.

Ryan's mind was mush. He saw the Glock spinning away on the asphalt. He felt the tightness across his chest and neck where fists gathered his shirt. He felt the hot breath and the spittle blast against his nose. He felt the tremor in his thighs, the warning sign that his legs were failing. He rubbed at his ears and worked his jaws as if that would wipe away the silence.

". . . idiot almost kill . . ."

The words sounded far away, like the hint of distant music. Ryan's brain finally put the pieces together. The pressure on his neck and throat was Raphael throttling his collar. The heat and spittle was Raphael red-faced and shouting.

"Raphael," Ryan said, his voice sounding thin in his own ears. "Please, stop. I don't know what happened."

Raphael was tall for a South American, but Ryan still had him by inches and pounds. He looked to Ryan's eyes, the heat in his demeanor fading, a flash of uncertainty in his face. "Do no yell at me and I tell you what happened. You almost kill my child with negligence."

"I am not— I'm not trying to shout. I can't hear."

Marco wrestled Raphael away. "He's in shock."

"I do no care! He almost kill you," Raphael said. He let go of Ryan's collar with a shove and grabbed the weapon off the ground. "You do no know how to use this. You can no have this weapon!"

Ryan raised his hands in surrender. "Okay, Okay. I'm sorry. I don't know what I did."

"This *es* unacceptable to no know what you shoot at. You can no be negligent when you have a weap—" Raphael's gaze shifted and then everyone followed his eyes.

Ryan saw the boy, about thirteen, standing amid the garbage and the bodies and the shattered glass. And then he saw the blood covering the boy's hands and stomach. "Oh God . . . did I shoot him?"

3

Global Infection: ≤ 29.9002%

"Please help me?" the boy said. "My mom's been shot." The boy ran to a panel van, its windshield and front riddled with bullet holes. He waved his arms as if he were pulling everyone by a rope.

Simone ran toward the van.

"Simone, stop!" Raphael said, his rifle snapping to his shoulder. "It *es* a trap."

"I can see her," Simone shouted. "There are no guns."

"*Muchacho tonto,*" Raphael said, scanning the street.

Marco limped to the van. "Let me look at her," he said as he crawled through the sliding door, grimacing as he twisted over the bleeding woman.

Ryan opened the driver side door and the stench of unwashed body, urine and something else, something a touch fetid, slid into his nose.

A man in his mid thirties crouched over a woman, his hands pressed on her chest and neck, the blood oozing between his fingers. "Marie, help is here. Please live, my love. God, there is so much blood . . . so much blood!"

Marco asked, "What is your name?"

"Gus. Gus Blanco."

"You are doing fine, Gus. Keep your hands where they are," Marco said as he pulled a headband out of a pouch in his tactical vest. He withdrew a Surefire torch, fastened it to a clip and put headband around his head. "Poppa, get in the back. I need more light and another set of hands."

"Simone," Raphael said. "Keep watch at the intersection. You do no shoot. You report. *Entender*?!"

"Why me?" Simone said. "I want to watch."

Raphael leveled his gaze.

"Okay!" Simone said and sulked to the intersection of First Avenue and Smithfield.

Marco rummaged through Lieutenant Bathgate's medical pack for scissors and cut open Marie's shirt.

"So much blood," Gus said.

"Just keep your hands where they are, Gus," Marco said. "Your wife has had the Eternity Vaccine, right?"

"Of course," Gus said.

Marco said. "Poppa! I need you in here!"

"The doors . . . they are locked," Raphael shouted from outside.

Marco crawled over a pile of blankets and flipped the lock. Raphael threw the doors open wide to let streetlights push back the darkness. And then they saw the boy: sweat soaked and fever-shaking, lying in a fetal position on a pile of blankets, moaning softly, clutching his arm.

"That is my son, Dakota," Gus said. "He's sick."

Raphael inspected the arm and then moved him gently out of the way. Then he knelt with Marie's head between his knees. He fixed his Surefire torch into a headband, lighting everything like an operating room.

Marie looked at Raphael's face and tried to talk but her words came out as a gurgle.

"Oh God, baby. Oh God. Please don't leave me," Gus said.

Marco twisted and pain shot through his body. He crumpled against the van wall. He dropped the scissors on her belly. "Ryan, cut for me," he said as he tried to fend off the pain.

Ryan squeezed between the front seats, trying to find a space amid the clutter of plastic water bottles filled with piss and potato chip bags and food wrappers, and started cutting. "Cut away her pants too," Marco said as he collected himself and started checking bullet wounds.

"I told you we needed help . . ." Marie said, looking at Raphael

"Don't talk, baby," Gus crooned.

". . . my boys . . . need help," Marie gasped. "You knew we were there. I know you heard—"

"Baby, we should have left," Gus said, tears rolling down his cheek. "I told you we needed to leave."

A spasm rolled through Marie's body.

"Gus! Gus!" Marco said. "Hold her. Gus, hold her!"

"Goddammit! We should have left."

"Focus! I need you to keep pressure on that wound."

"So much blood," Gus said.

"That is one of the advantages of the vaccine. The body repairs itself very well. It is already working for her. I've seen guys on the battlefield with wounds like this and . . ." Marco rolled Marie so he could see her back and his voice faded. He slouched against the panel van wall. He shook his head.

Marie looked hard at Gus. "I told you he couldn't keep me away . . . Get Dakota inside. Get to the drugs. Get the water cooler. The . . . get the doctor cooler." Marie worked her jaw like she was trying to spit. "Why . . . can't I . . . talk?"

"Shhhhh, baby," Gus cried. "Just be still. They are trying to help."

"Is Mom gonna be okay?" the boy asked.

"It's gonna be okay, Darien," Gus called back. His eyes cut back to Marco. "Right?"

"Gus, I lov—I love—" Marie said, "I love . . ." Then her face turned white and her eyes focused into a distance beyond human sight.

Gus bowed his head and patted the hair gently back from Marie's face, tears dripped from his nose and chin like a stream running over rocks.

"Dad?" Darien said. "Dad?!"

"Oh baby. Oh baby," Gus whispered, "We should have left. We should have—"

"We must get off the street," Raphael said, as he stepped out of the van.

Marco nodded, his body shaking from exertion. "I need help getting up."

Ryan pulled, but had no leverage. He shifted and his knee crushed a bottle. "Damn it." He swore softly as the bottle of yellow liquid burst. He felt the cold piss saturate his pants. Ryan pulled Marco toward the door. They slid out the front.

"Dad?" Darien said.

Gus held Marie against his chest, rocking and crying.

Raphael met Marco and Ryan by the van's front bumper. "We must go. We can no take them in," he said, his voice brooking no dispute.

"We cannot leave them here," Ryan whispered, "Gus is useless and his youngest one is in the back sick."

"Always with the arguments," Raphael said, "His son has been bit. He *es* infected."

Darien came around the van. He was a slight boy with dark hair and wide brown eyes. "Please help me get my brother into our house. I can't carry him."

"You should go check on your father," Raphael said.

"Wait," Ryan said. "Where is your home?"

Darien pointed to the top of the tower. "The twenty-sixth floor."

"You live here?" Ryan asked, looking at Raphael. "In this tower?"

"Yes."

"And your mother was trying to get in?" Ryan asked.

"Yes, she said her key didn't work anymore so we were waiting for someone to come to the door."

Ryan flashed Raphael another hard look.

Raphael's dark eyes betrayed no emotion. He said, "I told you that Daniel took care of the families that live here. They leave because they want to. He gave them much money so they could save their families."

"For God's sake, Raphael, they *live* here." Ryan ground his jaw. "And you told me you didn't recognize anyone who came to the door—"

"Please," Darien said. "My brother is sick. He needs medicine."

"There *es* no medicines in this tower," Raphael said.

"Yes, there is. My mom said that Dr. Beth might have some antibiotics."

"Dr. Beth?" Ryan asked.

"Don't you live here?" Darien asked. "Everyone knows Dr. Beth. If you don't live here, you can't keep me out."

"A lot has changed since your family was here," Ryan said. "Does Dr. Beth live on your floor?"

"No," Darien said. He looked at Raphael. "He knows we live here. He has talked to my mom."

Raphael frowned. "I do speak to your mother, but you do no live here any longer."

"I've had enough of this," Ryan said as he turned toward the van.

Raphael grabbed Ryan by the arm. "You can no bring this infection into the tower!"

Ryan drew himself up to his full height and looked down at the hand gripping his arm. Then he looked hard into Raphael's eyes. "This is the second time you have laid your hands on me like it is your right."

Raphael stared hard into Ryan's eyes for a hard count of ten and then dropped his hand. He said, "The boy has a human bite and his arm *es* infected like Marco. The medic say that the infection will kill Marco without antibiotics. It will kill this boy, too. But even if the boy survives, he has been bit. He will have the 2091 infection. He will go mad, and then he will bite peoples. We can no bring this into the tower."

"Did you forget that your boys are immune to the RVCJ-2091 virus?"

"That *es* no the point."

"It is *my* point," Ryan said. Then he asked Darien, "Has your brother bitten you or your father?"

Darien shook his head. "No, he's been too sick with fever to bite anyone."

"How long ago did he get bit?" Marco asked.

Darien shrugged. "I don't know. Maybe a week ago. Maybe more?"

Marco nodded and lowered his voice. "We have maybe three or four weeks before the RVCJ-2091 infection eats into his brain."

Raphael added. "His arm *es* septic. He will no live that long."

"What about the drugs in the doctor's apartment?" Ryan asked.

Raphael looked away and said, "I know nothing about these drugs."

"Why do I find that hard to believe, Raphael?" Ryan said. "They are coming inside."

Raphael crossed his arms.

Marco said, "The merciful thing here would be to put the youngest one out of his misery. And it will protect the rest of you."

"Look, I get the problem we have," Ryan said, "And here is how my thinking runs. That sick boy is too feeble to hurt anyone right now. Gus is useless from grief, and this boy is going to be on the street by himself in a van filled with piss bottles—"

"You can no save everybody," Raphael said.

"Did I say anything about saving everybody?" Ryan asked, "And I didn't get to the rest of my point. And that point is . . . they *live* here and I know we already had that conversa—"

Raphael said, "But Daniel—"

"Stop interrupting me," Ryan said. "I don't know what Daniel did or didn't do. But I know what I am going to do. I am going to respect their right to live in their home. And since this whole building is *my* private property, I expect you to do the same."

Raphael breathed hard through his nose. "I know if you see these peoples out here, you would open the doors. You are too soft."

"Raphael, I guarantee that my problem has nothing to do with being soft."

"They cannot come in," Raphael said.

"Popp—Poppa, do you cop—?" Simone said, his voice coming through the maintenance walkie-talkie unit clipped to Raphael's tactical vest.

"Simone? Simone?" Raphael said. "Say again . . ." He looked down the street. "I can no see you."

"At the . . . intersection," Simone said. "Do you . . ." the radio crackled.

"Fucking radios," Marco said as he tried to fine-tune the channel. "These pieces of shit are useless."

Raphael scrambled atop a car. "Simone! Simone?!"

"Here!" Simone said, waving his arms at the intersection of Boulevard of the Allies, "I think someone is coming."

Raphael keyed the radio. "Get back to the JLTV."

"But—"

"No but. Come now!" Raphael said. He frowned at Marco, then at Darren and then at Ryan. "You carry the boy."

4

Global Infection: ≤ 29.9003%

Dakota Blanco was delirious with pain, moaning and screaming the whole way to the twenty-sixth floor. Gus fumbled for his condo keys in his pants, and his hands shook as he put the key in the lock, but finally the door swung open wide. He shuffled into the living room and collapsed into a leather recliner, filthy, bloody and smelly, with eyes mute and distant.

Ryan lay the boy on the kitchen table and Raphael slowly cut away his rank clothes and then looked at his festering arm. Marco returned from searching Dr. Beth's condo with a bag full of drugs. He cut a 40 mg Oxycontin in half and helped Dakota drink some Lipton's cup of soup. Minutes later, Dakota fell asleep. Raphael carried him to a bathroom.

"Is my brother going to be all right?" Darien asked.

"I'm sure he will be," Ryan said. "Why don't you go clean up?"

Darien walked into the kitchen. "I'm hungry," he said, opening the refrigerator door.

Ryan saw that it was empty but for condiments, sodas, and a single container of vanilla yogurt.

"They cleaned it out before we went to Colorado," Darien said, but he kept staring.

"Darien, get cleaned up and I will get food."

"There is food in the pantry." Darien nodded toward a louvered door.

Ryan found shelves filled with canned goods.

"I like gumbo," Darien said, still holding the refrigerator door open. "Gumbo sounds really good."

"When was the last time you ate?"

"I don't know. My mom and I were sneaking out to see what was in the shops along the street, but they had been looted. I think I had some peanuts and some almonds yesterday."

Ryan grabbed a cup of soup packet: Chicken noodle. "Let's start with something not so spicy and not so heavy."

"But I really like gumbo," Darien said still staring into the refrigerator as if it held the meaning of life.

"You can close the door, Darien."

"I can't."

Ryan frowned. "Why."

"The door is shiny. I can see myself. I can see my mom's blood."

"Okay, then look at me," Ryan said, using his finger to gently turn the boy's chin. "Just walk that way and go clean up. I'll close the door."

"I don't want to take a shower yet."

Ryan closed the refrigerator. "How come?"

"Can't I just get some soup?"

"How about we start with washing your hands," Ryan said, stirring tap water into the freeze-dried mix and starting the microwave. "How long were you on the street?"

Darien tilted his head like he was trying to make an idea fall into his right ear. "I don't know. I can't remember. Four days, maybe. No, three, I think." He went to the sink and washed his hands. He watched his mother's blood swirled down the drain. Then he said, "The government safe zones didn't have any drugs. Well, my dad said they did, but they were lying. So we left the camp and tried to get in here." He kept watching the water swirl down the drain.

Ryan turned the faucet off. "Do you want to sit?"

Darien nodded. He turned his head as he walked past the refrigerator. "I don't remember you when we lived here. When did you move in? Or did you just take over this building?"

The microwave pinged. Ryan stirred the soup in the bowl and put a few crackers on a plate. "I haven't been here long, but I didn't just take over the building."

Darien climbed onto a stool, pulled the cup near his chin, and started blowing, but his eyes never left Ryan's face.

"I bought the tower from the owner about a week ago."

"You *bought* the tower?" Darien said. "What was the owner's name?"

Ryan smiled. "From the look in your eye, I suspect you know already. Richard Ryder owned this place. His father's name is Daniel."

Darien sipped. "What was the sale price? The real estate market around here is depressed, but it was still worth over a hundred million."

"A hundred million . . . I'm not sure if I got a bargain or not."

Darien slowly chewed on a cracker. "So what was the final price? Eighty million?"

"Nope," Ryan said. "I bought this tower for a chair, or rather for a seat on a helicopter."

Darien frowned. "I don't understand."

"Hard to explain," Ryan said, suddenly unable to ignore the smell of urine. He unbuckled his pants. "I don't suppose your dad would mind if I borrowed some shorts?"

"Sorry about the pee in the van," Darien said. "We could only use the toilets during the day. It was too scary to go into the deli across the street at night. I tried to go between the cars sometimes at night, but there were a lot of people coming to the tower. So we had to hide and do number one in empty water bottles."

"So your mom waited by the door to talk to somebody, right?"

"My mom talked to a security guard."

"Security guard?"

"She said she talked to someone patrolling the lobby. I thought that meant security guard, but I think it was Mr. Paguero."

"So you know Raphael?"

Darien scraped the cracker crumbs into a pile as they fell from his mouth. He said, "I've seen him. He worked for the building owner. Does he work for you now?"

In the van, Marie's reaction seemed like pain-filled delirium, but now Ryan knew Marie recognized Raphael. She had talked to him. And Raphael had ignored her. "No, he doesn't work for me. And he didn't work for Richard. He worked for Daniel."

Darien sat back in the stool and crossed his arms. "That's right. Mr. Peguero worked for Mr. Ryder. But he and Richard were friends, I think."

"No, they are not friends. But you already know that, don't you?"

Darien appraised Ryan like he was judging ballroom dance. "Were you and Richard friends?"

"No," Ryan said. "Were you and Richard friends?"

Darien made a face like he smelled a skunk. "He was always looking at my mom funny."

Ryan could not remember seeing Marie in the security cameras, but then he'd not been able to watch around the clock. He and the Pagueros had taken turns, or to be more exact, Ryan and Raphael took turns. Marco's fever kept him in a recliner, and Simone's commitment to watch the cameras was dubious. But there was no question that Raphael knew the Blanco family was just outside the door.

When the first wave of people came to the tower looking for haven or loved ones, Ryan asked Raphael if he recognized them. Raphael said an emphatic no and added that Daniel Ryder paid tower tenants to break their lease and find a safe place to live. Ryan remembered Daniel saying something similar, but Daniel had also mentioned that he had been unable to locate some tenants. Ryan told Raphael that the people who had not been compensated had a right to return to their property. Raphael thought Ryan's idealism was foolish and said so with his patented South American face—lips drawn down into a pensive muse, eyes cold and dark. It was impossible to save everyone; this was Raphael's impenetrable argument. Ryan didn't want to save everyone, but he did want to make sure that people who had their own resources could save themselves. If the people on the streets lived in the tower, Ryan expected Raphael to let them inside.

"I'm still hungry," Darien said. "Could I get some more?"

Ryan said, "Go get a shower first. You haven't eaten much in a few days. Let's give your belly time to get used to food. If you can keep it down, I'll feed you all night if you like."

Darien nodded and dropped off the stool. He made it five steps and puked. He started to cry. Ryan snapped off some paper towels and helped the boy wipe his face. "It's okay."

"I want my mommy," Darien said, tears rolling down his cheek.

Ryan reached out to hug the boy, but Darien held up a hand. He stood shaking until he wiped his chin. "I miss her," Darien said. "She was the one who hugged me."

"I'm sure she did," Ryan said.

"I'm going to get a shower now," Darien said, and walked out of the kitchen.

Ryan was cleaning up the mess when Raphael carried a sleeping Dakota, wearing Superman pajama bottoms, into the kitchen and laid him on the island. Marco turned on all of the lights and gave him a shot of lidocaine. For thirty minutes they worked to drain the puss-filled wound and cut away rotting flesh. Finally, they closed the wounds with Skinfuze and put a dressing on his arm. When they finished, Raphael carried Dakota to the couch and wrapped him in blankets.

Marco slumped into a kitchen chair and looked at Ryan putting away the mop and emptying the dirty bucket. "When was the last time you looked in the mirror?" he said.

"Why?" Ryan asked and then caught his reflection in the refrigerator door. He saw a man in his underwear wearing a blood-spattered shirt with clots of blood, bone and brain in his salt-and-pepper hair, neck, and face. Then he saw the bruises down his forearms, shoulders and chest. "I didn't even notice," he said as he ran his fingers through his hair. "How is Dakota doing?"

Marco's face was grave. "Not good. If he doesn't have it already, he will have blood poisoning soon. He is probably going to die before the RVCJ-2091 virus turns him mad."

Raphael said. "Flesh *es* rotting. To save him, we must take the arm at the elbow."

"You want to cut off my boy's arm?" Gus said, standing in the kitchen with dried blood from chin to shins.

"That is a hard part of the conversation to walk in on," Marco said.

Ryan said. "Here, sit down. Do you want some soup or something?"

"No, I don't want any soup," Gus said. "I want to know why you want to cut off my boy's arm."

"We don't *want* to cut off his arm," Marco said. "We are saying that the infection has spread, and we only have a handful of medical supplies that won't cure the infection."

"But what about Dr. Beth's place?" Gus said, the stench of long unwashed body rolling off him in waves. "That is why we came here. That is why Marie was staying outside the door." His voice rose in pitch. "She said that there were drugs in Dr. Beth's place. Are you saying that there aren't any drugs? Did she get that wrong, too?"

"I found a dozen ZPacs," Marco said. "Those are probably her stash for family flu. Azithromycin won't help."

"But we can try? Right? We can give him the antibiotics and see if it helps," Gus said. "I mean, that is why Marie is dead. Right? So we have to try, right? She said the safe zone doctors were wrong. They should have antibiotics. But they didn't. They said that the next camp would have them, but we couldn't wait. It was crazy to stay in the camp. So Marie said we should come back here. She said Dr. Beth had antibiotics. That is why we came here . . . because Dr. Beth would have green Skittles. Why can't you find those Skittles? Did you even look for them?"

Ryan and Marco exchanged looks. Finally, Marco said, "Gus, you are exhausted. Why don't you get cleaned up?"

Gus walked out of the kitchen toward the condo windows and stared into the darkened city.

Marco followed. "Look, it isn't as bad as it seems. We give Dakota a shot of morphine. We remove the arm, and then we give him one of these." He held up a red Syrette for Gus to see.

Gus didn't turn.

"This is Combat Medic. Have you ever heard of it?" Marco asked. "It will close up the stump and start to re-grow the arm. We'll have to keep Dakota on drugs because it will hurt, but the arm will grow back. It might even be use—"

"Marie, she loved to look out at the city," Gus said. "She said it was soothing. I never understood it, really. She made me pick this side of the tower. We could have had the southwest corner and looked out over the river and see the setting sun. She didn't want that view. She always said, 'Why do people want to see water? I want to see people.'

"I hate this fucking city," Gus said. "It is so gray here . . . so cold. Marie used to say that it was just as gray and cold in Manhattan. That was true. She was right, but I thought we were happy in New York. She didn't want to spend the money to stay there."

Gus banged his head against the glass. "Money . . . I have more money than I could spend in three lifetimes," he said, "but she wanted to be near her family . . . near her beloved Steelers. Fucking Steelers fans . . . insufferable pricks. I saw what they did to my Marie with their terrible towels. When the bullets started firing, where were those towels then? Where was that Steel Curtain?"

"Ryan?" Darien said, "I'm still hungry—" he stopped. His dark hair was a towel-tousled mess, dressed in Batman pajamas. "Dad?"

Gus banged his head against the glass again. "Was it too much to ask for those towels to help her? Was it too much to ask?"

"Raphael," Ryan said. "Why don't you take Darien to get some food?"

"*Si, es* good idea," Raphael said. "Darien, *hablas español?*"

"*Un poco,*" Darien replied. "Only what I have learned in school."

"We will have to fix that," Raphael said and waved for him to come.

"Gus," Ryan said, walking to the window. "Maybe we don't need to make this choice tonight."

Gus banged his head again.

Ryan shrugged to Marco. "Do you think we can wait through the night?"

Marco shrugged back. "He's resting. There is no reason to do anything tonight."

"Gus, you also have to think about Darien," Ryan said. "You've got to take care of your other son. He needs you."

"If you cut off his arm, there will be so much blood," Gus said, and suddenly, he saw his wife's blood in the window's reflection. "So much blood," he said, ripping at his shirt. "So much blood." The shirt finally tore. "So much blood," he wailed. Gus thrashed out of his pants, his feet getting caught in the legs. He fell to the ground struggling to pull them off, revealing stained boxers. He finally freed himself and lay on the floor, panting and whimpering. "Why didn't you look for the Skittles? Marie came for the goddamned Skittles!"

Darien came running into the room. "Dad? Dad?"

Ryan knelt, his voice low. "Gus, Gus, look at me. Gus, you have to get yourself together. You have two boys who need you right now."

"Leave me alone!"

"No. Get up and get a shower."

"I can't," Gus said. "Marie was the strong one."

"Gus," Ryan said, leaning closer. "Your son is watching you. He is learning right this minute what it means to be a man. Is this the lesson you want to teach him?"

Gus rolled to meet Ryan's eyes. Behind those eyes was hate. "Damn you!" he said. But he rolled to all fours and crawled to a chair and pulled himself up. Without another word, he walked deep into his condo.

5

Global Infection: ≤ 29.9004%

Ryan put his blood-caked and urine-soaked clothes into a bag, stepped into a pulsing stream of hot water, and tried to scrub away the night's memories. Then he found a T-shirt and sweats in an empty bedroom. He walked back into the Blanco kitchen, tugging the bottom of the shirt over his belly. "This is an amazing place," he said.

Marco frowned. "This from the man who owns a penthouse as plush as the TajMahal?"

"The penthouse is ostentatious," Ryan said. "This is more my sense of décor. More . . . I don't know . . . simple?"

"That shirt is a good look for you," Marco said. "You could get a job at Hooters. Did you get it out of Marie's closet?"

"You are hilarious . . . but not really," Ryan said, his tone dry. "Beggars can't be fashion critics. I hope Gus doesn't mind, but he's asleep, and I didn't have the heart to wake him."

Marco shifted in the chair. "He might start talking about Skittles again."

Raphael picked up his weapons and inched toward the front door. "We have much to do."

Ryan asked, "Where is Darien?"

"I'm right here," Darien said, as he stepped into the kitchen.

"We are going up to the penthouse. Do you know where that is?"

"Yes," Darien said. "I've been to parties there. Are Jenna and Melissa still there?"

Ryan frowned.

"Daniel's granddaughters," Raphael said.

"Ah . . . uh . . . no. Mr. Ryder took them someplace," Ryan said. "It's just me and Raphael and Marco and Simone."

"And you are Ryan?" Darien asked.

Ryan nodded and started writing his phone number on the white-board attached to the refrigerator. "If you need help, you can call my phone." Absently, he patted at the sweats and then felt through the bag of clothes looking for his phone. "Shit! I think I left the phone under the security desk."

Raphael said, "The tower security app *es* on this phone, yes? If peoples find that phone, they can get into the building, yes? With this phone, they can open the locks and turn on the elevators."

Raphael already knew the answer to these questions since he was the one who helped Ryan set up the tower management app. Evidently a negligent discharge also meant Ryan should be criticized for every failure. He raised a brow and said, "Anyway, Darien this is direct number to the penthouse. It is the inter-tower extension. Just use the kitchen phone if Dakota or your dad has a problem."

"And this *es* my cell phone," Raphael said with a smile, writing his number on the whiteboard. "Remember our Spanish lesson? Area code *cuatro, uno, dos*. Practice saying these in Spanish."

"Yes," Darien said. "I remember. Thank you. My dad is sleeping. And Dakota is sleeping. I should be all right . . . but . . . if I want to see you, could I . . . come up?"

"Yes, please come," Raphael said, a rare smile bending his face.

"You want someone to stay with you now?" Marco asked, "I could sleep in the chair—"

Raphael shook his head, emphatic. "You must sleep in your bed. You are too sick. You must rest."

Darien said, "I can sleep beside Dakota. It will be all right."

Marco limped to the counter. "I told your father that Dakota will need pain meds every four hours. Your brother needs to have these pills to keep the pain away or it will be bad. Give him half the pill with a cup of soup."

Darien said, "I'll set an alarm clock."

Raphael took three hard strides toward the master suite. "A man needs to be doing his job."

"Poppa," Marco said. "Leave him. We can come down later and check on them." He moved to the front door.

"If I lock the door, no one can get in, right?" Darien asked.

Raphael ruffled Darien's hair. "No peoples can get into this place. We are very far above the street. And the doors cannot be opened."

Darien took a step and hugged Raphael and for a brief moment Raphael hugged him back.

"Looks like you made a friend," Ryan said as they stood waiting for the elevator.

"He *es* a good boy," Raphael said, thumbing a tear from his eye. "But I still do no think you should have let them in."

Ryan shrugged.

"Speaking of good boys," Marco said, "I don't suppose Simone got the weapons and the JLTV into the tower?"

"He do what I ask," Raphael said.

"Riiiiight," Marco said. "Sure he did. Let's all think positive thoughts and chant to the universe."

Raphael frowned. His instruction had been short and specific. Pick up the weapons and bullets and pile them into the JLTV, and then take the vehicle to the loading dock underneath the tower.

Raphael fiddled with the radio knob, keyed the mic and said, "Simone, do you copy? Simone, do you copy?"

Radio static . . .

"Simone . . . Simone . . ."

Radio static.

Marco shook his head. "I keep telling you that those radios are useless."

Raphael said, "This *es* better than nothing. Simone?"

Marco sighed and looked around, impatient. To Ryan he said, "Did you push the button?"

"Three times," Ryan said. "But you can push it for me if you don't think I did it right."

"*Mierda*!" Raphael said. "I turn the elevators off to keep the peoples from coming up here." He pulled out his phone, tapped the app that worked with the Renaissance Tower smart system and a moment later the elevator opened.

Marco said, "My brother is a pain in the ass, but we should check on Simone before we go get the phone. He's usually complaining into the radio. The silence has me nervous."

Raphael pursed his lips. "Yes, it *es* good to find him."

Richard Ryder was obsessed with security—specifically his security. Richard Ryder, defender of the people's state and the workers' paradise, wanted to limit his exposure to the *hoi polloi,* so the penthouse elevator only stopped on three floors: the top floor, the eighth floor promenade level and ground level VIP parking garage. Getting to the penthouse from the 26th floor required effort.

First the three men rode the public elevators to the eighth floor. Then they walked to an alcove away from the public elevator bank where Ryan used a security badge to open an outer gate looking like it should be protecting a bank vault. Once inside, Raphael pressed his right palm to a bioscanner. Three seconds later the unit gave a soft chime, and the screen lit green. The elevator rose in seconds and opened to the penthouse landing lined with stone statues—idealized depictions of the South American Incan emperor Atahualpa and Aztec ruler Motecuhzoma Xocoyotzin, Simon Bolivar, Isabel Perón, Hugo Chávez, Che Guevara, Pablo Escobar, and Genevieve Chuquisengo. The walls were painted with socialist realism murals—portrayals of brown-haired, brown-eyed people surrounding their patrician heroic leaders. A security desk sat behind bulletproof glass to the right of the penthouse door where, in days past, Molitor Group security kept watch.

Ryan used his security badge to open the penthouse door and walk into foyer covered in Italian White Carrara polished marble. Overhead hung three Elegant Lighting, *Maria Theresa*, 85-light, five-tier crystal chandeliers.

"By the way," Ryan said, "don't let me forget. We need to get my bio scan profile set up."

"I ask you two days ago to do this," Raphael said, "and you did no have time."

"And two days ago I didn't have the time, but now I do."

Raphael closed his eyes like he was practicing patience and then said, "Simone? Are you here? Simone?"

Silence . . .

"Simone?"

Silence . . .

"*Mierda!*"

They fanned out through the 20,000 square foot penthouse, calling his name.

Silence . . .

Raphael was mere feet from the front door, mere moments from storming back down to the street to find his son, when they heard Marco on the radio. "I found him. He's in the security room."

The Molitor Group headquarters were in Texas, but three years ago, Daniel Ryder chose to move his operations to the Renaissance Tower to finish the work his son Richard had abandoned. So Daniel built a duplicate Molitor Group operations center: an office suite, global communications infrastructure and security headquarters in the tower.

The Molitor Group staff took up residence in the tower and commuted up a dozen floors. The Molitor Group private security team had a barracks on the thirteenth floor and a command post just off Daniel's main office. To keep the security team from interrupting Daniel while in meetings, they had their own exit through the penthouse public space.

Raphael found Simone slouched in a chair, trying to wake up. "Where *es* your radio?" he said. "I have been calling."

Simone, was a lean, muscled teen with wispy facial hair and a touch of acne, brown hair and brown eyes. He yawned. "The radio is heavy. And I was tired of wearing the tactical gear. I put it in my room.

The phrase, "my room" stuck in Ryan's craw.

The first night in the tower, Ryan assumed he would make his home in the master suite, where Daniel and Lisa Ryder had made their sanctum. Instead, he found Simone Paguero sleeping on 1200-thread-count sheets. Ryan decided to deal with the boy later and wandered the tower until he found the *au pair* suite: a cozy space with narrow windows along the top walls that let soft moonlight filter in, a bathroom, a sitting area, a wall closet filled with a young woman's clothes, a desk and lots of bookshelves. But even though he had found a place to call home, the fact that Simone had dubbed the master suite *his* room—without asking—was a misapprehension Ryan was going to address.

"It was heavy?" Raphael said. "You wear pads for football and a little radio *es* too *heavy*?"

Simone said, "If we are in the penthouse, we all take off our radios. What is the big deal?"

"The big deal *es* I was calling you and I do no know if you are all right. You could be hurt."

Simone shrugged. "Then you should have come with me." There was an edge to his words. It was as if the lone mission he'd been sent to accomplish had offended his soul.

"Where *es* these weapons?" Raphael said.

"Out there," Simone said, heaving his thumb toward the connected office like the weight of his hand was too much to lift. He shifted his slouch and adjusted his feet on the desk. His eyes focused on the security monitors, but he wasn't watching the cameras. He was watching a movie that he had streamed into the security room from the penthouse entertainment system.

Raphael walked to the door. Ryan looked over Raphael's head and saw four guns laying haphazardly on his desk—two M16s and two Berettas. And then he saw the gash in the desk surface.

Little twerp!

Raphael said, "What? What do you mean this *es* it? There should be many weapons."

Simone shrugged again. The protagonist was shooting bad guys and the camera was whirling and tilting and flashing as if that made the action interesting. "Those guns were the only ones that were good."

Raphael shook his head like he hadn't heard right. "There were many peoples in the firefight. I walk past many guns."

"Then *you* should have picked them up and put them in the JLTV."

"Un-fucking-believable," Marco said. "You can't possibly be this stupid."

"Bite me," Simone snapped. "Mr. High-and-Mighty Ranger Man! Just bite me. No one asked you."

"So you did no do what I ask?" Raphael said.

"I picked up some guns that I thought were good. We have guns. And it's not like you are going to give one to him," Simone said, flipping a thumb toward Ryan.

"*Muchacho tonto,*" Raphael breathed. "This *es* no the point. I ask you to do this thing."

"Do you not understand that there are no more guns?" Marco snapped. "Do you not understand that we need every bullet we can find?"

"What do you mean?" Simone said, confused. "We can always go back to the range. We have bullets there. And you and Mom have caches, right? She's the one who taught us how to do black market deals, for God's sake. We can dig up your caches and bring them to the tower."

"Do no use the Lord's name in vain," Raphael scolded.

Marco was shaking, maybe from exertion, maybe from the lingering fever or maybe from rising fury. And then he spoke, "You fucking shitbird! Days ago we almost died fighting our way to the tower and you want to fight your way back to the range, get more bullets, and then go try to dig up our weapons cache while some madmen are trying to chew off our face when all you had to do was to pick up some guns lying around! At! Your! Fucking! Feet!"

"Marco!" Raphael snapped. "*Es* enough!"

Marco rolled his eyes. "Right, I'm the bad guy here." He tossed up his hands and limped into the executive office and did three laps around the walls.

Raphael's jaws worked in the same rhythm of his clenching hands. "Did you take the JLTV to the loading dock?"

Simone crossed his arms and slouched deeper into the chair. "I couldn't get it down the street."

"Unbelievable. That thing had a .50 cal on top!" Marco shouted from the office. "That would have been . . . oh my God! I cannot believe this. If you were scared, you should have said something."

"I wasn't scared."

Raphael said. "It was easy. You pick up the weapons and then you drive to the underground. This place *es* locked. There *es* no one down there. You have many guns. You always say you want to fight. You can defend yourself. But you can no go into the underground? And then I asked you to bring up the weapons and clean them, but I can see that you did no clean them—"

"I couldn't find any gun-cleaning stuff," Simone huffed. "Now that you are back from playing with that man and his kids, we can go out and get the stuff. No one has been around. I've been watching the monitors. Nobody came."

Ryan slid into a second chair and worked through the system to bring up the security feeds.

Simone asked, "You don't believe me?"

"Simone, see these green flags with the time stamp?" Ryan asked. "The security system is telling me that it recorded something. And by the number of flags, it was a lot of somethings."

6

Global Infection: ≤ 29.9007%

Ryan was sure that he was going to see a swarm of people piled into the lobby hammering away at the stairwell doors. He clicked the mouse and the playback started. Two Humvees and two JLTVs rolled into the frame on the camera that showed the intersection of Smithfield and First Avenue. The security footage chronicled the movement of twenty soldiers, their movement through the street, putting their fallen comrades in body bags, putting bullets in the heads of anything stirring to life and collecting the weapons and ammunition.

Then came the order to search the tower and twelve soldiers breached the wrecked vestibule and moved through the lobby. Flashlights mounted to their weapons filled the tower with light as they swept through the space until they arrived at the locked stairwell doors. A few soldiers backtracked to the elevators and jammed the call button.

"Oh shit," Ryan said, as he saw a soldier move his light behind the security desk.

"What?" Raphael said.

"He's gonna see my phone." Ryan pointed with his finger at the object lying amid the shattered glass, wood, stone and metal scattered throughout. He held his breath, but the order to fall back to the rally point crackled over the radios and the soldiers retreated to their vehicles taking the Lieutenant's JLTV with them. "Look, I left it there. Just give me my Glock and I'll get the get the phone."

Raphael shook his head no.

"No?" Ryan said.

"You do no know how to use this weapon. I will no give it to you."

"Cut it out, Raphael. I'm not asking for permission. I understood why you took it from me on the street, but—"

"A negligent discharge *es* unacceptable," Raphael said with resolve. "You can no be armed when you are so negligent."

Simone Paguero gave a perfect adolescent smirk and crooked a finger like he was shooting. "Negligent discharge," he said.

Ryan ignored the comment. "Raphael, give me the gun."

"No."

"Poppa," Marco said.

"I will no give him this weapon," Raphael said, his arms crossed.

Ryan nodded and started working at the security console, clicking through the tower interface. He turned on the lobby lights, eliminated Raphael's security badge access and then locked down the system. He rose, walked to his desk and grabbed both Berettas.

"Stop!" Raphael barked.

Ryan kept walking through the Molitor Group offices and out of the penthouse.

It wasn't the smartest thing he'd ever done, riding an elevator down 30 floors to apocalyptic Pittsburgh armed with two handguns and a healthy dose of aggravation. But it seemed that smart decisions were as elusive as finding the answers to life. He'd lost track of the choices he'd made, the alternative courses of action he'd taken to arrive in a strange city, without family or friends or money just as the single greatest plague in history punched humanity in the brain. Each choice seemed like the best option considering the available information. It seemed like the best choice to come to Pittsburgh to be with his sister, but she descended into criminal insanity. It seemed like the best choice to avoid the US government's endless persecution, but that branded him a federal fugitive. It seemed like the best choice when he traded a seat on a plane headed to a distant safe haven for ownership of the Renaissance Tower, but in the days following he'd been in more gun fights than he wanted to count. It seemed like the best choice when he agreed to take in the Paguero family so they could ride out the fall of western civilization like brothers in arms, but now there was a dangerous power struggle emerging. It was apparent that Raphael was used to getting his way by sheer force of will mixed with no inhibition about lying. Their relationship was going to deteriorate fast if Ryan didn't enforce boundaries early and often.

Getting to the ground floor was not easy, which was why living in the penthouse was so secure. If it was hard to get from the top of the tower to the ground floor it was equally hard for monsters to rise to the top. Ryan took the penthouse express elevator down to the eighth-floor promenade and then entered the public elevator and rode to the lobby. He had turned on the lobby lights to drive back the gremlins lurking in the murk, but those same lights could attract things that don't need darkness to perpetrate mayhem. The doors opened and Ryan was ready to do battle, but found the Renaissance Tower lobby empty. Bullet holes riddled the walls. The marble floor was strewn with chunks of wood and stone and glass. A planter had exploded, layering the walls with dirt and leaving flowers spread about like fish at low tide gasping their last breaths.

Ryan rushed to the security desk and snatched the phone from the detritus and sprinted to the elevator.

Something moved, and then came the sound of rhythmic crunching like boots on gravel.

Ryan jabbed the button like he was speed typing a business report.

The door slowly slid shut and seconds later the elevator rocketed upwards.

Ryan willed his heart rate to slow as he tapped through the tower security app to find the elevator lockdown settings. The door chimed and slid open on the eighth floor; he stepped out and killed the power.

Ryan walked to the penthouse elevator alcove and rode it to the top. He walked past the South American dictators to the security station, tempted to review the lobby security feed to see what was moving, but then decided it didn't matter. There was nothing he could, or more important, would do. He certainly wasn't going to ask Raphael to see if the boogie man was hiding under the bed.

Ryan reached for the penthouse door and stopped. "I'm an idiot. How in the hell does Darien get up here with the elevators off?" For a full five minutes he stared at the statue of Isabel Perón and Genevieve Chuquisengo, unable to solve the puzzle that didn't end up with an elevator powered and able to travel from the ground level to the upper tower floors. "There is the old-fashioned way," he said and walked to the stairwell.

Richard Ryder fancied himself a connoisseur of fine cuisine and built a French Restaurant called *Mon Pierre's* on the twenty-ninth floor. According to Daniel Ryder, the restaurant served American bistro, but the master chef could make any food from any country taste like heaven. And since Ryan had been living on the chef's leftovers for a week, he knew it was true. It was very unfortunate that the master chef had left with Daniel.

Richard's passion for great food was secondary to his obsession with security. Ryan badged through three gates before he could exit the twenty-ninth floor stairwell. When the world was sane, the restaurant had been open to the public, but the public would have had an easier time getting into Fort Knox than climbing up that single flight of stairs.

Ryan walked past the elevator bank, past *Mon Pierre's* entrance, to the far stairwell and continued his trip down to the Blanco condo. He rang the doorbell, but got no response. He knocked and got no response.

Ryan looked around the floor for a place to hide a security badge so the Blancos could climb the stairs past Richard's security. "But if you hide the badge, how will they find it?" he said to himself. "And do I really want an unrestricted security badge lying around?" He rolled his eyes, shook his head and trudged up four flights of stairs. He only had to stop and catch his breath twice.

Goddamned Italians.

But even as Ryan cursed them, his mouth watered for that savory combination of capicola, pepperoni, salami and provolone, with olives and banana peppers, slathered with mayo, oil and a hint of seasoning, all sitting atop a perfectly toasted roll. He opened the penthouse door and headed straight to the family kitchen.

7

Global Infection: ≤ 29.9012%

IT geek hard on!

That was the subject line for an e-mail.

It seemed that not even the apocalypse could stop spam. The creators of the ARPANET would be so proud.

Ryan was a mouse click away from banishing the missive into the ether when he realized it was from Patrick, one half of Team Bruptrick. The other half was Bruce. They were the Molitor Group domain administrators. In the Molitor IT pantheon, these two ruled all with the capricious might of Loki. The downside of a Team Bruptrick interaction was their adolescent social skills. The upside of a Team Bruptrick interaction was that they were brilliant IT talent. Since Ryan had spent over a decade building a very successful Information Technology Managed Services business, he'd known dozens of guys just like Patrick and Bruce, and keeping them happy was a good management policy.

Mr. Sage,

Good to hear from you. Had to fight any zombies yet? Bruce wants to know. I told him to go play outside and maybe one would wander toward him.

About rsagespeaks.com. Blue Pill is a hacker friend of ours. Well, he's not really a friend. Well, he sort of is, but well, it's hard to explain. Anyway, he already moved your site. He says that it will remain live as long as there is sunlight.

This is a big deal. He doesn't like governments. Blue Pill likes you.

How is that for a bonus?!

Oh, and he did something really cool. He hacked the root DNS servers. Every twenty visitors to a government site get forwarded to your site. I'm getting an IT hard on just thinking about that feat of magic. Blue Pill is a god!

Root,
Patrick

Ryan had forgotten that he'd even asked for help with his blog. In a fifteen year writing career, he created almost twenty thousand blog pages, close to four million words in articles and essays. It made him physically ill to think that all his intellectual capital would vanish when the power went out. Creating a backup and saving it to a local drive was easy enough, but Ryan didn't want to just save the data. He wanted it publicly accessible forever and that was a very different technical challenge.

The government assault on the First Amendment prompted him to move his blog hosting to Sweden years ago, but the continents would soon be isolated. The first step to keeping his website publicly accessible was to bring it back to North America. He asked Bruptrick to solve the remaining technical challenges and he hadn't thought about it since. Indeed, it seemed absurd to worry about blogs and articles. Basic survival had a way of shifting a man's perspective.

"Blue Pill hacked the root DNS? Is that even possible?" Ryan said as he typed in the URL and found his site available for the world to see. And for kicks and giggles, he went to a government website and refreshed the page until it forwarded to Rsagespeaks.com.

"How cool is that?" Ryan whispered.

Patrick,

Blue Pill hacked the root DNS servers? He is a god. IT hard on worthy!

Ryan

The Italian sandwich was an inch from his mouth when a soft buzzer signaled that someone was at the outer doors to the office suite. Since the Molitor offices were intermixed with the residential space, getting into the office required being buzzed through a checkpoint. While Daniel was in residence, Mora, his longtime executive assistant, played gatekeeper to the inner sanctum, but Ryan didn't have a gatekeeper.

Marco was waving into the camera. Ryan clicked the intercom. "What's up?"

"Uh, my badge doesn't work, and the door is locked," Marco said. "Do you want privacy?"

"What? Try it again." A moment later, Ryan could hear the telltale buzz-beep of a failed access. He hit the Lock Release button. "Sorry. Come on in."

"Thanks," Marco said.

Ryan sighed. He did not need a technological puzzle added to the to-do list. How in the hell could the badging system break—. "Shit!" he swore, suddenly knowing the problem. *He* was the culprit.

Marco Paguero was twenty-six, but he looked like he had lived a hundred years. His face was hollow from days of malnutrition and sickness. The crow's feet around his eyes were etched into his skin by long hours of squinting at a battlefield as the sun beat on his senses. His shoulders were broad, but they slumped as if carrying the weight of the world. And this was all an improvement. He had arrived at the tower doorstep starved, fever ridden, with multiple puss filled human bites. A medic drained the wounds, stitched the skin together and banished Marco to bed rest with IV antibiotics dripping into his arm before leaving the city forever.

Marco limped into the office pulling an IV stand and laid the Glock on Ryan's desk. "Peace offering."

"Is that right?" Ryan said and took a bite.

"The outer door usually isn't closed, let alone locked. I can come back."

"No, sit. But I feel funny about eating in front of you."

"I'm fine. I ate something to settle my stomach, but when I have these damned antibiotics running through my body . . ." Marco made a sour face. "I'm concerned it will all come up," he said easing into a chair on the opposite side of the desk. "What a day, right?"

Ryan nodded, chewing.

"Locking my father out of the security system, was, how to say, very smart and maybe a little stupid."

Ryan swallowed and took a drink. "Is that right?"

"The moment you walked out the door, he tried to lock down the elevators. He was so mad that he might have left you there all night."

Ryan nodded and kept eating.

"Pretty impressive that you knew what he would do next . . . Most men can't outthink or outmaneuver my father."

Ryan nodded and blew on his steaming soup.

"My father thinks that men who can do that are . . . dangerous."

Ryan nodded and took a sip.

"I'm just saying that maybe you should not antagonize him."

Ryan nursed the piping hot soup in his hands contemplating the answer to the implied threat. "Do you realize that it has been twenty years since I had calluses?"

"What?"

"I worked for years in construction, framing houses, building high-rises, doing drywall. Twenty years ago I had calluses. I didn't sit behind a desk and get soft." He sipped his soup. "Of course, you don't know how long ago it was that I had calluses, because you don't know me, and neither does your father."

"I don't care about riddles," Marco said, "I'm just here offering a little friendly advice with a word of caution."

Ryan took a bite of sandwich and then another and finally sipped on his soup. Then he said, "And a man that assumes that what he sees is all there is to know is always blindsided by what he cannot see. He is always destroyed because he never seeks to learn what is beyond the moment."

Exasperated, Marco said, "So what is it you really want to say here?"

"Marco, you misunderstand. I don't really want to say anything to you. My conflict is not with you. And I won't be using an intermediary. My problem is with your father. And when it serves my purpose, I will take up the conversation with him. My point now is you don't know me. Neither of you do. And neither of you have made an effort to know me. Maybe some of that is because we've only be together for a few days, but I think the real problem is that the Paguero gods of war see a fat old man who is dead weight. You persist under the notion that I'm a guest in your military world and that I am beholden to your ability to fight."

"I wouldn't say that."

Ryan shrugged. "You don't have to. It radiates off all three of you in waves. It is revealed in your word of caution right now. Your assumption is that I should tread lightly around your father. It never once occurred to you that maybe he should be cautious around me."

Marco paused considering. "Well, if you want us to see something other than a fat old man . . ." he pointed at the plate with his nose.

"Hey!" Ryan said after he swallowed. "You should be proud of me. This is *half* a sandwich. And you have no idea how hard it was to forego the Mike-Sells rippled potato chips. Besides, I haven't eaten in what . . . I don't even remember when I ate last."

Marco nodded like he was having a conversation with a crack addict. "If you want help with a diet, I can point you in the right direction."

"Believe it or not, I know the right direction, but my excuse—at the moment—is that this food will spoil if it doesn't get eaten."

"Okay, true enough, but you have to admit that you don't know anything about guns and combat. It is foolish for you to think otherwise. You were talking a moment ago about what kills men. I can't tell you how many men I've seen die because they know nothing about war."

"Marco, I've never said that I knew anything about war. And I have been grateful to have your skills when the bad guys came to kill. I would probably be dead if you hadn't been here. But treating me like a child is never going to go well. But more important, your military skill does not automatically put you in charge of anything."

"I read you," Marco said. "You do you realize that by locking down the security, he really can't go out of the penthouse. Actually, none of us can. We won't be able to get in or even use the stairwell."

Ryan finished the last bite of his sandwich and took a drink. "Is that right?"

8

Global Infection: ≤ 29.9806%

Ryan Sage woke up at 8 a.m. thinking about cutting off Dakota Blanco's arm. He rolled his feet to the carpet. Yesterday's accumulated aches and pains ripped through his body like someone punched him in the soul. He had showered before bed, but suddenly he could feel the blood and brains and bone chips from the carnage itching into the side of his neck and throat. He ran to the shower and turned the knob to H until he couldn't stand it.

Ryan shuffled to the kitchen and found it empty. Raphael and Marco seemed hard-wired to rise before the sun no matter when they went to bed. They were usually up and drinking coffee by now. He made oatmeal, doused it liberally with Craisins, sprinkled in a dusting of brown sugar and a tap of cinnamon. He poured a glass of cranberry juice and hobbled through the outer offices into his. He sunk into the zero-gravity chair. The first bite of oatmeal hit his tongue and went down pleasantly, warm and smooth. He closed his eyes trying to let the throbbing drift away.

His eyes popped open.

Who was watching the security system?

He spun around his desk and opened the security room door.

Empty!

Ryan went back to his chair and his fingers raced across the keyboard—the security feeds started popping the HD televisions lining the office walls. In the six days since they had been in the tower, the security cameras had been under constant watch which is how they saw all five attempts to break in, and that had been when the tower was locked. Last night they suffered a full breach, and no one had taken over when he went to bed.

For thirty minutes, Ryan watched the security recordings spanning the night. It seemed impossible that nothing had come into the tower. His heart rate slowed, and he started eating. He was scraping three stray Craisins into a final bite when a video chat prompt trilled. He clicked Answer and the two-hundred-inch video conference display hanging from the office ceiling dropped down and adjusted toward the desk. The screen flickered three times and resolved on a pleasant face.

"Ryan Sage," Daniel Ryder said. "Good to see you."

"Daniel?"

Daniel Ryder looked like a cross between an aging GQ model and a politician with his perfectly coiffed black hair and distinguishing touches of grey. Indeed, Daniel reminded Ryan of a feckless presidential candidate from Massachusetts that the national Republican Party insisted on foisting on the people for four election cycles. But looks was the only similarity; Daniel Ryder, international construction mogul, was anything but incompetent.

"You have been getting my e-mails, right?" Daniel asked.

Six days ago, Ryan Sage bought the Renaissance Tower from Richard Ryder, Daniel's edifice erecting dilettante son. Daniel offered Ryan a spot in what he cryptically referred to as a summer home, which was in fact a doomsday pepper's wet dream: a long-term survival facility designed to house over a thousand people for generations. The Ryder family drama was unrelenting when Daniel refused to allow one of Richard's many paramours to flee with them. Names were called, guns were drawn, shots were fired and in the end Ryan traded his seat in the survival facility for the whole of Richard Ryder's estate.

"Somehow, I didn't equate e-mail with you being where we could video conference," Ryan said, "Anyway, so are you safe inside your summer home. You haven't given me much news from your end. But your lawyers are another matter. I think they are determined to kill every tree on the planet with the paperwork."

"Safe is a relative term, but things are progressing here."

Ryan studied Daniel's face on the large screen and he saw the deepened worry lines and the bags under his eyes. "When was the last time you slept?"

"Sleep is overrated," Daniel said. "But let's not talk about me. How are you?"

"Funny you should ask. I was about ten seconds away from overcoming a heart attack."

"What?" Daniel said. "Does your arm hurt? Your chest? Are you having shortness of breath?"

"Sorry, bad metaphor since I probably do look like a good candidate. I just realized that no one has been monitoring the security cameras. It seems impossible that Raphael and Marco are still asleep since you can set your clock by them waking up."

"Marco?" Daniel said. "Is he all right? You two getting along?"

"Getting along? Of course. And he was fine last night. We talked for a couple hours while his IV finished. Maybe the antibiotics made him too sick to get out of bed."

Daniel's brow furrowed like he'd just been told the Pittsburgh Steelers were best pals with the Cincinnati Bengals. "Wait, you were *talking* to Marco? Last night?"

"Yes, we talked until the day's excitement caught up with him. I assumed he would get up and take the security shift but evidently not." Then Ryan had a thought. He clicked into the security system looking for the setting that sent out phone alerts. "Ahh, now I understand. That is why he went to bed."

"So what did you two talk about?"

Raphael being a pain in the ass!

"We covered the spectrum."

"And he's doing all right?"

"Yes, he is all man. Amazing, really. I can't imagine being able to function like he does, up and around in two weeks after being eaten by 2091s. He is still able to grab a gun and kick ass . . ."

Daniel bit his upper lip. Then he said, "I've always been suspicious of the Eternity Vaccine and the Maksimov Therapy. But when you see it work for a loved one, it is hard to be part of the conspiracy crowd. It is good to hear that he is recovering." He paused again as if to work through some mental calculus. "My medic said he gave Marco a grim prognosis. Beyond the infection in his wounds, he might contract hepatitis. How's he doing with the treatment?"

"The bite wounds have closed up but a low grade fever persists."

"He should have already finished the IVs. Why has he put it off?"

"In Marco's defense, he stopped the IVs because he knew we needed him to help fight. He couldn't fight with the drugs and he's been the difference maker."

Daniel nodded. "He was part of the 75th regiment, a Ranger. But Raphael is no slouch. He was part of a special force in South America. And his wife, Leona, she is a special breed of warrior."

"Yes, it has become clear that I'm the only one without warrior gene."

"So, how are . . . things?"

Ryan shrugged. "I suspect you have seen more news than I have, but it is as bad as we thought it would be. I haven't been able to see much real-estate beyond the front door but it seems like Pittsburgh is in free fall. I see more and more infected roaming the streets when I look out the window, and fewer and fewer real people. I can only imagine that it is the same everywhere."

"That is not what I'm asking."

"Are you asking if I regret staying? Are you asking if I think I should have come with you? That is a useless question."

"No, that is not what I'm after."

"Okay, I give up. What *are* you after?"

"I asked for you to let the Paguero family stay as a favor. I'm just interested in knowing how things are going inside the tower."

And then the details started to click together. Ryan had specifically talked about needing Marco to help fight and Daniel had never asked for specifics. He listened like he was hearing about a softball game, not a fight to the death with looters and soldiers and 2091s. That meant he knew about the gunfight, which meant he had talked to someone, and Ryan would bet a large portion of Richard Ryder's money that the someone was named Raphael.

Ryan sat up and paused for an uncomfortable three minutes. Finally he said, "Daniel, why don't you go first?"

Daniel tried to rub the smile off his face as he looked off-camera. Then he looked back. "I really wish I had met you ten years ago. I would bet a lot of my money that we would have made a devastating team. What gave me away?"

"You didn't ask for details about the gunfights."

Daniel smiled in spite of himself. "And who called me?"

"The obvious choice is Raphael."

"Yeah, I guess it is obvious," Daniel said. "So what *is* going on?"

Ryan shook his head. "You realize that this comes off like a kid tattling to daddy, right?"

"I told him as much."

"And yet you called on his behalf anyway?"

Daniel said, "It seems important to head off a major conflict before it becomes irreconcilable."

"Is that what he told you?"

"Among other things."

"Look, I'm not doing this. The conflict, such as it is, is between Raphael and me. It does not bode well that his method of dealing with it is to first send his son and then to try and get daddy to scold me. Raphael misunderstands the nature of our relationship."

"You don't think you are overreacting?"

"Daniel, I don't owe you a justification for anything," Ryan said.

Daniel flinched like he'd been slapped. And then he sighed. "You are right. Let me start again. I will tell you what he said and you can comment . . . or not."

Ryan shrugged, his aggravation bubbling just under the surface.

"Raphael called me at roughly 1 a.m. my time, which means it is close to 4 a.m. your time."

Ryan did the math in his head. That put Daniel somewhere in the Pacific Time zone and it also accounted for why Raphael took the late shift to monitor the cameras. "This isn't the first time he's talked to you, is it?"

"No," Daniel said. "Your desk phone connects to the satellite uplink, so he's been calling my sat phone asking about Leona. I thought you knew."

Ryan shook his head. "No, I didn't. Not that it matters. I guess I should have expected he was checking on her. Even though the cell networks have been flooded, he kept his phone in his hand waiting for a call. Eventually, the landlines started ringing with people looking for you and he camped by the phone. He checks the message service every time he sees the light on the house phones."

Daniel nodded and said, "I didn't think when I took the sat phone that it was her only contact with Raphael. Fortunately, or unfortunately, it hasn't made a difference. No one has heard from her. Anyway, this morning Raphael called to ask if there is anyone that can work on the security system."

Ryan nodded. "He wanted someone to remote in from . . . wherever you are, right? And you told him that he already had a guy who could do technical support in the tower, right?"

"Yes and yes." Daniel said. "His reasons didn't make sense, so I pressed him, and he finally said that he has some worries. That he's unsure of your mental stability. That you locked him into the penthouse. That you are letting infected people into the tower. He is afraid for himself and his boys, and he would be afraid if Leona were there. He said you almost shot and killed Marco with a gun, but he took it away from you before you could do it."

"Ah, that is cute," Ryan said as another piece of the conversation fell into place. "That is why you looked confused while I was talking about my long and glowing review of Marco Paguero. It made no sense, because Raphael had implied that I had actually tried to kill him."

"Son, I swear you are a mind reader."

"I'm scary sometimes. I know it," Ryan said, like he was admitting he was tall. "So you were saying."

"He said he wanted to control where the infected could go in the tower, and since he didn't have access to the system, he was in danger."

Ryan said, "And you promptly pointed out to him that since both of his sons are immune to the RVCJ-2091 virus, and since it is a genetic resistance, he is likely immune, and that the only one at risk was me, right?"

Daniel said, "Ah, no, I didn't think about it. However, I want to point out that no matter how much compassion you have, it is a bad idea to let the infected into the tower. Spreading the infection is secondary. The biggest problem is 2091 violence. We had one guy go over the edge and it was mayhem. It took four people to put him down.

"We've had a riot over letting people—those in the early stages of infection—into the facility. So by comparison, Raphael's reaction has been temperate. Here, people are refusing to enter for fear they will be trapped. Many are demanding to be flown someplace else. We are scrambling to get an isolation location set up. There is a small city, a village really, about fifty miles away that we are negotiating with for living space.

"And Ryan, I shouldn't need to tell you this. You saw how violent the infected could be. You saw what it did to your sister and brother-in-law and your nieces. Plus you sat at that very desk and read the reports. You know that the purpose of the virus is social instability. You know it wrecks impulse control.

"Son, Raphael has a legitimate concern."

9

Global Infection: ≤ 29.9807%

It made sense that Daniel Ryder would default to presuming Raphael Paguero's actions were reasonable. They had been longtime friends and if Ryan understood the relationship correctly, even surrogate family. Ryan was the odd man in this dynamic, because beyond the apocalyptic circumstance—buying the Renaissance Tower from his son and reading a government dossier on Ryan's "subversive" behavior—Daniel really didn't know him. Daniel held Ryan in some esteem because buying the tower saved Richard his pregnant girlfriend's life, but if Daniel ever thought the Paguero family was in real danger from Ryan's actions, there was little doubt he would abandon all loyalty.

"Daniel, the people I let into the tower were the Blanco family, or what is left of them. Dakota is the one who was bit. Did Raphael actually tell you that he's weak as a kitten with an arm that is turning gangrenous?"

Daniel rocked back in his chair. "Oh, dear God in heaven. How is Dakota doing? Are Gus and Marie with hi—"

"And did Raphael tell you that Marie was shot full of holes less than two hundred feet from the tower front door?"

Daniel started crying. "No."

"And did Raphael tell you that Marie was trying to get back into the tower so she could get antibiotics from Dr. Beth's condo for Dakota's infection?"

"No."

"Daniel, in those frantic hours when you were trying to bug out of this tower to take your family to safety, you mentioned making an effort to compensate everyone who lived in the tower. You were trying to give the tenants money so they could flee as well. But you also told me that there were people you couldn't find, right?"

"Yes."

"Here is what I was really trying to do. I thought maybe the people you couldn't find might not have anywhere to go. I intended to honor their leases. Raphael knew that."

Daniel wiped his tears. "I was never able to talk to the Blancos. We tried, of course, but since he has so much money, so many resources, it never occurred to us to press. Frankly, I'm amazed that he didn't run to . . . well, anywhere. He's not a billionaire, but he's got more money than he could spend in three lifetimes. How is Gus?"

"He is a mess," Ryan said, "Darien is holding it together better than his father . . . at least on the outside. I suspect that the calm is a combination of suppression and shock, but if it hadn't been for Darien getting out of the van and asking for help, they would probably all be dead."

"Wait," Daniel said, "I haven't heard this part."

Ryan summarized the fight and then the discovery of Marie bleeding out in the back of the van. "And to veto the fight, I picked up Dakota and carried him into the tower. I think the military showed up maybe an hour later. I expect they would have been executed on the spot."

Daniel bowed his head. "I don't know what is wrong with me. I haven't cried this much . . . ever." He sighed. "So have you spoken to them today?"

"No, they are probably sleeping. But even if they aren't, they can't get to the penthouse. Wait, can Gus use the bio scanner?"

"No," Daniel said, "only my family and a couple of men on my security team and Raphael were set up. Speaking of the biometric . . . did Raphael get you into system?"

"Raphael asked me to do it, but I was busy at the time."

"You must get validated. If anything happens to Raphael, you are in a world of hurt."

"I've got access badges," Ryan said. "Matter of fact, I've made two dozen master badges and hidden them all over, just in case I lose one."

Daniel nodded. "Under the circumstances, that is probably a good idea. The badges will get you into about eighty percent of the building, but you need the biometric to get into the other twenty percent. And you *will* need to get into that twenty percent."

"What do you mean?" Ryan asked.

"To get set up on the biometric, someone with credentials needs to validate the new user. It is a security measure," Daniel said. "Without one of those people to validate a user, it is imposable to create a new profile. Had Raphael left with me, you would never be able to use the biometric."

"So what does it get me access to?"

"Anyplace you see a biometric reader. But the most crucial areas are the Main Distribution Frame on the thirteenth floor, primary security room on the thirteenth floor, the armory in the security barracks, also on the thirteenth floor, my private parking area, the VIP express elevator and the tower roof, which is the failover Intermediate Distribution Frame, and of course the helipad."

Ryan said, "You really did go overboard on the security."

Daniel snorted. "You only say that because you've never had a billion dollars. The word billion changes the game in ways that are hard to fathom,"

Daniel said. "If your enemies are coming to the rooftop to get into the tower, they are not coming with a lock pick."

"That sounds like paranoia."

"You are a billionaire now, Ryan. You might try on some of that paranoia."

"Daniel, I'll never see a fraction of your son's wealth. I'm struggling to hang on to this little corner of real estate I'm standing on."

"Son, in the world of the blind, the one-eyed man is a billionaire. If you survive, the tower will be invaluable and people are going to want to take it from you."

"Good point. Second good point you've made this morning," Ryan said.

"I like being right," Daniel said. "What was my first good point?"

"The part about the real purpose of the RVCJ-2091 virus was unrestrained violence. The issue is not spreading the virus, but the spread of social instability. If Dakota gets violent, it will only add to our internal problems. In that context, Raphael has a legitimate complaint."

"I told him you were a reasonable man. So now that we have that worked out, what was the issue with shooting Marco?"

"There was no *issue* with shooting Marco. I was careless. Raphael calls it a negligent discharge. I don't remember the event well enough to tell you for certain that Marco was or was not in danger." Ryan pointed to the cut and bruise on his forehead. "I pulled the trigger when the gun was near my head and the slide about knocked me out. I was an idiot, but Marco was never in any *deliberate* danger from me."

"Negligent discharge is a big deal," Daniel said. "When you pick up a gun, you must be responsible for every round that comes out of the barrel."

"Yeah, I got it. And I understand that to a bunch of military types, what I did is an unpardonable sin. I even understood why Raphael took the gun. I was a mess. I had just gotten done beating three human beings to death—no wait, or was it just two?" Ryan shook his head trying to banish the images. "Anyway, I won't go through the rest of societal collapse unarmed as penance to Pope Raphael. Negligent discharge or not, the truth is I don't answer to him."

"He didn't mention any of this," Daniel said.

"Of course not." Ryan said, shaking his head. He looked away from the camera. "The deceit in this man knows no limits . . ."

"I'm sorry I didn't hear you."

"Nothing."

"So, are you going to make sure Raphael has access?"

"This pisses me off," Ryan said. "The lockout wasn't intentional. It was a secondary effect of an immediate solution. We have been working for days inside the tower management software to pare down the electric requirements so that when the power dies, this building doesn't suddenly suck the power stored in the battery system down to nothing. In a fit of network administrator laziness, I dumped Raphael into a network admin organizational unit, so he—"

"I'm sorry. What is that?"

"An organizational unit is tech speak for a folder with permissions. Instead of applying permissions user by user and object by object, you can apply them to the folder and put objects into the folder to let it inherit permissions. It was easier to give Raphael administrator level of permissions so he didn't have to constantly ask me to make the changes to power management. Since I assumed we were on the same team, I had no concern. But that management system also controls building magnetic locks *and* . . ." Ryan paused for effect, "the elevator system."

"But why does this matter? Why was this necessary?"

Ryan took three deep breaths while he fumed. "I needed my gun back. I asked Raphael for my gun and he said no. Wrong answer.

"Instead of fighting him, I decided to take other guns. I knew the moment I picked them up he would try to stop me to make a point. The easiest way to do that was to turn off the elevators and leave me there until he thought I'd learned my lesson. Dumping Raphael into the lowest level permissions took away his trump card which is exactly the card he tried to play."

"Wait, how do you know he tried to do this?"

"Isn't that the sob story he told you? That I locked him *in* the penthouse?"

"Yes. Good point."

"Damned right, it is a good point," Ryan said, "Raphael was going to escalate the issue. And that would not have gone well for one of us."

"Okay, I get the picture."

"And Daniel, just for the record, I'm insulted that you didn't see the absurdity. Raphael crying to you that he'd been locked *into* the penthouse. That should have made you laugh. It is the penthouse for God's sake. It is twenty thousand square feet of the most plush, most friendly space in apocalyptic Pittsburgh. Oh God, the hardship. I'm such a monster."

"What did you need the guns for?" Daniel asked.

"That is what you got out of what I just said? Daniel, why is this so hard to understand? I don't owe anyone an explanation for my actions, wants or desires. If Raphael really and truly thinks me a danger, *he* is free to take *his* ball and go *home*. *He* is free to seek safety *away* from me. But he has no right to seize my weapons or physically prevent me from bearing arms. Raphael and his family are guests. Somehow that particular fact has been lost."

"Maybe he called me before you had done it," Daniel mused.

"Daniel, I understand he is your friend, but continuing to give him the benefit of the doubt is wrong. Think a minute. He called you after I was asleep, right? I had already reapplied the permissions. The badges, the bio scanners were all working correctly."

"Raphael Paguero has worked for me for almost thirty years. I'm grandpa to his kids. He's never lied to me, Ryan."

"Evidently he has."

"To what end?"

"You would have to ask him, but if I had to hazard a guess, he wants you to think I'm a bad guy."

"Why would he do that?"

"Again, you should probably ask *him*."

"I'm asking you."

"Look, I don't know what is going on in Raphael's head but here is a good guess. He disarmed me thinking that put him in charge. The fact that I demonstrated the ability to render this tower useless inspires him to think tactically, looking for a way to gain total control. He knew you would not endorse his actions . . ." Ryan paused for effect.

Daniel breathed deep. "Correct."

"Well, then there is your reason for him to lie to you."

Daniel shook his head and rubbed his eyes, the weariness coming through the video chat like a physical wave. "I can't believe . . ."

"You told me to try on paranoia? Try this on for size. He called you so he could find a way to plan a coup d'état."

"Oh, let's not jump that far down the path. Raphael is a good man."

"Well, if that biometric setup is as important as you say and Raphael realizes it is a real value, I guess we will see if he's still motivated to help me set up my profile."

10

Global Infection: ≤ 29.9807%

"You know that the purpose of the virus is social instability. You know it wrecks impulse control in the brain."

In spite of their argument, Ryan liked Daniel. In a different time and circumstance they would likely have become longtime friends, but then it was a unique circumstance that brought them together; without the circumstances, it is likely they would never have met.

Six months ago Ryan Sage was in Pittsburgh for a double funeral—Bexley Stepford, his brother-in-law, and his niece Georgia. Grief hung over the Stepford estate like a blanket. Tess Stepford, Ryan's sister, sat in a wheelchair, floating in an Ativan and Percocet stupor. Lenna, his youngest sister, looked after Tess because the Stepford servants had fled the manor. Ryan worked sixteen-hour days managing lawyers, benefactors and collectors. Bexley's death signaled blood in the water—the sharks were schooling around the $400 million Stepford estate.

But economic opportunists were not the only predators. The federal government was increasing its effort to silence Ryan Sage. The power brokers in government never let a crisis go to waste; the Stepford family meltdown was one more weapon in their arsenal. The message was passed from a president's aide to the Pennsylvania governor's office, to the Pittsburgh mayor's staff, and eventually to the police chief suggesting the PPD should take a look into Ryan Sage's "involvement" with Tess Stepford's conspiracy to kill her husband. They were co-conspirators in a plot to obtain the family fortune.

There was nothing incriminating, nothing implying probable cause and nothing even suggesting the appearance of impropriety, but equal protection under the law in American jurisprudence had all but vanished. After a not so distant presidential election, the governing cabal learned all it took to condemn a man was to mount an unrelenting campaign through the media; the evidence be damned. And of course, the evidence for Ryan's innocence was damning because the evidence that Bexley first killed Georgia and then put a gun to his head was irrefutable. But in the way of all political corruption, guns and badges are really for hire to the highest paying government puppeteer. The PPD called Ryan in for questioning.

In the spirit of political theater, the detectives thought it useful to show Ryan nanny cam footage of the attack that preceded Bexley's decision to put a bullet in Georgia's head. The tiny harmless thing that spent time on Ryan's lap, snuggling close and asking little girl questions had turned into a dervish of bloody destruction. What she had done to her sister and mother left the mind numb from brutality. The PPD purpose was to horrify, to hit Ryan deep inside his composure, to shake him so they could trap him in a misstatement. If they couldn't get him by manufacturing a murder charge, they would get him for a process crime. And since the average American committed multiple felonies a month because bureaucrats could write any capricious law they chose, and because the Constitution had deteriorated into a polite suggestion to be dismissed at a tyrant's whim, Ryan knew that every minute he was in that interview room he was in real danger.

He left Pittsburgh in an act of self-preservation. Lenna remained to look after Tess and the day-to-day Stepford drama and Ryan managed the big picture from home. And for a few weeks the arrangement seemed to work, until Tess bit Lenna and killed her surviving daughter. No one knew Tess was infected with the RVCJ 2091 virus because the general public didn't understand that aberrant violence was related to a deadly infection. It was the same infection that drove Georgia mad. It was the same infection that Bexley was trying to stop spreading when he killed his own daughter.

Lenna called Ryan from the hospital to do what she always did—bitch and moan and demand that someone else fix her world. The thirty-minute-conversation, filled with vitriol and hate, ended with Lenna's declaration that she was leaving Pittsburgh. She checked out of the hospital and flew home before Ryan could board a plane. Ignorance was a partial explanation for why BOHMeC doctors never considered holding Lenna in quarantine.

Ryan arrived back in Pittsburg and found Tess in a Duquesne hospital ward for the criminally insane and those same detectives continuing the political theater. They called him in for an interview again and showed him Stepford estate security camera footage of what Tess had done to her daughter. Again the footage had no investigative function, but it did confirm the depths to which a despotic government and a mercenary police force would stoop to achieve its corrupt ends. He told them that the only criminals in the interview room were the ones hiding behind their badges. They replied by emailing him the video files with a note that said criminal behavior was genetic. It was a public safety issue to get the genetically criminally predisposed off the streets.

The following weeks were spent visiting Tess as she descended into total insanity, planning a sparsely attended funeral for Xyla Stepford and side-stepping legal traps. So Ryan was isolated from broader cultural events until he checked out of his hotel to return home. He found the world degenerating into chaos: streets clogged, airports shut down and buses no longer running. When Daniel Ryder invaded his focus Ryan was holed up in a sub shop desperately strategizing a way to flee. Both men were prone to direct conversation, so social niceties soon moved to a deep conversation about the causes of American societal turmoil. Ryan's analysis inspired Daniel to dig deep into the violence that boiled at the edges of American culture. The government was perpetuating a hoax called African Rabies, but the truth was something else, something far more sinister.

Daniel could have dismissed Ryan's words as the ramblings of a mentally imbalanced conspiracy theorist, but instead he used his wealth and influence to tap sources at the highest levels of government both foreign and domestic. And once he asked the right questions, the people who knew the truth unburdened their souls with speed. Top secret documents poured into the Renaissance Tower, and within hours he had endless evidence of government corruption and detailed information that the RVCJ 2091 virus would likely destroy the human race. Daniel Ryder executed his plan to take his family and friends to his summer home. He credited Ryan with the information that would save the lives of many Daniel offered to let come with him.

The day Ryan Sage bought the tower from Richard Ryder was the same day he read the true story about the RVCJ-2091 infection. The Chinese created a virus to wreck the world, but they were not alone; many governments were complicit in the spread. The documents detailed a depravity that vindicated George Washington's immortalized words: government was fire and it should *never* be left to irresponsible action. The RVCJ-2091 virus was what happened when the people allowed government to indulge in irresponsibility.

Even after the Ryder family fled to points west toward the summer home, the two office fax machines ran nonstop for three days, drinking paper like desert nomads and spitting out top secret documents detailing the greatest scandal in the history of human government. Every morning and evening, Ryan pulled the documents from the machines and piled them into a box. Before the fax machines fell quiet there were ten boxes lining the credenza behind his desk.

Ryan flipped open box tops, feeling helpless. He only wanted one piece of information—the factors that determine immunity—but the data within the boxes had no order. He pulled out the first stack with the intent to organize, but worries gnawed at his concentration. His eyes strayed to the security monitors, and his thoughts rehearsed the argument he would soon have with Raph—

Raphael barged into the office. He said, "Where *es* Simone?"

11

Global Infection: ≤ 29.9820%

When Ryan and Raphael stepped through the Renaissance Tower rooftop door—a door that looked like it was designed for the White House nuclear bunker—onto the landing and saw what was happening to Simone, they were speechless.

"Tag him! Tag him!" Darien said, his transforming adolescent voice squeaking.

Dakota pump-faked. Simone dodged and spun. Dakota threw the Nerf football just before Simone touched a Doric column, drilling him in the chest.

"Out!" Darien crowed.

"He got me," Simone said and fell onto the overgrown sod, throwing his hands above his head.

The Renaissance Tower roof was a rich man's oasis. Built in the center was a horseshoe shaped fifteen-foot granite wall marking the oasis's perimeter. The walls were designed to hide the mechanical units, maintenance sheds, air handlers, satellite dishes, antenna towers, and a crane battened down underneath an industrial grade tarp. The architects had done a masterful job creating a veranda of solitude thirty stories above Pittsburgh's *hoi polloi*.

The wall was decorated with wildlife frescoes spaced between Richard Ryder's effort to create a family crest consisting of two Rs in the center of a hammer and sickle design. Planters filled with chrysanthemums, impatiens, lavender and roses were angled along the stone walkway that wound through the sod from the helipad to the glistening gold rooftop door with the double R hammer and sickle crest molded into the metal. A hot tub stood to one side of a stone path, with steam rising off the water flanked by four Horizon teak and sling chaise lounge chairs with personal shades. On the opposite side of the path was a two seat swing suspended under a dome built over narrow Doric columns for those moments when a Roman senator might choose to recline as he waited on dignitaries.

Dakota pumped his right fist. "Told you I'm deadly," he said as he adjusted the blanket on the swing over his left arm.

"You all right?" Simone said, sitting up.

"I'm good. Let's keep playing," Dakota said.

"Simone," Raphael called. "We have been looking for you."

"I left a note," Simone said, working to get Dakota tucked under the blankets. "My radio is on. Why didn't you call?"

"I do no see this note," Raphael said.

"Then how did you find us?"

"I have to ask Mr. Blanco."

"I'm in trouble no matter what I do," Simone mumbled.

"What?" Raphael asked.

"I put the note on your door."

Raphael closed his eyes and breathed deeply. "It *es* okay. You are safe. But . . ." He looked at Dakota. "He *es* here?"

Simone lowered his voice. "So Marco asked me to sit with them this morning. Dakota found out about his mom and he was crying. Well, both of them were crying a lot and I didn't know what to do. I think what Marco did worked, because his arm is doing a lot better. I thought maybe if they got outside in the sun it would be good . . . you know, to distract them. It's not like we can go out on the street so I thought about this place. They are both doing better."

"That was good thinking, Simone," Ryan said.

"What Marco did?" Raphael asked, not understanding.

"He gave him the industrial strength meds," Simone said pointing toward the IV bag hanging from the swing's upper support.

"Oh, *Madre de Dios*," Raphael breathed. "He did no do this."

"I did do it," Marco said shuffling past his father, his face haggard and sleep still hanging around the edges of his eyes like a delinquent. "My patient looks better today." He sat beside Dakota checking the IV line. "Throwing a football and IV needles don't really go together," he said, adjusting the tape holding the line in place.

"He's doing much better," Darien said. "I gave him the pain pills, and he ate. He got Simone out like five times."

Simone said, "It was like *three* times."

"Five," Dakota said. "I told you my arm was deadly."

Marco checked under the bandage on Dakota's arm. He frowned. It was still festering, but some of the flesh around the outside edge looked healthy. "We need to clean this out some more."

"Will it hurt?" Dakota asked.

"Maybe a little," Marco said. "But Dr. Beth has something to help with pain."

Darien said, "You are not going to cut off his arm, are you? I told him that is what you were talking about yesterday."

Marco shook his head. "I don't think so. We are going to hope this medicine works. I saw you flinch when I touched your arm. How long before your next pill?"

Dakota shrugged.

Darien said, "It should be at ten o'clock."

Marco checked his watch. "Almost time." He touched Darien's forehead. "He's a little hot. This is enough playing for today. Why don't you guys get him down to the condo?"

"But I want to play some more," Dakota said.

"Come on. I'm tired," Simone said. "I need to sleep."

"I'm kinda hungry," Darien said.

"Oh right," Simone said. "They don't have much food that isn't in cans. Can I take them to the penthouse?"

Ryan said, "Take them to *Mon Pierre's*. There are lots of food and juices that need to be eaten before they go bad. I think three teenage boys can make a dent."

Simone nodded. "Come on guys. The guy who used to cook in this place has some amazing leftovers." He helped Dakota walk. Darien grabbed the blankets.

"And don't make a mess," Ryan called.

"Whatever, Negligent Discharge," Simone called back as they piled the blankets onto a lumber cart where Dakota lay down. They disappeared into the tower arguing about how many times Simone was out.

Marco gave Ryan a sideways look. "Did you just turn three teenage boys loose in a kitchen and ask them not to make a mess?"

Ryan frowned. "Now that you mention it, maybe not my smartest—"

"You did this thing?" Raphael interrupted. His gaze bored through Marco with a mixture of confusion, grief and anger.

Marco shrugged. "How many battlefield amputations have you done?"

"This *es* no the point," Raphael said, his voice cracking from emotion.

"It might not be your point, but it is my point," Marco said. "I've done three amputations, and it is bloody and messy, and the screams are something I never want to hear again. And even if we get his arm off without him bleeding to death, without antibiotics, the chances of infection are high, which means we are right back where we started."

"But now we have two peoples that will die from infection," Raphael said. "You know what the medics say. The Army teaches you these things. The Rangers teach you medicines. You know you must finish antibiotics."

"I know, Poppa. But that stuff was kicking my ass. And I need to be able to operate when we have a fight. I got through all but two rounds of antibiotics, so I should be all right. The fever has gone down, and my stitches have healed, and there is no infection in my arm or hand." Marco held up his left hand showing the pink healthy flesh around the stump of his little finger. "I'll use the Z-Paks from Dr. Beth's. I will be fine."

"But he *es* infected. You know this. All you did *es* make him healthy. What happens when he can move? What then?"

"I couldn't watch this kid suffer."

Raphael's chin dropped to his chest. "I can no watch you die again. I put you in the ground once. I can no bear this twice."

A year ago, Raphael stood in Arlington National Cemetery as his wife was handed a folded flag. The official Army report said that Marco saved a platoon while fighting against Caliphate forces in Italy. And just like so many government official reports, it was a lie. Just days ago, Marco showed up at the Renaissance Tower alive—barely—with his sixteen-year-old brother Simone in tow. Marco's brief explanation was that he was immune to the RVCJ-2091 infection. This made him top-secret property of the U.S. government. They staged his death to keep him hidden.

"This *es* your fault," Raphael said, wagging his finger at Ryan.

Ryan should have seen that accusation coming and for a snappy rejoinder he said, "What?"

"If you do no bring them into this tower—"

Ryan laughed. "Raphael, stop. Don't embarrass yourself."

"You speak to me this way?" Raphael demanded.

"Raphael, how did you forget that the only reason you even have your sons is because I also saved them? Remember? You couldn't be bothered to listen when you thought I wanted to save some stray kid off the street? And that kid turned out to be Simone. Remember?"

Raphael's mouth opened and then it closed, his hands clenched at his thighs. "Would you have given the boy these antibiotics?" he demanded.

Ryan said, "His name is Dakota. And it never crossed my mind that Marco should do what he did."

"See!" Raphael said like he won the argument. "He would no do this thing. I would no do this thing."

"Poppa, it is already done."

"You must stop the IV and take the last for yourself."

"Poppa, I'm not going to do that," Marco said. "And you need to stop worrying. I will be all right. Everything happens for a reason," he said. "Maybe this is why the antibiotics made me sick. Maybe that is why I stopped. Maybe that is why the looters came. So I would have them later for him. Right, Mr. Sage? You saved him from the street, and I can save him from his infection."

Ryan shook his head. "Don't drag me into this, please."

"You are already in this," Marco said.

"Fine. Then honestly, I think you should do what Raphael said. Take back the IV I was going to start researching—"

"You are thinking of putting them back on the street?" Marco asked.

Ryan shook his head. "Marco, I didn't get to finish. I am not going to put them on the street, but the problem I have is you. I was trying to find the factors of immune—"

"Me? How am I the problem?"

Ryan was beginning to think that Paguero interruption was hereditary. He paused until no one spoke. "The fact that you and your brother are immune is the problem. I'd rather not kill someone who is immune. If there was no immunity, then Raphael is right. I have brought someone very dangerous into the tower, and he should be put down."

"But you said there was no danger last night?" Raphael said.

"No, I said that I was the one at risk for infection. But I forgot about the purpose of the virus. Daniel, of course, reminded me of that this morning."

"You speak to Daniel?" Raphael asked as if this was news.

"Raphael, don't pretend you didn't know about Daniel. He told me you asked him to intervene. Let's not add more deceit to the list."

"Wait," Marco said. "You have both been talking to Daniel? What did he say about the virus? What was its purpose?"

Ryan frowned. "I thought you had been working with the government on the virus for the last year."

Marco's gaze shifted like he was looking into the past. Finally he said, "No, I . . . The work I did . . . it was top secret. I wasn't told any details about the virus. You say you have a box of reports?"

Raphael nodded. "Daniel, he have much power with peoples. That *es* how he know to leave."

"So, now we are confronted with the dilemma," Ryan said. "If there is a chance that Dakota is immune, then I'm right to give him a chance to heal."

"And if you are wrong," Raphael said, pulling Marco toward him in an awkward hug, "you will have killed my son."

12

Global Infection: ≤ 29.9877%

Ryan intended to leave the tower roof, walk down four flights of stairs and address the Dakota infection issue with Gus. However, the Paguero family IV antibiotic drama delayed him until well after lunch. When détente was finally called, all three men made the trip to the 26th floor.

Ryan raised his hand to knock when the door burst open.

"Where the hell have you been?" Gus said, "I've been waiting for hours and you didn't come till now?"

Raphael and Marco exchanged looks.

"Uh . . ." Ryan said. "Good afternoon, Gus. Nice to see you, too. Would you fill us in on this meeting that no one but you seems to remember having?"

"We need to go outside and get Maria," Gus said, his eyes wide and his brown hair a rolling mess. "We can't leave her out there."

"Slow down please," Ryan said, "Take a breath and tell us what you are talking about."

"Marie," Gus said like he was talking to a toddler. "You remember her? My wife. The woman who died last night? She's not here. *You* left her down there. And *you* locked the elevators and the stairwell. I couldn't—"

"Did you forget that she *es* dead?" Raphael said, his hard eyes radiating disdain.

"If you had tried harder, she wouldn't—"

"Gus, stop." Ryan said. "You need to get yourself together. I understand your pain, but you—

"No, you don't!" Gus insisted. "You don't understand what I'm feeling."

The images of his dead nieces and his sisters, Tess and Lenna, flashed across Ryan's mind. His compassion vanished. "Bullshit!" he said. "Where do you get the notion that your pain is somehow entirely unique in the whole history of the world? Now calm down."

"But I loved her so much! And she's down on the street all alone," Gus said, his voice tremulous and broken.

Ryan said. "We've all lost people—"

"We need to go get her. She deserves better. She can't stay on the street like this. What will people do to her?"

"Gus, you need to hear me. There is nothing you can do for her body."

"We could put Marie into the grocery store refrigerator. They have those downstairs, right? We can put her in there and she will keep until I can find a way to give her a proper burial."

Ryan hadn't thought about the grocery on the ground floor since he bought the tower. It was originally scheduled to open about now had the world remained normal. Who knew what was down there. "Gus, while it was probably true there is a freezer in the grocery; Marie's body is not coming into this tower."

Gus pushed Ryan against the hallway wall, throttling his shirt at the collar. "We are not leaving her on street. We are going to go get her. We are going to get her now!"

"Hey! Hey! Gus, stop!" Marco said, stepping between them.

Ryan looked into Gus' eyes. "Gus, stop. Please. I understand that you are hurting. But you can't—"

"No, you listen to me," Gus said. "It is unacceptable for you to—"

"No, Gus. The only unacceptable thing is for you to use force to make me do what I've already said I won't do."

Gus pushed Ryan harder against the wall. "You *are* going to help me bring her into this tower so she is safe from those things. You *are* going to help her more than you did last night. She wouldn't be dead if you had helped her. Since you failed, you *are* going to make sure she gets a proper buri—"

"Come on, Gus," Marco said, loosening the man's grip on Ryan's collar. "Just relax, I'm sure we can work something out."

"The only thing to work out is you are all going outside to get Marie!" Gus snarled. "You are going with me now!"

Ryan said, "Gus, you have about thirty seconds to let me go. You are being unreasonable. There will be no such thing as a 'proper' burial."

"First, you want me to cut off my son's arm," Gus said, "and now you want me to leave my wife on the street. You are a monster!"

Ryan kept his gaze fixed and even. "Twenty seconds."

Marco did a double take at Ryan and then stepped back.

"What are you going to do to me?! What?" Gus said shoving Ryan into the wall again. "What are you going to do that hasn't already been done? Just kill me. Kill me now!"

"Dad!" Darien said as he ran into the hall. "What are you doing? Mom is dead. And you can't go back out to the street."

"You can't keep me here," Gus shouted, pushing his forearm into Ryan's chest. "You can't keep me locked up."

Ryan sighed and nodded. "Gus, time' up." Abruptly, he rolled his hand through Gus' arms, twisting harshly and violently, slamming Gus face first into the tan painted drywall. Ryan held Gus' right arm in a joint lock behind his back. "Gus, please stop fighting me. I know you are frustrated. I know you are upset, but this can only get worse."

"You can't keep me here!" Gus said, thrashing. "You can't keep me away from Marie!"

Ryan pulled a security badge out of his pocket. "Gus, I'm not keeping you here. This security badge will get you through every stairwell door and down to the street."

"But what are we going to do with Marie's body once we get her?"

"Gus, there is no *we*," Ryan said. "There is only you. *We* are not going to do anything with Marie's body. *We* are not going to get the body and *we* are not bringing that body inside this tower. It is important that you understand the distinction."

"But why won't you help me?" Gus said, thrashing.

Ryan tightened the joint lock until Gus went still. "Gus, there is nothing we can reasonably, safely do to help. You are free to do as you see fit, except bring her body into this tower. Do you understand?"

Gus paused for a long minute and then said, "Yes."

Ryan held up the badge. "Do you want this badge?"

"Yes."

Ryan let go and held out the card.

Gus turned, took the card and started rubbing his arm. "But I need you all to come with me. I don't have a weapon."

"Gus, again, we will not be going out to the street," Ryan said, looking at Raphael and Marco. They both frowned and shook their heads no.

"I can't go out there without a weapon," Gus said, his anger rising again.

"Darien," Raphael said, "do you have a baseball bat?"

"Yes, I have a Louisville slugger that I used for Little League."

"Get it pore favore?"

Darien ran into the condo.

"You want me to go out there with a bat?!" Gus said.

Raphael took three hard strides and stopped, his nose inches from Gus' face. *Muchacho tonto.* I want you to get your shit together and stop this craziness. You have two boys that need a man and they have this little boy throwing a tantrum."

Darien came running back, two bats in his hands. "Here," he said, handing one to Gus. "I'll go with you to get Mom." He held the bat on his shoulder like he was waiting for a fastball over the middle.

Gus clutched the bat, his mind trying to run out of the cul-de-sac of crazy. "You have to stay here. . . . You have to be safe. . . . You can't . . . I mean . . ."

"But I can help you," Darien said.

"Who will watch Dakota?" Gus asked.

"We won't be gone long, will we?" Darien said. "We just want to say goodbye, right? We are coming right back up. I don't want to leave home."

"I . . . we . . ." Gus dropped the bat and pulled Darien into his arms, crying.

Ryan's phone chimed at the same time that Raphael's phone gave the *Star Trek's*, Enterprise red alert.

They both tapped through their phone apps until they got to the security feed.

"*Mierda!*" Raphael swore, "Do no go outside. If you do go out, you and your boy will die."

13

Global Infection: ≤ 29.9878%

Raphael and Marco were a swirl of activity in the penthouse foyer, donning tactical gear, loading ammunition and slinging rifles. Ryan was given the job of waking Simone from his slumber in the master suite. Simone barked and snarled until Ryan told him that he might have to shoot people. Simone rolled out of bed and into his gear with admirable speed and was standing beside his father, locked and loaded.

"You can stay or you can go, but you will no have a weapon," Raphael said, pausing at the penthouse door.

"You want me to go into a fight without a gun?" Ryan asked.

"I do no want you to shoot me in the back," Raphael said.

"I won't shoot—"

"This *es* no argument," Raphael said. "Stay or go, but you will have no gun."

"Neg Dis!" Simone said, crooking his finger with a smirk.

Ryan looked at Simone like he was a bug. "What?"

"It's your nickname," Simone said. "Negligent Discharge." And he crooked his finger again like he was pulling the trigger.

Ryan opened his mouth to offer a snappy comment and then remembered the primary rule of adulthood—never argue with the teenage retarded. He looked into Raphael's coal-black eyes. "We will talk about this. You don't get veto power, but now is not the time. And I will be damned before I let you defend this tower alone." He stepped toward the door.

"Grab those two ammo cans and this bag of magazines," Marco said, nodding toward the items on the marble floor.

"So I'm a pack mule?"

"Your job is to load until the ammo runs out," Marco said with a shrug. "Then it won't matter what you are. We will probably all be dead."

Five soldiers kept a vigil at the intersection of First Avenue and Smithfield looking north south, east and west. This is what the security cameras recorded and why the system sent out a notification. Then three more soldiers joined, then four more and then two by two they kept coming.

The Pagueros took up positions inside the wrecked Reissuance Tower lobby behind anything solid. The goal, Raphael explained, was snipe at anything trying to come through the door for as long as it took. A protracted siege might make the soldiers go somewhere else. That was the plan until the numbers grew from squad strength to platoon strength.

"*Mierda!*" Raphael swore.

"Do we just surrender?" Ryan asked. "It is better than dying, right?"

"We already fight for this tower. We will no stop," Raphael said. "Do you have those magazines loaded?"

Ryan did not have them loaded and he felt like an idiot. He'd opened the ammo can the moment they had gotten to the lobby. He loaded three magazines and went to open the next box of ammo and the bullets were not the same size. The rounds in the first ammunition box had .223 stamped on the top. These rounds inside the box were much smaller and had .22 LR printed on the packages. For a frantic minute, Ryan dug through the bag thinking there must be a different magazine to load.

"Uh . . . No, I haven't finished loading the magazines."

"You need to hurry the fuck up," Marco said. "You see those soldiers? I guarantee they have plenty of ammo."

"Look, I can't fin—"

"Shhhhh!" said Raphael. "You load magazines and do no talk."

"Yeah, Neg Dis, they can hear you," Simone said and crooked his finger.

"Look! At! Me!" Ryan snapped. "This bullet," he said holding up a .22 LR, "does not go in this magazine. I'm not a gun guy, so maybe there is a trick. But these bullets do not go in this clip."

"What?" Marco said, scrambling to the ammo cans."Fuck!" he said as he rooted to the bottom of the can like a pig after a truffle. "Fuck! Fuck! Fuck!" he said as he snapped open the second ammo can. "Fuck!" He closed the lid and ran his finger over .223 stenciled on the lid. He opened the can back up and started rooting again. "Fuck!"

"Shhhhh," Raphael hissed. "They will hear."

Marco slumped to the ground. Then he looked at Ryan. "Run back to the penthouse and get the other cans." He held up a .223 bullet. "Make sure they look like this."

Ryan turned to crawl back toward the stairwell.

"Do no move," Raphael said. "They are coming."

And for a heart-stopping minute, the Pagueros focused on repelling an invasion.

The captain gave a command and the platoon moved out: It headed east down First Avenue . . . away from the tower.

And for thirty seconds Ryan, Raphael, Marco and Simone stood in the lobby blinking at each other like a dog with a new bowl. Then Raphael led them onto the narrow streets, slinking between cars and hiding behind vans until they confirmed that the streets were empty. The trash swirled in dust devils, and the streetlights blinked through their primary colors while the four men watched down First Avenue for a glimpse of movement.

Simone broke the silence. "Where did they all go?"

"That way," Marco said, like his brother was dim.

Simone rolled his eyes. "*Muchacho tonto*. I'm talking about the bodies from last night," he said sweeping his arms wide. "Do you see the people we killed last night?"

But no one gave an answer because just to the east gunfire filled the Golden Triangle with the sounds of war.

Ryan dove behind a car, sprawling on the asphalt.

Marco glanced down. "That is nowhere near us."

"Of course it's not," Ryan mumbled "Because if they had been shooting at us, I would have looked smart."

Raphael and Simone sprinted to the construction site just across First Avenue, a high- rise under construction by the Molitor Group, whose progress halted when the world went sideways. The building site was a little more than a deep hole with four levels of super structure peeking over the top of 25-foot-tall concrete barriers—barriers that were similar to the Jersey wall often seen dividing traffic. When construction stopped, Daniel Ryder lined the building site with Alaska barriers along Smithfield and Boulevard of the Allies, and he used oceangoing steel shipping containers to block off the First Avenue and protect the valuables within.

Simone climbed the ladder integrated into the shipping containers.

"Report," Marco said into the maintenance radio on his left shoulder.

Simone keyed his mic. "Can't see anything from here. I'd have to be higher. You want me to climb up there?" he asked, pointing toward the crane used to build multistory buildings.

"Yes," Raphael said and jogged west past the job site to a concrete-walled area locked behind a steel gate. He fumbled with his keys until he found the right one.

The gunshots grew dim like distant pops behind a pillow.

Simone ran through the gate to the base of the crane and scampered up the ladder. He stopped halfway. "They are coming back," he said quietly into the radio.

"Come down," Raphael said, "before they see."

"No, freeze!" Marco said. "They will see the movement. Just go still and don't look at them."

"Yes," Raphael said. "And turn your radio down."

Simone wrapped himself into the ladder and dropped his chin to his chest.

The area at the base of the crane was surrounded by fifteen-foot concrete walls on three sides. The west side was the exterior wall of the Renaissance

Tower's parking garage. A switchback walkway, like the walkways in football stadiums designed to give Americans an easy path to the upper decks, rose from the ground to the parking garage top level.

Raphael swiped his security badge at a security pad and the switchback entrance gate swung open. They ascended the switchback until they could see the platoon moving west on First Avenue past the *Banco Federal* headquarters to the rally point on Smithfield. Raphael and Marco pressed deep into the shadows while watching the soldiers through the security fence designed to keep the motivated from climbing into the switchback and bypassing the security gate.

No one spoke. No one moved

14

Global Infection: ≤ 29.9879%

The platoon loitered at the First Avenue intersection. The captain stepped away from the main group and talked to three other soldiers privately for ten minutes. A few soldiers moved toward the tower entrance and peeked inside, but a sergeant called them back, scolding them for hunting trouble. Finally the four seemed to come to an agreement and the order was given to mount up. JLTV and Humvees started and the captain bellowed, "Move out!" The vehicles rolled west, past the Pittsburgh Post Gazette, to I-279 and into the Fort Pitt Tunnel. The city fell silent.

"They are gone," Simone said, his voice crackling in the radio.

"Copy that," Marco said. "Meet us at the top."

"Copy that," Simone said.

Ryan, Marco and Raphael walked up the switchback and Raphael badged through the last gate. The parking garage's top level was a vast slab of concrete lined with six "K" Line shipping containers and sundry building supplies hastily dumped in piles. Raphael moved to the building's edge, scanning the streets below to the west. Marco did the same to the east and then as if choreographed, they did a simultaneous sweep on opposite sides.

The switchback security gate buzzed and Simone ran toward his brother, breathing heavy, sweating and smiling as if he'd just won the World Series. "They're gone," he said, pointing toward the mountains. "I did great, didn't I, Marco? I went still just like you said. They didn't see me."

Marco let his rifle relax in its sling as he regarded his brother, his face suddenly etched with anger. "Glad you listened . . . this time," he said.

Simone's face fell. "What? What do you mean this time?"

"What the heck just happened?" Ryan said. "Where'd the military go and what were they shooting at?"

"That was an extermination," Marco said.

"I don't understand," Ryan said.

"The Allegheny Correctional Facility is the only thing down that street worthy of military attention," Marco said.

"Marco, what do you mean . . . this time?" Simone asked. "I did what you said."

Raphael said, "They do no release criminals into the population after total loss natural disasters. The jails are purged."

Ryan nodded remembering research for articles he'd written some years ago. The public policy required that inmates in areas that suffered a disaster and could not remain in the place of their incarceration were to be moved to locations outside of the affected area. But if the disaster was too widespread and there was no place to put the criminals, some people advocated public policy that required the extermination of prison populations. The last thing survivors of a national catastrophe wanted was a bunch of violent criminals roaming the countryside. Ryan wrote a series of articles detailing the singular problem with this public policy: seventy five percent of America's prison populations were nonviolent offenders.

"Why won't you tell me what you mean?" Simone said. "I did what you said and it worked."

Marco looked at Simone hard. "Because I'm an inch from ripping off your head, and I am trying I cool off."

"What the hell did I do?"

Marco said to Ryan, "Would you please go back and get the ammo cans and magazines and meet us in the penthouse?"

Ryan lugged the ammo and magazine bag into a room to the right of the penthouse foyer that was filled with museum grade paintings, sculptures and antique furniture from some period of history that made them ridiculously expensive. The room was designed to impress the socialist wine-and-cheese crowd as they mingled and murmured their contempt for capitalist excess just before they sat down to a fifty-thousand-dollar-a-plate, invitation only fundraiser to save the wild-eyed newt. But today the room was transformed into an armory. Spread across every flat antique surface lay some form of weapon and ammunition. Ryan dropped the ammunition cans on an antique table.

"Why in the hell have markings *on* the ammo can if you are not going to put the correct ammo *in* that can?" Marco raged.

Simone slouched in a wingback chair, mute.

Marco continued. "This is the ammunition can that Mr. Sage was so kind to retrieve. I want you to notice the black stencil on the outside says 2 2 *3*," he said, pointing to the green box. "Now notice the ammunition in the box says .22 LR."

Simone huffed. "I didn't see the three."

"That is the problem," Marco said. "There is a three on the ammo can. See 2-2-3. The problem is when you look inside the can what we see is just 22." He held up a box of .22 long rifle ammunition. "See, it is *missing* a three. The reason to label the can is so that when you have to run into battle, you grab the right ammo. Why the fuck is this hard to understand?"

Ryan tried to be inconspicuous as he slumped into a matching wingback chair but he couldn't hold back the sigh that squeezed out: Ammunition was heavy and he was not a good pack mule.

Damned Italians.

"You haven't been here," Simone snapped. "You don't know. You were dead. You weren't king shit anymore!"

Marco closed his eyes and shook his head. "Well, there you have it. The ammo is in the wrong can because I was dead. Brilliant!" he said. "So, we are sitting on thirty thousand rounds of Eley Tenex Ultimate .22 ammunition which would be fucking fantastic if we were competing in the goddamned Olympic Biathlon!"

Most kids play baseball, basketball, or football, but the Paguero brothers had long ago decided that their sport of choice was shooting. They traded in their balls, bats and bases for lowers, barrels and triggers. From the time they were old enough to hold up the end that goes bang, the Paguero boys had been delivering lead into targets.

And where do young marksmen go to practice when the federal government infringes on the right to keep and bear arms?

They find an old manufacturing plant and set up a secret shooting range.

What do they do when the federal government seeks to outlaw ammunition? They apply for a federal sporting waiver that lets competition shooters obtain match grade bullets. Three-gun shooting was built around handguns, shotguns, and carbines requiring competitors to navigate courses under time constraint. Before Marco went into the army to use his talents to fight Caliphate forces, he signed a contract with Eley Tenex and then his brother Timoteo—the next brother in the Paguero lineage—followed in his footsteps and got a sponsorship from CCI. They abused their sponsors and reloading suppliers to fill up their ammunition stockpile.

A week ago, Marco found Simone hiding in their secret gun range, exhausted, and scared. Three months prior, Simone Paguero was bit by a schoolmate that went mad during lunch. Simone decided that he was going to turn into a zombie. Everyone thought him crazy, but before he would be publicly vindicated, Simone ran away. By the time he realized he was not going to turn into a walking nightmare, he returned to the Paguero Pittsburgh home to find that it had been ransacked and Raphael was gone. Fearing that his father was hurt, he spent days going to hospitals, but found them beehives of chaos with no record of Raphael. He called Miami, Florida trying to locate his mother, but neither she nor his brothers, Timoteo and Lucas, answered the phone. He thought he was alone in the world.

Marco, almost dead from poorly healing human bites, found Simone curled up in his sleeping bag, deep in the bowels of their practice range. It was then they thought to find Daniel Ryder in the Renaissance Tower.

They loaded up a truck with ammunition and guns, strapped on tactical gear and fought their way into Pittsburgh's Golden Triangle. On that day they found Daniel and they were reunited with their father. But today Marco discovered they lost their ammunition.

Simone slouched farther into the wingback chair. "We left ammunition there remember? We didn't have enough room, and you were too tired to load it up? We can go back and get it. What is the big deal?"

"I was too tired? Is that how you remember it?" Marco held up his left arm and showing ragged flesh and a missing pinky finger. "I was too tired? Okay, genius, when we go back to get the other bullets, what are we going to fight with?" he asked. "Harsh language? These bullets will do little more than piss someone off."

Harsh language . . . that is a pretty good line, Ryan thought. His mind wandered to the array of art. He smiled as he thought about the decorator's heart attack upon seeing these priceless treasures used like a Bill Goodman's gun show display. Ryan didn't know the price of such things, but considering the penthouse décor theme was Marxist ostentatious, he would be willing to bet that the furniture alone was worth enough to buy an armory three times the size of the current exhibit.

"What are you smiling about, Neg Dis!" Simone snapped. "You can't laugh at me."

Ryan looked at Simone then back at the table full of guns. He opened his mouth to explain and then closed it. He shrugged but he kept smiling. The thought of some fussy art dealer using a hanky to wipe up gun oil made him want to howl.

Raphael leaned against an antique table, its frame groaning and swaying under the strain. "So how many rounds *es* this?" he said, nodding at the ammo cans.

"Rough count," Marco said, "about two thousand .223, 360 rounds of 9mm, 411 rounds of .45, 930 rounds of 7.62 and fifty double zero buck."

"That doesn't seem too bad," Ryan said.

"That is because you don't know anything, Neg Dis," Simone said pulling an invisible trigger.

"It *es* not much," Raphael agreed. "We use almost 3,000 rounds in three fights. This *es* barely enough for one more fight."

"Okay then. Yeah, Marco is right. We are in trouble" Ryan said.

"Shut up!" Simone snapped.

Ryan smiled and went back to looking at a large painting that was all white in the center with a strip of indiscriminate color perfectly painted around the outside edge. The placard under the painting read, Sam Francis, *Untitled, "The painting reflects Francis' interest in silence and space generated by the color white."*

Silence? That isn't what it reflects, Ryan thought.

"I have more 7.62 in my apartment downstairs," Raphael said. "Maybe 300 rounds."

“And all you had to do was pick up the fucking guns on the street,” Marco said.

“All right already,” Simone said. “Get off my back! I’m tired of everyone laughing at me.”

“I’m not laughing,” Marco said, “This is my sergeant, ‘You’re a shitbird’ voice. I even told you to check the cans to make sure they had the right ammo, and you gave me shit. You told me the labels were right. We could have been sitting on fifteen thousand rounds of .223. We could have had a fucking .50 caliber mounted on a Jellytelly. We could have—”

“Marco, enough!” Raphael commanded. “Stop bickering.”

“This is not bickering,” Marco said. “This is me, a half an inch from ape shit.”

Raphael raised his hands in surrender. “Please, Marco, please. We must no be this way.”

Ryan shifted in the wingback chair wondering how anyone ever thought it was a good design. In all the years he’d sat in a wingback chair, he’d never found one that was comfortable. But somehow, for the moment the discomfort didn’t matter. He wasn’t in this fight. He wasn’t the one under fire from the Paguero gods of war . . . until he was.

“Well, Neg Dis is not going to need any bullets because he can’t have a gun,” Simone said. “So that is more ammunition for us.”

“Could you leave me out of this, please?” Ryan said. “And just for the record, my days of going around unarmed are at an end.”

Raphael leveled a long gaze at Ryan. Ryan looked back, impassive. Finally Raphael said, “How much ammo *es* at the range?”

Marco sat on an antique that groaned and shifted under his weight. “I don’t know. I was too out of it to count . . . but at least another twenty cans and maybe half a skid. But that assumes they are full.” He rubbed the back of his neck. “We should have grabbed that ammo when we had the chance, but I was so weak I didn’t have the energy to repack the truck.”

“How about down where the Molitor security team lived?” Ryan said. “Daniel said there was an armory down there.”

Raphael nodded. “That *es* a good idea. We will look now.”

Marco said, “And while we are down there, let’s get some different tables. These old things are crap.”

15

Global Infection: ≤ 29.9999%

Raphael went into craftsman mode once the decision was made to turn the mini art gallery into an armory. And Ryan knew they were in for a prolonged project when he said, “Let’s just store the paintings and statues in an empty bedroom.”

Raphael looked at Ryan like he was a true philistine and said, “These works suffer enough indignity. Everyone know that you do no display a Pat Steir’s *Border Lord* beside Nhat Tran’s Urushi art *Unexpected Compromise*. We will treat these with respect.”

For the next two hours, they fastened paintings into specialized crates and then transported them to a climate-controlled room packed with enough artwork to fill a wing at the Louvre.

Halfway through the project, Gus came to the penthouse clutching Dakota in his arms and Darien walking behind. With a wan smile, he said that it was a friendly neighbor visit, but the reality was Dakota had spiked a fever, Darien wanted someone to play with and Gus didn’t want to be alone. They set up a place for Dakota to sleep in a nearby room. Gus divided his time between helping with the art room-to-armory project and fussing over Dakota like a mother hen. Darien pitched in doing whatever Raphael asked. Marco found saline in the security barracks and started an IV, fearing that Dakota’s fever was exacerbated by dehydration.

At dinner Simone suggested that Gus and the boys remain in the penthouse. Gus made the simple observation, “I won’t be able to hide Dakota if things go bad.” Marco seconded the motion. It was better to have everyone keeping an eye on Dakota’s fever. Ryan saw the logic and gave his consent. Raphael relented as if it was his decision.

By nightfall Simone settled into one of the far-flung penthouse entertainment rooms to play a console game. Marco collapsed into a recliner to watch a romantic comedy while occasionally checking on Dakota sleeping fretfully on a nearby couch. Raphael and Darien sat at the kitchen table playing chess during an ongoing Spanish lesson.

Gus vanished. Ryan searched the penthouse but didn't find Gus until he reviewed the security cameras: Gus was standing on the helipad. Ryan grabbed his iGlass, exited the penthouse and badged through a door just past the security desk. He walked up the incline to a security gate.

The Renaissance Tower brochure touted thirty floors of prime business and residential space, but the tower was, in actuality, thirty-two floors. Like most high-rise buildings in the twenty-first century, superstition and science collided on the architect's drawing table. Tenants didn't want to inhabit a thirteenth floor, and architects couldn't build a fourteenth floor without something in between. The solution was to banish an entire floor from existence and remove the number thirteen from the elevator bank. The tower's thirty-second floor was the level directly above the penthouse. It was the home of data network infrastructure, mechanical rooms, the art storage vault, the tower maintenance office, and a seemingly endless succession of security gates. Ryan badged through gate after gate after gate until he got to the rooftop door. He stepped behind a small security desk and tapped through the security interface. The blast door slid open, and Ryan stepped into a pleasant spring night.

"So I guess this means that you are not afraid of heights," Ryan said as he walked across the helipad. Photovoltaic landing lights ringing the pad's outer edge gained brightness as the last sliver of sunlight fell behind the western mountains. They spilled their light across double R hammer and sickle design.

Gus stood on the southeast corner of the helipad looking down at the street, occasionally lifting his eyes to stare across the Monongahela River. He was standing very close to the edge, suicide close. "Marie loved to go mountain climbing," Gus said without turning around. "She would love this view. She would have her toes hanging over the edge. She was fearless. She taught me how to climb. Can you believe that the first time we went climbing I peed my pants?" He shook his head. "A grown man peeing his pants."

"I'm about to pee my pants just standing here," Ryan said, still a good twelve feet from the helipad edge. "Could I persuade you to come over here?"

Gus turned to Ryan and tried to smile, but the message from his brain capsized in a wave of grief. "Her favorite place to climb was Lumpy Ridge in Colorado. She always said she wanted her last hours to be spent climbing a mountain. I was supposed to take her ashes and let them go at her favorite view."

"And I'm sure you would have done that for her if you could," Ryan said. "I can tell you loved her very much."

Gus looked back at the street, his head bowed. "Love? She's dead because I didn't love her enough."

Causeless self-recrimination was one of humanity's greatest vices, evidence of a profound conceit, and totally impossible to argue with. Ryan said nothing.

"She's dead because I couldn't keep it in my pants. God is punishing me," Gus said. He wept quietly. "I'm so sorry, Marie. I'm so sorry."

God was punishing him by killing Marie?

This was where vice crawled aboard the crazy train and chugged into the rabbit hole after Alice. Nothing but the vilest form of self-absorbed indulgence could account for a logic that said God destroyed the innocent to recompense the guilty. Ryan couldn't decide which was the greater monstrosity—a God who would actually do such a thing or a mind that thought such causality represented cosmic justice.

Ryan had to derail this train. "Gus? Gus? Come over here by me, please. I'd feel better away from the edge."

"Do you know I didn't even love her?"

"Marie? You didn't love your wife?"

But Gus didn't seem to hear. "She was beautiful and fantastic in bed. I respected her, I guess, but I didn't love her. I didn't even feel sorry for her even though she married an ass. Her husband . . . God, he was a piece of work. That is why I didn't mind doing what we did. He was such a fucking dick, saying I made my money on the backs of the poor. He was such a fucking hypocrite. He had money and he didn't work. I worked. I worked my whole life to get what I had. Third generation immigrant and I rose to the top one percent. And I'm the bad guy? Fuck you! Just fuck you!" Gus shouted into the night, his fist beating against his thigh.

"Gus, I'm struggling to follow—" Ryan said.

"The sick joke is I even met her because of Marie. Marie was always having these parties. Fundraisers for some cause. She loved giving my money away. She said it was my duty to give back, as if I had taken something that wasn't mine. And I met her at one of these fund raisers, her and her asshole husband. And those long legs! God, those legs! That should have been the end of it. I should have just been content to look at those legs in that dress. I wish to God that had been the end of it. But she had two girls. Beautiful girls and my boys loved playing with them." Gus looked at Ryan with a tight smile and said, "Do you know how many quickies you can have during a play date?" he sighed and looked at the sky. "What kind of parent am I?"

Ryan was struggling to picture any woman thinking this unshaven, rumpled, pitiful man was desirable. "Whatever happened between you and Mar—"

"I finally persuaded Marie to go to our place in Colorado. I wanted to get away. I wanted to leave Pennsylvania. There was so much shit happening in Pittsburgh. That was my excuse. The riots and the looting is what I told her. But I was really trying to get *her* out of my head. We were going to take a break. She was leaving with her husband. He was going to speak at some conference. And I just wanted to get out of here. Marie complained that the cabin was too small. As if you can call four thousand square feet small," Gus said, his voice derisive. "But I loved Marie when she said yes. I loved her like the first day I saw her. I saw her on Broadway. It was the opening night for *Cats*. God, the way she carried herself, the poise." He closed his eyes, remembering some distant memory. "You gave up dancing for me. I wrecked that dancer body with children, but you wanted me more than dancing. And what did I do to you? What did I do to you?" Gus took a step toward the edge of the helipad.

"Gus! Gus!" Ryan said, taking a step. "Hey, come back this way. Come on, man. You are giving me a heart attack."

Gus stopped. "You don't think I deserve to die?"

"You are not the first man to be unfaithful. You are not the first man to make bad choices. The better question is why do you think what you did is worthy of death? And more important, you need to think beyond this moment. You have two boys who need their father."

Gus breathed deep and looked east down the Monongahela toward the smoldering ruins of South Side Flats. "Raphael is a good man. He would take care of my boys."

"No, Gus, stop! You don't get to do this. You don't get to check out on your boys. Marie gave up her dancer body for you and your boys. You can at least give up your self-pity for them."

"I couldn't even find a pilot to fly us back here," Gus said. "I thought it was a sign that we should stay in Colorado. But Marie begged me to come back. I'm not even rated for that goddamned plane. I about killed us on landing. And you know what is really sick? Marie thought it was a sign that we were doing the right thing . . . that because we lived, we were where the universe wanted us. Can you believe that shit? The universe wants us in Pittsburgh because it is our moral duty to suffer with the people. She never knew that I broke the landing gear. I knew the moment we hit the ground that we were stuck."

Marie got exactly what she was looking for. Ryan thought, but even as the words went through his mind, he heard the nagging voice of his mother demanding he keep those words tucked inside his head. "Gus, come on. You can talk all you want over by the swing. I'll listen to you all night if you want."

"You think talking will fix this?" Gus said, walking toward Ryan. His fist was clenched like he was going to swing.

Ryan kept stepping back until they were standing in the middle of the Richard Ryder crest.

"Do you?!" Gus raged. "Do you think *talking* will fix this?"

Ryan paused until Gus simmered. Then he said, "The only way to fix anything is to stop and think."

"This is a world gone mad. How can we live like this?"

"You are right. We can't, because no one is thinking."

"Thinking? How can you think in *this*? How? How can you think in *this*? How can you think that *this* is worth saving? That life is worth living!?"

"Gus, here's the problem. If you need persuaded that living is good, then the moment I'm not around you will find another time to come back up here and jump. I don't want that responsibility, and I am not asking for the job. You have to want to live. You have to find a reason that keeps you from the roof edge. Maybe find this woman and her two girls. She obviously meant something to you. You obviously meant something to her. Maybe live long enough to find out if she has survived. Maybe you can help her and her girls. Or maybe live because life is a better choice.

"I don't know what else to say. If it were just you, I would politely walk off this helipad and see if you were still around tomorrow, but it isn't just you. You have two sons who need a father."

"I have one son." Gus snorted. "And another who is going to turn into a monster."

Ryan nodded. "Maybe it is true that Dakota will become a monster. And we have to figure out what to do if he does. But you also have Darien. And he will need a father."

Gus nodded and then turned to look into the night. "Darien is a good kid. He's strong. He takes after his mother. I wonder if he knows he can see the van from here. Maybe I should show him."

"You have to be alive to show him. So let's go sit down. It's a nice night—"

"You want me to kill him, don't you?" Gus said.

"Kill who?"

"Dakota. You want me to kill him. You have no idea how hard that would be. You don't have kids."

"Gus, if I wanted that, I could have left you on the street."

"Good point. So what do you want?"

"Uhhh . . . how to say this? Dakota is little danger when he is weak but if he gets stronger . . ."

"Assuming he has this infection; if he is healthy, he is more of a danger."

"Do you know much about the infection?"

"Just that it makes people go crazy violent."

"Basically, yes."

"And there is no cure?"

"I don't know if there is or not, but I do know that Marco and Simone are immune. They were both bitten and neither of them has gone mad. That is why I was willing to risk bringing Dakota inside."

"Immune? Really? How?"

Ryan shook his head. "I don't know. Marco says it is genetic. And a report I read said the creators of this virus tried to build in genetic resistance, but I'm not sure how it is possible for there to be a genetic resistance to a viral infection, but maybe it is true."

"And because I'm of Spanish descent, my Dakota might be immune also?"

"Maybe that is true," Ryan said.

"Oh, wouldn't that be the biggest irony?" Gus said, looking at the stars. "Her ancestors were from Germany, so she was as white as they come. But she always acted like I was white because I made so much money. She said I was white and privileged. You'd think a name like Gustavo Blanco would be a clue, right?

"I didn't even have the advantage of growing up in the barrio overdosing on Carlos Santana. I had no street cred at all since I grew up in Toledo,

Ohio. The only thing that mattered was that rich meant white. I am the poster child for that ridiculous government racial category called White Hispanic." He sighed as his thoughts drifted down an unpleasant memory. Then he said, "So what do we do about Dakota?"

"Well," Ryan said, "I want to show you something." He held up his iGlass, "I want you to understand what it means if and when Dakota turns. I suspect it is hard to think about . . . putting down a loved one without knowing the danger they really pres—

"Wait, do you hear that?" Gus said, "Looking toward Mount Washington. "Helicopters!" he grabbed Ryan's arm. "Run!"

16

Global Infection: ≤ 30.0000%

Gus took the nine steps down from the helipad in two strides. "Follow me," he shouted as he dashed to the right, running behind the granite wall beyond the veranda perimeter to the roof's darkened outer edge. He pulled Ryan under a large industrial tarp. "Did they see us?" he asked in ragged breaths.

Ryan ducked and banged head on metal. "Damn, that hurt," he said rubbing hard. "What is this damned thing?"

Gus peeked out. "It's a rooftop crane. Did they see us?"

"I have no idea," Ryan said, trying to find a place under the tarp where he could stand upright. "What the hell is a crane doing up here?"

"They use it to get the mechanical units to the top," Gus said, "Did they see us?"

"How the hell should I know? And who is they?"

"They is the guys in helicopters and helicopters mean guns. Anyone not in the camp they shoot on sight."

"What?" Ryan rubbed his head.

"You have got to get those landing lights turned off," Gus said, still eyeing the sky. "That is a big, fat welcome mat."

"Why didn't we just run inside?" Ryan asked, looking through a seam in the tarp, spotting the helicopter running lights far away against the night sky.

Gus nodded toward the photovoltaic lights lining the walkway. "We would have been seen."

"We could have been inside by now and it wouldn't have mattered?"

"Trust me. I'm a pilot. If we could hear them, they could see us. Movement on the ground is very easy to see at low altitude particularly when there is light. You really have to get those lights shut off."

"How did you know this space was under here?" Ryan asked, his eyes finally adjusting to the darkness. The space was just enough to fit two people.

"What? What are you talking about? Under here?" Gus stammered, like he'd been caught unhooking his prom date's dress. "Whatever. Whatever. It doesn't matter how I know. You need to get those landing lights shut off."

"I'll get right on that."

"You really don't know, do you? You really don't know what is going on down on the streets. You're living up in the penthouse as if everything is normal, like some big shot and you don't have a goddamned clue—"

"Uh, no. The idea was to stay *off* the street, because it isn't normal anywhere. If it were *normal* I would be in my hometown doing whatever I would be doing on a Thursday." Ryan said. "The idea was to hide long enough to figure out how to get back *to* normal. So no, I don't know what is going on. And I didn't know there was a damned prescription for how one was *supposed* to live in the face of societal collapse!"

"Right! Sorry! Sorry! I just sounded like Marie criticizing the rich," Gus said, "Okay, so the military has been coming into Pittsburgh for weeks. I heard they were going to make Pittsburgh a command center for the east coast so they built two camps, one at Heinz Field and the other by the convention center. We thought that if we could survive the chaos of lots of people being stuffed into a small space, we would be all right. And then they started putting people on trains forcing them to relocation camps out west. Lots of people didn't want to get on the trains. One night a group of people just walked away and a helicopter crew just mowed them down."

"Were they infected?" Ryan said.

"No, they weren't infected. Don't you get it?" Gus said. "One second they were walking, the next minute they were hamburger. That is when you learned to fear Big Brother's helicopters." Gus looked between a seam in the tarp. "Shit! They saw us."

Ryan ducked out from underneath the tarp. Six Black Hawks flew from the east, along the Monongahela, over Duquesne University, and the last helicopter adjusted toward the Renaissance Tower helipad. "We have to make a run for the door."

"Did you not hear me tell you they shoot everything?"

"And this from a guy who a minute ago needed to be talked out of jumping? If they land and we are out here, do you think they are only going to use harsh language?"

"Funny!" Gus said.

Gunfire echoed through the Pittsburgh skyline: distant pops followed by the rip of an automatic weapon. The landing Black Hawk seemed to hang in the air over the river for an endless minute, and then it tilted left and flew over the Pittsburgh Plate and Glass buildings. Ryan and Gus ran the rooftop's outer edge until they edge they could barely see Heinz Field's upper deck.

"There are almost a hundred thousand refugees in that place," Gus said. "The governor's designated safe zone. I tried to get us into the convention center. At least that place had a real roof and some climate control. But it might have been good that I didn't. I heard that is where the crazies were. I heard they locked everyone in to keep the crazies from getting out."

Ryan's face went slack. "They locked the infected in the convention center? How many are in there?"

Gus shrugged and leaned his forearms against the half wall. "Fifty thousand, but I don't know if it is true or not. We were in the camp there," he said pointing toward the glowing temporary lights off in the distance. "I was trying to get us on the trains. They were packing people onto Amtrak like it was 1937 Germany. I almost waited too long."

"What do you mean?"

Gus was quiet for a minute and then he said, "We'd just gotten out of line. The queues to Amtrak were getting more and more dangerous. Dakota's arm was really starting to hurt. He couldn't handle the constant pushing and shoving and the people fighting when the infection finally saturated their brain. There is no way to know if someone is sick until they just go berserk. So we were trying to get on the train. We waited for a whole day in line but I decided to risk one more night in the camp. We snuck out of the lines when the guards weren't looking. We were squeezing between the buses when we heard the machine guns and the screams. We hid in a city bus forever and when we snuck out we saw all the bodies."

"They wiped out everyone in the queue? Why?"

Gus shrugged. "I have no idea. But that's when Marie finally knew that we could never stay in the camps, that it was foolish to suffer with the masses. She finally knew that we should never have left Colorado."

Both men fell quiet, lost in their own thoughts. The firefight continued near Heinz field. Streetlights far below winked on and off. The breeze smelled like a campfire mixed with burning plastic. A dog barked to the west, beyond the river, along the mountain ridge. A car, using nothing more than parking lights, sped across the bridge toward the Fort Pitt Tunnel.

Gus said, "You ever watch those old zombie movies? *Night of the living Dead* and *Dawn of the Dead*?"

"My dad wouldn't let me watch them when I was younger."

Gus gave a half smile, "My mom wouldn't let me watch them either, but in college they played these old movies at the student union. *Dawn of the Dead* scared the shit out of me. Hard to believe that George Romero was a prophet."

Ryan chuckled. "I haven't heard that name in ages. I remember my father having an argument with one of his friends at the house. He said George was just another Marxist filmmaker who loved to tell metaphorical stories about the masses consuming the rich and powerful."

Gus looked at Ryan like he was seeing him for the first time. "I've never met anyone else who knew that."

"Most people don't care about such things, except my father."

Gus sighed and then said. "I'm ready."

"Okay, Gus, I'm having trouble keeping up with you."

"You were going to show me something. Something that would help me make a decision about Dakota."

"Oh, right, I was going to show you some video clips and pictures. They are of . . ." Ryan's voice caught in his chest as he thought about his niece.

"She was the one committing the horror on the first video. Then in the second part of the video you will see her mother doing . . . well, you will see what it looks like." He tapped on the iGlass until he got to the right place. "They are graphic. But I want you to realize that a young girl did this. She was Dakota's age. It is a nanny cam so there is no sound. Be thankful."

Gus took the iGlass. "You are showing me this to horrify me."

"No, not horrify you. Well, I expect you to be horrified. But I want you to get a sense of proportion. If your son is infected, he will be capable of what you see. You have a healthy son. This is the danger you put him in if you decide to keep your sick son alive."

Gus breathed deep and touched play. Frame by agonizing frame, he took in the details.

Ryan's mind wandered as the silence dragged on back to the night when Daniel Ryder's Black Hawk helicopter faded into the western horizon toward safety. Ryan stayed in Pittsburgh while it burned. That night a whole swath of land along the Monongahela River's south shore, from the Tenth Street bridge to the Birmingham bridge, was ablaze; and to the north two skyscrapers had flames pouring out of upper floors. Smoke clung to the air like a leach. The streets were mayhem and clatter. The Monongahela and Duquesne Inclines ran the face of the mountain shuttling the populace from Mount Washington down into the valley. The military and police worked like they were herding kittens: a fever pitch of motion and claws.

Tonight Ryan looked at the silent streets and saw a different city, a city in its death throes. South Side Flats burned down to embers. The high-rise fires were gone, but they smoked like aircraft carriers after the Battle of Midway, covering downtown in an acrid fog. Pittsburgh's historically impressive skyline rose into the darkened sky, black and forbidding. The Monongahela and Duquesne Inclines were frozen halfway down the mountain. The sounds of mayhem had dimmed like they had been smothered under a blanket of fatigue. Scattered pockets of survivors skulked between streetlights, seeming to have no specific direction. A single train sat dark, its passenger cars empty on the rail just across the river.

"What the hell?" Gus whispered. "What the hell?"

"It is hard to watch, isn't it?"

"Is this a sick joke?" Gus said, his voice shaking. "Are you some devil sent to torment me? Are you really Satan in disguise?" He devolved into groans punctuated by invective.

Ryan considered himself a perceptive man, but no amount of prescience could have prepared him for the words coming out of Gus' mouth. The world seemed to twist and turn like a picture that refused to resolve into clarity as he tried to catch up with the thinking buried under a sewer of profanity.

Gus wound up as if to pitch the iGlass over the edge, but Ryan's hand shot out and plucked it out of his hand. "What are you doing?" Ryan demanded. "Just when I think you might actually be sane, you totally flip."

Gus pushed him in the chest. "How do you have pictures of *her*? How do you have pictures of *her*? And why would you show me that hideous video . . . of *her*!"

And then like a kaleidoscope, the pieces twisted into a complex and fantastic image. "You have got to be kidding me," Ryan said. "Tess, what in the hell did you do?"

17

Global Infection: ≤ 30.0001%

In retrospect Gus' reaction wasn't that strange. He was a man deep in the throes of guilt-fueled grief, inclined to find a grotesque causality perpetrated by supernatural sources. It made sense that he would jump at mystical shadows when a man he did not know suddenly appeared with horrifying pictures of a woman who was the source of his guilt. What other explanation could there be but that Ryan Sage was a demon sent to torment him?

Of course, the answer to Gus' question was much more commonplace. Tess Stepford had been stepping out on her husband, Bexley, and Ryan Sage happened to be her brother. The answer was mundane, but that didn't mean it was easy to grasp. An hour- and-a-half passed, and Ryan still struggled to wrap his head around the facts. And Gus swung between incredulous and overly apologetic as if his infidelity was a specific affront to Ryan.

They returned to the penthouse and parted company, their minds spinning down their own paths until Gus came to Ryan's office asking a flurry of questions about the RVCJ-2091 infection, none of which he could answer, so Ryan pushed ten boxes across the desk while explaining that the information was in no particular order.

Gus shrugged like he'd just been told the grass was green. "That is how I made my money. I eat information."

Ryan nodded, created a network login and mapped the drive so Gus could access the tower storage, then left the office and found Marco watching a romantic comedy in his recliner. Ryan dropped into the matching Hancock and Moore leather couch and watched the 200-inch super high definition screen for an hour and twenty minutes. When the credits rolled, they both gave a polite nod and headed toward their rooms.

Ryan walked through the outer offices. His goal, among other things, was to see if Gus was still working on his self-appointed task. He walked to

Mora's office—the grandmotherly woman who was Daniel Ryder's chosen gatekeeper—and that was where he found Gus, sitting behind her desk, a single lamp light splashing down. "What are you doing out here?" he asked.

Gus blinked and stretched. "I got kicked out about a half hour ago," he said, nodding at Ryan's office door.

"Kicked out? That's not possible since that is my office and I didn't kick you out."

Gus shrugged. "Dakota isn't doing very well, and I wanted to keep a better eye on him," he nodded toward the sleeping boy. "This office has a couch; your office doesn't."

Ryan remembered falling asleep on that couch. It was pretty comfortable. "Is he doing better?"

"I don't know," Gus said. "His temperature is 102. We tried to keep him drinking through the day and Marco kept the IV fluids going, but now he's wetting himself while sleeping. I found some adult diapers. That will keep him from destroying the couch if you are worried about it."

"I hadn't thought about it, but keeping pee off the couch is a good idea. Were you able to get him to eat tonight?"

"He nibbled on some crackers and had about three sips of soup, but that is all. The antibiotics really messed up his stomach," Gus said, "Speaking of messed up, how much of this have you read?"

"Enough to get the gist."

Gus picked up one pile and said, "There are at least ten senators named in these documents who used their position to advance the virus or suppressed measures to control its spread." He picked up another pile. "An entire congressional committee report on the virus almost a year ago." He picked up a third pile. "The Director of the FBI sent memos to the Attorney General stating that he refused to recommend prosecution for related acts of treason." Gus slumped back in his chair, his voice rising. "It was all intentional. All of it. They thought they could control it and now my boys are likely to die because of what these pricks did in the name of my government. If I could find them, I would kill them."

"Yes, and that is exactly what should happen to these men and women—"

Dakota stirred and mumbled. "My arm, my arm is deadly, Simone. Got you."

"Sorry," Ryan said. "Go back to sleep. Didn't mean to wake you."

"Nerfed you like 100." Dakota mumbled, then rolled away. "One hundred."

Ryan and Gus exchanged a smile. Ryan opened the office door. He took a stride in and saw Raphael sitting behind his desk talking on the phone. Raphael raised his palm abruptly. And when Ryan didn't leave he said, "Not done."

Ryan opened his mouth and then closed it, stepping back into Mora's office and shut the door.

"Did you get kicked out of your office, too?"

"I'm not sure what just happened."

Gus frowned. "I think you were too nice," he said and continued reading.

"I think you are right," Ryan said and opened the door ready to face Raphael's displeasure and found the room empty. He slid into his chair and logged himself in. Then he powered on the bank of televisions that adorned his office walls. Daniel Ryder used them to monitor global financial markets and international news agencies. But now Ryan used them to monitor the security feeds throughout the Renaissance Tower. He worked through each angle, stopping to listen at each camera that was also equipped with audio. The city streets were quiet, and the building was silent. The irony continued: since the front door had been broken out, no one even tried to walk across the threshold. Marco's theory was that people now feared that something was already inside. Maybe that was true, but eventually curiosity and bravery would combine in someone's soul.

Ryan's attention focused on an e-mail from Patrick. The subject line read: *Blue Pill says you need to post. The people on your blog are worried about you.*

"How in the hell do people have time to read?" Ryan said to himself as he logged into his website. Sure enough, people were concerned that the government had snatched him off the street. They were demanding that officials identify his whereabouts.

Ryan felt his eyes getting misty. He'd always had loyal readers, but the outpouring of concern, during a time when so many people were fighting for their existence, but still took the time to comment, touched him deeply and viscerally. Blue Pill was right. He needed to give his readers some feedback, but it had to be more than a quick note; it had to be something that his readers would know came from him. Four days ago when the President of the United States put a capstone on his longstanding criminal behavior, Ryan wrote a brief article in a few spare minutes in response, but he'd not had time to proof and post.

> Dear Readers, thanks so much for your comments and concerns. Know that I am well and, at least for now, free. Well, as free as a people can be under political autocracy.
>
> The following are my thoughts on how we, the people should know and act.
>
> Ryan Sage

The Dissolution of Civil Government

> We have now completed the cycle: A nation born from a rebellion against tyranny has now become a government of tyranny.
>
> And where are our modern day patriots to rise up and destroy the tyrannical force pervading the land? Do not be deceived that these are Americans and as such, deserve sanction based on nationality. Indeed,

our forefathers fought against fellow Englishmen and fully understood that nationality was not immunity from the consequence of tyranny. And do not fall prey to the political sleight of hand that these criminals deserve due process. No government agent can abolish the Constitution and then demand the protection of the Constitution. Upon using the force of government to alienate you from your liberty, they have abandoned the protections of civil society; they are deserving of the consequence of their crimes a thousand fold. And do not succumb to the lie that they are only acting out of necessity. As I have echoed in many places, necessity is always the tyrant's plea. He always insists that his despotism is in service to the greatest good. But there is never a necessity to seize individual liberty. Taking people's liberties is always a crime of an illegitimate government. Do not confuse might for right. Learn from history the fundamental truth that John Stuart Mill pointed out in his work *On Liberty*:

> "Throughout history rulers have held an antagonistic position to the people whom they ruled. They consisted of a governing One, who derived [his] authority from inheritance or conquest, who, did not hold . . . the pleasure of the governed, and whose supremacy men did not . . . contest . . . [His] power was regarded as necessary but also as highly dangerous; as a weapon which they would attempt to use against their subjects, no less than against external enemies."

This is the way of all power amassed in the name of necessity. That it will be used against those for whom it was originally acquired to protect. And this is precisely where we are in American history, consumed by the might of government, because Americans have been seduced by the age-old lie: that they must capitulate to the beak and claws of government, that we must not contest federal supremacy.

John Stuart Mill said:

> "But as the king of the vultures would be no less bent upon preying upon the flock than any of the minor harpies, it was indispensable to be in a perpetual attitude of defense against his beak and claws. The aim, therefore, of patriots was **to set limits to the power which the ruler should be suffered to exercise over the community; and this limitation was what they meant by liberty.**"

Indeed, the limitation of government action is the root of individual liberty. It is the delimitation of government action, the restraint of government action that defines civil liberty. But to our great shame,

Americans have come to believe that "civil liberties" are the permission granted to the people by the government. We have sunk back into the primordial ooze of despotism, because patriots have allowed this perversion to twist the American Republic into the American oligarchy.

The Founding Fathers cleaned themselves of the tyrannical filth by changing the root premise: government is organized for the singular purpose of defending the individual. And as such, the individual enters into a social contract that grants government delimited permission to act on his behalf. A civil liberty is the specific and narrow freedom of the government to take action. In 1776, for the first time in human history, the government had to ask permission. This is the true meaning of civil liberties.

But now we have reached the pinnacle of perversion. Days ago, the Executive branch of our government gave an Executive Order declaring the government as the sole arbitrator of all resources. The president has declared himself king and the other two branches of government have chosen to candidate their power by remaining complicit. The establishment has claimed for itself the power to seize the whole of our existence, to dispose of us as it sees fit, because of "necessity."

Liberty is inalienable. Remember?

I will say it again, because somehow Americans have decided that inalienable really means negotiable. Liberty is inalienable. Any government agent, any judge, any senator, any congressman, any governor, who declares the power to alienate individuals from their liberty has declared war on those it was appointed to protect.

You, dear reader, already know of my admiration for John Locke. Without his insights, the greatest political achievement in human history would likely have never come. So I will point out how John Locke's ideas apply here and now. From his seminal work the *Second Treatise of Government*:

> . . . governments are dissolved from within when.
>
> Sect. 214. That when such a single person, or prince, sets up his own arbitrary will in place of the laws . . . [and] introduces new laws, not being thereunto authorized by the fundamental appointment of the society, or subverts the old, disowns and overturns the power by which they were made, and so sets up a new legislative.
>
> Sect. 216. When, by the arbitrary power of the prince, the electors, or ways of election, are altered, without the consent, and contrary to the common interest of the people . . .
>
> Sect. 217. The delivery also of the people into the subjection of a foreign power, either by the prince, or by the legislative,

And here is the point.

Government for the people and by the people can never become government by dictatorial decree. Presidents, judges, governors senators and congressmen are stewards of the government power, not owners of people's lives. Therefore, a Presidential declaration subordinating the whole of our existence to the executive branch is the formal dissolution the American government. The declaration of martial law is the declaration of war against a free people, and all men who take up arms to enforce the order are soldiers in a war of usurpation. The social contract of the U.S. Constitution has been usurped by criminals . . . criminals who cannot appeal to constitutional protections for their crimes because *they* dissolved the agreement and seek to alienate that which is yours by birthright—your life, liberty, and happiness.

Patriots have a moral responsibility to resist tyranny as only tyranny can be resisted.

18

Global Infection: ≤ 30.0001%

Ryan leaned back in his chair, exhausted, but his mind rolled through an avalanche of thoughts. No matter how he dug toward the surface, he couldn't seem to find the top. He wanted to sleep, but he needed to talk to Bruptrick. The thought of starting the conversation caused dread to fill his soul; it could be a very long night.

He took a deep breath and pressed the video chat button. It rang once.

"So what is the zombie kill count?" Bruce asked without preamble.

Ryan said, "And hello to you, Bruce."

"Who you talking to?" a voice asked off-camera.

"It is Daednu calling us from Maladomini to make good on his offer to play Dungeons and Dragons."

"Mr. Sage?" Patrick said, popping into the chat session. "You gonna game with us? We got our dice ready. We are waiting on Smokey to dungeon master."

"Uh . . . yeah. You two do realize I'm actually trying to survive real bad guys, there is no dungeon master to mediate, and there are no dice rolls and chances to hit?"

"That is so fucking cool," Bruce said. "IT guys rule. How many have you killed?"

Ryan really didn't want to think about the men and women he beat to death with his shotgun. He didn't want to think about the teenage boy whose head he'd crushed with a two-by-four. He didn't want to think about the ten people he'd obliterated with a shotgun. But the question made all those things roar to the front of his mind. And Bruce was going to pepper him until he gave a number. He rubbed the crease in his forehead just above his eyebrows and told the truth. "Fourteen, but I might not have the count right," Ryan said.

"Is that all?" Bruce said, sounding disappointed.

That is fourteen more real live human beings than I ever thought I would kill.

"That's it," Ryan said.

"Tell me how you did it," Bruce persisted. "Did you shoot them with a crossbow? Did you stab them with a knife? Did you make a baseball bat with nails and spikes in it? Or maybe you picked up a mower and mowed them down?"

Ryan said, "Sounds about right."

"IT guys rule!" Bruce said.

"Shut up, Bruce," Patrick said. "You are such a doob."

"Am not! You're the doob."

"Shut your smoke hole," Patrick said. "Mr. Sage didn't call about this." He looked at the camera. "What did you call for? You usually just e-mail."

"I need your technical expertise."

They instantly sat up straight. "What do you need Team Bruptrick to do?" they asked in unison.

"You know the bio scanner system here in the tower? I need to know if there is a way to reset the system and add new users?"

"Why do you want to do that?" Bruce asked.

"Well, the short story is, I need to add myself to the bio scanner."

"But why do you want to do that?" Bruce asked again.

Ryan sighed. This is what he dreaded—that Bruptrick was going play gatekeeper. "Is there a reason that I shouldn't be able to add myself to the scanner?"

"But there are protocols as to who has access to biometric system," Bruce said. "We just don't give that access to anyone."

Patrick said, "He owns the tower."

"So what? We need to know why he wants access."

Ryan's greatest fear was forming in reality. He was going to lose an entire night's sleep persuading Bruce that he needed access. *Oh, Dear God in heaven, please help me.*

And God answered Ryan's prayer immediately.

"*We* don't even have access," Bruce said. "Only Samuel's had a biometric profile on that system."

Ryan put on a coy smile. "Did I understand correctly that you don't have access to that system?"

"Nope," Bruce said like it was an affront to the universe.

There was nothing like dangling an IT toy in front of an IT nerd. "So how about if you had access *and* I had access?"

Bruce bit his lip. "Really?"

"Yup," Ryan said. "You figure out how to reset that system and then we can all have access."

Bruce's eyes glazed over. "And we have the bio scanners here. If we figured out how to reset the Molitor system, maybe we could figure out how to reset the system here, and then we could get to the lower levels. But we'll have to figure out how the ACL is configured—"

"Do we have the infrastructure schematics?" Patrick said. "That was on a dedicated port, right? I'll bet there is a factory reset." His fingers started slapping at a keyboard.

"We'll have to—"

"So you will do it?" Ryan said.

"Hell yes," Bruce said, "I'm going to need some—"

"Hang on, guys. Daniel Ryder is calling."

Bruce and Patrick went white. "Mr. Ryder is calling you . . . now?" they both said in unison.

"Yes, I have to take—"

Ryan's video chat went black. "Okay," he said to himself and answered Daniel's call.

19

Global Infection: ≤ 30.0002%

I knew I was in trouble when Raphael actually said Urushi art and Nhat Tran in one sentence," Ryan said, his laughter making the last words come out with a stutter.

Daniel laughed deep and pleasant, thumbing a tear out of the corner of his eye. "I remember the first time he walked in and saw that room. I thought he was going to burst a blood vessel. After Simone ran away . . . you knew he ran away, right? Anyway, we decided Raphael should stay in the tower instead of going crazy at his house. When we went to get his things, Raphael was more interested in retrieving his two Jackson Pollocks and his six Joaquin Torres-Garcia paintings from his house than his pants."

Ryan smiled. "I don't know who they are, but I'm sure my priorities would be different."

"Speaking of priorities, did you get set up on the biometric?"

"I'm guessing you already know that I haven't. This has been framed like it is a showdown at the O.K. Corral, but I don't want to mislead. We did finally make an attempt to work on my profile, but we ran into some technical snags and Raphael ran out of patience."

"Technical snags?"

Ryan said, "I had to figure out how to program the system and he didn't want to wait. Raphael did put me off, but to be fair we did have other things to do."

"Okay, good. I put you on the spot when I asked you to let the Pagueros stay at the tower as a favor and now I feel responsible to help make this amicable."

"At the moment we are amicable," Ryan said, "but we are far from pals."

"You are both strong-minded men," Daniel said. "It is to be expected."

"No, Daniel, this is not two hardheaded men failing to get along. Raphael is deceitful and presumptuous. I know he's been close to your family for decades and I understand why you want to give him the benefit of the doubt. But I can't afford to ignore what I have right in front of me."

"Very well, but I want you to know that I made him promise to make sure you had everything you needed."

"Well thanks, but I shouldn't need you as mediator," Ryan said. "I don't want to talk about that anymore. But are you sure I need the bio scan to get to the roof? The badge gets me through the security checkpoint on the thirtieth floor and through the half a million security doors on the thirty-first, which means I can get outside without using the scanner."

Daniel chuckled. "You exaggerate. There are only ten."

Ryan snorted. "It's overkill, whatever the number."

"How should I describe my son's relationship to the world? For all of his love for the poor people of South America, he has many enemies. That is what happens when you are the esteemed guest of dictators and cartel leader with visions of political power. He had some real troubles about four years ago with a very scary, very powerful South American cartel. He was building the Renaissance Tower during that time, so he built the upper floors like a compound. He has security features up there that you can't even see. Since he mostly came and went by helicopter, he thought of the roof as his front door."

Ryan struggled to wrap his mind around the world of billionaire Marxist revolutionaries. It was a trending business and there were a lot of them, but he never understood how such internal treachery could be so appealing across the globe. "Well, there is a flaw in the security. If I can get to the roof, then what difference does it make if I'm on the biometric scanner? Someone with a badge can open the door."

"No, we only had four such cards. Mine, Richard's, Raphael's and my chief security officer. Only those people could open the door from the inside, but unless someone is set up on the biometric they can't get through the door from the outside."

Ryan's eyes got big. "Ohh, that could have been a problem."

"What?"

"Gus went up there too."

"Went up there to do what?"

Ryan waved the comment away. "I was just thinking he went to the roof and no one knew he was there. He would have been stuck."

"Son," Daniel said, "You are not the only one who can be perceptive. What did Gus go up there to do?"

Ryan looked at the door. "Wait one second." He got up and checked Mora's office. The desk light was on but Gus was lying on the couch beside Dakota, sleeping. Ryan pulled the door shut and sat back down. "I think he went up there to jump."

"That doesn't sound like the Gus Blanco I know. He was a great husband and a great father and a fantastic investment banker. I've known some great money men, but Gus is a wizard."

Ryan said, "Gus is eaten up by grief and guilt. The man that is here in this tower is a half inch from unhinged. And I still can't figure out what she saw in him."

"Gus is a very charming man," Daniel said. "Marie was totally smitten and gave up a very promising dance career in New York to marry him. It is just the stress of the moment. I'm sure he will come around. I'm sure he will find a way to be an asset. And I'm sure he will do the right thing with Dakota."

"Did Raphael talk to you about Dakota?"

"And he told me what Marco did." Daniel shook his head. "I think Marco's heart was in the right place, but the medic was adamant that if he didn't complete all the antibiotics, the chances were strong he would die."

"So here is a question," Ryan said. "What are *you* doing with people who have been bitten?"

Daniel nodded his face grave. "A few have been shot. A few have been driven off into the wilds. A couple families just packed up and left."

"But you are not outright killing them, correct?"

Daniel shook his head no. "We were going to. But after our conversation, I decided to hold off. But now our biggest concern is the family members who will try to intervene when we need to put someone down. We made it clear that we are willing to wait to see symptoms of the disease, but if any family member tries to prevent putting the infected down, we will kill him or her too."

"What if a kid gets in the way?"

Daniel's face was adamant. "These creatures are too dangerous to have any human shields."

"Good point."

"I do have a message for you though," Daniel said.

"Haven't you figured out that I don't like intermediaries?" Ryan asked, his irritation bubbling to the surface. "I'll talk to Raphael when it suits me."

Daniel raised his hands in surrender. "I'm sorry I should have introduced this better. It is from Ahou."

Ahou, the beautiful, gloriously naked Persian goddess that almost stole his heart, but turned out to be her own brand of deceitful. There were few things that Ryan hated more.

"Anyway, she is doing well. She asked about you. Actually, she has not stopped asking when everyone can get to e-mail. She wants to keep in touch."

"E-mail?" Ryan said. "I don't understand. Your network is up. Why don't you just let them get on a computer?"

"Well, beyond the security issues of letting a thousand people get on e-mail and tell the world where they are, we seem to be missing our IT administrators. Bruce and Patrick? Do you remember those two idiots? Well, they were supposed to be here. They were going to be instrumental in getting this facility up and running. We have a big challenge because they are very likely dead."

"Dead you say," Ryan said. "How terrible."

"I don't want to talk about those two clowns," Daniel said. "Ahou wanted me to tell you that her father is praying for you and she has not forgotten one word you said. As soon as she can, she will start sending you e-mail."

Ryan's stomach twisted. He'd made a photo album from a collection of pictures at Ahou's house and every night before bed, he thumbed through her pictures and smelled a pillow from her bedroom.

Daniel said, "She has become a Ryan Sage acolyte. One of the biggest reasons she wants to get back online is so she can read your articles. Twice she has gone up against Richard in the cafeteria when he started in with his progressive revolution rhetoric."

Ryan shook his head and looked away from the camera.

"What?" Daniel said. "You don't think she should?"

"I don't want to get into it."

"Don't be shy now."

Ryan regarded Daniel and then said, "You won't like what I have to say here."

"I can handle it, son."

"Okay, I think *everyone* should be going up against Richard when he starts that nonsense. But more important, I think *you* should be going up against him. He shouldn't be getting a free pass to speak on your dime. I've never understood why capable, successful capitalists cower away when Marxist progressives and socialists start spouting off about the greater good when the capitalists are paying the bills. Richard can't hope to survive without you paying for his life. Indeed it is because of you, because of your capitalism and because of my capitalism that he is alive.

"He has no moral ground to advocate an ideology that undermines what you have done, but the person challenging him had never heard of dialectic materialism until I told her maybe three weeks ago. Are you kidding me? That is like sending the freshman squad to play against the professionals in a game where they don't know the rules."

Daniel chuckled. "That is the man I remember from the sub shop. Blunt to the point of painful."

"You think what *I'm* saying is painful? You have no idea what is coming," Ryan said. "I need to repeat what I told you on the helipad just before you left. Richard is a viper who will murder to get what he wants and his ideology is pure poison. If you let him go unchallenged and unchecked, he will destroy what you have built.

"But Richard isn't the problem. You are. You are a cowardly capitalist and committing ideological treason. I've never understood how CEOs keep giving money to the very universities that teach young minds to hate individual production. I've never understood how they finance political parties who will pass legislation that destroys their industries. It is the highest rational treason to aid and abet the very people who will cut their throats the second they have the political power. Appeasing Marxists has never worked. Treating Marxists like misguided adolescents has never worked. They will kill faster than you can say, "Needy children." And yet producers like you—free, capable, morally superior capitalists—continue to indulge them. Wake up! If you keep indulging Richard, keep financing his ideology, if you keep pretending that he is not a murderer, you will get what you deserve."

Daniel sat back in his chair breathing deep, his face inscrutable. This was the face that had created an international construction company and wrangled deals with presidents, despots, and sovereigns all over the globe.

Ryan didn't flinch.

Finally, Daniel said, "Can we talk again soon?"

"Of course," Ryan said. "Have a good night."

"Be safe." And the video chat went black.

20

Global Infection: ≤ 30.0003%

Ryan slumped in his chair. That was the second conversation with Daniel Ryder that had ended in a fight. That couldn't be a good thing. Ryan didn't want an intermediary between himself and Raphael, but he did want Daniel as an ally and even a friend. For a few minutes Ryan spun his mouse cursor over the video chat button trying to decide if he should call back and apologize, but the problem was he was right. Richard's ideology was pure poison and Daniel was letting that toxic mess into his home. Then he heard the voice of his mother, at first dim and distant, but growing louder until he said the words out loud, "You can be right or happy." And then Ryan said to himself, "How come you can't be happy and right?"

Then he saw Gus standing in the doorway.

Ryan jumped. "Oh shit, you scared me."

"Sorry, I didn't mean to eavesdrop," Gus said, "but I must confess that I was so taken by what you were saying and to whom you were saying it that I didn't want to move."

"Yeah, well, my voice tends to get loud when I start hammering away at Marxists and cowardly capitalists. I suspect I was hard to miss."

"You are," Gus said, coming to the desk holding some folders. "And those were some of the most impressive words I've ever heard come out of someone's mouth. I've never heard anyone go after Richard Ryder like that. And I can't imagine anyone has ever spoken to Daniel Ryder like that for indulging that useless turd of a son. I'm impressed."

"My mother just thought I was rude."

"I knew Richard," Gus said, "He came to the parties that Marie had. He hit on her, of course. He was a lady-killer. He probably slept with eighty percent of all the women on the social circuit." He paused, realizing what he just said. "He didn't sleep with Tess though."

"Thank God for small favors."

"No really, he didn't. Tess hated Richard. Seems she must have gotten that from you."

"Tess and I didn't see the world the same at all. Ideas were inconsequential to her. If she hated Richard, it was because she thought him a creep."

"You are right. That is what she called him," Gus said. "I will say this for Bexley. He didn't like Richard either, even though they supported the same things politically. Those two would never leave me alone if I was at a party. Used to piss me off the way they ganged up on me," Gus chuckled to himself. "You know what is funny? I was always trying to be the good host and not cause trouble. Marie was always mortified when I said anything back. Somehow it was my job to be quiet. They could run their mouths about the greater good and the evils of capitalism and corporate welfare, but if I pointed out their idiocy, somehow I was the one who should apologize.

"But anyway, one night I'd had enough and I let Richard and Bexley have it. And when I was done, Bexley said something like, 'Have you been listening to my brother-in-law? You sound just like him.' And I said, 'In that case I'd like to meet him.'" Gus shook his head. "Small world, huh?"

"Yeah, small world."

"Hey, are these bullet holes?" Gus said, running his finger over the drywall.

"Yes," Ryan said.

"Wonder what the story is with that?"

Ryan snorted. "That is where Richard Ryder tried to kill me."

"What?"

Ryan raised a pausing hand. "Another story for another time. I'm about to go to bed."

"Okay, I need to get Dakota to his bed. But before I go, I wanted to say something about this." Gus held up a folder.

Ryan recognized the report that Daniel Ryder had uncovered where government agents had tried to strong-arm Bexley Stepford into framing Ryan for molesting his nieces, Xyla and Georgia. "Yeah, that was in one of the boxes. I didn't think to take it out."

"I'm glad you didn't. I learned a lot. I learned that you are much more than meets the eye. You have powerful enemies which means you are a player. I haven't met too many players in this life. And someday you need to explain how you became the owner of this tower. Darien is suspicious. He thinks you didn't pay market price."

"How does your son even know about real estate market prices in Pittsburgh?"

Gus smiled. "Like father like son. It is what I talk about, so he listens and reads like he is studying for his securities license. So since Daniel Ryder is talking to you via video conference, it must mean you really did buy this place. What price did you pay for the tower?"

"I paid the market rate."

"You had $75 million in spare change lying around?" Gus asked.

"It's a long story that I'm too tired to tell tonight."

"Okay, but promise me you will tell me," Gus said. "One more thing before you go to bed. I wanted to tell you . . . but I'm not sure how to say it. I know you probably don't like your brother-in-law, but I learned something else about Bexley Stepford.

"What is that?"

"He is one of the most courageous men I've never really met," Gus said. "I really thought he was an ass. And if what Tess said is true, he really could be. But what he did by standing up to the government for you, that is, well, that is amazing. And then I went back and read through the police report you had for Bexley's murder-suicide and got some insights from some test results in a government report.

"The infection rate for the RVCJ-2091 strain is off the charts. When Bexely went to China to speak at that human population control conference, he knew that his family had been infected. Somehow he figured out that he and his daughter were a danger.

He understood this long before anyone knew about the 2091 strain. He knew there was no cure. He knew she was a danger. He knew that he had to keep her from hurting anyone else."

Gus' voice broke as tears leaked down the side of his cheek. "The bravest, hardest thing he could have ever done . . . stopping Georgia and himself before . . . before they spread the disease.

"Tess was a rare woman. Few men were worthy of her. On that day, Bexley showed what kind of man he was. He was worthy of Tess. And I wonder if I'm that kind of man."

ACT 2

21

Global Infection: ≤ 30.3009%

Marco's face got big on Ryan's laptop. He was standing close to a security camera, the noontime sun washing out his complexion. "Where do you want us to put these keys?" he asked.

Ryan and Gus were in the master chef's kitchen hip-deep in food processing. The laptop was tied into the tower's security system. Ryan wiped his hands on his apron. "Why not just bring them up here?"

"If I bring them up there," Marco said, "and we lose them, then these doors remain locked forever."

"Forever, huh?" Ryan said.

Marco raised a brow. "You ever tried to cut through a titanium security bar?"

"In a former life I had to do that once. It is a pain in the ass," Ryan said.

"Oh," Marco said. "Of course you have." He rolled his eyes like he resented the game of one-upmanship. "Would you like a suggestion?"

"Always."

"How about I put them on a hook close to the door?"

"That is stupid," Simone said in the background. "If someone finds them, they can open the lock."

Marco ignored his brother and spoke to the camera. "If they are able to get these keys, then the keys don't matter, because they are already inside the building."

"True," Ryan said, pausing to think about options.

Just after breakfast, Simone came into the penthouse family kitchen and said someone was trying to break into the tower. The cameras revealed four people hammering at a metal gate that was the last line of defense between the public parking garage and the grocery store skywalk.

When Richard Ryder obtained permission to build the Renaissance Tower and put a grocery in its bottom levels, the city required dedicated parking and egress that did not cross a street. The solution was to isolate the bottom three parking garage levels from the tenant parking and attach the parking garage to the tower with a skywalk across First Avenue. It was an elegant solution to an everyday urban problem. But today that skywalk represented yet one more way the tower could be penetrated.

The Pagueros loaded up for war and Ryan stayed in the security room watching the cameras. By the time Raphael, Marco and Simone were standing in the skywalk, weapons drawn, ready for a firefight, Ryan had a plan that didn't require bullets. Ryan told them to pause while he played a newsfeed that captured the 2091s strange tortured moaning. "Rattle the doors," he whispered and Simone banged against the doors like a madman.

The intruders paused, listened and then fled.

Everyone assembled in the penthouse security room and for an hour they debated how to close off the skywalk.

The best option was to seal the entrance from the parking garage side, but neither Ryan or Raphael was motivated to go to the street. Simone suggested blowing a hole in the skywalk floor with the det cord they found in the Molitor security barracks on the thirteenth floor. Blowing stuff up had been his solution to pretty much every problem since he'd found it. Raphael suggested using a jackhammer to take out a section of the skywalk floor too big to casually jump over. Ryan was not crazy about blowing holes in his building or jack hammering holes into floors, so he decided that Gus's suggestion to "pile a bunch of heavy shit in the skywalk" was the best course of action. And that is exactly what they did. While Dakota slept, everyone followed Raphael to the tower floors where building supplies were stored. They loaded drywall on carts, and after an hour they had one large stack of very heavy gypsum board piled high in the skywalk.

After three more loads stacked in the skywalk, Gus bowed out to check on Dakota and then reported that the boy's fever had spiked and he needed to remain in the penthouse. Just before lunch, Ryan checked on Gus and found him in the penthouse master chef's kitchen—the kitchen used by *Mon Pierre's* chef when the Ryders decided to host the very important people—prepping food for freezing.

Dakota's fever had risen to 104 and to cool him down, Gus chose to put him on a cot in one of the kitchen walk-ins. Moving a cot inside required moving food outside which inspired him to prep food for long-term storage. While Dakota napped, Gus worked at freezing, canning and vacuum packing.

Ryan called the Pagueros on the maintenance radios to explain he was going to help Gus with food prep, but they proved useless. Instead, he connected his laptop to the security system.

"Are you guys done?" Ryan asked. "The camera angle makes it hard to tell."

"I'm not moving anymore drywall," Simone announced.

Marco shut his eyes and shook his head like he was trying to muster the patience of Job. "So, the keys . . . what do you want me to do with them?"

"Leave them on a hook close to the door," Ryan said.

"That is stupid. Someone will find them," Simone said, flying his middle finger at the camera.

"Simone, you do understand that just because you can't see me doesn't mean I can't see you, right?"

"Oh," he said and stuffed his hands into his pickets.

Marco waved his hand toward the drywall piles. "No one is getting through without a lot of really hard work. I'm gonna put a chain through the grocery doors in addition to the titanium bars. It is overkill, but it will help me sleep at night."

"I trust your judgment," Ryan said. "Come on up for lunch."

"Do you trust *my* judgment, Neg Dis?" Simone said, mugging for the camera.

"Please ignore him," Marco said.

"Bite me," Simone said.

Marco said, "If we really want to sleep well at night, I say we park cars in front of the gate or fasten metal over the outer door. I think we should do that now."

"And I want to shoot zombies!" Simone said, photobombing the security camera.

"I'm gonna let the zombies eat you if you don't shut up," Marco said.

"Bite me, douche!" Simone said, starting to bob and weave and throwing a flurry of air punches.

Marco brushed his brother off like a fly. "You see what he is like when he has a good night's sleep?"

"Where is Darien?" Gus asked leaning into the laptop.

"He's been a good helper," Marco said. "Poppa and Darien headed up to the penthouse a few minutes ago. Poppa is determined to make him fluent in Spanish."

Gus smiled. "I'm glad he has been a help."

"How is Dakota?" Marco asked.

"His fever was 104 earlier, but I found a way to help bring it down," Gus said. "We are out of antibiotics, right?"

"Yes, just keep giving him liquids," Marco said. "I'll be up in a few minutes. "Come on, butt-munch. Let's get this place locked up."

"I'm not the butt-munch," Simone said, still bobbing and weaving on camera. "You are."

Gus smiled. "I never thought I would say this, but I can't wait for my boys to be like that again. Used to drive me nuts listening to them snipe at each other all the time, but now," he thumbed a tear off his eye. "That would mean they were both healthy."

Darien rushed into the kitchen, "*Hablas español, Padre?*" he said.

"What?" Gus said, wiping his hands on a towel.

"I said, 'Do you speak Spanish, Father?'" Darien asked, looking sly. "Listen, *uno, dos, tres, cuatro, cinco, seis, siete, ocho, nueve, diez.* That is one through ten in Spanish." He held up his hand for a high-five.

Gus returned the high five. “Sounds great. Now go get cleaned up.”

“But I’m hungry,” Darien said.

“You are always hungry. But before you can eat, get a quick shower,” Gus said. “Now get moving.”

Darien trotted out of the kitchen and vanished beyond the swinging doors.

Gus cringed, waving his hand in front of his nose. “I think it is about time I explain deodorant to my son.”

“That *es* the smell of a young man who worked hard,” Raphael said. “You should be proud.”

Gus nodded. “I am proud. They are good kids in spite of everything.”

“It *es* also good that they learn the language of their heritage,” Raphael said.

Gus laughed. “I know the name is Blanco, but the English version of my name is White. And since I grew up in Ohio and the boys have grown up in Pennsylvania and New York, English *is* their heritage.”

Raphael wrinkled a brow and leveled a flat look but didn’t reply. He laid his AK-47 on a stainless-steel table, snatched the kitchen phone into his hand, and dialed the messaging service code listened, sighed and put the receiver back with a little too much force.

“You think Leona’s in trouble?” Ryan asked.

Raphael’s mouth turned down at the corners. “It *es* nothing. She will call if she need to.” He unzipped his tactical vest, the magazine clattering together as he slung it over his shoulder. “I will clean up before we eat.”

“I’m beginning to think that he is only nice to kids,” Gus said.

“His wife, Leona, and their two other boys are coming to the tower. They were somewhere in Georgia when we talked to them just over a week ago. Her last words were that the police were pulling them over. Southern Georgia hasn’t been ten days travel from Western Pennsylvania since the horse and buggy was replaced by Henry Ford’s model T.”

“What is he going to do?” Gus asked.

“He has no way to know where she is.”

Gus gave a low whistle. “I *know* where my wife is and I’m about to lose my mind. You mind if I ask you a personal question?”

“I always think it funny when people preface their questions like that. What am I supposed to say?” Ryan took the pot off the stove and poured its contents into a serving bowl.

Gus collected plates. “You want to eat in the fine dining room or take this to the other kitchen?”

“It will be fun to eat in the big fancy dining room,” Ryan said. “Besides, Dakota is in the walk-in. We don’t want to leave him by himself, right?”

“Good point,” Gus said, exiting the stainless-steel swinging doors that served to separate the working class from the world of the rich and Marxist. He started putting dishes on the table. “So do you know what happened to her?” Gus asked.

“Leona?” Ryan said. “No. We’ve not heard—”

"No," Gus said. "I meant, do you know what happened to Tess?"

Before Ryan could answer, Simone shouted from deep in the penthouse. "Hey, where's the food?"

"We are in here!" Ryan called. Then he said to Gus, "I assume that she is still locked in the security ward at UPMC Mercy."

"Do you think she has anyone feeding her? Or taking care of her?"

Ryan bowed his head. There was something horrifying about picturing Tess locked in a room slowly wasting away. "Honestly, I can barely stand to think about that."

"Why are you guys in here?" Simone asked, dropping his AR-15 on the table, shrugging out of his tactical vest and dumping it on a two-thousand-dollar carved wood chair.

"Variety is the spice of life," Ryan said. "Grab whatever you want to drink. We are going to eat as soon as Darien gets here."

Marco said, "That doesn't go there, butt-munch." He was nodding toward the vest full of ammunition and sundry effects of war. "Take it back to the armory."

"Bite me!" Simone said. "I gotta get Darien to move. I'm hungry. Darien?! Darien?!" Simone turned into the adjoining room and ran into his father.

Raphael was cool and impassive, squeezing his son firmly on the shoulder and pointing toward the tactical vest and the weapon.

"But I'm—"

Raphael put his fingers to his lips and then pointed again.

Simone rolled his eyes. "Fine!" he said and snatched the vest off the chair making sure that every hard surface dragged across the crafted wood.

"Are you going to try and get her out?" Gus asked as he and Ryan walked back into the kitchen for the rest of the food. "I mean she *is* your sister."

"Gus, I have no way to do anything about it. And the thing she became . . . wasn't my sister. It was her body maybe, but *she* was gone. It is hard to explain, but I was sitting beside her bed and I saw what made her . . . *her* fade out of her eyes and what took her place was . . . madness."

Gus said, "But what if she is all right? What if it isn't that bad? Maybe we could help her."

Ryan squeezed his eyes shut. "Look, Gus, I get what you are asking, but it was worse than I ever wanted to believe. You have to remember Tess was a ward of the state and was probably going to spend her life in a location for the criminally insane. And there was a strong possibility that she was going to be one of the few women executed by the State of Pennsylvania. What she did, what that *thing* did . . . it would have been hard for me to object. Nothing and no one that dangerous can be allowed to live in civil society."

Darien ran through the swinging door, his shirt damp but his hair dry. "Dad, can I have a peanut butter and jelly sandwich?"

"No, the food is on the table," Gus said. "Wait, did you take a shower? Your hair is dry."

"I did," Darien said. "But I was trying to be fast because I heard Simone."

"And you used soap and everything . . . under your arms?"

"Dad!" Darien said, blushing.

"All right, but if I smell you while we are eating, I'm throwing you in the shower myself. Now, do me a favor. Your brother is in that walk-in over there."

"You put him in the refrigerator?" Darien said.

"He has a really high fever. I'm trying to keep him cooled down," Gus said. "Check on him for me."

Darien pulled the walk-in door open. "Dakota? Dakota, how are you doing?"

Gus grabbed more food and headed to the doors. "You know, I asked your brother-in- law once why he gave up medicine to do what he did. You know what he said?"

Ryan filled his hands with the remainder of lunch. "No."

"Dakota?" Darien said as he tried to keep the door from shutting, "Are you cold? You're shaking."

Gus paused before he pushed through the swinging kitchen door. "Bexley said, 'They outnumber us.'"

"Who outnumbers us?"

"The poor," Gus said. "And then Bexley says, 'And if they ever figure it out, they will kill us all. Can you believe that? His real reason for all the social justice rhetoric was self-preservation." He pushed into the dining room.

Just before the walk-in door clicked shut, Ryan thought he heard the word *bleeding*. He paused to listen but didn't hear anything beyond the door. "Darien," he called. "Is your brother all right?"

Silence . . .

"Let me check on Darien," Ryan said, setting the dishes on the dining room table.

"Can you believe that? Self-preservation?" Gus said again.

"No, Bexley was a true believer. I don't know why he said—"

The scream came from the kitchen like a horror movie soundtrack muted by a pillow.

Ryan spun.

Gus clawed his way toward the sound.

Raphael rushed around the dining room table and Marco thrashed out of his chair and through the kitchen, slamming against stainless steel tables and food racks until Ryan yanked open the walk-in door. Darien's keening seared into their ears like white hot slivers of metal.

Dakota lay on the cot, his body twitching and rocking, his jaw savaging Darien's hand like a pit bull, blood dripped down the sides of his mouth. Darien punched and punched with his left hand. "Let go! Let go!" his voice growing more shrill with each strike.

"Oh dear God!" Gus shouted. "No! No!" He took a step and slipped. He clawed his way to his knees. Marco strode over him and wrapped Darien's arms.

Raphael drew his sidearm and pointed it at Dakota's head.

"No!" Marco shouted. "It's a seizure. It's a seizure. Pull his mouth open. Pull his mouth open!"

"Let go! Let go!" Darien screamed as he thrashed in Marco's arms.

Raphael held Dakota's head and pressed hard on his jaw. The teeth parted and Darien snatched his ravaged fingers from the mouth of destruction. Gus pulled Darien from Marco's arms and slumped to the frigid floor. "Oh, baby. Oh, baby. This is my fault," Gus said, his breath coming in hot steaming gasps. He rocked and rocked as if that would drive the pain from the world. "This is my fault. This is my fault."

22

Global Infection: ≤ 30.3037%

Ryan held out a cup filled with his favorite smoothie recipe. "I know it doesn't look too good, but it tastes pretty good."

"Not real hungry," Dakota said, his jaw stiff and his words coming out like his mouth was full of cotton. "And it will hurt to eat." Hurt and eat came out like hurth and eath.

Ryan nodded. "That is why I made a smoothie—so it wouldn't hurt, at least not as much." During Dakota's seizure, he'd bitten deep into his tongue. "We've got to get something in you. You haven't really eaten much in days. Your body is exhausted. It needs fuel."

"How is he doing?" Marco said, sitting down on the couch.

"The fever is down, which is good, but he's reluctant to eat," Ryan said. "I made him this, so we could get something into his belly."

Marco looked at the green frothing liquid and wrinkled his brow. "You serious? You want him to eat that?"

Dakota tried to smile through his swollen face.

"Hey, this is pretty good," Ryan said, giving Marco a look that made it clear he was not helping. "This is one of my best recipes."

Marco made a show of looking at the glass with suspicion. And then he took a sip. "Mmm . . ." he said with appreciation. "That is pretty good, but it needs alcohol." He looked at Dakota. "I don't suppose you are old enough to drink alcohol?"

Dakota laughed and then he winced. "Don make me laugh. It hurth."

"Okay, too bad for you," Marco said. "But here is the important part. You got your vaccines in school, right?"

"Yeth," Dakota said.

"Well, those little robots in the Eternity vaccine are trying to repair your body. They can do it super fast if they have building blocks to work with. The more nutritious food you have in your body, the more they can use those building blocks. So, you need to try and eat something. That will help them fix your tongue."

"Okay," Dakota said, trying to sit up. He flinched when he bumped his arm, grimaced on the first sip but as soon as the liquid hit his belly, he started drinking in earnest. "Could I have more, please?"

Ryan was already filling the cup from the blender pitcher. "As much as you like."

"I had a guy in my platoon that swore by juicing," Marco said. "But his stuff didn't taste like that. That is pretty good."

"I used to drink these by the gallon," Ryan said. "When I was training for track and field, I learned dozens of recipes."

"Track and field?" Marco said. "You? What did you compete in? The potato sack race?"

"Yeah, yeah, yeah. Pick on the fat kid," Ryan said, dropping into a chair beside the couch.

"Well, if you drank these all the time, you wouldn't be fat," Marco said with a wink.

Dakota finished the second cup and leaned back. "How's Darien?" His brother's name came out sounding like Arian.

"He will be all right," Ryan said. "We got him fixed up. You don't need to worry about that."

"Can I see him?"

"He is sleeping right now," Marco said.

"Buth I had part of his fingers in my mouth," Darien said, a tear in his eye.

Marco held up his left hand and showed his pinky stump. "Look at my hand. I had it bitten off a couple weeks ago. This is how you become part of the new cool kid club. See this pink flesh right here. That is the stump growing back. That is what those cool robots are doing in your body, and that is what it will do for Darien. He will be fine."

"You donn have to call them roboths" Dakota said, "I know what nano-boths are, and I know how the vaccine worths. My mom broke her arm last year mountain climbing. The docther explained it then."

Ryan nodded. "Then you know your brother will be all right."

Dakota turned his head away. The silence passed until Dakota said, "I have tha go to the bathroom."

"You feel sick?" Ryan asked.

"No, I have tha go number thoo, thoo," Dakota shook his head, "I have tha poop."

Marco smiled. "Do you need some help getting there?"

Dakota nodded and Ryan and Marco helped him walk down the hall. "I'm good from here," he said and closed the bathroom door.

Marco took a few steps away. "This is so totally fucked," he said trying to keep his voice down. "Darien was just trying to stop him from biting his tongue off and loses the tips of two fingers for his trouble."

"Are we sure it was a seizure?" Ryan asked. "Are we sure it wasn't the 2091 infection?"

"I know a seizure when I see one and if it was the virus we wouldn't be having a reasonable conversation with Dakota."

"Is seizure a sign of infection?" Ryan asked. "The reports I read made no mention of it, but it seems logical that it would be a side effect of an infection that eats away at the brain."

"I don't know." Marco said with a sigh. "When I was first bitten, they had me in a ward with fifty-three other men and women. All but three of us went mad. I don't remember any of them having seizures. I think the seizure was from his high fever and some dehydration."

"Three of fifty-three?" Gus said."That is 0.0566 percent immunity rate." He stood, feet planted in the hallway. "That is worse than the immunity rate I read in the reports."

"I didn't mean for you to hear that," Marco said. "I'm sorry."

Gus's face was pale and haggard. His grief had returned and hung on him like a coat. "No need to apologize. It's what we have to deal with, right? This is the reality before us, right?" He gave Ryan a meaningful look.

"I was just in one group," Marco said. "There were other groups. I don't know if their immunity rates were any better."

"You warned me," Gus said. "And I didn't want to listen."

Ryan said. "Marco thinks this was a seizure, not 2091 inspired aggression."

"But can we be sure?" Gus said, "And does it really matter? The fact that it was unintentional doesn't change the outcome. Dakota is infected and he bit Darien, and now . . . well, we know what that means."

Ryan cast a glance toward the bathroom door. "You really want him to hear this?"

Gus checked himself and dropped his voice. "No . . . no I don't."

"I'm looking for some hope," Ryan said. "Are you sure that the person who bit Dakota was infected?"

Gus slumped against the wall. "I don't know. He struck me as crazy at the time. He was some firefighter in the camp from Boston or Philadelphia. He kept complaining about being hungry . . . really hungry. He had a broken arm and kept chatting up Marie. Men always tried to chat her up, so I didn't pay much attention until she was going to give him our rations. And I was like, 'Have you lost your mind? You have two teenage boys. You want to hear someone complain about being hungry? Just wait.'

"The firefighter kept going around asking for food, but the people had the same reaction that I did. They told him to get lost because there just wasn't much to go around. He came back to talk to Marie, and I thought I saw him eyeing Dakota, but again I didn't make too much of it. And then it seemed to come out of nowhere. He grabbed Dakota's arm and took a bite out of it like it was a sandwich. I wouldn't swear to it, but somehow I have it in my head that he was salivating just before he did it. Maybe I just made that up, but . . . I don't know."

"Okay, that sounds crazy. But does that mean infected?" Ryan asked. "What happened to this firefighter afterward?"

"I have no idea," Gus said. "I was too wrapped up in trying to keep Dakota from bleeding to death. I think they dragged him away, but I don't know what happened to him."

"Firefighter you say?" Marco asked.

"Yes, is that significant?" Gus said.

"Only because firefighters don't tend to have mental problems," Marco said, "If the attacker had been a street person, then you might be able to chalk it up to crazy, but an otherwise normal man in a stress-related job deciding some kid's arm looks like dinner. . ."

"You think that means infected?" Ryan asked.

Marco shrugged like the answer was obvious.

"But he was talking," Gus said. "I thought the infected couldn't talk any more. That is why they moan and babble. You said you were with them in a ward. Could they talk?"

"I don't know," Marco said. "We were in isolation. I was able to talk to a couple of my friends for a while and they said some strange things, but they were always taken away. The ones who I came to know well were the ones who stayed. They were the ones who didn't go crazy."

"But what was this thing with needing food," Gus said. "He was constantly talking about being really hungry, but that doesn't seem crazy. There wasn't a lot of food in the camps. Most people just thought he was being an ass."

Marco shrugged. "Complaining about being hungry probably comes from his broken arm. One side effect of the Eternity Vaccine is that it makes demands on the metabolism which makes people ravenous. The army started issuing these super dense protein sticks to counter this effect. They tasted terrible but if you were wounded in combat, you couldn't eat enough of them."

"So . . . so . . ." Gus' voice hitched with grief. "What you are telling me is that my son is most likely infected with this terrible disease." His breath seized in his chest, the grief on his face, a living thing. "If the firefighter was infected, then Dakota is certainly infected, and if he is, then Darien—"

The bathroom door cracked open and Dakota took a step out. Tears cascaded down his beaten and swollen face. "I deserved this, didn't I? I deserved this . . ." he said, pointing to his face. He turned and looked into the mirror then back at his father. "I deserved this, didn't I, for what I did to Darien . . . I deserved . . ."

Gus rushed to Dakota and scooped him into his arms. "No, son. This is my fault. This is all my fault."

23

Global Infection: ≤ 30.3042%

The calamity sucked the motivation to work out of everyone. Simone retreated to his favorite gaming console, the boys slept, Gus pored through the boxes of reports, Marco and Raphael disappeared and Ryan was left to fill his time with busywork. He found some interesting things in the new armory and decided he didn't know how to use them. He need a tutorial from the gods of war. He found Marco and Raphael in his office. "So how are these things supposed to fit?" Ryan asked, reapplying the Velcro strap on the body armor.

Raphael was sitting behind the desk. He fell silent as Ryan stepped into the room and casually turned toward the color printer on the credenza next to the fax machines and pulled a handful of documents out of the tray. Then he slid the papers into a folder.

The combination of Daniel Ryder's encouragement toward an ongoing state of paranoia, the fact that Ryan was normally observant and the fact that the Paguero men fell quiet like they had been caught raiding a panty drawer led Ryan to conclude that whatever was on that printer, they didn't want him to see. "This feels a bit short," he said, trying to pull the vest down closer to his hips. "But it's the biggest one I could find."

"The kids have already starting playing with the new toys," Marco said.

Raphael leaned back in Ryan's office chair and frowned. He said, "It *es* fitting right. But you need to make the sides closer. Pull the straps tight so the bullets do no go through the space."

"Closer?" Ryan said. "I'm barely breathing as it is."

"Lose weight," Raphael said.

"Come on, Raphael," Ryan said. "I'm a big guy but I'm not morbidly obese. And besides, I have actually lost fifteen pounds. That is what a few weeks of manual labor interspersed with mortal terror will do for a man."

"Where did you lose it?" Marco asked with a sly smile. "Certainly not in your legs. I think we should call you floods."

"Keep it up you two," Ryan said, tugging at the vest trying to make it more comfortable. "But beggars can't be choosers. Fortunately, one of

Daniel's friends had my waist size. I found these jeans in the baggage they left behind. Unfortunately, he was short, like some people I know." He winked at Raphael.

Raphael frowned.

"I wondered what we were going to do with all of that stuff?" Marco asked. "It looks like a bomb went off in those rooms. Are we going to leave it all over god and country?"

The day Daniel Ryder planned to evacuate his family to his secret doomsday retreat, one of the escape helicopters was shot down by the military in Perry, Florida. The helicopter loss meant the bug out plan suffered a serious blow. With only one remaining helicopter, Daniel required everyone traveling with him to abandon their earthly possessions and they had all arrived at the tower packed as if they were moving their house. Luggage and suitcases were stacked up like the baggage claim at Pittsburgh International Airport. And when the command to ditch everything was issued, people dug through their luggage like dogs rooting through a garden for their favorite bone. Bags and suitcases and clothes were strewn everywhere.

"You want a job?" Ryan asked. "I'll let you put it back in the suitcases and haul it to a bedroom if you like." He tugged at the neck of the bulletproof vest. "It is no wonder people get shot. This is seriously uncomfortable. And damn, I'm already sweating."

"The choice is sweat or a bullet," Marco said, standing up. He turned Ryan around and manipulated the Velcro straps. When he was done, he said, "Is that better?"

Ryan nodded. "Yeah, that is better, with the exception that I can't breathe."

Marco laughed. "Like Poppa says, lose more weight."

Ryan squirmed against the vest as he dropped into a chair. "So what is the powwow about?"

"Powwow?" Raphael said, wrinkling his brow.

"Indian word for meeting, conversation, planning session," Ryan said. "What are you two cooking up?"

"I know what powwow means," Raphael said as if he should be insulted. "It *es* nothing. We were just talking."

And with that answer, Ryan was 90% sure that whatever they were talking about was in fact *something*. It was *something* they didn't want him to know.

"We were talking about all of this data," Marco said, nodding toward the stacks of papers piled neatly on the desk and the three legal pads laying just to the left of Ryan's computer filled with notes penned in Gus' very impressive script.

Liar, liar pants on fire, Ryan thought. But he said, "So what is the prognosis? What is Gus's conclusion?" he pointed towards the notepads.

From the time Dakota and Darien fell peacefully asleep, Gus came into the office and pored through the documentation like a mad man. Every stack was neatly arranged by subject matter. The notepads were the compilation of his endless observations. This was the product of his tireless work to organize the data on the RVCJ-2091 virus.

"It must not have been good," Marco said. "He was crying when he left the room."

"Crying?" Ryan asked.

Raphael handed him the top pad. "He *es* grieving for his sons. So yes, he *es* crying."

Ryan thumbed through the first five pages trying to understand the endless list of equations.

"Either of you any good with numbers? Gus's math is beyond me."

"I'm good," Marco said, "but he's the math wiz."

"Yes. That *es* my job, working with numbers."

"When you looked at these," Ryan said, "did you understand what they meant?"

"I did no look at these numbers."

"I thought you said you were talking about this stuff?" Ryan handed the pad to Raphael.

Raphael's coal black eyes flashed and then he thumbed through the pages, at first disinterested, and then his focus becoming sharper.

"Maybe the numbers aren't important," Marco said.

"Well, since Gus wrote The End, underlined it and put stars beside it," Ryan said, "I think that these numbers told him something."

Raphael put the pad down and sifted through the neat stacks. He pulled a stapled bundle of papers out and began reading. Something in those numbers caught his attention.

"So I see that you put locks on all the guns," Ryan said.

Raphael had done a great job turning the art room into an armory. It was now lined with heavy-duty tables and shelves, gun racks and places to hang MOLLE tactical vests, body armor and the other accoutrements of war. And the finishing touch had been to lock the guns into their racks.

"Yes," Raphael replied. "I do no want curious boys to have problems." His eyes remained on the papers. He started running calculations on the margins.

"Speaking of curious boys," Marco said. "You have your weapons laying on your bed stand. Maybe stick them in a drawer."

Ryan hadn't really thought about those guns. He still had the two Berettas and the Glock. He'd put all three in his room where they had remained. He hadn't had the need or the nerve to wear them. "Maybe that is a good idea. But since I am not a child, you will be giving me the other gun rack key."

Raphael frowned, not looking up. Finally he said, "It *es* a problem to be locked out?"

"Since I didn't get stuck in an elevator, I guess I wouldn't know if it was a problem," Ryan said.

Raphael paused, giving Ryan a flat look, started collecting papers and Gus's notes and started for the door.

"Raphael, two things I want you to think about. First, do you honestly believe that I am going to take a gun and shoot you—"

Raphael interrupted "You do—"

"And," Ryan continued as he stood, "just because you leave doesn't mean this conversation is over." He faced Raphael, his hands at his sides, calm and waiting.

The muscles in Raphael's jaw clenched and corded under his skin. Then his eyes focused on the desk. He took a step and snatched up the folder into which the mysterious color prints had disappeared and added them to his pile. He turned and walked out.

Ryan walked around his desk and took his seat.

Marco remained slumped in his chair, his chin in his hand. "You have 30 seconds to prove to me that you are connected to reality," he said.

"What?" Ryan asked.

Marco said, "That is what you said just before you whipped out some Brazilian jujitsu on Gus. You remember when he was losing his shit? When you said that, I thought it was cool. I'm going to add that to my list of things to say before I put a beat down on someone. And now I'm going to have to add, 'Just because you walk away doesn't mean this conversation is over.'"

Ryan laughed. "Among the many pithy comments I make, you could probably find better ones." He arranged the stacks of papers on his desk so he could move his keyboard.

"For a brief second, I thought we were going to see some more jujitsu. Could have been interesting."

"No, the only interesting thing would be for your father and I to actually finish the conversation like reasonable men." Ryan logged into the computer.

"So where did you learn jujitsu?"

"I read about it in a book once," Ryan said and clicked through the computer. He brought up a remote desktop and navigated to the print server.

"You are a puzzle, Mr. Sage."

"Start with the boarder pieces, that will make it simpler," Ryan said.

"You do realize that my father has been in places that you couldn't manufacture in a nightmare. You know he's done more than most men do in a lifetime and killed more men than some kids tally on a video game. You do know he has a particular ability that comes in very handy in times like these?"

"I do realize that, but I also realize that our fight is not over his ability."

"So what is this fight over?"

"Liberty and tyranny."

"What in the hell are you talking about?"

"Come on Marco, don't let your brain go tilt just because I don't connect the dots. Your father pretends he is in charge of me. That would be the tyranny part. I don't want him to be in charge of me or mine. That would be the liberty part."

"Now you are just being dramatic."

"You only say that because you see your father's actions as benign and I'm just some guy you met a few days ago. If it were me disarming you, in your own home, would you say it was being dramatic?"

Marco narrowed his eyes. "You are not disarmed; he let you have two guns."

"And that is the point. I don't need his permission."

"My father is concerned that you are dangerous and he is keeping you from potentially doing someone else harm."

"Potential harm? Meaning that because I *might* do something harmful he is justified in preventing what I haven't done? Where does that logic go? I am obviously no direct threat. Whatever accident happened on the street has nothing to do with me being able to keep and bear arms now. Your father knows this, but yet keeps me disarmed because it serves his purpose." Ryan said. "That would the tyranny part."

"You don't think he has the right to be safe?"

"Do you really want a conversation about rights?" Ryan asked, "Or do you think saying *rights* is like an argumentative trump card?"

"Humor me."

"Okay, here is the answer. There is no such thing as a right to be safe, because no man can exempt himself from the dangers of this world. Rights are a consequence of existence. You have a right to life because life *is*. You have a right to liberty because you cannot live without freedom to act in your own behalf to sustain your existence. You do not have a *right* to demand that other men satisfy the requirements of your life. One man cannot impose an obligation on other men for what he cannot secure for himself.

"So the principle applies like this. Your father does have a *right* to remove himself from a threat, real or fantasy. For example, he is free to go back to his house, away from me, if that is what he thinks defines safety. He has the *right* to go to private property and a right to freedom of action and a right to freedom of association. If safety is his primary concern, then he has the *right* to leave."

Marco narrowed his eyes. "You do realize that you will not last by yourself? You realize you will die here if you are alone. You need what we have. You need my father and his skills."

"Marco, the issue is not death. The issue is life. And specifically, the kind of life that I'm being compelled to accept. History is filled with examples where the weak deferred their lives to the warrior. In the beginning, it seems like a good, pragmatic, even superior choice, but inevitably those same people are enslaved to the warrior, because he soon uses his violence against the very people he was protecting.

"Your father wants me to bow to his will merely because he is a warrior. And now that I think about it, this is the very same logic all governments use to disarm the masses. Those who control government power insist that because the people are *potentially* dangerous the people are not worthy of their right to keep and bear arms. Because the people in charge have the *right* to be *safe,* everyone else must disarm. How has that worked out for us?"

Marco's jaws clenched and in that moment it was impossible to miss the paternity. He and Raphael were the same man separated only by the years and the accumulated scars of war. "So we are free to leave? Be careful what you wish for," he said and walked out of the office.

"No," Ryan said, "You better hope I get exactly what I am trying to achieve."

Ryan clicked through the print server interface and found Raphael's last print job and sent it to the high definition HP print device. Ryan looked at the first image, splotches of green and gray and brown with ribbons of red, blue, white and yellow dots, thinking briefly it was an abstract painting. He turned it in his hand once, then twice, looking for the proper orientation. He pulled the second one off the printer and then the third. And that was when he saw the familiar lines of the three rivers: Monongahela, Allegheny and Ohio.

"Maps?" Ryan said. "Why in the heck is he printing off Google earth?"

24

Global Infection: ≤ 30.3073%

Simone stood at the refrigerator, door open, staring at the food like he was studying for law school.

Ryan sat at the table eating leftovers and looking through the tower security settings on his iGlass. He took a drink of Sprite and said, "You know the reason they made refrigerator doors out of glass is for teenage boys."

"Huh? What?"

"Glass, you can see through it," Ryan said.

"Oh right," Simone said, but he kept looking at the food like voices were calling his name.

And then like a cannon shot from the far reaches of the penthouse, Raphael shouted, "How could he do this?!"

Simone jumped. "What did I do now?"

"Maybe he felt the cold air from the refrigerator," Ryan said.

"You're not funny," Simone said.

"No, I'm hilarious. You just haven't figured it out yet." He turned toward the sounds of Raphael's voice having a heated exchange with someone. Raphael had been grumpy since the conversation. That was the reason Ryan was eating an early dinner by himself. The sound of the conflict was heading toward the kitchen. Ryan said. "I think I'm on your dad's list."

"Yeah, I heard what you said to him," Simone said, his face grave. "I think you might have a death wish."

Ryan swallowed a bite of potato, cheese and hamburger casserole: It wasn't the best dinner, but they were trying to eat through the mounds of potatoes that would eventually rot. It seemed that everything the Pagueros cooked had *papatas* in the recipe. The upside to the cooking arrangements was that the Pagueros were pretty good cooks.

"Nope, no death wish," he said. "But now that I think about it, I can't imagine that I'm the focus of his wrath. I've been sitting here minding my own business, trying to figure out what this security alarm code means. So you better run. I won't tell him I saw you."

"Really?"

"Cross my heart," Ryan made an X over his chest.

Simone cast furtive glances toward the Spanish rant. "Do we have bolt cutters?"

"Bolt cutters?"

"Do we have some or not?"

"I'm sure there are some. There is a utility room. Did you look—"

"I already looked there," Simone said.

"Okay, how about your father's room. I think he keeps one of everything in there."

Simone faded to the opposite side of the kitchen. "I looked there, too."

Ryan looked over his shoulder. "My only other suggestion is to go to one of the maintenance offices. I'm pretty sure there is one in the substructure. We passed it a couple of weeks ago when your father was showing me how to keep the solar cells from feeding the grid."

Simone sighed. "I didn't want to go down there. It's dark."

"What do you want to break into?"

"I don't want to break into anything," Simone said. "The bolt cutters were for Gus— Shit! You haven't seen me," he said and ran from the kitchen.

Ryan took a bite of casserole, and tapped the iGlass trying to find the explanation for code 67!#911. The security system kept pinging his phone with the code for the last forty minutes, but he couldn't find the explanation for the alert. Every other code came with a description or a reference number so it was simple to identify what was wrong. He'd seen the code before but he couldn't remember when or where.

"I can no believe you would put childrens in danger," Raphael said, stomping into the kitchen, Marco two steps behind.

Ryan looked up from the iGlass and then around the kitchen expecting to see Simone trying to hide in the corner. When he saw no one, he said, "Me?"

"Who else *es* in this kitchen?"

Ryan almost said Simone but they were bonding.

Raphael stomped to the table and slammed his hand into the back of a chair.

Ryan spoke first. "So why did you hide the explanation for the security alert 67!#911? You want to make sure people can break into the tower, right?"

Raphael tilted his head. "What? Why did you accuse me of this?"

"Oh, I'm sorry. I thought we were making arbitrary accusations. You accuse me of endangering children. I accuse you of messing with the security system."

Marco suppressed a laugh.

"Do no laugh," Raphael snapped. "This *es* serious."

"Poppa, why don't you just ask him?"

"Yes, Raphael why don't you just ask me," Ryan said. "The conversation would go something like this. 'Ryan, you *es* a dipshit. You want to kill little childrens, but did you try to hurt them?'" It was a pretty good imitation.

Raphael's eyes narrowed. "One day you will mock me and it will no be a good thing."

"Raphael, I don't have to mock you. You do a good job of making a fool of yourself all by yourself. So why don't you tell me what you think I have done."

"You already know what you did."

Ryan rolled his eyes and turned his attention back to his iGlass. He cut out a fork full of casserole and took a bite.

Marco said, "He thinks you tried to saw through the lock on the gun rack."

Ryan took another bite, swallowed and washed it down with a sip of soda. "Well, okay, but even if I did do it, I don't owe you an explanation. This is my house and I get to do what I want in my house, and if I decide that there is a lock preventing me from getting to an objective and I can't find some bolt cutters—"

Ryan paused.

Is that why Gus wanted bolt cutters?

"So you did do it," Raphael said, triumphant.

Ryan rose from the table and looked around the corner. He found Simone standing in the next room listening. "I thought I'd find you here."

"What?" Simone said. "What did I do?"

"You didn't do anything," Ryan said, waving him into the kitchen. "But I didn't rat you out so you are gonna help me get out of trouble. When did Gus ask for the bolt cutters?"

Simone came into the kitchen. "I don't know. A few hours ago. Dakota and I were playing video games. Well, I was playing and Dakota was watching. Gus said that Dakota needed to rest so he was going to take him down to his own bed. As he left, Gus asked if I knew where to find bolt cutters."

Taking him to his own bed?

"See, Poppa, you just needed to ask," Marco said. "You didn't need to yell."

Raphael crossed his arms. "He still do no say that he didn't do it."

"Gus took Dakota to his own bed?" Ryan said. "Like, he took him down to the Blanco condo?"

Simone shrugged. "Yeah, I think that is what he meant."

It was like someone had plucked a base string and it was vibrating low and ominous in Ryan's soul. "Did he say anything else?"

"Not really," Simone said. "Actually, he just sat in the chair watching us. He cried but he didn't say much. He just thanked me for being a friend to Dakota and Darien. Oh, and he said something about talking to Poppa. Something about the numbers don't lie."

Raphael's phone pinged.

Ryan nodded toward the sound. "What is the alert on your phone?"

Raphael dug the phone out of his shirt pocket. He wrinkled his brow. "What *es* this? 67!#911?"

"Raphael, what did you and Gus talk about after you left my office?"

Raphael shrugged. "We talk about his calculations. Then he talk about this woman, Tess. He have an affair with her. He say he love his wife, but I think he love this Tess more."

"Ryan," Marco said. "You look pale."

"When was the last time anyone saw Darien?" Ryan asked.

"He and Poppa were trying to play chess a little while after the incident and speaking Spanish," Simone said.

Raphael gave a rare smile. "I was trying to distract him from some pain. He *es* learning his native language very well."

Simone rolled his eyes. "You mean English?"

"Do no be smart," Raphael said.

"So the last time we saw Darien was when?" Ryan asked.

25

Global Infection: ≤ 30.3074%

Ryan's thoughts were a jumble. Gus talking about Bexley's courage. Gus talking about deserving Tess. The calculations on the page. Gus' parting words to Simone. Taking Dakota to sleep in his own bed.

Why go back down to the condo?

"Simone, do me a favor," Ryan said, "You know where the boys were sleeping. See if you can find Darien, and then go down to the Blanco condo and look for Dakota."

"Why?" Simone asked

"Just go check on them for me, please. Take a radio and call us when you find one of them."

Simone looked from Ryan to Raphael. Raphael nodded.

"Talk to us," Marco said.

"Tess was my sister," Ryan said. "Gus had an affair with her. But something Gus said to me about my brother-in-law, Bexley, has me nervous."

"What? What did Gus say?"

Ryan raked his hands through his gray hair. "This is so hard to explain. Before everyone knew what the 2091 virus was, or that it was very dangerous, my brother-in-law shot his youngest daughter and then put the gun in his mouth and pulled the trigger. He did it because he knew they were both infected."

"*Madre de Dios*," Raphael said. "This *es* a damnable sin. He will forever be in hell for this suicide."

"Oh shit," Marco said. "You think that Gus is going to kill his boys—"

"Because they are infected. That is why he tried to cut the lock—"

"He can no do this. This *es* no courageous. God will damn him to hell. We must find the boys. We must find Darien."

Ryan held up his phone. "Raphael, think. What does this security code mean?"

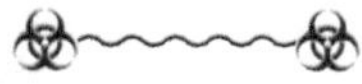

67!#911 meant that the rooftop door was open and the Renaissance Tower was vulnerable to the world. Ryan had seen the code on the night he found Gus Blanco at the edge of the helipad, and that is where he found him again. Gus was sitting cross legged holding Darien in his lap rocking and singing softly into his son's ear mere inches from falling.

"Gus, let's think about this." Ryan said as he walked slowly across the double R hammer and sickle design.

"It is a beautiful evening, isn't it, Ryan? My only regret is that I gave him too much Ambien," Gus said continuing to rock Darien in his arms. "I wanted him toremember his mother one more time."

"Gus, where is Dakota?" Marco asked.

"Dakota needed to rest," Gus said. "He's fine now. I know he didn't mean to hurt anyone. It is like Georgia, right? She didn't mean to hurt anyone. I'm sure it just happened. She was such a sweet girl. She loved playing with my boys. I loved it when she would crawl into my lap and sleep on my shoulder. She always smelled like flowers."

"Gus, come on man," Ryan said, "This is not—"

"I lied to you," Gus said. "I said I didn't love your sister." Tears started leaking down his cheek. "She was a wonderful woman. She wanted a divorce. She wanted us to marry. She said she wanted to have my babies. That is when I knew I had to leave Pittsburgh. I knew if I stayed one more day, I was going to break Marie's heart."

"Daddy?" Darien mumbled and stirred.

"Shshshshhhh, it's okay, baby. Daddy's got you. Just take your time waking up."

"Why am I so sleepy?" Darien said, his words sounding like mush.

"You will be fine in a minute. When you wake up, you can see your mom."

"Mom? Really?" Darien said trying to sit up. "I thought she was . . ."

Marco walked closer. "Gus, where is Dakota?"

"Simone? Simone?" Raphael said into the radio. "Can you hear me?"

"Every third wor—" Simone said into the crackling radio. *"Dak . . . not in penthouse. Going to Blanco . . ."*

"Simone," Raphael said. "Say again? *Es* Dakota in the condo?"

"Not here," Simone said.

"Where *es* Dakota?" Raphael said. "Tell me what you have done with Dakota?"

"Bexley had such balls," Gus said. "I thought about it a lot . . . how to put a gun in my mouth and pull the trigger. I even tried to get a gun, but Mr. Gun Safety over there put a lock on the rack that even God couldn't get through. But in the end, I didn't think I could actually do that to them."

"Dad, I'm cold," Darien mumbled, trying to force his eyes open. "I want to go inside."

"He's waking up now," Gus said. "So I can't really say much more about Tess. I guess I could, but I don't want that to be the last thing he hears. But Ryan, I wanted you to know that she wasn't some slut that I used and tossed away. She was a woman that a man had to earn. I thought Bexley was an ass most of the time, but his last action as a father and as a husband . . ."

"No, Gus, this is not the same thing," Ryan said, taking a few more steps forward. "Bexley already knew that Georgia was dangerous. We don't know that about Dakota or Darien."

Gus made eye contact with Ryan and then Raphael. Then he said, "Yes, we do. Ask him. We worked through the numbers twice. Mr. Spanish Lesson is also very good with math. He knows. I showed him the other documents. I showed him what the numbers mean. It is madness to stay here on this earth. I think the scientists call it an ELE, and Extinction Level Event"

"Dad, why are we so close to the edge?" Darien said.

"Stand up with me son," Gus said. "I want you to see your mother. I want you to see where she is."

"But I don't want to be this close," Darien said, trying to push back.

"I told your mother that it was a bad idea to come here," Gus said. "But she wouldn't listen to me. She kept saying that it was our duty to be with the people, that we should suffer just as they suffered. Look down there, son. We have suffered, haven't we? We are part of the people, aren't we?"

"Dad? Dad?" Darien said, his voice rising as he tried to push back, but the drugs in his body made him sluggish.

"Your mom said that our white privilege was immoral." Gus shook his head. "But did your mom tell you that the Blancos have a heritage that goes deep into the tribes of Peru? Maybe it was good that Raphael was teaching you Spanish. Or maybe he should have taught you the language of the Incas. That would have been our true heritage. But she didn't tell you that, did she? She told you that because the Blancos came to American and spoke English, we were participating in the evils of white privilege. She told you that because your father made money, he was a white man." Gus took one more step closer to the helipad edge.

"Dad! Dad, stop!"

"Do you see the van?" Gus said. "That is where your mother is. Do you see it?"

"I see it," Darien said, squirming. "I see it. But this is too close. Please let me go."

Gus looked deep into Ryan's eyes. "But I see the truth now. Tess never condemned me. She thought my money was a virtue. She thought I had virtue. You were wrong about her. She did see the world like you see the world. One of the last things she told me was that I reminded her of her brother. I knew it was a compliment."

"He's gonna jump," Ryan breathed. "Shoot him."

Raphael was confused. "What? This *es* sadness. I see this before. We can talk him to come here . . ."

"No, this is not grief. Shoot him. Gus is going to jump."

Gus took one step closer.

Darien said, "Dad? Dad?"

"Shoot him now!"

"Don't move! Gus, don't you move!" Marco said from behind, his weapon drawn down on target.

"Do no shoot! You will hit the boy!" Raphael said.

"Raphael," Ryan rasped. "I'm telling you he is going to jump. Shoot him in the leg now."

Gus flashed them a pained smile.

Raphael reached. "No! No!" he barked. "Come here now!" he said stepping closer and closer to Gus. "You come here now!"

Gus tightened his grip on Darien. "Raphael, you of all people know it has to be done. How many times did Marie beg you to let us into the tower? This is why you wouldn't let us in, right? You knew the danger and that is why you didn't want us in the tower to begin with. I hated you for locking us out until I realized, that with a disease this dangerous, it was the right thing. I couple hours ago I forgave you."

"Dad?" Darien said, his body rigid, his voice high and shrill. "Dad?"

"Maybe there *es* another way," Raphael said. "Maybe he does no have to be sick. He *es* my best student. Maybe . . ."

"He's here," Simone said in the radio. "He's in the . . . ub. Blood . . . washed away bu . . . wrists— You copy?"

"Damned radio," Raphael said. "Say again."

"Dakota is dead!" Simone's voice came through loud and frantic.

Gus raised his leg toward the edge.

Darien screamed.

Raphael tipped toward the precipice, his hands groping like a wide receiver reaching for an errant pass.

Darien clawed at the air.

Raphael caught his hand.

Gus tilted forward . . . farther, farther, farther.

Darien bent at the waist, pulling Raphael toward the edge like a drowning man killing a lifeguard.

Raphael lurched under the abrupt pull of gravity.

Ryan dove, grabbing Raphael's belt.

Marco dove, grabbing Ryan's legs.

And for an agonizing second, they all tilted toward the street thirty-two stories below.

Gus smiled into the sky. "I love you, Tess," he whispered.

Darien shrieked, his voice warbling like a horse brought down by a pack of wolves: his scream piercing, desperate and visceral, his hands clawing, ripping, digging for something to catch hold.

Raphael fell face first, his chin bouncing off the edge of the helipad, his chest slid inch by inch. His grip failed and gravity won.

The screams faded like a train passing on a track.

The sound of wet laundry, shattered glass and twisting metal filtered up to the helipad.

Raphael lay on the helipad, chest hanging over the edge. Ryan lay on his legs holding his knees like a linebacker and Marco piled on pinning them to the helipad.

"Oh, *Madre de Dios! Madre de Dios!*" Raphael wailed staring down at the street. "*Mia Madre de Dios.*"

"Can I move?" Marco demanded, not daring to look up. "Tell me if I can move. Tell me, god dammit! Will he fall if I move?"

Ryan opened his eyes. "Pull his legs. Pull his legs."

Marco shifted and pulled Raphael's heels.

"*Madre de Dios,*" Raphael cried, the tears pouring down his face as his chest slid away from the horror below. Marco and Ryan dragged him six and then eight, and then ten and then twenty feet from the edge until they collapsed. Ryan sat back, his arms and legs shaking like he had Parkinson's. Raphael curled into a ball and sobbed. Marco dropped himself over his father and lay still.

26

Global Infection: ≤ 30.3411%

Three stairwells accessed the ground level to the eighth floor promenade and Ryan was in the middle stairwell. Sweat dripped down his nose as he lay the plywood in place. He paused to grab a red shop rag, wiped his brow, then picked up the ITW Ramset and faced the barrel toward the plywood. He angled the tool so the anchor bolt would catch the stair tread below. He pulled the trigger and the sound of the gun slapped against his ears and echoed up the well. He moved the Ramset over three feet, braced himself for the sound and fired. He slid up the incline, wedged his foot on the exposed stairs, angled the Ramset and pulled the trigger once and then twice. Ryan tested his work to make sure the plywood was secure. Satisfied, he picked up a shop rag and the Ramset and slid up the fastened plywood until he could climb the stairs to the midpoint landing.

Ryan wiped his face, feeling tempted to open the ground floor exit and let the natural draft sweep up the stairwell like a chimney to cool off. But he didn't have the nerve. The ground floor was where the monsters lived. The ground floor was where things lurked in the shadows and tried to eat you. The street level was where the dead people were.

Gus . . .

Darien . . .

If the ground floor stairwell door was locked and barricaded, there was nothing to fear. Or at least that was Ryan's logic and besides, the heat and the sweat, the pain of aching muscles felt good. It gave him something to think about, to focus on, to distract his mind from the image of Darien Blanco's face as he started to fall, to erase from Ryan's psyche the scream, the pitch, the tone, the timber of pure terror—the dread of an innocent soul that had done nothing but love: a boy who just tried to relieve his brother's suffering.

☣~~~~~☣

Raphael and Marco lay on the helipad, hugging and sobbing. No one dared move as if they feared the concrete under their bodies would magically disappear and follow Gus and Darien to certain death. They lay in the dull gray afternoon with the cold wind tormenting their skin, the tower's energy producing wind turbines spinning and spinning, driven by the acrid breeze carrying the smells of death and destruction down the Monongahela Valley.

Marco spoke first but Raphael started shouting first. Then father and son raged in Spanish. Ryan could follow a general conversation, but a heated exchange that rolled off the tongue like a machinegun was lost on him. Not that it was hard to get the gist. Ryan caught the accusatory looks and the acrimonious tone. He heard the words Tess and Bexley and affair. Somehow Gus killing Darien was Ryan's fault because Tess was his sister.

Marco called Raphael *muchacho tonto* and would have said more, but Simone interrupted. He climbed to the helipad, tears streaming down his face. "Dakota is dead," he said.

Raphael rushed to hold his son.

Indeed Dakota was dead. He'd been laid in the bathtub, in Superman pajamas, his damp hair combed, his hands crossed over his lap, his eyes closed. It looked like he'd fallen asleep except for the slits at his wrists, the small trail of pink tinted water that pooled under his feet near the drain, the pile of water-logged bloody towels, the empty glass of orange juice and the small line of crushed Ambien that failed make it into sleep cocktail.

Raphael found a sheet in the linen closet, wrapped Dakota with the affection of an embalmer and carried him, clutched to his chest, down to the grocery. The world, it seemed, was filled with vicious ironies. Ryan was wrong. Dead bodies *were* going to be stored in the freezers until they found the time to bury them outside. Raphael stood over Dakota and prayed in Spanish, his breath puffing steam into the cold. Simone and Marco crossed themselves when he finished. The freezer door clicked shut, and Ryan turned off the lights.

They returned to the penthouse in silence. Simone vanished into the deep warrens. Raphael collapsed in a kitchen chair and stared at the chessboard as if he were waiting for Darien to make his move. Marco slid into his recliner and the penthouse smart system started a romantic comedy. Ryan joined him in a matching recliner and stared at the screen, trying to banish reality behind the thin veil of mindless entertainment until the female love interest started a third insipid fight.

Disgusted, Ryan pushed himself to his feet and walked to his office. He paused at his desk and then kept walking through Mora's office, through the outer offices, toward his bed thinking that he might sleep maybe for a few minutes or maybe for a few years, whichever came first. But Ryan walked past his room and continued his tour, walking into suites and rooms he didn't know existed. He explored the workout room and the small dance studio and a second entertainment room and the library with tall dark oak shelves that required a ladder to reach the top shelf. He climbed the stairs to the penthouse's second floor and found an endless line of bedrooms for when the Hampton and French Riviera friends came to hang out with Richard Ryder in the Steel City. And it was on the second floor among the endless spare bedrooms where he found where Dakota and Darien had slept. Like two adventurers, they'd staked out an obscure bedroom in the far corner of the penthouse with bunk beds. But instead of sleeping in the bunks, they pulled the mattresses down to the floor and strung blankets over their heads. Flashlights were scattered around amid the empty chip bags and soda bottles.

The memory clawed through Ryan's chest and grabbed his lungs. His breath came in hitches and gasps as he thought of Xyla and Georgia staying at his house, making a fort in the living room when it stormed and the lights went out. They begged him as only young girls can to have a slumber party under the blankets. Every cushion in the house ended up on the floor and half dozen sheets were commandeered to make the top of the tent. They cuddled close to his shoulders clutching flashlights to their chests like they were a lifeline. They said the sheets would keep him safe if the roof blew away in the storm.

They just wanted me to be safe from the storm. They just wanted . . .

Ryan started walking as he mopped the tears from his cheeks with the tail of his shirt. He walked back to his room, pulled the Glock and holster off the night stand, fastened it to his belt. He left the penthouse, descended the stairs to *Mon Pierre's* and then down more stairs and then more stairs and then through the empty tower floors.

When Daniel Ryder said the building was only about a third rented, Ryan didn't realize that meant only a third of the building's residential floors were built out. But floor after floor was empty but for the piles and piles of building supplies neatly stacked, merely waiting for the general contractor to give the word.

He walked down more stairs and still more until he arrived at the eighth floor. The building map on the wall called this floor the promenade level. It was the transition level between the commercial space below and the residential space above. Arrows to the left pointed toward the pool and the workout rooms. Arrows to the right pointed toward the telecommute offices, the executive meeting room, and clubhouse. The arrows pointing toward the main exit said Running Track. Ryan exited the tower, went down the handicap ramp and passed the picnic tables where the office workers could come for lunch, past the small toddler playground with its maximum security fence decorated in clowns, bunnies and puppies, and onto the running track where mothers in yoga pants could push their strollers.

Ryan paused to look west toward the Ohio River but as soon as he stopped moving, Darien threatened to rush back to his mind. He continued south and dared not pause to look at Mount Washington, because he knew his eyes would want to look down. And if they gave into their lust, they would see Darien's body just a few stories below, broken open like a watermelon maybe staring sightlessly toward the gray and forbidding sky.

Ryan finished the circuit around the tower running track, returned to the tower and went down one flight of stairs onto the seventh floor. And it was here that he found another stash of building materials and tools and small industrial machines, spools of wire, power cords, hammers, tape measures, boxes of nails, boxes of screws and bags of concrete scattered hither and yon in piles, in chaos, in disarray. It was like people had dropped everything wherever they could . . . and ran.

He leaned against a contractor table littered with five carpentry pencils, two rolled-up architectural plans, a pack of cigarettes and two red shop rags. Sweat rolled off his forehead and into his right eye. He mopped his face with the rag, only vaguely aware that it smelled. The clutter bothered him so he put a hammer into a blue Lowe's jobsite storage box, followed by a screwdriver and an orange electric cord. Then a builder's tool belt went around his waist and he tucked a tape measure in the front and a hammer in the loop. He saw the pile of plywood and his mind thought of Builder Bob, a man who gave himself that name and laughed every time he said it.

Builder Bob was a man with theories about the RVCJ-2091s.

> *"These African lunatics, they're mean as shit and act like ants, but they don't have a queen bee," Bob said. "Them lunatics, they just keep coming and coming just like them ants in Africa. Must be why they call it the African Rabies. Am I right? But them African lunatics were stymied by ladders and trees and," Builder Bob was sure, "they would not be able to climb up slippery, plywood-covered stairs. They would have to fill up the whole stairwell to pile over the upper floor, and by then no more could get in from the bottom."*

At first Ryan thought he would just stage some plywood in one stairwell, but staging became arranging and arranging became the need to build. But building required being on the ground floor and being on the ground floor seemed the height of daring. For fifteen minutes Ryan stood at the landing midway between the first and second floor, feeling as if he taunted the fates. He used the security app on his phone to confirm that the magnetic lock was powered on and then reconfirmed and then confirmed again. But somehow that didn't make him feel safe, so he duplicated Raphael's elegant but effective barricade, the same one used to secure the tower's exterior doors. The only difference was that Ryan's version was made of plywood, not steel.

The first drumming echo of the Ramset blasting cap slapped off the walls and echoed up the stairwell. Ryan's ears rang. He almost made the tedious trip back to the seventh floor to rummage through the gang boxes for earplugs, but he knew if he walked out of the stairwell, the project would stall. He had to keep working. He had to keep focused. He had to keep that face, that scream, that terror, out of his mind.

Soon the first stairwell was covered from the ground floor to the midpoint landing. To test his handiwork, he slid to the bottom only to regret the splinters that ravaged his butt as he scraped over the plywood seams. The climb back up proved wonderfully treacherous: a smooth forty-degree incline was pure hazard. 2091s couldn't hope to rush up the slope.

Ryan was in rhythm by the time he got to the second stairwell, feeling good, feeling pleasantly fatigued and feeling productive, feeling the edges of grief move off into the distance. As he slid the plywood into place, he heard the footsteps in the stairwell above.

Ryan used the Ramset to send an anchor into the tread and then moved the tool over two feet and pulled the trigger again.

The footfall grew closer.

Ryan slid up the slope and quickly set two more anchors.

The footfall stopped.

Ryan climbed back to the landing and looked up.

Raphael stood at the second-floor door, dressed as he was always dressed when he left the penthouse: sprouting guns like a porcupine. "What *es* this?" he said, nodding toward the plywood.

"You can come on down and see what I've done."

"You are armed?"

"What?" Ryan said, confused until he remembered that the Glock was on his hip; he had forgotten it was there. Somehow the poking into his muffin top had faded into an irrelevancy. "Yes, I'm armed. Do you honestly think this weapon is going to jump out of the holster and shoot you?"

"I think it *es* my right to take my ball and go *home,* yes? I am being safe away from you, yes?"

"Okay, whatever."

"You will lock me out again?"

"I'm pretty sure you know the whole context. Don't pretend to be stupid."

"Yes, I hear this context."

And suddenly Ryan didn't care to fight. "It doesn't matter. You can come down here and look at it by yourself if you want. I'll be done in a few hours."

"But why did you do this?" Raphael said. "Peoples can't use these doors with this plywood."

"Well, that is the point. We are trying to keep the infected from getting up these stairs, and I speak from experience that this is a pretty effective technique."

"But what if we want to get out? You have blocked the doors."

"I used the exact same design that you used on the external doors. I liked your design *because* it was easy to take down from the inside."

"You should speak to me about this. This may not be the best plan. Maybe we need this plywood for other things. Maybe we need those tools for other things."

"Hang on," Ryan said and started to climb up the stairs. He was not having this conversation looking up. "Raphael, I would be glad to talk to you—"

"You can stay there," Raphael said, nodding toward the gun on Ryan's hip.

Ryan paused, sighed, and finally said. "Very well. But eventually we'll have to find a solution. I am not going through the rest of my life unarmed merely because you are angry at me."

Raphael remained impassive.

"I'll be done when I'm done." Ryan walked down stairs to the unfinished project. He fiddled with the plywood and then paused when he saw Raphael's shadow, leaning over the railing.

"My family goes back to Marcial de Lorenzana," Raphael said, "the legend *es* that my seventh paternal grandfather was a Jesuit priest who live in San Ignacio."

"What?"

"He fell in love with a Spanish princess, and he broke his vows to be with her. But she was engaged to a prince. She flee Spain because she do no want to marry him. They do no have the family blessing, so the Jesuit and the princess remain in Paraguay to raise the boy."

"Raphael, I'm sure this is going somewhere, but I confess I'm lost."

Raphael frowned at the interruption and said, "The Jesuit and the princess, they live in one of the Indian *reducciones*. In America these are named reservations. But as they live there, the *mamelucos*—I do no know what this word *es* in English—they raid the reservations for slaves. Their home *es* burned and their goods destroyed and their friends murdered. The princess think it *es* God's judgment for sins, but the Jesuit, he tell his wife that she should no worry about what she cannot control. He tell her that it *es* family that *es* important. They leave Paraguay to sail back to Spain. She never go home and she never tell her family that she have a son and two daughters. The son grows up and becomes a Jesuit and sails back to Paraguay. And he live in the same *reducciones*, in the same house he build again."

Ryan slid to a step and leaned against the wall, trying to figure out what this had to do with anything.

Raphael bent his lips down in a muse as if the thoughts in his mind had a bad taste. "It is said that the Jesuits conquered Paraguay with no war, but this *es* a story that peoples tell. To conquer requires war. It was during the war for independence from Spain that the son also meet a woman from Spain, from Castile. She was raped by a soldier and the Jesuit love her. But he will not break his vows. He flee Paraguay. He leaves what he knows so that they can be safe, to take those he love to live in peace. Later they return to Paraguay, but they do no return to the *reducciones* because they are no more. They live in a city, and they never be with each other. But the boy, he grow to be a handsome man, a university professor who want to marry a European woman. But *de* Francia forbid the Spanish to marry the Spanish. He say that peoples must marry the Indians, and so this man become an enemy of José Gaspar Rodríguez *de* Francia. The priest and the woman were killed by *de* Francia, but the man, he flee to the mountains where they live until *de* Francia die."

Raphael paused, his eyes shut, his brows knit like he was putting ideas together, ideas that he'd been considering but had yet to speak. "Paraguay have war. It have lots of war. I meet my Leona in war. And like my sixth and seventh grandfather, we leave to be safe. We leave the peoples we love so that we can live and raise our son Marco. We learn what the Jesuit tell his wife, that we can no worry about what we can no control. The death of peoples . . . the death of little childrens . . ." his voice caught and his eyes watered. "The deaths that we see, we must not grieve for them because it *es* God's will. . ." his voice caught again, "even if we pray to the Holy Mother and it does no happen . . ." he tried to hold back the tears. "It *es* God's will."

And for minutes, Raphael leaned against the railing, tears dripping down his nose. Finally, he wiped his face with the back of his hand, made eye contact with Ryan, nodded and turned to walk up the stairs. The door opened and then banged shut sounding like a drum.

27

Global Infection: ≤ 30.8071%

The vibration woke him at 6:15 a.m. The iGlass vibrated until Ryan pulled it from under his pillow. He vaguely remembered watching a video before he fell asleep, but the details were fuzzy. He slid his finger across the surface to answer the call. He saw Bruce's face and winced.

"Bruce?" Ryan croaked, his eyes squinting hard against the light. "What is going on?"

"Mr. Sage, hey, we need you to do some things. Team Bruptrick has figured out how to reset the biometric security system. We need you to go the central reader and get us the serial number, and we need you to confirm the port it is connected to, and we need you to take your laptop and a crossover cable to verify that the ping command is enabled on the box, and then we—"

"Patrick, hang on," Ryan said trying to drag himself awake, putting his memory on rewind. He remembered collapsing in his bed after a shower, feeling like he'd accomplished something. He remembered putting the tools away in the Lowes gang box and trying to decide what to do next. He remembered the quiet late-night snack and being vaguely disappointed that the Pagueros were scarce—"

"I'm Bruce," Bruce said.

"Oh, right. Look I'm still asleep. For all I know I'm dreaming."

"Mr. Sage! This is no dream. This is Team Bruptrick. We have solved the problem." Bruce was all excitement. "We were able to find some proprietary documentation on the scanners, and we think we can trick them into doing a factory reset. The company insists that it is not possible, but we are IT gods."

Ryan sat up and pinched his eyes. "Well, Your Worship, can't this wait until us mere mortals have woken up?"

"Sleep?" said Patrick off-camera. "Sleep is for pussies." Then his face popped into the video conference. "Need to get moving, Mr. Sage. We've got this beat."

Ryan's mind finally started clicking and it looked like they were sitting in some kind of command center. The backdrop was consoles with readouts and dials and switches. And every spare flat surface held Mountain Dew and Five Hour Energy bottles and empty Doritos bags and Hostess cupcake wrappers. Their unshaven faces loomed large in their cameras, and the dark spots under their eyes made it look like they had both put on eye shadow. "Oh dear god, you guys have not slept since we talked, have you?"

"I slept less than he has," Patrick said.

"You have not!" Bruce said. "You were sleeping for like an hour after you did that blunt."

"I was not sleeping!" Patrick snapped. "I told you I was just thinking with my eyes closed."

"You were toasted and you were *sleeping*," Bruce snapped back.

"If I was sleeping, then how did I come up with the idea to have Mr. Sage check the ports for us?"

"I came up with that idea, you doob, like yesterday."

"You are the doob. And no, you didn't."

"Guys! Guys! I don't care who slept less," Ryan said. "I am encouraging you to sleep *more*. Like *me* sleeping more while *you* sleep more. And then maybe tomorrow afternoon, after we have all slept you can call me. That sounds like a truly elegant technical solution."

"It's not like we have anything else to do," Bruce said.

"Or go to work in the morning," Patrick said.

One of the reasons Ryan hired guys like this was because they never quit working. The downside was he got calls at six in the morning to listen to them crow about their latest technical miracle. "I think Daniel Ryder would disagree with that last comment," Ryan said.

Team Bruptrick suddenly started looking around as if uttering Daniels name would summon him into a pentagram. "You talked to him?" Bruce said, his voice a squeak.

"About us?" Patrick asked.

"No, he talked. I listened. But it seems that you two are AWOL. Actually, he thinks you are dead."

"Dead?" Bruce asked. "Why would he think that?"

"I'm sure that if you had a couple hours *'sleep*," Ryan said, "you would understand his conclusion."

"You are such a doob," Patrick said. "It's because we are not there, and he expected us to be there."

"Oh," Bruce said. "I guess that makes sense. Did he cry? Were there any tears?"

Ryan knew that the right answer was yes. Bruce wanted to be missed. Ryan said, "I'm sure you could stop the tears if you would get in touch with your old boss."

"You didn't tell him we were alive?" Patrick said.

Ryan shook his head. "Nope. Not my secret to tell."

"See, I told you he was cool!" Patrick said, looking off-camera. "I told you he was cool! Us IT guys have to stick together. Isn't that right, Mr. Sage?

When you have time, we are going to get Deadnu out of the nine hells. And that is a promise."

It had been almost a small Ice Age since Ryan Sage played Dungeons and Dragons, and the last time he played his favorite monk character, Deadnu, he ended up banished to some part of the Forgotten Realms world. He couldn't remember where Deadnu was supposed to now reside, so maybe it was to the nine hells or maybe it wasn't. Not that it mattered, and not that he cared. All he cared about was getting back to sleep. But the faces of the two men in the camera looked so expectant, so excited, so determined to please that he didn't have the heart to say no. "All right, I'll tell you what. You need me, my laptop and a crossover cable near the bio scanner's main interface. I'm going to need at least twenty minutes to get my act together. I will call you then."

"It's been like forty-five minutes," Bruce said, as soon as the video chat connected.

"We were worried," Patrick said.

"Yeah, sorry. I could not find my phone anywhere. I could have sworn it was on my nightstand, but . . . I don't know. Plus, it is pretty damned creepy walking around this tower in the middle of the morning. And there is no easy way to get to the thirteenth floor. So, anyway, what do you need me to do?"

"We need the serial number. It is going to be inside the housing somewhere," Bruce said.

"And we need you to check the number on a chip for us," Patrick said. "That will be on the motherboard."

"He knows where the chip is, you doob," Bruce said.

"Why are we doing this?"

"We have to trick the system into accepting our palm prints as the master print," Patrick said.

Bruce said, "But we can't find it on the network."

"It's gotta be there," Patrick snapped.

Having worked on PCs most of his adult life, Ryan was smart enough to have arrived on the security barracks with tools. "Hang on for minute. The unit is fastened to the wall. I'm going to have to take the casing off to get your numbers."

"Hey, Mr. Sage, is that a gun on your hip?" Patrick asked.

"Yup," Ryan said. He'd been fretting for five minutes about whether he should wake one of the Pagueros before heading down to the barracks. He was surprised that he didn't find anyone in the security room watching cameras, but grief had so permeated the penthouse that it made sense that everyone collapsed as soon as the sun went down.

"We gotta get guns," Bruce said.

"You'd shoot yourself in the foot," Patrick said and laughed like it was the funniest thing he'd ever heard.

"You are such a doob," Bruce said. "Hey, Mr. Sage, is that the gun you killed zombies with?"

"Nope," Ryan said, pulling the last of the wall mount away. Not wanting to talk about that, he said, "Why don't you two tell me what you figured out?" IT guys rarely got to tell people how they worked their magic because most people just didn't understand.

Patrick said, "The system had to be programmable, right?"

"I mean you have to program it the first time without a palm print, right?" Bruce said.

"So, we found out that once the system has a master account, it locks the root account," Patrick said.

"The scanner merely reduces the palm print to ones and zeros," Bruce said.

"We think we can spoof one of the signatures, but first we need to be able to touch that system from our end," Patrick said.

Bruce continued. "But it is pretty well hidden from your end. We can't see it. I mean, if you have a security device that is on a network and everyone can see it and it can be hacked, that would be stupid. But for the authentication to work on a network, it has to have some access to the whole security network. So we were like, 'Where would we hide this device—'"

Patrick interrupted. "Because we weren't around for its installation."

"I was going to tell him that," Bruce said.

"I'm just saying," Patrick replied.

"Anyway," Bruce said as if he were making a demand on cosmic patience. "We figured the best way to hide this was to put it behind a tasteful firewall and then route all network traffic through dedicated ports on all other routers. This would make it almost impossible to see."

"Tell him the next part!"

"I'm getting there!" Bruce said, "But when we started looking at the network layout, we found like eighty ports that were configured for dedicated traffic. So then we were like, 'Which one is the right one? Where is the firewall hiding?'"

"And this is the cool part," Patrick said.

"I'm telling this," Bruce said. "I had the idea to eliminate all of the ports where ping traffic actually worked."

"That was my idea. That is when I was thinking with my eyes closed, remember!"

"No, that was my idea. You were sleeping. Then we kept testing and found only six potential ports that have no traffic whatsoever."

"Maybe there is nothing on those ports?" Ryan said as he pulled the last of the housing away, revealing the scanner's internals.

"That is what you are going to verify," Patrick said. "Instead of tracing every line to every patch panel, you just need to verify where you are connected. And then we will be able to tell if that line is behind the stateful firewall, because it shouldn't show traffic."

"Okay, the face plate says MDF 13-A22-47 Blue," Ryan said. "If I had to guess, that means it runs to the main distribution frame here on the thirteenth-floor rack 22 A port 47."

Patrick beamed into the camera. "I told you he was the real thing! I told you!"

Bruce pinched up his face. "That's not what you said—"

"Shut up!" Patrick said. "Can you see the traffic now?"

"Go smoke a blunt or something while I do the real work," Bruce said. "I gotta get into the system. Okay. Mr. Sage, can you take the crossover cable and try and ping that NIC? You will lose connectivity when you unplug, so you can call us—"

"Oh ye of little IT faith," Ryan said. "There is a computer here in the room." He ran the command and got the replies. "Ping is enabled on this machine. Your data traffic is controlled on your switches."

"I fucking knew it!" Patrick said. "I fucking knew it!" His fingers clattered over his keyboard. "I'm in the switch. Why didn't those idiots notate? Fucking CCNA goons! They know better. You see this? You see this?"

"Fucking CCNA goons," Bruce chimed in. "Yeah, why didn't they notate their setup?"

Ryan wanted to say, *"Probably because they were trying to keep the purpose of those specific ports a secret? To make it as hard as possible for people just like you from doing exactly what you are doing right now."* But he kept quiet.

"Now we need you to find a chip on the motherboard. It should have a prefix CAZ231. We need all the numbers that follow. And we need you to identify the dip switches on the south side of the board."

Ryan said, "I have a better idea." He took his iGlass and tapped his way to the camera function and took pictures. "I just uploaded pictures to the M drive. You can see what you need from there."

"I see them," Patrick said. "I got you, you bastard. Now I'm going to fuck you!" His fingers clattered over the keyboard like it was personal.

"Uh, Mr. Sage. Do you know you have a security alarm going off in your building?" Bruce said, "Like lots of them?"

28

Global Infection: ≤ 30.8072%

What? Security alarms?" Ryan asked, patting himself down for his phone and then remembering he couldn't find it. He was terrified that he'd left it in one of the stairwells or maybe amid the clutter on the seventh floor. It could take forever to find it. "Where are the alarms?"

"One of them is door 1LD," Bruce said. "And . . . wait a minute. Why can't I see the camera? Did someone break that camera? It's 22LD."

"The camera on the loading dock?" Ryan asked. "No it is almost impossible to break the outside cameras. They are very well hidden, set into the walls or ceiling. All exterior cameras are like that."

"Oh, it's just been turned off," Bruce said. "Why did you do that?"

"I didn't," Ryan said as he started working through the security interface on the iGlass. The loading dock door mag lock had been disabled.

"A bunch of doors have been left unlocked."

"What the hell is going on?" Ryan asked. "Guys, do me a favor. Start watching the security cameras. Tell me if you see anyone or . . . anything wandering the halls. I have to wake up the cavalry."

"It took you long enough," Patrick said as soon as the video feed connected. "What is wrong?"

"They're gone." Ryan said. Raphael, Marco and Simone's room were empty. Indeed, it looked like they had never slept in their beds. They were not in the penthouse and not on the roof. He tried to raise them on the maintenance radios but got nothing but static.

"Who is gone?" Patrick asked.

"The Pagueros."

"The Mexicans that were staying with you?" Patrick asked. "They just up and left?"

Ryan scanned the armory, noticing that Raphael's Kalashnikov, two AR-15s and six handguns were missing. His confusion deepened when he saw that the Pagueros' tactical vests on hooks. "Why did they leave these?"

Bruce said, "Why did they leave without you?"

Ryan ran his hand through his hair and finally looked into the iGlass. "Maybe because I'm a hard ass and they called my bluff."

"What do you mean they called your bluff," Patrick asked?

"There has been a power struggle between Raphael and me. I wouldn't back down."

"Fucking Mexicans," Patrick said. "I've never met a beaner that was worth a damn."

Ryan pinched the bridge of his nose. "Their skills are really important."

"No! Fuck them. Fuck them. You don't need them," Patrick said.

Ryan kept brushing his grey hair out of his face, suddenly bothered by it drifting down over his forehead. "Thanks. I need a cheerleader, but I need to go make sure that nothing came into the tower."

"I don't see anything on the cameras," Bruce said. "But you have most of the lights off. People could be in the shadows."

"Do you two know how to use the power management system?"

"It can't be that hard to learn," Patrick said.

"Remote in for me and turn on the lights in the lower levels. I'm going to get some guns. I have to check—" He took one step toward the gun rack. It was locked. "Damn!"

Ryan's logic was simple. The fastest path to ground level was to use the penthouse elevator to the VIP parking garage. He assumed that this was the path the Pagueros used and it had the added benefit of being secure. The elevator doors parted, and Ryan looked through a gate designed like a bank vault. Nothing short of a nuclear explosion would breach the gate and give access to the elevator. When he was sure that the area beyond was empty, he pushed the gate open.

The VIP parking inner sanctum was where penthouse tenants parked, and the cars in the sanctum were worth a lot of money. There were fifteen parking spots and all but one was filled. There were two limousines, one white and one black. And there were two BMWs, three Acuras, two Escalades, two Infinity SUVs, one refurbished Hummer, one Ferrari, and one blue Lamborghini.

The inner sanctum was separated from the outer parking area by a heavy, motorized gate. Tenants like Gus Blanco, tenants that rented five to ten thousand square feet in the Renaissance Tower's upper floors, parked in the reserved spaces just beyond the inner sanctum. Ryan found an Acura unlocked and the gate opener fastened to the sun visor. The gate trundled open, rattling and clattering its way back into the wall. Ryan inched beyond the gate farther from the security of the penthouse express elevator, searching around corners, pointing the Glock and the flashlight into the shadows. He juggled the gun, the iGlass, and the flashlight and bent to look under the parked cars.

He was alone.

He walked to the blood-spattered late model Chevy truck with a bed cap that smelled like road kill. The truck was parked exactly where it had been left almost two weeks ago, right in the middle of the exit. Ryan had been part of the frantic fight to clear a path for Simone Paguero to drive this truck into the garage. Simone gunned the engine, fishtailed through the outer door and skidded to a stop. He crawled out of the cab, ducked under the chassis and shot two of the infected clinging to the under carriage. It hadn't moved since, which meant that whatever the Pagueros drove to leave the tower couldn't have come from the garage.

"What is going on?" Bruce asked. "We're getting dizzy, and we can't see anything."

Ryan fished the iGlass out of his pants. "I'm trying to figure out how in the hell the Pagueros got out of the tower. I expected to see this truck gone, but obviously it's—" His words seized in his mouth when he heard the subtle whine of motors and the definitive sound of a lock snapping firmly in place. "Shit!" he said. "I just locked myself out."

"Locked out of what?" Bruce asked.

Ryan turned the camera toward the penthouse elevator. "Do you see the bio scanner to the right of the gate? Without a bio scan, I can't take the *safe* way back to the penthouse.

"Damn!" Patrick said.

"Damn!" Bruce said.

Ryan sighed. "Look, here is the plan. You guys can't keep asking me what is going on. First, because it makes noise and I am trying for stealth. Second, it is hard for me to keep a running dialogue. And third, I can't hold on to the gun, the flashlight, and the iGlass. So here is what we are going to do. You watch the cameras ahead of me, and if you see something, make a sound and then *wait* until I ask for the details."

"What kind of sound?" Bruce said.

"I don't know, but something soft."

Ryan tucked the iGlass into his pants at the small of his back, and then put the flashlight under the Glock like he'd seen in so many cop dramas. He moved through the garage and through the door that led into the tower.

As he walked the halls, he puzzled over the Pagueros' actions. Leaving the tower did not require subterfuge or leaving doors unlocked. The obvious path was to take the elevator to the lobby and just walk out the door standing wide open to the world. And if that was too much trouble, why not exit the tower's eighth floor and walk across the skywalk to the parking garage?

But the answers to these questions were squeezed from his mind by the tower's oppressive mass hanging over his shoulders. It seemed like a living thing with the sounds of distant rattling, muted tapping, and the faintest moaning swirling past his ears. His running shoes seemed to sound like horseshoes clattering on asphalt, and his breathing felt like he had a bull horn next to his mouth. The hallways were closed, and the air was thick and musty with a faint hint of sewage. Suddenly it occurred to Ryan that the infected always seemed to smell of feces and urine. He sniffed trying to discern a direction, but the stench seemed to be everywhere and nowhere. And then he realized he was standing beside the restrooms, where the smell of sewage was strongest.

In the movies, zombies were always in bathrooms.

29

Global Infection: ≤ 30.8073%

Ryan watched the bathroom doors, sure that something—that someone—was going to stumble out. He moved quickly to the next hallway and badged through the door.

Bang!

His legs went rigid, and his heart ragged against his ribs. He pressed his back to the wall swiveling his head, sure that something or someone was moments away from biting him on the blindside.

Bang!

The sound was a deep drumming thud that reverberated down the hall.

Was it a door slamming shut?

Was it someone beating their fists against a bathroom stall?

He tried to make his legs move but his thighs were weak and his knees refused to bend. His hands felt moist, and the Glock's polymer frame felt slick. Sweat dripped into the corner of his right eye. His hand rose, coming closer to his head, finger on the trigger, hand throttling the grip.

And Ryan froze. He'd seen this before. He'd seen what terror does to a man holding a gun. He pushed the barrel down toward the floor as if exaggerating the motion made up for his failure to pay attention. This is exactly why Raphael objected to him carrying a weapon; Ryan was a hot mess waiting to create a disaster.

He felt the ducts above his head start moving the musty air and he understood the noise. The power had been off, but when Patrick turned on the light circuit he also turned on the air handlers.

Ryan breathed in short sips while he waited for his heart to cease its escape attempt.

When his legs would finally move, he made the short trip to the loading dock. He started to swipe the badge but paused. He rolled his shoulders and his neck and massaged the back of his head. He fished the iGlass out of his pants and asked, "Can you hear me?"

"Yes," Bruce said.

"Do you see anything on the other side of the door?"

"I didn't make a sound, right?"

"True," Ryan said, still breathing deep. In . . . out . . . in . . . out. He rubbed his head; it felt painful from ear to ear. "I don't like being blind . . ." his voice trailed off as a thought niggled at the back of his mind.

"What is like being blind?" Patrick asked.

"Uh, sorry. What?"

"You said it's like being blind . . . something."

For a moment, Ryan couldn't remember what he'd been thinking, but then the thought invaded like Islamic insurgents. *Blind? Blind? Why in the hell did the Pagueros shut off the cameras and then open the locks? Why would they want to be blind when they left?*

"Look through the security tapes and see if you can figure out when the Pagueros left."

"Will do," Patrick said.

"I came up with a sound," Bruce said. "I'll go like this, 'Buzz!'"

"You will say buzz?"

"No, you are going to have to buzz like for real," Patrick said. "Bzzzzzzt! Like that. That is what we agreed on."

"Why can't I just say buzz?"

"That's not a sound," Patrick said. "That is a word."

"What is the difference?"

"You are such a doob. You need to make a sound."

"Guys," Ryan said, trying to keep his voice down. "It's all right. Buzz works. It's short and sweet and all I need."

Bruce looked like he'd been appointed king. "See, he likes it. You're the doob."

"It's not a sound," Patrick said.

"Patrick, do you have the security logs yet?" Ryan asked. "Bruce, can you get the lights beyond the door."

"It's not a sound," Patrick muttered.

Ryan tucked the iGlass into his pants and opened the door doing the gun over the flashlight scan like he'd seen in the movies, wondering if it was Hollywood fiction or a real technique. Not that he needed the flashlight. The receiving dock was bright and clean. The floors were painted light gray, the walls were white and the LCD lights blazed away overhead at eleven hundred lumens. The shelves were neon yellow so that they stood out like lighthouses on a foggy cliff and filled with boxes and crates and bags of all shapes and sizes. The forklifts were bright blue and parked where they'd been left.

The dock was empty.

Ryan walked to the people door labeled LBD1 in the security system, and he immediately knew where the Pagueros exited the building. Raphael's barricade was disassembled. He looked out the one-foot-square security window and saw an empty street. Ryan pushed the panic bar and the door swung open. He stood straddling the threshold as if keeping one foot in the building kept him safe. He looked east and west along First Avenue, but only saw trash and dust blowing in the early morning breeze. He pulled the door closed and froze. After the first incursion against the tower, Ryan and Raphael parked two panel vans in the loading dock to add a layer of obstacles to keep people away from the dock doors. Then they parked cars around the steps up to the door. It wasn't a foolproof method for keeping the 2091s from flooding the door, but any obstacle was a good one. Ryan pushed the door open and looked. One van was missing.

"What in the hell . . .?"

"Buzz!"

Ryan pulled the door shut. He drew his iGlass form his pants and leaned it on the receiving desk. "That was pretty good."

Bruce smiled. "See, I told you that was the right sound."

"It's not a sound," Patrick muttered.

"We found them," Bruce said.

"Not really," Patrick said. "They left the penthouse at about 1:30 this morning, went passed that restaurant and about ten minutes later, they appeared on a camera named LL East-12."

"They used the stairs?" Ryan asked? "Were they carrying anything?"

Patrick shook his head. "Just a shitload of guns," he said.

Ryan looked out to the street as if he might have hallucinated the missing van. "Do you see them anywhere else? Uh, maybe down by the grocery hauling stuff out to the loading dock?"

"The grocery security system is different than the tower security system," Patrick said. "I can't see those cameras. I think the Mexicans turned all the cameras off. They just forgot those two."

"This makes no sense," Ryan said. "If they are they are going to steal my stuff and leave, why do they care if I can see them on camera?"

"What are you going to do?" Bruce asked.

"I don't know, guys. The truth is I am a big chicken. The idea of searching through this tower by myself with this silly gun strikes me as a horror movie cliché. This is usually when I start shouting at the screen, 'Too stupid to live.'"

"But you already killed all those zombies," Bruce said. "You can just kill the rest of them, right?"

"Shut up, Bruce," Patrick snapped. "Mr. Sage, just go back to the penthouse. We can watch the cameras."

"At the very least, I need to be better armed," Ryan said. "I need to get my hands on a shotgun, and I hope to God they left me more ammo than one box of shells. And then I need to have a plan on how to search this place without getting killed."

"Do you think something is inside?" Patrick said.

Ryan raked his hand though his hair again, even more frustrated that it was hanging down over his forehead. "I don't think so, but there is only one way to be sure. Now all I have to do is figure out how to get back to the penthouse."

"Can't you go back the way you came?" Bruce asked.

"I locked myself out, remember? That is why I need you to hack that bioscan system."

"Ohhhhh," Bruce said as if he just heard the answer to the meaning of life.

"We could guide you through empty hallways," Patrick said.

Ryan picked up the iGlass and peeked out on the street. "Maybe I could make a run to the front. I could get to the elevators." His eyes scrubbed the streets looking for wandering monsters.

"But you will be on the street," Bruce said, "with all those zombies."

"It's not that far. Pittsburgh streets are really short and tight. I could run to the front in a minute," Ryan said, and then his eyes focused across First Avenue on the gate for the tenant parking garage. Its bottom three levels were dedicated to grocery patrons, and the entrance was one street north off the Boulevard of the Allies. But the tower residents and the commercial tenants accessed private parking from First Avenue sealed by a heavy gate, twenty strides across the street.

"I have an idea."

"You can't go on the street," Bruce said, sounding worried. "All those zombies . . ."

"If this works, I will be fine." Ryan stepped through LD1 onto the landing. The sun was climbing into the morning sky, but the shadows were deep behind the towering buildings. With the power off, the magnetic lock failed open. All he had to do was pull the latch. Ryan said, "Re-engage the mag lock, please."

"Will do," Patrick said with a flurry of keystrokes. "Done!"

Ryan tested the door and it didn't budge. Then he used his badge and heard the lock click. "Okay . . . good deal. See you guys in a second."

He went down the steps and around the parked cars. With the van gone, the makeshift barricade was incomplete.

The word avenue inspired images of broad streets with cars traveling with glamorous people inside, but in Pittsburgh the name was misleading. First Avenue, like all similarly named Steel City streets, was narrow and would be considered little more than an alley in most cities. Ryan squeezed around a passenger van that Raphael parked to prevent a determined looter from crashing through the metal gate and passed his access badge over a reader; the gate started to grind inch by inch into the ceiling.

Ryan pulled the iGlass out of his pants. "Okay, I'm good," he said.

"Say agggg . . ." Bruce said, but his image pixilated, and his voice was digital chatter. Ryan took three steps toward the tower.

"Can you hear me now?"

"Brea . . . up," Bruce said.

Ryan walked to the loading dock. "I should be good—" And then he saw the connectivity bars on his iGlass cycle. The tower Wi-Fi connection dropped. "Damn," he said, and swiped his badge to step back inside. Then he realized he'd left the parking garage gate open.

He was in the middle of the street when he saw them.

They came from the west in a churning disjointed gallop: fast-moving 2091s.

Ryan swiped the security pad as he squeezed by the van.

Inch by inch the gate trundled down.

The infected people slammed into the van's front bumper rocking its shocks.

Four feet to go . . .

Ryan grabbed the gate to help it down . . . and froze.

What if it had a security setting that made it reset with resistance?!!

Three feet . . .

Bang! Pop! Slap! The bodies hit metal sounding like . . . Gus and Darien falling from the helipad.

Two feet . . .

A window shattered as a man battered through the van's passenger side and raged through the interior until his face slammed into glass.

One foot . . .

A skinny woman slid around the van bumper. She tripped—

Six inches . . .

She groped toward Ryan's feet, her arm under the gate . . .

30

Global Infection: ≤ 30.8073%

Ryan kicked the skinny woman's hand as the gate came down and locked into place.

For a long minute, he stood watching the mayhem: the infected hammered against the van, breaking limbs and spattering blood.

Ryan ran.

The grade to the tenant parking area was steep. His breath was hard and heavy, coming in gasps as he passed the sign stating, *Parking Closed Beyond This Point*. He slumped over, hands on knees, breath heaving. He continued, slow and shaking the last twenty yards up to the seventh floor parking area. The space was filled with tools, machines, building supplies and company trucks. He turned in circles looking for a rout to the top; a path that led to the skywalk that spanned the street and connected the tower promenade level.

But there was no auto ramp.

Ryan turned in place once, twice, then three times looking for a way to the top. Finally he saw the stairwell hidden behind two tool sheds, a front loader, and a backhoe. He ran to the door, swiped the badge plate and pulled.

Locked!

The security pad had been disconnected.

Ryan moved to a tool shed looking for a screwdriver, but it was locked. Then he checked a row of tan colored Knaack job site chests: Three were locked, the fourth was open. Ryan removed the front plat and found the power lines and twisted the wire nut back in place. The light came on and he passed the badge over its face and heard a satisfying buzz-click; the door popped open. He climbed the stairs two at a time, exited onto the broad expanse of concrete and the door latched shut.

Ryan walked the eighth level's outer edge, around the fifty-three-foot Hanjin shipping containers, past the piles of rebar, and skids of shrink-wrapped building materials, looking for a way for cars to drive up, but there wasn't any. Indeed, there were only three ways to the top: the elevators, to which Raphael disabled the power, the stairwell whose ground floor door had been covered with sheet metal, and the switchback that was locked behind a series of security gates. He was safe.

He badged through the skywalk doors. The covered walkway across First Avenue was almost ten feet wide and lined with Plexiglas.

He pressed his face against the glass. First Avenue had been turned into a charnel house floor—blood was everywhere. Bones stuck out from flesh. Body parts hung at odd angles. He slumped against the opposite wall. Thoughts tumbled around his mind like *Cirque du Soleil* acrobats, until one idea struck a final pose.

I'm alone . . . again. I have a real gift for driving people away.

He banged his head against the wall.

The iGlass chimed.

Ryan dug it out of his pants. "I—"

"Oh my God!" Patrick said. "Are you all right? You had us scared to death. Your connection dropped, and we saw you run, and then there were like a thousand zombies. And we couldn't see where you went. And we saw a girl and a boy run around the van, and we thought they got inside, and then we didn't hear—"

"Patrick, I'm okay."

"Why didn't you call us back?"

"I told him you were killing all the zombies," Bruce said. "IT guys rule, right?"

"Shut up," Patrick said. "He should have called us back."

"You are right. I should have. I just wasn't thin—"

A machine gun went full automatic, shattering the city's silence. Ryan rolled to his knees and then he saw them . . . and the world made no sense at all.

"What was that?" Patrick said.

"The Pagueros are about to run into an ambush!" Ryan said as he set the iGlass down on the window ledge. "Don't move. I'll be back."

The Pagueros were running. They were a hundred yards from the intersection at Smithfield and the infected—too many to tally—roiled thirty yards behind their heels. Every twenty strides a Paguero would stop, pivot, pull the trigger taking down the creatures that surged to the lead, and then peel out to the right.

The 2091s below untangled themselves and moved toward the three men.

"Look out!" Ryan shouted.

The Pagueros crossed Smithfield, past the Alaska barriers surrounding the jobsite, past stacked shipping containers, past the contractor's trailer, down First Avenue. They were coming to the loading dock.

"Contact front!" Marco shouted.

Raphael and Simone stopped, raised their weapons and sent a barrage down range. It sounded like a thrash metal concert—indiscriminate thundering riffs punctuated by ear-wrecking echoes. Simone sprang up the stairs and yanked the loading dock door. It didn't budge. He pulled and pulled and pulled . . . frantic.

"Badge through the door," Ryan yelled. "Badge through the door!" But his words were drowned out by Raphael's thundering AK 47.

Marco pushed his brother out of the way and pulled.

Simone patted his hips. Marco patted his pants pocket. Marco and Simone started firing. Raphael riffled through his pockets. The infected surged.

Ryan ran for the skywalk. "Patrick, open the door. Open the door. Patrick . . . Bruce can you hear me? Open the door." He pushed his face in front of the iGlass camera. "Open the door! Do it now! They are going to die!"

"We are trying," Patrick said, fumbling at his keyboard, his light speed key strokes slowing as if he was in a temporal distortion.

"Open the door," Bruce squealed. "Open it! The zombies are by the cars! Open it!"

"Shut up," Patrick said.

The explosion made Ryan's knees buckle.

Bruce and Patrick stared at their screens.

"Talk to me, guys. I can't see what you see."

"Uh, Mr. Sage," Patrick said. "They just blew the door open."

The Paguero gunfire continued, muted inside the tower.

"I just opened the locks on the inside," Bruce said. "I hope that was all right. But they look like they are bleeding and the zombies are coming after them. Well, they were coming. After they went through the doors I locked them before they could follow"

Ryan's mouth hung open, a thousand things threatening to fly out at once. "Yeah. That is fine. Uhm . . ." and then it made sense. "I tell you what. Go ahead and get some sleep. But when you wake up, I'm going to need that bio scanner as soon as you as get it reset."

"But what about the zombies?" Bruce said. "They are in the tower."

"The zombies are the least of my problems," Ryan said. "I'll call you later."

Ryan closed the connection and turned toward the tower: across the running track, past the picnic tables and planters and maximum security toddler playground. He badged through the tower promenade doors, walked past the darkened shops that lined the hallway to the elevator bank. He turned toward the penthouse elevator and swiped his badge, riding it to the top. He took two strides out of the elevator and waited for the doors to close. He listened to the motors take it down, pause and then reengage. Thirty seconds later, the elevator doors slid wide revealing three dirty, exhausted men, the smell of cordite and the stench of battle rolling onto the landing.

All three men wore Dragonskin body armor and all three had bullet holes. Raphael's arm was bleeding. Marco's left side was bloody from his hip down to his knee. Simone was shaking and pasty white.

Ryan stood stalwart, letting the seconds tick by. No one moved. Finally, he said, "So ... which one of you is the thief who took my phone?"

31

Global Infection: ≤ 30.8075%

Here," Simone said, handing Ryan his phone.

"Thank you," Ryan said, turning the phone over in his hand. It seemed a miracle that it had survived a gunfight. He wanted to be angry, but Simone looked so scared, boyish, and shaken it was impossible to muster outrage. Not to mention that Simone wasn't the real culprit. Raphael was the mastermind; his goal was to keep Ryan from hearing the endless alarms created by disabling the locks and cameras.

All three men stumbled into the penthouse and shed their body armor in the foyer.

Simone tried to pull his sweat-soaked T-shirt over his head, but he couldn't raise his arms.

"Would you like some help?" Ryan asked.

Simone nodded and Ryan helped him peel it off. The boy had two baseball sized bruises on his chest and one on his back the size of a softball. Bullet-proof vests stop bullet penetration, but they do not stop the bullet mass and velocity slamming into flesh.

Stripped down to boxers and briefs, Raphael and Marco shuffled to the kitchen. Simone split off to get medical supplies. Marco turned on every light, and Raphael cut his T-shirt into strips and then washed his hands and arms with steaming water. His chest was a bruise from nipple to nipple; his back looked like he'd been beaten with a bat. A tattoo of a rosary wrapped around his left shoulder and two stars like a general adorned his right. He sat on a stool alternately dabbing the wound on his bicep and casting Ryan a jaundiced eye.

"What is taking you so long, Simone?" Marco called as he untied the battlefield bandage wrapped around his right hip, blood seeping through at the entry and exit point, just above the bone.

"I'm here," Simone said, dropping the medical bag on the island with a handful of maxi pads.

"Wash your hands," Marco said, putting a pad over the holes and retying the field dressing to hold them in place. He dug through the medical bag, pulled out supplies, motioned for Raphael to take a seat on a stool and gave him a shot of Lidocaine. Then he washed and dried his hands and put on rubber gloves. A few minutes later, he was digging for a bullet.

"You think this *es* funny?" Raphael said to Ryan.

"I was smiling because I was impressed with how you handle pain," Ryan said, noticing these were not Raphael's first combat wounds. Two holes looked like they should have been fatal. "But if it will make you feel better, I can change to raving outrage or crying."

Raphael snarled. "You deliberately lock us out."

"Oh, Raphael, now I am going to laugh. I thought you guys were gone. There were no letters, no note, no nothing. I wake up and find the penthouse empty and a whole series of doors left unlocked. You obviously shook the Grim Reaper's hand tonight, what the hell should I have done? Leave those doors unlocked, pining for your return?"

"But we did no die," Raphael said. "You lock the doors just like before."

Ryan rolled his eyes. "Raphael, you are far too smart to be such an idiot. You almost got *yourself* killed because you were too busy making a point."

"Isn't this what you tell Marco," Raphael asked. "That I have the right to leave if I think you are dangerous?"

"You had your son steal my phone so I wouldn't receive security alerts. You disabled the cameras. You snuck out of here and tried to erase every trace. So why don't we have a real conversation. What *are* you trying to hide?"

"This *es* no the point," Raphael said.

"Hold still," Marco said. "And answer the man's question."

"You are taking his side?" Raphael asked.

"Just hold still," Marco said. "I almost have the bullet out."

"We had to unlock all the doors because you block off the stairwell," Raphael said. "I tell you that you should have talked to me about your project. I would not have to open all those doors."

"What you just said makes no sense. Somehow I'm supposed to read your mind about a plan to leave the tower that you don't want me to know about?"

Raphael said, "You would have been no help tonight. You would have got us killed. You can no shoot in a firefight and you could no run because you are old and fat. I did no want to take you, and I did no want a fight with you over this negligence."

Ryan got up from his stool and got some orange juice. "Raphael, the only reason we are fighting is because you treat me like a redheaded stepchild. You give me edicts and commands and pretend to have veto power on my life. You think my opinion is beneath you, which is confusing. I remember a certain phone conversation with your wife where you gave me a glowing review and told everyone that the Holy Mother was looking out for me. I'm not sure how I went from God's chosen to a piece of shit, but whatever.

"Under normal circumstances, after the first time you showed me contempt, you would have gone home, never to return as a welcome guest and I wouldn't have given you a second thought. But we don't have normal circumstances. I'm aware that I need your skills, but the problem is I'm not willing to let you rule me like a dictator.

"I haven't figured out the solution yet, but I can say this with certainty. Had you talked to me before you went on your nighttime raid, you would not have been in a fight."

Raphael scowled. "You are loco. How can you know such things? Do you see the future? Do you think you are God?"

Ryan finished the orange juice. "You were so busy trying to be deceitful it never occurred to you that I might have something to offer."

Raphael said, "*El Papa* does not know the future. Even the Holy Mother can no make such a claim. Even she intercedes, but her son do as he wills. What happened tonight *es* because God will it. You are not God."

"Oh this is rich. Uh . . . Raphael, if circumstance is God's will, then why are you blaming me for locking the doors?"

"Do no twist my words," Raphael said.

"I just pointed out that they were already twisted, Look I know better than to argue theology after a gunfight. I can't speak for the Virgin Mary or how she fares when asking Jesus to do things, but here is what I do know. If you had come to me and said, 'Ryan, I think you are a dipshit, and we are going on a dangerous mission to do some macho bullshit, and people will have guns, and I know you will shoot me in the back, and we do not want you to go.' I would have said, 'Gee, Raphael, that makes me sad that you think that, but since it is a good thing to avoid getting shot, I won't go. But since I'm sure you want to live, why don't you take a Stryker? I hear that they are bulletproof.'" Ryan paused and winked. "I'm sure your superior tactical mind can see that a Stryker would have done just what I said . . . keep you out of a fight."

"Wait," Marco said. "There is a Stryker . . . here in the tower?"

"Three of them," Ryan said, cracking eggs into a pan. "I've never seen them, but Daniel said they were parked down where the tractor trailers unloaded for the grocery, someplace underneath the street level."

Stryker combat vehicles were originally named in accord with the military's endless preoccupation with acronyms, an IAV, or Intermediate Armored Vehicle. But realizing this moniker did not do the vehicle justice, the Army changed the name to Stryker after two Medal of Honor recipients, Pfc. Stuart S. Stryker, who served in World War II, and Spc. Robert F. Stryker, who served in Vietnam. The Stryker was a nineteen-ton, eight-wheeled armored vehicle that could switch between four-wheel and eight-wheel drive. It was designed to maneuver in urban terrain or blaze a path in open terrain. It sustained speeds of 60 miles per hour, traveled more than 300 miles on one tank of gas and the modern version had a hybrid propulsion system that let the vehicle travel up to five miles in tactical quiet mode. It comfortably seated nine and sported a Remote Weapon Station with an M2 .50 caliber machinegun on the top of its hull, so it engaged enemies without exposing anyone from within. The Stryker hull provided protection from 14.5mm projectiles and 152mm artillery airbursts and could be upgraded with Rocket Propelled Grenade armor. The Stryker combat vehicle was an eight-wheeled beast that combined firepower, mobility, survivability and versatility. It was the ultimate zombie apocalypse recreational vehicle.

Marco pointed the tube of Skinfuse into the bullet hole, squeezed, pinched the skin and waited while looking hard at his father. "We have Strykers and we didn't fucking take one?" he asked. "We took a fucking truck instead?"

Raphael's eyes darted left and down. He did remember the Strykers that the Molitor Group security team used to retrieve Richard Ryder from the northeastern United States. "Do no speak to me in this voice."

"Are you serious?" Marco said. "We almost died tonight because you are too goddamned proud to have a reasonable conversation with him. And you are concerned with my tone of voice?"

"Do no use the Lord's name in vain," Raphael said, his eyes narrowing. "The Holy Mother, she save us tonight. You must have respect, or you will have to confess your sins."

Marco shook his head and checked the wound, making sure the skin was mending. "Confess my sins? How about your sins? You want respect, but refuse to give any to him."

"Leave Poppa alone," Simone said. "The reason we almost got killed is because you lost your shit when the zombies showed up."

Marco spun. "Let's take a trip down memory lane. The reason we had to go out tonight is because you are too damned lazy to pick up bullets lying at your feet. The reason we had to go out tonight is because you were too damned lazy to make sure the bullets *in the box* are the same as the label *on the box*. We got shot tonight because you opened your fucking pie hole and told the whole fucking world where we keep a stock pile of ammunition. It's the fucking zombie apocalypse, Simone. Where did you think all those people were going to go? What about a *secret* gun range is unclear? Secret means you don't tell *anyone*!"

"But I didn't tell them," Simone said.

Marco started shouting. "Simone, they knew your goddamned name! Remember when we were crawling on our bellies begging God to make our buttons smaller so we could get lower? Remember when we were laying there praying to God that they wouldn't shoot anymore and they called your name? Remember when the man said, 'Simone? Simone? Is that you?' Or did your forget that part? They called your goddamned name."

"They knew yours, too!" Simone said. "You could have told them."

"Shit! For! Brains," Marco said, "Where have I been for the last three years?"

"Oh," Simone said and slumped into his chair.

"So who was it that called your name?" Marco demanded.

"That was Steve's dad," Simone said. "His mom was beside him. She was the one who told them to stop shooting."

Marco held up his hands like that math was obvious. "And how does Steve's dad know where our *secret* gun range is located unless you told him the *secret*?"

"I didn't tell him," Simone said. "I took Steve to the range, but he was always blindfolded."

"Unbelievable. What was the first rule? What was the goddamned first rule for the range?"

"Bite me!" Simone shouted and stomped deep into the penthouse. Seconds later they heard the pop of the master suite door.

Raphael said, "He *es* only sixteen."

Marco snorted. "He is plenty old enough to have a brain in his fucking head."

"You do no remember what you were like then."

"Whatever I was like, I never hit Momma," Marco snapped and limped out of the kitchen.

"Do no walk away from me!" Raphael yelled.

"You can yell at me after I get back," Marco called. "I need a beer before you start sewing me up."

"Stitches will take too long to heal," Raphael said. "You must use the Skinfuse."

"No fucking way," Marco said, his voice fading into the penthouse. "That shit itches like poison ivy and poison oak combined. That is why I dumped a shitload into your arm!"

Raphael spun toward Ryan. "Are you happy now?"

Ryan slid the folded omelet onto the plate. "Happy? Hell no. You blew a hole in my building and now I have the infected wandering the inside of my tower." He pushed the plate across the island. "You like salsa with your omelets, right?" he held out the jar.

Raphael looked down at the food. "*Si*," he said and gingerly slid onto a stool. "*Gracias*."

"*De nada*," Ryan said.

32

Global Infection: ≤ 30.8907%

Ryan could have predicted a general course for the rest of the afternoon, but he did not expect that by the end of the day he would have a gun pointed at his head.

Marco's wound was not serious, but it still took forever to sew it up. Mostly because Raphael demanded that he use the Skinfuse, but Marco refused. Raphael finally gave in and Marco suffered through Raphael's sewing, but bitched that the stitching looked like it was done by a blind seamstress on crystal meth. Raphael threw down the forceps and needle holder and stomped out of the kitchen. Marco finished the last two stitches himself, ate an omelet without saying a word and went to his room.

The penthouse was silent.

Ryan had been up since before the roosters but he was still keyed up. He called Bruptrick but they didn't answer. Even IT gods come down off a rush of Doritos and Mountain Dew. He worked through the security system to verify that every door was locked. He stared at the security feeds covering the loading dock and the hallway where 2091s stumped in circles. Finally, futility sent him to bed.

When he woke, Ryan found Simone in the family kitchen eating cereal. "Where is your father and brother?"

Simone crunched through a spoonful. "Getting the infected out of the loading dock."

"Why aren't you with them?"

Simone slurped milk from the bowl and shrugged.

Ryan found Raphael and Marco putting the final touches on the door barricade while tracking through puddles of blood. The loading dock's pristine paintjob was splattered with gore, but there were no bodies.

"Wow, how did you get them out?" Ryan asked.

"People are attracted to sound so it turns out 2091s move toward noise," Marco said, "We turned a car stereo on outside and most of them wandered out. Then we put that Elay Tenex ammunition to use."

Ryan stepped over some intestines and then saw the loading bay door was open and the panel van was loaded with dead bodies. He suppressed a gag. "You got a place for this meat wagon?"

"We should leave it," Raphael said, "It will keep peoples away."

Nasty smells rolled out of the panel van. Ryan felt his stomach roll. "Ohhh . . . please tell me . . . ohhhh." He slapped at the bay door close button. "Please tell me you are making a joke."

"Puke outside," Raphael said with a smirk. "You do no like being near them? Other peoples will be like you."

Ryan forced his stomach to calm and looked at the damage to the door to keep his mind away from the stench of bodies. The explosion had been small, a shaped charge from the C4 found in the barracks.

"I took out the mag lock and the hinges," Marco said, "It was easy to put the door back in place."

"Are you sure you got all the infected out of the building?"

Raphael fit his metal plate barricade across the door and dropped the wedge into place. It wasn't perfect, but nothing was coming back through the door.

"So you had the other panel van," Ryan said, "Why did you have to run back?"

"The panel van got shot up in the fight," Marco said

"Why didn't you boost another car?"

Raphael snorted and walked to a utility closet, turned on the water and soap dispenser and filled up a mop bucked.

"I really don't ask questions to hear myself talk," Ryan said.

Raphael rolled three buckets full of steaming water into the loading dock. "We clean," he said pointing with his nose toward the puddles of drying blood and gore.

Ryan grabbed a mop and worked in silence until he couldn't tolerate the mystery. "So, Raphael, what were you trying to hide? You took my phone and shut off the cameras because you didn't want me to know something. What didn't you want me to know?"

"Always with the questions. You are worse than a child." Raphael threw down his mop and walked away.

Ryan poured the last bloody bucket of water down the drain and rinsed it out.

"You want to take one last look through the building?" Marco asked. "See if we missed anything?"

"Sounds like a good idea." Ryan tapped through his phone and turned on lights as they ventured through each new hallway.

"So we got to the gun range," Marco said, "And fortunately for us, Steve and his family can't shoot for shit or we would have been dead in the first exchange. They let us go but the radiator had been shot all to hell, so it overheated. My dad boosted another car, but it was on fumes and we only got about another mile."

Ryan tested a door, then another, found them locked and kept walking. "Why didn't he boost another one?"

"It died right in the middle of a mob of 2091s."

"Sounds exciting."

"It wasn't," Marco said, pushing a door open with his foot and sweeping the room beyond with the muzzle of his weapon. "We had to run from that group for maybe three miles. I kept thinking that they would get tired and drop off, but God, they just kept coming. You know how long you have to train to run three miles? It makes no sense that they could keep up."

Ryan walked passed a restroom. The smell of sewage wafted into the hallway. "I want to check something," he said and waived Marco forward. The bathroom was empty. "Damn."

"What is the problem?"

"The traps are drying up. The toilets are venting sewer to gas into the building." Ryan flushed each unit.

When the noise subsided Marco said, "You know you can't do that, right?"

"Why not?"

"You will run out of water."

"Double damn." Then Ryan asked, "So what were you all trying to hide?"

"You thought if you asked me quick I would answer?"

Ryan shrugged.

"You should talk to my father about that."

Triple damn!

33

Global Infection: ≤ 31.0003%

Ryan cleaned his dishes, fixed a large soda with lots of ice and sipped on it as he wound a path through the penthouse. He paused at the south-facing windows and looked out over the Duquesne Incline at the world frozen in time. The city looked like someone had pushed the pause button and everything stopped.

Ryan turned, but a blur of pink streaked between cars parked on the Smithfield Bridge, jumping out in an ocean of stillness. He did a double take; the color snapped his mind to a memory of a young girl in a pink coat. They'd spoken briefly just before Ryan stepped into the cool afternoon air for a walk that almost killed him. Over the next few days, he'd seen the girl near where he hid as the world went to hell. He saw her one last time on his frantic run to the Renaissance Tower slouched in a snack shop eating chips and drinking a soda like she was watching afterschool cartoons. They had been less than fifteen feet apart but he'd still been unable to help; the drive to survive had driven them apart one last time.

Ryan thought of the girl in the quiet moments between the fire fights, but the flash of pink thirty stories below grabbed his mind in an iron grip. He strained to see if there was blond hair flowing behind a pink coat, but the angle was wrong. He dashed from window to window, room to room, trying to see more and finally he lost track. He leaned his head against the window feeling foolish.

It could have been the girl, or a plastic bag catching the orange glow of the late day sun, or a thousand other things. The Vegas odds favored that the girl was dead—either a victim of the 2091 virus or government tyranny. He'd been on the street a total accumulated time of an hour and shook death's hand every minute. Certainly she wasn't still wandering the streets looking for dollar bills for vending machines.

Ryan's phone pinged in his pocket. It was an email from Patrick. The subject line said: call ASAP. He hung his head. He didn't have the energy for another Team Bruptrick conversation, but he had promised they would talk. He crossed his fingers that the chat would be quick as he wound the path toward his office—through to the outer Molitor Group offices, through Mora the gatekeeper's office. Ryan crossed the threshold and saw Raphael sitting behind his desk.

"*Un momento*, Daniel," Raphael said, raising a pausing hand toward the video conference screen. He flashed Ryan flat eyes. "This *es* private," he said and flicked his fingers for Ryan to leave.

Ryan turned, then stopped, then frowned, and then, like an earthquake starting deep inside, his outrage tore through the tectonic plates in his soul: The casual dismissal, the underlying disdain, the presumption all rumbled and churned to the top. He took three strides to the desk and met Raphael's eyes. "Then *you* should have had the conversation somewhere else."

"But this *es* the only place I can talk to Daniel."

"Raphael, you—"

"Boys! Boys!" Daniel interrupted. "Do I have to send you to your rooms?"

Ryan spun to the video conference screen hanging down from the ceiling. "I am in *my* room and you can stick your condescension up your ass. If you two want to continue this conversation, then you can ask nicely. Or, Raphael, if you want privacy, you can walk outside through that hole you blew in my building and shout really loud."

Raphael bolted from his chair. "You speak to me this way?"

"Yes, I do speak to you this way," Ryan said, feeling Raphael's hot breath and seeing for the first time the faint outline of three teardrop tattoos on his left cheek.

"You do no get to speak to me this way!" Raphael's hand dropped toward his holster.

"Raphael!" Daniel called from the video conference.

Ryan laughed without humor. "And now we see the truth. After all the Holy Mothers and *Glory a Dios*, all you have is threat and intimidation. After all your appeal to faith, all you really have to offer is force."

"I do no make threats," Raphael said, his voice low, the deep underbelly of his soul laid bare.

"Raphael!" Daniel barked.

"You want to know what we say?" Raphael asked. "You want to know what I talk about in *your* office, in *your* building, on *your* computer? As soon as my Leona come here, we are leaving. Then you can have *your* building and *your* office and *your* computer. It *es* madness to stay in the city. This *es* what Gus Blanco figure out. We can no survive with so many infected. There are too many peoples. We will die here. This is what I also learn from Gus. I see his boys die and I will no let my sons die here. This tower *es* a death trap. We take the Strykers and we leave."

Ryan shook his head, emphatic. "Raphael, you keep trying to take my shit to save your ass. You can't take my shit. Period."

"Those Strykers are not your shit," Raphael said with triumph, "They are Daniel's. I can take them."

"No, they are not. They are mine. He gave all of his—"

"It does no matter what you say!" Raphael drew his sidearm pointing it at Ryan's head. "We take them. You can no have all of this when we have this much need. You do no do the right thing. You do no sacrifice. In times like this, we all must sacrifice. But if you can no do right, we will take the Strykers and you can no stop us."

"Raphael!" Daniel shouted, leaning into the camera as if he could crawl into the room.

Ryan said, "After all of the recrimination, after all of your snide comments about Richard Ryder, you are really no different than he is. But this is no surprise. Catholics always act exactly like Marxists. They always resort to force when they can't bully people into guilt." He took a slow step forward until the barrel of the gun rested on his chest. "So what is next, Raphael? Are you going to pull the trigger so we can see if the Holy Mother is still protecting me?"

Raphael rocked back as if he had been punched in the face.

"Raphael Paguero! Look at me!" Daniel said, his voice thundering in the office. "I gave Ryan everything. You will stop acting like this!"

"*Es una locura aqui*. We die here. We can no stay. This fat old man, he *es loco*. This *es* a bad plan. You will send me what I ask for. I will find another way." He turned toward Ryan. "We leave as soon as my Leona come." He paused as if to say more, but then his eyes strayed to the bullet holes in the far wall. Raphael swallowed and walked out.

"You should not provoke him," Daniel said. "He is dangerous, very dangerous. And you need him. You need his sons and Leona. They are all fierce warriors. And maybe you could try not being so abrupt."

Ryan sighed. "You know . . . Daniel, my mom tried to fix me and it didn't work, so you are wasting your breath expecting me to act different and besides, blowing smoke up people's asses doesn't make them loyal, and no, I don't need Raphael."

"That is foolish, son. You can't hope to make it alone. You will be dead by yourself."

"No, you misunderstand. I didn't say anything about alone. I said I don't need Raphael. I don't need anyone who will kill to take what he wants in the name of sacrifice. The way to make sure that I fail spectacularly is to let people treat me and this place like they are entitled."

"He is just trying to protect his kids. If you had children, you might think a little—"

"Don't," Ryan said. "I've heard this bromide my whole life. As if not having children stunts the ability to understand values. The comment is as condescending as it is evil. Having children is not a license to despicable behavior, and adults that hide behind children are vile creatures that have no principles."

"Son, you are wrong. Raphael is a man of great principles. The only thing keeping him away from church is there are no priests holding Mass."

"Yeah, everyone thinks that the gods are the source of morality but that same morality shifts with everyone's whim. The fact is Raphael lies and steals when it serves his purpose and when he doesn't get what he wants, his moral standard *is* to use force to make sure someone else sacrifices for his greater good. Since I'm not part of his family, he will sacrifice me for the greater good of the genetic code in a minute."

Daniel shook his head. "Don't be so quick to judge."

"Quick to judge? Daniel I've been slow to judge. I should have kicked him out of here days ago. I have been foolish to ignore who Raphael really is. The only thing that saved me this time was he thinks that the Holy Mother made the bullets pass through me when Richard tried to shoot me. But when that piece of mysticism finds another explanation, the next time the shit hits the fan, he will have no hesitation about putting a bullet in my head. If I don't judge reality now I might not have the chance tomorrow."

"He does think the Holy Mother protected you. And he wouldn't kill you—"

"Did you miss the part where he just put his gun on my head? Or was threatening me with a gun deemed a justifiable act of asset redistribution in *el Papa's* recent Encyclical?"

"Don't be a smartass. Just know that it is unwise to provoke him."

"Amazing. After all you saw take place, I'm the unsympathetic one? Because I make a judgment about the bad ideas driving bad actions I'm the one provoking *him*?" Ryan rolled the tension out of his shoulders. "So, what does Raphael want you to get for him?"

"He wants me to get more satellite photos," Daniel said.

"I don't understand."

"They are recon photos. He wants to see if there is a clear road to the Adirondacks. That is where their camp is."

And the last piece of the puzzle fit into place. Raphael didn't print out Google earth. He was printing out satellite images. They needed to be able to see the best path to their secret shooting range. Raphael was scouting the roads.

Brilliant!

Ryan said, "Camp?"

"Yes, remember when we were on the phone with Leona? They talked about going to their camps?"

"No," Ryan said, trying to remember back to the day when he agreed to let Raphael stay in the tower. So much had happened in the days following that the details faded into a pile. "Yes, maybe. I don't know."

"The Pagueros built a series of camps in the Adirondacks for when the Marxist revolution broke out so they could use it as a place to stage guerilla war. They also have a primary camp in Maine. The one in Maine is very remote. That is Raphael's goal. They could last a long time in Maine. Maybe you could salvage this," Daniel said. "Maybe if you apologize, they would let you go with them."

"You do realize that the reason to keep their trip to the gun range secret was because he didn't want me to know he was planning to leave. He was going to leave me alone."

Daniel nodded. "I was hoping to change his mind before he did that. We can salvage this."

"No we can't. Pragmatism is a deadly killer and almost more destructive than altruism. Going with them to save my ass in the short term will end up killing me in the long term."

"Goddamn, you are stubborn," Daniel Ryder said.

"Can you get them these recon photos?"

"Yes."

"How? How can you get such things with everything falling apart?"

"Because I'm a rich and powerful man." Daniel answered like he'd just been asked his height.

"All right, Great and Powerful Oz," Ryan Sage said. "Get him what he wants. Let's get this Catholic murderer for the greater good out of my tower."

34

Global Infection: ≤ 31.0011%

Minutes after Daniel Ryder ended the video call, Ryan started shaking, because he knew that Raphael's hot breath on his face was the feather touch of the Grim Reaper dancing across his soul. Ryan collapsed into his zero-gravity office chair until his body settled, but then he could barely muster the energy to turn on the security monitors. So that is where Ryan stayed, his body spent and his mind roiling through the events. The Paguero nighttime secret raid still didn't make sense. It seemed that Raphael didn't want Ryan to know they were leaving and had the raid gone well, that they had more bullets. But then, what did it matter if Ryan knew about the details? If they had guns and ammo, all they had to do was pack their stuff when Leona showed up, point their guns, tell him to sit like a good dog and leave. There had to be something more to this story, but for an hour and a half Ryan couldn't puzzle out what was really behind the subterfuge.

Marco knocked on the open office door dressed in a blue T-shirt, blue BDUs, and bare feet. His face was finally filling out from eating. In fact, his whole body seemed to be inflating, but his shoulders only came from miles and miles under a rucksack followed by thousands of pushups. He said, "I guess that is the second time you have stared down the barrel of a gun and didn't mess yourself."

"Oh, I did. I just cleaned up before anyone could tell," Ryan said. He shifted in his chair still feeling the subtle shake of his legs.

"I don't know too many people that have made my father that angry and lived," Marco said. "I can't decide if I should be impressed or appalled."

"I'm sure there are other choices," Ryan said. "Aghast, dismayed, vexed or even awe-stricken."

"Even under pressure he makes jokes."

Ryan managed a smile.

Marco looked at the televisions lining the office walls, each with its own security camera view. He finally settled on the two-hundred-inch video conference display hanging from the ceiling. "I thought you said that government news will rot your brain?"

"I did say that," Ryan said. "But at the moment I need a little brain rot."

"I think the rot happens faster, if you watch with the sound on."

"I couldn't stand listening to the propaganda. After the second broadcast cycle, I could recite what the teleprompter readers were saying. I'm watching the live footage to pick out what the censors are missing. Besides, I prefer listening to the city. At least the streets tell the truth."

"What does Pittsburgh sound like?"

"Occasional distant screams and the even more distant gunshots," Ryan said. "The important part is that it is *distant*. So, Raphael sent his mediator again?"

"Mediator? No this is a fact finding mission." Marco dropped gingerly into a chair; the bandage seeping under his shirt.

"Make yourself comfortable," Ryan said, trying for ironic but it came out as solicitous. Something about Marco's bearing made him cautious. He was different but Ryan couldn't figure out how.

Marco watched the government feed that showed Chicago under siege. The streets were violence, fire, and destruction. "What did Gus say? It is madness to stay in the city?"

"Is there supposed to be a message in there for me?"

Marco shrugged and watched the screen through the next segment: Men wearing DHS emblazoned vests and hats in a shootout at the Vonderhaar farm in Preble County, Ohio. The scroll along the bottom said: *Federalized forces battling a local domestic terrorist uprising . . .*

"Just making an observation. It does seem like madness to stay in a city full of chaos."

"Subtle, Marco, so very subtle. I understand why I look like a fool, but dare I point out that you haven't left for your family home and you're not leaving the city until your mother gets here."

"You're only a fool if you keep on the path of folly."

"That was very Zen."

The government broadcast transitioned to beautiful people talking pleasantly into the camera. The scroll underneath said: *Federal law requires citizens to report to their FEMA zone*. The footage changed to a report at a shelter where people were eating and smiling. The scroll under the video said: *Shelters providing gluten-free and vegan menus*.

"What did you expect to happen?" Marco asked. "When you decided to stay here?"

Ryan shrugged. "The plan was to huddle in here as the city boiled and burned into social collapse. I don't know how I could have projected what happened next. Two gun fights in how many days?"

"Four firefights in about seven days not including the fight at the gun range."

"Has it been that many?" Ryan shook his head, trying to separate the prevailing terror into specific instances. It seemed impossible that the Renaissance Tower should become a focal point. It was an obscure piece of real estate—one of dozens of tall buildings that blended into the Pittsburgh skyline. The city was filled with so many buildings, so many restaurants and sundry stores that it seemed statistically absurd for people to notice a darkened, mostly empty office and residential high rise among the buildings crowded into the Golden Triangle. "I thought we would quietly survive until our little corner of the world settled down," Ryan said, "but that has proved to be a delusion."

"Can I ask you a question? Why did you stay?"

"Stay? Here in Pittsburgh? My house was destroyed, so I didn't have any place to go. Well, that plus a few weeks ago it became almost impossible to leave Pittsburgh. You've seen the cars cluttering the streets right?"

"No I mean, you could have left with Daniel. Did you just want your own penthouse?"

"The price was right," Ryan said, deadpan.

Marco knit his brow. "You are being funny again, right?"

"I don't have the energy for serious right now."

"Well, the situation is serious," Marco said, "I'm wondering if you are failing to see the gravity. I don't know too many men who willingly walk toward someone holding a gun. You've done it twice. Considering your reaction is to joke, that seems a little crazy."

"My *reaction* is the problem? Really? Where is it written how you are supposed react to having a gun to your head? How do you get to make that judgment and fail to call into question the mental balance of the instigator? How is it you forget that your father was going to murder me. I would be plenty sane to drive that murderous thug into the street and you and your brother with him, but I'm *sane* enough to know that you will kill me where I stand. Does that sound sane enough for you?"

"If he wanted you dead you would be dead," Marco said, "So maybe you are exaggerating. Maybe what we are seeing is the effects of a persecution complex? All he asked for was a few minutes of privacy. You could have given him that, but you chose to get in his face. My father won't bow to your edicts, so you decide to escalate a problem. You pop off about governments. Hold everything you see on TV in suspicion. And tell the whole world they are patriots for resisting the authorities. Maybe you just have a problem with authority."

"Exaggerating? Persecution complex? A problem with authority? What the hell are you talking about?" Ryan said, and then sighed. "Look, I don't want to know. But to be clear, I have many problems with your father. Not least of which is that he doesn't have any authority. It is obvious that we fundamentally disagree about the nature of my relationship with your fa—"

Marco shifted and groaned, his face flushing with pain. He unscrewed a bottle of pills and popped one in his mouth. After the pain subsided he said, "I'm just trying to understand what makes you tick. Why did you stay here?"

"I don't think that is what you are really after here. And at the moment I don't really care what the Pagueros think of me."

Marco fixed his eyes on Ryan and said, "Pretend that my opinion is important."

And Ryan saw the change in demeanor again, an expectation that he should be heard and obeyed. A military bearing that said, 'You will regret fucking with me."

Ryan didn't want another fight so he said, "Why did I stay? Because . . ." his voice faded. Finally, he said, "No answer I give will seem sufficient, I think. There has been so much loss, so much grief, and so much conflict that my reasons will seem trite."

"Humor me."

"One reason was . . . there was a young girl. I wanted to help her. I knew I couldn't if I left."

"A *young* girl?" Marco said like a marble suddenly dropped into a slot. "Who was this young girl to you?"

"No one, really. Just some girl, maybe twelve or thirteen: I about stepped on her when I was exiting a sub shop. It was maybe three minutes of happenstance, but something about the way she looked at me, something in her eyes said she needed help. I saw her again and again over the next few days, on the streets, alone."

"You wanted to help a young girl who was alone?" Marco asked, "Why just her? Couldn't you find others to help? Didn't you find any boys for instance?"

Ryan put his palms up. "I never thought I'd have to justify who I wanted to help, so I don't have an answer for you."

Marco frowned. "You stayed so you could help a young girl? That does seem foolish."

"Is that another word for trite?"

"You had the option to go with Daniel Ryder. Had you gone, you would be safe. In that context and with your reason seems . . . very strange."

Ryan breathed deep. "I think I already said that."

"Come on, no matter how cute a girl is that doesn't—"

"Marco I don't like what you are implying. I didn't stay because she was attractive—"

"So what is the reason? Do you just want to keep picking fights with the government? Did you fall in love with the comfort of the penthouse? Do you have a secret death wish? You could have had a cushy life in Daniel Ryder's refuge. You could have run from the government and they would never have found you. If he builds anything, he builds it well. So why didn't you go with Daniel?"

Ryan frowned. "I don't think Daniel's solution will work. Closed societies deteriorate into tyrannies, because the nature of a closed society requires the imposition of individual liberty. And it does not bode well that Daniel is willing to look the other way while Richard tried to murder me." He indicated the bullet holes in the far wall.

"My father said that Richard Ryder shot you. He said the bullets passed right through you. He said that the Holy Mother protected you that day."

"I think the more obvious explanation is that Richard is a very bad shot."

Marco looked at the bullet holes and then back to Ryan. "My father knows a little more about shooting than you do. I'm inclined to believe him."

Ryan shrugged. "Whatever Richard's shooting skill, his ideas are the dangerous part. He thinks he is a right murderer in principle. Progressives, also known as Marxists, think that killing on behalf of the greater good is morally justified. And Progressives always think they are the rightful recipient of the greater good."

Marco said, "About three years ago, my family had some problems that took them down to Paraguay. They needed some military intelligence. I had the ability to help them. But that intel revealed some nasty shit about Richard." He shook his head. "I never understood how Daniel could ignore those reports."

"And that is my point," Ryan said. "There is no way that Daniel Ryder, politically connected, globally respected billionaire, doesn't know who his son really is, and yet, in the face of irrefutable evidence . . . watching him try to murder me in this very office, Daniel has shown no ability to condemn his son's actions. Daniel shows no willingness to penalize Richard. So by default, Daniel confirms his son's actions.

"Richard has wasted no time in advancing his ideology. I suspect he will speak unopposed, because cowardly capitalists refuse to defend the single greatest social organization ever achieved by men. Twelve hundred people packed into a human vault for years with an unchecked ideologue like Richard to provide philosophical direction is a recipe for bad, bad, bad things. Cowardly capitalists who tolerate such things get what they deser—"

The silence made Marco double take. "What? What happened?"

"I think I just figured out what this conversation is really about. I think I just figured out the only thing keeping me alive is that you are not inclined to swallow your father's masterful manipulation whole."

35

Global Infection: ≤ 31.0012%

Exhaustion will make the mind work like it's filled with molasses. Fear will make the mind go tilt. And it seemed that both exhaustion and fear made the brain totally useless.

Which is why Ryan could barely hear the warning bells tinkling every so lightly in the back of his head. The conversation made no sense, filled with accusations and recriminations that had no context, until he saw the converging lines: Raphael.

Marco leaned forward and pointed his finger hard. "Stop calling my father a liar and a manipulator. We are not talking about him right now. We are talking about you."

Ryan met his gaze then turned to the credenza and started shifting through the organized piles until he found the correct file. It was black and thick with papers and exhibits. He thumbed through the first few pages in silence and then he said, "Raphael was talking to you about killing me wasn't he? He wanted your blessing, but you won't condone outright murder, at least not yet. So my guess is he first implied that that I had been investigated for molesting young girls. You couldn't buy into Ryan the molester so he switched to something dear to your heart: my criticism of our government. It is a nice hot button with a military man. You spend your life prizing obedience to rank, so any man failing to obey orders is a man you can't trust, right? And then what, he portrayed my objection to government as paranoia, right? Did he show you some out of context excerpt or did he just imply I was some right wing nut? You stewed in your uncertainties and moral outrage for about an hour and then came here to confront me, right?"

Marco's face moved from indignant to offended to incredulous and finally settled on wide-eyed petulant—the same look that a boy gets when his mom catches him with a skin magazine. "What are you talking abou—"

"Don't dishonor yourself, Marco. I understand siding with your father at first, but don't lie. I've had enough Paguero lies."

Marco fidgeted in his chair. "How did you know? Do you have the penthouse bugged?"

Ryan laughed. "Now who is being paranoid? I figured it out by how you acted and what you talked about. He tried to talk you out of coming to talk to me didn't he? He didn't want you to be able to check the story."

Marco turned away lost in thought. Then he said, "But what about you being investigated?"

"Bring me the man and I will find the crime" Ryan said, fiddling with the folio under his hand. "Do you know who said that?"

"No."

"Andrey Vyshinsky. He was the state prosecutor for Joseph Stalin. He said those words, but those words could be spoken by pretty much any special prosecutor the US Congress foists on America. Special prosecutors operate the same way; they find crimes to use against political opponents, and if they can't find a process crime they make one up." Ryan pushed the file across the desk. "Read," he said. It wasn't a suggestion.

Marco looked at the first page noticing the official government seal, flipped to the second and third. He paused, his eyes focused and read.

Ryan watched the television; the segments once again rolled through the footage around the Preble county farm. The camera cut to a dead terrorist wearing a green John Deere hat, a Carhartt shirt and a farmer's tan. The scroll underneath said: *Federalized forces battling a local domestic terrorist uprising. Forces gain control of essential food supply. Destroy GMO contaminated crops.*

Marco stopped reading and said, "Holy shit? Who did you piss off?"

"That should be obvious."

"You know what is really fucked up? I knew these guys," Marco said, spinning the folio and tapping the pictures of the government investigators who tried to force Bexely Stepford to accuse Ryan of molesting his daughters or suffer government displeasure.

"I trained with him at Fort Benning and he was deployed to the same company I was in Italy. This other guy I met about a year ago. He was not a nice man."

Ryan wanted to talk about those two men at length, but he had a more pressing problem with a nasty man in this tower. "If the cosmos ever delivers those two men to me they will both die, maybe quickly, maybe horribly. I haven't decided yet which. But we need to finish our conversation about your father. Considering how this night has transpired he's not much better than those two."

"What about your efforts to overthrow the government? Is my father right about that?"

"Marco, I'm done justifying myself today. I've just handed you overwhelming evidence that your father's implications are a total fabrication, so that should call everything he told you into suspicion. And then I need you to give me your word that I won't be murdered in my sleep."

Marco shook his head. "You won't be. Look, maybe we can salvage this. I'll talk to my dad. We can work something out. Maybe you can come with us."

"The events of this evening don't make me inclined to kiss and make up. Had this been an isolated heat of the moment thing, then maybe we could hug it out, but Raphael has acted as if this tower was his property from the start. There has been no respect for me or mine since day two. I've been treated as a guest in my own house. He—"

Marco waved his hand like it would wipe away the chatter. "Forget the tower and your property. This issue is bigger than all of that. This is just stuff. We are talking about life. We are talking about escaping the city and going where we can live. The Maine camp is well supplied with vehicles and food and fuel. If we take all three Strykers we could be there, in worst case scenario, in a month."

"Marco, there is no distinction between human life and material property. Man's life is *not* divided between some supernatural perfect moral existence and an inferior immoral material existence as Saint Augustine would have everyone believe. Man is an integration of his spiritual existence *with* his material production. If you steal a man's stuff, you steal his life, precisely because man must create his own wealth to live. Man must produce material stuff so he can satisfy every facet of his life. Man cannot trot off into the wilderness and expect nature to provide him anything. He must choose his values to sustain his life, and then he must think and work to achieve those values. If he doesn't, he dies. It is that simple, and it is that serious. So when you make light of my material possessions, you are participating in the same presumption as your father."

"Okay, I understand," Marco said. "You, we, are all entitled to our private property, but you can't take this tower with you."

"Marco, you are not thinking in principles," Ryan said. "It wouldn't matter if I have a tower in Pittsburgh or a pointy stick in the wilds of Maine. Your father does not see my existence as a sacred trust. He sees me as something to pillage for his own use in the name of sacrifice for his tribe. He treats this tower as if it is his to do with as he chooses. He would do the same thing with the pointy stick if he thought it was in his tribal interest."

"Well, you have to understand that my family has been here for a lot longer than you have. This has been my family's second home for years."

Ryan chuckled without mirth. "And you just made my point. By that standard, I should be able to go back to England where my ancestors walked the earth 500 years ago. I should be able to walk onto any piece of land and declare it mine because my ancestors hunted and gathered on tribal lands."

"Don't be absurd."

"I'm being absurd to make a point," Ryan said. "There is no such thing as ancestral property. Property is not defined by geographical familiarity. And a man is not entitled to dispose of whatever resources strike his fancy because he slept a few nights in the State of Pennsylvania.

"The fact that you can so blithely dismiss my right to private property tells me I would never survive your family. Your familial loyalty would always trump my claim to anything."

"Is getting stuff the only important thing?" Marco said, exasperated. "What is your obsession with property? You don't think that in times like this, people need to work together?"

"Marco, again, you try to diminish my point by implying there is a moral failing with property. How is it you fail to grasp the principle? The conflict is not about my stuff. The conflict is because your father sees no moral problem with *taking* my stuff.

"I already said this, but I will keep saying it until you get the point. Man's life and property are connected, because man uses his life . . . his heartbeats and his brain . . . to create property. He uses that property to live. Property and life are inseparable. So when you take a man's stuff, you are taking the heartbeats used to make that stuff and all of the heartbeats he will use to replace that stuff. Property, things, material goods are not morally inferior chaff. They are the morally essential means by which man satisfies the needs of his life—"

"But people should work together in times like this," Marco interrupted.

"Your definition of working together is that I give you my stuff on pain of death without any complaint. That is not working together. That is slavery.

"And 'times like these' is merely a catch phrase tyrants use to justify their despotism. The phrase implies that the circumstantial nature of crisis justifies increased dictatorial power. This is a lie. The world has always been dangerous, and expediency is not a justification for abolishing liberty.

"Inalienable rights are not conditional to tragic events anymore than they are conditional to someone's whim for security. The individual is always the social and political primary. The state is not sovereign. The community is not sovereign. The tribe is not soverei—"

"But I'm not talking about all of that," Marco said. "I'm talking about my family and you."

"So am I," Ryan said, "I am trying to point out your father's deepest assumptions.

He believes that his families' *needs* trump everything. My point is that until the Paguero tribe changes the foundation of its thinking, it won't matter if we are in this tower or in the great state of Maine. The Paguero tribe will always demand I sacrifice for the tribe. And if I won't, they will murder me for the greater good."

Marco snapped to his feet and then winched with the sudden movement. When he recovered he said, "This tower will likely be the death of us all. You need us. You need our combat skills. You will die when we leave. "

"Marco, what I am talking about is far more important than guns and ammo and fighting. If we don't know what we are fighting for, then we will be reduced to barbarism . . . a life that is nothing but war and warriors. History tells us that that kind of society is a terrible society. It took man thousands of years to crawl out of the tribal world ruled by strong men. And no rational man, no sane man, has a wish to return to such a culture.

"It is useful to have the skill to shoot bad guys, but it is much more important to understand the criteria of civil society. One of man's greatest achievements was the discovery of civil society. But to discover civil society, man first had to discover the primacy of the individual and the corollary private property."

Marco walked to the door and stopped. "I know you don't like my father, but you should know that he is a good man. I know you think him irrational, but he is a rational man. Only rational men can become mechanical engineers. But he has also survived in worlds of total chaos. He will survive this world and he will make sure his family survives. And if you would give just a little here, he would be willing to sacrifice for you."

Ryan said, "Oh no. I don't want anyone to sacrifice. In fact, I am counting on Raphael's self-interest. I am counting on his rational self-interest. So it is my sincere hope that he is as rational as you say."

Marco was confused. "What do you mean?"

Ryan said, "Tomorrow should be an interesting day."

36

Global Infection: ≤ 31.3006%

Ryan woke late because he slept deep and well—a curiosity since it was possible that a man sleeping just down the hall might kill him before he woke. After Marco left the office Ryan walked into his bedroom, a group of rooms dubbed the *au pair* suite, locked the outer door and stuck a chair under the knob, closed the bedroom door and did the same. The shower was quick and hot, his head hit the pillow and REM sleep came immediately. He woke to a distant knock followed by the jarring sounds of his ringtone. He didn't recognize the number, but guessed it was Raphael and crushed the reject button. He dressed and as an afterthought tucked a Beretta into the small of his back and went to the family kitchen. Raphael stormed in, demanded they talk and saw the weapon, which inspired Raphael to go full tactical for a two o'clock meeting in Ryan's office.

Raphael Paguero sat on the opposite side the desk in his vest, side arms in their thigh holsters and a Kalashnikov resting across his lap. He was overdressed. "It *es* like Gus Blanco say. It *es* madness to stay here. The camp in Maine. We can live there. It will be hard, but we can survive there. There *es* nothing you can say to change my mind."

Ryan leaned forward and said, "Raphael, you misunderstand. I am no longer interested in you staying here—"

"What?" Simone said. "You are kicking us out?"

Ryan said to Raphael, "I don't foresee a long-term relationship. I think it is better that we go our separate ways amicably."

Raphael's eyes narrowed and he wagged his index finger. He winced and put his hand down. Raphael pulled a bottle of OxyContin from a pocket flicked a pill into his mouth and swallowed. "Are you sure we can no have a long-term relationship? But would you say this if maybe Daniel persuade me to take you with us? He know that you will be dead if you are alone in one month."

"I appreciate what Daniel tried to do, but our current interaction is based entirely on Daniel Ryder's goodwill toward each of us individually, and it is very apparent that *his* goodwill is not enough to sustain *our* interaction. We have barely lived together for two weeks and that hasn't gone well, because we don't share common goals or common values."

Raphael shifted forward in his chair, his face hard. "You say to me that I do no have values? I have faith in God. I pray to the Holy Mother for guidance. I have values."

Ryan leveled his eyes for ten heartbeats. "Raphael, I don't care where you get your values from. I only care that we don't share them. You value the tribe and sacrifice, and you consecrate your values with your religion. In contrast, I value the individual. I reject sacrifice as man's highest virtue. I will not sacrifice you to myself, and I refuse to be sacrificed to you. These two world views are irreconcilable; therefore it is better that you leave."

Raphael leaned back in his chair and straightened the tactical vest like he was primping his suit. "All peoples must sacrifice for the good of everyone," he said. "Every wise man already know this."

Sacrifice as the highest moral ideal had been burned deep into the American psyche, so it was almost impossible to argue against the altruistic disaster. Ryan said, "You think the Stryker is the best way for your family to survive. So, you think that I am morally obligated to sacrifice to your need to protect your family. You think that I am morally required to give away my property because you have a need."

Raphael wagged a finger, again stifling the pain in the shoulder. "But you do no understand times like this. You have so much of the Strykers. You cannot keep them when peoples need them."

"Raphael, let me ask you this," Ryan said. "When the first raiding party attacks your camp and they say you have too much and you can't keep what you have because they have a need, what will you say? How will you defend your right to keep your stuff? How will you justify your right to live for your own sake? Will you sacrifice your wife and children for the sake of *their* tribe? Will you cut your own throat to fulfill *their* need?"

"This *es* no the same thing," Raphael said with a dismissive wave.

"You called what I did a negligent discharge? I call what you just did negligent thinking. My question is the exact same scenario, but the difference is you are the one with the stuff. So how can you defend your right to keep your stuff if the moral standard is sacrifice based on need?"

"This *es* no the same thing!"

"Raphael, your lack of intellectual honesty is further proof that we do not share values. You not only lie to other people, but you lie to yourself. It is impossible to have a productive relationship with a liar."

"I have values!" Raphael roared, his veins throbbing in his forehead.

"Then prove it. Do you believe theft is wrong? Do you think murdering a man to take his stuff is wrong?"

"Yes, yes, of course," Raphael said, "The Bible says that man should no do these things."

"If that is true, then you are forbidden to murder me to take the Stryker," Ryan said, "Right?"

"But you can't have all those Strykers!" Simone shouted. "It's not fair. It's our only chance to survive the trip."

"Simone, shut up," Marco snapped.

"Simone," Ryan said. "I am talking to your father. And for the duration of this conversation, I will be talking to him and him only. But you raise a point I want to address. The Stryker is not your *only* chance to survive. It represents maybe your best chance to travel from here to wherever your camp is, but it is not the only means to get there. And this is an important point. You can find another means to get to the camp without stealing from me. You still have Raphael's SUV in the garage or the truck you drove here. And if that won't work, I will gladly give you the Lamborghini. And if those don't work, there are thousands of abandoned vehicles scattered all over the city."

Simone crossed his arms. "You say not to steal, but now you tell us to take someone else's car."

Ryan leaned back in his chair. "If you are going to absolve yourself of stealing from me in the name of need, then certainly you can absolve yourself of taking from someone who may not even be alive. But the point is, there are many options that do not require you to steal from me to achieve your goal."

"You just want us to die!" Simone snapped.

"Hush, Simone," Raphael said. "The grownups are talking."

Ryan said, "My point is that having the Stryker is not an issue of metaphysical danger."

"Neg Dis," Simone sneered. "Use English."

"Simone, be quiet," Marco said. "Really, little brother, you are way out of your depth and don't know it. Do yourself a favor and keep your mouth shut."

"You shut up," Simone snapped and then he added, "I'm just saying, he uses big words and he doesn't need to."

Raphael shook his head. "What does this mean? Metaphysical danger?"

"It is easier to give you an example," Ryan said. "You are on a boat at sea. The boat sinks. You swim to the only island. You get to the shore and a man meets you and says that this is his property and you cannot be on the island. To respect his property rights means your destruction. This is an irrational moral standard. In this instance, a person has the right to defend his life against someone's property right. That is an example of metaphysical danger. And now here is a contrasting example—your boat sinking near hundreds of islands and hundreds of boats within swimming distance. The private property owner has a moral right to ask you to leave because there are other options that make survival possible, even if there are sharks in the water. In this context, you are no longer in metaphysical danger. Your existence may be dangerous, but your death is not certain.

"Our specific conflict is like the second example: You are not drowning, and there are many other means of travel, even though those means represent different levels of danger. The Stryker might be the most desirable means of travel, but it is not the only means by which you can get to your camp."

Raphael's gaze slipped out to a thousand yards, and then he focused. "Yes, this I understand. We can take something else to get to the camp. This *es* true. And the Stryker *es* the best way to be safe on this trip so I would be a fool to take something else when it *es* here."

"I am glad that it represents that much value to you," Ryan said. "That will make my proposal simple."

Raphael frowned. "Proposal? What *es* this proposal?"

"I will sell you a Stryker for—"

"All he wants is money?!" Simone said. "This man is crazy. The world is falling apart and he wants money? You have Richard Ryder's millions and you want more? You are crazy!"

Raphael smirked. "Maybe it is as you say. We do no share values. I could never be so greedy. And I can tell you I do not have three million dollars. You are godless. I was wrong to think the Holy Mother should protect you. She would not protect such a person. She would not protect a man who does not understand love. She would scorn the greedy."

37

Global Infection: ≤ 31.3007%

Ryan held his chin in hand, elbow on arm rest. He had been called worse many times, but he always found it fascinating that *his* moral credibility was called into question when challenging the moral right to steal in the name of the greater good. What did it say about a culture that tacitly approved of force to compel those who have stuff to give to those who claim to have a need? What did it say about a people where attitudes adopted from mythology were more reasonable than someone appealing to reality? What did it say about a person who thought the looter was morally superior to the man defending his right to private property? What did it say about a person whose definition of *good* was what *other* men gave away?

Finally Ryan said, “You interrupted me again, so I didn’t get to explain. But since you brought up the issue of sanity, morality and the definition of godly, then let me respond. It is to your shame that I should even have to make this defense, but since your religion seems to make your memory faulty, I will remind you that just a few days ago I saved your sons’ lives. It was then that you credited my actions to divine endorsement.

“I think what we are learning here is that your religion is merely a way to sanctify your own actions. And I think the contrast could not be starker. You have offered me little more than contempt and unfulfilled threats and demands of sacrifice. By contrast I have offered you reason, safety and a peaceful means to solve our problem. I have given you a safe place to live and food to eat. You have offered me disdain, disrespect from your teenage son and death. If this is what it means to be godly, then I thank God I am not.”

Simone jumped from his seat. “You talk to my—”

Raphael’s hand shot out and grabbed Simone’s collar. “Shut! Your! Mouth!”

“But—”

Raphael looked deep into Simone’s eyes. Simone sat. Raphael ground his jaws and looked at Ryan.

Ryan waited.

Raphael shifted in his chair. Finally he said, “Please continue.”

“What you so casually call greed is what I call free men honoring the other’s life. I have something you want. I want something you have. This gives us an opportunity to exchange and to align our goals. There are no bullets here. There is no compulsion. There is no sacrifice. So while you condemn me, I am the one offering peace. If offering peace is immoral, then I am willing to be immoral.”

“But what if I do no want this offer?” Raphael said. “What if I think your price *es* too high? Then you are no offering peace. I am compelled to give you what I cannot.”

“Raphael, your necessity is not my compulsion,” Ryan said. “The fact that you find something valuable does not mean I enslave you by expecting an equal value in return. If you do not accept my offer, then you are free to look for another solution. And we have already established there are many other options.”

“What *es* this proposal?”

“Before I go on, I need to make something clear. Your choice to leave is a family decision?”

Simone rolled his eyes. “What a knob.”

“Yes, we will all be going,” Raphael said.

“Okay, I am negotiating this agreement with you as the representative of the family. There will not be separate agreements with each person. I agree with you, and you are responsible to provide the resources to achieve the outcomes. Agreed?”

“How can I agree to such a thing when I do no know what you want me to do?”

“It doesn’t matter what the work is for this part of the agreement. All I am saying is that I will not be negotiating say one Stryker for each of you based on individual work. You are leaving as a family; you take on this agreement as a family. That means you must speak for your wife and kids.”

“Yes, this I can do.”

“But wait. I want a Stryker,” Simone said.

Ryan spun a piece of paper toward Raphael. “So that there is no confusion, please read this and sign it. The paragraph merely summarizes what I just said.”

Raphael read the document handed it to Marco who also read. Simone stood behind looking over his shoulder. “This is fair,” Marco said and handed it back.

Raphael signed and spun the paper back. “But I still do no have money.”

“That is good, because I do not want money. Money is only a medium of exchanging value. I want your brain. I want Marco’s brain. And I want Simone’s brawn. There is no way for me to calculate exactly what I will need. I don’t know enough about this building, or about the days to come, or what opportunities will arise over the next few weeks. So here is what I am asking for. As we said, the Stryker represents the best opportunity for secure travel. It represents your best option for survival. Right?”

"Yes," Raphael said warily.

"That is what I want here. I want you to help me fortify and stock this building. I want you to give me the best options for survival, and I want you to teach me combat skills. This will require your highest and best abilities. I have here a list of things that I think need done, but this is only a starting point. What I am asking from you is this. You say you know times like this: That you know what it takes to survive?"

"Yes, I know these things," Raphael said.

"Then I want you to plan what you would do to give yourself the best option for surviving in this tower. This will give me the best chance to survive. The Stryker represents your best chance; I will trade you for my best chance."

"This is good, Poppa," Marco said.

Raphael tugged at his chin. Then he said, "Yes, this I think *es* good."

Ryan said, "Before you sign this agreement, you will give me a high-level plan, then you, myself, and Marco will prioritize each item."

"But it could take months to do what you ask," Raphael said. "And we will not be here for months. We are leaving when Leona gets here."

"Yes, we will look at your list and make decisions based on time constraints. And this goes directly to what I am asking from you. There is no way that I would get enough value from you in a couple of days to justify you taking the Stryker. So, my proposal is for you to remain for thirty days after your wife and sons arrive to complete whatever can be achieved."

"Will we be doing dangerous stuff?" Simone said.

Ryan gave Simone a flat look. "You mean like a nighttime raid on a weapons cache in that ends up in a shootout where you blow a hole in my building?"

Simone shrugged. "Well, yeah, like that."

"The world is dangerous," Ryan said. "We will have to go outside for obvious reasons. One thing that we must do is travel roughly a mile and a half to the east to clean out a store for supplies. I expect that to be plenty dangerous."

"Cool. I will get to kill zombies."

Marco smacked Simone in the back of the head. Simone threw a half dozen air punches.

Raphael rubbed his jaw. "We may not live for thirty days here."

"True," Ryan said. "We might not live through the evening. You might not live the first night in the Stryker. There are no guarantees and I am not offering any. I am asking for unrestricted access to your expertise and your labor from now until Leona's arrival. When she arrives, the clock starts on the thirty days. You expect her soon, right? Maybe even tomorrow?"

"And we can leave after thirty days no matter where we are in the projects?" Marco asked.

Ryan nodded. "You will give me your expertise and energies until Leona and your other sons arrive, and then all of you will work for 30 days to complete whatever we have planned and then you are free to go. If you are men of values as you say, then we will have gotten done most of what needs done. If you are not, then you will probably be putting a bullet in me anyway."

Raphael kept pulling on his chin, thinking. "And I want diesel fuel, a full tank and three more barrels," he said. "And I go down and look at the Strykers. There are three: two M1126 and one M1132. I want to take the—"

"No, I am not pulling parts and pieces from the Strykers. You pick one as is. I will provide one full tank of gas, and you can fill the weapons to capacity from the other vehicles, but all other ammunition stays with me. As for more fuel, I don't have it to spare."

"One tank of diesel will not be enough," Raphael said. "There *es* the generator fuel. There *es* two drums in the sublevel."

"I didn't know there was a generator in the tower," Ryan said, "so I will take your word for it, but remember I am looking for the highest chance of survival. If I give you that drum, will I not be crippling my energy production for the tower?"

"But if we only have one tank of gas, we can no get to the camp."

"I tell you what. We both need the fuel, but it doesn't have to be a deal breaker. How much is a full tank in a Stryker?

"Fifty-three gallons," Marco said. "Diesel."

"I do not have an immediate solution," Ryan said. "It seems that fifty gallons of diesel fuel represents a lot of power for this tower. The ability to recharge the energy system multiplies that production so I cannot just give fuel away."

"But you have an advantage," Raphael said. "The generator *es* flex fuel. It can run on natural gas and gasoline fuel. You have many options."

"Okay, like I said, this does not have to be a deal breaker. I am willing to look into options so that we both get what we want."

Marco nodded. "We can figure this part out, Poppa."

Raphael nodded. "*Es* good. You say this *es* a free market. How about if we find another way to travel that does no require this thirty days."

"It is a free market, Raphael, but my offer is for the next twenty-four hours. This should give you time to prepare a proposal or find an alternative method of travel. If you choose a different solution, my hospitality will be at an end. I will expect you to pack your things and only your things, hand me your security badges, and withdraw to wherever you choose."

"But we can't go back to our house!" Simone snapped. "It isn't safe."

"Then I expect you to treat living here like it is valuable," Ryan said. "I will no longer let you presume on my hospitality. If you want to be here, then you will earn that privilege."

ACT 3

38

Global Infection: ≤ 32.4301%

Ryan tried to act like he wasn't tired, but the façade was crumbling. When Ryan offered the deal, he expected Raphael to need at least a day to get a proposal together, expecting for him to look for an alternative way to travel, but Raphael returned an hour later with a list of things that needed to be done and two points of negotiation. He wanted two weeks worth of food and two paintings: *Orange, Red, Yellow*, and *Salvator Mundi*. Ryan countered with one week, because food for four people was a lot of food and declined to part with the paintings. He didn't know art and didn't value the paintings specifically, but he suspected the paintings under negotiation were worth at least a full year's salary. He decided to hold the paintings for a later negotiation point.

Ryan, Raphael and Marco spent an hour prioritizing a backlog and then they went to First Avenue. The best method to secure the tower exterior was to block off the street at the Smithfield and the Wood Street intersections. They used the construction crane to rearrange Alaska barriers from around the construction site perimeter, and then they butted a shipping container against the tower wall on the Smithfield end. They duplicated the setup on the building's west end, but this meant there was no way to get a vehicle out of the tower without using the crane to lift the container.

Marco suggested putting wheels under it so it could be rolled back, and Simone rolled his eyes and said, "Buses already have wheels." It was a great idea to replace the shipping container with a bus that could be pulled back and forth across Smithfield—a mobile barricade with one drawback. They didn't have a bus.

They ate an early dinner and worked until the sun set behind the mountains. The day of labor had pushed Ryan beyond fatigued, but it was a good, productive day and he only had one more job: deliver gun cleaning supplies to Marco.

Ryan found Marco sitting on the edge of his favorite recliner in the entertainment room, wearing a sweatshirt, watching a romantic comedy, leaning over a TV tray covered with an old towel littered with springs, screws, a trigger and a barrel. A row of weapons was neatly organized on top of a coffee table to his left that very likely cost more than his military salary (the coffee table not, the guns).

"Don't worry about the wood," Marco said. "Underneath the towels, I have a layer of cardboard."

Ryan handed him the orange bottle of Hoppe's and a bottle of Shooter's Choice. "I'm sure it's fine," he said.

"You just sounded like my mother," Marco said. "That is how she says fine."

"From what I've heard about your mother, that should make me a superhero."

"She is a super hero," Marco said, "but a super hero that is fussy about her furniture. I can set up somewhere else if you prefer."

"I'm too tired to care," Ryan said as he unzipped his mostly empty tactical vest and slouched onto the Hancock and Moore couch. He thought he should hang the vest in the armory, but the message from his brain got short-circuited before it reached his legs. "If I had a woman here, she would probably care. But I don't, so she can't care. Just keep the utility work on the fine furniture to a minimum and we should be *fine*."

"I'd swear you have already met my mother." Marco smiled, but the good humor seemed like a façade. His face was flushed, with a thin sheen of sweat along his forehead. Marco had begged out of working about two hours prior, saying he needed to tend to his injuries.

"You are wearing a sweatshirt and it's not cold. Is the fever back?"

Marco waved off the question. "My father said you had a woman. But you let her go." He twisted off the black bottle cap and the pungent odor of Hoppe's No. 9 bore solvent filled the room. "My dad said she was a very pretty woman from the Middle East."

"We haven't already learned our lesson about gossip? Really?" Ryan said. "Did the gossip include the fact that she was engaged to some Scandinavian Adonis who makes me look like the much older man that I am?"

"You're not that old," Marco said, picking up the gun barrel and rubbing it with the cleaner. "And my dad said you didn't ask her to stay."

Raphael would not know this factoid. That information had to come from Daniel who could only have gotten it from Ahou.

I didn't ask you to stay? Really? That is how you are portraying our final few minutes together?

"It doesn't really work like that," Ryan said. "Talking a woman into doing something that she may not want to do is a very bad idea. That guarantees she blames you for everything that happens next. And how does everyone seem to miss the fact that she had a fiancé?"

"But still . . ." Marco said and took a drink of orange juice.

Ryan shook his head and ignored the prompt. It was a useless conversation. Ahou Derakhshan was miles and miles away, locked in Daniel Ryder's apocalyptic getaway where she would likely remain for the rest of her life with Thor the Scandinavian underwear model. They would probably be miserable, but they would still have children and grow old together. To stop thinking about Ahou, Ryan stared at the Bang & Olufsen super high definition television and let himself get pulled into the movie playing on low volume. At least in this story, the woman acted like an adult, which was a lot more than could be said for the male lead.

Ryan shifted on the couch as the waves of mental, emotional, and physical exhaustion rolled over him like he was adrift in the Arctic Ocean. Trying to stay awake, Ryan said, “How did you and Simone become such good shots?”

Marco smiled ruefully and said, “I'm not good. My brother Timoteo, he is eight years younger than me. He is a god with a weapon, any weapon.” He paused to pull the sweatshirt over his head and set it off to the side. “What are my father and Simone doing?”

“Hot flash?”

“I'll be fine,” Marco said, sounding distinctly like a woman who said the word fine but meant exactly the opposite.

“When I left, Simone was complaining about siphoning the gas by himself. I think he went to look for more gas cans. And your father was determined to boost that truck and get it down to the Strykers.”

The deal almost fell apart four hours after Raphael signed the agreement. He came up from the tower substructure fuming that Ryan knew there was no diesel fuel. That he had deceived him. All three Stryker's fuel tanks were down to vapor; the tower reserve fuel drums were empty and the flex fuel generator only had four gallons in the tank. Ryan listened to the rant until Raphael took a breath. Finally, he said, “Raphael, I didn't even know there was a generator in the tower until you told me. So how could I lie?”

Raphael fussed and swore until Marco told him to get his shit together. There was no lie. There was no deception, and he was looking for problems where none existed. After he cooled off, Raphael offered this proposal: They would siphon the gas out of the abandoned cars to fill the flex fuel generator, but he got the first one hundred and ten gallons of diesel for the Stryker.

Raphael then created an assembly line. He boosted the cars on the street with a slim jim and a bagful of tools that would make a Grand Theft Auto gamer envious. Then he drove the cars one by one to the underground loading dock where they drained the tanks into a five-gallon gas can. It was Simone's job to walk the gas can deep into the substructure to the generator and back.

Ryan said, “I don't suppose you will tell me how your father happens to have tools to steal cars?”

Marco smiled he fitted a Glock's barrel assembly back onto its polymer frame. “When you asked my father that question, what was his answer?”

"I was no always an upstanding American citizen," Ryan said in a good imitation.

"That is the only answer he's ever given me." Marco pulled the slide rod and spring out of a different weapon. "Pull up a chair. You are going to strip these down, clean them, and put them back together."

"Really? Tonight?"

"The more you learn before my mother gets here, the more you will know by the time we leave."

Ryan shook off a yawn, groaned as he stood, found a card table and a folding chair in a small closet. "I'm supposed to know how to do this? I don't suppose there are instructions?"

"The first instruction is that a gun is always loaded," Marco said, "You should check the weapon."

Ryan struggled to pull back the slide on a .45. His hands hurt and the spring was stiff. The slide snapped back twice, pinching his fingers before he held it open long enough to see nothing in the barrel. "I am sure I made that look harder than it was."

"Is the weapon empty?"

"Yes."

"Are you sure?"

Ryan looked again wondering if it was a trick question. "Uh . . . yes."

"Are you positive?"

Ryan looked at Marco and then back at the weapon. He hit the button to pull the magazine and looked and then turned the weapon over and over and then ran his finger into the barrel. Finally, he said, "Yes, positive."

"Good. Positive is the only acceptable answer. And to be positive, you do exactly what you did. Drop the magazine out of the weapon and then look in the barrel and run your finger in it. This is how you will be positive that the weapon is empty. Until you are positive, you treat the gun as if it is loaded. Keep your finger off the trigger until your weapon is pointed down range. Don't shoot anything you can't positively identify and know what is behind your target. And last, never point a weapon at anything you don't intend to destroy. Repeat that back to me?"

"Treat a gun as if it is loaded. Keep my finger off the trigger until it is pointed down range. Don't shoot anything that I can't positively identify, and never point a weapon at anything I don't want to destroy."

"Now take the weapon apart, wipe every part with these patches and this solvent until you do not see any black." Marco paused, and took a drink of orange juice. "Then wipe the gun parts with this oil, and put it back together. When you are done, we will continue."

It took Ryan until the boy and girl finally traded the inevitable final passionate kiss before he could present the weapon fully reassembled, clean, and gleaming with oil back to Marco.

"At the rate you are going you will still be cleaning these in thirty days."

"Yeah, yeah, yeah, pick on the slow kid in class. Hand me the next one."

"You are done cleaning for now. The downside of our gunfight, beyond being shot, is that we burned through a lot of ammunition. We don't have enough bullets for you to practice with, but we have plenty of .22 rounds, and a negligent discharge with this weapon is less likely to kill somebody."

"Gee, thanks," Ryan said.

"You are welcome, and the goal here is for no one to die because of stupid mistakes."

Marco said. "This is a GSG 1911, .22. If you want to be a good shot, here is what you will do. Unless you are sleeping, this weapon never leaves you. It is either in your hand or in a holster." And then for the next five minutes he explained how to manipulate the weapon and detailed the difference between center fire and rim fire. This was a distinction that was lost on Ryan, but he ultimately understood that letting the hammer fall on his unloaded .22 was a bad idea. Marco explained the concept of a sight picture, and demonstrated a draw and dry fire drill with his Heckler & Koch P30L. Finally he demonstrated how to load a magazine with snap caps so Ryan could duplicate the drill.

While Ryan practiced the basics, Marco walked slowly out of the room. A few minutes later, he came back with a SERPA holster attached to a Black Hawk thigh rig. "Some people prefer a holster on the belt. After you use this for a while, you can see which you prefer. But this version will keep the weapon from poking you in the muffin top."

Ryan fumbled his way into the thigh rig holster and fastened it to his belt. The GSG slid into the SERPA with a satisfying snap.

"Slow is smooth and smooth is fast," Marco said. "Now do what I showed you slow a thousand times."

"I'm pretty tired."

"Tired is good. Tired is how you will be when you are in a battle. Do it slow. Do it smooth. Start now. Maybe in five years you will be good."

Ryan sighed. *I'm the guy that gave them thirty days.*

Before he got to two hundred repetitions Ryan had to find duct tape to cover his thumb. The GSG thumb safety was square and sharp and cut mercilessly into the skin, but he loved how the weapon felt in his hand. He lost count how many times he worked through the drill during the first hour of the next romantic comedy before he got sloppy. Marco gave a sour look and a terse headshake.

Ryan shook himself awake and resumed.

Sometime during the first act of the third movie Ryan leaned back on the eight-thousand-dollar Hancock and Moore couch with the GSG .22 resting across his stomach, thinking that the couch was comfortable. And then he thought he saw Ahou walking toward him with her fabulous rolling stride. She sat down, curled up beside him, and leaned her head on his shoulder. "I should have told you I wanted to stay," she said.

At 9:41 Ryan woke to an empty room and a row of guns gleaming fresh oil. The GSG 1911 was duct-taped to his hand, the index finger dutifully fastened off the trigger and flat against the side of the gun. Marco called this position trigger discipline. A sign was taped to his arm: *In your holster or in your hand while you are AWAKE!*

Ryan laughed at Marco's teaching methods until he felt the hair on his arm rip out with the tape. His hand was raw and swollen from the days of manual labor and the last few hours of weapons drills. He filled a bucket with ice water, plunged his hand deep underneath, and went to his room.

Ryan took a shower, laid out some clothes in case he had to fight a horde of zombies at a moment's notice, piled up the pillows just like he liked, snapped off the light, and sighed towards slumber.

I should check the cameras. The front door is still open . . .

But his body hurt.

I should check the cameras . . .

But his legs were heavy.

I should check . . .

But his hand throbbed.

I sho . . .

Ryan's eyes popped open.

. . . should check the cameras.

Ryan rolled toward the bedside clock: 7:33 a.m.

39

Global Infection: ≤ 32.6101%

Ryan swung his feet to the carpet, but it took forever for his mind to engage. He finally limped to the bathroom, took care of business and got dressed. He strapped on his GSG 1911, went to his office and brought up the security cameras to do a quick review. He saw no disasters.

He logged into his e-mail hoping to see a reply from Team Bruptrick, but his inbox held no such missive. It also seemed that the apocalypse was finally having its effect on junk mail. The electronic fruit flies seemed to have been doused with pesticide, because their numbers had dwindled to a few stragglers. He deleted a few pests that had survived extermination until he flash read a subject line: *It's me Ahou.*

But the e-mail address was from Cheryl Rosen.

Cheryl Rosen?

He read.

Ryan,

I miss you. And I am so very sorry that I lied to you.

Ahou

Ryan leaned back in his chair.

What do I say to that?

Nothing came to mind as he idly watched the cameras. His stomach growled once, and his hand went to his keyboard. His fingers hovered over the keys, but he couldn't shape a word. He leaned back in his chair, his gaze returning to the cameras. His stomach growled again.

I'm sorry you did too?

His right hand scrubbed through his hair until he had a glimmer of something to say.

Ahou, I—

Motion on the security feed caught his eye. Someone was in the lobby. "What the hell?" Two men were bent over near the security desk. They had guns. Ryan clicked through the interface to bring the camera up on the main monitor. The image expanded and Ryan sighed. It was Marco and Raphael.

He looked at the e-mail one last time, clicked the red X to cancel, and headed to the kitchen. He ignored the dirty dishes scattered around and fixed a quick breakfast, ate standing, grabbed his tactical vest, feeling silly that it was still empty, but he was determined to get into the habit. He made the trek from the penthouse to the ground floor. The elevator pinged, and Ryan walked into two men holding firearms.

"Whoa, whoa, whoa! Why are you both so jumpy?" Ryan asked. "The danger can't be coming from the elevators."

Raphael holstered his weapon and turned to the papers on the desk.

"Can't be too careful when we are here and enemies may be close," Marco said, sliding his weapon back into his holster. "Sleep well? I see you got the tape off."

"Tape?! Piffle!" Ryan said. "And yes, I slept well. But you look terrible. You are the one who should be in bed."

"I'm fine. Anyway, speaking of sleep, my brother seems determined to sleep enough for all of us.""

"I tell him to get up," said Raphael.

Marco said, "Did he tell you to fuck yourself too?"

"This boy," Raphael said, shaking his head.

"How did he get to take the master suite?" Marco asked, looking between Ryan and Raphael.

Ryan shrugged.

"You do no care he *es* in the master suite?" Raphael asked.

"Yes and no," Ryan said. "He should have asked. But I won't be sleeping in there, so I haven't said anything."

Raphael nodded.

"So, right now I'm carrying a gun with snap caps," Ryan said. "Do I start a major fight if I get the real bullets?"

Raphael continued making notes on the paper.

"Get loaded up," Marco said. "There are six or seven magazines in a box in the armory. We'll start shooting lessons a little later. But now we are trying to get a plan for this area."

"We make a fence across here," Raphael said to Marco, but pointed at the elevator bank. "This will keep the peoples away. And we put boards across there." He indicated the wrecked exit.

Ryan looked down at the architectural plans and Raphael's notes. "What are your thoughts for securing the glass?"

"Tactically, this *es* too much space to defend," Raphael said.

Ryan said, "We can't . . . I can't have all this open to the world. It will be too easy to get through that glass. It's already shot to hell. It seems like it would take nothing to smash right into the lobby."

"No, you listen," Raphael said. "We seal off the bottom floor here and here. We drop this security gate to the residential elevators. It *es* strong. If you *es* still scared, we seal the elevator shafts with metal. The devils will no be able to get to the upper floors."

"They are not devils, Poppa," Marco said. "They are people."

"Anything that can no be killed must be a devil."

Marco pressed his eyes shut. "They can be killed. They are not devils."

"The Holy Mother tell me they are devils," Raphael snapped. "And do no interrupt me."

How did this become a theological fight? Ryan thought. "Look, I'm all for all those things you said, but all I'm asking is that we find a way to block off the front. How about if we use some of the shipping containers? Put them in front here?" he said, pointing along the windows.

"The crane will no reach," Raphael said. "We have no way to do this."

"Okay. How about if we park cars along the front?" Ryan said. "All those cars right out there on Smithfield can be parked on the terraces. That would at least stop someone from just driving up the stairs and through the glass."

"We were going to use those cars to block the grocery parking garage," Marco said. "We really need to keep people out of the skywalk."

This made no sense, because the streets were clogged with vehicles. Two weeks ago Pittsburgh came to a standstill when people abandoned cars by the thousands, desperate to escape the violence brought on by the RVCJ-2091 infection oozing like pus out of hospital wards and makeshift jails. "Okay. Then we can use *other* cars," Ryan said. "The streets around this building are full of cars. For god's sake, the Smithfield Bridge is filled with cars. We are not going to run out of cars by parking some on the terraces."

"You cannot save this space," Raphael said. "You ask for my expertise. I am giving it."

"No, I'm asking for a *solution*! I'm asking for something that makes it harder than walking through that broken out door to get into the tower."

"This place here," Raphael said with a sweeping hand, "*es* no important. We block the elevators and the grocery doors. We build a fence or maybe something out of wood and steel. No one can get to you. Why can you no understand this?"

Why is he fighting this so hard?

"If I concede this atrium," Ryan said, "then whoever gets this far can wreck whatever we build. If they can run a truck through the window, they can use that same truck to smash down whatever barricade you build. And if that happens I'm fighting a siege in the heart of the building with no hope of getting them out. And I'm cut off from any resource that is in the lower floors, which would include the sublevel parking garages where two Strykers will be parked, mechanical rooms that control the power systems, and the tower generator."

"The streets are already filled with cars; that should be enough," Raphael said.

"Raphael, we already know that isn't true. You remember the looters that drove a truck right up those stairs and attached a chain to the door? If it can happen once it can happen again."

"My father's point is that you can't claim territory you can't defend," Marco observed. "This lobby is a lot of territory to cover," he said to Raphael. "But he has a point."

"But it will take too long," Raphael said. "To barricade all of this space will take much time."

"Raphael, I'm not asking you to build the Great Wall of China," Ryan said. "I'm just asking that we find some passive defense. How about Simone's idea, only we park a big bus right up next to the glass, then disable it so it stays where we park it.

The elevator chimed and everyone jumped.

Marco and Raphael both shucked side arms.

"Jesus!" Simone shouted. "It's just me!"

"Where have you been?" Raphael asked.

"Why are you guys so jumpy?" Simone asked.

Marco slipped his weapon back into its holster with a sly smile on his face. "We were talking about farming. It has everyone on edge."

Simone looked at Marco like he'd turned into a turtle. "Farming? We have zombies to kill and you are talking about farming?"

Marco laughed. "You are so gullible! If you had gotten up when Poppa told you, you would know what we were talking about."

"Shut up! You're the one who's gullible."

"You don't even know what that word means."

Raphael stared daggers at Simone. "I tell you to get up an hour ago."

Simone rolled his eyes. "Just because you signed your life away doesn't mean I have to get up before dawn. I made a hundred trips to that stupid gas tank. I had to sleep," he said. "Hey, I have an idea. You know what we should do?"

Marco said, "Let you sleep till noon every day?"

"Bite me!" Simone said, throwing air punches. "We need to kidnap an Amish family with their cows."

"Amish family? Kidnap?" said Ryan.

"The world really will come to an end without cheese," Simone said.

Marco tried to swat his brother's head. Simone ducked easily and came up with a smile, fists ready for a mock fight. They threw a half dozen shadow punches until Marco winced in pain.

"We work on this kidnapping after you do what I say," Raphael said.

Simone said, "Hey, I had an idea—"

"This could be dangerous," Marco said.

"Shut up! God! You are such a douche!" Simone said. "As I was saying . . . why don't we use the gas tanks on the cars in the VIP garage. I saw like a dozen limousines in the special parking space. I'll bet those gas tanks are huge."

"You wanna drive a limo out on the street so you don't have to walk your lazy ass into the basement."

"No, you idiot. Well, yes. I want to drive the limo out there, but then we only have to drive one car down to the generator."

"You still have to siphon the gas out of the tank once you get it into the substructure," Marco said.

Simone shrugged. "Oh, well, I just thought it would be easier."

"That is not a bad idea," Ryan said. "It would be faster to fill the cars, and if I had to drive a limousine I would have a full tank."

"See, I told you it was a good idea," Simone said.

"This *es* okay with you?" Raphael said. "To fill the cars and not the generator?"

Ryan nodded, if for no other reason because he didn't want to go back to the previous fight. "That works."

40

Global Infection: ≤ 32.6344%

The construction crane held the gently swaying shipping container above Wood Street like the sword of Damocles while a white limousine idled underneath, with a Ford F150 rumbling beside it and Simone stood in between. Ryan sat in the cab monitoring the gas gauge drain down to E. A few seconds before the pump ran the truck dry, he gave Simone a thumbs-up. The pump paused, the hose rattled out of the truck and Ryan drove the it into the public parking garage right around the corner.

The parking garage's walls were built of injection-molded concrete with rows and rows of decorative half circles that let sunlight in, but kept people out. If the metal gate blocking off Boulevard of the Allies had still been in place, the garage would be a fortress. But someone smashed through the gate and then ripped the parking validation machine off its post. As Ryan drove the truck into the garage, he thought about using the gate as a cautionary tale. Could there be a better object lesson than a wrecked a gate designed to keep cars out? How could a chain link fence in the lobby hope to survive?

These were great questions, but Ryan thought that maybe he should wait to make his case. The pot of conflict was already simmering.

Before coming to the street, Ryan loaded six GSG magazines, but somehow being armed with a .22 didn't seem sufficient. The Pagueros sprouted guns like they were appendages, so it seemed right that Ryan have more than the itty bitty thing for protection. He put the Glock and holster on his belt and rode the elevator down. Raphael noticed and the pot started to bubble until Marco whispered in his ear. Raphael frowned, shifted his gaze between Ryan and Marco, gave a mighty *harrumph* and walked away.

"What magic words did you say?" Ryan asked.

"I told him the truth," Marco said.

Raphael work his auto larceny magic. The slim Jim opened the door. Seconds later he was cracking the starter code with a handheld device, and the car purred to life. Raphael moved to his next conquest, and this time he ducked under the dash, twisted wires, and the car engine turned over.

It took him a little over two minutes to get the cars started. By the tenth vehicle, the time dropped to under sixty seconds.

Some vehicles were useless, because they lacked fuel, had flat tires or dead batteries. So, Raphael prowled the streets farther and farther from the tower. Marco and Ryan retrieved the idling vehicles and drove them to Simone so he could drain them like a vampire. As a tag team, Ryan and Marco drove the vehicles to their final resting place inside the grocery public parking in an interlocking pattern in front of skywalk outer doors.

"There *es* . . . north . . . Wood Street," Raphael's voice crackled in the tower maintenance radio.

"What?" Marco said. "Say again? You broke up."

"A car *es*—"

"Fucking radios," Marco said.

"I think he said that there is a car ready on Wood Street to the north," Ryan said.

"I'm not gonna get it," Simone said, crawling on top of the limousines hood. He leaned back against the windshield, rested his rifle across his arms, and closed his eyes.

"I'll go," Marco said and started limp down the street. He was moving slow and sweating more than the labor required.

"Stay put," Ryan said. "You are not doing so well."

"Neg Dis," Simone shouted. "Don't get eaten!"

Ryan felt a keen urge to raise his middle finger, but he remembered the number one rule: don't argue with teenage retarded.

The streets were quiet like a library. Every running footfall echoed off the asphalt making Ryan slow to a walk. Surely the librarian would rain down wrath for disturbing the silence. Leaves and trash swirled. Streetlights swayed on their cables and the crosswalk signal *beep, beep, beeped.*

Boulevard of the Allies was only one block north of First Avenue, but every footstep felt like miles in hostile territory. Vehicles clogged Wood Street like boulders in a river. Ryan saw the green Toyota, driver's side door open, a block further north.

Ryan was thirty feet from the car when he saw . . . him . . . a man with an unruly, matted beard, wearing a Philadelphia Eagles jersey and grimy jeans. The jersey was ripped off the right shoulder, and there was a chunk of flesh out of his chest. For a dozen heartbeats, Ryan stopped breathing. His mouth dried, and his palms sweated. The wind blew between the buildings, kicking up dust and detritus. The crosswalk beeped its warning.

"Slow is—" Ryan said, but his words froze in his mouth. He worked his jaw trying to drive moisture into his throat. "Slow is smooth . . ." his voice came out hoarse. "Smooth . . . is fast."

The 2091 lurched.

Ryan groped at the holster, his index finger jabbing at the SERPA release trying to draw the weapon. He pulled . . . and pulled . . . and pulled . . . but the weapon would not come loose.

The 2091's stride was a stumbling awkward gait, but he came with a will for mayhem.

Eighteen cars.

Ryan pulled and . . .

Sixteen cars.

His index finger finally caught the release button, and the weapon slid out. His hands shook. His fingers slapped against the trigger, but the gun would not fire.

The safety!

Ryan's thumb crushed the safety down. He pointed the muzzle, hasty and trembling, emptying the magazine in a flurry, the .22 rounds giving a small bark like lively firecrackers.

Ryan missed . . . all ten shots.

Fifteen cars.

His thumb mashed the magazine release, but the magazine would not drop. He pulled it out with his left, pawed for a new magazine in his tactical vest, and bobbled the fresh magazine in to the gun butt.

Twelve cars.

Ryan wracked the slide and pressed the trigger as fast as he could. Philadelphia man flinched three times as the .22 rounds struck his shoulder. Ryan dropped the GSG and grabbed for the Glock.

The radio crackled. "Ryan?! Ry—?! A—you shoot—?!"

Eleven cars.

"I'm com—" Marco said. " . . . coming!"

Ten cars.

Ryan forced himself to be slow. He forced himself to be smooth.

Eight cars.

Ryan's hands shook and the Glock's polymer frame felt slippery from sweat.

Six cars.

The weapon's front site settled on the green and white Eagles jersey. Ryan paused and pressed the trigger.

The gun clicked.

It was the sound of a firing pin falling on an empty chamber. It was the sound of a dry fire.

Four cars.

Ryan looked at the gun like it was an alien.

Three cars.

Ryan's brain engaged. He wracked the slide expecting that action to load a bullet into the barrel. He pushed the weapon toward the infected bearing down on him.

Sight picture! Sight picture!

Click!

He dropped the magazine and saw the malfunction.*Not loaded?*

Two cars.

Ryan ran.

"Get down!" Marco shouted, his AR-15 aimed down the street.

Ryan dove. The weapon barked once. The 2091's head exploded and the body dropped.

Ryan stood, his jaw grinding hard.

Marco limped up beside him. "You all right?"

Raphael sprinted around the car, his Kalashnikov scanning Wood Street. "Are you okay?"

Ryan regarded them both. He walked back to the GSG. He dug out another magazine from a vest pouch. He didn't try to do it fast. He knew he couldn't because his hands shook. He slapped in the magazine, wracked the slide to chamber a round, pushed the safety, and returned it to its holster. "Am I okay? No, I am not okay," he said, thinking back to the night of the negligent discharge, thinking about Marco later handing him Glock as a 9mm peace offering.

"When did you take the bullets out of the gun?" Ryan asked.

Raphael frowned and Marco said nothing.

"I could have sworn there were bullets in this gun when you gave it back. I could have sworn it was loaded when I put it on my nightstand. So, when did you take them?"

Both men remained quiet.

"You humored me by letting me carry an empty gun?" Ryan shook his head. "When are you going to treat me like an adult? This passive aggressive bullshit is a bad plan, gentleman. A very bad plan."

Ryan walked past them both.

"Mr. Sage," Marco said. "You say we were not treating you like an adult? I think that is exactly how we were treating you."

"I don't see how."

"That gun was empty the night I handed it to you."

Ryan's stomach flipped. He had carried an empty gun to search the tower.

Marco continued. "In my first lesson last night . . . didn't I tell you to check a weapon every time you picked it up? Didn't I emphasize that you must treat every weapon as if it is loaded until you are positive?"

Ryan nodded.

"You could have known that I handed you an empty weapon the moment it touched your hand. Maybe I am an ass for the way I went about it, but you are the one who carried an empty gun," Marco said. "I wasn't really trying to teach you a lesson, but it turned out to be one. No one should ever have to tell you that a weapon has no bullets."

41

Global Infection: ≤ 32.6702%

In the early days of Pittsburgh's collapse cars, trucks, semis, panel vans and self driving vehicles clogged the city arteries like a sclerotic heart. And when the military invaded the city, their first mission was to clear a path. They performed a triple bypass with all the finesse of a Tijuana, Mexico cosmetic surgeon—hacking, smashing and slashing metal like so much dead tissue. And when they were done they had opened up two main paths through the city, and one route was the eastbound lane of the Penn-Lincoln Parkway.

Raphael drove an extended cab truck—yet another vehicle that he boosted on a moment's notice—easily through the clogged streets, over side-walks and around snarls, ever watchful as they traveled. Simone and Marco sat in the back. Ryan sat in the passenger seat, smoldering. He was tired of the Pagueros' smugness and after two grueling hours listening to Simone laugh about carrying an empty gun, his Neg Dis meter was pegged. He wanted to find a corner of the penthouse to sulk in private, but Ryan knew he'd lost enough man points that he was dangerously close to losing his club card. His solution was simple: if he couldn't outshoot them then Ryan was determined to set the work pace. With a few hours of daylight left, Ryan made a defiant display of loading his guns, adding a Mossberg shotgun to his arsenal and announcing they needed to embark on a dangerous mission farther into the city. After a brief reconnaissance of the streets from the penthouse windows they were all loaded into the truck, everyone blessedly silent, traveling toward Firouz Derakhshan's sub shop and minimart.

Firouz Derakhshan was a Persian Christian who fled persecution in Iran and became the model American success story: an immigrant with the barest language skills who carved out a great life without govern-ment subsidy or handout. In two decades he'd acquired a sundries store, a sub shop, a nice home, and put two daughters through school. And for a few hours Firouz and Ryan's life collided in a common quest for survival. Firouze fled Pittsburgh knowing he would never return, and also knowing that Ryan had no place to go, he gave Ryan the title deed to his business and his home. The minimart location was a mere mile and a half from the Renaissance Tower, but direct travel was impossible; the through streets would take weeks to clear. However, Daniel Ryder's satellite photos showed a path, but it took them miles to the east before they could double back.

Raphael stopped at the intersection of Fifth Avenue. Trash rolled like tumbleweeds, soda cans clattered down the sidewalk and the power lines swayed overhead. A steady *beep, beep, beep*, signaled the blind to cross. The streetlights were stuck on flashing red. The air was a mixture of charred wood, garbage and the cloying reek of road kill. Two cop cars, a burned-out SWAT vehicle and a fire truck were pulled into a circle like wagons on the prairie to defend against Indian attacks. Inside were mangled corpses, axes, and batons lying beside piles of spent brass and discarded guns.

Fifth Avenue was impassable to the west so Raphael drove down a parallel side street until he stopped the truck. "Mercy Hospital *es* just there. Leona say the hospitals were no safe. Marco check the photos."

"Where is this place you want us to check first?" Marco asked, trying to orient photos with a Google map.

"It's called Saint Joseph's. I don't know the street, but it is right up the road from some old school building," Ryan said.

"Okay, I see it. Poppa, turn here. Keep going two blocks, then take a left and then the first right," Marco said. "So how do you know this woman? Is she why you let the Persian goddess go?"

"Yeah, is she hot?" Simone said, winking. "She must be hot."

"Simone, you might find her hot if you are into grandmothers," Ryan said.

"You're such a knob."

"I *don't* know Shaniqua," Ryan said for the fourth time since he explained what he wanted to do. "When I was looking for a place to stay, she was one of the few people who was nice to me. We talked on the phone a couple times. I'm just trying to figure out how to help someone. If we see any infected, we will leave."

"Are you going into the building?" asked Marco.

Raphael nodded. "We do no go inside. We do no fight. The contract say to help you clean out the grocery. No save peoples."

"I got it, Raphael. We are not here to fight. I just want to drive by. It is very close to the minimart, so it shouldn't take but a minute. Okay, turn left here. Yes, this is the street. Go forward slowly."

Raphael stopped in the intersection of Manila and Bedford, craning his neck. "What if she *es* there, and wants to come?"

"I won't be saying no," Ryan said. "I *am* coming to help."

"You do no learn this lesson the first time?"

"Obviously, if she is bitten, she won't be coming."

"It is a shelter, right?" Marco asked. "How about if there are ten people?"

"Gentlemen, did you forget you are leaving? Who I ask to join me doesn't concern you. But for now, let's see if she's here. Not every woman will jump at the chance to come live in the tower with four strange men, not even grandmas." He checked his phone; it had full bars. He dialed Shaniqua's number and listened to it ring and ring and ring.

"You want to check inside? She might be scared to answer the phone," Marco said.

"Marco doesn't want to go," Simone said. "He's scared of the zombies."

"Shut up," Marco said. "No one asked you."

"It's true," Simone said. "You lost your shit when we were running back from the gun range."

Marco pushed his door open. "I'll go with you."

"No, stay put. This is my deal. I'll run up to the door. You guys can cover me from here."

"I will go," Raphael said. "Marco, you drive. Simone, watch the street behind." He got out of the car, weapon at low ready, eyes probing.

Marco slid out of the backseat and stood beside the driver's side door watching the street like he expected jihadists to breach the perimeter.

"But I want to shoot zombies," Simone said.

Raphael said, "*You* obey me. Now keep watch!" He looked at Ryan holding the shotgun. Then he silently demonstrated mounting the AK-47 into his shoulder and pointing the barrel toward the ground. He held up the side of his weapon so Ryan could see his index finger. He made a point of wiggling the finger along the side of the gun. "This *es* where your finger stay until your weapon goes to your cheek." He demonstrated and the finger only dropped to the trigger when the butt stock met the side of his face. "Understand?"

"Yes," Ryan said, imitating what he'd been shown.

They walked through a wrecked fence and then around three white passenger vans pulled into a barricade under the portico. The front door was off its hinges, and the building beyond was lit like someone had left for a quick errand and hadn't bothered to shut off all the lights.

"Knock?" Raphael asked, scanning Saint Joseph's broken out ground floor windows revealing bent blinds and ragged curtains fluttering in the afternoon breeze.

Ryan cradled the shotgun in his arm and pulled out his phone. He heard it ring in his ear first and then ring deep inside the shelter. "Damn, no one—"

"Find any zombies?" Simone asked, coming around the van.

Ryan jumped. Raphael swung his AK toward the voice and pulled the muzzle skyward at the last second.

"Shit! It's me!" Simone shouted.

Raphael's face was hard, and his coal black eyes points of menace. "I tell you to keep watch."

"I just came to—"

"You disobey me! Go! Now!"

From deep inside Saint Joseph's came the sounds of movement followed by nonsensical moaning and babbling: a combination of a toddler trying to form his first words mixed with underlying despair.

"We move," Raphael whispered, peeling out to the right. Ryan followed.

Simone stopped at the door, his weapon trained inside. He took a step forward.

The AR-15 thundered under the portico. "Got 'em!"

A 2091 crashed through the fifth-floor window. She hit the ground with a pop and crack as her legs bent to odd angles, but heedless of pain she clawed toward Simone. He fired. Her head exploded. "Take that!"

Suddenly the building looked like a dog with flees jumping off its back as more infected flung themselves out windows.

"Contact," Simone said, dropping to a knee, his rifle stock to his cheek. He squeezed off rounds, delivering a flurry of destruction. "Moving!" he shouted.

"Move!" Marco bellowed.

Simone stood and peeled out to the right, sprinted for the truck, and slid into the rear cab, whooping. Ryan got in the opposite side, and Raphael backed into the passenger seat. The doors popped shut as Marco hit the gas.

"I guess your hottie is one of them now!"

Ryan said, "Yeah . . . that is something to celebrate. Marco, take a left here. The minimart is just down this road."

Raphael turned in the passenger seat, staring deep into Simone's soul.

"What?" Simone said as if he were a perfect angel.

Raphael's jaw ground and his fist clenched.

"See the minimart sign?" Ryan said to Marco. "See where the iron fence stops? That is the street behind. Yeah, take the right here."

"More zombies!" Simone said, jumping from the truck before it came to a halt. He drew down on a 2091 stumbling through the trees on the Washington Plaza Apartment grounds.

Marco stomped the brake.

Raphael jumped out, and in the blink before Simone could trigger a shot, he yanked the barrel toward the sky and slammed Simone against the truck bed. "You do no think!" he rasped. "The noise draws them."

"But they are behind the fence—"

Raphael slammed Simone against the truck bed again, then shook his finger left and right, left and right.

Simon's head dropped to his chest. Then he stole a quick look at Ryan, his face flushed. "Sorry!" he said, sullen.

Ryan pressed an automatic opener, the security gate trundled open and Marco drove inside. The courtyard behind Firouz's grocery looked exactly as it had been left: empty but for a catering truck and Ahou's car. Marco parked the truck, bed towards the loading dock, and killed the engine. He stepped out of the truck and winced as his feet hit the ground.

"What if we get stuck here tonight?" Simone said.

Raphael said. "You will work fast."

"You always say I have to work fast."

"That *es* because you work slow."

Simone rolled his eyes. "I'm just saying, what happens if we get caught out here?"

Raphael pulled a pack out of the truck bed. "We can walk to the tower from here."

"But it will be dark."

Ryan unlocked the mini-mart loading dock door. "If we get stuck here, we will spend the night behind secure doors with plenty of food and cozy beds."

"But in the movies," Simone said, "it is always at night when and the good guys do something really stupid and that is when the zombies get them."

"People who do stupid things during a horror movie are too stupid to live," Ryan said. "We won't be like those people, right?"

"Yeah, none of us do anything too stupid to live," Simone said like he had invented wisdom.

Ryan flipped on the stockroom lights. "This is the key for that door," he said to Raphael. "Behind that door is a hallway that leads to the sub shop. Would you mind checking for unwanted visitors?"

"It is better that your woman wasn't there," Simone said. "We'll need the food."

"Simone, you need to learn when to keep your mouth shut!" Marco said.

"I'm just saying we need this food. What are we gonna eat when we are traveling to the camp?"

Raphael snapped his fingers. "Simone!"

"But—"

Raphael's look brought the words to an end.

Ryan unlocked the minimart, shotgun ready. Marco came up behind, resting his hand on Ryan's right shoulder. "You focus left. I take the right. Keep your shoulder connected to my hand. Move systematically through each door and down each aisle. If you see something, identify the direction by saying 'contact front' or 'contact left.' If you see nothing, say 'clear.' Understand?"

"Okay," Ryan said, and together they moved through the grocery verifying they were alone.

"My father must be right," Marco said. "The Holy Mother does protect you. No one has broken in and emptied this place."

Ryan shrugged. "Right, that must be it."

"How else do you explain a grocery story that hasn't been looted and the electric is still on?"

"The grid is still live, so it seems logical that someone is still running the power plant. 2091s don't break into stores and if Gus is right, the government shipped most of Pittsburgh's people out of the city." Ryan shrugged. "But since we are talking about divine intervention, I've been meaning to ask. They buried you a year ago. How did you come back from the dead?"

"Come back from the dead," Marco snorted as he sifted through a magazine rack, his face melancholy. "You realize that these magazines will never be published again?"

Ryan said. "Did you just sidestep explaining your resurrection?"

"I was never dead," Marco said, his gaze fading into the deep distance, and for a minute he started to shake. Then he snapped back. "So what are we taking out of here?"

"Perishable food is top priority, then canned goods, then anything that might be used for survival."

Marco walked down a refrigerator aisle and stopped. "Not enough time to clear this place out tonight. How about we take the last of the milk, eggs, cheese and the meat?"

"Yes, and everything in the sub shop. And we should even take the outdated milk. After Simone kidnaps an Amish family, maybe they can make things out of sour milk."

"My brother thinks cheese should be a food group," Marco gave a tired smile. "This is more than a few hour project. We have to come back with a much bigger truck."

"Maybe we could make it harder to get inside."

"I'll go take a look around. Maybe my father and I can figure out how to make this place much more unattractive. If we can keep Simone from shooting zombies, he can empty the sub shop." He paused, looking back toward the front register. "So, uh . . . do you mind if I get some of those magazines? I really like People and Star and I haven't read much of anything in a while."

42

Global Infection: ≤ 32.6708%

Ryan opened the manager's office door and paused as the memories washed over his mind: the chaos and panic inspired by Daniel Ryder's e-mail, scrambling around Builder Bob's apartment, almost killing himself climbing the fire escape down into the courtyard, gathering all his belongings in the world and dumping them into Ahou's duffel.

The manager's office was just as he left it: the box of Firouz's deeds and legal papers on the desk, the office safe door open with bank pouches and a register drawer full of money. Ryan picked through the safe and realized there was over sixty thousand dollars inside. He had worried over Ahou's photo album more than the money in the safe. It was the right choice the first time, but he couldn't bring himself to abandon the money twice. As he stuffed the money into bank pouches, a twenty floated to the floor and the fluttering bill reminded him of something.

Ryan closed the box of money and papers and took it to the truck, running into Simone tossing vacuum-sealed meats into the truck bed. "Simone, we have a lot to put in the truck. You need to put those meats in boxes. You can't just toss them in the bed."

Simone rolled his eyes. "But they are in plastic."

"Simone, I'm not negotiating. Please put everything in boxes."

"You're such a knob," Simone muttered.

Ryan made a dozen trips with a cart and had yet to see Raphael and Marco help empty the food and after their initial conflict, Simone made himself scarce. If this was going to be done before next year, he needed help. Ryan headed toward the sub shop.

Firouz Derakhshan left the protection of his grocery and sub shop in Ryan's hands to run home and protect his wife and two daughters on the night that the 2091 infection seeped out of the hospitals. The first night alone Ryan cowered in the manager's office, sure that someone was going to breach the building to plunder and pillage. The next morning he worked with the single purpose to fortify the entry points. He built a barricade across the sub shop's front doors with plywood, shelving and fifty-pound bags of salt piled high on a pallet. It would have taken a truck to bring it down. But when he walked into the shop he found his barricade dismantled and the front door unlocked. Raphael and Marco were outside talking like they were on a coffee break.

"What's going on?" Ryan asked.

"This will take hours to empty," Raphael said. "We must secure this place."

"Okay, so what is the plan?" Ryan said.

Raphael pointed. "We park these vehicles along the sidewalk in front of the windows and doors just like in the parking garage."

"Uh . . . I seem to remember making that very suggestion to block off the front of the tower," Ryan said.

Raphael made a sour face and moved toward a truck and performed larceny.

"I told you he would come around," Marco said.

You did?

"And somebody died out here," Marco said, pointing with his nose toward the bloated, festering corpse in the tall grass across the street.

"Yeah, that was the first one I killed," Ryan said. "He was just a kid maybe fourteen or fifteen. I dropped the body off the roof thinking it would keep people from trying to get in."

"Biological warfare?" Marco said, his tone approving. "I've seen biohazard signs painted on houses all over town," he said. "I say we paint one on the door. Propaganda is a good wartime strategy."

Ryan nodded and then remembered the twenty-dollar bill floating to the floor. "And oh, I know this is a long shot. But you remember that girl I told you about, the one I wanted to help? This is where I saw her. So if you see a girl in a pink coat wearing those boots that all the kids wear, maybe we try to talk to her."

"You really think she is still alive?" Marco said.

"Seems absurd, right?"

"So you like this girl?" Simone goaded from the doorway.

"I don't really know her," Ryan said. "She is young. Maybe twelve or thirteen."

"You are a pervo!" Simone taunted.

Ryan paused and just looked.

"What?" Simone said. "It was a joke."

"Little brother, please learn to shut the fuck up," Marco said. "Why don't you go find a can of spray paint. That will make you useful."

"I'm not your slave," Simone snapped and stomped back into the sub shop.

"Sorry about that," Marco said. "He really is just sixteen."

"I vaguely remember sixteen," Ryan said. "I think I was probably that clueless too."

"Speaking of remembering?" Marco said. "I remember this place. I remember the two girls that worked in this place. Damn, they were good-looking."

Jealousy pinched at the edge of Ryan's stomach. Marco had the looks that made women melt and their panties catch on fire, and Ahou said she dated . . . a lot. "Did you know them well?"

"I wish. The summer before I went into the Army, I was working construction here in the city on one of the Molitor Group jobsites and Daniel sent me to get sandwiches here. I met the oldest one, I don't remember her name. All I remember was her yelling at her sister because she had to leave for class and was pissed that she had to make my sandwiches. The younger one was shy and could barely get out five words. But she did make some good sandwiches. I kept going back and finally got the youngest one to talk to me. What was her name?" His eyes filled up. "Can't remember her name. Ironic, since I fantasized her doing all kinds of things."

"Ah," Ryan said.

Raphael backed a truck down the narrow sidewalk right next to the building to cover the storefront. He looked at both men and said, "*Mucho trabajo*," and then walked back down the street for another car.

"So how did you get the keys for this place?" Marco said.

"Long story, but the owner, Firouz, is Daniel Ryder's friend. Firouz went with Daniel. And since he knew he was not coming back, he left everything with me."

"Wait," Marco said. "Is his daughter the one who you didn't ask to stay?"

"Ahou, yes, that is the one," Ryan said. "But somehow the fact that she had a fiancé never seems to register in anyone's mind."

Marco scowled. "Fiancé? That is barely a step up from fuck buddy. If you let her go, you need your head examined."

Ryan rolled his eyes. "I'll go get that spray paint."

Raphael tapped the horn so that Ryan would move. Ryan stepped into the door, and Raphael pulled the car close to the wall. He killed the engine and got out. "Are you going to work?" he asked, looking at Ryan and Marco.

"I'm guarding the street like you asked," Marco said.

"Hey, I was loading the truck with food and found that the project had expanded," Ryan said. "I—"

Something in the distance smashed through a window, and a trashcan clattered onto asphalt.

Raphael grabbed his AK-47 out of the idling car. No one moved, waiting. A minute ticked by and then another, and then they saw four infected stumbling up Stevenson Street.

Raphael leveled his weapon.

"Don't shoot," Marco said. He took a potato out of the cargo pocket and pressed it onto the AR-15 muzzle. He waited for the ghouls to turn the corner."Identify yourself!" he said. "I will shoot if you do not respond."

The reply was incoherent gibberish.

The report was little more than a pop and a hiss as the bullet slammed into the creature's head: a priest in a collar. "Forgive me, Father," Marco said, crossing himself. Marco added another potato and took aim at a teenage boy missing a sneaker. One more potato and one more shot: a fat man in a business suit who didn't seem to have a mark on him. One more potato and one more shot.

Marco took aim one more time. "Mr. Sage, do you see this?" he said, nodding toward the last target. "Is . . . uh . . . is that your girl?"

Ryan's breath came in small sips as he squinted into the late-day sun. He could see that it was a girl but little else. She was in a short skirt, long socks, dirty knees, and a white blouse with dried blood spilled down her collar. Her hair was dark blond and matted with something foul, her right hand groped toward him, and in her left claw was a bright pink cell phone. "No, it's not her," Ryan said with relief.

"You sure?" Marco said. "You said she was blonde."

"Yeah. This one is in a Catholic uniform. And it's hard to tell with the shape she's in, but I think she is too old."

Marco nodded, aimed, and dropped her. They went to inspect the body.

Ryan stared at the girl, taking in the details, trying for a memory of the little girl's face, but it wouldn't seem to come. Not that a memory would have helped: Marco's shot had turned the skull into pulp.

Marco chuckled.

"This seems like a bad time to laugh."

Marco tried to wipe the smile off his face but failed. "But what is it with teenage girls and their cell phones?"

"Oh yeah," Ryan said, "Till death do us part?"

Raphael was searching through his backpack resting on a car trunk. He scowled when they got close. "I will start the cars, then *you* drive down the sidewalk. We will line the sidewalk with cars. Yes? We will all work, yes?"

"It *es* a good plan," Ryan said with the accent.

Raphael frowned and slipped the slim jim between the glass and the weather strip. A second later, the door lock popped and he ducked under the dash. The car roared to life. For the next half hour, they worked to pack cars along the building's length, from the abandoned storefront with the HAYEK sign mounted on its overhang to the other end at Friouz's minimart front doors. When they were done, the entire south side of the building was covered by cars, and the sun was fading behind the horizon with the streetlights coming on.

"Hey, look what I found," said Simone coming to the sub shop door. He was leaning over a car hood holding out an iPad Feather.

"You *found* that, did you?" Ryan said.

"You didn't pay for that," Marco said. "Put it back."

"Pay for it? I found it."

"No, you stole it," Marco said. "That is Mr. Sage's."

"What?" Simone said. "How can it be his?"

"The man you keep calling a knob owns these stores," Marco said.

"When is he going to pay me for all the work I've been doing on *his* store?"

"It *es* no yours," Raphael said, "Put it back."

"But . . ."

Raphael's eyes narrowed.

Simone looked down, dejected. He started to turn back into the shop. Then he stopped like he had walked into a door and spun back to the street. "Hey! She's got Poppa's bag!" He dropped the box and sprang across the car hood like a cop on a crime drama. Simone sprinted down Pride Street. He kept running toward Mercy Hospital.

All Ryan saw was a blur of pink coat.

43

Global Infection: ≤ 32.6709%

I've got her!" Simone shouted, as he dashed between cars, a relentless hound after a blur of pink. He ran past the yawning opening of the chain pharmacy at the corner of Fifth and Pride Streets. A red truck hung out of a darkening plywood barrier, looking like a lewd tongue between rotted ragged teeth. Simone sprinted past a looted Starbucks, past an old store front that said Renaissance Publications, and then right down Marion Street—directly toward UPMC Mercy.

"Simone, stop!" Raphael shouted.

Raphael and Ryan dashed to the corner of a brick building that had Hot and Sweet Sausage painted over its doors. They looked down an alley with lots of places to hide bad, bad things. And then they saw a splash of pink sprint under a streetlight, girlish laughter rising in the evening air.

"This is a game to her," Ryan said.

Raphael ran through a church parking lot just in time to see the girl plunge into a darkened doorway of a six-story brick building, seconds before Simone followed into its depths.

"Oh, Holy Mother! He did no do this," Raphael said, scanning the street, spotting three people lurching toward them. "Identify!" Raphael said, pausing, his weapon sighted. "Identify!"

The creatures shambled forward in a drunken lurch. They walked under a streetlight revealing blood and gore spilling across their faces and chests. Raphael fired. The Kalashnikov clacked like a jackhammer three times.

The infected dropped like three instant rag dolls.

"*Mierda!*" Raphael said as he ran toward the darkened door, breathing hard and listening for the sounds of the RVCJ-2091s within. But all they heard was Simone's feet slapping the stairs and then . . . silence. The crosswalk started a two-tone *beep-beep, beep-beep.* Raphael spun toward the street, his Kalashnikov scanning for the horde that was sure to come.

Raphael keyed the radio. "Simone? Simone? Do you read?"

Silence . . .

"Marco? Marco?"

"Did you . . . that little pri—"

"Marco do you follow?"

"Say again?"

"Do you follow us?"

"Fuck . . . adios! . . . second," Marco said. "Can you read me? I had to climb on a fucking truck."

"Yes, I read. Do you follow?"

"Follow? No, I can barely fucking walk. Did you find that little prick?"

"He *es* in a building. He do no answer his radio. I need you here."

"I don't know where you are. But do not go in that building. He will have to come out."

Raphael muttered a Spanish invective as he fished his phone out of a shirt pocket. He hit speed dial and put it to his ear. Then he looked at it like it had just sprouted an arm. His face drained of color. "Oh Holy Mother, pray for me," he whispered to himself. Frantic, he hit speed dial again, his jaw clenched in frustration, his knuckles went white. "*Mierda! Mierda! Mierda!* Leona pay this—" he closed his eyes. "I did no think to pay."

Ryan pulled out his phone. "What is his number?" He tapped in the digits. *This number is temporarily out of service* . . . "It is a family plan, right?" he said, stuffing the phone back into a pocket. Ryan adjusted the shotgun to his shoulder. "I have your back."

"You can't clear a building. I do no want to get shot. I am going in. You *stay* here."

"In the movies this is when everyone splits up and they all die. Just wait a second. I have an idea," Ryan said. "Simone!" he shouted.

"They will hear," Raphael hissed, his eyes immediately started scanning the streets.

"Simone, you just did what gets everyone in the movie killed." He paused for effect. "Are you too stupid to live?"

It took a hard count of ten, but then Simone's voice called from deep inside. "But she has Poppa's bag! She is in here somewhere. We need to get that bag!"

"Too *stupid* to live!"

Another hard count of ten and then they heard his footsteps. Simone saw his father's face and wilted. Raphael's hand shot out and grabbed his ear. "*Eres un moron*," he said and dragged Simone toward the sub shop.

Ryan paused, listening at the door until he heard shuffling. He said, "Little girl, I think we met once before. I was the guy who almost ran over you at the sub shop when you were with your dad. I won't come in after you because I'm a big chicken in the dark, but I will wait where you took the bag for a little while longer. I would like to help if I can. I can get you some food."

Silence . . .

A bottle clattered in the street behind him.

Ryan spun, his shotgun raised.

Beep-beep, beep-beep, beep-beep . . .

The wind whispered through the street. Ryan could feel movement just under the darkness, just out of sight. Raphael was already a half block away haranguing Simone like the hound of hell.

"I'm sorry, little girl. I've got to go! Please come if you can."

Ryan started toward the minimart. Each step seemed to last for days; the shadows were alive, tricking the mind into seeing swirling malevolent creatures. The hair on the back of his neck rose and his scalp pulled painfully tight. Something behind him hit the ground, heavy and wet. He spun. His breath caught in his chest. He couldn't see beyond the pools of streetlight splashed on asphalt, but something was churning just behind the darkness.

He ran.

Ryan ran up Pride Street past the Banco Federal and the pharmacy. He didn't stop until he slumped against a car outside the minimart.

Marco stood atop the truck, an endless sentinel against the monsters. "Was that your girl?"

"I . . . think . . . so . . ."

"If I can no trust you to think," Raphael shouted from within the sub shop, *"I stand over you and tell you what to do."*

Ryan started toward the sub shop door.

"I wouldn't get in the middle of that," Marco said. "Besides, he deserves it."

"Raphael can yell till his heart is content, after I close the shop door. You okay here by yourself for a few minutes?"

"I'll keep a watch for your girl."

Raphael decided it was Simone's job to purge every rotting, moldering, fouled thing from the sub shop's walk-in refrigerators and haul it to the loading dock dumpster.

Ryan left them to their father-and-son moment on his way to the grocery. After suffering a series of break-ins, Firouz Dirakhashan had taken a page out of the Richard Ryder manual of security; the name on the page was called overkill. To get the mini mart front door open required unlocking three separate gates. The final one was an exterior heavy metal gate that covered the windows and was lifted by a motor into its housing. Marco was standing atop a car hood watching the streets, and that is where he stayed while Ryan adjusted cars into a strategic barrier, posed the four dead bodies along the store front for maximum effect and created some spray paint propaganda. Between bio hazard symbols he wrote, "Keep them inside!"

A half hour later Raphael stood in the minimart doorway his hand holding Simone by the collar. He said, "This one finally get the sandwich shop empty. But it *es* late and we must return. I have much work for him."

"I think I should stay," Ryan said.

“Mr. Sage,” Marco said, “there is nothing else you can do. She wouldn’t even see you in here. And if she can get to the door, then certainly the 2091s can.”

“Yeah, stupid idea,” Ryan said, his mind raced around the cul-de-sac of his dilemma. “If there was a way for her to call me. Maybe she has a pho—”

Ryan dashed to the electronics display, grabbed a prepaid cell phone, and went into the manager’s office. To activate the phone he logged onto the computer and navigated to the carrier website, but it was down. “Shit,” he said, “How the hell do I talk to this girl?”

“She’s a teenage girl,” Marco said. “She probably has her own phone. Leave her your number.”

“You are a genius!” Ryan jumped from the chair, ran to the front door, crawled over the cars and jogged to where he’d laid the body and pried the cell phone out of the Catholic schoolgirl’s hand, pressed her thumb to the print reader and watched the phone open. He ran back to the grocery.

“Are you *loco*?” Raphael said. “The streets have the devils everywhere and you run out there by yourself?”

“It has bars and half of a battery,” Ryan said, as he disabled the finger print login and set a new password. And then the phone chimed as text messages flooded in. Little blue and green balloons populated each side of a conversation. “That is a good sign. That means it is on the network.”

Ryan started to read the texts. “Her name was Karen . . .”

(Monday/12:11)
Karen: Mom ... w/ Sarah
Mom: She driving?
Karen: Yes.

(Monday/3:42)
Mom: Where r u?
Karen: Won’t let us out of school
Mom: ??? Like hell the school will keep you. Leave now!
Karen: Locked school dwn. Crzy peeps in hall. Scared.

(Tuesday/8:21)
Mom: Police blocked the roads yesterday. Dad is coming today!

(Tuesday/11:41)
Karen: Where Dad?

(Tuesday/2:02)
Karen: Sarah and I are going to sneak to her car.

(Tuesday/2:39)
Mom: Calls don’t go through. Are you getting these?

(Tuesday/6:17)
Karen: Sarah's not feeling good. Her stitches are bleeding. Can't find help. Hiding in nurse's office.

(Wednesday/10:56)
Karen: Mom? Where r u? Where's Daddy?

(Wednesday/6:33)
Mom: Baby, you need to hide. Insane people are running the streets. Get somewhere safe. We will find you.

(Wednesday/7:21
Karen: Had to leave nurse's office. Went to cafeteria to find food. The crazy people got in. I'm trying to hide but Sarah wants to fight them. I'm scared

(Thursday/9:03)
Karen: Sarah can't get a hold of her mom. Phone doesn't work. Can you call her?

(Thursday/9:07)
Mom: Get out of the city, Karen. Run! Head to Grandma's.

(Friday/10:08)
Karen: Sarah's dead. No one would help her. Freaking out!!!

(Saturday/9:15)
Karen: Mommy!! Please come???!!!

(Saturday/9:41)
Karen: Why won't you answer?

(Saturday/9:44)
Mom: At Grandma's? Are you coming??! Call me!

(Saturday/9:47
Mom: Call me from a regular phone. I have no idea if you are getting any of these messages. Cell phones are out. It is crazy out here. Get out of the city. Get away from people.

(Saturday/9:47)
Karen: Mom, are you getting my txts? Really scared.

(Sunday/6:02)
Mom: Worried. Call me ASAP! Find a pay phone

(Sunday/6:35)
Mom: Oh baby please call. Daddy is fighting to the school

(Sunday/8:30)
Mom: Baby, your dad sdcrtgjahey

(Sunday/11:01)
Karen: Finally got your text. Taking forever to get to me. What is the gibberish?

(Sunday/11:05)
Karen: Mom? What about Dad?

(Sunday/11:14)
Karen: I thought Sarah was dead. Sarah bit me! She's a bitch!

(Sunday/1:02)
Karen: Mom, sooooo hungry.

(Sunday/2:49)
Karen: They are in the science room. Can you get me, please, Mommy? Can Daddy come? Please!

(Sunday/2:59)
Karen: I hear them. Shut myself under the lab table. Can't lock the door from the inside. Afraid to sleep.

(Sunday/3:06)
Karen: Battery dying. Shutting off my phone. Will turn it on in the morning

"Hey, that's fucked up," said Simone as he finished reading over Ryan's shoulder.

"Yeah . . . that is fucked up," agreed Marco, from the other shoulder.

Ryan let Raphael read. Raphael finished, handed the phone back, turned and wiped his eyes.

Ryan tapped his number into Karen's phone.

The ragged they come and
The ragged they kill!
You pray so hard on bloody knees.
The ragged they come and
The ragged they kill!
Down in the cool air I can see

"That is your ring tone?" Simone asked.

"Yeah, it was one of my mother's favorite songs."

"But you like that old music, too?" Simone said like he was seeing Ryan for the first time.

Ryan put together a bag of food, put the phone inside, grabbed the spray paint, and told the Pagueros to lock up. He stepped outside. The minimart security gates rattled shut. He painted two arrows on the side of a truck pointing to the bag sitting on the hood. Ryan sat atop the truck cab, his shotgun across his lap. He watched the Fifth Street traffic light turn from yellow to red to green. He could hear the distant bark of a lone dog and the faint sounds of music lingering in the warrens of Pittsburgh's Hillside neighborhood. He smelled wood smoke, but could see no firelight. The UPMC Building sign glowed high in the sky, somehow inspiring foreboding and despair.

They had worked for hours defying bad things to come out of the shadows. But now sitting alone in the silence, the barest noise seemed pure arrogance. The hush pushed down on Ryan's shoulders like a living thing. And then he saw something move by the pharmacy. Someone ran behind the malevolent tongue hanging out of the ragged plywood like the sign of the devil.

Ryan mustered his courage and raised his voice: "Little girl, I don't come here often. I have some food in a bag here, and a phone. My number is the last on the call list . . ."

His voice seemed to offend the stillness. He paused, hoping she would respond.

Silence . . .

"I wrote the pass code and my number on a piece of paper in the bag. You can call me any time. Or you can come to the Renaissance Tower. It is on the south side of the city by the Smithfield Bridge. I wrote the address on the paper, but it is the big tower with the crane beside it."

Ryan's voice faded, and once again he could hear the barking dog and the faint music. He suddenly felt stupid talking to himself in the middle of a dead city. He waited as the traffic lights worked through red, yellow, and green four times, wondering what was taking the Pagueros so long.

"If you want help . . . maybe I can. . ." Ryan said, but this time his voice was barely above a whisper.

44

Global Infection: ≤ 32.6715%

The Pagueros pulled around the minimart minutes before the infected trickled down the streets like neighbors for a friendly visit. Raphael retraced the long path back to the tower and pulled up to the shipping container on Wood Street. He ordered Simone to climb the crane and open the way. He told him to hurry. Food was thawing. Simone started to object, but Raphael's look closed his mouth. Simone slid out of the extended cab, climbed the ladder built into the shipping container, scanned First Avenue with his weapon, and then dropped out of site. Minutes later, the crane lifted the container into the air.

Raphael used his badge on a security plate and a section of the parking garage wall parted in the middle—the upper part sliding up and the bottom folding down—revealing a passage that led into the darkness below the streets.

Inner cities often lack chain grocery stores for two reasons: floor space is expensive and bulk shipments are limited to narrow busy streets that prevent tractor trailers from making deliveries. The result is that city dwellers pay higher prices at selectively stocked local convenience stores and subsidize their essential needs with frequent trips to the suburbs. Richard Ryder designed the Renaissance Tower to solve the high price and limited availability problem by building a subterranean loading dock that could accommodate bulk deliveries. The tower substructure was designed to allow tractor trailers to drive down to a three-bay loading dock where they were met by forklifts that could empty the wares into shelves and coolers for later distribution to the grocery above.

Raphael drove the truck through the massive concrete pillars that served as the foundation for everything above, passed three Strykers—two M1126 and one M1132—and backed into the loading dock.

Ryan exited the truck, climbed the stairs and walked deep into the staging area past a long row of storage racks lined with shrink-wrapped pallets. He dialed Karen's phone. It rolled to voice mail. Karen was trying for sultry, but she couldn't keep the giggly schoolgirl out of her voice: *You've reached the B&D Hotline. All our operators are tied up right now. So if you leave a name, number, a list of transgressions, and bark like a dog, we'll get right back to you with your penance."*

"At least she kept the theme Catholic," Ryan said.

"Where are you going?" Raphael asked Simone.

"What?" Simone asked. "I'm going to the same place Neg Dis is going."

"No, you have work," Raphael said. "All of this must be taken to the penthouse freezers. You did no know to put meats in boxes. You just dump them in the truck. And since you do no know how to do simple things, I am watching so you know how to act."

"But—"

"There *es* no but," Raphael snapped. "There *es* only listening."

"But, Poppa, she had your pack—"

Raphael spun. "*Hablen menos trabajen mas.*"

"Best to stay out of this," Marco said, grabbing a stack of magazines from under the truck seat.

"You keep saying that like I plan on intervening," Ryan said as he pulled Firouz's box out of the cab. He and Marco rode the freight elevator up to the grocery and wound through the service hallways to exit at the tower elevator bank and then up to the penthouse. They dropped their weapons into a rack, hung their vests on a hook and then went into the kitchen to find leftovers of choice. With a nod, Marco took his plate and magazines and headed to the entertainment room. Ryan took his food and the box and headed toward his office. He slumped into his chair and dialed Karen's phone.

"You've reached the B&D Hotline. All our operators are tied—"

It seemed a miracle that the girl in the pink coat was still alive.

So why hadn't she called? Did we make all that noise and now she is—

Ryan stood and walked the length of his office. Then he walked back.

The minimart is close. She could have beat us here . . .

He clicked on the security feeds focusing on the front cameras. But after twenty minutes of staring at the cameras and seeing nothing but blowing trash, Ryan was ready to pull the gray hair out of his head. He accessed his e-mail looking for a distraction, looking for something to take his mind off worrying about the girl. He scanned new e-mail and saw that Bruce and Patrick had still not replied. He typed out a quick missive asking for an update on the bio scanner reset and hit send. The task was far too short to banish the worry from his mind. He clicked on the solitaire button and the cards shuffled across the screen. He worked at the game for a minute but could not focus.

Ryan clicked back to his e-mail and saw the distraction he was looking for. Someone with a Molitor Group official-sounding title wanted Ryan to do paperwork: lots of paperwork. Ryan Sage signed the sale documents with Richard Ryder, in the presence of witnesses, and on digital recording prior to everyone leaving. The process seemed final and comprehensive, but evidently transferring the assets for an empire required more than just a few hours. The Molitor Group important person wanted Ryan to sign and biometrically validate a list of documents. Biometric validation required a small blood sample that created a totally secure marker that attached to documents like an eternal watermark. Ryan had already given blood to the machine once, so he didn't have to repeat the process.

The process took two hours of Ryan's life, but finally he clicked send on the confirmation e-mail and sat back in his chair, thinking that it all had to be an exercise in futility. Who cared about such things during societal collapse?

Ryan's e-mail pinged. It was a reply from the Molitor Group important person. Ryan was instructed to find an envelope in the wall safe behind the desk.

The night Daniel Ryder left, he handed Ryan a folio filled with information. This was how he learned of the penthouse's four hidden safes. And in the first few days of ownership, Ryan looked inside each safe and found a fortune: four fortunes to be exact. But he didn't know about the secret safe behind the credenza.

He locked both office doors and then found the release built into the credenza that let a panel shift that opened a door that revealed another switch that opened another panel to reveal the safe. Ryan's heart beat like a kid at Christmas. He entered the code and the wall safe gave a satisfying click and swung open.

Ryan's mouth made a small o.

The content within made Firouz's grocery store sixty thousand dollars packed into bank bags look like lunch money. In addition to cash, he found twenty 400-ounce gold ingots, a black felt sack of diamonds, and another felt sack with rubies and yet a third sack with emeralds. Other valuables were inside, but Ryan focused on finding the leather folio. It held a list of accounts, passwords, and a dozen credit cards with Richard Ryder's name on them. According to the Molitor Group important person, it was easier to add Ryan to Richard's existing accounts than to create his own and transfer the money.

Ryan logged into the various bank websites. His heart skipped beats when he saw all of the zeros. Then he gave a mirthless chuckle, knowing he would never see a penny within those accounts. When the power died across the world the digital ones and zeros would fade into the ether and the record of the wealth would vanish. Maybe for kicks he would hit every ATM he could find for the max withdraw until they stopped giving money. If nothing else, he could use the bills for lighting fires through Armageddon.

And then he thought about Raphael and his suspended cell phone account. Ryan logged into his cell phone provider, clicked through a half dozen screens that said the provider was really sorry for the fluctuations of service and they were working diligently to keep their systems running during these serious times.

He verified that the auto renewal was on. And then just because he could, he used a platinum card to pay five years in advance. He leaned back in his chair, and the worry rushed to the forefront.

He dialed. *"You've reached the B&D Hot—"*

Ryan paced the length of his office pausing at each monitor to check the security feeds and then watched them all again as he paced back to his chair. He picked at his food until he saw another e-mail from Cheryl Rosen with the subject line: *Ahou here . . . How to respond to Richard?*

He clicked open and read.

> *Ryan,*
>
> *I wanted to say a couple things. First, I suspect that you read my first e-mail and struggled with how to respond. That is all right. You don't need to respond, but I did need to say it. Maybe someday I will say it in person. Hopefully, I will be able to start a video chat soon. Second, I heard that you had a candid conversation with Daniel. What you said to him lit a fire under his pants to get more people access to the Internet. I know he's been reading your stuff because he has joined me in the cafeteria to address Richard's proselytizing.*
>
> *I wanted to summarize what I've been saying and am hoping you will give me some feedback.*

He read the first few lines of Ajou's comments and then pinched the bridge of his nose. *I don't really have the time to think about this.* He stood and paced back to the monitors. He watched the empty streets feeling impotent. He walked back to his desk. Ryan sat and read through Ahou's argument and then she finished with the following question.

> *I'm trying to figure out how to answer this. Richard insists that because man is a "social animal," he is part of the broader society, and it is for the good of society that he must work. Each of us has different skills and therefore when we withhold those skills for selfish gain, we are robbing everyone of the ability to survive. When a man works for himself he is robbing all other men of what is rightfully theirs. And for everyone to successfully work together, men must sacrifice their selfish desires to assure that everyone gets an equal share.*
>
> *I'm summarizing his argument, but I think that I gave you the gist.*
>
> *I miss you,*
> *Ahou*

45

Global Infection: ≤ 32.6717%

Ryan immediately clicked reply, cut and pasted content from his website into a larger document and started writing.

Ahou,

Your question really requires a much broader conversation so I'm going to break this up. I will give you the short answer and then in the attachment give you a more detailed explanation for when you have the time to wade into the political philosophy weeds.

The short answer:

As a Marxist/Progressive, Richard assumes that the social ideal is a collectivist ideal. His argument is designed to morally validate a collectivist social order.

> *Social animal = collective animal*
> *Collective = morally superior social order*
> *Animal = genetically determined behavior*
> *Society = the primary collective entity*

Therefore,

> *Society is the rightful recipient of all labor.*

Therefore,

> *Man's moral ideal is self-destruction.*

For the philosophically uninitiated, Richard's logic is a potent argument against individuality. The formal presentation of these ideas come from B.F. Skinner: Because man interacts in a social context, man is really a "collective" animal. And since man is merely an animal, man can only act within the determined confines of his biological nature. Any action outside of these criteria is an aberration of natural order. Or simply said, man is shaped by nature to benefit the herd, therefore the herd is the rightful "owner" of individual production.

The list of errors here are legion, but the central error is in accepting the premise that man's consciousness is helpless against his environment, or said another way, man's consciousness has no causative power. If you accept that man has no volitional power, then it follows that man merely inherits his life from his environment and the herd is as much a part of the environment as the trees and rocks and rivers. There is no individuality qua individuality, so there is no such thing as private property.

Ryan's fingers froze when he saw movement on the security feeds: Sublevel 1-17. He clicked through the interface and found sound settings and turned them on. Raphael was midstream in a relentless harangue: "*You will clean this floor until Marco can eat off it. You will clean this floor until Mr. Sage can eat off it. You will clean this floor until I want to eat off it. And since you can no listen to what I say, I will be right here.*"

Simone was standing beside a mop and a bucket, tears streaming down his face, looking at the loading docks' broad expanse. Suddenly he collapsed into sobs and ran out of frame. Ryan caught a flash of the boy running past security cameras until he got to the elevators, and stabbed the button trying to force it closed. When the elevators started to rise he dropped to his knees and wept.

Ryan clicked off the sound, shut off the feed and sat in his chair until his thoughts returned.

There is no individuality qua individuality, so there is no such thing as private property.

He hit the backspace key and added to the sentence.

There is no individuality qua individuality—individual thought or action—so there is no such thing individual production, which means there is no such thing as private property.

Skinner's behaviorist determinism says that because man acquires knowledge from society. Society provided the individual with a first grade teacher who gave him knowledge, but the student can't make a claim to possess what he is given. His consciousness is impotent. The student exercised no volition in the acquisition of knowledge.

Why did society decide to create first grade teachers?

Don't bother yourself with such questions. Society does what it does just because people had "good feelings" when they shared their knowledge with six-year-olds. The six-year-olds get "good feelings" when they continue to participate in society or they suffer pain when they fail to integrate. And so it goes in an endless cycle of reinforcement or aversive action that man endures until he dies. Or said another way, man starts life as an infant and remains a metaphysical infant beholden to society for his "good feelings" until life ends.

But never forget the purpose of the argument: determinism (in all forms) wipes out all claims to individual identity, sufficiency, or action.

So here is the method to Richard's madness; he is trying to destroy the concept of volition—the intentional individual choice to pursue values. If he can persuade people that self-originated action does not exist, then he can eradicate achievement as such. Achievement is merely individual attainment of values, so if there is no such thing, then no man can make a claim to his ability. If the individual has no proprietary interest in any outcome, he has no moral authority to object when "society" comes to take his stuff. No one has a "right" to their own production, because there is no such thing as "individual" production.

This is a vile and profoundly evil objective. And speaking of profoundly evil objectives, I need to close this email with the following.

Ahou, it is exciting that you are taking on this important fight, but you must understand this is not an academic exercise. You might think you are arguing with a professor in class, but Marxists, Socialists and Progressives are all cut from the same cloth; they are all the same creature by different names and they ARE NOT interested in rational discussions. Their singular objective is to establish the moral right to seize production by force. Ahou, you must never forget that the end game is force.

Endgame players:
*Lenin = Marxist/Progressive \ Socialist = est. killed **1M***
*Joe Stalin = Marxist/Progressive \ Socialist = est. killed **50M***
*Pol Pot = Marxist/Progressive \ Socialist = est. killed **1.7M***
*Mao = Marxist/Progressive \ Socialist = est. killed **(49M-79M)***

*Fidel Castro = Marxist/Progressive\Socialist = est. killed **200,000** (compare this number to a total population of roughly **6M** people through the **1960s**)*

Make no mistake. Killing for the "good of society" is standard ideological operating procedure with Progressives. You already know that Richard will kill to get what he wants. He just happens to be a bad shot.

Ahou, never forget that he is pure poison. So, arm yourself with ideas and then arm yourself with a gun. Because if he sees you as a threat, I have no doubt that he will inspire his recruits to remove the obstacle.

Ryan

Ryan clicked send, leaned back in his chair and checked the security feeds and his phone. The evening passed, restless and worrisome.

The Attachment:

Ahou, now that you have the time and want more details on how to answer the Progressive's justification for collective property, here is a more detailed rebuttal.

> So let's now evaluate how Progressives manipulate words to shape the argument.
>
> **Man = animal.** True, but he is not determined. Man is an animal, but with a specific kind of consciousness—a volitional consciousness that he must use in a specific way to acquire his survival. He must think to shape his environment for his own use.
>
> **Man = social.** True, but he is not a cog in a collective wheel. Man is social in the sense he cooperates toward common goals and in pursuit of common values. The ability to share knowledge is man's greatest means of expanding prosperity and quality of life. Since it is impossible for one man to know everything about everything, it is to his advantage to specialize and then share what he knows and what he produces in exchange for someone else's expertise and production. The process of trading specialized values—production or knowledge—in pursuit of common goals is the essence of social interaction.
>
> **Man = socially dependent.** Not true. Richard's social dependence ignores the source of production—individual men—and merely asserts that man's life is the consequence of group existence, i.e., if the tribe doesn't exist, then the individual would not exist. He is saying that the group begets men. Therefore, men owe the group for their existence.
>
> This is demonstrably false. Men can live by themselves. And also notice that there is no group without the individual members existing first, so individual men must exist before they join a group of other men. A man is the primary unit of all groups: individual men are the constituent parts of all groups. This was John Locke's extraordinary observation that ultimately set in motion the single greatest manifestation of political liberty in the world.
>
> So how does social "dependence" actually work?
>
> Say for example, I want a peanut butter and jelly sandwich. But to have one, I must first invent fire, the wheel, the wheat mill, and sliced bread. Such a lengthy process of invention and development would prevent me from having a PB&J.

So instead, I trade my knowledge of fire with the inventor of the wheel, who shares his knowledge with a guy who invents a mill, who invites the grower of wheat to grind his production at his place of business, who sells his flour to the grower of peanuts, who sells his Jiff Crunchy peanut butter to the jelly manufacturer, who one day decides to spread peanut butter and jelly on his bread. This long chain of social "cooperation" is what makes it possible for me to have a PB&J whenever I want.

But Richard reverses this process. He says "society" created fire, the wheel, the wheat mill and sliced bread. Therefore "society" is entitled to all PB&Js because "society" needs PB&Js to "survive." Therefore, individual men must give away their production in service to society's "need." By reversing the starting point of production, Richard can position individual wants, desires, and action as a direct threat to society. Individual men acting "selfishly" are therefore at moral odds with the collective.

To refute this, first understand that "society" does not exist. "Society" is a generalization to encompass individuals based on geography (sort of) and common culture (sort of). Second, it is important to grasp that groups don't live or die. Only individual people live or die, so groups do not eat PB&Js. Only individuals eat sandwiches. Or said another way, societies do not eat; only people eat.

It sounds warm and fuzzy to talk of the "good of society." But since it does not exist, society is never the recipient of food. Society is never the recipient of a value. Only individuals receive values, which is why in the Marxist/Socialist social organization, a select number of individuals, end up with all the PB&Js and the rest of the people starve. *Some*-**one** receives all those sandwiches in the name of the people.

If you see through the bait-and-switch, you can understand why "society" cannot be the measure of moral value. Measuring morality by the yardstick of society is like defining morality by the yardstick of Santa Claus. They are both myths. By contrast, individuals do exist and human life—the specific means and methods of life—is the measure of moral action.

With this in mind, you can understand that production is the essential function of life. If a man does not produce food, he will die. If a man does not produce knowledge on how to produce food, he will die. His choice is to find someone who has knowledge for survival, or to develop knowledge for survival. But in either instance, he must employ the knowledge such that he produces the requirements of life.

This is inescapable: individuals must think to produce to live. And now you can understand the disaster of what Richard is advocating. He is specifically saying that non-producers have the moral authority to enslave the producer. Richard is advocating the moral justification of slavery.

Richard's implied question is, "Why should the producer have the *right* to keep what he makes?"

But the real question is, "Why does a non-producer have the moral *right* to anything?"

But do not expect Progressives to answer the question, because they cannot.

46

Global Infection: ≤ 32.8888%

It was sweltering on the Pittsburgh byways, and it wasn't even noon. And the infected were coming.

Marco said, "Okay, draw, shoot two to the chest, then one to the hip, then holster and repeat. And this time it should be faster. We want a double tap *bang-bang . . . bang.*"

"My grouping goes to hell when I double tap," Ryan said, trying to wipe sweat from his face with his T-shirt, but it didn't do any good; his shirt was soaked.

Ryan watched the cameras for the girl in a pink coat into the evening, until he was so hungry his mouse looked like a snack. He went to the kitchen for food and heard Marco and Raphael in the game room shooting pool. He was in the game room eating while Marco bitched about Simone's behavior and Raphael lamented being cut off from Leona. With nothing to add to the conversation Ryan returned to his office, watched the monitors until he couldn't keep his eyes open and finally programmed the system to send alerts for the camera zones covering First Avenue and Smithfield. He collapsed into bed but woke every few hours to check his phone.

Raphael pounded on the *au pair* suit door much too early. At breakfast he announced their new project: filling the terracing in front of the Renaissance Tower with cars. It was a good short-term solution to protect the glass windows.

"What the hell?" Ryan said as Raphael walked out of the kitchen.

Marco whispered, "I told you he would come around."

They exited the tower lobby at 7:15 a.m. and Raphael organized the work: "We build a ramp to the terrace. Then we can drive a bus along the front windows. This will stop peoples."

"I think I said that yesterday," Ryan mumbled.

They opened up First Avenue and then moved the contractor trailer to pillage a pile of gravel inside the building site. Marco drove the front loader while Simone and Ryan shaped the ramp. Raphael applied the finishing touch by laying concrete forms over the stone and anchoring everything together with rebar spikes. It was now a simple task to drive vehicles to all terrace levels.

The noise brought visitors, and Marco decided to turn the occasion into a training exercise. But Simone thought it a game to shoot the 2091s before Ryan could squeeze off a shot. When reason wouldn't stop Simone, Marco resorted to yelling, and when yelling failed, Marco and Ryan left to find a quiet corner of the city.

At 9:45, Marco and Ryan found two police cars crudely jammed together on Smithfield in front of a Third Avenue law firm in a building with exquisite eighteenth century stonework with arched single paned first floor windows. Six police officers put the large stone walls to their back and held off the infected until they ran out of ammunition. Their torn bodies lay on the asphalt, among piles of brass and shotgun shells and empty firearms. The last officer tried to flee by crawling up a low-hanging fire escape bolted into the masonry, but the counterweight hung and the ladder stayed down; the 2091s followed him to the landing. He'd been ripped apart while beating their heads to mush with a baton.

Ryan and Marco pushed the police cruisers into the gaps along Smithfield to create a snare for 2091s coming toward the sounds of work, and thus began the shooting lessons in earnest.

"You are slapping the trigger a little, but the grouping is fine. You are shooting combat effective," Marco said. "The goal is to get some speed."

Ryan nodded, squared his shoulders, and peeked at the SERPA on his thigh.

"Stop looking at your holster," Marco said. "It hasn't moved. Keep your eyes down range. You should be able to get your weapon out of your holster and back in without looking. Find the SERPA with your thumb and then roll the weapon back into place." He demonstrated sliding his gun in and out in a blink, never once taking his eyes off his targets. "Now kill those first three working around the cars." Marco inched back with each step forward.

Ryan drew the gun slow and smooth, the front site driving toward the first target, left thumb along the slide, wrist locked down, sight picture on the businessman's tie pin.

Pop . . . pop . . . pop!

The GSG .22's report sounded like firecrackers, but the noise amplified as the echoes bounced against the buildings.

Ryan's hand dropped to his thigh. His wrist found the holster, his thumb found the opening. The weapon clicked into place. He drew and fired.

Pop . . . pop . . . pop!

"Faster on the double tap!" Marco yelled.

Holster. Draw. Sight picture.

Pop, pop. Pop!

"Better!" Marco shouted. "Faster!"

The infected finally shifted around the cruiser's trunk. There was nothing between him and Ryan.

"Reload!" Marco shouted as he took a step back.

Ryan's thumb hit the mag release; his left hand slipped a magazine out of a pouch, eyes focusing on the target. The magazine slammed home.

Pop, pop! . . . Pop!

"Faster!"

Holster. Draw. Sight picture.

Pop, pop! . . . Pop!

The 2091 was ten feet away.

"Finish him," Marco said, taking yet another step back.

Holster. Draw. Sight picture . . . the bridge of the nose.

Pop, pop!

Instant ragdoll.

"Excellent!" Marco said with a smile. He watched the two remaining infected like a cat scrutinizing a dog from a perch. Finally, he said, "Much better speed, and your groups are tight. They are still inside eight inches. That is combat effective. With a bigger caliber bullet, you will be putting big holes in people."

"But these guys can soak up lead like a sponge," Ryan said.

Marco nodded. "A few to the chest will still put the 2091's down, but they will eventually get back up. I've seen it happen. So remember, headshots up close. But a headshot at eighteen feet is tough. Shooting the hip is much easier and a great way to slow them down. A heavy slug breaks the hip bone, and they are not as mobile. That was the pep talk," he said. "Now for the critique. On your reload, did you know how many rounds you had shot?"

"Uh . . . sort of," Ryan said.

Marco's lips drew down in disapproval. "Not sort of. You must know. And after your last shot, what must you do?"

Ryan said, "I have to scan for threats."

"Yes. You must perform your after-action drill. You must keep your situational awareness at 360 degrees. As soon as you have neutralized a threat, you immediately scan. And in this environment, you want to look up and down. There are a lot of places for people to hide and lots of places from where a 2091 can attack. You finish your scan. You refocus on your target to confirm that he is down. Then do a magazine check and chamber check. Confirm that you have ammunition in the chamber. Finally, when your world is safe, the gun goes on safe."

"All right," Ryan said, picking up the spent magazine. He reached into his pouch for a handful of ammunition and started recharging.

"Now let's run through three more magazines, then finish these last two off. We'll go back to my father and Simone. He's probably ready to kill him by now."

Ryan returned to the drill.

Holster. Draw. Sight picture . . . Center mass.

Pop-pop! . . . Pop!

Holster. Draw. Sight picture . . . Center mass.

Pop-Pop! . . . Pop!

“Say again?” Marco shouted into the hand unit. “You can’t hear a fucking thing with these,” he groused. Again the walkie-talkie screeched and warbled. “Damn it! Cease fire! Cease fire!”

Ryan scanned the street, practicing a threat assessment. He performed his after-action drill and then holstered his weapon without looking.

“Need . . . ba . . . to . . . age—” Simone said.

“I have no idea what he said, but we should head back,” Marco said. “Finish them.”

Ryan stepped forward and put the sight picture on the bridge of the nose. *Pop-pop! Pop-pop!*

“Good job,” Marco said, picking up a backpack lying beside a light pole. It was filled with the empty weapons recovered from the fallen policemen and a thousand rounds of Elay Tenex .22 LR ammunition. “Okay, let’s move.”

Ryan took the lead, his shotgun in hand. Marco hung back just a few feet off Ryan’s right shoulder giving him instructions. “Remember what I told you. Slow is smooth—”

“Smooth is fast,” Ryan finished. He’d heard this phrase about a thousand times in less than an hour.

They moved down Smithfield and turned right onto the Boulevard of the Allies.

“Do you see the one on the right? Behind the blue VW.”

“Got her,” said Ryan. This 2091 was a girl, maybe sixteen, in powder blue shorts, no shoes, bloody feet, and a black zippered, hooded sweatshirt. It seemed that hunting the infected was like trying to clean up mercury; no matter how hard they tried to scrape them together, some always squeezed through their fingers.

“Drop down into your legs like I showed you. There you go. Bend your knees,” Marco said, walking Ryan through shooting on the move. “That will take the wobble out of your sight picture. Roll your shoulders into the butt of the shotgun.”

They approached her from behind and saw the dried feces on the inside of her leg from when her bowels let go. Ryan was twenty feet away when she turned and that was when he saw her throat. What should have been an open gash surrounded by ragged teeth marks looked matted over, almost like the skin had tried to heal. “Identify yourself!”

The girl moaned and lurched.

Ryan squeezed the trigger. The shotgun roared. The girl’s head vaporized. He checked his peripheral for more targets and dropped the shotgun to low ready.

“Bravo Zulu!” Marco said with enthusiasm. ”Now check your nine and three. Always perform your after-action drill. Good. Let’s keep moving.”

“One sec,” Ryan said. On a whim, he dropped to a knee and dug through the girl’s sweatshirt pockets, trying to ignore the stench of shit and piss dried to her body. “How did I know?” he said, pulling a cell phone out of the right pocket.

“You guys coming?” Simone asked, his voice crackling in the radio. “We need your help.”

Marco keyed his unit. “Be right there. Mr. Sage is feeling up a zombie.”

“I told you he was a pervo!” Simone taunted.

Ryan stuffed the phone into a pocket, and they started walking again, moving between cars, eyes scanning. But even with his focus turned up five notches, Ryan still missed the two infected stumbling from behind a U-Haul van.

“Contact right,” Marco said to get Ryan’s attention. “Just watch!” He let his carbine go slack in its sling. “Identify yourself!” he shouted and then paused a beat.

The 2091s rushed forward.

And then it happened: hand to thigh, gun to chest, a two-handed push out to sight picture, *blam-blam!* Marco’s Heckler & Koch P30L delivered one shot for each head.

“That might be smooth, but it looks like lightning.”

Marco gave a cocky smile and holstered his weapon. “You gonna check them for cell phones too? Or are you only molesting girl zombies?”

“Bite me,” Ryan said, as he dropped to a knee checking pockets. But he came up empty, and they continued their tandem movement down the street.

“We need you and the old guy to push these cars,” Simone said.

“Old guy?” Ryan said with a raised eyebrow?

Marco snarled, “You called us down here to push cars?”

“That girl stole poppa’s bag. And you know what is in the bag?” Simone asked. “His starter hacking tools and his picks, which means we can’t start some of the cars, which means we push the ones we can’t start out of the way so he can drive the cars he can hotwire. So guess what? If you guys had helped me catch her, your lazy butt wouldn’t have to do this.”

“You have got to be kidding me,” Marco said.

“He *es* no kidding,” Raphael said, sliding out of a car. “The bag have some tools. They are gone. I must find older cars, so I have to hunt farther away.”

“How about if we use some of the cars that we put in the parking garage?” Ryan asked.

“This means we do work over,” Raphael said. “It *es* better—”

“There she is!” Simone ran and dropped down to all fours. “I got her right here! She’s under the U-Haul.”

The girl inched away from Simone but shied back from the two dead men draining blood onto the asphalt.

“I can get her. The little thief stole another pack. This one has got our lunch in it!”

“Simone,” Ryan barked, “leave her be. Let me talk to—”

“No!” The girl screamed. “Let me go, you dick wad!” Then came the heavy thud of a punch. “Get! Off! Me!” each word punctuated another blow.

The girl kicked at Simone until he backed up and then she bolted down the street.

"She bit me! She's a zombie!" Simone said, his left hand covering his nose has right hand groping for his side arm.

Before he could draw Marco took a big stride and swatted Simone on the head, hard. "Idiot! She is talking. She beat the shit out of you because you grabbed her."

"But—" Simone said, but another swat to the head stopped him.

"No but!" Raphael said. "You listen! You draw a weapon on a girl?! What have I say? You no draw a weapon unless you kill. You want to kill a girl for defending herself."

"No," Simone said withering under Raphael's glare, alternately holding his nose and nursing his throbbing hand.

"Tell her you're sorry!"

"Did you hear what she called me?" Simone said. "Besides, she ran away."

"Then speak loud."

"Sorry, girl."

Raphael kept glaring. "I do no hear you, and I'm standing here!"

"I'm sorry, little girl," Simone said. "I'm sorry."

A moment later, her head peeked around the car bumper showing her ragged blond hair and dirty face. She flipped him off.

Ryan laughed.

A smile forced its way across her face and she started to laugh. It was deep into her belly and rich—the kind of laugh that girls were supposed to have as they played with friends.

Ryan crawled under the van and retrieved the bag of food. "Tell you what. I will keep watch here. You three keep working."

"Come, Simone, *mucho trabajo*," Raphael said.

"But she—"

"Think, boy! Now come."

47

Global Infection: ≤ 32.8890%

Ryan stepped into the shade created by the Renaissance Tower, laid an apple on the van hood as he made a show of looking up and down the street. He saw the girl sneak around the U-Haul front bumper. He shifted.

She slid farther back behind another car.

He waited.

She came toward the food.

Ryan saw two 2091s two blocks east. He put the food pack over his shoulder. "I've got to practice shooting, so I'm going to put those bad guys down. If you want more food, you will have to be here when I get back."

The girl stood and put her hands on her hips.

He walked until he was about thirty feet from the 2091s, he raised the shotgun, and took a bent-knee stride. "Identify yourself!" he said, but it was all formality. They were not going to respond. Reflex took over and his finger squeezed through the eight pounds of trigger pull. He was surprised when the shotgun bucked against his shoulder: The 00 buckshot vaporized the head, and the body dropped like a sack of laundry. Ryan wracked the shotgun and pulled the trigger. The second body dropped. He patted the corpses for phones and found two useless devices.

He caught a glimpse of movement. The girl had followed and was finishing the apple behind the bumper of a car. "Whatcha doin?" she said.

"Feeding you. You look skinny."

"You've never seen me before."

"Yes, I have."

"Nuh-uh."

"Yuh-huh."

"Nuh-uh."

"Yuh-huh." Ryan laughed. He pulled an apple out of the bag and set it on the hood of a truck. "You don't remember me from the sandwich shop?"

"I don't know. Maybe," she said, moving toward the trunk, trying to be sly about getting near the second apple.

"You were with your dad. I was probably shaved," Ryan said, feeling the beard on his face.

"That wasn't my dad. So you just go around killing zombies?"

"You are full of questions."

"Nuh-uh."

"Yuh-huh," Ryan said. This riff was always a hit with his nieces, Georgia and Xyla. It worked on her as well. She smiled and then boldly, she grabbed the apple from the hood and took a bite.

"So did you get the phone I left for you?"

"Yup. Thanks."

"Why didn't you call me?"

"You guys made a lot of noise and woke up a bunch of zombies. It was past ten when I snuck out and got the phone and my mom always said I couldn't call after nine."

"My mom told me the same thing, but you could have called anytime this morning."

"The phone ran out of battery," she said. "I was playing this new game called Galaga where these monsters come from outer space, and you have to try and shoot them with your spaceship."

"That is a new game, huh?"

"Yup. And it is pretty fun. I got like a high score, but I fell asleep. And when I woke up, the battery had died."

"I see. So do you live in a building over by the pharmacy?"

She shrugged and kept eating.

"Guess there are no zombies in there, huh?"

"There are some," she said, as if he should have known.

"So why haven't they eaten you yet?"

"They know I wouldn't taste good," she said, deadpan.

"You're hilarious," Ryan said.

"No, I'm not!"

"Yes, you are."

"No, I'm not!" She paused and then said, "Wait, I might be thinking of another word. What does hilarious mean?"

"Hilarious means you're funny."

"Yeah, I can be funny when I want to be."

"No, you can't."

She giggled. "You're worse than my brother!"

"Brothers are supposed to torment sisters. What is your name?"

Her eyes were suddenly wary. "Why do you want to know?"

Ryan made a show of thinking for a minute. "I guess I don't. I'll call you Puddintane."

"That is a stupid name."

"Ask me again and I'll tell you the same."

"You're weird!"

"No. You are!"

"Nuh-uh!"

"Yuh-huh! So where is your brother now?"

The girl shrugged.

"You said I was like him."

"No, I said you were *worse* than him."

"No, you didn't."

She put her hands on her hips. "You're not gonna get me with that again."

"Yes, I will."

"No, you won't!"

"Gotcha!"

"Hey!" She crossed her arms, pouting. But the corners of her mouth threatened to turn up in a smile.

Ryan continued his act of watching the street, and she edged closer and closer to the pack on the truck's hood. "Puddintane, I don't mind feeding you. But it isn't good to be a thief."

She put her hands on her hip in the universal pose for twelve-year-old girls that said some bad shit was about to go down. "But if I don't steal, how will I eat?"

"That is a good question. It is hard to know what to do about such things right now. But if you know the person standing there, maybe you could ask?"

"But what if they say no?"

"Well, they can say no. But you won't know the answer until you ask."

"So if I asked you, would you say no?" she said, her hands tugging at her coat sleeves.

"I guess you will have to ask me and find out."

She put her hands on her hips again. "You're mean!"

"No, I'm not!"

She rolled her eyes. "If they say no, what should I do then?"

"Puddintane, maybe the best way for them to say yes is to offer them something in return. Maybe you could ask them if they have a job for you."

"My name isn't Pudding Tame!"

"Ask me again and I'll tell you the same." Ryan laughed.

"You're really weird."

"I think you said that already."

"So, can I *please* have some food?"

"If you tell me your name, yes."

"It's Hailey. All right?!"

Ryan offered his hand. "Hailey, nice to meet you. My name is Ryan."

Hailey thought it was a trick. She shook her head and put her hands in her coat pocket.

"Okay. Well, I have some more apples and four more sandwiches." He pulled them out of the bag. "Would you like these?"

"But I don't want to eat all of your food. Do you have enough to eat?"

"I do have more. So where is your mother? Is she in the city?"

Hailey's eyes strayed to a point in the middle distance. Then she said, "So could I get more food, please? It is for Tim."

"Is Tim your brother?"

"He's just a friend of mine. He's skinny, skinnier than me."

"Why don't we go get Tim and then you could come live with me?" Ryan said. "I've got a nice, safe place, and you could have more than just a couple of sandwiches."

"You're lying. No one has more than one sandwich a day," she said, "Except Moe. He gets the extra food, because he let us stay with him and he keeps the zombies away. I get stuff out of the vending machines in the office buildings. But they are getting empty."

Ryan said, "Who's Moe?"

Hailey shrugged. "I just want the sandwiches. I'm okay by myself."

"You sure you don't want to come with me? It is pretty nice."

"You can't make me come!"

Ryan could see her spoiling for a fight. He raised his hands in surrender. "All right, suit yourself." He was suddenly sure that if he didn't find a way to keep her coming back to him, she would disappear forever. "Tell you what. How about if I give you a job? You do something for me every day and I will get you some food every day."

"A job, huh?! And what would you want me to do? Are you one of those maniosos?" Hailey said, suddenly exuding sexy.

Ryan wrinkled his brow trying to match the attitude with her age but they didn't go together. "I'm not sure I know what that word means and I don't think I want to know. Here is the job I was talking about. You've been all over downtown, right? Been into the buildings to find vending machines, right? You know where the zombies are and what buildings are empty. Right?"

"Yes. . ."

"Can you write?"

She rolled her eyes. "Do I really look like I was on the short bus?"

"Okay, this job has two parts. Can you get some maps of downtown? Take the maps and make notes about where zombies are and every day you come, you tell me about one building."

"And what do I get?" Hailey asked.

"What would you like?"

She eyeballed his backpack. "How about sandwiches? Maybe one a day? No, two. Tim needs one."

"So, just two sandwiches a day? That is all?" Considering this was a lot more than she had been eating, this probably sounded like a lot. "Like I said, you can come live with me if you want. I have a safe place."

"No. I'm not coming with you!" Hailey said.

"Okay, okay. So, two sandwiches for every time you bring me one map with notes about where the zombies are and where stuff is."

Hailey nodded, the fight draining out of her face.

"And I need to be able to read the notes. And I want to be able to discuss what you know. Deal?" Ryan stuck out his hand to shake.

She started to take his hand but pulled back. Her face told the story. She was too sly to be tricked. "I'll do it. But can I get an advance on the sandwiches?"

"Can I trust you?"

She paused considering her answer. Then she said, "Yes."

"You can have this backpack. It has sandwiches and apples and some sodas."

Hailey smiled like it was Christmas. "I'll do a good job for you."

The earnest tone reached into Ryan's heart and squeezed. "I'm sure you will." He turned back down the street walking toward the Pagueros. It killed him to walk away, but he didn't know what to do but let her want to come. He hoped if he walked away, she would follow.

"Hey, how will you find me?" She asked.

Not quite what Ryan hoped to hear, but it was a start. "Give me the phone. I will see if I can charge it. I will leave it for you right inside the building. There is a security desk just inside that broken out door. I can leave it for you there."

Hailey shook her head. "I don't want to go inside there. It's dark."

"I can turn on some lights. There is a phone on the security desk you can call me from ther—"

"I'm not going inside."

Ryan sighed. "Ok, how about on top of the shipping container there. That metal thing that is across the street? See the ladder? Can you climb up there? If you can, it is a safe place, and I can leave stuff there for you. I will put it in a cooler or something."

"How will you know I'm here?"

"Well, after I charge this phone you can just call me," Ryan said.

"But what if I don't have the phone?" Hailey said.

"That is why it would be good to just go inside and call me on the security desk phone," Ryan said, but her face hardened to granite. "If you won't go inside . . ." He had an idea. "Okay, try this. On the other side of that shipping container is a loading dock. Walk up the steps and just talk to the ceiling. The security cameras have microphones. They are hidden, but I can hear you."

"If they are hidden, how will I know where they are?"

"It is hard to explain, but just trust me. Go to the loading dock, move around for a minute and that will trigger an alarm I can hear. If I don't answer in a few minutes, move around some more and then talk again."

Hailey nodded. "Okay, I saw the shipping container earlier when I went to the front door. That was the address you gave me on the paper. I can climb. That is how I stay away from the zombies. I can sneak and I can climb. That is easy." She handed him the phone.

"I will get this charged. It will take a few hours. Okay? Will you come back today?"

"Yeah, I want to play some more Galaga."

"I really want you to call me when you get the phone, even if it is past nine, okay?"

"Okay," Hailey said. "I have to get this food to Tim, but I'll come back with a map."

48

Global Infection: ≤ 32.8904%

When I'm not with you I lose my mind, Give me a sign, Hit me baby one more time," Ryan sang, watching the school from behind the corner of a house. Over a dozen infected coeds milled about in klatches. If it hadn't been for the limbs at odd angles or dried blood splattered over white shirts or the indiscrete intestine hanging down over pleated skirts, it might have been a typical lunch hour at Saint Somebody's Catholic High School.

They finished the packing cars on the terraces and Raphael announced that they needed a centerpiece for their barricade: A Port Authority bus to park right in front of the plate glass windows.

Marco made eye contact and said, "I told you he would come arro—"

Ryan cut him off. "No, you didn't?"

They drove from the Renaissance Tower and wound through nearby streets, scraping through passable spaces or backtracking when they were stopped by makeshift barricades. Finding no buses close, the search required they travel farther and farther from the tower's shadow. Simone mentioned seeing buses near Firouz's grocery, so they retraced their path from the day before along the Penn-Lincoln Parkway, past the circled police cruisers with the SWAT vehicle manufactured by Lenco gleaming in the hot sun. They drove side streets looking for buses, but only found another location where cops and firemen had circled the wagons to fend off an attack. It was the same story played out over and over: the fight raged in growing piles of spent brass until the guns locked back, revealing empty chambers and then the 2091s overran the barricades, leaving behind rotting dismembered corpses.

Marco demanded that they stop and for Simone to collect the empty guns, police batons, brain-crusted axes, and blood-stained machetes. As they searched farther and farther to the east, they found three similar last stands. By mid-afternoon their arsenal boasted weapons from axe to Winchester.

The search continued but they never found Simone's bus; however, something caught Ryan's eye and a few minutes later he and the Paguero men were huddled a block away from the truck, looking through binoculars at a Catholic school while Ryan sang pop tunes from decades past.

"This *es* for cell phones?" Raphael said, rubbing his stubble.

Ryan said, "Marco keeps complaining about being able to talk to each other. Maybe we find a few working phones for a temporary solution. I think luring those girls this way has promise, even if it does have a drawback."

"What drawback?" Marco said, the lingering low grade fever making his face flush.

Ryan shrugged. "They might eat us."

"That isn't a drawback," Marcos said holding up his left hand.

"This is stupid," Simone said.

"Only because it's not your idea," Marco said.

"Bite me! And no, he's the one with the weird moral thing about stealing stuff. And here he is talking about taking shit from those girls. I think that is called hypocrisy."

Ryan laughed. "Wait, I'm the one morally suspect? And what is your social solution? Everything is fair game in the apocalypse? There is no morality?"

"I'm just saying it seems like a double standard."

Ryan wrinkled his brow. "Simone, do you really not understand the difference between looting and scavenging?"

"What's the difference?"

"There are three obvious differences. Stealing is taking from living person. By contrast the dead are, well, dead. The living use things to improve their lives. The dead don't use things, because they are, well, dead. The living own the product of their labor. The dead don't *own* anything, because they are well, dead. You see the common theme right?"

"Well, you're the one who bitched about us taking a Stryker."

"Yes, and that would be the, 'Stealing is taking from a *living* person' part."

"Well, *they* are alive," Simone said with triumph, pointing toward the klatch of pleated skirts. "And you are going to take their phones. Actually you are going to kill them and *then* take their phones. So does that make it right for us to kill you and take your Stryker?"

"No, you are dropping the broader context. We kill the infected because they will kill us if we don't kill them, because their disease poses a direct threat to our life. We would kill them no matter what they had."

"Well, what if there is a cure and then you killed all those girls and then they would have been able to use their phones."

"Simone, do you have a cure right here right now?"

Simone snorted. "What a knob! Obviously not."

"Then what are you talking about?"

Simone gave a perfect adolescent shrug. "I'm talking about you being a hypocrite."

"For a second I thought you really wanted to understand the distinction between looting and scavenging, but this was really just teenage gotcha, right?" Ryan said.

"Anyway," Marco interrupted, "We have to do something about communication. These radios are useless. We have to be able to talk farther than two streets. Phones would be great. Many cell towers have solar panels, so they will work for a while, but—"

Ryan said, "We have found three phones. And they were all from teenage girls."

"But none of them worked except the one you gave to that *girl,*" Simone said. "And you didn't even tell her to bring poppa's bag back."

Ryan did forget to ask for the bag, but there was nothing he could do about it now. "Whatevs," he said, trying for teenage vacant. "Like, like, like, who cares? Duh?! Look, if we are mining for cell phones, there's gold in them thaaar hills. Uh . . . err . . . I mean . . ."

Marco laughed.

"I don't get it," Simone said.

"That is because you haven't gotten to second base," Marco said, "and don't know about all the things women keep in their bras."

"Oh, that's stupid," Simone said.

"But . . . as I was saying, aren't we supposed to be looking for a bus?" Marco asked. "I mean coms are important, but are we really going to bait a bunch of 2091s to come chase us and hope we can double tap them before they bite us?"

"You never minded double tapping the Catholic girls before," Simone said, snickering as he ducked and Marco's backhand sailed over his head.

Marco smirked. "But this is a different kind of gun and a different kind of tapping."

"That's not what Mary Carmichael said. She said it took you about ten seconds to empty your magazine."

This time Marco didn't miss. Simone doubled over sucking air, but laughing between gasps.

"I count thirty 2091s," Raphael said, "That *es* all I can see, but maybe there *es* more in the school."

"When did you talk to Mary Carmichael?" Marco whispered.

"Who do you think took over after you left?" Simone said ducking, bobbing, and weaving throwing air punches.

"Here is the plan," Ryan said. "If we lure them this way, they limp and moan and shuffle down this street. We get them around this corner. We stand behind the cars. They file through, and we take them one at a time. If there are too many of them, we run away like big fat chickens down that empty street toward our truck."

Simone rolled his eyes. "You are what you eat."

"I'm good with running," Marco said. "I'm good with running now and we go find that bus so we can get off the streets."

Raphael pursed lips. "No, this *es* a good plan, but we must be quiet," he said, looking at Simone.

"What? I haven't done anything."

"I make sure you understand quiet means no shooting," Raphael said.

"Then how are we gonna kill them?" Simone said. "With Marco's bad breath" He ducked and came up bobbing and weaving and landing two punches on Marco's side.

"Ow!" Marco said. "Damn it. Did you forget that I got shot?"

"It was just a scrape—"

"Boys, you must be serious," Raphael snapped. "Come, I show you how we do this quiet." He walked back to the truck and pointed to the weapons. He shifted the AK-47 on its sling so that the weapon was on his back and picked up a machete and spun it in his hand like he'd done it before.

Marco slung his rifle and grabbed an axe.

Simone slung his rifle and puzzled over his choice like he was a surgeon preparing for brain surgery until he selected a machete. He looked at his father and smiled. Ryan shrugged and plucked the last machete. Its blade was stained dark red, and tufts of hair were stuck on the pommel.

"The only way you will ever get any Catholic school girl action," Marco taunted, "is because you are zombie bait. Go on out there, Romeo, and charm those ladies to come down the street."

"Bite me!" Simone snapped.

"They will," Marco said.

"Wish me luck," Simone said, with a dashing smile, like he was about to hit on a girl in the school lunch line.

"You need luck!"

Simone talked low, and then waved his arms, and then did some dance steps and a few hip thrusts. The girls didn't notice.

"I told you so!" Marco taunted.

Simone flipped him off.

"You want my help?"

Simone raised both fingers.

"You want to go help my son get some girls?" Raphael asked, poking Ryan in the shoulder.

Ryan snorted. "I haven't been on a teenage girl's radar in thirty years. Send the Latin Adonis."

Marco smiled, almost bashful, and walked toward Simone, his steps slow and wobbly. Simone pushed him. Marco almost fell over, recovered, struck a pose and whistled. Then as one, the girls turned.

"No way!" Simone shouted. "No way!" he elbowed in front of Marco. "Hey, girls! Over here! Over here!"

"What is Spanish for, 'We do this quietly'?" Ryan asked.

Marco took one more step. "Hey, ladies. My name is Marco."

They moved. Some trundled along, dragging a broken limb, arms outstretched, inch by stumbling inch, inexorably coming to kill. Some moved like drunks stumbling in disjointed haste, but with single-minded determination toward mayhem. But the leading group had coordination and moved with speed, not a full sprint but galloped at a pace that could overtake a slow jog.

The four men fell back through the snarl of cars and for thirty seconds, the leading wave collided against metal, sounding like a hailstorm as the fast movers slammed into the cars as they clawed toward their prey.

"Get them," Raphael said, jumping to a car hood swinging, cleaving arms like weeds.

"Damned thing keeps getting stuck!" Ryan snarled, trying to haul the blade out of a groping arm.

"Swing harder!" Raphael said.

"Harder?! I'm about to throw my own shoulder out of joint!" With a backhand like he was playing at Wimbledon, Ryan drove the machete through an arm bone that also separated the head from its neck, his momentum carried him away from the arterial spray. The body froze, wobbled and then fell like a tree.

Ryan swung at another 2091, the head severed and the body fell. "Oops! I did it again!"

The next few minutes were a blur of sweat and heavy breathing until the last coed dropped with a gash in her forehead. The four men gasped, hands on knees.

"Lord of the Rings my ass. Where is Gandalf when you need him?" Ryan said, sucking air. "This melee shit is hard work."

"You ever notice that Gandalf almost never uses magic in the trilogy?" Marco said, as he dug through bodies. "He uses a sword in the Battle of the Five Armies and the Return of the King. How fucking stupid is that!"

"I'm the one that told you that," Simone said. "But if this is Lord of the Rings I'm Legolas. I'm cutting off zombie heads like he killed Orks. Oh, I got one, a phone!"

"I have one," Raphael said.

"Here they come!" Marco said.

The second wave started pushing through the car maze like water bursting its banks.

"I thought you said there were only thirty," Ryan said.

"I *count* thirty!" Raphael said. He swung into the sea of white blouses, pleated skirts, and knee socks.

When the last body fell, they tiptoed through the carnage.

"How many do we have?" Ryan asked working his way through a girl's purse, handbag, and bra cups.

"I have two!" said Marco.

"I have *three*," said Simone.

"Two," said Raphael. "But I no know if they work."

"It doesn't matter. I don't I have it in me to go another round," Ryan said.

"That is because you're a fat kno—oh shit!"

One by one they saw the gathering horde at the other end of the street.

"Get down!" rasped Marco. "They haven't seen us."

"But *they* have," Ryan said pointing.

The last wave of draggers rounded the corner, and they were joined by a new group—men, women, firemen, policemen, priests, and nuns.

Marco said, "We have to go!" drifting toward the side street.

Ryan took two steps and saw a pink nugget clutched in a zombie hand. He crouched to pry it away, but the phone was throttled in the girl's claw.

Simone leveled his AR-15. "Contact!"

"Hold!" Raphael shouted.

"Ryan!" Marco shouted as he looked left and right, his feet dancing toward the escape route.

"One second," Ryan barked.

"There are no seconds," Marco said, his voice rising.

"Forty feet," Simone called, his finger dropped to the trigger.

Ryan picked up the machete. "Sorry, baby," he said. "I need your digits." He swung.

Ryan felt like when he was a little kid, standing between houses, throwing snowballs high into the air, timing them so they would splat onto the hood of a passing car, one driver always gave chasing. Eleven-year-old Ryan and friends ran like the devil was on their heels. At first, the rush was terror. But after they dove into their hideout and the angry driver was lost, they laughed like kings. And that was how the four men made their retreat from the moaning mini horde: shouting, yelling, and giggling until they tumbled into the truck and Raphael punched the gas.

"That was awesome!" Simone said looking for high fives. Everyone left him hanging.

Marco stuck his finger out the window. "Yeah! Fuck you!"

Ryan looked at the two phones in his pouch. Now that he could concentrate, it was obvious that they were useless, cracked, and mashed piles of electronics. He picked up the hand and pried the phone out of the death grip. The girl had changed the phone skin to bright glittery pink and then lovingly wrapped it in a bright pink OtterBox. He held the power button and watched it boot, then acquired a network and then bars. He used the girl's fingerprint to get past the security prompt, not bothering to look at the messages and texts that pinged down from the network. He reset the phone password and then dialed his number . . .

The ragged they come and
The ragged they kill!
You pray so hard on bloody—

Ryan killed the call and reached over the seat to hand Raphael the phone. "Here, tough guy. It matches your colorful disposition."

49

Global Infection: ≤ 32.8965%

The bus recon was successful . . . finally.

It took them until dark to get the battery charged, two intersections uncluttered and send a 2091 mob to the afterlife. Wedging the bus between the lobby glass and the exterior pillars was a terrifying forty-five minutes. But in spite of the noise, visitors never arrived.

Before they left for the bus recon, Ryan charged the phone, packed two peanut butter and jelly sandwiches, some apples, two packs of raisins, two cans of chicken noodle soup and a bottle of multi vitamins, along with a spare phone charger he had found in the office. He wrote a note with instructions on how to make the soup and charge the phone, encouragement to take the vitamins and an explanation of where they were and a request that Hailey call as soon as she got the phone.

Hailey never called.

By the time they returned to the tower, Ryan was fearful that she'd been waiting in the dark by herself. He climbed atop the shipping container found that the cooler and phone gone—and no Hailey.

Then he saw Raphael's bag leaning against the Alaska barrier with a note attached with a clothes pin. He couldn't read in the dark, so he rushed to his penthouse office. The note was written in neat looping cursive on lined paper, complete with hearts at the top of every "i."

Ryan,

This is more food than we said, so I will have to get more maps for you. You told me that you wanted to discuss the locations so I waited for a while, but you weren't home. I was going to call you but I didn't want to bother you because you seem busy.

I'm sorry I took your pack . I was looking for food. I ate the power bars. But the other stuff you will want back. Besides I can't eat electronics and lock picks. By the way, what do you need lock picks for?

Anyway, since you wanted to know where the zombies were, I put some z's on the map where there are like a billion of them. The one street is 21st Street, I think. It is hard to explain, because it isn't really a street. We can talk about it tomorrow maybe.

I gave Timmy the soup, because he got hit in the jaw so he can't chew very well. He said thanks. Plus he likes grape jelly, but I love the strawberry. That is my favorite!

And you are so lame for giving me vitamins, but my mom wanted me to take them too, so maybe we can be friends.

Sincerely,

Hailey Katharine Vasela

P.S. I KNOW how to make soup. Duh?! I don't ride the short bus!

P.S.S. You can call me if you want.

"Girl, I want you to bother me!" Ryan dialed the number with his phone on speaker. Hailey picked up on the second ring.

"Hello?" she said her voice quiet.

"Hello, Hailey. This is Ryan Sage."

"I know. You are the only one who has this number."

He laughed. "I wanted to call and see if you were all right."

"I'm okay, I guess," but her voice left the truth of that open to discussion. "Did you get the map?

"Yes, this is good work."

"Thank you," she said, her voice filled with pride. "I was hoping that I did a good job for you."

She was killing him. "Well, you have. So, are you safe where you are? You're talking very quiet."

"Oh, I'm okay. I'm locked in a room. It's safe. There aren't any zombies in here or anything. But it just . . . I don't know. I like to talk quiet at night. I guess because I can hear better. Do you know what I mean? I can hear what is going on around me if I talk quiet and maybe if there is someone listening, they won't be able to hear me."

Ryan pinched the bridge of his nose. *Out there all alone!* "Well, I am glad you are safe. What time will you come tomorrow?"

"That depends on how easy it is to get past the zombies. They group together and move around in packs. They wander around during the night, so when I wake up I have to be careful."

"Why do they wander around?"

"I think they are looking for food, but I'm not sure."

"Speaking of food, you are welcome come eat anytime."

Hailey didn't reply.

"Hailey? Are you there?"

"Oh, I was just listening. I can call you, right? If I want?"

"Yes, of course."

"Okay, but I won't be a pest or anything. And I won't call past nine o'clock. Like my mom said, that would be rude. And you have been nice to me."

"Hailey, you can call me any time you like. If you want, I will stay on the phone until you fall asleep."

"Really?"

"Yes."

Again, she fell silent.

"Hailey? Are you listening again?"

"No, that time I was thinking about things." She yawned. "I'm sleepy. I want to play one game of Galaga before I sleep. I will call you, okay?"

"All right, Hailey."

"Goodnight."

"Goodnight."

Ryan slumped in his chair, feeling the need to tear the hair out of his head. That is when he saw Raphael standing in the door to the security room. "How much of that did you hear?"

"I hear everything," Raphael said, coming to the desk and taking a look inside his bag.

"She brought this back."

Ryan nodded. "This girl is a mystery to me."

As Raphael studied the map, he pulled a bottle of OxyContin out of his pocket and swallowed a pill. Then he browsed the letter. "A billion zombies? This explain why we do no fight all the time on the street."

"I already thought there were a lot of infected on the street," Ryan said. "But Gus did say that the camps were dangerous with more and more people showing signs of the infection."

Raphael nodded. "The military put many peoples on the trains, and they clear the prison. Marco thinks the military *es* gone, and they leave the devils to wander the streets."

"If what Hailey says is true, then we know where *not* to go."

Raphael looked at the map again and oriented it on the desk to correspond with the compass. "This *es* the north camp."

"I see your tactical mind working."

"I see parts of the camp from the penthouse windows. I see fuel barrels."

"Fuel? As in diesel? You know that a *billion* zombies is twelve-year-old speak for a lot, right? You understand what she is saying, right?"

"I see some of these devils," Raphael said. "I do no see the whole camp, so I do no see a billion zombies."

Ryan frowned. "So this is you telling me we should go check out this camp?"

Raphael shrugged but said, "If the military leave fuel, then we must see if it can be recovered. This *es* part of our agreement . . . that we can get diesel for the Stryker."

"No, Raphael. Our agreement is that the fuel we do find, you get the first 150 gallons. That is very different than taking on a billion zombies to *get* diesel."

"You will no honor your agreement?"

Ryan narrowed his eyes. "No, I pointed out that there is a distinction between our agreement and what you are proposing. And I'm not saying that I'm against it. What does Marco think of walking toward a billion zombies?"

"He has a fear from when he was attacked," Raphael said. "But he *es* a warrior."

"Well, warrior or no, he is not looking too good. And for that matter, I can tell the bullet wound in your shoulder is bothering you. That is why you are popping oxy like it is candy. What happens when we end up in a fight?"

Raphael frowned. "My shoulder *es* healing. The Skinfuze heal it fast. I only use a little bit of drugs to help with the discomfort. I will be fine. And Marco, he will be with us. He know that war does not stop for anyone. And now he know that he should no have given Dakota his medications. The fever *es* coming back. He know we must look at the camp."

"Okay," Ryan said. "So is this you telling me that you want my company? Or am I not invited."

Raphael paused, his lips pulled down in a sour face. He spun Hailey's letter under his fingers. "Marco think that you should come," he said. "It would be training."

"That is what Marco thinks? Or is that what you think?"

"You did well today, but . . . if you fear to go . . ." Raphael looked in his bag again. Then he said, "Maybe you want to stay?"

"Okay, I think I see the problem. You are not sure which I want to do, and you are trying to avoid a fight?"

Raphael sighed and nodded his head slightly.

"Okay. Do I fear to go to where there are a billion zombies? Yes, I think that is a healthy fear. But I also see the value of finding diesel fuel."

"Then you will come?" Raphael said.

Ryan put his chin in his hand to think. The fuel was very important. The more fuel the Pagueros had meant they were gone as soon as the contract ended. Every gallon he had for the tower meant hours and hours of battery life in the months and years to come. He needed the fuel as much as the Pagueros did. So if there was fuel to be had, he needed to be in on retrieving it. And besides, Marco's healthy fear of the 2091s would put a logical limit on the potential danger. Finally, Ryan nodded. "I'm in training, right?"

50

Global Infection: ≤ 33.0785%

Ryan was pleased he avoided a fight with Raphael in the office, so he slept well, woke and exchanged pleasant banter with the Pagueros during breakfast, but thirty minutes after their last sip of coffee the ledger sheet balanced out.

Raphael commanded everyone to mount up in the truck. Marco insisted they take a Stryker. It was impenetrable, powerful and had guns. Raphael said they must save fuel, because they only had three gallons of diesel. Marco said that with the hybrid power train and three gallons of diesel that was more than enough to drive a couple of miles and back. Ryan made the mistake of siding with Marco and suffered Raphael's wrath until Ryan raised his hands in surrender. Raphael won the argument by force of will—Marco's will undermined by his increasing sickness.

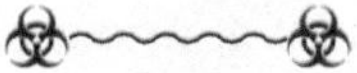

The military opened a path through the Fort Pitt tunnel, down the 276 off-ramp to Boulevard of the Allies into the heart of downtown Pittsburg's golden triangle. Their goal was speedy travel to the north side. To achieve the goal, they cleared Boulevard of the Allies to where 376, the Liberty Tunnel Bridge and 579 converged. In civil times, city traffic planners built large concrete barriers to control the traffic pattern through the twisting and turning junction separating the routes and keeping passenger cars flowing in the right direction. But the military held no concern for traffic patterns. They smashed walls and placed metal street plates over the holes. In a single act of destruction they connected the south side of the city to the north via the overpass called Crosstown Boulevard to Grant Street via the Seventh Street exit to the convention center. Following the military's rout, it took minutes for Raphael to drive the truck from the Renaissance Tower to Seventh Street.

He drove down the off-ramp to street level and hit the brakes. The street was clutter and death and disaster.

The entire Port Authority fleet was parked nose to tail like a line of wiener dogs. The buses had shuttled the greater Pittsburgh population to the Amtrak station on Liberty Avenue. The passengers unloaded at the entrance of long, winding, chain link queues that guided tens of thousands of citizens toward the trains. But countless people never made it: bodies lay like toppled dominos, held in line by the ridged fence, piles of meat festering under the blistering morning sun.

The four men studied the milieu in silence until Raphael rolled the truck forward between the tall buildings that flanked Grant Street casting deep shadows, making the morning look like twilight. The truck tires crunched over bone, the pops sounding like firecrackers in the stillness. Raphael braked gently to a stop twenty yards from the intersection of Liberty Avenue.

"What is it?" Simone asked.

Raphael held his finger to his mouth. He shut the ignition off and quietly opened the truck door and stood on the running board.

"What—"

Marco's hand shot out and grabbed Simon's mouth. "Be quiet," he rasped into his ear.

Raphael pivoted toward the back, looking down the street and then to the front, toward Liberty avenue, toward Hailey's billion zombies. He sniffed the air and then slid back into the driver's seat, turned the ignition and backed up. As he finished a three-point turn, Ryan saw the mob close off the end of the street in the mirror.

Raphael drove to 7th street and then turned on William Penn Place until they saw the David Lawrence Convention Center looming dark and forbidding. William Penn Place turned into 10th Street and ran under the convention center like a train track into a mountain. And what he saw in the darkness under the building made him stop: people churning in the darkness—the infected, the undying infested the street. Two tanks flanked 10th Street and each tank was guarded by a sandbag-lined gunner's nest holding a .50 caliber machine gun tipped skyward.

Marco said, "Do you notice that those corpses are all facing away from the guns."

Ryan said, "They were running away."

"That means they weren't infected," Marco said.

Simone asked, "How do you know they weren't infected?"

"2091s run toward guns," Marco said. "Sane people run away from them."

And then they heard a pop, distant and faint like a stray fire cracker on the Fourth of July. A few seconds later they heard another pop and another and another. Each spaced out by a few seconds.

"Someone is shooting," Simone said.

Pop . . .

Pop . . .

Raphael tried to orient himself to the sound, but the reports bounced along the buildings. The gunfire could have come from inside the Convention Center, or it could have come from across the Allegany.

There was a long pause and then *pop*.

"Turn around," Ryan said, his voice hushed. "We have to find another way."

Raphael put the truck in reverse and did an efficient three-point turn. They retraced their path back to the Crosstown Boulevard until they arrived at the exit to Route 380. Raphael stopped the truck.

"Poppa, how did you know to stop?" Simone asked. "How did you know those zombies were going to come down that street?"

"Because I am not always talking," Raphael said, and then he turned to look at Marco. "There *es* another way around, but the girl may have been right. Many infected."

Marco sat with his head leaning against the window, his skin tone sallow, a subtle shake rising in his limbs. "We've got to look."

Raphael nodded and turned down the inbound lane of 380, then wound through back streets to the Twenty-Eighth Street Bridge and parked the truck in a nearby park lot.

Marco looked Ryan in the eyes. "I need to know that you can jog a mile there and back. If things get hot, I need to know you can keep up. We will not be dragging your ass back here."

"I can do that."

"No bullshit?"

"I can get it done," Ryan said.

Marco nodded and then leaned against the truck trying to catch his breath. Then he said, "We take the train tracks. It's less likely that we will encounter 2091s. Poppa, you take point. Ryan, you will follow. Simone, you will follow me. You will not shoot. Do you read me?"

"But what if—"

Marco's hand shot out and grabbed Simone by the throat. "You will shut your fucking mouth, and you will do exactly what I say, or I swear to God that I will shoot you myself. Do you read me?"

Simone's eyes went round, his chin trembled. "Yes . . . yes . . . I read you."

Marco nodded. "Let's move."

Hailey's map showed lots of Zs around a big box on the Allegheny riverbank by 21st, but they had to move west before they could travel north. The train tracks running west toward downtown were clear. They made good time until they were parallel with the location on Hailey's map. They wound through the trash-strewn side streets looking for a better vantage. Raphael climbed the fire escape of a building at the corner of Mulberry Way and 22nd.

Marco dropped to one knee like a football player during a time out.

Ryan handed him a bottle of water.

"Thanks." Marco said.

Raphael slid down the fire escape ladder. “I can no see the camp from here. The church *es* blocking. We move closer.”

They crept to a building with a loading dock sporting a sign saying, *Tom Ayoob, Inc.* and climbed to the roof.

Everyone low-crawled to the edge.

“Oh, fuck me,” Marco said, his voice was barely a whisper.

51

Global Infection: ≤ 33.0787%

Ryan, Raphael, Marco and Simone clung to the roof watching. The sound washed over their ears like the roar of the surf. Beyond the roof edge was a sea of 2091s milling, sluggish and vacant around the vast parking lot that made up downtown Pittsburgh's north shore. From where I-579 crossed the Allegheny River to 21st Street was a vast stretch of asphalt used in decades past for who knows what. But in the last month, it had become a government-designated refugee camp and a staging ground for the military action.

Marco and Raphael exchanged whispers and then Marco motioned for everyone to follow. Raphael led the way to the backside of St. Stanislaus Church where he produced a lock pick set from inside a vest pouch. He winked and said, "The Holy Mother know that I was not always an upstanding American citizen." The lock clicked, the door swung open. Raphael crossed himself before he slunk inside.

The church's interior was musty in the way of all old churches, and quiet like a library. They searched for infected, but found that even the mice were gone. Raphael had chosen the building because it had a bell tower that rose high above the streets. But after twenty minutes of searching, they could not find the access. They left as they came in, and Raphael led them around the block until they found a fire escape on the back of an old apartment building across the street. Ryan and Raphael stood on a dumpster and hoisted Simone to the ladder. The counterweight dropped and the ladder slid down. They climbed seven stories until they walked onto the roof. It was a perfect panoramic view of the refugee camp and military staging ground.

At the far west edge, under the I-579 overpass, three tanks sat in silent vigil, flanked by empty gunners' nests smashed down to useless piles of sand and burlap, their bulking menace useless against friend and foe alike. The chain link fence, concertina wire and HESCO bastion walls started at 15th and extended under the David McCullough Bridge in a roughly rectangular shape. A row of 200 Porta-Potties demarcated the camp's north edge.

The area within the wall was what the government had mistakenly called a safe zone; tents and hardened emergency shelters within were ruined as if the Pamplona running of the bulls had come to Three Rivers Valley.

Large, temporary lights stood at intervals around the camp perimeter. Some were toppled and smashed, others stood dark and impotent, their generators exhausted and silent. A dozen guard towers—their bases surrounded by wire mesh cubes filled with rock and sand—rose fifteen feet above the camp, the weapons behind the sandbags facing outside.

The military's staging area started just past the refugee camp's east edge. The expanse of ragged and broken asphalt was glutted with tractor trailers, shipping containers, transport trucks and construction equipment, and shrink-wrapped supply pallets that never got moved to their final destination. It seemed that someone tried to impose order in the early stages, but as time passed he abandoned all pretense. The last few shipments looked as if they'd been dropped with the precision of a Jackson Pollock painting.

The disaster scattered across the two square miles was compelling like a train wreck, but the curiosity overshadowing the whole tableau was the fort. At the easternmost end of the asphalt expanse, along the Allegheny River's edge, stood an L-shaped, three-story warehouse. The long side ran west to east along the river; the short side ran north to south along 21st. The warehouse made up two sides of a fort. The rectangle was completed with a 30-foot-high HESCO wall for the long side; the short side was closed off by three stacks of oceangoing shipping containers.

From their vantage seven stories above, the men saw inside the fort: tents, temporary buildings and medical huts. They saw a white RV with a large caduceus over a bright red plus sign painted on the side and a trailer that said, "potable water," fed by a hose attached to a water purification system and shrink-wrapped pallets filled with boxes that read, *Meals Ready to Eat—Do Not Rough-Handle When Frozen.*

The fort seemed a perfect defense with high walls, water and food rising like a stone pillar in an ocean of 2091s.

There was only one problem.

The inside was a blood spatter theater; a three-act horror story with temporary lights blazing down on center stage.

Act one: medical tents, wrecked from the inside out, the beds broken and smashed, the linens bloody, bodies in lab coats with their bellies ripped open and their bowels strewn on the ground like an impressionist painting.

Act two: barricades, fights and flights—people scrambling to the top of the walls to find that the camp beyond was overrun with 2091s. They lay dead, scattered across the top of shipping containers, where they fought to the death over canteens and plastic water bottles.

Act three: two firefighters' final desperate gambit to flee the terror within. They used a military M939 transport truck to punch through the concrete warehouse wall.

It almost worked.

The military transport broke the wall penetrating to the front wheels, making a small hole above the hood through which to crawl. Both men squeezed out of the cab's back window mere feet from escape. While crawling toward freedom, one firefighter slipped and his legs were trapped between the cab and the trailer. He dangled face down, his neck and arms eaten down to the bone. The second firefighter got stuck in the hole, his legs ravaged from behind.

"That is serious Charlie Foxtrot," Marco said, his binoculars traveling slowly over the camp.

"Charlie Foxtrot?" Ryan asked. "I'm guessing that is like FUBAR?"

Marco nodded. "The very same."

"Why did they hang all those blankets from the roof?" Simone asked. "And over all those tents?"

Marco wiped the sweat from his eyes and said, "Those aren't blankets, little brother. Those are REPPS systems solar power battery chargers. They usually come with a portable wind turbine. See there on shipping container? Ones like that."

"But why did they hang them up?"

"It is a south-facing wall," Ryan said. "Solar energy is best captured facing south."

"You don't know everything," Simone said, rolling his eyes.

Marco said, "It's a treasure trove. I see a tactical operations center. Military-grade communication beats this shit any day." He tapped the walkie-talkie on his shoulder.

"Fuel," Raphael said. "Many barrels—" He paused and shifted his binoculars studying something of interest. "*Armado*," he whispered, his eyes suddenly shifting toward Ryan.

"I'm sorry," Ryan said. "What?"

Raphael shook his head. "*Es* nothing." He leaned close to Marco, and for five minutes they talked in whispered Spanish pointing and plotting.

Simone said, "Look, the woman there." A woman had locked herself into a cage with four sections. The cell to her right still held a 2091; the other two cells were empty. Her body was pressed away from the pawing horde outside. "She killed herself while we were coming. That is pretty fucked up."

"Charlie Foxtrot, right?" said Ryan.

Simone gave a half smile and said, "Yeah, Charlie Foxtrot." He scanned the camp with binoculars. "There's someone in the Humvee," he said. "Oh, wait. No . . . that is a zombie. The lower jaw is gone."

"There," Ryan said, pointing. "Is that someone alive?"

"No," Simone said. "He's dead. I can see blood on his shirt."

Ryan adjusted the binocular focus. "Pittsburgh started out as a fort, and it ended as a fort," he said. "I suppose there is a metaphor in there somewhere."

"I suppose there is a metaphor in there somewhere," Simone mocked. "You're such a knob."

"I thought I was clever," Ryan said.

And then they saw the temporary halogen camp lights flicker once, twice, three times and fade to black.

"We have *got* to get in there," Marco said.

"Right now?" Ryan said.

"What a knob," Simone muttered.

"Quiet!" Raphael snapped.

"ASAP," Marco said. "Tonight if we can, but no later than this time tomorrow."

"Could we shoot our way in?" Ryan asked. "You said we have a lot of .22 rounds, right?" said Ryan.

"Much shooting," said Raphael, considering.

Marco looked west studying the street and buildings far into downtown. Then he did the same methodical study of the streets to the northeast. Finally, he looked over the roof edge at Smallman Street below, then toward the fort and then back to the building as if to measure something. "I think shooting is a great idea. And besides, Mr. Sage needs the practice."

Of course, Simone would say the bad things that came next were all Hailey's fault.

52

Global Infection: ≤ 33.0857%

Sometime during the city's panic, a Port Authority bus driver walked away from his green vehicle while it was still in drive. That bus trundled down Smallman Street, careening left and right, scraping off cars and knocking down parking meters until it veered, somehow missing all traffic, jumped the curb, and rolled under an old stone overhang that served as a marquee. The bus stopped inches from a store's plate glass windows behind which was an impressive display of lifelike female dolls dressed in thongs and nipple-showing bras in a rainbow of colors.

If the store owner ever returned, she would be thrilled to see that the bus blocked the doors and prevented looting. Either that, or people living in societal collapse don't consider vibrators, lubricants, and lingerie survival essentials. The bus, the overhang, the store and the building were roughly four hundred meters away from what Ryan dubbed Fort Pitt, at the corner of Smallman Street and 21st.

Ryan stood between the bus front bumper and the plate glass window under the overhang, waiting. The overhang was originally built as a second-story porch for premium renters, but at some point in the last hundred years, a railing had been removed and mismatched brickwork was used to reduce a doorway to a window. Now the porch served as the mounting place for signage: H U S T L E R blazed five feet tall in red letters across the front.

The Pagueros could have climbed the fire escape, smashed out a window on the building's far side, found the front-facing apartment from inside the old tenement building and then crawled out the windows. However the Paguero men—either because they could, or because their sense of danger was totally misplaced—chose to rappel down the building's brick north face. Their logic was that they didn't want to risk entering a building full of 2091s and end up in close quarter combat. According to Marco, that CQB required a high degree of skill—skills that Ryan and Simone didn't have.

The rappelling gear came from the Renaissance Tower security team barracks. The know-how came from the Paguero family's determination to master all military skills. In keeping with that theme, Simone thought it a great time to practice rappelling down the building face first, like Delta Force. "I'm your ninja," he said to Ryan over and over as he dropped over the side.

However, there was no way this side of the warm and smoky afterlife that Ryan was going to rappel down seven stories. The Pagueros pointed out that his choices were to either brave the inside of the apartment building by himself or climb up from the ground. Since Ryan had even less interest in walking into the dark and scary apartment to face homicidal monsters alone, he chose to climb up from the street.

Climbing the bus looked doable from a distance, but after the third time of only making it halfway, he had to wait for help. He wanted to blame his failure on a lack of handholds, but the truth was he didn't have enough upper body strength. So he huddled in the very small space between the bus' front bumper and the Hustler glass doors, terrified that the ocean of infected just a few hundred yards away would see him. And to make a point, Simone and Raphael took forever to hoist him to the bus roof. Ryan crawled to the porch under his own power. "Thank you," he said, but when Marco and Simone exchanged looks, he almost preferred a fight with zombies.

Ryan continued to feel like an enormous, useless, dork watching Raphael and Simone work in their harnesses, using cordless drills to fasten ten-inch plywood boards into the window sills. They remembered how the 2091s jumped out the windows at Saint Joseph's, and they didn't want a repeat performance. The strategically spaced plywood was designed to prevent zombies from crashing through and dropping down to the porch. Full sheets of plywood were too unwieldy to handle that far above the ground, so they spaced narrow boards over the windows for maximum effect using three-inch screws to anchor into the sill. Screws wouldn't back out like nails, and the average adult 2091 would only be able to reach an arm through. It wasn't foolproof zombie construction, but it would certainly slow them down long enough to shoot.

Raphael finished driving the last screw home and returned to the top floor with an impressive display of climbing. Simone made a snarky comment about fat, old men and then emulated his father's skill. A few minutes later, Simone lowered three cargo bags down to the Hustler Store overhang containing five-thousand rounds of Elay Tenex .22 LRs, magazines, a magazine speed loader, gun cleaning supplies, food, water, sleeping bags, duct tape, athletic tape, gloves, and two AR-15s, one with a night scope.

Marco looked toward Fort Pitt. "No paper targets for you. You won't be killing from two hundred meters, but you will be able to hit targets once they start moving."

Ryan surveyed the street. "So tell me why I am not shooting from that building?" he asked pointing to the Pennsylvania Railroad Fruit Auction Sales Building just across Smallman Street. The building ran from 21st Street to 16th Street and looked like an old shipping terminal with hundreds of truck loading bays on its north and south sides. That building separated the refugee camp from Smallman Street. "Or why can't I shoot from inside the church? We would have four walls around us."

Marco gave Ryan the look he used to give recruits in boot camp. "We talked about this. That building across the street is not far enough away. If the horde merely shifts from one side of the camp to the other, nothing changes. We need them to move away from the HESCO wall, which means we need them to come to this side of that building.

"And for them to move *en masse*, they must see you. They will not be able to see you in the church unless we break a window. And then what stops them from coming in the window?"

The Pagueros had retreated back to the Renaissance Tower to plan out the rest of the day, but somehow Ryan failed to grasp the logistics. "Okay. So why not break out some of that stained glass window? They are high above the street. Maybe we build a platform on the inside. That way I'm above the street and I have walls around me."

Marco shook his head. "But then we would have to spend time building a platform, and I don't think St. Stanislaus would like his window broken. He might tell the Holy Mother to stop interceding for you."

"If the goal is to get them to move then why not get a car, crank the music and lead them away? I can learn to shoot some other time."

"And where are you going to drive that car? You see the streets. The moment you drive into a dead-end and they swamp the car, what are you going to do then? And besides, there is no way to know if they would all follow the car. Trust me. Given our choices, this is the best place."

Marco reached into the cargo bag and pulled out an AR-15. "This carbine is my training weapon; it shoots .22 LR rounds, but operates like its 5.56 big brother. Here is what you are going to work on: shooting without support." He demonstrated pulling the weapon to his cheek. "Resting the weapon on a support." He placed the carbine on top of the T. "And then shoot from sitting." He knelt, sat back onto his right shin, and propped his elbow onto his left knee. "Remember to use bone on bone to remove muscle twitch and heartbeats from the shot. And last, you will practice prone." Marco lay flat. "Practice your after-action drill. Remember 360-degree situational awareness. Don't let this building behind you seduce you into believing you are safe. Always check your blind side, then confirm your target is down, and finally perform a mag check-chamber check."

"Okay," Ryan said.

Marco said, "My brother put two 50-round magazines in one of the bags, but don't use them unless it is an emergency."

"Okay."

"You are about four hundred meters from the front edge of the mob down there. You see that semi-trailer sticking out there?" Marco asked, "That is about two hundred meters. You probably won't be able to kill them at 200 meters. Pick parts of the body and try to keep your groups tight.

When they get seventy-five meters and closer, these weapons should be able to penetrate the skull. Remember, the human head is mostly bone from the nose up and very hard to hit from a distance. So your primary objective is to work on the skills around the gun and on your tactical vest. Here is what I mean."

Marco stared firing. He was a blur—firing, dropping a magazine, reloading, policing his spent mags and rotating them in their pouches. Marco's weapon did not have full auto but he put 240 rounds down range in minutes, smiting any 2091 that wandered into the range like he was playing whack-a-mole.

When the last shot faded, Ryan said, "So, that is how fast you move in combat?"

Marco frowned. "No. Faster."

Faster?

"Okay, practice, practice, practice," Marco said, fastening himself into his climbing harness.

Ryan's stomach got tight. "You're leaving?"

53

Global Infection: ≤ 33.0858%

"You have the easy job," Marco said, checking the climbing gear one final time. "You are the distraction. We have the hard job . . . cleaning out the warehouse and the camp."

The entire discussion in the tower had implied that Marco would remain and teach. "Actually, I thought *we* were the distraction. I distinctly remember your father insisting you needed to do very little and watching me shoot was the very little part," Ryan said feeling a twinge of panic crawl out of his gut and into his spine. "When did the plan change to just me?"

"I'm sorry you misunderstood, but we never said that I would stay here with you. This is a good, fortified position. You have food and the weather should hold even though it's hot. Right now it sucks, but that will mean the night will not be too cold. But remember, war is fought in the worst conditions."

"Here all night? By myself? Since when?"

"You aren't scared of the dark, are you?"

"Marco, I am way too old to feel any need to measure up to some macho bullshit. I got comfortable with my abilities and *inabilities* long ago, and I couldn't care less about impressing you. So if you are messing with me, fine. Got it. I can't climb the building. I'm stuck. Joke's on me. Just tell me when you will be back and the snipe hunt ends.

"But if the plan really is for me to stay here all night, then I sure as shit need more than a smart remark and a pat on the ass to man up like I'm sixteen. It is way too dangerous for us to pretend this is some ghost story and we are acting brave to measure our Johnsons. Now explain to me why I have to spend the night with a billion 2091s a half-mile away."

"A billion zombies? Let's not exager—"

"Don't be obtuse, because you don't like hyperbole," Ryan snapped. "You are smart enough to understand my point."

Marco squared up. "Here is the truth. My father didn't want the fight because we didn't have time for another hour-long battle. Securing what is inside that camp is as important as anything we have done to the tower."

"Marco, this is *why* we keep having fights. At best, you treat me with indifference and at worst, you treat me with contempt. You assume that because I don't have your combat skills that my opinion is irrelevant. Your father does not suffer questions or for that matter anyone else's considered opinion. The argument is unavoidable because he refuses to hear what I have to say. The fight comes from treating me like a child and trying to bully me into submission. But here is a newsflash: I didn't back down from the onslaught of federal tyranny. I've stood up to some of the greatest despots on the planet, so I guarantee that neither of you will make me flinch.

"This smacks of the horror film cliché—people making choices so obviously ridiculous that they are too stupid to live. I understand that I need to learn to shoot, but there are much safer ways for me to do that. If the 2091s climb that bus, I'm dead.

"So unless you can make a compelling case for me to remain here all night, it is not happening."

Marco nodded. "I chose here because you are above the ground. Which means you should be safe."

Ryan frowned. The second day in the tower he'd seen news footage—a government broadcast showing thousands of infected pouring out of New York City through the streets of Yonkers. It was mesmerizing to watch the creatures pile up like army ants and swarm over buildings. He'd shown the video to Marco and Raphael to solicit their opinion about being safe thirty stories above the streets. Ryan asked, "Remember that video of Yonkers I showed you? Remember I told you about that guy called Builder Bob? What if the 2091s pile up around the bus and climb up here?"

Marco wrinkled his brow, thinking. "Uh, no . . . not really. I was barely conscious when you showed it to us, so . . . Look, it doesn't matter. The fact is you couldn't even climb up here. The 2091s are not superhuman. They have the same limitations that you have, maybe even more because they are crippled. Those creatures look like they can barely stand up, let alone climb thirty floors up the side of a building."

"It's more like twenty feet," Ryan said.

"Mr. Sage, I've fought these creatures all over the world, and I never saw anything like what was on that video. For God's sake, how many Hollywood movies have shown scenes just like that? Have you ever been to Yonkers? Can you identify it from a video? For all you know, it is old horror movie footage used as propaganda."

"No, I can't identify Yonkers from video . . . but propaganda . . . to what end?"

"Who is your favorite villain?" Marco said. "What better excuse to declare martial law than to portray a mob of humans acting like an unstoppable colony of insects? How many people saw that video and demanded that the government take over everything?"

That sent a chill through Ryan's soul.

"Look," Marco said, "here is my best argument for getting behind those walls. The reason we can't take our time is because the lights went out."

"I don't understand."

Marco's passion over the last few minutes seemed to have tapped his strength. He staggered toward the windows and caught himself. Finally he said, "The lights were attached to a Solar Stik generator system. That system is like your tower's power system. It uses solar and flex fuel generators to charge batteries. When the batteries are empty, it means that generator is out of fuel. But that system was keeping the camp's refrigeration units cold. I saw two refrigeration units. I'm hoping that they have medicines that I need."

Ryan got it then. The fever meant that the antibiotics failed to fight off his infection. Raphael's worst fear was coming to life: giving the antibiotics to Dakota was going to kill Marco.

"I am running on fumes," Marco said, "This sickness is going to put me in bed soon and the next step after that is in the ground, this time there will be no resurrection. Mr. Sage, we should fear the 2091s. If we do stupid shit, I have no doubt that we will die. But right now, for me, being too stupid to live is walking away from that camp."

Ryan nodded. "All right. But how does that require me to be here all night alone?"

"The issue is not *you* here all night," Marco said. "The issue is manpower and limited daylight. There are only a few hours until sundown. If we have to stop work to come get you or spend our time watching over you, that severely limits what we can accomplish. And we have a *lot* to do even before we get into that warehouse.

"I estimate maybe fifteen thousand infected over there, and as long as they are packed tight against those walls, it is highly unlikely that we can close the breach. We can exterminate the few hundred 2091s inside, but we can't hope to exterminate the whole population in a few hours. We must pull the 2091s away from the containers so we can close the gap. You remember what my father said? Mass is mass. And if we have to move the mass of human bodies *and* the mass of those shipping containers, we will fail."

Ryan nodded. "Yes, okay. I get it. But how does that require me to be the goat tethered to a stake?"

"If you had a better idea on how to get the 2091s to move, you should have told us in the tower."

Ryan frowned. "That is the problem of not letting me in on the details before we get this far. I didn't know I needed to offer a different solution, and even if I did, no one wants to hear my opinion."

Marco said, "I am not trying to be an ass, but I fought my way out of New York City and then through the mountains." He held up his left hand to show the stump of his pinky finger. "I have been much closer to these creatures than you will ever be tonight. I survived. You will too." He tugged the rope. A moment later, Simone and Raphael started pulling him up.

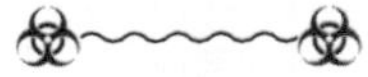

The hours crawled by as Ryan drilled the basics slow and smooth, slow and smooth: lollypop, slow breath, press the trigger like he was snapping a glass rod, pop. He rotated magazines, cleared misfeeds—s p o r t s—and reloaded over and over and over and over. The work kept two worries at the back of his mind: the foreboding that a 2091 was going to crash through the windows above and take a hunk out of his liver, and Hailey. He'd left food and a note and then sent a text explaining that he was looking at the billion zombies. She didn't need to find the street signs, and she should give him a call. But the phone remained silent.

After three hours, the gunfire only attracted the 2091s by ones and twos and threes and fours. They shuffled toward the bus like stroke victims, awkward and disjointed but with single-minded purpose. And then it was like someone made an announcement that the after party had started and the horde bolted for the doors. Ryan changed to the rifle without the scope and created a game to see if he could stem the flow. But they kept coming and coming and coming, the little .22 slug barely causing a flinch as it bounced off skull bones.

The first 2091 to reach the corner of the Pennsylvania Railroad Fruit Auction Building was a petite brunette dressed in a New York Giants coat. Suddenly it seemed that putting her down meant success or failure. Ryan sighted and shot and sighted and shot, chipping pieces off her shoulder and chest and neck and ear, but he couldn't put a shot into the head. Disgusted, he slapped in a third magazine. After ninety rounds, the coat was riddled with little holes leaking blood like a cartoon character. His concentration drained as he emptied the magazine. Ryan lost the game as the Giants fan lumbered closer followed by many, many friends.

Ryan slumped against the wall exhausted. He wanted to sleep, but fear rippled through his stomach. He recharged magazines as fast as his fingers could move. When he looked up, the bus was surrounded by 2091s babbling like lunatics and their stench so very, very close. They stood with arms outstretched, grasping like toddlers, awaiting mommy to pick them up. He watched to see if the pawing, groping mass would start pouring over the bus. He measured the passing time in heartbeats, waiting, waiting, waiting and firing and firing and firing until he couldn't hold his focus or his body. Physically spent, he dropped to the deck and couldn't make himself move. He lay on the porch staring at the distant clouds, his mind turning them into animals and faces and things. And then, unbidden, a new worry gnawed on his head like a rat into cheese.

"You are a billionaire now. You need to be paranoid too . . ."

54

Global Infection: ≤ 33.0867%

Paranoid.

He was now.

Ryan sat against the brick wall between two boarded-up windows, letting his thoughts unravel. He rubbed his knees, suddenly appreciating why pictures of Special Forces always showed them in kneepads. The zombies under the porch seemed to calm when they couldn't hear him, but their stench was agitated by the heat: body odor, urine, feces and the faint hint of rot. Pittsburgh had been boiling under the early summer sun for the last couple days, and there was no relief on the horizon.

What the hell am I going to do?

He'd left the tower never once thinking the whole exercise was to get him *out.* Something made Raphael reconsider outright murder but Ryan was suddenly sure that Raphael had no moral qualms about letting events take an unfortunate course. If Ryan died in the middle of a city by himself, suffering the misfortunes of the moment, how could that be his fault?

Wasn't that Raphael's rationale for Marie?

He pulled out his phone to access the tower security app. If he could get to the interface, he could shut down the tower. Of course, the app was unresponsive, because it was not connected to the tower systems. Ryan pinched the inside of his nose. He felt the air in the corner of his eyes squeak under the pressure. A warm breeze blew down the street, but only managed to send a chill across his sweaty body like he was naked.

"You are now a billionaire. You need to be paranoid too." Daniel Ryder's words resonated in his mind.

It was no wonder Raphael didn't want to discuss the plan. Ryan would have seen through the ploy. He pulled out the maintenance radio. "Marco? Raphael?" he said, keying the mic.

Static . . .

Did they change frequencies?

He stood and looked over the edge for a way to reach the ground but only saw a mob of carnivores, their ragged nails, their filthy hair, the sunburn blisters on their faces and arms, and the dark stains around their mouths. If he jumped the 2091s would certainly make him a feast. Ryan tried pulling the plywood away from the window sill. It didn't budge. He looked for something to remove the screws but found nothing.

Ryan looked through his call log and saw the number for the pink gem he'd given to Raphael. The phone rang and rang and rang, and then . . . "This user's mailbox is full. Goodbye."

"Of course he won't answer," Ryan said.

Maybe Team Bruptrick could bring down the hammer and lock the tower. He tapped through the settings to add the phone to the Molitor Group domain and pressed the last button. The connection was rejected. Who knew what security those two techno tyrants had put on the system?

He brought up his personal e-mail on a free account and typed in Patrick's e-mail. The subject line said. It's Ryan Sage. Call me ASAP!

He stared at his phone for thirty minutes willing it to ring but it seemed that team Bruptrick wasn't monitoring email.

His skin felt like sandpaper, and the sharp bite of cordite scratched at his nose. He poured some water into his hand and tried to wipe away the grit and gunpowder from his face. He took a bite of power bar, drained a water bottle, started the second bottle, then put them both on a windowsill, and finally he took a leak over the porch.

He sat down, finished half the power bar and his head slumped forward as a ripple of tired pulled him toward a nap. He shook his head and did a rough ammo count thinking that he should be close to running out, but he had only gone through twelve hundred rounds. That meant he had a lot of ammo left, but it also meant he sucked at shooting. There were nowhere near 1200 bodies lying on the asphalt.

Ryan applied athletic tape to the sore spots and worked his handgun technique trying to thin down the infected around the bus. The GSG 1911 felt good in his hand. He practiced drawing his weapon, finding a sight picture, squeezing off three rounds, and returning the gun to its holster. When the slide locked back, he practiced reloading exactly how Marco demonstrated. He worked patiently, reloading . . . shooting . . . reloading . . . shooting. He took a break to remove the old gunpowder-blackened athletic tape and reapplied a fresh layer over blisters. Then he went to the windowsill for his power bar and water.

They were gone.

Laughter echoed, stifled and distant like a sinister horror movie soundtrack.

Ryan froze.

He drew the GSG looking for a threat.

Laughter . . .

Ryan scanned the crowd of 2091s.

Can zombies laugh?

Fear clawed at his bowels. Ryan triggered off ten shots into the writhing pack. He was midway through a magazine change when he heard the laughter again. He forced himself still, listening to the city. The ever-present drone of the infected, the *caaw, caaw, caaw* of crows tolling like a church bell at a funeral, the distant bark of a frantic dog, the screech of cats, the tumbling of a glass bottle, the groaning sway of crackling electric cables overhead. Ryan tried to shake off the certainty that someone was looking at him. He jammed a new magazine into the butt of his weapon and started shooting to drive the gremlins away.

Slow is smooth, smooth is fast.

He found a sight picture and squeezed off shots.

Pop! Pop! . . . Pop!

Pop! Pop! . . .

Laughter . . .

Pop!

Ryan's heart leaped back into his throat. He dropped down behind the T, searching. He crept close to the boarded windows, terrified at what might be looking back. He listened hard, but heard . . . silence.

Was Simone messing with him? He looked up.

Ryan low-crawled to the edge and looked underneath the porch, fearing he was about to see a 2091 giggling like an evil clown.

No laughing zombies or evil clowns . . .

He leaned against the brick to have something solid at his back and willed his mind elsewhere.

Lenna.

Unbidden, the forever sullen and unhappy face of his youngest sister flashed into his thoughts. As a baby, she was colicky. As a toddler, she was a screamer. As a preadolescent, she was a curmudgeon beyond her years. As a teenager, she was determined to smoke and drink and screw her way to oblivion. Lenna was the reason Easton and Betsy Sage never had more children.

The drinking and screwing was how she met Steve, an alcoholic who did nothing but sit in his chair. He neglected his wife, his job, and his boys. If Lenna ever needed a reason to hate life, she'd found the perfect cause. She managed to clean up her life to raise two boys, but misery clung to her family like wet dog fur.

Ryan's patience for his sister's life ran out long before Easton and Betsy's, but that was the way of parents, forever clinging to the hope that their love will be the catalyst for peace and harmony and health. While Ryan had never been close to Lenna, he did care about her boys: Stephen Jr., and Aaron. They came to his house often until Steve put the kibosh on visiting Uncle Ryan. It had been almost two years since their last visit, and suddenly Ryan's heart squeezed as he realized he was struggling to remember their faces.

They would be what? Fifteen and sixteen?

Ryan tried to do the math.

Lenna had her kids first . . . Xyla and Georgia had been ten and twelve? Why can't I remember how old they are?

Ryan always assumed that he would marry and have kids, but it never happened. When he was younger, he focused on a track career. He had two near misses in his twenties, but both relationships had catastrophic flaws. And if the women were to be believed, the flaws were his—dating a professional athlete came with its own unique challenges. And as he got older, his focus went to social and political commentary. It seemed absurd that in America, frank discussions about limited government and individual liberty should be a verboten, politically correct conversation. But it was. Any criticism of any group, any problem, any error was labeled hate speech, and on a whim the government could slap the *terrorist* label on anyone they sought to silence. The social costs were high and no woman Ryan met could handle the heat. He had been seeing Stacy Twist when the government finally shut down all dissenting voices on radio and sent many hosts to Guantanamo Bay—at least those who had not escaped to radio-free Russia. He thought Stacy was the love of his life, until she looked at him in the kitchen and made the choice clear: stop talking about the government or she would leave. Ryan breathed deep, fought back his tears and packed her bags.

He didn't have anything to offer that was movie star obvious, and the closer to middle age he got, the less he exuded that intangible something that made women go weak in the knees. It didn't help that he totally lacked the social patter that translated into dates. If he started talking about anything other than drinking Cosmopolitans, the women's eyes glazed over: *Knock, knock . . . nobody home.*

Ryan tried casual relationships, but that never worked; someone always moved toward serious. Twice he was caught in a pregnancy scare with women who were never, ever going to be long-term interests. The first time, he sucked down antacids like they were Halloween candy for two weeks before she peed on a stick. The second time, he realized too late that the woman he'd bedded was unstable—and unstable was the polite adjective. He scheduled a doctor's appointment to get Prozac during those three months of terror. He never kept the appointment, but afterwards he'd concluded that was enough. Abstinence made life so much easier. It was lonely, but it was the only sane solution.

So Ryan Sage jogged into middle age with no wife, no kids, and an abiding emptiness.

Ahou Derakhshan . . .

One night by video chat, they talked easily and endlessly. She had so much to say about things that Ryan cared about. She was attentive to what he said. Never once had they mentioned alcohol. She never checked out even when Ryan jumped into the intellectual pool. Indeed, she had been inspired, even aroused. They shared something . . . a transcendent something that, for a brief moment, made Ryan think "I'm almost home."

And yet—

Suddenly he had to go to the bathroom.

"Oh shit!" Ryan said. His mind cascaded down the precious few options and the absence of toilet paper. But there was no putting it off. He walked to the far end of the overhang and unbuckled his pants. He took a quick look to see if infected were underneath; a face full of feces seemed an indignity that even the undying should not suffer. He dropped down, holding on the H support hoping for two outcomes: that he didn't tumble to the street and everything came out . . . cleanish. But balancing over the abyss made him clench up. He hovered, trying to make himself relax. He took a deep breath and looked forward.

And that is when he saw the window. It was open a few inches. And there sat the power bar and bottle of water.

Ryan's butt puckered and his stomach flipped.

55

Global Infection: ≤ 33.0867%

Ryan jumped. He caught himself with the H support. He fell forward, pawing at his briefs and jeans.

The laughter rolled from inside the building in waves of girlish mirth.

"Hailey?" Ryan said, trying to zip his fly.

She lay inside the window holding her side, giggling deep into her belly. It was a wonderful laugh, the infectious kind, the kind that Ryan wanted to hear over and over. Hailey finally sat up, cleared the tears from her eyes, and raised the window flush with the plywood barricade. "If you are gonna poop on a zombie, I'll go away for a few minutes."

"What . . .? How . . .? Did you see me—" Ryan shook his head. In a city full of dead, the population of living souls near statistical zero, he'd managed to put his butt on display to the one remaining person. "You could have told me you were there."

"But that wouldn't have been as funny." She dropped back to the floor, laughing and gasping.

"You took my water and my power bar just to see if you could make me crazy?!"

"You were gonna poop on a zombie!!"

"I was not going to poop—you almost killed me. I almost fell off the roof." Ryan wanted to be mad, but he couldn't. "I, uh . . . how did you get in there?"

"The door," she said, like she was talking to a toddler. She recovered and moved back to the window, her face radiant.

"Isn't it dangerous in there?"

"You are the one outside with them, duh," Hailey eyed Ryan's bag of food.

"So there are no infected in there?"

"There is one on the top floor," Hailey replied with a shrug. "But she is locked in an apartment. She bangs when she hears me or when she can smell me."

Ryan sniffed. "That wouldn't be too hard," he said. He was trying to be funny.

"Hey! You're mean!" Hailey pouted.

"No, I'm not," Ryan shot back, trying for his former gag.

Hailey rolled her eyes and groaned

"I need new material, huh?"

She looked at him like he had six heads. Then in a blink, she batted her eyes and gave an dazzling grin. "Could I have a sandwich, please?"

And then Ryan saw her actions in all their manipulative glory. This wasn't the first time she had gotten her way flashing those blue eyes and that smile. Ryan almost said no just on principle. "You have been waiting all this time just to ask me that? You could already have eaten the power bar."

Hailey shrugged. "But that wouldn't have been as funny. Besides, you told me it was better to ask if the person was standing there." Then she brought out the full wattage of that smile again. It was the same smile that all supermodels have, the ability to show all their teeth. It was genuine and that made it impossible to resist.

Ryan handed her a sandwich through the window. But the shock of the moment was wearing off, and he was feeling that pressure again. "Uh . . . I . . . need to go. I don't suppose there is a bathroom that works in the building?"

"Yup," she said, taking a bite.

"Could I come in and use it?"

"You are the one who boarded up the windows."

Ryan paused in sudden despair. Nails would back out easily, but screws, no, they were not going anywhere.

"Uh . . . could you do me a favor?"

"Yup," Hailey said, taking another bite.

"Could you go get me some toilet paper?"

"Yup," she said but didn't move. That ornery glint was back in her eyes.

Ryan rolled his hand to hurry her along.

"Could I have something to drink?"

"This is blackmail, pure and simple." He grabbed a bottle of water out of the bag. "Here! Hurry!"

She reached handed him a roll through the window.

"You already had it with you?"

"Yup." She took a drink. "I knew that eventually you would have to go, and I wanted a sandwich and something to drink. See, I gave you something you wanted and you gave me something I wanted." And with that, she was gone from the window, saying something about pooping on zombies.

Ryan finally relaxed, things moved, and eventually he put himself back together, beyond thankful for toilet paper—such a simple creation, but for most human history unknown to man. Ryan determined he would raid every bathroom in the city for a stockpile. The apocalypse would surely have come if they ever ran out.

"I'm done," Ryan said through the window, but there was no reply. He started shooting, then reloaded and shot again. While he recharged his magazines Hailey came back in the window.

"Is that fun?" Hailey asked.

"I wasn't sure you were coming back."

"I had to finish eating and didn't want to be anywhere near . . . you know."

"It is fun. I'd let you try, but I'm not sure you can squeeze out here."

"You'd let me?"

"Sure."

Hailey went to a different window, took off her pink coat and squeezed under the board. "Why did you put these on the windows? How are you gonna get off this overhang?"

"The idea was to keep the bad guys from coming through the window."

"But there aren't any zombies in here. Didn't you look at my map?"

Ryan opened his mouth and then realized there was no good answer. "Uh . . . good point."

"Oh, but we didn't have the opportunity to talk about what I wrote. I'm sorry I was so sleepy last night. Do the boards come off?"

"I don't think so. Maybe if I had a hammer or something."

"Having a hammer would have been good, right?"

Having a hammer would have been really good. If he'd had some tools, he wouldn't have been stranded in the middle of the city with a few thousand carnivorous mouths between him and finding out what the Pagueros were really doing.

Ryan motioned for her to stand behind the H. He said, "If you want to be a good shot, here is what you will do. One, treat every weapon as if it were loaded! Two, keep your finger off the trigger," he said with emphasis, "until your weapon is pointed down range and your sight is on target. Don't shoot anything you can't positively identify; know what is behind it. And four, never point a weapon at anything you don't intend to destroy. Do you understand?"

"Yes," Hailey replied and took the rifle in her hands. She was attentive and focused, but was determined to keep two feet between them. Her eyes were wary; she cringed at sudden moves and balked when he reached out to adjust her hold on the rifle. Not that Ryan wanted to get too close. She smelled of unwashed body and the faint traces of urine.

Over time, the AR-15 proved too heavy for Hailey to hold up. She was tall, but she was in need of food and sleep. They spent most of the afternoon with the rifle resting on the middle part of the H. The recoil on a .22 was trivial, and after an hour drilling through checking the chamber, raising the weapon for a sight picture, controlling her breathing and squeezing off a shot, Hailey was clipping zombies in the head as well as any junior assassin. Eventually, she asked to take a break, but the break proved to be her stopping point. She crawled back through the window and yawned as she rested her head on the sill.

"So is your mother in this building? Is she the . . . zombie?" Ryan asked as he worked a bore snake through the barrel.

Hailey shrugged. "This is old man Renfro's apartment. He used to let me come down and read books with him when my mom was busy."

"Where is Mr. Renfro now?"

"I dunno. I haven't seen him since the soldiers built that camp. But he gave me keys a long time ago so I can come in when I want. So why are your pants so short?" Hailey asked. "You planning for a flood?"

"Ha ha! Smarty pants. If it rains, I'm gonna blame you."

"I already did my rain dance. So it probably is my fault. But at least you are prepared."

Ryan laughed.

"Guess who I saw today."

"Who," Ryan said, genuinely puzzled at whom she could have seen that he would know.

"Everybody I looked at," she said, deadpan.

Ryan laughed again.

"Are the zombies ever going to go away?"

"Is this another joke?"

Hailey shook her head. "Not until I can think of a punch line."

"No, Hailey, they are here with us until, well . . . until we have gotten rid of them in every city. Not just here."

"Every city? In the whole world?"

"I was only thinking about America, but yes, in the whole world. But I figure we start with one street at a time."

"Yeah, it's like what one math book said to another."

"What's that?"

"I've got my own problems to solve."

Her delivery was flawless. "You are a funny girl."

"I know," Hailey said, with a weary smile. "That is what my mom used to tell me all the time."

"You getting tired?"

Hailey shrugged. "Are you here all night?"

"Yes. You don't stay here, do you? Are you going to go back over by the store?" Ryan said, suddenly realizing that she had traveled all the way here. "Wait, how did you get here?"

"Duh?! I walked. Well, I have a bike that I rode, and then I hid the bike and walked here. But it's not like there is anyone around who will steal the bike. The only people in the city are the zombies, because the army guys made everyone get on a train, but I hid it anyway. I got your text and then saw the note and the food, so I had to take the food back to Timmy before I rode over here, and I had to kinda go the long way to stay away from zombies, so it took me longer. I thought I was gonna miss you, but it's not that far."

Ryan guessed that was true. It was a mile-and-a-half from the tower to the minimart, and if the map in his head was right, it was only a little farther north to Fort Pitt.

Pittsburgh was a maze of narrow streets, a cluttered grid of asphalt sliced into the side of the Pennsylvania foothills that seemed to only allow two directions: up or down. If it wasn't for the two ridges that run along the sliver of land between the Monongahela and Allegheny, it would be a brisk walk from river to river. Ryan had trekked through downtown on foot only three weeks ago. He had walked the maze of streets inside the golden triangle and then up the ridge to St. Joseph's. That was how he found himself having breakfast in Firouz Derakhshan's sub shop. That was how he met Ahou Derakhshan.

"So, I usually see you over by the sub shop," Ryan said. "If this is your home, why do you stay over there?"

Hailey looked at Ryan like he had six heads again. "Duh?! The zombies are over *here*."

"So are you gonna go back?" Ryan said. "It is going to be dark soon. If you have to ride back, you need to get going."

Hailey paused for a few minutes. Then she said, "I stay a lot of places. This is just one of them."

"Well, isn't there someone looking after you? How about those men I saw you with? Don't they worry about where you are?"

Hailey's countenance changed in a flash, wariness poured out of her eyes full force.

"When I was at the sandwich shop you were with a man. And then a day later, I saw you with three men outside the pharmacy. There was a fight, and you ran into the store and came back—"

"Oh no, I don't stay with them," Hailey said. "Well, I used to. One of them is Timmy. I still see him. I told you, because I give him the soup and stuff. But the other two are Moe and Kurt. I don't stay with them." Her tone made it clear that this subject was closed.

The sun began to sink below the western mountains, and the street-lights started to come on. "I'll stay with you tonight," Hailey said.

"You don't have to stay on my account," he said.

"If I go, you will be all alone."

"I will be fine, Hailey. You need to go. Be safe, okay? And you can come find me tomorrow. You know where I live. And you can *call* me."

Hailey was quiet again, resting her head on her arms, her expressive face suddenly unreadable. She stayed quiet long enough that Ryan finished reloading while he sat with his back to the wall. He pulled out the scoped AR-15 and took a shooting position, building a bone bridge: elbow on knee, leg planted on the ground, and took aim down range. He was tired, but his focus was back. With the help of the scope, he picked off 2091s with ease.

He turned back to the window and found that Hailey had left. Ryan reloaded again and worked to thin down the mob around the bus. Ryan cycled through his ammunition, recharged the magazines, and continued his extermination. He stopped at full dark, teetering toward exhaustion. The porch was covered in brass, so he swept the casings into a pile near the far end and laid out the sleeping bag. He drank some water, ate a sandwich, and cleaned his weapons while cycling the maintenance radio's preset frequencies.

The radios had always been terrible, but assuming the Pagueros were actually in the warehouse, they were less than a half mile away with no tall buildings to wreck transmission. The signal should easily travel the open distance, but he got nothing. He sighed. He was here all night no matter what. In the morning he would find a way off the porch. The battery indicator showed low. He clicked the power off, pulled the unit off his hip, disconnected the hand unit from his tactical vest, and stuffed it into the cargo bag.

As quietly as she left, Hailey returned, her face in the window.

Ryan jumped. "You are a quiet somebody!"

"Duh, that is how you sneak past zombies," she said, like the fact was as obvious as the sun, moon, and stars.

"I thought you had gone home."

"No, I told you that I have lots of places and I was going to stay here tonight. This is as safe as any of them. I went to look for some stuff," she said and handed a big blue square of plastic through the window. It was a folded, large, heavy tarp. "I was trying to find a hammer. I thought maybe you could pry those boards off, but I couldn't find one. That is in case it rains."

Rain had never been a consideration, but now that the word had been spoken, it seemed like a certainty.

"Thank you, Hailey," Ryan said and realized she was making a small nest of blankets and pillows. She handed him three couch cushions that smelled like smoke and dog, but it would be better than lying on stone. He took a few minutes to wedge the plastic into the boards and duct tape them down along the windows. Then he weighed down the bottom with the remaining ammunition. The sloping tent wouldn't stand up to hard wind, but it might keep a drizzle manageable. Ryan pulled the rifles and the three cargo bags under the tarp and arranged his sleeping bag on the cushions. He recharged magazines and readied his weapons. His hands were sore and his cheek was raw from the butt stock rubbing against his beard stubble. He was done shooting, but if something with teeth came out of the dark, he wanted to be ready.

"Are you sure you are safe in there?"

"Uh-huh," Hailey said. She was on her knees, her face poking out of the bottom of the window, chin resting on her folded arms. "The doors are all locked. And I sleep quiet. So no one is going to know I'm here." And then her voice dropped in reverence to the night. "Why don't skeletons fight each other?"

"Why?" Ryan whispered, matching her tone.

"Because they don't have the guts," she giggled. "What did Geronimo say when he jumped out of the plane?"

"I don't know."

"Meeeee!"

56

Global Infection: ≤ 33.0872%

Hailey fell asleep mid-sentence, the punch line forever lost.

Ryan listened to the night and the relentless, shuffling, milling horde. As his sweat dried, a chill ran through his body, so he wrapped himself in the sleeping bag sitting on the couch cushion, determined to stay awake.

He wasn't sure what pulled him out of sleep first: Hailey's voice or the thunder.

"Ryan! Ryan!"

He bolted upright. Loose ends from the plastic sheet chattered in the gusting wind. Ryan felt the belligerent air screaming its threat of rain.

"It's gonna storm," Hailey said, her voice a whisper like she was trying to hide.

"I'm not awake yet. Hang on."

"You need to get inside."

"Hailey, I can't fit between the boards on the windows, remember? I'll just have to pull the plastic down over me. It will be okay."

Lightning flashed.

"One, two, three, four," Hailey counted. Thunder rolled. "No! The storm is really close. You have to get inside!"

"Hailey, I can't get those boards off." Ryan pulled the tarp down. The makeshift tent held in the body heat but with the plastic down the cold bit at his skin. Ryan pulled boards on the right window and then the boards on the left but they were tight, the three inch screws deeply imbedded in the frame. "Leave it to the Paguero wizards to build to last."

Lightning long, wicked and deadly flashed just to the east.

"One, two, three, four." Thunder "You *have* to get inside!"

Ryan put the butt stock between the boards and the sill, but with the first pull he could tell the gun would break before he moved the plywood.

Lightning.

"One, two, three." Thunder. "Ryan!"

"Stop counting. I know it's close." The first rain drops hit him like bee stings. The wind grabbed the tarp and it took flight like a kite without strings.

"No!" Hailey screamed.

Ryan took aim at the screws to shoot the boards into splinters.

One second he was pulling the trigger, the next second he was staring up at the sky and Hailey was on top of him shouting his name. Ryan shook his head trying to get his thoughts to engage.

"You're bleeding. Did lightning hit you?" Hailey's voice was shrill.

"No," Ryan said, rolling to his side feeling the crease in his scalp where the bullet hit on ricochet. "I did something really stupid."

Lightning . . . thunder.

The Hustler sign swayed like a tree limb about to break. The wind tore through the street bouncing electrical lines and tossing stoplights around like a dog ravaging a chew toy and the rain washed over streetlamps, consuming their light like a swarm of locusts.

"Hailey get back inside. Go!" He scrambled to the window and started shoving the sleeping bag and the remaining ammo in the bags and the AR-15 with the night scope through the open window.

"Where are you gonna go?" she asked, her voice brittle.

"Don't worry about me!"

Hailey grabbed his sleeve. "Nooooo! I don't want you to leeeeeeaaave!"

Ryan turned her toward the storm. "You see that? The wind will blow you off."

Hailey was squeezing under the plywood before he finished his sentence. Ryan wedged himself between L and the T. The letters shivered in the rising gale rocking toward the street below. The rain hit like a fire hose. Ryan dropped over the edge.

"Noooo!!!" Hailey screamed.

Ryan stood on the bus roof. "Hailey! I will be right here! I am going to be right under here!" He crawled around the rooftop mounted air conditioning unit and rolled to his back, the underside of the porch pressing down on his face like an MRI machine.

Trash cans slam into the Port Authority bus sounding like cannon fire; it pitched and rolled like a ship at sea, vibrating like it was going to break apart under the onslaught of Poseidon's fist. The glow warbled as streetlight pole suspension arms swayed like willow trees. Some 2091's rolled with the wind like tumble weeds, some buried their faces in a fresh kill, feasting in gluttonous bites, and still others stood with their mouths open catching raindrops on their tongues.

Lightning!

Even in his peripheral vision it left a mark on Ryan's retina and the immediate thunder hit his bowels like he'd been punched.

And then it was quiet.

Rain fell and the wind blew, but the storm's intensity dropped below half. That is when he saw a shape fall on top of the bus.

Did a 2091 get blown up here?

Ryan groped for his GSG, and then he saw her. "Hailey! What the hell are you doing?"

She grabbed onto Ryan like she was trying to crawl into his skin. He pulled her close, feeling her tremble and hearing her sob. They lay unmoving, unspeaking for agonizing endless minutes, the claustrophobia growing in proportion to Hailey's chattering teeth.

It was the rhythmic strobing light that pulled Ryan out of the safe space. He saw the transformer, the telephone pole and the high voltage line swaying overhead. It took him seconds to do the geometry. "Oh God!"

"What is it?" Hailey whispered.

The wind rose again. The high voltage line groaned and jerked.

"The flashing is an electric line coming loose from a transformer. It will fall across this bus. If we are here when that happens, it will kill us."

Hailey's face went slack.

"Get back into the apartment."

"Nooooo, I want to stay with yooouuuuu!"

"I know . . . but we can't stay here."

"What are you gonna do?"

Ryan paused, thinking. "How do you get into the building?"

"The door," Hailey said, like Ryan belonged on the short bus.

"Where is the door?!" Ryan snapped, "How do you *get* to the door?!"

"Oh, it is the delivery entrance on the other side of the building. If you go to the corner and turn left, the next street, well, it is more like an alley. It is about halfway down."

"Okay, I will meet you there."

"No, there are lots of zombies. You have to sneak by them and there is no way you can do that."

"Like how many?"

"It doesn't matter. You can't sneak like I can."

The transformer glowed and crackled.

"We have to go. Now!" He climbed to the porch. Hailey slid into the apartment.

"Hand me that bag," Ryan shouted above the wind. He plucked out the two, fifty-round magazines and fit one of them into his AR-15. He stashed the second one into the empty magazine pouch on his hip. "You go down to the door. You wait for me. You will probably see me before I see you. I will be running. I will be shooting."

"Nooooo, don't goooo!"

"Hailey—"

The transformer sparked, the cable swayed.

"I will be there!" he said, jumping to the bus roof. He tightened the tactical vest, checked the flaps and fasteners and pressed the GSG 1911 into his SERPA. The storm had scattered ghouls hither and yon, but dozens had resumed their teeming, groping, vigil around the bus.

Ryan leaped.

He threw himself toward the back row of hands flattening his body like he was splashing into a pool. He expected it to hurt. He expected to get the breath knocked out of him, but he wanted to avoid twisting an ankle or wrecking his knee. And he learned something that day that most people will never know; zombies are soft.

Ghouls took the force of Ryan's body in the arms and chest as he rode them down to the asphalt. He felt bones break, but they were not his. Ryan rolled to his feet and started that fast moving heel-toe crouch that he'd seen Raphael demonstrate.

He didn't think when the first 2091 lurched; he reacted—stock on shoulder, cheek on stock, sight picture. *Pop!* Instant ragdoll. All the instruction, all the practice, all the tediously slow-moving training blossomed exactly as Marco said it would: slow was smooth, smooth was fast.

Pop! Pop! Pop!

His rifle barked and the infected dropped.

Moving and dodging, he made it to the alley and saw the zombies. Hailey was right. There were a lot—more than he could count.

Ryan shot ten and checked his six.

Lightning flashed, filling the night with a preternatural strobing, turning everything into an amorphous, malevolent roiling hallucination. The hoard was coming, stumbling, churning and lurching with single-minded purpose. The rolling mass of Fort Pitt had spotted prey.

If he dashed for the delivery entrance he would be caught between the two mobs.

"Hey here! Here!" Ryan shouted down Mulberry Way, waving his hands. "Come on damnit, move!"

He waited . . .

The Fort Pitt mass stumbled closer and closer.

Twenty feet, nineteen feet, eighteen feet . . .

The alley zombies moved fast.

Ryan ran west toward downtown, past 19th, 18th and 17th streets. Driving rain battered his eyes and the wind savaged his soaked body. He jumped atop a car, waving his arms. The fast movers came at a trot and he shot them as he waited for the hoard to catch up. As the leading edge came to a kill, they dropped to their knees to feed until the river of infected flowed around them like stones. The human menace glided toward him, determined, dogged, impervious—slithering around cars and through the narrow streets. When the head of the snake was near the intersection Ryan bolted.

He dashed across Liberty, turned left out of sight and snuck through the side streets until he was back at Mulberry Way. He peeked down its narrow length. His plan had worked . . . almost. Six 2091s were on all fours, feasting on the bodies he'd killed minutes ago.

Ryan raised his riffle, took slack out of the trigger—and froze. The gunfire would bring the horde down on his head. He snuck down the alley.

Two security lights stood vigil like all-seeing eyes.

Ryan slipped around the outer darkness.

Two 2091's looked up.

Ryan froze.

They returned to eating.

He gave the first door a tug. It was locked. Then he gave the barest knock.

No answer.

He moved to the second door, but it was obvious it hadn't been opened in years.

He passed a high chain-link fence that closed off a walkway that wound back out of sight. Barbed wire covered the top, and the gate was secured by a heavy lock.

The last door was fifteen feet farther, bathed in light right beside the 2091's.

Could Hailey sneak past that?

Ryan ducked between two dumpsters lined against the chain-link fence. "What the hell?"

"I'm here."

Ryan jumped. The dumpster thrummed.

"Come on," Hailey said, pushing on a corner of the fence.

Ryan squeezed under the chain link and stood in a delivery walkway. Hailey led him by the hand through building to the second floor. She locked the apartment door and led Ryan into a front room with old furniture that smelled of smoke and dog and urine. From the boarded window, he could see the Hustler sign, the sparking transformer, and the bus.

He slumped against the wall opposite the windows and furniture, body shaking, breathing hard, dripping puddles.

Thunder crashed. Lightning flashed. Wind shrieked.

Hailey dropped to her knees and crawled under his arm.

Outside, the high voltage cable gave a shriek, a hiss, and jumped toward the bus like a viper. Streetlights went out and the room faded to black.

Before he fell asleep, Ryan smelled roasting pork.

57

Global Infection: ≤ 33.2672%

The *Superbeast* ringtone blasted him from sleep.

During the night, Ryan woke to shed sodden clothes and hang them to dry. Old man Renfro had not been concerned with clean, but he found sweat bottoms and a T-shirt a size too small that didn't seem hazardous to wear. Ryan found Hailey shorts that fit her like pantaloons and a T-shirt that was too big. She was half asleep and fully reluctant to be near Ryan as she changed. She hid in a bedroom, handing wet clothes through a small crack in the door, then locked it.

He used detergent to rinse out her pants and underwear and socks in the sink and made a makeshift clothesline. The old building had registers built into the floor with good airflow, and put their shoes upside down over them.

He noticed the time on a battery-operated wall clock just before he lay back down on his sleeping bag.

It's only ten?

That was Ryan Sage's last thought before the muffled refrain:

The ragged they come and
The ragged they kill!
You pray so hard on bloody knees.
The ragged they come and
The ragged they kill!
Down in the cool air I can see.

woke him from a nice dream.

From the sleeping bag, he rolled to all fours, soreness screaming down his body. He stood with a groan, walked to the kitchen and plucked the phone off the counter. "Yes!" he said, not bothering to take the edge out of his voice.

"You are alive?" It was Raphael.

"The Holy Mother is watching out for me, right?"

"We tried to call, but you do no answer."

Annoyed, Ryan pulled the phone away from his ear and tapped the call log. It was true. There were over a dozen calls in the last two hours.

"Where were you when I was trying to get you on the radio?" Ryan said to himself.

"What?"

"Nothing. Where are you? You in the tower?"

"The tower? No, we are in the warehouse. How did you survive? How did you get all those devils to move? We can no believe how you did this."

Ryan rolled his eyes. "Of course you can't."

"The Holy Mother, she intercedes for you. She *es* protecting you," Raphael said. "Marco es driving to you. He es bringing the Stryker."

"Wait. Marco is driving *to* me? Why is he doing that?"

"We are stuck in the warehouse for many hours, and Marco was getting sick. He have to go back to the tower to sleep and get the Stryker. Simone and I stayed to work. Marco, he call me early and tell me to call your phone. When you do no pick up, he es worried about you. He *es* coming now."

Ryan went to the window and squinted in the early morning sunlight. The horde was scattered down the full length of Smallman Street and along the vast expanse of the refugee camp. "No, the horde is still out there. The moment he drives anywhere near me, they will mob us. He needs to get that breach closed."

"*Es mui importante* to get you. If we cannot make it work today, *es* okay."

"Since when? Marco is getting sicker, right? He still needs the meds in the camp, right? I did my part of the plan; you finish yours."

"Yes?"

"Tell him to close the gap."

Ryan heard the maintenance radio crackle in the phone. Raphael spoke in rapid Spanish and Marco's brief response was heated. "Marco say he *es* coming anyway."

"Like hell he is. I'm not behind the sign. He doesn't know where I am. I will get to the fort myself. Tell him to close the breach. I'll be at Fort Pitt in a few minutes." Ryan hung up.

Ryan felt his clothes. They were damp but tolerable. He started to dress.

The ragged they come and
The ragged they kill!

Ryan jammed the phone to silence and pushed his feet into cold damp shoes. "Hailey? Hailey?! I've got to go."

Hailey opened the bedroom door a crack, her hair had dried in a jumble of blond waves and sleep was hanging on her eyelids like a ten-pound weight. The shirt and shorts made her look like a cross between a gangster wannabe and an Oompa Loompa from the Willy Wonka and the Chocolate Factory. "Where are you going?"

Ryan shrugged into this tactical vest and checked his weapons. “I have to get down to the place you showed us on the map. That map you gave us will probably save someone’s life.”

She rubbed her eyes. “But what about the zombies?”

“They are spread out, so I can run to the walls. You won’t be able to keep up if I run. Do you think you can get there by yourself?”

“Of course,” Hailey said.

“Okay. But if you change your mind, you can meet me at the tower. That would be much safer.”

“No, I want to come too. I will get to the fort. I will get dressed. I won’t be long.”

Ryan reached into a cargo bag and grabbed a Power Bar and a bottle of water and handed them to her. “Breakfast of champions,” he said with a wink.

He cinched the cargo bag strap down tight. He moved through the building, under the fence and crouched between the dumpsters. His friends were still in place, maintaining their mindless vigil. The fifty-round drum magazine was more than half full, but he chose discretion. He rose, walked the opposite direction, around the block down Penn Avenue. He crossed Smallman on the far side of St. Stanislaus.

The Port Authority bus was half buried in a mound of dead . . . undead. The cable lay across the bus, snapping and sparking, and anyone could predict the culinary result: two parts wind, four parts rain, one stick of metal tube, add sardine-packed 2091’s, cook at seven thousand volts for seven hours. Breakfast is served.

2091s shambled up Smallman to kneel at the buffet as if they had manners. Others didn’t bother with formality, grabbing a leg to rip it from its socket and gnaw on a thigh bone. Ryan moved past the feast at a brisk walk. Twenty infected stared at him, fathomless eyes turning with his movement, their bellies distended like African famine children standing idle in their misery. But not everyone was satisfied with the breakfast bus, choosing free-range human over processed.

The first 2091 ran; then two, then three and then the dominoes started toppling, and they seemed faster than yesterday.

Ryan dashed between semis and over debris and plowed through the small crowd at the HESCO wall. He climbed using the wire mesh cells for hand holds until he pulled himself over the top and collapsed in a gunner’s nest with a dead body in a military uniform leaning against the machine gun stand.

Ryan rolled to his back, gasping.

The top of the HESCO wall was almost ten feet wide. The gunner’s nest was built with sandbags and plywood for a base. The nest was littered with spent brass, a 7.62 caliber machine gun tilted muzzle to the sky on a motorized tripod, its ammo box empty.

Ryan kept watch on the corpse and shed the heavy cargo bag. He’d seen enough horror films to know that the moment he looked away, it would come to life and eat his face.

The large hole in the soldier's stomach and the crusted pool of blood on the plywood explained the cause of death, but it seemed that humans were suddenly able to survive untold trauma. It wasn't right to call them the undead, but rather the undying. Just to be safe, he put three rounds into its skull.

The south side of Fort Pitt was constructed of HESCO wall, interlinking heavy wire cubes lined with high-grade plastic sheeting that expanded like an accordion to be filled with dirt or stone. Each five-foot by five-foot cell was filled, and then another row of cells was stretched on top and filled and then another to create a wall forty feet wide at the base and thirty feet high. HESCO barriers were a fast means to control a flooding riverbank, build a temporary shelter, a bunker in the theater of combat or, as it turns out, a brilliant solution to keep 2091s from eating brains.

The HESCO side of Fort Pitt was four hundred feet long with gunner's nests at intervals along the top. The west side of the Fort Pitt was lined with three stacks of three shipping containers with names like Hanjin, "K" Line, Hapag-Lloyd, and Maersk adorning the sides.

It was at the intersection between HESCOs and a stack of Hanjin containers where the gap opened Fort Pitt to the world. Maybe the gap had been designed to give egress, a flaw in the fortress design, or maybe the gap had been opened in a desperate attempted to escape the horror story within. Whatever the cause, it was this passage that needed to be closed.

Ryan stood in a HESCO cube indifferent to the mass of groping hands just two dozen feet below his ankles as the Stryker M1132 Engineer Squad Vehicle maneuvered through the maze of security outposts and tractor trailers until it rolled to a stop.

Marco sat inside a small hatch. "Oh my God," he said above the engine noise. "I thought you made a liar out of me and got yourself killed."

A dozen snappy comments flooded Ryan's mind, but 2091swere squeezing through the opening into Fort Pitt. "Get this closed," Ryan shouted, rolling his hand to signal *let's get a move on.*

Marco put the massive vehicle in gear and pushed the Stryker's IDE clearing blade against the stack of three shipping containers. The eight-wheel machine with the Caterpillar C7 power plant closed the gap, but the objective required Marco to flex some diesel engine muscle and lean on the gas, and then leaned on it some more, and then still more. Inch by painful inch, the triple stack of shipping containers moved. As the engine grew in pitch, it became clear that the Paguero plan had not merely been some ruse. Getting the horde away from the fort had been essential. The Stryker would never have been able to push three loaded containers through a wall of meat.

Ryan's mind worked through the implications and conceded Raphael's concerns as he waved Marco off when the gap closed. But that still didn't mean that Raphael hadn't considered the happy accident of his death.

Marco turned the Stryker and cut a path through the lingering 2091s with the surface mine plow. Stryker tires are the size of an average woman, and vehicle bottom is built like a boat with ground clearance. Without the

IDE blade, the infected would have been knocked down and suffered little. But the blade was shaped like a snow plow designed to clear bombed-out vehicles and sweep away explosives. It turned a swath of 2091s into mush as he retraced his path back through the wrecked camp toward downtown route before doubling back to the warehouse.

Assuming Ryan could lure the hoard from Fort Pitt's walls and they could close the gap, the Paguero part of the plan was to infiltrate the warehouse from the Allegheny River side undetected. Eliminate any 2091's inside and finally build a way to control the flow of infected through the wall for systematic extermination. And finally, they would expand the existing hole with a shaped charge.

Raphael's plan had only one requirement: save the transport truck. An explosion so close to the engine would destroy it. Father and sons offered up a dozen ideas to rescue the truck that all ended with fighting the 2091s inside the fort. After they had nixed the last option as another suicide mission, Ryan said, "Too bad we don't have a ninja."

Simone called him a knob.

"Ninjas could climb down from the roof unseen because Ninjas are magic." Ryan was being absurd.

But the Pagueros didn't think it was ridiculous at all.

Rappelling is done butt first by hopping down the wall. But Special Forces, from Delta to SEAL, learned to rappel face first so they could shoot as they descended. Rappelling face first was the very skill Raphael Paguero taught his sons in the quest for paramilitary mastery. Rappelling face first was the skill Simone practiced yesterday down the face of the brick tenement. "I'm your ninja," he said over and over, treating the exercise as a lark, a joke to be had at Ryan's expense.

Today, Simone moved across the warehouse roof strapped into his climbing gear where he tested and retested the ropes. He was dressed in BDUs, leather jump boots, and Carhartt jacket in case 2019s got within biting distance. He was sprouting weapons like he was fertilized with gun powder. He waited patiently for Raphael's signal.

Ryan heard the distant purr of the Stryker's engine on the northeast side of the warehouse and then go quiet.

Simone tilted his head to talk into the maintenance radio. He walked to the roof's edge and gave Ryan a thumbs-up. He took his face first step down the warehouse wall. Simone took five slow, quiet strides down the building.

And he slipped.

ACT 4

58

Global Infection: ≤ 33.2674%

One second Simone looked like an action hero; the next he was tumbling like a stupid stuntman in a home movie. He spun and jerked and twisted in the ropes and then landed on his shoulders.

Ryan started shouting and then started shooting. Any 2091 that looked like it was headed toward Simone got a bullet to the head. He triggered through the drum in less than a minute, his kill rate dropping toward zero under pressure.

"Raphael!" Ryan shouted. "I need some help out here! Simone is down. Simone is down!" For a minute, he thought he could keep the zombies entertained, taunting them from the top of the wall, but he was wrong, very wrong.

At first Simone didn't move; he didn't seem to breathe. But suddenly he let out a wail as he rolled on a depleted sand pile about ten feet from the truck cab. It wasn't soft, but it wasn't asphalt. Had he spun the other direction Simone would have cracked his skull on the Army truck and broken his neck.

The 2091s at the back of the mosh pit turned but could not see anything resembling breakfast. From ground level, the scattered crates, tents, boxes, cots and stray carcasses camouflaged Simone's prone body.

And then Simone moaned again.

Watching the 2091s shift was like watching dance moves in a music video: jerking, halting, and twitching images with no synchronization, rhythm, or context.

"Do you hear me?!" Ryan shouted. "Simone has fallen!" He slapped in a new magazine and started shooting. But Ryan could not keep his hands still. He missed, only taking chunks out of the creatures that lurched toward the sound.

"Simone! Stop moving. Simone! Go still!" But the boy could not hear through the fog of pain. He kept touching the parts of his body that hurt. He started to cry.

Ryan sprinted to the gunner's nest and grabbed the M16 off the body and all the full 5.56 magazines he could find and stuffed them into ammo pouches. He pulled the M9 from its holster and dropped the magazine. It was full. Then he raided the soldier's remaining 9mm magazines. He ran the length of the HESCO wall and climbed down. The back side was tiered like an Aztec pyramid. He jumped down level by level until he could leap the five-foot gap to the roof of the Army transport.

Ryan dropped to the ground. "Simone is down!" he shouted through the small hole.

"I'm coming!" Raphael shouted between smashing the concrete with a sledge hammer. "Get down!" Raphael snapped, raising his rifle into the hole.

Ryan dropped.

Raphael opened up with his Kalashnikov. His weapon belched in three round bursts, 2091 heads turning to puree with each report.

At first the 2091s moved at glacial pace. The camp was in shambles, filled with endless makeshift barricades that created a maze. The infected wound through the jumble, churning, moaning and groping toward two choke points. The one to the left was between the end of the truck bed and a pile of crates. The choke point to the right was between the crates and two skids stacked with 55 blue five-gallon water drums. Ryan scrambled to the right, butt stock to shoulder, cheek to stock, sight picture . . . *Crack!*

But this was a different kind of crack! This had kick. He was used to the little pop of the .22 round, but the NATO 5.56 was closer to being a killer. The first seven shots were wild as he learned to lean into the weapon and hold the muzzle down. He advanced to within twenty feet and shot level with their heads.

Skulls exploded.

Ryan's shots were like the slow staccato of a metronome clicking off 80 beats a minute for a waltz. Raphael's shots came like thrash metal, clusters of destruction, pounding the 2091s into oblivion.

The M16 ran dry as four creatures surged through Ryan's choke point. He pulled the Berretta, took two strides forward and pulled the trigger. From eight feet, it was impossible to miss: a firefighter, a nurse, an EMT tech, and a private. The M9 bucked in his hand eleven more times, each pull of the trigger sounding like a sledgehammer strike against concrete until the chamber locked back empty and smoking, the bottleneck filled with bodies.

Ryan groped for magazines and finally slammed one into the gun butt and racked the slide. "Simone! Simone! Can you hear me?" he shouted as he holstered the Berretta and replaced a magazine in the M16.

"*Es* he all right?" shouted Raphael.

"He is hurt, but I can't tell how bad. He is moving his arms and legs. I need some help out here."

"Marco *es* coming. He *es* on the roof. *Es* anything broken? Check arms and legs." Raphael shouted between the *clang, clang, clang* of the beating sledgehammer.

"I don't feel anything out of place," Ryan shouted back. He looked up just in time to see the right choke point fail. He strode forward to engage at point blank range. He fired 30 rounds from the M16, pulled his GSG, fired ten more, pulled the Berretta and fired fifteen more. But still they kept coming, pawing their way over the bodies.

"Marco, where are you?!" Ryan scrambled back to Simone and pulled the machete off his belt thinking it a wonder the kid hadn't impaled himself. He strode back to the chokepoint and started swinging. He decapitated one ghoul on the first swing. On the third swing, it got stuck in a fat doctor's skull. "Just for the record," he said, putting a foot into her chest for leverage. "Machetes suck!"

A 2091 lunged for his ankle.

Ryan fell back and crab-walked away. And that was when he noticed Marco hanging ten feet off the ground, clinging to the rope like a kid stuck in a low-hanging tree.

"Marco! Are you okay? Marco!" Ryan shouted as he fumbled magazines into his weapons.

Marco thrashed his head from side to side. "Nooooooo."

"Marco! Marco, listen. Can you get back to the roof? Can you get up? You can shoot from there."

"I can't," he said, barely above the noise. "I can't move."

"What? What *es* happening?" Raphael shouted through the hole. "Where *es* Marco?"

"Raphael, can you get through that wall? Can you blow the charge?"

"I can no blow the charge with you close. You must get away."

"There is nowhere to go!"

"Where *es* Marco? What happened to Marco?"

"I can't . . ." Marco moaned. "I can't move."

"Behind!" Raphael shouted. Ryan dropped. His Kalashnikov delivered a barrage of devastation.

The choke points were coming apart against the driving mass of malignant humanity.

"One magazine," Raphael said.

Ryan pushed a mag through the hole.

"No. This *es* Kalashnikov. I need different ammunition."

"Where the hell do I get commie bullets?!" Ryan said. He pushed his M16 through the hole. "You shoot. Don't miss."

The muzzle pressed back through the wall.

Feeling naked, Ryan scrambled to Simone, unsnapped his AR-15 and raided his magazine pouches.

"Out!" Raphael called.

And that was when they heard the bark of another rifle. Ryan glanced up thinking Marco had returned to the roof, but he still hung in the air. Ryan scanned the Fort Pitt of death and saw Hailey with the .22 resting on the gunner's nest firing into the crowd. "Hey!" she shouted. "Over here, zombies. Come eat me!"

Ryan pushed five magazines through the hole. "Here!" he said and turned to do battle. Every time they stopped firing, the tide of zombies surged. He burned through three magazines.

"Hailey! Hailey!" Ryan said. "Come here!" She dropped the rifle and ran toward the truck. When Raphael stopped to reload, Ryan climbed halfway up the cab. "I need you to look in those gunner's nests for magazines that look like this. Make sure they are full of bullets!" He held up the 9 millimeter and the 5.56 magazine. He threw the empties at her feet. She picked them up and in a flash, she was searching.

Ryan scrambled back to Simone. "Can you hear me? Simone, I need to get you up on the truck. Can you hear me?"

Raphael's weapon started chattering again.

Ryan had to move Simone to the truck. He pulled him by his tactical vest, trying to right him.

Simone screamed.

It could have been his back or his ribs or a collar bone. It didn't matter. They had to move.

Ryan hoisted him into a fireman's carry and Simone screamed again. "Raphael, cease fire. Cease fire." But he hadn't moved fast enough.

"Behind!" Raphael shouted.

And that was when Ryan felt something grabbing at his thigh. Ryan's heart seized. Certainly, that was a zombie ready to take a bite.

The GSG fired behind his head.

Simone was shooting. He emptied the magazine. "I'm out," he said, his voice coming out with strain. "Give me another. I can shoot." It took seconds to lean him against the wall. Ryan put a weapon in his hand.

"Get my shotgun," Simone said. "There!" It had fallen off his back and slid to the far side of the sand pile.

Ryan scrambled to the shotgun as the infected closed in. He rose as the front six zombies reached for his throat. He pulled the trigger. The shotgun choke was set to deliver an arc of destruction; the 2091s lost their heads in groups. Each pull of the trigger beat back the surge by a body length.

"Out," Ryan said, fumble shells into the loading port.

"Reloading," Simone said, slapping a magazine into the GSG. "Give me the shotgun."

"Last magazine," shouted Raphael. "Marco! Marco! Get in this fight. Do you hear me! Get in this fight."

Marco moaned from above, his head thrashing back and forth. "I can't be near them."

"Marco!" Ryan said. "Drop your ammo. Drop it now!"

"Ryan!" Hailey called. "Here!" She heaved the cargo bag. It landed on the truck's roof.

Raphael reloaded.

Ryan stepped up on the truck's fuel tank and pulled the bag down just in time to drop out of Raphael's line of fire.

"God damn, that man can reload fast!" Ryan said. The roar of the weapon over his head pounded his mind like a cage fighter. Hailey found ten magazines—six 5.56 and four 9 millimeter.

Simone speed-loaded eight shells in the shotgun and moved a step forward. The shotgun belched thunder once. He caved in on himself, dropping the shotgun and clutching his sides.

Ryan slammed a magazine into the carbine and stuffed two 5.56 and four 9 millimeter into his pouch. The rest he pushed through the hole in the wall. He pushed a Beretta into Simone's hand and scrambled for the shotgun. Seven times he pulled the trigger, and rows of 2091 heads exploded.

"Out," Ryan said.

"Out," Simone said, finishing the last round from his sidearm.

They traded weapons. Ryan filled the M9 with a magazine and Simone loaded the shotgun like he was dealing cards from the bottom of a deck. They traded back and the destruction followed. The two repeated the cycle three more times. They burned through the ammunition as fast as the infected advanced, the pile of dead inching closer and closer, growing higher and higher. Each man, by turn, announced he was reloading until . . .

"Out," said Simone, slumping down the wall holding his side.

"Out," Ryan said.

"Raphael, we are coming to the truck. Hold your fire. Hold your fire!"

Three shots later Raphael said, "Out!"

Ryan pulled Simone toward the truck and tried the door.

Locked!

The window was down a few inches, but Ryan could not reach the release. The side of the truck had built-in handholds, but climbing them might as well have been ascending Mount Everest. Simone could barely stand, barely breathe, screaming in pain every time he raised an arm.

"I can't lift you Simone," Ryan said, "You have got to help me."

"Behind you," Raphael shouted as he tried to squeeze through the hole, but he didn't fit. "Get on the truck now! Get up!"

"Ryan! Ryan! Ryan," Hailey screamed. "The zombies!"

It was then that they heard the scream from above, like a wounded animal retaliating against an attacker. Marco dropped into the fray, his back pressed against the concrete. He was a blur. Firing, reloading, and firing again. When his AR-15 was empty, he drew a Sig Sauer P229 TB like he was in a Wild West showdown, triggering through six magazines like the pistol was on full automatic. As the last echo faded into the Allegheny River valley, it looked like a tidal wave had come to a halt at his feet in a small arc like he was a superhero with a force field that covered a circle around Ryan and Simone.

No one moved. No one breathed.

Finally, Ryan crawled to the truck's back window and slithered like a snake into the cab. His hands and legs shook as he tried to turn the ignition key. He finally started the engine and pulled it back. He rammed it into the wall twice: the concrete cracked and then caved and Raphael climbed through. When Ryan stepped down to the ground, Hailey was standing by the door. She threw her arms around him.

"Thank you," Ryan said, hugging her tight.

Raphael tended to Simone. Marco slumped against the wall, hugging his knees to his chest, his eyes focusing into the distance.

Ryan's stomach rumbled. He climbed into the truck bed looking through the supplies. He found boxes of MREs and a few cases of bottled water. He passed out brown packs and said, "Breakfast is served."

59

Global Infection: ≤ 33.2676%

I still see Greg's face when they come like that. I can't get this shit out of my head. How they tore him apart," Marco said. He was sitting on a bucket inside the warehouse, his body slumped in on itself, his face waxen. His eyes trailed out to the rows and rows of industrial shelving, but he saw nothing.

"Greg?" Ryan said as he scraped a bit out of the MRE Mylar bag with the spoon provided in the pack.

"He was my best friend in the whole world and a kick-ass operator. He was with me in New York. We were the only ones in our section to survive."

"What happened in New York? Is that where you got attacked by 2091s? Is that where you got bit?"

Marco shook his head. "No. It was so fucked up. We made it out of the city and made our way to Allentown. We were trying to get here, because so much had gone to shit. I thought it best if we hooked up with my parents. Who would have thought that Allentown would be overrun? Who fucking goes to Allentown? But the city was full of them. Those fuckers tore him apart right beside me. I told him to run . . ."

Not sure what to say, Ryan looked at Hailey sitting on a bucket beside him finishing her second MRE like it was fine cuisine. "Tastes good, huh?"

Hailey bobbed her head, mouth full.

"I'm sorry about your friend," Ryan said, "But you saved our bacon this morning."

"No, I almost got you and my brother killed. Actually I almost killed you twice. At the Hustler store yesterday and now here today."

"I wanted to punch you yesterday for the attitude," Ryan said. "But you didn't almost kill me. You made a good argument. I accepted the risks."

"Yeah, I laid the attitude on pretty thick," Marco said, looking at Simone lying on rubber mats that Raphael found in the warehouse. The teenager protested every time Raphael felt around his ribs and shoulders. "But I did almost kill him."

"You sure that would be a loss?" Ryan asked with a wink.

Marco just stared into the distance.

"Too soon?"

Marco smiled briefly. "I lost my shit just like he said I would."

Ryan asked, "Was it like that when they bit you? They just kept coming and coming and coming?"

Marco's eyes stared out to a thousand yards. He started shaking. Marco hugged himself until he stopped. "Yeah, it was exactly like that."

"Having gotten close to getting being eaten twice in twenty four hours, you won't get any criticism from me," Ryan said. "If it happens again, I will be the first to run away."

Marco appraised Ryan. "Why did you do it?"

"Do what?"

"If it was such a good idea, why didn't you run this time? Why did you jump into the pit to save my brother?" Marco asked."It's not like he's your greatest fan."

"Where else was I going to test the Paguero training methods?" Ryan asked.

Marco smiled, and this time it stayed.

"Could I have another one?" Hailey asked, finishing her MRE and rubbing her hands on her pants.

"As many as you want," Ryan said, standing up. "I'll get you one."

"I can get it." Hailey walked toward the hole in the wall and climbed the makeshift human cattle shoot and started to drop over to the other side.

To create a kill box inside the warehouse the Pagueros disassembled some industrial grade shelving often seen in big box home improvement stores, and reassembled it into a long walkway. They built a gate to control the flow of infected and outfitted warehouse forklifts with makeshift scoops to haul the bodies away. It would have been a good plan.

"Hang on girl," Ryan said. "Let me catch up."

"It's just out there," Hailey said, pointing.

"Yeah, but I will feel better if I make sure nothing is going to eat your toes."

Hailey rolled her eyes, headed through the hole in the wall, and scaled the truck into the bed. Ryan squinted into the morning sun as he watched Hailey rummage through boxes and then return holding two MREs like they were trophies.

"Is your leg hollow?" Ryan asked.

"No, my belly is."

Raphael was standing beside Marco when they returned to their buckets. "I do no think anything *es* broken. But Simone, he have a rib out of place and a concussion."

"But it hurts," Simone said, lying on his back on a pile of mats covered by cardboard. "You sure it's not broken?"

"War does no stop for anyone," Raphael said. "Get up. We have much work."

"Here, try this one," Hailey said, handing Simone an MRE. "I think this is my favorite, but maybe I'll try another one and maybe that will be my favorite."

"What is this going to do for me?" Simone asked. "I just fell off a roof."

"It might make you feel better," Hailey said, sitting on her bucket and unscrewed the cap on a bottle of water. She puzzled over adding water to the MRE heater.

"Let me help," Marco said. "You don't want to overfill. See this line here?" he said, pointing to the line on the clear plastic bag. "That is how much water you put in."

"Are you sick?" Hailey asked. "You look like you have a fever."

"Yeah, but I'm not contagious," Marco said, adding the right amount of water. "Now we put the food inside the bag, and then we put all of this in the box. You see how I did that?"

Hailey nodded, already digging into the quick cereal contained in the MRE Blueberry Granola with milk. "This is really good," she said. "I think this is my new favorite. Can't you take medicine?"

"That is why we are here," Ryan said, "to get him medicine. Speaking of, what is the plan to get from here to there? There are a lot of bodies out there."

Marco said, "There are some stragglers that we need to put out of our misery. And we are so fucked. We have no bullets. That firefight so fucked us," he whispered, holding his head in his hand. "I so fucked us."

"Marco," Ryan said. "We'll figure it out—"

Raphael stepped beside Ryan scrutinizing him, his mouth pulled down into a frown, like it was the first time he'd ever seen him. His dark eyes remained inscrutable. Finally he nodded and said, "We will go look for the medicines, yes?"

Ryan frowned. "You and I go look? Out there? Sure."

"We can't wait." Marco pushed himself to standing, but wobbled and caught himself against some shelving.

"You are wrung out," Ryan said, sliding a half-dozen large new cardboard boxes into a pile on the cold concrete floor. "You lay down and rest. Tell us what you are looking for; we'll go."

Marco swayed, and then slowly dropped onto a makeshift bed; his tremors started to subside. He reached into his pants pocket, pulled out a piece of worn paper and handed it to Ryan. "When the medic worked on me he said that if the first course of antibiotics did not work, I should look for these."

The paper was tattered, damp form sweat and the ink was faded. "Imipen . . . Impenem cil . . . astatin . . . cilastatin," Ryan said.

"Imipenem cilastatin," Marco corrected. The other two are ceftriaxone and Ampicillin sulbactam. The Ampicillin was what I was taking that made me so nauseous. The other two are broad-spectrum antibiotics. The medic wasn't sure which would be best. You are looking for bottles, not pills. Also, the medic said if I became septic, maybe I should do a blood transfusion. I really hope I don't have to do that. But if I do, my blood type is A positive, so we should find type O and A positive in that blood bank. Also in the blood bank, you will find some WFEVMT. That will help Simone with the concussion, and it will help me improve cellular repair."

Ryan shook his head. "I'm never going to remember these, and they're hard to see," he said and moved to a nearby tall desk lined with papers and inventory stickers. He turned on the light and picked up a pen. "Hailey, while you are waiting for your food to heat up, could I borrow you a second?"

Hailey finished the last bite of granola and blueberries.

"By the way, everyone, this is Hailey. Hailey, this is Marco, Raphael, and Simone."

Marco said, "Hello, Hailey."

Raphael nodded.

Simone grunted.

Hailey shifted behind Ryan, tugging on her shirt-sleeves.

"I need you to write these out on two pieces of paper so Raphael and I can read them," Ryan said. "Can you do that?"

"Or course," Hailey said, then took the pen and paper and started copying.

"So what is the plan?" Ryan asked Raphael.

Raphael paused for a moment and then pulled the machete off his hip and gave it a deft spin. "Find a weapon and we finish the rest of the devils."

By the time Ryan got back with a fire axe, Hailey was done copying. The letters were big and clear. "Good job," he said. "I bet your breakfast is done. Eat and I'll be back in a few minutes." He handed one of the papers to Raphael.

Hailey gave Marco and Simone a suspicious look. "I want to go with you."

"You know they won't bite, right?"

Hailey tugged at her coat sleeves. "Please?"

"Okay, come on." He held up the paper. "You should make one of thes—"

Hailey held up her own list.

The three climbed the cattle shoot and exited the hole in the wall. No one wanted to crawl over the mound of bodies, so they skirted the Army transport by squeezing through the space between the truck and the HESCO wall. They climbed over detritus until they found a vague path deeper into the fort that led them to the first straggler. Raphael offered to let Ryan kill the blond nurse in filthy scrubs, but suddenly all Ryan could see was the wedding ring. He couldn't burry the ax in her head.

Raphael nodded, knocked her to the ground, planted his boot on her shoulder and gave a quick, decisive thrust into the brain pan. Then he ended the miserable existence of the jawless 2091 in the Humvee, the two behind the crates in the corner of the warehouse L, the three still caged in the temporary jail, and three others that were tangled in places they couldn't escape.

There was so much chaos it was impossible to divine where to move next.

The three stood surveying the carnage when the wind shifted and the coppery odor of blood-soaked death swirled into Ryan's nose. He and Hailey gagged. Raphael smirked like he had a stomach made of iron, and then Ryan caught the smell of menthol.

"Quit holding out, tough guy," Ryan said.

Raphael produced a jar of Vicks, and Ryan and Hailey stuffed it up their noses like cocaine.

Hailey found a box of rubber gloves and passed them out like they were candy, and the search for drugs began, but it didn't go far. Looking in a crate required lifting a broken cot. Looking at a bottle on the ground required dragging a bloody blanket off the bottle. It seemed every goal had obstacles that had impediments that had hurdles.

Ryan and Raphael started with an easy objective: wrestle a 55-gallon fuel drum five feet to the generator, attach the fuel line, and hit the ignition. The engine purred to life. The camp lights flickered once, twice and stayed on. The refrigeration condensers cycled. Three industrial fans moved the air through Fort Pitt. Lights inside the mobile doctor's office lit up and the camp filled with the sound of a dozen alarms.

"You guys are taking too damned long," Marco said, leaning against the Humvee bumper. His eyes trailed toward the corpses as if he expected them to rise.

"We have no been able to move," Raphael said.

"Hey," Hailey said, crawling over a makeshift barricade. "Is this what you are looking for?" She held up a small bottle and the paper.

Marco read the label, rubbed his eyes, and read it again. "Oh, thank you!" He reached out to hug her, but she flinched. He raised his hands and said, "I won't hurt you."

Hailey fidgeted with her coat sleeves as she shuffled toward Ryan.

"Where did you get this?" Marco asked.

"It was over there by those tents," Hailey said, pointing. "I saw the dead doctors and thought maybe the medicine was close."

Marco said, "She found the antibiotics, but I need saline. There should be some close to where she found this."

Hailey led the way. "Right here." She pulled open the lid of a hard-shell case revealing rows of medicine packed in hard foam.

Marco took three more slow steps knelt. "This is a gold mine. We've got to save this case and any others like it. But I still need saline."

"What is that?" Hailey asked.

"You've seen IV bags before? That is what we are looking for. I have to mix this," Marco said, holding up the antibiotics, "with one of those bags."

Raphael stepped over a body in a white lab coat and spun the fasteners toward him. The box was secured with a bronze-colored Master Lock with a combination.

Ryan said, "I don't suppose the doctor there happened to write down the combination for us?"

Raphael looked at Ryan like he was insulted. He pulled out a small case and turned the lock so he could see the numbers. He slid a pick with a small hook into the gap above the fourth number wheel and gave a small twist. The lock popped open. "Who needs a combination?"

Ryan said, "How did you do that?"

Raphael gave a half smile. "You want to steal from peoples? What of private property?"

Ryan rolled his eyes. "Cute, Raphael. This from the man who treats the apocalypse as his own personal free-for-all. What do you think the Holy Mother thinks of you pillaging this place?"

Raphael frowned looked at Ryan, then scanned the camp. "When governments take from the peoples, when they do not follow the Constitution, they are stealing. When the government takes from the peoples to make communism they are stealing. So this place . . . I am taking back what is mine. Taking this stuff *es* no theft. Taking what has been stolen *es* called reparations, and the Holy Mother knows this. She know that we need these medicines to help Marco."

Ryan suppressed a hearty laugh. Like most mystics Raphael was a basket of intellectual contradictions. Pretty much every Papal Encyclical in the last 200 years had upheld the premise that the haves must forfeit their property to the have nots but here was Raphael, rejecting church decree to denounce the only logical social organization in harmony with the doctrine. And he was correctly identifying the US government's criminal activity, whose apparatus of power employed many methods to defeat and defy the Fourth Amendment. RICO being the leading scheme, but there were many variations of civil forfeiture. Ryan had written extensively about the despicable practice of the government confiscating assets prior to ever proving a criminal case. All the government needed to do was hold a suspicion and then preemptively take anything it deemed the product of ill-gotten gains; that logic proved to be endlessly inventive, empowering the government to take whatever it wanted whenever it wanted. So the government was able to enrich itself under the pretense of law, which made the US government the greatest organized criminal organization in the world. When a government violates the Fourth Amendment and seizes property, it is armed robbery. Everyone who participates in civil forfeiture, from local sheriffs to federal law enforcement, to judges and governors, are guilty of criminal conspiracy and have abandoned any claim to legitimacy. Any government that seizes private property with impunity can never make a claim to own anything.

Ryan nodded his approval. "Raphael, I think the Holy Mother would be right to agree with your position. And I think we finally found something that we agree on."

"I will show you how to defeat this lock. It *es* simple."

60

Global Infection: ≤ 33.2677%

Raphael picked five more locks, but still didn't find the IV solution.

"Shit," Marco said, looking around the camp, "This could take all day."

"We are looking," Raphael snapped.

"Look faster!" Marco snapped back.

Ryan said, "The RV is a doctor's office, right?"

"Yes, this *es* a good place to look," Raphael said and began climbing over barricades. He picked the lock, pulled out his machete, and opened the door. The smell of death rolled out like a fog: a nurse and a doctor, by their dress, had died horribly. The RV interior was spattered with blood and viscera. Someone had relieved themselves in the corner.

"Gross!" Hailey said and ran outside, breathing deeply.

"God dammit!" Marco whispered. "Everything in here is contaminated."

"Do no use the Lord's name in vain," Raphael said.

"You are concerned about what I say and not the fact that I need to get medicine in me?" Marco rasped, leaning against a counter.

Ryan held his hand over his mouth, breathing slow and shallow, popped the fastener off the cabinet and looked inside. He did the same to the next door and the next. "Most of the medical stuff is sealed in packaging."

Hailey stood in the threshold. "This is so gross," she said, covering her nose.

"Why did you guys leave me?" Simone pushed past Hailey.

"Hey!" Hailey snapped. "I'm *standing* here."

Simone looked at her like she was a bug. "Well, move. I want to get in."

"Ooookaaay," she said, making herself small.

Simone lost his balance and stumbled forward. He tried to catch himself, but his ribs protested and he fell on to the floor with a moan, his face slapping against a coagulated pool of festering blood. "Oh, nasty!" he said, and wretched.

"Outside," Raphael snapped. "Puke outside!"

Simone crawled to the door and down the steps and puked at the bottom. "You did that on purpose," he said between heaves.

"Duh?!" Hailey said.

Marco winked at Hailey.

Raphael smirked, opened a door latch and looked inside.

Ryan opened another cabinet. "Marco," he said. "Is this what you are looking for?"

Of course the Paguero gods of war knew how to start an IV. Marco and Simone lay down on their temporary beds—rubber mats covered with a thick layer of cardboard boxes—and Raphael started an IV for them both. Then Raphael stomped around Fort Pitt scrounging for ammunition like a heroin junkie.

Ryan said, "If we get rid of the bodies, it will be easier."

"We must find ammunition," Raphael said. "We are vulnerable if the devils come into the warehouse. How will we fight so many of the devils without guns? You should know this *es* true."

"How about Marco's training weapons? I still have a bunch of .22 rounds. I left them up on the w—"

"That *mariposa* gun *es* like a kiss. You want to kiss the devils to death?"

Ryan was pretty sure that *mariposa* meant butterfly, but he didn't have the energy to debate the merits of ballistic lethality, so he let Raphael to stew in his own futility. And after an hour of shuffling one body after another to dig through spent brass only to shuffle them back to clear more asphalt to sift through more spent brass, Raphael threw up his hands and declared they had to move the bodies first.

But they had to have someplace to move the bodies to. They disassembled parts of the human cattle shoot and then Raphael ushered everyone deep into the warehouse and detonated a shaped charge to make an opening large enough to drive the Army truck through.

There was a brief discussion on whether to load the bodies in one of the semi trailers parked in the warehouse loading bay, but they feared the noise would bring the horde to the northeast side of the warehouse—the same side that had doors and ground floor windows. The alternative was far less tidy, but much more convenient.

Raphael, the master of engineering and process efficiency, started the assembly line by putting Marco and Hailey in charge of scavenging valuables from the dead. Empty magazines were dumped into buckets. Guns were laid in a box. Ops Core ballistic helmets with mounted cameras and body armor were put in a pile. Communications headsets were put in a plastic crate. An array of units that looked like a cell phone from the 1980s wrapped in green ballistic plastic were put in another box. Dog tags and identification cards were put into large plastic jars. And the most precious commodity—bullets—were immediately loaded into weapons. Simone ran the forklift, because sitting kept him from complaining. He waited while

Ryan and Raphael loaded the dead onto the makeshift scoop. Then he drove a few feet to the HESCO wall, raised the lift to its full height, and tilted it forward. Bodies tumbled outside Fort Pitt.

"You notice how many of the infected have an axe stuck in them?" Ryan said, as he and Raphael dropped the body into the scoop. He snapped the fifteenth pair of rubber gloves off his hands. The gloves deteriorated quickly with the manual labor. He tossed them into a pile that they intended to burn.

"A few decades ago," Marco said, kneeling over a body, "the Army started issuing tomahawks to infantry. They are a great field tool and double as a melee weapon."

"They can't be too good. They get stuck," said Ryan, watching Hailey climb over a skid of Red Cross emergency kits as he doused his hands with sanitizer and put on another pair of rubber gloves. Removing the bodies would have taken half the time if they hadn't spent every few minutes trying to scrub the heebie-jeebies out of their skin.

"This does no get stuck," Raphael said, holding up his machete. To illustrate his point, he took a swing at a doctor's arm dangling off the scoop and it dropped to the ground with a wet thud.

"We need swords," Simone said, as he drove to the wall and tilted the scoop forward, watching the bodies roll out.

"You'd cut yourself on a sword," Marco said, checking the IV line taped to his arm and then slowly pulling his IV stand toward another body. "I knew guys that were swordsmen. They trained for a lifetime just to be good."

"I'd be good in a day!" Simone said.

"Bring the forklift here, Zorro," Raphael said.

"Zorro!" Hailey laughed, standing on top of narrow HESCO barrier surrounding the Fort Pitt command center: a hard shell center building with soft shell extensions on the left and right.

"Better than you!" Simone shouted.

"At what? Falling off roofs?" Hailey said with a sly smile as she climbed down into the labyrinth of crates and boxes and shrink-wrapped pallets.

"Shut up!" Simone said with a little too much force. He bent over, holding his ribs.

"*Hablen menos trabajen mas*," Raphael said, waving Simone to pull the fork lift closer. "We fill this two more times."

"But I'm hurt," Simone said. "Can't I go lie down?"

Marco said, "Let me look at your meds, little brother." He limped over to the forklift and checked the IV hanging from the roll cage and then checked the line into his arm. "It's only half done. When it's finished we can talk about sleep. Do you have a headache?"

Simone shrugged. "A little."

Marco popped a cap off some ibuprofen he found in the remains of a wrecked medical tent. "Take two of these."

"But I need to sleep," Simone said. "I've been up all night."

"War does no stop for the wounded," Raphael said, his tone unbending.

"Look what I found," Hailey said, holding out her hand to Ryan. She had a box of bullets. "When are we going to eat?"

"Where do you find this?" Raphael asked.

Hailey pointed and said, "Can we have some more of the MR thingies? They are really good, but Simone ate the one I was going to eat. So I'm kinda hungry again."

Ryan looked at his phone. "It's about noon, and we got an early start. I think we should all eat."

Raphael looked at the direction of Hailey's point. "There was more like this, yes?"

Hailey shrugged. "I think there were more. I saw some of the boxes that said Spaghetti and Meatballs. Do you think those would be good? I kinda like spaghetti, but I also saw one of them said Beef Stew. Maybe that would be good."

Raphael's knuckles grew white around the box of bullets.

Ryan said, "Why don't you show us where you found that box and then we can get some food?"

Raphael let out a breath. "Yes, show us this place, then you can have many meals."

Hailey slouched. "But I'm really hungry."

Raphael's face clouded over. "These bullets are *muy importante*—"

"Hailey, it will take one minute to show us . . . please?"

"Okay!" Hailey huffed. "It's just over here." She wound through the camp, behind the command center and then around a satellite dish protected by a narrow HESCO wall. She pointed at dozens and dozens of green cans.

Raphael knelt and put his forehead in his hand like he was praying. "We have ammunition."

Hailey looked at Ryan and whispered, "Is he going to cry?"

61

Global Infection: ≤ 33.2969%

Raphael didn't cry, but Hailey almost cried for joy when she dug into her second MRE. Ryan adjusted himself on the black crate and leaned back against the bottom level of the HESCO wall watching Raphael and Simone inspect the front of a Pittsburg Police Department SWAT vehicle. The truck was black, ornamented with standard blue and red emergency lights along the top and the manufacturer's name—Lenco—blazoned across the front. The Lenco had suffered much during the apocalypse; the left rear tire was flat, the sides were riddled with bullet dents, the spotlight on the left front was hanging by a wire, and the front left windshield was a mash of spider web cracks.

Simone winced as he slowly dropped down on all fours to stick his face underneath the Lenco's front bumper. He touched something with his fingers and rubbed them together. He looked at Raphael and said something, shaking his head. Raphael banged his fist on the hood.

Hailey picked up the M&M's that came with the MRE. "Hey, do you want these?" she said, holding out the bag. "I like them, but I've had too many. It's like all I've been eating for like days. So you can have my other candies from the other one too if you want."

Ryan reached for the bag. "Thank you."

Considering that the Bureau of Optimal Health and Medical Compliance (BOHMeC) controlled America's dietary standard with the zeal of a banana republic dictator, MREs supplied to the U.S. military were curiously unhealthy, filled with candy, snack foods and comfort entrees.

"What is your favorite M&Ms?" Hailey asked.

Ryan ripped the edge of the dark brown bag. "Peanut," he said.

Hailey swallowed. "That is my favorite too. I like regular M&M's, but I like the peanut kind better. And I like Almond Joy candy bars, but I think my favorite candy is Mentos."

Ryan frowned. "Really?"

"You don't like Mentos?"

Ryan chuckled. "Not really. But my father did. He loved them. My mother and I used to run from the room when he started eating them. We didn't like the way they smelled."

"I would have liked your dad. We could have been friends. But I'm not sure about you though."

Ryan laughed. "My dad would have liked you too. I'm sure he would have enjoyed a partner in Mentos crime."

"Hey, it's not a crime if you get away with it," Hailey said with a wink. She wiped her hands on her pants. "I gotta get back to work."

"Doing what? Looking for more magazines and bullets?"

"No, Mr. Raphael doesn't want me to do that anymore," Hailey said, "He wants me to Saran wrap that stuff on the wood thingy." She pointed at the pallet filled with medical supply crates and ammunition cans, a spool of shrink wrap sitting on top.

"You mean he wants you to put shrink wrap around that stuff on that pallet?"

"No, I have to put Saran wrap around the boxes to keep the bullets fresh."

Ryan laughed loud and long. "You are a nut."

"I know," Hailey said. "Nuttier that peanut butter."

Marco limped close. "Hate to break up the party, but I think you should see this. There are two 2091s in the Lenco."

Raphael and Simone shaded their eyes, looking in the SWAT vehicle.

Hailey grabbed Ryan by the hand. "Come on, we gotta see the zombies in that truck."

"Slow down," Ryan said. "Raphael is very good at this stuff."

"No, you have to help him kill it."

Raphael tested the front door, then the passenger door, and finally the rear doors. They were locked. When he saw Ryan, he looked at Marco and frowned.

Marco shrugged and said, "He needs to see this."

Raphael pulled out his lock picks.

"Try the hatch," Marco said, pointing with his nose to the top of the SWAT vehicle.

Still scowling, Raphael crawled up the bumper and over the bullet-riddled window. He held his weapon in his right hand and pulled the latch with his left.

Hailey tapped Ryan's shoulder and whispered, "Why is Mr. Raphael mad?"

"I don't know."

Simone made his way to the roof and looked in. "Damn." He said, "That is fucked up. There are two of them, but they are just twitching. I can't tell if they are infected or if these are two people that need help. Hey! You! Can you hear me? Hey!"

"They are devils," Raphael said.

"But I don't see any wounds," Simone said. "And I don't see blood."

"You do no smell that?" Raphael said. "No one can live like this."

"Ryan, come up here and look inside," Marco said.

Ryan stepped on the running board and looked inside. "They look like they are having one long seizure."

Raphael said, "Ryan, hand me your sidearm."

"Me?" Ryan said, reaching for his Beretta.

"No, the 1911, *por favore*," Raphael said.

Confused, Ryan slid the .22 caliber gun from the holster, checked the safety, and spun the grip to Raphael. Raphael aimed for their heads and pulled the trigger twice. He dropped inside, opened the rear hatch and pulled the bodies to the ground. Raphael spun the butt of the weapon back to Ryan without eye contact and crawled back to the driver's seat and turned the key. The battery was dead. He slammed his fist on the wheel.

Why is *Raphael so angry?*

"I think they died of heat stroke," Marco said, kneeling by the bodies.

"They stink!" Hailey said.

"You should know!" Simone mumbled.

Hailey flipped him off from behind Ryan's hip.

"Simone," Raphael called, popping the hood. "Come look at this."

"Simone, do this. Simone, do that," Simone mumbled. "I already told you that there is no coolant. They shot the hell out of the radiator. Looking again isn't going to change that."

The Lenco rear area was filled with a half dozen LAWs rockets, ten claymores, two Remington 700s with scopes, two Mossberg shotguns, two M4s and six M9s, 5,000 rounds of 5.56, 4,000 rounds of 9mm, 500 rounds of .308, and 500 00 buck. They also found a pile of empty water bottles, a dozen water bottles filled with piss, twenty plastic bags filled with something suspiciously brownish green, ten uneaten MREs and mounds of brass scattered across the floor.

"I think I know what happened." Ryan said. "This was supposed to be their Alamo. They were going to wait out the chaos and then shoot their way out."

Marco nodded toward the bullet holes and the damage to the truck and said, "And someone took serious offense at a plan that takes everything for themselves."

62

Global Infection: ≤ 33.3123%

The warehouse breakroom was on the second floor with windows that looked south and east, and it had become the staging ground for electronics and other valuables that needed evaluation. One table was lined with weapons: M16s, Berettas, Mossberg shotguns, Remington 700s with scopes and three SAWs—Squad Automatic Weapons. Another table was lined with technology. Marco had named each as they carried them to the breakroom two hours before—Nett Warrior units, Rifleman Radios, and ORACLE Huds.

"Marco? Marco? Your dad asked me to—" Ryan said as he walked into the breakroom. He stopped talking because he couldn't process what he was seeing. "Marco, what in the world is that thing?"

Marco stood at the counter wearing an exoskeleton, the frame outlined his body up to the base of his head. He swapped a power cell out of the hip. "Officially, it is called a Lockheed Martin Human Cargo Universal Carrier. Unofficially, the soldiers call them the Tony Stark."

"Tony Stark?"

"As in Iron Man, the comic book character," Marco snapped another cube into the right hip.

"I thought his suit was red and covered his whole body. That thing barely covers your chest and back."

"Picky, picky. This one augments the soldiers carrying weight and improves jumping and running and increases his combat endurance by a factor of ten. The titanium shell, the miniature arc reactor and flying was supposed to come in the next model, but then the world decided to go crazy."

"First they stop printing gossip magazines and then scientific development dies. What is a soldier to do?"

Marco gave a melancholy smile and said, "We got these in the European theater about two years ago. Some very smart people finally solved the power problem. They were lifesavers. They gave us the edge we needed against Jihad Johnny. Without them, the Caliphate would have driven us out of Italy." He looked out the window above the counter. His gaze faded into the distance. "Jihad Johnny would come at us jacked up on amphetamines and adrenaline. You could fucking butcher them and they kept coming and coming . . ." His metal-clad hand thumped the countertop. ". . . and coming . . ." The microwave jumped to the rhythm. " . . . *Allahu Akbar!* . . . *Allahu Akbar*!" The counter cracked.

Hailey rushed through the door. "What happened? I heard a crash!"

Marco shook his head like he was trying to wake from a dream.

"Nothing to worry about," Ryan said. "Marco was testing this equipment and he had some trouble."

"Oh," Hailey said. "Simone needs a pop."

"Did my brother send you up here to get that for him?"

"No, his head is hurting because, well you know, he fell." She went to the soda machine, pulled some bills out of her pocket, and put four dollars in the machine. "My mom used to have migraines and she always wanted me to get her a Mountain Dew. She said the caffeine helped." She pressed the button and a bottle rumbled out of the shoot. She put in four more dollar bills and pressed the button. "Ryan, you're coming back outside, right? I'm trying to find all those black thingies that go into guns. It's kinda fun looking for them, but it's a lot since the camp is so big. Mr. Raphael said he doesn't want me to look everywhere, but just near like where Simone is sitting. Anyway, I got to get back down there, because this is getting warm." Hailey bolted out of the breakroom and down the stairs.

"Speaking of caffeine," Ryan said. "I think she has had too much."

"And God, can she ask questions." Marco said. Hailey peppered Marco every time she found him standing still. "She even made notes about those MREs." He opened a small compartment in the Stark's left chest plate and fastened an IV bag inside. He flicked the tube that ran through the mechanical arm into the needle in his vein. He picked up an M16, slapped a magazine into the weapon, pulled the charging handle and snapped it into the sling integrated into the exoskeleton.

"They thought of everything, didn't they?"

"The goal is to keep war fighters killing even when they're wounded. If you get shot to hell, the corpsmen starts the WFEVMT IV, pats you on the ass and sends you back to the war."

"You know I have no idea what WFEVMT means, right? I don't speak military acronym."

"WFEVMT," Marco said, starting for the breakroom door, the servos in the exoskeleton a mere whisper as he walked. "War Fighter Eternity Vaccine Maksimov Therapy, but it's different than civilian treatment." He paused at the top of the stairs trying to keep his balance.

Ryan put a steadying hand on Marco's shoulder. "Why don't you lie down?"

Marco shrugged. "What is my father's favorite line? War does no stop for the wounded."

"I think he says that to whiny teenagers," Ryan said "Not grown men who are trying to ward off death."

Marco said, "I'm doing better. The drugs are working, and I also found some stuff to help with the nausea. And the Stark will keep me from exhaustion. It will do most of the lifting for me." They walked down the stairs, through the warehouse and exited the hole in the wall and stepped into the midday sun. The weather was mild with a breeze blowing from the west helping the fans to carry the stench out of Fort Pitt.

Simone sat leaning against the warehouse wall with buckets of empty magazines lying around his feet. He was slowly pressing rounds into the magazines.

Marco looked at the bucket with full magazines. "You haven't gotten any more done than that?"

"Bite me," Simone said. "And you're the one who lost his shit. We wouldn't have empty magazines if you had come to get me, because we wouldn't have had to shoot all those zombies. We could have done the plan."

Marco's eyes drew down into hard points.

"What?" Simone said. "I'm just saying . . ."

Marco breathed deep, shook his head, and walked toward Raphael.

Hailey came with a handful of handguns and magazines. She stacked them neatly in bins at Simone's feet.

"Gee, thanks," Simone said.

"You're welcome," Hailey said, "Hey, why does history repeat itself?

"Don't care," said Simone.

"Because it doesn't listen," she said and ran off to continue the hunt.

"She is just trying to make you feel better," Ryan said.

"But she stinks," Simone said, taking a drink of Mountain Dew. "How can you stand to be near her?"

"Simone, we all smell ripe right now. And that includes you," Ryan said. "That girl has lasted by herself in this city for who knows how long."

"Well, tell her to take a bath."

"Be nice. I know it is tough for you. But be nice."

Simone squinted at Ryan and then pressed two more bullets into a magazine. "Why do you even care?" he said. "She's just gonna die."

Something hard and wicked stabbed at Ryan's heart; it was like the Oracle of Delphi had spoken an evil portent and the future was set. His breath caught for a minute before he could speak. Finally, he said, "Why would you say such a thing? That girl saved your life."

"She's the reason I'm hurt. Without her stupid map, none of this would have happened," Simone said. "And I'm not going to be the one who has to go find her when she's . . . when she's . . . in a tub . . ." He used the corner of his T-shirt to wipe his eyes.

63

Global Infection: ≤ 33.3784%

The camp beyond the walls of Fort Pitt looked even more wretched as the sun started to set on the western horizon; the reddish orange glow doused everything in the color of dried blood, inspiring Ryan to calculate mortality as he leaned against a gunner's nest atop the HESCO wall. The night running the streets with monsters and surviving waves of malignant humanity suddenly seemed trivial in light of the future. A shiver made him hunch, but it wasn't from the evening breeze; it was from the weight of reality crushing down on his mind. In the penthouse the unraveling world had been an abstraction as if it was a television show; something crafted in the mind of a mad genius to be visited at leisure. But the brutality and savagery writ large in the wrecked camp was a hard punch to the jaw: staggering and sobering in one blow.

"You look pale," Marco said, climbing the last HESCO cube to the top.

Ryan jumped. "Holy shit! You startled me."

"I've been calling you for ten minutes. You're a jerk for making me crawl all the way up here."

"Where is your Stark? That would have made the climb simple."

"I had some problems with the batteries. It is charging now."

Ryan looked around, his awareness of the world expanding past his rumination: Raphael at the far end of Fort Pitt taking a count of some crates, Hailey crawling down the shipping containers spelunking into new places and Simone laying atop the Humvee hood. "You know, they make little brothers for just such menial errands. You should have sent him up after me."

"His solution was to shoot you to get your attention. Fortunately Hailey made it crystal clear that would be a bad idea."

"I'm glad I have one ally." Ryan stood trying to shake some life into his limbs. He'd sat long enough that his butt was asleep. "So is your father finally ready to take the first load to the tower so we can sleep in our own beds?"

"I asked him to wait for a few minutes, because I wanted to talk to you."

"About what?"

Marco looked towards the Pittsburgh skyline, thinking. Then he said, "Before I get to that, would you mind telling me what you were thinking on so hard? You obviously didn't hear us calling you and you really did look pale."

"Do I lose man points if I confess that I'm scared?" Ryan swept a hand wide indicating the tableau of horror spreading into the distance. "I came up here to take a break, but my mind doesn't seem to sit still. The more I looked at the city the more I realized what has happened. Civil society is dead . . ."

"No, you don't lose man points. That is probably the sanest thing I've heard you say yet," Marco said. He watched the infected fight over the carcasses dumped outside the walls. "Maybe now you understand why going to Maine is the right choice."

"Yeah, I understand why Raphael thinks it's best to leave the city," Ryan said, the evening breeze blowing his gray hair in swirls.

"You know we have two locations, right?" Marco asked. "The closest is in the Adirondacks. We can probably be there in a week. The long-term camp is way up by the Canadian border. That place is like being on the moon and we could survive out there forever. There are lots of resources . . . water, wild game, and fish for eating. There are plenty of trees for heating fuel, but we do have a generator and gasoline for the important things. The winter climate is rugged, but the growing season will keep us in staples. We have a secondary place across the border with vehicles. This would give us access to the Atlantic coast and I heard that Nova Scotia sealed its roads, its air space and its shores, so there is a good possibility that it will remain uninfected. The population is right at a million people, so maybe in time we can make some friends. "

"I always did think the Canadian accent was sexy," Ryan said.

"And I can tell you from experience that the ladies are very, very warm and welcoming."

Food, security, and women: Ryan felt longing gnaw into his belly. He'd declared his independence while sitting far removed from reality. How much of that had been bravado? How much was commitment to principle?

"This fort is a treasure trove," Marco said. "We are going to want to take what we can to our camps."

"There is plenty here to take." Ryan saw Hailey emerge from behind stacks of fuel drums. She showed something to Raphael, then pointed back the way she'd come. After a minute Raphael shooed her away. "The big challenge will be finding a path that will let you drive a Stryker and a truck all the way to Maine. That is your fathers plan, right? That is why he didn't want to blow up the military transport. He thinks it is his part of the spoils."

"My father has many plans. That is his strength and his weakness I think. He's always calculating," Marco said. "You know the best part of going to Maine? There won't be any 2091s, or at least not many. The terrain and the climate will keep the infected away. Most of them will freeze long before they get to us. And that assumes they can even walk through the mountains."

Ryan forced a laugh. "Are you trying to rub it in?" Feeling a twinge of frustration he said. "You know, there are some problems with your father's plan.

People are leaving the cities, which means in six month those mountains you think are empty will be filled with roving bands of hungry barbarians who won't freeze because they know how to make fire and drive cars. They will be stalking through the mountains looking to loot every camp they come across."

"I don't think that is true," Marco said, "Did you read through Gus's notes? The total global infection is somewhere around 30 percent. He projects it will double in less than eight weeks and inside four months the global infection will spread to 93.6 percent. In six month the species known as man will be near extinction. Statistically speaking, the only thing walking through any mountains anywhere will be 2091s."

"Wow. No. I didn't read that part of his report." Ryan rubbed the crease in his forehead as if to wipe away a headache. "But if those numbers are right then maybe it isn't a good idea to be on the back side of the moon."

Marco frowned. "How can you say that with those . . . things feeding less than a few feet away? Every day we are here. Every minute we are on the streets we are in danger of being torn apart."

"I'm not dismissing the danger here. In light of Gus's numbers I was just thinking that there is an unforeseeable danger in going to the wilds of nowhere." Ryan shrugged. "I was just talking out loud. I guess it doesn't really concern me."

"What unforeseeable danger?"

"By the time you get all the way to Maine it will be the middle of the summer and you won't be able to grow anything. It seems unlikely that you will be able to plant food this year. The first winter will be subsistence living."

"We have supplies," Marco said. "My parents have prepared for this."

"For this? Or was she preparing for a civil war?"

"All right, not this, exactly. Who could even think to prepare for this? She was convinced that America was going to descend into a Marxist revolution. She grew up listening to the pre-revolutionary propaganda in Paraguay as a young girl, so when it started here she thought it inevitable."

"Right, but a civil war is not a total collapse. A civil war would cripple American production, but it would not destroy it, at least not in the beginning. So supplies might be scarce, but you could get them. With a 93 percent infection rate all production is going to end in six months. There isn't going to be anything to get, because there isn't going to be anyone to make it. Marco, we are weeks away from being plunged into the Dark Ages. Living in a building with 2091s just a few streets down is dangerous, but maybe heading deep into the wilds might be a one-way trip."

Marco's jaws worked like he was chewing through a tough steak. "Look, I don't know what the future holds. But it seems that staying here alone is death. I'm trying to save your life. I'm hoping that you and my father can fix things. I started out talking about the good things, because I was sort of making a sales pitch. I didn't get to the point directly and maybe if I had you wouldn't have been so critical. But I want you to reconsider coming with us. If you can't swallow your pride for yourself, then maybe swallow it for Hailey."

64

Global Infection: ≤ 33.5214%

Ryan told Marco he would think about the offer and climbed down the wall, ready to head to the tower. It had been a long two days and he was past ready to leave. Marco talked to his father, presumably to discuss the offer, and the minutes ticked by as the discussion became more animated. Ryan couldn't hear the words but the sideways glances and gestures made the disagreement clear. And it was during this time that Ryan realized they could easily get the mobile doctor's office out of the camp. All the work done to clear and organize the camp had opened up the path, so when Raphael finally declared they were ready to leave, he said so.

"I'm not going to drive the plague mobile," Simone said. "It smells like shit."

Ryan said, "Hailey can drive it."

"Duh?! I can't drive."

"Are you sure? Let me see your driver's license."

"Okay, officer," Hailey said. "Let me get it out of my purse. Oh, that is right. I don't *have* a purse! Because I don't have a *license!*"

"You *are* nuttier than peanut butter."

"That was stupid," Simone muttered.

"We need to leave this here," Raphael said. "It *es* better to have this RV in this place. It will take disease to the tower."

Ryan asked, "What do you mean? Why wouldn't we take it to the tower? It has Marco's meds and all kinds of medical supplies."

"It *es* better here."

Ryan's confusion deepened. "You already said that. And in response I pointed out that its value is best transferred to the tower. It will give us time to clean it out and recover the stuff inside."

"It *es* better to clean it here, but we do not have the time."

Marco looked at his father and then at the ground.

"I'm not cleaning it out," Simone said.

Ryan said, "I'm not talking about cleaning it now. We can clean it at leisure in the tower where there are no 2091s."

"Poppa, we could do a much better job of cleaning in the tower," Marco said. "If we do it here, we risk contaminating the medical supplies."

Raphael looked hard at Marco. "It *es* too much work to take this from here. We have to make a path, and that will take too long."

"Raphael, we have maybe ten minutes of work to get a path to the hole in the wall," Ryan said, "And once we get the RV moved, we open up the rest of the camp. If nothing else, we can get those two skids of diesel fuel with a forklift. And I know you have been looking at that SWAT truck back there. If we get the RV out, you can get that out too."

Raphael shook his head. "This will no fit through the hole in the wall."

"This RV is the same size as the army transport, and we already know that the truck fits through the wall. Then we have thirty days to clean and figure out what to take."

"See," Marco said. "We can take what we want with us."

Raphael's mouth pulled into a frown and then he said, "We will make a path, but we will no drive this RV."

"Okay," Ryan said as he opened the door and poked his nose inside. He flinched. "I feel like I need a biohazard suit just standing beside it."

"Too bad we can't use those suits that were on the zombies," Hailey said.

Ryan looked at Hailey and paused. "You're a genius."

Thirty minutes later, Ryan was dressed in a disposable biohazard suit and gloves. Hailey refused to ride with anyone else, so she put on a suit and crawled into the passenger seat, looking like she was wearing her father's clothes. Ryan drove the RV out of the warehouse without knocking down a fifty-foot-high industrial storage shelf, but for a minute it didn't look good.

The warehouse loading docks were built along the northeast side, and there was a bay door that allowed trucks to back into the warehouse and stage under a lift that put shipping containers on trailers. The convoy, led by Raphael in the Army truck, followed by Ryan in the RV and then Marco in the Humvee with a .50 caliber gun turret—Simone manning the gun like a warlord—drove out of the warehouse and down the vacant streets, winding toward the 28th Street bridge to the inbound lanes on Route 380 and on to the Renaissance Tower.

Ryan scraped the RV along a concrete pylon once as he drove into the tower's sub structure as he parked the vehicle on the opposite end of the vast underground area. They got out of the RV fast: Hailey was shrugging out of her suit as Ryan snapped off his gloves. Marco met them with a trash bag in hand so the suits barely touched the concrete. They used sanitizer on any exposed skin and went straight to the dock restroom.

They returned to find the Humvee empty and the transport truck half unloaded. Marco pushed a pallet loaded with four diesel fuel drums under a shelf in the receiving area. Simone drove a forklift back to the dock to retrieve a skid of MREs and Red Cross aid packages. And Raphael lined a third skid of ammunition outside the freight elevator. When the truck was empty, Raphael slid the pallet jack under the last skid and said, "We take this to the penthouse, and then we have dinner."

"High five," Ryan said, holding his hand up for Hailey. "Good work, girl. What do you want for dinner?"

"I like those MREs. Can I have spaghetti?"

"We will have stew," Raphael said. "We do no need to eat these MREs when we have fresh food. It *es* very good. Come, you will see." He motioned toward the elevators.

Hailey froze. Her eyes darted toward Ryan. She took a step back. "No . . . I mean . . . I . . ."

"Hailey?" Ryan said.

"I can't go into the tower," Hailey said, clutching at the collar of her coat.

"What do you mean you can't go into the tower?" Simone said. "You are already *in* the tower."

Suddenly Hailey's breath was coming in heaves. She looked around. "Can I go out, please? I just need to go out!"

"Hailey?" Ryan said. "Stop. It's okay. What is the problem?"

"I don't want to go into the tower." She took another step back.

"Hailey, you will be safe here. It will be okay."

"No! I won't! And you can't make me." She ran to the loading dock doors slamming them open and running into the substructure. She spun in a circle and started to cry.

"Hailey," Ryan said as he drew close. "It's okay. If you don't want to stay here. I won't make you."

Hailey choked back her tears. "Could you stay with me at old man Renfro's apartment?"

"I would be glad to stay with you, but you know there are a lot of zombies there."

Hailey dried her face on her coat sleeve. "Yeah, that's true. But if I can find another place that is safe, maybe you would stay there?"

"I tell you what. I have an idea. Can you just wait a minute? I need to make some arrangements."

Hailey tugged at her coat sleeves. "Okay."

Ryan walked back to the Pagueros.

"What happened?" Marco asked.

"I have no idea. She went from amicable helper to a feral cornered animal in less than a minute," Ryan said.

Marco looked at Simone.

"What? What did I do?"

"What did you say?"

"Nothing! I was with you," Simone said.

"I don't think it is Simone," Ryan said. "I think she feels trapped by being in the tower with us. She asked me to stay with her. She has a place that she stays, but it will have too many infected around it. I was thinking I take the Humvee back to Fort Pitt, and she and I camp out in the warehouse offices, or no, we can lock ourselves into the Stryker."

"We can no split up!" Raphael said.

"She's stupid," Simone said.

Marco looked at his watch. "We can still work this evening. It seems like a waste to stay here tonight. I say we all go back."

"But I want to sleep in a bed!" Simone said.

"Yes. My son, he needs to sleep so that he can recover. Both of my sons need to recover. It *es* better that they are in beds," Raphael said. "We will go back when they are better."

"It's all her fault," Simone rasped. "If it hadn't been for her, I wouldn't have—"

"Don't!" Ryan said. He checked over his shoulder to make sure that Hailey couldn't hear. "That girl is most likely the reason you are alive."

"But if she hadn't—"

Marco swatted his shoulder. "You fell because you fell. It had nothing to do with her. Now hush!"

"Ow!" Simone said, clutching his side.

"Look, I know Marco and Simone need to heal so I'm not asking you to go," Ryan said. "I will go back. There are lots of weapons to retrieve and more ammo. Hailey and I can get some of the air mattresses and blankets and lock ourselves into the Stryker. It will be fine."

Raphael shook his head. "You can no be in this place by yourself. It *es* too dangerous."

"What do you suggest, Raphael?" Ryan said. "She is not coming in here. I can work, and she can maybe learn to trust me."

"You can no be in this Fort Pitt. We must all stay in the tower," Raphael said. "You have fuel for the generators and ammunition and some emergency food. This *es* good. This *es* more then you have before today. It *es* no safe to be there."

First, he fights over the RV, and now he is fighting going back? What the hell is going on?

Marco said, "I'll go with them."

"No, I forbid it. You must rest."

Marco sighed and stretched the tension out of his shoulders. "Poppa, I am too old for you to be forbidding me anything. This is the right thing to do," he said, meeting Raphael's eyes. "It is right to keep working to bring more stuff back to the tower. It is right that we keep helping Mr. Sage. It is right that I go back. I can sleep anywhere, and as one wise man said, war does not stop for anyone."

"Can I speak to you over here?" Raphael said to Marco.

"No, Poppa," Marco said. "If you want to speak to me, you can come to Fort Pitt." He turned to Ryan. "Let's head back."

Raphael sighed. "Wait, I will pack food. Simone, come with me."

Raphael's stew was exceptional. They ate in the warehouse break room, washing it down with sodas left in the refrigerator with the name Tom written on each one in black Sharpie.

65

Global Infection: ≤ 33.2668%

Ryan and Hailey felt like Goldilocks when looking for a place to bed down. Hailey liked the idea of spending the night inside the Stryker until Simone crawled in, said his father was coming soon, lay down in the middle and promptly went to sleep. The Stryker was too crowded. Ryan suggested sleeping in the Lenco armored truck, but Hailey took one sniff and said no. That SWAT vehicle was too smelly. The breakroom was on the second floor behind two locked doors, but an exit door—a door that led to the world of 2091s—was at the foot of the stairs. Even after Marco wedged a metal case between the door and a pallet filled with car parts, Ryan couldn't shake the fear of being cut off. The breakroom was too close.

Out of ideas, Ryan stood in the warehouse while Marco made his case that any of the second floor offices would be fine. Hailey called his name from the storage shelf 50 feet above his head. While Ryan had been talking, Hailey had been working, raiding the camp; Fort Pitt was a trove of blankets, clean and folded in hermetically sealed American Red Cross emergency kits complete with air mattresses. Ryan drove the fork lift with the scoop to the storage rack and rode it to the top like an elevator. Hailey wanted Ryan to make his bed on the other side of a pallet of grass fertilizer. This spot was just right.

But the comfortable bed and the isolation far above the warehouse floor didn't banish his fears. He kept waking to noises: the creaking of phosphorous lamps swaying in the rafters, the settling catwalk that ran around the warehouse perimeter, and things shifting in the dark that seemed to have no cause. He second-guessed turning out the lights for the hundredth time, but neither he nor Hailey had been able to sleep with the buzzing just a few feet above their heads. The roof skylights were spaced at intervals, but the moonless sky condemned the world to blackness. Two exit signs and four security lights stood like lonely lighthouses along a stormy coast, but they failed to drive back the gremlins that skittered through the vast dark ocean.

For comfort Ryan reached above his head to touch the backpack of twenty 5.56 magazines. His tactical vest was beside the bag, as were two M16s and an ORACLE HUD. They found 33 ORACLES in the camp—some on the heads of 2091s and some stowed in cases. ORACLE was military speak for Optimal Recognition, Anticipation Combatant Lighting System. The ORACLE looked like heavy sunglasses, but they were in fact a Heads-Up display that gave the soldier infrared, heat and low light visual capabilities. With a click of a button on the temple, Ryan could turn the darkness into twilight; with a second touch, he could see the white signature of body heat, and with a third touch see infrared.

As Ryan lay in the dark listening to spirits shift and move in the warehouse, listening to the muted gabbling of the infected beyond the walls, he resisted the temptation to put on the ORACLE and scan the concrete floor for threats. He rolled to his left trying to make himself relax, trying to focus on Hailey's rhythmic breathing.

"Ryan," Hailey had said quietly after her last joke of the night. "Thank you . . . for being nice to me."

Those were her last words before she fell asleep.

He smiled at the memory: Hailey having a grand time searching through the camp for magazines. She glowed with pride as she showed off her every trophy. She climbed the shipping containers like she was scaling Mount Everest and dropping into remote parts of the camp. She came out of the northwest corner, excited and smiling, and ran to Raphael with something in her hand. He took it and then shooed her away.

And just then something bothered Ryan about that exchange. He hadn't thought much of it when it happened. But in retrospect, Hailey stopped the hunting game soon after, suddenly preoccupied with some other task: tasks that Raphael assigned through the evening.

He didn't keep after Simone that much.

I'm making shit up . . .

He breathed deep, trying to still his mind, but Daniel Ryder's words bubbled in his thoughts: *"You are a billionaire now, you need to be paranoid."*

And paranoia over Raphael's behavior bubbled back to the surface. Marco had made the invitation to travel to Maine, but Ryan was pretty sure Raphael was not on board.

Should I leave? For Hailey's sake? Has anything really changed? Raphael has never recanted his actions. Maybe I should go and then at the first opportunity look for someplace in Nova Scotia. More people . . . better opportunities . . .

Ryan sighed and tossed to the left. And suddenly he had to pee.

"Damn!" he whispered. For a few seconds, he considered dropping his fly and relieving himself over the edge. And just as quickly, he decided against it. He put on his shoes and shrugged into his tactical vest, but cringed as it rattled and clattered. He feared waking Hailey, so he only grabbed his rifle. He could see the forklift platform outlined by the faint glow of the exit sign, but it was barely enough light to move by. He slid the ORACLE onto his face, feeling the uncomfortable weight press against his nose, brow and ears. He touched the power button and watched the HUD work through its boot process. Five seconds later, the warehouse looked like it was lit with the dull green glow of fireflies. He tapped the temple and saw the heat indicator blink in the lower left corner. He scanned the floor and nothing. He put the single point sling around his neck, snapped the rifle on and stepped onto the makeshift scoop.

"Where are you going?" Hailey asked, her voice thick with sleep.

"To the bathroom," Ryan whispered. "Go back to sleep."

"You are coming back, right?"

"Yes, Hailey I will be back. I will always come back."

"Okay. When you come back, can you bring Pogo's bowl? He'll be thirsty."

"Go to sleep, Hailey. I'm sure Pogo will be fine."

"Okay."

Ryan pressed the hydraulic lever and the forklift dropped quietly to the floor. He took a few steps toward the warehouse restroom and paused: zombies, bathrooms, horror movies. They always went together. Ryan did the pee-pee dance as he tried to make up his mind if he should brave the bathroom or go outside in the camp. And that was when he saw light spike in the HUD.

The camp lights are on?

Curiosity made the choice for him. He turned toward the hole in the wall to investigate.

He practiced sweeping his weapon for targets as he moved down an aisle and then to the hole in the concrete wall. He paused just inside, in the shadows, scanning the camp for invaders. One lone temporary light burned at the farthest end of the camp, the generator cycling to charge the battery array.

Raphael was so fuel conservation-conscious that throughout the day he killed the power to anything that made the generators run. The camp had been dark when they bedded down for the night.

Wasn't it?

The camp was empty and Ryan felt the urge building in his bladder. The twenty camp Porta Potties were full and disgusting, but they had found one unused unit—Marco said it was reserved for the command staff—behind a pile of crates. Ryan navigated his way to it, positioned just behind the command bunker.

The command bunker was a modular hardened structure, expanded with two tent additions on its left and right side. The bunker survived the carnage because the military surrounded it with narrower and thinner versions of the HESCO walls, similar to what towered 30 feet above the Pittsburgh streets. The narrow cells were filled with stone and sand shielding the command center from the rolling tide of destruction.

Ryan pulled open the Porta Potti door and stooped inside. He paused halfway in trying to figure out how to juggle his gun and his zipper in a small space. He heard Marco and Raphael talking in the command center, their voices muted behind the wall. Ryan let the door close without making a sound, tugged all the important things in the right direction and relaxed.

"It's not right," Marco said, stepping out of the command bunker.

"Shusshushushhh," Raphael said. "We do no need a fight."

"A fight? Really?" Marco said. "Of course there is going to be a fight. You made an agreement."

"Come inside," Raphael said. "You need to make these work."

"I already told you," Marco said. "I don't know how. My training was medical. You want to know how to patch up a blown off leg or treat a sucking chest wound, I'm your guy.

What I know about this system I just showed you."

"You are always complaining about the radios we need . . ." Raphael's voice faded as they stepped back into the command center.

"What the hell?" Ryan said, tucking everything back to where it belonged. He exited the Porta Potti, keeping the door from popping shut and walked to the command center door. He pressed against the HESCO wall that flanked the threshold, trying to decide if he should walk into the conversation. Finally he shook his head. Ryan's fight quota was maxed out, and besides, he'd know soon enough.

He took three steps toward sleep when he heard the tail end of Raphael's sentence:

". . . Sage will be greedy with ammunition."

Ryan's feet froze to the broken asphalt. His mind put the pieces together in crisp, clear images: Raphael standing on the wall looking through the camp like Francisco Pizarro surveying the Inca Empire before he killed the Atahualpa; Raphael chasing Hailey away from the shipping containers at Fort Pitt's west end; Raphael's resistance to driving the mobile doctors' office back to the tower; refusing to load the two skids of diesel fuel onto the army truck when there was plenty of room; his effort to keep Ryan in the tower.

Ryan walked toward the blazing temporary light through the medical tents, around the toppled cots and the blood caked blankets, over the dark splotches of asphalt that looked like shark chum. Finally, he stood about where Hailey had been when she climbed up the shipping containers to show Raphael her prize. The container in Fort Pitt's farthest northwest corner said Maersk. It was in the one part of the camp Ryan had failed to investigate. It was a tight space, perfect for a young girl to go spelunking where the adults couldn't go.

And then Ryan saw what did not belong—the remains of a bloody medical tent hanging up like a shower curtain. He squeezed around a MEP 1000 Tactical Quiet Generator and double-stacked pallets of 55-gallon diesel drums. He pulled the tent away, revealing a door built into the side of the shipping container and an electrical cable running inside. He lifted the latch and stepped into the light. The container was filled with ammunition and crates of weapons. It was like someone had emptied an armory. And then Ryan remembered how hard it was to close the gap between the

Hanjin container and the HESCO wall, how much horsepower they needed to push it into place. The containers were heavy because they were full.

If all nine containers are filled with guns and ammunition . . .??!!

"Unbelievable."

And then Ryan stopped breathing. "Oh no," he said. Raphael's actions finally made sense. The whole point was to get Ryan away from Fort Pitt so that he wouldn't see what was in this container. Raphael wanted all of it for himself.

"Shit! Shit! Shit! Shit!" He killed the light and the darkness wrapped around him like a shroud, his mouth going dry and his legs feeling heavy.

He snuck out of the container and quietly closed the latch. He moved forward a step, his heart raging in his chest, his tongue feeling like a slab of leather. He had no hope of surviving a shootout with the Pagueros. He looked for a way to sneak through the darkness, but the only path was to retrace his steps through the camp light.

Ryan tapped the ORACLE to reveal heat and scanned the shadows looking for the telltale white glow of body heat, then again to see infrared.

How would they explain my death to Hailey?

And the answer struck him in the heart. Raphael watched Marie Blanco and her family die on the street without so much as a fuck you. He wanted to leave Dakota and Darien behind because it served his purpose. And when opposed, Raphael was quick to point a gun at Ryan's head. Raphael would feel no obligation to say anything to Hailey: he'd just kill her.

Ryan moved from fuel drum pallet to fuel drum pallet until the next step would take him into the blazing light. He looked up at the shipping containers trying to see if there was a way to climb into the darkness above. If he could get to the top of the wall, he could run the perimeter and drop back into the building. But the ladder built into the shipping containers was lit like it was on center stage.

Get to Haile—

"Mr. Sage, put the gun down, please." Marco's voice came from the darkness above.

66

Global Infection: ≤ 33.2670%

He who knows when he can fight and when he cannot will be victorious.

Sun Tzu

Ryan's breath stopped. His muscles went slack, and he felt his sphincter start to fail. Marco's face and the barrel of his weapon were barely visible atop the shipping containers.

Ryan had no shot and nowhere to go. "I'm not going to let you kill Hailey."

"What?" Marco asked. "We are not going to kill Hailey. We are not going to kill you. No one has to die tonight. This is just a misunderstanding. I know it looks bad, but just put the gun down."

Ryan willed his legs to stop shaking, but his right foot pounded up and down like a sewing machine.

"Mr. Sage, if I wanted you dead, I would have shot you when you came out of the container. I understand how this looks. And I would probably be thinking the same thing if this was reversed. But it really is a misunderstanding. I don't want to shoot you, and my father does not want to shoot you. He is grateful that you saved his son so he feels he owes you something. And I'm hurt that you think we would harm Hailey. Now put the gun down so we can talk."

"You think I give a shit whether I hurt your feelings? You Pagueros are a bunch of thugs. And that ass-hat that you call a brother speaks to her like she is less than a dog. He already tried to shoot her once for biting his hand. Who knows what he will do to her when I'm gone?"

"Mr. Sage, this is not our finest hour. I can't argue with that, but please, put the gun down."

Ryan finally got control of his body. He stood. "If you cowards are going to kill me, then there is nothing I can do about it. Maybe when she hears the gunshot she will run."

"Mr. Sage, put the gun *down*."

Ryan yelled. "The Pagueros are cowards! The Pagueros are cowards!"

Come on, Hailey. Wake up and run!

"I am no coward," Raphael said from the darkness, slowly stepping to the light. He held his rifle above his head. Leisurely, he knelt to place it on the ground. "I will speak to you as a man."

"While your son has a gun trained on my back? Right, that is all man, Raphael, all man."

"Let's just talk," Marco said, his voice filtering down into Fort Pitt. "It really is a misunderstanding."

"What am I misunderstanding? How you were planning to keep me out of Fort Pitt so you could take everything?"

"It *es* no what you think," Raphael said.

"Just listen," Marco said.

"All right," Ryan said. "Talk, but I'm not putting my gun down."

Raphael said, "What Marco say *es* true. You do some things to help save Simone. For this, I am grateful. But as you say, we can no have a relationship. You say that we must leave the tower. It *es* true that we must leave. I pray to the Holy Mother to give us a place to stay, and she provide this place. God give this place to us. My son suffer when he fall, but then God give Simone strength to fight, and God help Marco overcome his great fear so that we can have these things. He gave it to us so that we can do good things for many peoples. We will take these things to our camp. There are many peoples in Maine where we will go. God knows that we will give and we will not ask for anything in return. So, you can have the tower," Raphael said. "We will stay here. We will use this place and when Leona come, we will leave."

Ryan said. "Let me get this straight. I didn't have anything to do with getting in here? God gave you this place because you will give stuff away? So I have to leave?"

Raphael nodded. "Yes. God say you will go back to your tower."

"God said that, did He?" Ryan asked. "And did God forget about my part of the fight? Did he forget about me spending the night playing a goat tethered to a stake to draw the infected away?"

Raphael shrugged. "All you do is sit on a building, and the devils come to you. Sitting *es* no work? And how would you fight unless we teach you? You ask for our teaching, and you learn to fight."

"So I don't get any credit for what I did because you taught me how to fight?" Ryan asked.

"This is what we agree," Raphael said with a shrug. "You say you wanted our knowledge. You get this when Marco teach you. Coming to here was training, yes? This is what we say, yes? Without this knowledge, you would no survive. Without us, you could no fight these devils. To want more from this is to be paid twice, yes? This was the terms of our agreement, yes?"

Ryan said, "Raphael, that same agreement committed your family to a month of work after Leona comes to Pittsburgh. We agreed that you would provide the best opportunity for my survival, and now you want to go back on that?"

"I do no need the Stryker, because I have these vehicles. And your agreement *es* foolishness," Raphael said, like he was giving the sum of 2 + 2. "It *es* greed how you want to live. You tell me that it was a free market. This *es* how the free market work. I have this option now. I already give you ammunition and six barrels of fuel. You have the bus in front of the windows and the street secure. And I do this for free."

Ryan breathed deep and said to himself, "This is what I get for expecting a Catholic to understand capitalism."

Raphael narrowed his eyes. "What *es* this thing you say?"

"Never mind," Ryan said, shaking his head. "Dare I point out that nothing here was yours to give?"

Raphael frowned. "God gave these things to me, so they were mine to give."

"Right. Of course a mystic would want credit for what he didn't earn to get paid by that which God decreed was already his." Ryan said. "Is this some bad joke? Am I supposed to take this seriously? Did you just claim a piece of Pittsburgh like a conquistador for the Queen of Spain? And what, I'm supposed to accept the declaration like the Incas of South America?"

"These medicines *es* no yours," Raphael said. "These ammunition *es* no yours. These cars *es* no yours. You have no right to these things. You are just greedy. God give these things to me because he know I will give these medicines to the peoples."

The image of Raphael standing on the roof, his binoculars pressed to his face and the whispered word focused like a camera phone. "What does *armado* mean?" Ryan asked.

"What?" Raphael said.

"*Armado,* what does it mean?" Ryan said, confident that he already knew.

"It means armored," Marco said. "Why?"

Ryan shook his head. "You have been planning this since we were on the roof, haven't you? Or was it before you signed the contract? You knew you were leaving the moment you found a better way to travel, and then you saw that armored truck and the Humvee and the transport truck sitting in the middle of this camp, and you knew you had found it."

Raphael shrugged. "Everyone know that in times like these, men can no make a profit. They must sacrifice for the good of the peoples. Everyone know this but you. Maybe I tell a small lie, but it *es* for the best. And I will ask for forgiveness. But I will no do a bigger evil by helping you."

Ryan scrubbed his hand through his hair, exasperated. "I should have known not to make an agreement with a liar.'

Raphael's eyes narrowed. "You insult my honor. I am no liar."

"Whatever," Ryan said. "It doesn't matter. There is only one problem. I earned the right to be here. Your God might be afflicted with amnesia, but I remember the work it took to get in here. So I'm not leav—"

Raphael took a step forward but stopped when he eyed the rifle muzzle. Then he said, "God already say you *will* leave."

Ryan adjusted the rifle in his grip.

Marco said, "Mr. Sage, put down the rifle!"

"Let's cut to the chase, Raphael. How are you going to *make* me leave? How are you going to keep me from taking what I want back to the tower?"

"God gave this place to my family"

"No, he didn't."

"You do no believe in God?" Raphael snarled. "You are godless. You have no respect. And you are right that we do not share values."

"Yeah, blah, blah, blah," Ryan said. "So the question remains. How will you *make* me leave?"

"Mr. Sage, put the rifle down," Marco said again.

"Shoot me, coward, or shut up!" Ryan said. "So, Raphael . . . your move."

Raphael took another step forward, his fist flexing, his eyes on the muzzle of Ryan's rifle. "You are no welcome in *my* house like I was no welcome in yours. You will leave because you *will* believe that God gave me this place," he said, his posture projecting menace and pain.

"And now we get to the point," Ryan said. "Faith and force are handmaidens of destruction. The only way to deal with men by faith is by the use of force. Because I do not believe what comes out of your mouth, you can only resort to violen—"

The rifle shot shattered the night.

Ryan was surprised that he didn't react except to smile. *Hailey, wake up and run!*

"The next one will not miss," Marco said.

Ryan turned. "I was hoping you would give Hailey a warning shot. I want her to run away from you murderers."

"I am not a murderer," Marco said.

Ryan's contempt boiled over, and he threw the rifle at Marco's feet. "I guess we will see if at least one Paguero can tell the truth."

Marco lowered his weapon. "Now, let's just talk."

"Marco, we have been talking," Ryan said. "And we have just confirmed that Pagueros will use force to compel me to do whatever the tribe dictates." He held Marco's gaze.

Marco looked away. "That's not what happened."

"Did those antibiotics just make your IQ drop fifty points?" Ryan said. "Didn't you just fire a rifle at me to make do what you want?"

"Maybe you could just go back to the tower," Marco said. "We can't take everything. We will get what we want, and then you can get what you want. There doesn't need to be a fight."

"I refuse to negotiate at the point of a gun," Ryan said. "And more important, I don't accept the premise that the Paguero tribe has a divine title to this place so I will not leave and give sanction to the absurd." He turned back to back to Raphael. "So now what?"

Raphael was smug. “In the morning, you *will* leave,” he said. “You insult me and God. I will no teach you respect tonight, but I will teach you respect in the morning.”

“Raphael, you are not worthy of respect day or night.”

Raphael grabbed Ryan by the shirt, breathing menace and hate.

“What are you going to do?” Ryan said. “Punch me for saying the obvious?”

“This *es* no the ways of real men with the constant talking,” Raphael said.

Ryan said, “Real men are rational men, and rational men don’t make shit up.”

“Again you dishonor me. I would let you sleep the night. But now you will no sleep because of the pain. I will teach you respect that your mother did not teach.”

“Raphael, this is retarded. This won’t stay *mano a mano*. This is three against one. The moment you start to lose, your sons will jump in to help. And that will be a bad day for everyone.”

Marco laughed.

Ryan looked at Marco like he was a bug and then back to Raphael. “I might not know how to shoot a gun, but I’m smart enough to avoid fights I can’t win.”

Raphael frowned. “The Bible say fools will be beaten with rods. I think you are a great fool. I think you will need many blows to learn humility.” He unzipped his tactical vest. “I will no lose.” He slid the gun from his thigh holster, letting it fall. Finally, he dropped the machete with a clatter. “See, I have no weapons. And I will no need help.”

67

Global Infection: ≤ 33.2672%

A victorious army wins its victories before seeking battle.

SUN TZU

Raphael exchanged smirks with Marco.

Ryan hadn't been in a fight in decades, but he was no stranger to violence. He made the mental shift back to old habits, back to the mind-set of aggression, the place where the analytical mind stepped aside and his primitive brain took over: he focused on his breathing—in . . . out . . . in . . . out. His limbs loosened and his perceptions slowed, becoming aware of the stones under his feet, the texture of his jeans on his thigh, the breeze that caressed his cheek. His perceptions reached out farther, noting the camp clutter, the things that would trip his feet, the distance between the HESCO wall and the Lenco's front bumper.

Slowly, carefully, deliberately Ryan said, "No, Raphael, you *will* need help, and they *will* come to your rescue. I won't fight three of you. Not when you have guns and a son who is a trigger happy adolescent idiot. So just punch me so we can move past this macho bullshit and pretend that your honor is repaired."

"Simone *es* asleep," Raphael said.

"Well, at least we agree on who the adolescent idiot is," Ryan said, casting a critical eye at Marco. "But I don't believe you. I'd bet money he's hiding inside the command bunker chomping at the bit to kill someone."

"He is asleep in the Stryker, and he can sleep through anything," Marco said. "Poppa, stop this. There is no reason to humiliate him. Just let him leave in the morning. He can go back to the tower."

"This one *es* godless. He insult the Holy Mother. He insult my honor, and he insult Simone. He call him a retard," Raphael said. "This I can no ignore."

"All right," Marco said with a shrug. "I'm not jumping in even if you need help." Even as he said the words, he couldn't suppress the smile.

"What? Another *commitment* from a Paguero?" Ryan said. "I feel better all ready."

The smile disappeared from Marco's face. "If you are winning, no matter how bad you are beating him, I swear on my mother's life, I won't intervene. May God strike her down. But Mr. Sage, you really are a fool if you think my father is Gus Blanco and a move you learned in self-defense class will save your ass."

Ryan bowed his head and then said, "You are worried about the wrong man."

Raphael stretched and rolled his shoulders. "I will no need help. I am unarmed. No guns. No knives. Just these." He held up his fists.

"Raphael, one last opportunity to avoid this, so let me be clear. No matter how much you hit me, you are not going to change my mind. I will still think you are a liar and a thug. So maybe just live with that. I'll accept that you don't care for me and I don't care for you. We call it a night. We work around each other in the morning. But I'm not leaving."

"I will never let you work around me. I will never let you speak of my son this way. I will not let you disrespect the Holy Mother."

Let the games begin.

"What has me puzzled is Daniel Ryder. I thought he was respectable, had virtue, that he was a man of his word. I have no delusions that successful men are perfect angels. They are often their own brand of bastards. I was successful and I know I can be a colossal prick. But I cannot begin to fathom what Daniel ever saw in you."

Raphael stepped in close, flexing, breathing heavy and looking hard. The insult to Daniel Ryder struck a nerve . . . which was the point.

"Yes, yes, Raphael. I saw the teardrop tattoos when you threatened me in my office. I can see their faded outline after you tried to have them removed in a desperate attempt to become respectable. Did you really think that people couldn't see that you were really just a petty gangbanger? Did you think owning highbrow art would erase the thug in your soul? Did you think that some canvas with smears and blobs would cover over the fact that you are little more than a savage in mystic clothing? Raphael, strip away societal restraint and the real you comes roaring to the surface.

"But what I can't seem to figure out is how you hid this from Daniel. Are you that good of a liar, or is he that gullible? Oh no, wait. Maybe I have this all wrong. Maybe he knew exactly who you are. You were his pet pit bull, his *perro mascota*. Right? He trained you to sit and heel so he could take you out in public. But when he couldn't get his way, when he needed that edge in a negotiation, he'd let you off the leash to blather about the Virgin Mary, wave guns around and give them that Sinaloa Cartel stink eye."

Rage spiked in Raphael's eyes. He swung vicious and hard.

Slow was smooth and smooth was fast. The adage when practicing with guns was also true when practicing anything . . . and that included martial arts. The only difference was that Ryan had practiced slow and smooth fighting for decades. He was older and he was nowhere near fighting shape. But he had practiced the moves thousands of times through New Year's resolutions to get in shape. When he was bored with yoga and the frustrations of life scorched his psyche, he returned to the workouts of his twenties. And in the recent weeks in Pittsburgh, looking after Tess, living through the avalanche of death that buried her life, he took many opportunities to go to the hotel gym in the late hours to work off the steam that tried to vent through his pores.

Many years ago, Ryan Sage entertained the ridiculous idea to try MMA fighting. He'd been a terrible fighter. He hated the pain. He hated the injuries. He hated the recovery. It was during those two years of cage match combat that he learned he would never be a title contender. He also learned that trading punches with stronger, faster savages was a terrible idea. There had to be a better way to fight. And there was. He learned grappling and submission and from Helio Gracie's Brazilian Jujitsu. He learned joint locks and weapons disarming from a seventy-five-year-old Korean man who stood five-foot-seven and destroyed a room full of attackers with nothing but his hands guided by *Kuk Sool Won*.

The recent weeks of manual labor had hardened his hands, and Ryan slapped Raphael's blows away like flies. Ryan dodged, timing the strikes, gaining rhythm, patient . . . assessing. Raphael was enraged and shamed. Raphael thought that raw violence was indomitable. Raphael meant to hurt. He meant to maim. He meant to demoralize.

"*Coño*," Raphael taunted. "I can smell you from here . . ."

Ryan pivoted, keeping his base, keeping his body squared to the attack.

"You must douche," Raphael sneered as he threw a flurry of punches. "You slap like a woman. Marco will never help."

For all his military mastery, Raphael was reduced to a brawler by a few words that sliced open his ego. And that was exactly what Ryan intended; Raphael was exposed. Ryan struck—not to the head and not to the ribs where even brawlers know to protect—to the forearms, to the small bundle of nerves just above the elbows. He assaulted the soft spots of flesh to turn them into fine points of suffering.

Raphael flinched, trying to harden himself against the pain and the surprise. He swung, but his punch was slow as the nerve struggled against the throbbing. Ryan trapped the elbow against his ribs and drove his fist into the inside of Raphael's biceps, into the nerve that runs inside the arm. With a counterstroke, Ryan drove his elbow into Raphael's ear and slammed the South American face-first against the HESCO wall—against the wire mesh and the rocks. Raphael rebounded, dropped to a knee, but scrambled around like a wounded animal, uncertain, confused, and enraged. He leaped.

Ryan grabbed an arm, pivoted with all his height and weight, and let mass and force and vector do the rest. Raphael flew, and the crates and boxes and Lenco armored truck cut and bruised and beat him into a heap. He crawled on all fours, then to his knees, and finally wobbled to his feet. He shook his head; then shook it again—blood leaked from his nose and his right ear and he had cuts across his forearms. And then something dark and vicious and rancid poured out of the Raphael's eyes: murder.

Raphael reached down and slid a knife out of his boot and spun it to flatten down his wrist.

"Of course you would lie about that too," Ryan said, his head dropping to his chest. "Raphael, I'll only tell you once. But if you don't put it away, I will cut you with your own blade."

"Poppa!" Marco shouted, "Put the knife down. Put it down now!"

"Silence!" Raphael barked, "I will no tolerate this *mariposa's* disrespect. Where *es* your insults now? Where *es* these useless words? Have you ever cut someone?" He sneered as he slashed left to right, drawing nothing but air. "I have cut many peoples. I will cut you slow." He slashed right to left and drew more air.

Ryan said nothing, securing his base, checking his distance, feeling the asphalt under his feet.

"Why do you no speak?!" Raphael roared as he lunged.

Ryan's perceptions blended perfectly: as his mind ticked off the technique his body performed the actions.

The foundation of combat: foot work. Move from base . . . to base; shift at an angle to the attack and close the distance. Counter the knife strike at the apogee with left forearm: joint lock elbow, joint lock shoulder with the right hand. Drive hard. Shoulder pop. Shoulder rip. Ignore scream. Sweep leg. Drive attacker to the ground. Head bounces off asphalt. Air explodes from lungs. Knife clatters away. Look into the eyes. See the fear. See the terror. See the despair. Drive elbow into the throat: short, harsh, and violent. Listen to the ragged breath. Watch the dark eyes roll back into his head. Smash fist into left eye; hit the right eye. Head bounces off asphalt once and then again. Look into the eyes and see the fear, see the terror, see the despair. Raise forearm. Aim for the jaw. Break jaw. Break jaw. Give over to the blood lust! Wreck him! Wreck him! Lift higher. More force. More power. Maximum destruction. Explode through ja—

Ryan felt the cold steel of a barrel on the side of his head.

"Mr. Sage," Marco said, his voice trembling. "I won't let you kill him."

Ryan turned slowly, to meet Marco's eyes. "Like father like son. You swore that you wouldn't help no matter how bad I was beating him. You swore on your mother's life. I guess she's going to die now, right?"

Marco's face went white. His mouth opened, but no words came out. His eyes dropped. "My father can be a bastard," he said. "But I won't let you kill him."

Ryan's eyes narrowed. "I won't kill him," he said as he picked up the knife and spun it three times through his fingers.

"Don't," Marco said, emphasizing his word with the barrel. "Just don't . . ."

Ryan's gaze was cold and unmoving. "The difference between me and the Paguero family is that I mean what I say and I say what I mean. But I don't expect you to believe that. So again we get to see if you are a murderer."

Marco relaxed and the weapon muzzle slumped. He nodded and swallowed. He suddenly looked like a little kid. The military bearing faded into contrition and weakness and uncertainty.

But Ryan Sage was in destroyer mode, his mind traveling the fine points of balance and counterstrike and weapons disarming. He slapped the AR-15 muzzle away as he swept Marco's leg and the riffle flew out of his hands. For an instant, Marco's back was parallel to the ground and Ryan tried to drive him to China. Breath ruptured form Marco's chest and Ryan dropped his knee to his throat the knife tip barley above Marco's eye. He waited for Marco to gasp and struggle, waited for Marco to make his mind start working.

"Jesus, God," Marco said. "How? How did you do—"

"Now let us talk about misunderstanding," Ryan said. "This is the second time that Pagueros have pointed guns at me, and that is the last time a Paguero draws a gun on me and lives." He shucked the side arm from Marco's thigh and held it in his hand.

"Please," Marco said, his breathing labored under Ryan's weight, groping feebly for his arm. "I really just wanted to keep the peace. I saw you walk away from the Porta Potti. I knew you heard us. I knew what you would think when you saw the ammunition. I saw the rifle in your hand. I thought you would come out of there enraged and shooting. I just wanted to keep you from getting killed." His voice started to crack. "I told him not to treat you this way. I'm sorry," Marco groped weakly for Ryan's arm. "Please. Please don't kill him. I lost my family a year ago, and I only just got them back. Please."

Ryan nodded. "But it wasn't a misunderstanding, Marco. It was exactly what I thought it was. Your father set out to deceive me. And when that didn't work, he tried to invoke the name of God. And when that didn't work, he resorted to force. The fact that he didn't start with murder doesn't change the fact that he was willing to end with murder."

Marco gasped and gagged, the fight having sapped whatever strength he'd recovered. His resistance collapsed.

Ryan stood, checked the Sig Sauer P229 TB and found a full magazine and a round in the chamber. "As one wise man said, when a man initiates a state of war against civilized men, it is the responsibility of civilized men to make that choice an ill bargain. Your father, like all mystics, only understands getting what he wants by initiating a state of war. So as a civilized man it is my responsibility to make his choice an ill bargain." He knocked Raphael out with the gun butt and tucked the Sig Sauer into his belt. "I told him I would cut him with his own knife. And I want to make sure that the Pagueros grasp the concept of keeping their word." In a stroke Ryan Sage cut off Raphael's right index finger.

"Oh Jesus God!" Marco gasped, struggling to crawl toward his father.

Ryan went to Raphael's tactical vest and dug out the tower security card and then stood and looked down at Marco. "He can probably shoot just as well left-handed, but I figure I'll give myself an edge. When he wakes up, you tell him the tower is closed. You guys wanna stay here. You do that. But I have an equal claim, because I fought to get in here, and that means I earned my right to the things that will benefit me. Now, if you are going to murder me, put a bullet in my head in the morning. I'm going to sleep."

Ryan Sage dropped the finger on Marco's chest.

68

Global Infection: ≤ 33.8071%

Ryan smelled the sausage cooking just before the forklift started and the hydraulics engaged as the makeshift elevator brought Hailey to his bed. "Ryan, are you gonna get up?"

"Oh, maybe someday," Ryan said, snuggled hard under the blankets, an M16 cradled in his arm like a teddy bear. It was a good sign that he could actually wake up. It meant that during the night he hadn't been murdered.

He left Marco and Raphael and went to the perch and found Hailey fast asleep. Apparently, Simone wasn't the only one who could sleep through anything.

For all the bravado about remaining in Fort Pitt, Ryan fretted for an hour on how to wake Hailey and get back to the tower. It seemed prudent to put distance between the Pagueros and himself, but leaving Fort Pitt at night was a fool's errand. There was no good way to get back to the tower in the dark, running streets filled with the infected. And Hailey wouldn't come inside even if he managed to get there alive.

"Marco wants to see you," Hailey said, standing on the scoop. "And I made you breakfast. I made the sausage. It's really good. And I have some cereal with blueberries. I really like that too. So get up and eat. I've got the food for you on the floor. I mean it's not on the floor because that would be gross. It would be kinda funny, but I mean I made it down on the floor because I didn't think I should cook it up here. The heater thingy gets kinda hot. And oh, you should see Raphael. He got hurt last night. He fell off the wall. Cut his finger off and everything."

"He fell, huh?" Ryan said, trying to sit up.

"Yeah, his face is all swollen. It's kinda gross, but I can't tell him that because that might hurt his feelings. You won't tell him that I said that, will you?"

Ryan tamped down his bed head. "No, Hailey, I won't tell him that."

"Come on, the food is gonna get cold. Well, some of it is already cold 'cause it's like cereal. But the hot stuff will get cold."

“Hold your horses.” Ryan stood and stretched his hands, seeming to almost touch one of the metal beams. And then he caught a whiff of his body odor. “Two days without a shower.”

“Yeah, you stink,” Hailey said with no irony.

“Hey, you’re mean.” He shrugged into his tactical vest and zipped the front.

“I’m nice. But if you don’t get moving, I’m gonna be mean.”

“All right,” Ryan said, sliding the ORACLE on his face and donning his tactical vest and holsters. He snapped up the bag filled with extra magazines and his rifle and stepped onto the scoop and held on.

Hailey made him sit on a bucket while she laid out the food on an empty crate, making him wait until everything was done, and was sitting across from him. “You can eat now.”

Ryan dug in like he hadn’t eaten in a month. “Wow!”

Hailey beamed. “What are you gonna do with all those bullets?”

Shoot Pagueros?

“Oh, maybe shoot bad guys,” Ryan said. “So where are Raphael and Marco?”

Hailey shrugged. “They are in that place with all the computers. Mr. Raphael doesn’t look good at all. And Marco looks really sleepy.”

“Where is Simone?”

“He is in the strike thingy. I think he is still sleeping. Well, he was sleeping earlier. Mr. Raphael told me to wake him up, but I didn’t want to, because Simone is kinda mean. But I tried to wake him. I even yelled through the hatch but he didn’t hear me. I went and told Marco, and he said he’d take care of it. Did you sleep good?”

Ryan had slept very well all things considered. “Yes, I did. Even better than at Old Man Renfro’s apartment.”

“See, I told you my idea was fantastic.”

“I have a question for you,” Ryan said. “If there was trouble, how would you get out of here?”

“What do you mean? Like if the zombies come inside?”

Ryan swallowed. “Yeah, you have a plan to get out, right?”

“Duh! That is how you stay away from the zombies.”

“So how would you do it?”

“Why do you wanna know?” Hailey asked, suspicion dripping off her words.

Because I might be killed by three very angry South Americans, and I want to make sure you have thought about how to escape.

“Oh, because I can’t seem to figure out how to do it,” Ryan said. “You have good ideas. Like where to sleep.”

Hailey smiled large. One day she would bring all men to their knees with that smile. “Well, it kinda depends on where I am, but the first place I’d go is to that walkway up there,” she said, pointing to the catwalk that went around the top of the warehouse. “That is how I got on top of the shelves. I went to the walk and jumped down.”

Ryan did a double take. “You did what? You jumped from the catwalk to the storage shelves.” His heart did a flip. It was at least eight feet between the two.

"It was easy," Hailey said, like she was talking about riding her bike. "So I would get up to that place if they were following me. And then I'd jump on the shelves and the zombies are really stupid so they would jump after me, but they wouldn't be able to get on the shelf and they would all fall and . . . you know. Splat!"

Ryan nodded, impressed. That was a pretty good plan except for the jumping to an eight-foot wide shelf 60 feet above the floor.

"And then I'd sneak to the back and go out the doors," Hailey said, "'cause we blocked all the doors in the front. But that was smart, 'cause that is where the zombies are and we don't want them to come in."

"Back doors?" Ryan said, shaking the punch drink mix that came with the MRE into a bottle of water.

Hailey pointed and said, "Back there."

"Can you show me?"

Hailey shoveled three more bites into her mouth and grabbed her bottle of punch and took a drink. "See this shelf thingy? I would sneak to here, because I can hide behind those big boxes and plus it's dark. Which means, if I had to, I could get across the aisle, but this open space here is kinda tricky, because it is big and the light up above makes it too bright. I would distract them by throwing something. Thank God the zombies are stupid," she paused, considering. "No, this shelf won't work because they might see me from the other side. But that would be a great spot," she said, pointing to a shelf with a small space between boxes and a forklift blocking the view. "And then all I have to do is get to those doors. They lead to the rest of the warehouse and there are a bunch of places to hide."

The warehouse was an L. The short side was on 21st Street. That was where the loading bays and the doors and the offices were located and where all the work had been done. But Ryan was sure that no one had ventured into the warehouse's long side—anyone except Hailey.

"I thought those doors were locked," Ryan said.

"That is what you get for not looking, kemosabe." Hailey walked to the left of the doors and hit a button and a latch somewhere in the wall released. She pushed the door open. "Sometimes I think you went to school on the short bus."

"Smarty pants," Ryan said.

"No," Hailey said. "Smarty brain."

Beyond the doors the lights were off, but the morning light poured through the skylights. A half dozen forklifts were parked along the wall. And the remaining space was filled with shipping containers—the same kind of containers that lined the west side of Fort Pitt. Two massive cranes hung on the ceiling, their steel suspension system extending beyond large loading bay doors to the river. The doors were sealed shut, but if opened, they would give a full view of the Allegheny River.

Hailey led the way to the westernmost corner. "When I followed you, this is the way I came. But this door was locked from the outside." She pushed the door open. They stepped out to a concrete walk that was built above the shore. "We don't want to let this lock behind us, because then we couldn't get in like I couldn't get in yesterday. Anyway, I came around here because there aren't any zombies, and then I went that way," she pointed toward the camp. "And then snuck up to those big metal containers and that is when I saw you shooting and stuff. I tried to call you, but you were about to jump down into all those zombies. That was really stupid, by the way."

"You would have let the zombies eat Simone?" Ryan asked.

"I might have. He's kinda mean." Hailey winked.

"I wondered how you found the rifle," Ryan said, looking at the structure built out over the river. A barge floated, secured in its mooring, on a muddy river that was slowly receding back into its banks. The crane mounts ran out over the barge and rested on large concrete pylons. The system was built to take cargo right off a river barge into the warehouse and onto a carrier that could be driven right out of the building.

The Pagueros were onto something. This warehouse was a trove of resources.

Ryan looked over the edge of the concrete walk at the bike path twenty feet below.

"I wouldn't jump from here," Hailey said. "But there are some stairs over there. It's got a gate, but it's easy to get over the gate. And then I could just go any way I want to. But I'd probably go that way," she said, pointing east. "because the zombies are that way."

Ryan nodded looking down the river bank. Movement across the river caught his eye. Then he saw a line of people along the river's edge. They were on all fours with their faces in the river.

What are they doing? Drinking?

"Is that a good plan?" Hailey asked, like she was worried.

"That is a very good plan."

"Good. Then you can come with me."

"So listen. If we ever get separated, I want you do your plan. Get out of here fast, and don't worry about me."

Hailey's eyes went round. "Where would you go?"

"Look, we have a plan, but sometimes things happen. We need a backup plan. If we get separated, you can go to the tower. I will try to meet you there. I know you said you didn't want to go inside. I know you are scared of something. I'm not sure what it is, but it really is safe there. So if we ever get separated, or if you want a safe place, go to the tower." Ryan pulled out the access card he'd taken off Raphael. "This is a card that will get you into the tower. It is like a front door key. There are pads. I'm not sure how to describe them. But if you put this on the pad, it will open the doors. Go to the parking garage. One of those pads will let you in. Once you are at the very top of the parking garage, you will see how to get into the tower. Your goal is to get to the penthouse. That is on the very top floor. There is a special elevator on the 8th floor. It only works with one of these cards. If you can get to that elevator, you can get to the penthouse. It sounds complicated, but it's not. There is lots of food there, and no one could get to you."

Hailey looked at the card and then at Ryan, her jaw quivering.

"I'm just trying to help you. We . . . I won't be able to stay here forever. And there are like a billion zombies just over there, so it isn't safe, not even for you to sneak around."

Hailey looked out over the river, her hands pulling the sleeves of her coat down over her wrists. The wind blew a stray lock of blond hair over her eyes. Finally, she said, "Okay," and took the card, put it in her pink coat and zipped the pocket shut.

69

Global Infection: ≤ 33.8073%

Ryan did a magazine check-chamber check for the third time, making sure the rifle was loaded. Hailey chattered away in a perfect stream of consciousness, but he could barely hear her words as he approached the command bunker. He grunted at key moments, and it must have been the right moments, because she seemed content. He skirted a double stack of shrink-wrapped skids containing concertina wire and saw the entrance. He had a glimmer of hope that this wasn't an ambush when he saw the neat line of rifles, handguns, and tactical vests lying to the side of the entrance. He turned sideways and then ducked inside.

The command center was lit by LED lamps integrated into the structure and a thousand small points of blinking light—the telltale sign of switches and servers showing data traffic. Ryan heard a faint beeping coming from a server bank and noticed that a removable drive bay was loose. Out of habit, he reseated the drive. The beeping stopped.

Marco smiled. "I told you he would know what to do," he said to Raphael.

Raphael grunted and put a dark stick that looked like beef jerky into his mouth and sucked on it. The right side of his face was deep purple, and he looked like a raccoon around the eyes. Raphael seemed to have aged a hundred years in a few hours. He sat strapped into a Lockheed Martin exoskeleton on a pile of blankets, without a shirt and pants, a catheter tube running from the front of his boxers to a bag filled with yellow fluid. Without the Tony Stark supporting his body, he didn't look like he could hold himself upright. When Raphael saw Hailey standing just behind Ryan, he pulled a blanket over the catheter.

"But I don't see why I have to do it by myself," Simone said to Raphael.

Raphael took a long, slow drink from the hydration system built into the Stark, wincing as he put pressure on his mouth to suck. Finally, he said, "You will do this because I ask you." His voice came out as a rasping croak.

"But you said war does not stop for anyone," Simone said, like he'd just proved that the world existed.

"My son," Raphael rasped, "you must think before you speak. You must see what *es* happening before you open your mouth." He shifted in the exoskeleton, his movement labored with pain. "If you can no do this thing then go back to the Stryker and sleep. I will know that you are a lazy boy. You choose, but do not ask me more questions."

"You always think I am lazy," Simone said. "You always like Marco and Teo better than me."

Marco started to speak, but Raphael interrupted. "I love you Simone, as I love all my sons, but I have run out of patience to teach you important things. You want to be a man and do whatever you want? Then I will no longer tell you what to do." Raphael Paguero's head tilted forward and his body hitched. He was crying.

Simone started to cry. But when he saw Ryan, he choked back his tears. "Did you do this to him?"

Hailey came around Ryan's hip like a momma bear. "He didn't do this, dick wad. Everyone in your family falls."

"My Poppa didn't fall!" Simone shouted. "He—"

"Enough!" Raphael bellowed. And then seemed to collapse as the effort rippled through his ravaged body. "I tell you what happen. Leave Mr. Sage be."

"Say you're sorry!" Hailey snapped her left hand on her hips, her right finger wagging like a parochial school nun.

"Hailey," Ryan said, reaching out to touch her shoulder.

Hailey spun toward Ryan, all fight and fire. "But he said you did this—"

Ryan said, "It's okay."

Simone stepped up close, his eyes smoldering. "If you did this, I will—"

"You should probably do what your father has asked," Ryan said holding his gaze.

Slowly the look of revenge dissolved into adolescent fear. Simone's eyes went round and he looked to Marco.

Marco said, "If you want to be a good soldier, do what Poppa asked."

Simone's jaw quivered. "Okay," he said. Then he flashed a malignant look at Hailey. "Shut up!" he snapped and stomped from the command bunker.

"Dick wad," Hailey mumbled.

Ryan watched Simone walk into the warehouse. "Hailey, I'm gonna need some new clothes, so I can change. Could you see if you can find something for me to wear?"

Hailey stepped back, looking at him from head to foot like she was measuring him for *haute couture*. "You're pretty tall," she said.

"Look for extra large shirts. I'm sure you will find something."

"Okay," Hailey said. She took two steps toward the door, stopped, took two steps back, hugged Ryan's side and then left.

The smile lingered on Ryan's face until he turned to Raphael and Marco. "So you fell?"

"Yes, I did no want you to kill my son," Raphael said, taking a long drink of water. "He *es* a hot head. He would die. I know this now. And besides it *es* true. I fell many times." He tried to smile but couldn't make his face work.

Ryan noticed a splint on Raphael's right hand, and the Stark held his right shoulder immobilized. He looked at Marco. "You can reattach a finger?"

Marco said, "All I did was sew it back in place and splint it up. I just hope that I got it straight. There are no do-overs once the Combat Medic starts repairing bone."

A jolt of pain surged over Raphael's body like electricity.

Marco frowned. "Would you take some fucking painkillers?" he held up a green syrette. "we can survive without you for a few hours."

"I deserve this pain," Raphael rasped. "This *es* how God teach me humility."

Ryan said, "Raphael, you've been popping Oxycontin for a gunshot. Why in the hell wouldn't you take morphine now?"

Raphael sucked on a protein stick. "The morphine will make me heal slow."

"That is the trade-off," Marco said. "Morphine knocks a person out, and he can't eat. In a hospital, they would pump him full of proteins, sugars and liquids so the body can do the repairs. Combat Medic makes you eat and drink constantly. He needs the food to give the nanobots the fuel to repair the body and the water to flush his system."

Ryan looked at the tube coming out of Raphael's boxers. "Did you put the catheter in?"

"No," Marco said. "He did."

"I did no want to spend the day sitting in there," Raphael said, pointing toward the Porta Potti with his nose. "This *es* better."

There was no reasoning with Raphael to stop the self-flagellation. So Ryan said, "Hailey said you wanted to see me?"

Marco looked at Raphael.

"We have a proposal," Raphael said.

Ryan smiled without mirth. "Oh, isn't this cute?" he said. He stepped toward the bunker door and watched Hailey pick through the camp debris. Simone used the forklift to clear a path.

"Just hear us out," Marco said.

Ryan snorted. "I think the adage goes something like fool me twice and I'm a fucking idiot."

"We will no fool you," Raphael said.

Marco said, "There is a lot of stuff here, more than you can shuttle back to your tower in months of work. And that doesn't account for the 2091s. If they ever move to the other side of the warehouse, it is going to be a bitch to get back in here. So we still have interests that align."

"I already tried to *align our interests,* which I thought I did with a very effective and elegant solution. What really pisses me off is that beyond the mystical bullshit, there was no *reason* for the conflict. I never made an arbitrary claim on the content of this place. I never demanded that you take it all to my tower at your expense. I was even going to suggest that the paintings you asked for could be used to compensate for helping me."

"The paintings?" Raphael rasped. "You would have done this? You would have offered these things in trade?"

Ryan rolled his eyes.

Raphael sighed, his head fell forward. "Yes, I did this thing. That *es* why God needs to teach me humility."

"Marco, didn't I tell you that I would always be a second-class citizen in the Paguero tribe?" Ryan asked. "Didn't we have this very conversation in my office, and didn't you insist that I was wrong?"

Marco said, "Yes, you did say that."

"And you did exactly what I said you would do," Ryan said, trying to keep the rage out of his voice. "You sided with the tribe over right? This is inexcusable. The fact is I'm keeping my fingers crossed that we part company before anyone dies." Even as Ryan said the word, he took a look outside to find Hailey. For a heart-stopping second, he couldn't see her. Simone drove the forklift with a skid of four banded barrels of diesel fuel toward the hole in the wall. When the fork lift passed, he saw Hailey looking through a green duffel full of clothes.

"He will no hurt Hailey," Raphael said. "He *es* a stupid boy sometimes, but he is not like this."

"You mean like when he was going to shoot her for beating the shit out of him?"

Raphael sighed as deep has his body would allow.

Marco said, "Let me tell you what we want. This place," he said, holding out his hands, "is a battalion level communications center. For all practical purposes, it has the ability to talk pretty much anywhere around the globe. The thing that looks like a satellite dish outside is an uplink to the whole United States military communications structure." He held out something that looked like a cell phone from the 1980s. "This is a Rifleman radio," he said, and then he held up two devices. "This is a Galaxy Chronicle 5 and this is an Itronix Pip Boy 8000. This is what a soldier carries into battle. The ORACLE we have been using to see in the dark also integrates with the radio and the Net Warrior unit. The ORACLE is the HUD. You remember those video games where the hero could see bad guys through walls? This is almost like that. With this system, it is possible to see the whole battlefield and talk to anyone anywhere on the planet."

Ryan nodded. "And you guys can't make them work, and you think I can."

"Yes," Raphael rasped. "You are the computer wizard. Yes? This *es* your business?"

"I understand the principles of mesh networks. I even had a contract with the military some years ago to deploy a similar technology, but I have no specific knowledge of this system. And it would take me a long time to learn."

"How long?" Marco said.

"I have no idea. I don't even know if I could. It is a safe bet that this whole system has layers of encryption that makes it off-limits to the average jihadist. They take this stuff into combat, right? It would be really stupid if any stray Muslim with an AK-47 could hop onto the network."

"Can you make the Rifleman radios talk?" Raphael asked, frustrated.

"Poppa, I told you even if he can, they will not stay on the same network. These need to be reprogrammed . . ." Marco's voice faded. "I don't know what it's called. But the radios lose their connection over time."

"Yes, that is one of the challenges of a self-forming, self-healing mesh network. When a node drops from a network, there are some challenges in getting it to reacquire the network if too much time has passed, or if the encryption key has been changed."

"You do know how to do this?" Raphael said, hopeful.

"Again, I understand the technology, but I don't understand this command center."

Raphael was exasperated. "You just do no want to help us."

"Raphael, first, I have no obligation to do anything for you. Second, try pretending for a minute that I'm not always trying to screw you. Try just listening to what I say and pretend that I actually mean that. I am trying to be honest. I am trying to tell you that there are potential, even probable limitations. This may very well be beyond my abilities. I assume these servers are all secured by passwords. I don't have my log in cracking tools, and there isn't anyone here to—" Ryan stopped, his mind tripping down a stray path.

Blue Pill hacked the primary DNS . . .

"Did you hear something," Marco said.

"No, I just had a thought."

"These radios are very important," Marco said. "It is worth a lot for us to be able to talk to each other. In the weeks and months and years to come, this will be as important as any barricade. Since it is so important, we will help you get the valuable stuff to the tower." He paused and produced a piece of paper. "I made a list of things that we want and a list of the top ten things I think would be valuable to you." He handed the list to Ryan.

Ryan read through the list. "What is a TWPS?"

"It means Tactical Water Purification System," Marco said. "We have fresh water in both camps, but you will need a way to purify water. The system would mean endless fresh water."

It seemed a miracle that the water and power hadn't failed already. The city had been in decline for over a month and then the government started shipping the citizens to points unknown. Unless the water and power plants were on autopilot it was a mystery why anyone would stay behind to keep things running. "You guys want dibs on the transport truck, the Humvee? I didn't think the Lenco worked."

"You remember when we went to the grocery?" Marco said. "There was a SWAT vehicle at one of the intersections. The back had been burned, but we hope to scavenge parts from the engine."

"That is a good idea," Ryan said as he finished reading the list. He thought it was overgenerous, but he understood why the Pagueros thought they needed to sweeten the pot. "So let me guess at the original plan. With me banished to the penthouse you were going to load up as many of the abandoned semis as you could manage. What changed your mind?"

"I see that this *es* a bad idea," Raphael said. "It will be very hard to drive the semis to the camps. It *es* better to take less."

"So here is how my thinking goes. Every minute I spend on the communications system I'm not spending on my tower. And there are things in this camp that are much higher on my priority list. Global military communications sound like a great toy, but I already have satellite communications."

Raphael shook his head and immediately winced. "It *es* not like this. It *es* limited."

Marco said, "He is right. This would give you communications everywhere, because the system has the ability to take over networks. I heard one of my tech buddies tell me that it was like the thing was aware, that it was a very early form of AI. So if there is power and there is a network, you have coms. This would be invaluable in the decades to come."

Ryan said, "I'm not saying it has no value. I am saying that if I spend time on this and Pagueros do what Pagueros do, I am the one who suffers most. Time is my greatest commodity, particularly since I will be doing the work alone."

"We can still help you do it faster," Marco said.

"Here is some more honesty for you. This stuff is dead weight to you, so you won't take it. I have the time to come back and work on this later. It might be a month or a year from now, but I can come back. So the safe play for me is to decline, because I'm seriously screwed if I invest in this project and the Paguero tribe betrays me again."

Raphael tried to sit up against the pain. He tried to bring assurance to his bruised and battered face. "We will stock your tower first. Then you do this."

Marco said, "We will set aside what we would like to take. We take the rest, whatever you want, to the tower. Then you start working on this."

"There is only one very serious problem with this plan," Ryan said.

Marco nodded. "You don't want us back in the tower."

"Damned right I don't."

70

Global Infection: ≤ 33.8075%

But it's gonna rain," Hailey said. She was sitting cross-legged on top of the sandbags that made the gunner's nest, playing with the frayed edge of her boot. The wind at the top of the HESCO wall ruffled her matted hair.

"That isn't the same as a shower," Ryan said.

"But it's dark in there."

"Turn on the lights." He looked out over the camp, watching the infected. Somehow they seemed . . . different, but he couldn't put his finger on why. Twenty-four hours ago, the horde had been scattered over almost two square miles seeming to dither and twitch like they had the palsy. But now they were making their way back to the walls of Fort Pitt, as if on a Sunday stroll.

"But it's creepy in there."

"How about if I stand in the hallway outside?"

"Someone might come inside and peek."

"No one is going to come in."

"Uh-huh . . . they have already been in the shower. Well, Simone was in there, and Marco was too but not Raphael. He's still really hurt. When do you think he will get better? I think it will be like days, but that is kinda sad. Don't you think it is sad that he got hurt?"

"Don't change the subject."

"But I like you even though you stink."

"And I like you even though you stink, too." He reached out to touch her shoulder but she flinched. He paused until she made eye contact. "We've been handling dead bodies. I don't need to explain why that is a bad thing. I'm gonna take a shower just as soon as I can. Did you find me something to change into?"

"I found some shirts and some scrubs but they are not gonna match. The shirts are like baby poop green, but the pants are blue. I tried to find some pants that matched the shirts, but they weren't the same size."

"And did you find something for yourself to change into?"

"What's wrong with what I'm wearing?" Hailey asked, looking at her jeans and opening her pink coat, revealing a long-sleeved blue shirt.

"Duh?! They are *dirty*. That coat has seen better days. It's got a big rip in it. And it is getting a little small on you."

"But I like them. They are my force field to keep stuff away."

"Force field, huh?" Ryan said, thinking there was some truth to that statement. No one wanted to stand too close. "If you find a new camouflage jacket, you can be invisible and have a force field. And if you want to keep it, you can *wash* this coat."

"Where are we gonna wash them? I don't see a washing machine around here." She stood up and looked into Fort Pitt like she was a sailor on a ship's prow. "Nope, no washing machine there."

"I might just make you take them to the river and wash them on a rock."

"Oh, you're gross. There are zombies in that water!"

Ryan saw Marco climbing to the top of the HESCO wall. "Go find yourself some clean clothes. I'll come down in a little while."

"Ohhh," Hailey whined as she slumped, letting both arms hang down limp. "But—"

Ryan pinched his eyes shut. "Come on, girl."

"O! K!" She climbed down the wall.

Marco crested the top wearing the Stark, decked out in full combat kit and digital camouflage raided from Hailey's pile of clothes. He wore an Ops Core FAST helmet and an ORACLE darkened like sunglasses. He stood tall, his broad shoulders back, his face filled out, his complexion healthy, and his eyes sharp. Ryan had always seen hints of this man buried underneath the pain and suffering and sickness.

Since arriving in Pittsburgh, Marco had walked with one foot in the grave and one foot dragging behind, but today, even though he still had an IV attached to the Stark, feeding necessary meds into his arm, he looked like the Special Forces operator he'd trained to be.

"What is the occasion?" Ryan asked. "You are all dressed up looking for someplace to go."

Marco pointed his weapon down to the gathering mob. "They are the occasion. I was thinking I'd gotten lax. The last group of people who relied on these walls to protect them died."

"That is why this weapon is always close," Ryan said tapping the M16 with his index finger.

"You have been my most attentive student," Marco said. "Except for that first night in the penthouse, I don't think I've ever seen you without a weapon."

"Except when you disarmed me," Ryan said.

"Mitigating circumstances," Marco said, trying to put a smile at the end of that thought.

Ryan offered nothing.

"I had to watch my father for a concussion last night, so he really couldn't sleep much. We are past the critical stages so I persuaded him to take some painkillers and sleep. The body still heals best when it rests."

Ryan still offered nothing.

"I came to tell you that we have the transport loaded. This is our down payment, if you'll accept it."

"Yeah, I saw that Simone was packing a trailer. Does that mean you are calling dibs after all?"

"No, the stuff going into the trailer will go to the tower like we said. But my father is the one who can drive the semi. I don't have the confidence to drive it through the narrow streets without getting stuck. And Simone doesn't have the skill, so we will have to wait. But Simone can drive the military transport to the tower. Between the transport and the Humvee, we can take a load."

Ryan said, "Physically Simone looks like he is doing much better. But dare I say mentally, he seems . . . unstable."

"He's sixteen, under enormous pressure, with a big chip on his shoulder."

"He's been that way since I met him, and getting worse."

Marco's eyes scanned the infected gathering at the base of the wall. "I think I mentioned that my family had some trouble a couple years ago. My mother's brother, Miguel, was taken by a cartel employed by a dictator, Gaspar José de Francia, some wannabe world leader who thought naming himself after an 19th century ruler gave him legitimacy. Anyway, my mother is . . . how to say this . . . very outspoken against the socialist governments that dominate most of South America. They are almost always corrupt, and they are either in bed with cartels or impotent against them. She speaks out against the policies that prop up those governments."

"I would like to meet her, I think."

"Let us hope that my father is healed before that happens," Marco said. "Anyway, the Paraguay government, which is to say Gaspar José de Francia, took offense and had a cartel kidnap Miguel to silence her. They tortured him and sent pieces of him to her in the mail every time she showed up in front of a mic or after one of her articles was published. The U.S. government wouldn't help. So she and my father and Daniel Ryder's security team went to get him out. I told you my brother Timoteo is a truly gifted shooter. He was asked to go with them on the mission. He was a real asset. Simone wanted to go. Of course, he couldn't because he was fourteen and just as uncontrollable as he is now. As you can tell, my family makes a big deal out of being a warrior. When Timoteo came back a hero, Simone put the chip on his shoulder and has never taken it off."

"So that is why he is always spoiling for a fight," Ryan said.

"Yes. My mother is a legend. She was sixteen when she led a guerilla force against the Marxist oppressors. My father has always been a fighter. I went into the Army, and after a tour in the Middle East, I worked on my resume until I was selected for the Rangers School. After being assigned to the 75th Regiment, I did a tour in the European Theater against the Caliphate. Timoteo was going to go into the Marines. He wants to be a Marine Recon sniper, but I talked him into waiting until he was out of college before he went into the military. Brilliant kid, 4.0 grade point, patient, determined. I think he would be a junior this year, and he was scheduled to do OCS this summer . . ." Marco paused, and then shook his head. "Anyway, on the raid, Timoteo made three shots over nineteen hundred yards."

"I guess that is good," Ryan said.

"Doing it *once* with the weapon he had is damned near miraculous," Marco said. "Long story short . . . Simone is trying to live up to the Paguero warrior legend. Poor kid doesn't even know that it's nothing to aspire to." He looked out over the camp, his face tightening around the corners as if he were puzzling out a spelling word. "If Simone had been there last night, you could have taken all three of us, couldn't you? I mean, if we didn't have guns."

"Probably," Ryan said. "But who knows? If you had been healthy, it might not have been so one-sided. And I'm not motivated to cripple a sixteen-year-old kid even if I do think he's a mouthy little prick."

"But you would have hurt him, wouldn't you?"

"I don't fight for fun. Actually, I don't want to fight at all. I'm too much of a pussy. But if I'm pressed, my goal is to destroy. My goal is to make myself as safe as possible, as fast as possible."

Marco breathed deep as he chewed the inside of his cheek. "I remember I was in Army Mountain Warfare School and we were running an assault on a mountain emplacement. The scenario was that some *Al-Qaeda* high priority leader was there. The LT leading the platoon performed a textbook advance to the location, performed the assault, and completed the mission. There was nothing specifically wrong with what he did. I'd rarely seen better, but there was a Marine Corps Captain, or maybe he was a Lieutenant Colonel . . ." He paused trying to remember and then said, "It doesn't matter. He was overseeing the exercise. I don't know why this jarhead was at the school, but he did the after-action debrief. He said timidity was a combat disaster. Mission success was based on three things: speed, surprise, and violence of action. I remember what he looked like. I remember the look he had in his eyes. I remember thinking that was the kind of officer I'd go into battle with. And I can't believe I missed it."

"Missed what?"

"You had his eyes, and you did exactly what he said—speed, surprise, and violence of action. God, it was beautiful. I was so caught up in my father's *machismo* that I missed the important details. In hindsight, I can see it in the way you handled Gus, and I can see it in the way you handled my father. And then the way you disarmed me . . ." He shook his head like he was trying to wake from a dream. "You've wrecked people before, haven't you?"

"Yes," Ryan said.

"Against multiple attackers, right? How many have you fought at once?"

"In the *dojang,* I trained against maybe eight at once."

Marco gave him an appraising look. "Eight?"

"Don't be too impressed. Everybody pulls their punches in the gym."

"Mr. Sage, I saw you fight. I saw your face. You've seen the real thing. That wasn't dojo fighting. That was what it looks like when it means life and death."

Ryan said, "What is the most you've fought against?"

"Hand to hand? I went up against three jihadists at the same time. I had a knife. They all died."

Ryan raised an eyebrow. "Do you like talking about it?"

"No."

"Neither do I."

Marco looked away, traces of exasperation tugging at the corners of his eyes. "My dad didn't lay a finger on you. I've seen my father hurt people, and I know what I can do, and you went through us like butter. I want to know what else you are hiding from us."

Ryan laughed. "Hiding? Me? Are you serious?"

"I'm very serious," Marco said. "I can't make the pieces fit. I don't like the mystery. I feel like I, we, have been misled. That you are not what you have said you were."

71

Global Infection: ≤ 33.8076%

Okay, this is really going to make me laugh," Ryan said. "Your father casually betrays his word, and I'm the one who must be the liar?"

"That's not what I said," Marco said. "I didn't call you a liar."

"That didn't even make sense. Marco, I've never misrepresented myself. I told you that no one in your family made an effort to know me because everyone thought I was beneath you. Your father's mystical warrior ethos is what got him hurt. You both thought the fight last night was some raw recruit dick-measuring. You thought it was the alpha male proving his dominance . . . but you were wrong."

"But you didn't have to hurt him like that."

Ryan regarded Marco for a minute. "I didn't do combat school, but I got the same advice from a seventy-year-old Korean man. In broken English, he said that apes thump their chest to scare off a threat, but predators hide until they rip out the throat. His point was the same as your Jarhead. The purpose of a fight is to destroy. So if it was an effective *ambush* more is the better. I'm not going to apologize for being a better tactician. But you have forgotten a crucial point. I tried to talk everyone out of a fight. The fact that your father picked a fight with a man who had him by seventy pounds, five inches, and a will to destroy was his mistake, not my lie."

"So why didn't you kill us?" Marco said. "Why didn't you finish it? You had to fear that we would just shoot you in your sleep. Why not end the threat?"

Dark clouds rolled in from the distance. "That might have been the safe move but killing both of you would mean I'd have to kill Simone and no matter how much of a mouthy idiot I think he is, the boy doesn't deserve death because his father picks a fight. And besides, killing is hard. I've already got images in my head from killing infected. I know that they are sick, and I even understand the necessity of destroying the infection, but somehow killing them still grates on me inside. I don't need to add any more trauma to my psyche."

Marco appraised Ryan. "I know exactly what you mean. So, just to be clear, you're not some secret agent that is hiding his identity or some former navy SEAL sandbagging his shooting skills."

Ryan laughed until he realized that Marco was serious. "Oh no. I'm just a businessman with a particular skill for pissing people off with big ideas, trying to survive the apocalypse."

"You laugh, but what happened last night seems so inconsistent with . . ." Marco's eyes traveled Ryan's physique. "With this . . ."

"Okay, so this is good camouflage. But it's not really a mystery. Some years ago, I thought I was a badass. I think every kid thinks that. I was tall, strong as an ox, and wanted something to work on besides track and field. I thought mixed martial arts looked badass. But truth is, I was bad and I was an ass, but I was not a badass. I didn't like the pain or the recovery, and that kind of fighting required a fitness level that I would never maintain over decades. So I went looking for a form of fighting that could be sustained no matter what my physical condition or age."

"You fought MMA? That would have been a good detail to know."

Ryan snorted. "There was no need to know it if Raphael had acted like a rational human being and kept the contract."

"I don't like the fact that after all my training, I missed such an important detail." Marco's gaze faded out to a thousand yards. The birds sang, and the infected gabbled and yammered like babies trying to shape words. "So are you going to tell me about your fight with the biggest number? I'm a Paguero and a Ranger. So you can understand why I like that kind of macho bullshit."

Ryan frowned at the memory. "I haven't thought about this in years. I was in Dublin. We were at some mid-level track meet. My coach thought it was good practice as a lead-up to the rigorous schedule for Worlds. I won the gold in the 400-meter, and I think I missed the world record by like two tenths of a second. That is still an eternity in track time, but I was stoked. So two buddies and I went to a pub for drinks and to chat up some women. There is always a woman, right? Anyway, these ten guys come into the pub, rowdy and mouthy."

"Ten guys?" Marco said. "You took on ten men?"

"No, it was six," Ryan said, his face grim. "Fucking Irish football hooligans," he said.

Marco said. "Football hooligans? I'm guessing they didn't pull their punches."

"My coach was so pissed when he saw me," Ryan said. "He thought I'd taken a private cage match to make some money, which was stupid because I'd *never* done that, and my endorsement contracts specifically forbade fighting because they knew of my very brief MMA career. But I ran the 4 by 400 the next day all beat up, and we still took gold. So he didn't stay mad. In the post-race interview, the woman asked me and my teammate what happened to our faces, and I said, 'We were at a party and some very pretty women challenged us to a potato sack race and we fell.'"

"You didn't," Marco said.

"Yeah, I did," Ryan said. "I told her that the girls won fair and square. That bit of chivalry went over great. I had to make sure that my endorsements weren't in jeopardy, so I had to give a reason. But when the real story came out, the European press had a grand time. They thought I made a joke with the potato sack comment. I was in Ireland after all. And the real irony was my endorsements doubled."

"So what was the real story?"

"It's boring. It's the same bar story over and over," Ryan said. "Girls, beer, fucking Irish football hooligans, broken bones, blood, pain and suffering, hospitals, police, jail cells, and judges."

"You went to jail?"

"Yes, I did, which sucked because I really needed to sleep for the race the next day."

"If it is boring, why did the European media make a big deal out of it?"

"You're the one who reads gossip magazines."

"Come on. Just tell me."

"Look it up on the Internet."

"You really aren't going to tell me?"

"I don't know, Marco. I'm still trying to be pissed at you because of your part in last night's events. It's hard, because you are a likable guy. I even thought we might have been friends, but now I can't decide. I enjoyed our conversations. I respected your achievements. I knew a couple Rangers, and they were what everyone describes . . . quiet professionals. You handle yourself like them."

Marco sobered for a moment and then he said, "So does that mean you won't help us?"

Ryan looked down the length of the wall noticing that the infected had dragged the bodies away to feed. He tried to find a place for that factoid in the larger puzzle, but he couldn't make it fit within the borders. Finally, he said, "Marco, have you ever wondered why they built this place with these walls so high?"

"No."

Ryan looked at him with a question etched into his brow.

"My tactical brain is malfunctioning," Marco said. "I missed the threat you represent, and I've been around you for almost two weeks and you disarmed me like you were taking my lunch money. If my 75th Regiment CO knew, he would take away my tab—"

"What do you think they would do if they realized you were helping someone to break a contract?"

Marco opened his mouth and then shut it, his jaw grinding. "They drill into us that there is never an excuse for failing to get it right, but the axis of my world is on tilt. My loyalties and values have been challenged in ways I would not have believed possible. I was betrayed by the government I swore an oath to protect . . . that same government that demanded I sacrifice my connection to my family for the greater good of this country.

I knew the pain my family would suffer when they put that gravestone in Arlington, but I believed in the mission. My family was dead to me until twenty days ago. And my brothers in the regiment betrayed my trust when they hunted down my team. I know they didn't know who I was and that they were following orders from men they trusted. But they died that day about a month ago. I get here and my one touchstone to existence is a family that I thought was gone forever. So yes, I gave my father the benefit of the doubt."

"And therein is my problem," Ryan said, "How many more times will you give your father the benefit of the doubt? Or did you already give him that benefit? Maybe you knew what these walls meant and just left out the details."

72

Global Infection: ≤ 33.8077%

The wind kicked up, swirling dust and trash and stench through the heavy Pittsburgh air.

Marco narrowed his eyes as Ryan's accusation settled into his mind. "What are you talking about? I think this whole camp is a clusterfuck waiting to happen. I figure some REMF got a hair up his ass and decided to put real soldiers to work with shovels to fill up these HESCOs because he couldn't stand seeing them do something important. And then I think he hid his ass in that command bunker and let the world go to hell."

Ryan said, "Well, here is what I am thinking. The military had weeks to build this camp, and Fort Pitt is the only place like it. There are no other walls this high. But someone chose a tall building right on the water's edge with no windows and no doors. They made sure the enemy could only come from one direction. Through the eyes of modern warfare, it looks foolish. But if we were in the medieval age with knights and damsels in distress and castles to resist a siege of the barbarian hordes, this place makes sense. All we are missing is a moat."

Marco's eyes swept over the camp. "Okay, but I've never seen the infected climb over much more than a truck let alone castle walls. They never got to the top of the bus. So how does this castle—" he met Ryan's eyes. "Wait . . . you think I knew something. You think that when I left you on that porch, I knew they could get to you, and these walls are the proof."

Ryan said, "The moment Raphael saw into this camp, he was plotting how to get it all to Maine. So I can't help but think that it would be so very convenient if I just happen to die all by myself. And I can't help but wonder if his oldest son wasn't in on the plot."

Marco squared his shoulders and pulled the ORACLE from his face. He held Ryan's gaze and said, "I might be having a crisis of conscience, but I would not, could not do that. I know what kind of death that would be. I'm the guy who has been eaten by them, remember. I was the guy who tried to get you to reconsider coming to the camps, remember. I was trying save your life. And for the record, I spent a full day trying to talk my father out of his plan. We had been arguing for an hour when you heard us in the command bunker."

"No Marco, you asking me to come to Maine was a guilty conscience. You condemned me for a failure of pride, but you should have been condemning your father for a failure of morality. The bottom line? What difference does it make if you objected in theory, but in practice you side with him?"

"No. The only side I was on was trying to keep people from shooting each other. I thought maybe if I could persuade you to go to the tower, I could work on my father so cooler heads could prevail."

"My head was cool, Marco," Ryan said. "For that matter, your father's head was plenty cool, because his actions were calculated. He'd already pointed a gun at my head once. I had every reason to believe he would kill me on sight. And with the way your father treated Marie Blanco, it was logical that he would sacrifice Hailey in a minute. So, let's not pretend that I'm the reason things went sideways. And for the record, you could have held your father at gunpoint to avoid a gunfight, but you threatened me even though I hadn't initiated violence."

Marco shook his head. "My father was a known quantity. I knew he wouldn't shoot. I didn't know how you would act. Whatever error in judgment I made, my goal had nothing to do with furthering my father's actions. And as for what I knew about these walls and what they mean . . ." he shrugged. "I've been all over the world fighting these things. There have always been fast movers that are a bitch to kill in a pack, but I've never seen them crawl over obstacles this size so I thought you would be safe on the overhang, well, as safe as you could be under the circumstances."

Ryan said, "I saw how low that overhang was in comparison to this wall, and I said to myself, 'Self, how come the Paguero tribe didn't think I would survive? Why were they surprised that I showed up?' And then I decided that the most likely answer was because the Paguero tribe thought they had stranded me with certain death."

"God, you are paranoid," Marco said, exasperated. "And in your calculations, how did we plan for that storm? Is my *tribe* able to manipulate the weather? How about if we were amazed that you survived one of the worst storms we've ever seen? How about we were amazed that you managed to get off that porch? How about if we thought the Virgin Mary had saved your faithless ass again?

"When we boarded those windows, our one concern was making sure nothing could bite you from behind. We could see that you hadn't broken a window and crawled inside. I mean, my God, you could barely haul your fat ass off the street and then we see you the next morning dry and looking like you had a good night's sleep. We thought we'd witnessed our first fucking miracle."

Ryan nodded. "Okay, fair point."

"So, these walls and that porch and my knowledge is the conspiracy theory you've been thinking about for the last hour?" Marco asked.

"Conspiracy theory?" Ryan asked. "All things considered, can you blame me? But no, I came up here to get away from the smell of death and rot down there and talk to Hailey, but it seems prudent to figure out how the Paguero tribe will screw me if I agree to this deal."

"We won't," Marco said. "We are not playing an angle here."

"I don't think you are con men. I think your father's actions are a product of sincerity."

"Thank you."

"It's not a compliment. It is a deeper form of evil. Con men know they are doing wrong. They recognize their moral failing but enjoy tricking people. But your father thinks his actions are morally vindicated, even though his personal definition of morality shifts like the desert sands. He was going to *murder* me last night to vindicate the Holy Mother."

"If you had said half the shit you said to a Muslim about Muhammad, he would have cut your head off. You went after his religion, for God's sake," Marco said. "For that matter all you have done is whine and preach against his beliefs. What did you expect to happen?"

"Whine? Really?" Ryan rolled his eyes. "That portrayal of my objection for your father's criminal actions is so ridiculous that I won't dignify it with a response."

Marco snorted. "You are so damned self-righteous. You act like you have never done anything wrong."

"Marco, the dirty little secret is that there is no other kind of righteousness. No matter the Christian doctrine of imputed grace, you can't borrow someone else's moral action. To be sure, Catholic doctrine destroys moral action at the root. Pervasive depravity means man can't take moral action no matter what. To claim moral action is to steal from God so the only option available to man is moral bankruptcy, which means men are forced to write endless moral blank checks to be cashed by any evildoer. I refuse to write the fucking check, which is the real root of your objection. The Paguero tribe has treated civil collapse as a private free-for-all. You are insulted that someone would dare fault you for doing what you have to do to survive. As if the absence of police writing tickets abolishes the moral principles required for human life. But I won't absolve you of bad action. There is no moral equivalency between myself and the Pagueros, and I have judged accordingly. I expect individuals to act right because only individuals can choose moral action. The only kind of righteousness that exists is *self*-righteousness; therefore I judge and prepare to be judged."

Marco said. "I will grant that my father did some wrong things, but there has to be a compromise somewhere. You have to respect what people believe, and you didn't respect anything he said last night. You barely listened to him."

"Listen to him?" Ryan asked. "I did listen to your father offering up his religion as the justification for his actions. He offered his religion as the guiding principle of his actions. His religion told him that it was morally right to deceive, mislead, intimidate and then ask for forgiveness for bad actions from a dead woman. That is the definition of intellectual FUBAR. So I have no responsibility to take that seriously. I didn't accept the premise that I have to accommodate the irrational. The Paguero definition of compromise is me conceding their right to believe, say, or do anything they want and this is the root problem. I don't."

"You are wrong. My father is a moral man."

"No, I'm not wrong. Let me illustrate my point. Last night, it was Raphael's divine prerogative to use violence to teach *me* humility. Today, the beating is God's way of teaching *him* humility. The same event creates two moral rationalizations. How can a man claim to be moral if the ethical standard changes with a moment-to-moment divine revelation?"

"We all fall short sometimes. My father is a flawed man. He knows that. We are all flawed. That is the human cond—"

"Stop," Ryan said. "I've heard this refrain over and over . . . We're all just sinners . . . It is the human condition to do bad things. This is exactly what I was talking about and I won't tolerate it. I won't accept moral condemnation that I have not earned, and I will not absolve your father of moral vacancy because everybody does bad things."

"Are you really saying you don't make mistakes?"

"Obviously, I do since I entered into a contract with a man who thinks nothing of breaking a contract," Ryan said. "But don't drop the context. The issue isn't about my moral perfection. The issue is that you expect me to share moral condemnation to absolve your father's epic bad action. Again, I am being asked to compromise my virtue, and the beneficiary is Raphael. It is as if this conflict only exists because I demand better behavior. The expectation is that I must compromise my values to make it easy for the Pagueros. But what compromise is Raphael making? What value is he walking away from to achieve social harmony? Is he going to compromise his religion? Is Raphael going to abandon self-sacrifice as the moral standard?"

Marco sighed. "My father could never think like you do. He could never abandon the Church."

"Then why would I enter into another agreement with him? I have everything to lose by ignoring how he has acted."

Marco said, "No, you do have something to gain. You will gain our knowledge and help. No matter how much you would like to pretend otherwise, you can't do this alone. Just look at all of those 2091s and remember it is too damned dangerous for anyone to live alone."

Ryan breathed deeply. The refugee camp was an object lesson in what happened when men failed to sustain social commitments. "And that is my problem. That is what I can't figure out how to reconcile. The pragmatic choice is to evade Raphael's actions and accept this deal so I can get momentary help. But pragmatism is as deadly as altruism." His mind whirled and spun looking for a solution. "I am very aware that I need help. Living alone in this environment is probably a death sentence, but negotiating with people who are committed to sacrificing me to the greater good is the same outcome."

"Then make the agreement with me," Marco said. "I will never sacrifice you or your property to the needs of my family. I will make sure that my father and brother fulfill their responsibilities."

Ryan regarded Marco for a long minute, then his gaze returned to the infected coming in their inexorable march back to the Fort Pitt walls. "So you will load the tower first and then I work on the system?"

"Yes."

"What if I can't get the system to work?"

"You have already explained your concerns. I accept that you may not succeed. But it is to your advantage to try. And if you agree, I commit to the original contract until my mother gets here. We will even stay here in Fort Pitt if you prefer."

"And the Stryker?" Ryan asked.

"My father is the one who broke the contract. It's still yours."

73

Global Infection: ≤ 33.8079%

It started raining ten minutes before the convoy rolled out of the warehouse. They left Raphael lying almost naked and sweating on an inflatable mattress topped with a camouflage sleeping bag while he slept. The Stark kept his right shoulder and hand immobile while the Combat Medic worked its healing magic, but he was in no shape to move. They stocked the bunker with guns and ammo, food and water, and a waste bucket. Ryan made sure the pink phone was on a desk, and then they piled crates in front of the entrance.

Simone was behind the wheel of the fully-loaded military transport, with Ryan following behind in the Humvee packed with supplies and towing the mobile blood bank. The streets on the northeast side of the warehouse were clear but for a few cars and four Peterbilt semis parked along 21st Street. The cross streets to the northeast were clear of infected. And for a hundred yards, it looked like they were on a planet with no 2091s.

And then Simone passed the southernmost edge of the warehouse and came into full view of the refugee camp to the west at the intersection at Smallman Street. He stopped and waited.

He waited and waited and waited.

The infected rushed toward the truck . . .

"I said we wanted to lure them to follow us," Ryan said, to himself. "Not get in our cars." He hit the speed dial.

"Yes?" Marco said.

"They are getting a little too close," Ryan said. "And they are moving fast . . . faster."

"I thought you wanted them to follow us into town?" Simone said, his voice distant from the driver's seat.

"They are plenty close!" Ryan snapped as the first one slammed into the vehicle.

Hailey flinched in the passenger seat and screamed.

"Go!" Ryan snapped. "Go! Go! Go!"

"But they are not—"

"Marco?! Dammit!" Ryan shouted. "You promised me he would not screw this up!"

Simone hit the gas and turned right, gunning down Smallman toward downtown Pittsburgh like he was trying to qualify for the Daytona 500—the load in the back shifting and wobbling toward the truck bed edge.

"Too fast!" Ryan said. "Too damned fast!" He tried to control the loaded-down Humvee as the blood bank attached to the hitch fishtailed behind.

"Ow!" Simone yelped.

"Get your shit together, little brother, or so help me god, I will beat you," Marco shouted. "Now slow the fuck down and drive like you have some goddamned sense."

The truck slowed to an even pace, its front bumper parting the infected like Moses before the Red Sea, and Ryan drove through his wake. In a few blocks, they were clear of the mob.

The wiper blades swiped left and right, pounding out their own rhythm. "Okay, slow down. Let's let them catch up," Ryan said. "Hailey peek your nose up into the turret and tell me how close they are."

Hailey scrambled between the seats, her smelly pink coat scrapping past Ryan's face. "They are about four streets back."

"Tell me when they get to 15th Street and keep looking all around."

"Okay," Hailey said.

Marco stepped out of the truck and paced the street in front of the transport.

"How are you looking up there?" Ryan said.

"We are right as rain, pun intended," Marco said, "and there are 40 or 50 2091s dead ahead, but nothing we can't handle."

Hailey dropped down from the .50 cal turret, her hair and face soaked. "They are almost to that street."

"How many?"

"You want them all to follow right? Well, they are coming," Hailey said. "They are kinda running fast."

Before the convoy left Fort Pitt, Ryan and Marco took a hard look at the streets to formulate a plan. Option one was to take the Northeast to the 28th Street Bridge and then drive 380's empty inbound lanes toward downtown, but they feared that would pull the infected to the northeast side of the warehouse. Option two was to drive west through the mob and pull them away from Fort Pitt. They chose option two.

"Did she say running fast?" Marco asked as he stepped back into the cab and popped the door shut.

"Yes," Ryan said. "Let's get moving."

"Roger that," Marco said.

Simone continued his—mostly—sane driving to the crosstown connector and finally to Boulevard of the Allies. They pulled onto Wood Street, and Simone groused only a little when he was nominated to climb the crane in the rain and lift the shipping container, but in the end, he performed like a true Paguero warrior.

"You got it from here?" Ryan asked Marco, standing in the rain at the entrance to the Renaissance Tower's substructure.

"Yes," Marco said. "How much time do you need?"

"An hour?" Ryan said. "Does that give you enough time?"

"That will work. We will get these unloaded and get the blood bank hooked to power," Marco said. "Do you mind if we get some tools? There are some things we need to take apart."

"That is fine," Ryan answered. "See you in an hour."

Hailey sat in the passenger seat, water dripping down her cheeks, looking like a little drowned puppy. "I am going to the penthouse to get some things," Ryan said, "I know you don't want to come in, and I won't make you. So you have three choices. You can ride with Marco down to where you were before, or you can wait right over there up on those steps behind those cars." He pointed to the loading dock door. "It is covered and out of the rain. Or you can come with me."

"Can't I just stay in here?" Hailey asked

"They are going to unload the Humvee," Ryan said. "They are going to drive it down underground."

Hailey fidgeted with her sleeves. "I don't have to come in?"

"Not if you don't want to."

Hailey crawled out. Ryan walked to the tenant parking entrance, swiped his badge and squeezed behind the van while they waited for the gate to open. The rain had washed away much of the blood and gore, but patches of flesh were rotting inside the van. Ryan waved for Hailey to follow as he started up the car ramp.

"What happened with that van?" Hailey asked, her worn-out boots flopping on her feet.

"Oh, zombies tried to eat me," Ryan said.

"Nuh-uh!" Hailey said. "You're not that sweet."

"Funny girl."

"I know."

They made a quick trip through the parking garage across the skywalk and stood under the overhang at the tower's promenade level entrance. "Okay, this is where I told you to go if you ever needed to get into the tower. Remember?"

Hailey nodded, her hands working overtime pulling her sleeves over her wrists. "Yes, it makes sense now."

Ryan pointed through the double doors. "Right down this hall is that elevator I was telling you about. It goes to the penthouse. I am going there now to get things, and I will come back."

"What are you gonna get?"

"Food and my computer and some tools," Ryan said. "You can sit over there on the picnic tables or you can stand inside the door. They are both out of the rain, but it might be warmer inside. Your choice."

"How long will you be gone?" Hailey asked.

"I will try to be fast. So maybe a half hour, but you are safe here. There is no one up here. If you like I will take a lap around the track with you to make sure."

Hailey's eyes were looking for an escape route. "I'll sit over there."

"Okay." Ryan badged the door open.

"You are coming back, right? You won't forget me?"

Ryan looked into her eyes. "Hailey, I will always come back for you, okay?"

She sat on the picnic table cross-legged like an Indian and played with the edge of her boot.

Ryan hit the penthouse door running.

In the kitchen, he grabbed a pile of T-bone steaks and some prepackaged mashed potatoes, green beans, bread, lunchmeat, condiments, pancake mix, eggs, and two pounds of bacon. He found an electric skillet, spatula and grilling fork and bagged everything. He dithered in a circle for a minute trying to decide if he'd gotten everything he needed. MREs were great in a pinch, but there was nothing like fresh food. And with Raphael in need of huge volumes of protein, he thought the steaks would be a great dinner option.

He dropped the bags in the foyer and went to one of the Ryder granddaughters' bedrooms and found a pair of Nikes. He went to his office and gathered up his iGlass and computer. He logged into the desktop and brought up his e-mail.

He found nothing from Daniel.

Patrick had sent two e-mails. The first one said that there was a snag getting the bio scanner reset. The second asked if he'd gotten the first e-mail and closed by saying that the shit hit the fan. Patrick didn't explain what that meant.

And last, he saw an e-mail from Cheryl Rosen with an attachment.

Ahou?!

He clicked to open.

Ryan,

OMG! I don't know how you do it, but you inspire my mind and my body! That answer was great! I practiced saying it until I could make the argument for myself, and you were exactly right in what Richard would say. He acted like it didn't matter, but I know he was furious. And it was fascinating how people responded to what I said. It was encouraging. But I have one more question. I hope you will answer it before you click on the video. Because I think you will be distracted if you watch the video first. ;)

At least I hope you will be distracted.

Here is my question. Well, here is the question that I was asked. If man is not a social animal, then what is he? How do I answer that question?

Ahou
xoxoxo

Ryan smiled, his heart speeding up. "I wish I had that effect on more women," he said as his cursor rested on the attachment. *Distracted??* He could use some distraction.

Hailey is waiting . . .

Ryan cut and paste two links on related articles and then wrote:

Ahou,

Socially/politically, man is a contractual being. All of man's social interaction is based on contractual agreements. A contract is merely an offer of a value, an acceptance of a value and the consideration which is the "down payment" on the ongoing exchange of value. When you hear value, don't think money. Values can be a hug or a kiss, or good conversation. The consideration could be a meal, or a Valentine's card a stuffed animal or a wedding ring.

Most people are familiar with formal contracts that are written down, but most "contracts" are informal . . . the generalized give and take of small things: smiles, eye contact, social niceties, et cetera, that lead to the exchange of bigger values, or maybe I should say more personal values. With this in mind, you will easily see that social failures are really contractual failures, meaning someone did not follow through on an explicit or inexplicit commitment. Someone lied. Someone was deceptive. Someone defaulted on the exchange of consideration. Notice that all human virtues—rationality, truthfulness, justice, et cetera—are virtues because they are essential for successful contracts.

Anyway, that is the short version. Sorry to be so abrupt, but I've got some things cooking here. Hopefully tomorrow we can twist Daniel's arm for a video conference.

I'll look at the video now.

Ryan

Ryan clicked on the attachment, and the video sprang into the player and there stood Ahou, standing in front of a neatly made narrow bed with white sheets and black coarse blankets, a bed stand and institutionally gray walls, all lit with a stark overhead light. She wore nothing but a smile that radiated an invitation that made men want to sell their souls.

"Ryan, I hope you enjoy this," Ahou said, her voice thick with arousal.

Ahou was Persian, accounting for her dark hair and dark eyes, but her skin tone was white with a hint of darkness like the color of coffee filled with cream—smooth, flawless, and hairless. Her nose was narrow, and her lips were delicate, giving her an elfin aura. Her shoulders were back and upright, showcasing C-cup breasts with pert, tan nipples. She raised her arms and slowly turned, showing off every curve. She moved to the bed and lay down, her back arched showing her ribs and her narrow waist. Her fingers traveled across a nipple, then down to her navel heading toward the smooth cleft between her legs. Her knees parted and the camera shifted, slowly moving closer—

The ragged they come and
The ragged they kill!
You pray so hard on bloody knees.
The ragged they come and
The ragged they kill!
Down in the cool air I can see.

Ryan dug out his phone. "Hello? Uh . . . hello?" he said as he frantically tried to kill the sound on the video.

"You coming back down?" Hailey asked.

"Yup, just about ready to leave now."

"It's kinda scary by myself. It just thundered."

"I'm sorry. I'm sorry. I am coming right now. You should see me in like five minutes."

"Okay," Hailey said. "See you.

He took one last longing look at the still frame on the video, hovering the cursor over the play button. Ryan shook off the spell that threatened to seduce him and clicked on the red X to close the player. He gathered up his essentials, grabbed the bags in the foyer, and paused briefly at the door to think if he was forgetting anything. "Shit!" he said and put everything down.

He ran back to Mora's office and grabbed a pile of Post-it notes of various colors, tape and pens. Then he ran into the security room and riffled through drawers. "Camera, camera, camera," he said until he found it in the next drawer. He opened the case, assuring that the camera and lights were inside, snapped it shut, and ran back to the front doors. Minutes later, he was exiting the elevator and walking toward the promenade exit feeling like a pack mule.

Hailey was standing with her face pressed against the glass. She looked relieved.

“Okay, your turn to carry,” He handed her some bags.

“These are heavy.”

“It will give you muscles.”

“Yeah, I need muscles, too, so I can fight,” Hailey said as they walked back across the skywalk.

Ryan’s thoughts mulled over the video, to the details of Ahou’s body, the way it moved, the sound of her breathing—

The camera moved. Someone was working the camera? Who *was running the camera?*

“Did you hear me?” Hailey asked.

“Uh, what? Uh . . . what did you say?” He pulled himself back to the moment. “Fight? Who do you want to fight?”

Hailey tried to shrug, but the shoulder strap on the computer case weighed her down. “Bad people,” she said. “Do you think you could teach me to shoot some more?”

74

Global Infection: ≤ 33.8083%

The four returned to Fort Pitt wet, cold, and tired. They stumbled upstairs to the warehouse breakroom and dumped the supplies on a table. Simone complained that he was hungry and Marco nominated him to cook. Hailey stripped off her coat, draped it across a chair, dried her hair with a roll of paper towels, put a duffel bag underneath a table in the corner, wrapped herself in a green wool blanket, and promptly fell asleep. Marco checked on Raphael. Ryan wanted to kick himself for forgetting to change clothes. So, he went to Hailey's wardrobe pile and found things that looked promising. He grabbed a Red Cross hygiene kit and headed to the shower. Afterwards, he dressed in two layers of blue scrubs, an olive drab T-shirt, black socks and an orange sweatshirt with a firefighter's emblem on the left breast. He felt like a clown, but the clothes fit.

Ryan entered the breakroom and found piles of pancakes, eggs, and bacon on the table. Raphael sat, dressed in digital BDUs, tactical vest and a Tony Stark. His Kalashnikov hung on a single-point sling angled for his left hand. Five hours of sleep, a full round of Combat Medic and an additional course of the Maximov therapy had worked its healing magic. Except for the fading dull yellow bruising and his occasional hand flexing to work the newly knitted muscles and ligaments, Raphael looked the picture of health. Hailey roused to the smell of food and joined the men at the table. Everyone ate in silence until the last scrap of bacon disappeared into Simone's mouth. As he chewed, Simone announced he was going to sleep and left for an office down the hall. Hailey returned to her corner and slept while Marco, Raphael, and Ryan planned their next steps as they waited for the rain to pass. When they cleaned the dishes, Hailey woke. She stood beside Ryan, hair lopsided and rubbing the sleep out of her eyes. "Can I learn to shoot now?"

Marco said, "I think we can find a spot out of the rain. I can teach her."

"I'm all for it," Ryan said, as he dried a plate. "But one condition."

"What's that?" Hailey asked, yawning.

"You have to wash up and get clean cloths," Ryan said.

Marco said, "Good idea."

"No, it's not a good idea," Hailey said.

Ryan and Marco exchanged looks, shrugged and returned their focus to tasks at hand.

"That's it?" Hailey said, "You have nothing else to say? I really need to learn to shoot. I need to be able to defend myself."

Ryan said, "I agree and the condition to do that is to get cleaned up."

"You really do need to," Marco said.

Hailey's face flushed, pulled into sourness, and she stomped out of the breakroom.

They finished the dishes in silence. Ryan went to find the company's IT room and was completing his hack of the warehouse Wi-Fi system when Hailey came to him holding a Red Cross hygiene kit and an armful of clothes. She asked him to keep guard outside the women's bathroom. When he pointed to the co-ed shower, she was immovable. She disappeared into the bathroom for an hour, and when she emerged, her hair was wet, her face clean, and her teeth brushed. She wore a green T-shirt under a gray long-sleeved sweatshirt, a pair of camouflage pants that fit, gray socks and the Nikes. Underneath the dirt and smudge was blond hair and a light dusting of freckles on her cheeks.

"Very nice," Ryan said, reaching out for a hug.

Hailey flinched, her bright blue eyes wary.

Ryan held his distance and said, "Let's see if we can find you a shooting tutor."

"Oh no, I can't be seen like this," Hailey said putting on an Army jacket a size too big like it would hide her from the world. She pulled the hood over her head and hid behind Ryan as they walked to the command bunker.

The rain halted working in the camp so Ryan used the downtime to learn the coms system. He read through manuals while Hailey sat in a chair, spinning in circles, running a comb through her curls telling jokes to Ryan's grunts. He wasn't sure when she left.

Starting with the first Iraq War, the U.S. military faced a troubling reality: the pace of modern battle far exceeded communications. Ground force communications was still based on Vietnam-era technology, but combat operations moved at three times the speed. They could fight faster than they could talk.

To solve the problem, the military created the Joint Tactical Radio System (JTRS) and Ground Mobile Radio (GMR) systems to provide state-of-the-art communications to ground war fighters. But in the program's early stages, the military was confronted with a second troubling reality: the speed of government *procurement* was also operating at a 1945 bureaucratic pace. By contrast, the modern cellular communications industry developed at the speed of business. The lag between bureaucratic approval and implementation meant soldiers in the field were given technology that was already woefully outdated. The soldier went into combat with a radio and a computer weighing in excess of fifteen pounds, but owned a phone with ten times the functionality that weighed ounces.

The U.S. Army realized that it first needed to improve procurement before it could advance communications. In the early twenty-first century, the Army phased out the JTRS and GMR program and began a new initiative WIN-T: Warfighter Information Network-Tactical. Its stated mission was to provide secure and continuous communications from brigade command all the way down to a four-man rifle squad with their boots in hostile territory. The objective was to create a network that was self-organizing, self-healing, and path-optimizing: a mesh communications system that could provide voice, data, and video to the farthest reaches of the earth. It was a solution suited for modern warfare.

The Army set a long-range plan to deploy the WIN-T initiative in three increments so it could take advantage of commercial communications' technological lifecycle. By the end of the third increment, it had succeeded. The modern warfighter entered battle armed with his weapon, a one-pound radio integrated into his MOLLE vest, a Nett Warrior Situational Awareness/ Mission Command unit attached to his chest, and an ORACLE HUD on his face. Battlefield information poured into the Net Warrior system from drones, Sat Com uplinks and dozens of nodes distributed across the whole battle space—supplying the warfighter every tactically important detail. A soldier's training made him a killer, and the WIN-T system made him omniscient.

The success of the WIN-T system was on full display as the U.S. armed forces fought through six years of fighting the Caliphate's European Peace Initiative. Even with combat forces at levels far lower than WWII, the U.S. Military continued to dominate the European Theater.

The history and purpose is what Ryan Sage learned in the first few hours of investigation. It was almost impossible to walk into a network cold and figure out what the pieces did without understanding the system's purpose, so the WIN-T network details were essential for Ryan to understand the big picture. He paused, stretched and rolled his neck, then picked up his iGlass to start reading again. But a smell he'd not noticed before pulled him out of his technology haze: it lingered in the back of his mind, persistent and nagging. He sniffed and sniffed again, the smell seemed to swirl around the bunker like a swarm of elusive fruit flies. He finally identified the brutal stench of body odor and then he spotted the pile of sodden sleeping bags off to the far side. It seemed that as Raphael sweated through one sleeping bag, he dumped it into a pile and put down a fresh one. Ryan pulled the sleeping bags into the rain, and then ducked back into the command bunker.

He scanned the technology, studied the racks filled with routers and switches and the banks of servers and a dozen laptop computers encased in green ballistic hardened plastic. He traced cables and power lines to get an understanding of what connected to what, and finally followed a braided cable sheathed in rubber out of the bunker where it connected to antenna rising high above the command center, and then traced it to a satellite dish parked to the left side. Somehow all those pieces sent data into the heavens—to drones and satellites—which then relayed data back down to terra firma to the war fighters on the ground.

Now Ryan understood the puzzle borders, but he was left with a pile of pieces and no box cover. He looked through a crate filled with what looked like large smartphones wrapped in green ballistic polymer protective cases: these were the Net Warrior situational awareness units manufactured by Samsung and Itronix. There were two models: the Galaxy Chronicle 5 and the Itronix Pip Boy 8000. But these were not over-the-counter cell phones. The cellular function was off, and the units had been reprogrammed with a hardened Android kernel operating system and an NSA encryption algorithm. The Army didn't want some bored eighteen-year-old kid calling his best girl when Johnny Jihad was coming over the Alps.

Ryan grabbed the crate with the 42 rifleman radios and a 123 rechargeable power cells that had been recovered off the Fort Pitt dead. The radios looked like early '80s cell phones wrapped in army green polymer. The Rifleman radio had 100 preset channels with three talk groups per preset. The radios could adapt to all available communication carrier signals and act as a transmitter, receiver, and TCP/IP node. The Rifleman radio was the centerpiece of the warfighter's communications gear.

Ryan powered on the first radio. The goal was to find five radios that talked together, but he spent the next hour trying to figure out how the buttons worked. Finally, he cycled through radios in pairs looking for two that talked together.

He had no success.

He understood that the WIN-T system didn't broadcast voice by radio waves, but rather broadcasted data traffic—the computer speak of 1s and 0s—on specifically dedicated encrypted subnets. These subnets then—somehow—formed larger and larger networks. So, when he failed to find two radios that talked together, he was forced to investigate the programming functions.

"How in the hell do the coms guys know how to program these things?" Ryan asked. "Where is the manual?" He methodically looked through every binder again hoping that he'd merely missed the instructions the first time, but he had not.

He rolled the radio over and over in his hand. "This can't be complicated," he said. "Soldiers are kids in the field with guys shooting. It has to be simple, and the manual has to be in their head—"

Where did Marco serve? Army? What was it? Delta? Isn't that what Lieutenant Bathgate said Delta. No wait . . . Daniel Ryder said . . . Green Beret? Ranger?

Ryan picked up his iGlass and started searching. He typed into Safari: *Green Beret instruction manual . . . Rifleman radio programming manual . . . Ranger school training . . .*

He found a link to a PDF: Ranger Field Manual.

Could it really be this easy?

He clicked the link and the PDF opened. He browsed the table of contents: Chapter 7 Communications. His heart quickened as he scrolled through the PDF. And there it was: step-by-step instructions for programming the radios. It still took him forever to get it right, but he finally had two radios talking. He was programming a third radio when he heard:

The ragged they come and
The ragged they kill!
You pray so hard on bloody knees.
The ragged they come and
The ragged they kill!
Down in the cool air I can see

Ryan dug his phone out of a pocket. "Hello."

"Hello. This is Hailey Katherine Vasela. Can I speak to Ryan Sage, please?" she said, trying to sound serious.

"Let me check and see if he is available. One moment, please."

Hailey giggled.

"This is Ryan Sage speaking. How may I help you, Miss Vasela?"

"We are conducting a very important demonstration, and we would like you to attend."

"Let me check my calendar, Miss Vasela."

Hailey's demeanor broke. "Oh, come on. You were ignoring me earlier while you were working on the radio thing. I want to show you this."

It was true. Hailey tried telling jokes while he worked, but he was a tough crowd when he was concentrating. So she got off the stage and went to look for a better audience. "Okay, give me one second. I will come out." He put the two working radios in a bag and added two ear wigs, the kind of earphones often seen wrapped around a CIA agent's ear.

"Hurry up! Marco has been teaching me to shoot!"

Ryan exited the bunker, squinting against the sun. The day was cool and the rain saturated everything. Marco and Hailey were on top of the HESCO wall, standing inside one of the gunner's nests, talking over a rifle balanced on a sandbag. Marco tried to adjust her hold.

Hailey shied away until Marco backed up. She situated herself behind the weapon and squeezed off a shot. She paused, looking over the scope and then looked back at Marco who gave her a high-five. She saw Ryan, smiled wide and waved. Ryan climbed to the top of the wall. Hailey met him with a high-five.

"Look what I did! See, look over there, by that guard tower. See that zombie lying on the ground? I just shot that!"

"Wow!" Ryan squinted into the distance.

"She has skills," Marco said.

"Anyone can hit that while bench resting and using a scope!" Simone shouted from the pit where he was stacking boxes on a skid.

"Faker!" Hailey yelled back.

As if on cue, Simone cringed and held his chest like his ribs hurt. Since lunch he'd been complaining that his ribs were still out of place whenever he was asked to carry something heavy. To stop the bitching, Marco to let Simone wear the Stark. It didn't stop the complaining, but it did increase the production. Between Raphael and Simone, they had cut a large path through the camp minutes away from pushing the Pittsburgh Police Department SWAT vehicle into the warehouse.

Ryan said, "What is that? A hundred yards?"

"A hundred and thirty meters," Marco said. "It is a great shot for her."

Hailey's blue eyes sparkled. She did a cheer with a fist pump and ended with her hand on her hip. "Wanna see me do it again?"

"Yes," Ryan said.

"You are gonna wanna put on your headsets. The gun is loud," Hailey said.

"I'll plug my ears," Ryan said.

Marco made a sour face, bent inside the gunners' nest and handed Ryan a spare headset. "You will need these."

"Did you clean these?"

"Ohhh, gross! Of course I did," Hailey said. "They are cool. They let you hear everything but it keeps the report from hurting your ears."

Ryan slid on the headset, expecting the silence to press down on his ears like he was stepping into a soundproof booth. But the headset fit comfortably, and the sounds in the world seemed magnified.

Hailey adjusted the weapon on the sandbag and went through her routine.

"Put your cheek tight on the buttstock," Marco said. "Remember what I called that?"

"Uh, you called it welding your cheek to the butt stock." Hailey planted her legs and rolled her shoulder into the rifle. Her target was a 2091, its belly distended from gorging. "Breathe slow. Breathe slow," she whispered. "Deep breath. Let it out half . . ." And with the pad of her index finger, she slowly pressed the trigger. She jumped, surprised when the gun bucked hard against her shoulder. A half a beat later, the 2091's head blew apart.

"Wooohooo!" Hailey said, pumping her fist then turning for high-fives.

"She has skills!" Marco said.

"I'm gonna do it again! I'm gonna do it again!" Hailey said and immediately turned to work through the shooting ritual.

"Okay, I'm your spotter," Marco said, leaning close over her left side. "Do you see the 2091 by that white car? Twenty meters to the left?"

"Meters?" Hailey said, unsure. "I see the white car. Oh, there she is . . . but she is so far away."

"You can make this shot. You don't have to change anything. She is standing there all fat dumb and happy just waiting on you."

"Okay," Hailey said, her voice going flat with concentration. A moment later, the rifle roared and the infected staggered. The bullet struck just about the base of the throat and slammed into the windshield behind.

"Damnit!" she squealed, starting to turn and get sympathy.

"You don't have time for that," Marco said. "The bad guys are coming. You have to fix your aim. Look at your shot. Where did it hit?"

"I don't know. I—" she said, looking up at Marco.

"Don't look at me. Look at your target. Where did you think you were aiming and where did your shot hit?"

Hailey looked back through the site. "I was aiming at her nose, and it hit her in the chest."

"What does that mean?"

"It means that the bullet dropped."

Marco nodded. "It means that when you squeezed the trigger, the muzzle was lower. You were flinching against the recoil and the muzzle dropped. Hold yourself still and be surprised with the trigger breaks."

"But it's too fa—"

"Bad guys are coming. Shoot!"

75

Global Infection: ≤ 33.8084%

Hailey puffed out her cheeks but turned back to the scope and went through the ritual again. She paused for just a second longer and pressed the trigger. The zombie's head exploded.

"I did it!" Hailey said, unbelieving.

"High-five!" Ryan said.

And Hailey gave high-fives all around like she was in a dream. And then at the very last she threw her arms around Ryan and hugged him. It lasted for a minute, and then she broke the embrace and said, "I'll be right back." And without another word she scrambled down the wall and ran towards the Porta Potti.

"She is an amazing kid," Marco said.

"Yeah, she is a rare one. She has been surviving by herself," Ryan said, "But something has happened to her. She holds men in high suspicion. That usually has one source."

Marco nodded. "I was thinking the same. A beautiful girl . . . out in this, trying to survive. That is a recipe for bad."

"Back when I first saw her by the grocery, she was arguing with a man, trying to play peacemaker between him and some boy. I thought it was her father, but she called him Moe. Hailey is very tight-lipped, so I can't tell if he is someone close who died and she doesn't want to grieve, or if he is alive and she is afraid of him. I also saw her with another guy, college kid, but she almost never mentions him."

"Well, at least she doesn't look like she has been beaten," Marco shrugged. "You know, forced . . ."

"Yeah, anyway what are they going to do with the Lenco? I thought someone shot the hell out of it."

"Believe it or not," Marco said, "my little brother is pretty good with cars. He started working at a garage when he was fourteen to make money so he could buy guns and ammo. When he wasn't shooting, he was usually pulling an engine apart for a local race team."

"I have a hard time picturing that."

Marco nodded. "My father wants him to see what is wrong with the engine. He wants to know what parts they need."

Ryan looked at the clouds on the western horizon. Another storm was coming as were the 2091s. "The downside to the shooting is that the noise draws them back," he said. "Tell me, do they look like they are moving faster, or is that my imagination?"

Marco regarded the 2091s. "I think it is your imagination. I see fast movers like usual, but they don't seem special."

"You see those drinking out of that puddle," Ryan said, pointing into the distance. "I saw some infected across the river doing the same thing. It is disturbing that they eat and drink like we do."

"What I find disturbing is that we were not smart this morning," Marco said. "We did a good job of pulling them toward downtown. If we had thought about it, we could have made a raid on those tanks. Tanks carry about four thousand .50 caliber rounds and about ten thousand 7.62 rounds. We scavenged a little over 2000 rounds of the .50 caliber from these gunners nests and loaded the Stryker. And I only have about two thousand rounds for the SAW."

Ryan frowned. "What about all the ammo in the shipping container?"

Marco shook his head. "We haven't found any belt-fed ammo in the container, and the .50 and the SAW are belt-fed weapons."

The servos on Raphael's exoskeleton gave a whisper-quiet *whir* as he jumped from ledge to ledge, climbing the HESCO wall in six bounds. He paused briefly from the effort but soon stood upright. A weariness that surpassed tired hung around his eyes. He held up his right hand; the splint was off. "It *es* crooked," he said without preamble. The index finger was twisted just a degree to the right. The knuckles were misaligned with the rest of the hand. When he flexed the finger, it pulled in toward the palm.

"Damn!" Marco said, holding Raphael's hand inspecting. "It's not like I'm a surgeon. It was a bitch to get your hand still to sew it on."

"I can no feel the fingertip," Raphael said, rubbing his index finger.

"That part will take a little more time. The nerves are the last things to repair." Marco held up his pinky stump. "I've only gotten feeling in my hand I the last day or so. And look, I think the knuckle is starting to grow. But you need to leave the splint on. The bone is still mending."

"But the feeling will come back?" Raphael asked. "Because I can no feel a trigger."

"It will come back."

Raphael nodded, his face impassive, his eyes inscrutable behind the ORACLE darkened lenses. Finally, he said, "The trailer is loaded. We are ready to take it to the tower. I will—" he paused. "I will take Simone, yes?"

"Okay," Ryan said, realizing that Raphael was asking for permission. "How long will it take to make the trip?"

"You want to keep track of me like a father?"

"Raphael, I don't have a reason to trust you no matter what you tell me. But since we are doing the second sin of all horror flicks by splitting up, I figure maybe we should have some idea when to expect you. At least that way, we can mount a rescue instead of wondering what happened."

"Yes, this *es* true. If we unload the supplies in the loading dock, then it will take us maybe three hours. If we take the ammunition to the penthouse, it will take maybe longer."

"How about if we leave the trailer loaded and empty it later?"

Marco said, "We have other tractor trailers in the loading dock here. Have Simone drive the Humvee and use it to get back."

"This *es* a good idea," Raphael said. "We want the .50 caliber. If the devils give us problems, it will take us maybe one hour, maybe a little more, if we just leave it. But I want to take the ammunition to the penthouse. It *es* better that it is not left on the dock. This will take maybe one more hour."

"So you will be gone maybe three hours?" Ryan said. "Do you have room left for the antenna and some crates?"

"Yes."

"Okay, good. Clear a path, please, and we can take the satellite uplink to the tower. While you are doing that, I will disassemble some modules. When you take the ammunition to the penthouse, you can put the electronics in my office. I'll rebuild the system there."

"Did you get the coms system to work?" Marco asked.

"No, just the radios." Ryan handed him a Rifleman radio.

Marco's eyes went round like he was seeing a miracle. "How did you do it?"

"It is the power of Microsoft certification," Ryan said, making the sign of the cross like he was the Pope. "Just remember to be kind to tech support."

"Do you have one for me and Simone?" Raphael asked.

"For now I just have two."

Raphael said, "When we travel to the tower, I want . . . It would be something that I need to—. I know we say that we would work on this camp first, but Simone find that the radiator is good. But a hose has been punctured. I want to find this hose and bring it back."

Raphael's groping, almost incoherent words were really a request to take on a project that helped the Pagueros. Less than ten hours from offering an amended agreement and Raphael was already asking to deviate from the agreement. Ryan thought he should be mad on principle, but he had already prepared for this moment. He'd already decided that the first shipment to the tower was very likely the only shipment. Anything else was a bonus.

"How long will this side trip take?"

"Maybe one hour," Raphael said.

"Okay, so that means you are back for dinner?"

"Yes," Raphael said.

Ryan shrugged. "Okay, be safe."

Raphael pulled the ORACLE from his face. His eyes narrowed, studying. "Yes? This *es* okay? This *es* not what we agreed to? This camp *es* no empty, and we have much work to do."

If you knew it wasn't part of the agreement, then why did you ask?

Ryan reached into the bag and handed Raphael a Rifleman radio and an earwig. "You know what is at stake, Raphael. I know what is at stake. You will either do what you say or you won't. And one more working armored vehicle is a handy thing to have, even if you do take it when you leave."

76

Global Infection: ≤ 33.8086%

What Ryan assumed were more modules for the communications system were in fact claymore satchels stuffed in hard-shell server cases, operations manuals and a third Lockheed Martin Human Cargo Universal Carrier. Marco was like ten-year-old birthday boy when he opened the case and saw the Tony Stark. He pointed to the bird insignia etched into the shoulder and said, "This belongs to a colonel. Fucking thing is brand new. What's a REMF doing with one of these?" A few minutes later, he loaded the case onto a cart and pushed it to the breakroom and started doing diagnostics.

Raphael pulled away from the warehouse dock, deftly driving the Peterbilt truck through the side streets toward the 28th Street bridge route back to the tower. Ryan returned to the command bunker to continue programming radios, but this proved difficult because the constant, "Test, test, test," annoyed Raphael. And when Ryan was silent, it was hard to decide if Raphael was talking to him or Simone.

The cross talk meant that Ryan wasn't doing something right. There had to be a way to isolate radios while maintaining contact with everyone else, because the military didn't want extraneous chatter to clutter important things like calling in nuclear strikes. This could only mean that Ryan's radio programming skills were still in their infancy.

Unable to overcome the problem, Ryan stopped programming radios and shifted attention to other system components. He kept the earbud in his ear so he got moment-to-moment updates on progress as Raphael issued edicts, and then he heard Simone's monologue as he removed every nut and bolt and screw from the Lenco while Raphael stood watch. Finally, Raphael announced that they were heading back to Fort Pitt. Ryan said they needed firewood and then took off the earwig. His threshold for tedium was maxed out.

Ryan stood and stretched, feeling the pressure of technological frustration until he realized that the constant chatter had masked the silence in the camp beyond the command center. He hadn't heard a rifle or a handgun go bang in a long time. The bunker suddenly felt like the backside of the moon, and fear throbbed through his stomach.

Did the infected come over the wall?

Ryan peeked through the entrance and saw an empty camp. He took ten strides toward the warehouse when he saw movement beside the middle gunner's nest atop the wall. Marco and Hailey were kneeling, their Ops Core FAST helmets almost touching at the forehead, studying something like they were calculating the meaning of life. They finally stood, and Ryan saw the addition to Hailey's wardrobe: an ORACLE, a combat headset and a tactical vest with magazines filling the pouches. The vest was too big, but she wore it well.

Marco demonstrated opening his mouth and clamping his hands to his helmet and dropping to his knees. Hailey imitated Marco's actions.

What . . .?

Marco shouted, "Clear! Clear! Clear!" He dropped down and opened his mouth. Hailey did exactly what she'd been taught.

The explosion made Ryan's ears ring even from behind more than thirty feet of dirt. Hailey jumped up to peek over the edge, and suddenly she was a camouflaged cheerleader, her right fist pumped into the air, left arm bent at the hip, her leg doing a kick. It was a reflex from a day not long ago, when she had been celebrating a touchdown.

A tear leaked down Ryan's right cheek.

"Ryan! Ryan!" Hailey called. "Come see! Come see!"

Ryan ducked back into the bunker to grab his headset, and then climbed to meet her.

"Hey! Hey!" Hailey said, jumping up and down. "Marco showed me how to set up these s'mores things. You have to put these wires here and here." She pointed at the claymore in her hand. "And then you have to put this so it faces the zombies. See? It even says 'Front toward enemy.' And they're the enemy, so this side goes that way." She pointed out into the parking lot. "And then you shout 'Clear! Clear! Clear!' and open your mouth like this." She demonstrated. "And then you push this trigger like three times. Look what we did."

"She's gonna be a demolition expert," Marco said as he worked to reset his weapon of mass destruction. He attached a claymore to a long, heavy shelf post with a few loops of duct tape. Then he fastened the wires to the claymore. And last, he let the pole slide down the face of the wall by a cable. It took him a minute to jiggle the steel post into a gap between the infected and the wall, but when he was done, the claymore was about head height. He took up the slack to keep the post from falling over. He handed the trigger to Hailey. "Remember what I said."

Hailey puffed out her cheeks like she was about to attempt brain surgery. Then she practiced the order under her breath. Finally, she said, "Clear! Clear! Clear!" She dropped down, covered her head and squeezed the trigger: *Click! Click! Click!*

Ryan thought that Thor slapped the side of his head.

A wall of steel balls in a sixty-degree arc at 4000 feet per second took the heads off a few hundred 2091s in a single stroke.

Hailey jumped up and peeked over the edge. "Woohoo! They got decapped!" she said and did her cheerleader move again, dancing down the wall.

Ryan looked at the destruction: the mist of blood and flesh that hung in the air. He noticed the bodies that still stood, without a scratch from the shoulders down, twitching until they toppled left and right like bowling pins. He saw the legs and arms blown out to the semi-trailers a hundred yards away. He saw the bodies cut in half, the torsos groping, groping, groping in no direction in particular, like the wounded in the streets of Fallujah after Operation Phantom Fury IV. The only thing missing was screams of pain and the soldiers crying for their mommies.

Ryan said, "I guess this was your solution to drawing them back to the wall."

"Not until we found the claymores," Marco said. "All the claymores we had went to the tower in the first truckload. But when we found these, I was going to line them across this wall and put one to cover the hole in the wall, but Hailey wanted to see how they worked."

"Adding to the delinquency of a minor," Ryan said. "What other dangerous things can we teach a twelve-year-old girl?"

"I guess I didn't think about this being dangerous for her."

Ryan shook his head. "It wasn't a criticism. I was just thinking about the irony. A month ago, a father could be put in jail for child endangerment if he didn't cover his kid in bubble wrap and turn the world into a bouncy house. The world is dangerous, and if she's not learning something to defend herself, she's running the streets at the mercy of every predato—"

"What you are guys doing?" Simone asked. He jumped to the top of the HESCO wall. "I heard the explosions across town. Oh, cool. Look at that. They are eating that guy."

"That's gross," Hailey said, coming up behind Ryan. "You're sick."

Before Simone could pop off, Raphael said, "Hush now. You have work."

"But I want to blow up some zombies," Simone said.

Raphael pointed with his nose. "There are many of these devils, but there *es* only one armored car. Fix this first and then we will think of blowing things up."

"Besides, we're done blowing stuff up," Marco said. "The rest of these are for defense."

"Why does she get to have all the fun?" Simone asked.

"Because I'm nice," Hailey snapped.

"No, you're not—"

"Maybe you should listen," Raphael said. "Now, please, we have much work to do before we eat."

Simone sulked as he jumped down into Fort Pitt, the Stark controlling his descent.

Raphael said, "When I hear the explosion, I could no speak to you. Why did you turn off the radio?"

Ryan said, "I was tired and took a break."

"What good *es* communications if we do no wear them all the time?" Raphael asked.

Ryan raised his hands in surrender. "You are right. I've got two more radios. I have to test them to make sure they work, but I'll give one to Marco and one to Hailey."

"What of Simone?" Raphael said. "He *es* working. He needs the coms."

I'm the one fulfilling the agreement early and you want to argue who I give the radios to first? That is what Ryan thought, but he held his tongue; maybe his mother would be proud. "The reason I was going to give Hailey one first is because Hailey . . . being twelve—"

"I'm almost thirteen," Hailey said.

"Okay, Hailey being almost thirteen with no guns and no Stark has no way to fight if there is a problem. Your son has guns and a Stark and can fight. Plus, he is working almost right beside you. I expect to have another radio in a little bit, so I'm not trying to cut him out."

Raphael pursed his lips as he looked between Ryan and Hailey and then back. "Yes, this *es* good thinking. It *es* time to eat, right?"

"If you brought wood, then we just need to make a fire."

Raphael easily dropped down the wall.

"Hailey," Marco said. "You're going to help me wire these up."

"Wooohooo!" Hailey cheered.

Ryan winked at Hailey and climbed down. His descent was not so easy. His legs and arms shook from two long days of hard labor.

"You know why graveyards are so noisy?" Hailey asked.

"Why's that?" Marco said as he pulled a claymore out of a bag.

"Because of all the coffin."

Ryan walked into the command center, his mind whirling like a spring tornado: Hailey, 2091s, self-forming mesh networks, Rifleman radios, computers, cables, mystery devices . . .

He stepped over the threshold, and suddenly his mind twisted like a kaleidoscope: the infected trying to catch water in their mouths, infected feeding at the bus, the infected with bellies distended, infected hungry, infected sated, infected feeding below the wall, the infected seeking water. An idea worked around the edge trying to form a coherent picture, but it seemed to shift the wrong way. He tilted his head trying to will the thought to twist into a symmetric image, but nothing happened.

Then the thought scattered into chaos, and all Ryan could manage to think about was Hailey dancing down a wall, mere feet from carnivorous mouths: *Clear! Clear! Clear!* Her words played over and over like a warning.

77

Global Infection: ≤ 33.8090%

Raphael built a grill out of a barrel and a metal grate. He started the fire with cotton balls soaked in Vaseline and four-week-old newspaper. And for a few minutes, they stood around the fire smelling wood smoke and cooking beef, listening to Hailey talk about her new favorite things—a Berretta and an M16, a Remington 700, and s'mores.

The T-bone steaks were fantastic. Ryan forgot butter, but it didn't matter, because the mashed potatoes and green beans tasted perfect.

Sunlight cut through the clouds and splashed into the breakroom offering only the third reprieve from the day's murkiness. They sat around the table eating off mismatched plates, slicing their prime cuts with K-bar knives recovered from Fort Pitt and drinking sodas from the vending machine like it was fine Chablis. Raphael finished his first steak, started on his second and Hailey tried to keep up.

Simone pushed his empty plate away, yawned and his head slumped forward.

"You can no sleep," Raphael said, chewing on the left side of his mouth. "We must finish the engine."

Simone sighed. "Can't we do it in the morning? I'm exhausted."

Raphael chewed slowly and swallowed. "You work hard today, but we need to finish this. How much time will it take?"

Simone sighed. "Maybe an hour. But if I have to work on it tonight, we need to move the Lenco away from the Stryker. The Stryker stinks."

"Yeah, I could smell it all the way up in the rafters this morning," Ryan said.

"Blame him," Simone said, pointing a thumb toward Marco. "When he plowed through the infected, he got meat and blood all over the thing, and now that shit is rotten."

"You think blowing up bodies is fun," Raphael said. "Maybe you clean it after dinner."

"You are going to give me another job?" Simone asked, frustrated. "I'm the one who's supposed to fix the radiator hose. Why don't we dump a bunch of cleaner on it and park it in the rain? That will wash it off and save the planet."

Raphael raised a brow. "You want to sleep outside?"

Simone shrugged. "What's the difference? Nothing can get in once we lock it."

Ryan said, "I like the idea of walls between me and those creatures."

"You should like the idea of walls between you and my father's snoring," Marco said.

"It *es* not that loud," Raphael said.

"Yes, it is," Simone and Marco said at once.

Raphael almost smiled.

"That isn't a bad idea," Marco said. "If the Stryker is outside, then they can see if the infected are on that side of the warehouse. The Stryker has the M151 Protector Remote Weapon Station and a perimeter security system and night vision. It would be impossible to approach unseen. And since we have working coms, we will still be in constant contact."

"When do I get my radio?" Simone asked.

"I've got one for you," Ryan said. "I think I left the bag down by the fire."

"I got mine," Hailey said.

"Oh, great," Simone mumbled. "Now I'll have to hear her jokes all the time.

"That is good, for you because I'm hilarious," Hailey said, and then she smiled at Ryan.

"Little brother, her jokes are better than hearing you complain," Marco said.

Simone opened his mouth, but Raphael silenced him with a finger. "This *es* a good idea. We will guard this side of the warehouse."

"I was kinda thinking that the Stryker was our security blanket. If anything went wrong, we could get inside and run away like big fat chickens," Ryan said.

"You are what you eat," Simone mumbled.

Hailey rolled her eyes. "That wasn't funny since we are obviously eating steak." She fake whispered to Ryan, "I think he went to school on the short bus."

"Short bus?" Simone asked.

"See," Hailey said.

"Anyway," Marco said, "when Simone gets the Lenco fixed, then we can use that to run away like big fat chickens."

"But he is funny," Hailey said.

"You're stupid," Simone said. "He's not funny."

"Yes, he is," Hailey said. "I'm the expert on jokes."

"Yes, we will finish the truck," Raphael said.

"Come on!" Simone said. "I just want to sleep. And aren't we supposed to load up the rest of the computer equipment? We'll never get done."

Ryan said, "Get the Lenco working and then sleep. I'll get the rest of the command center broken down."

Raphael asked. "We agree that this would be done last."

The truth was that since he was already into the project, Ryan didn't want to let the puzzle go. His brain was already working through how to make the system work and it beat the hell out of humping crates into a truck. He said, "It's raining, so there isn't much to do in Fort Pitt tonight. There is no reason to lose the evening. Everything is modular, designed to be set up and torn down in the worst possible environments, so many of the connections are already labeled. If I'd set it up once or twice, it wouldn't be a problem. I am going to document the system. Once I'm done, I will load it up, and we can take it back in the morning."

Raphael nodded and turned to Simone and started planning how best to work on the Lenco.

Hailey leaned forward and tapped Ryan on the shoulder. "So, uhm . . ." she said, fidgeting with her coat sleeves. "Do you think I could . . . uhmm." She looked sideways at Marco then leaned closer. "I know I haven't found you maps, but maybe I could get some food anyway, like as an advance?"

Ryan matched her tone. "Hailey, you don't need an advance. You have worked with us, so you've earned whatever you like."

The tightness in Hailey's eyes relaxed. "I need to take some stuff to Timmy. He's probably out of food by now."

"Tonight?" Ryan asked. "It's going to be dark in an hour."

"He will be hungry," Hailey said.

"Who's Timmy?" Marco said.

Hailey ducked behind Ryan, suddenly shy.

"He's a friend of hers," Ryan said. "She wants to take him some food. Hailey, the infected are pretty restless. We've made some noise today drawing them back to the fort."

Hailey said, "They are still scattered toward downtown. Marco and I shot a bunch of them up close and then we used the s'mores. I can sneak out. What food can I take?"

Ryan said, "There is plenty. A loaf of bread, the lunch meat and cheese, and I brought some apples. We could probably find something to pack the leftovers in so you can have the steak and the mashed potatoes. Raphael picked the lock on the soda machine. You can have sodas and all of this, but the problem is heading out at night. How would you carry it all? If you'd said something earlier we could have made a run during the day."

"Hey, she can't have all that," said Simone. "That's ours."

Ryan ignored Simone. "Look, you've earned the food, but we need to be smart about taking it to Tim. If you must go tonight, let's go together."

Marco said, "We can ask him if he wants to come back with us. Then he could eat as much as he wants."

Hailey put her hands on her hips. "That's not the deal. The deal is I get sandwiches."

"She didn't even bring any maps in like two days," Simone fussed.

"Simone," Ryan said, "this doesn't concern you."

"If it wasn't for her and those stupid maps, none of this would have happened," Simone said. "I wouldn't have fallen, and my poppa wouldn't have been hurt."

"Stop!" Ryan snapped, his eyes flashing between Simone and Raphael. "It was wrong the first time you said it. She helped save your ass. You should be saying thank you." He turned back to Hailey. "Look, the food is yours; the problem is leaving now."

"Smelly little bitc—" Simone barely got the last word out of his mouth when Raphael grabbed him by the back of the Stark and dragged him out of the breakroom, Spanish echoing through the stairwell like thunder.

Hailey looked at Simone as he was being dragged away like he was a bug, then said to Ryan, "I will be okay. I just need to check on Tim."

Ryan asked, "Is there a reason that you don't want Tim to come here? You know we won't hurt you and we won't hurt Tim, so what is the problem?"

Hailey's eyes drifted toward Raphael's voice. "He doesn't have to do that. I've called Simone worse."

Marco hid a smile. "My brother needs an attitude adjustment. He'll be fine."

"Hailey, don't change the subject please," Ryan said, "Why can't Tim come here? Is he really a 2091 and you don't want us to kill him?"

"What? A 2091? You mean a zombie? No. He's just my friend," Hailey puffed a stray hair away from her eyes. "Look, you are not my dad. You can't keep me here. I just want to take some food to Timmy."

Ryan was surprised at how hard her words hit. Finally he said. "You are right. I'm not your dad and I'm not going to keep you here. But I am an adult who thinks of things you may not have thought about. I fully expect a teenage boy has figured out a way to eat without you, so it makes much better sense to take him more food in the morning."

"I've made the trip like a billion times and I can sneak best in the dark. I just want to take some food to Tim. I don't want to be a pest or anything."

"Hailey, do I treat you like you're a pest?"

Hailey met his eyes after a minute she said, "No." She looked into the refrigerator. "Maybe I could just take half of this." Then she went to the window and studied the street.

Ryan pinched the inside of his eyes. Marco put a hand on his shoulder. "I'll follow her," he whispered.

Thunder rumbled from the west, long and low like a drum roll from a distant amplifier.

"I'll take this to Timmy later," Hailey said. "Probably tomorrow after breakfast."

Ryan smiled, but before daybreak he would wish he'd driven her into the streets.

78

Global Infection: ≤ 33.8094%

By the time Ryan was able to work on the communications bunker, full dark had come to the Allegheny River valley. He stepped through the hole in the wall, feeling the cold wind rush through the fort and light rain spit against his face. He zipped up the fireman's coat and it felt good to have pants long enough to reach his ankles and clean socks. He looked to the sky but couldn't see past the temporary lights blazing over the camp. Their glowing intensity felt like an intrusion, so he went to the light base and flipped the switch. The lights popped and slowly faded to black, plunging Fort Pitt into darkness under a starless and moonless sky.

He could have walked to the command bunker by following the dim light that squeezed through the entrance, but he was concerned about tripping over a claymore. Ryan tapped the ORACLE at the temple and everything turned a faint green like a Marvel Comics Incredible Hulk movie. Marco and Hailey worked on their placement like they were going to repel the Japanese on Okinawa. She'd been proud when they finished stringing the wires into the warehouse to a last stand location that she called the *A la mode*. When Ryan explained it was called the Alamo she said, "Nuh-uh, s'mores need ice cream."

The wind muted the night; Fort Pitt was a cold, wet soundproof room.

Ryan stopped after twenty steps, his eye jerking to the top of the HESCO wall.

Movement?

Paranoia skittered up and down his spine like a spider climbing across his skin. He waited and watched.

The drizzle increased and the wind churned.

I should make sure that the monsters are still where they belong.

He walked to the wall and pulled himself up its hard, cold, wet and slippery surface. His legs and arms shook before climbing the first five-foot cube. He started to slip. "Shit," he said under his breath as he caught himself and let his feet drop back to the ground. He thumped the slick

HESCO cell, trying to talk himself into making the ascent. And then he thought that climbing the wall at night, in the rain, exhausted, and alone violated at least one of the horror movie seven deadly sins.

He took one last long look down the length of the wall and then turned to the communications bunker.

The system was modular, designed to be broken down and reassembled on a moment's notice, but that assumed the users had trained to execute the mission in their sleep. The manuals he found earlier showed Ryan nothing about the system setup. So the moment he started pulling cables, he was operating without a net. In the world of IT, once cables came out, there was no guarantee the system would work right again. What Ryan was about to do could turn a military grade communications network into a very expensive paperweight.

He pulled the camera out of its case, attached the lights and started shooting video. He made a systematic sweep around the command center with a running monologue of observations. Then he started the tedious task of labeling everything with color-coded tags.

Hailey came in a half hour later wearing her oversized Army jacket and an ORACLE, grunting under the weight of a box filled with cleaning supplies. She put it down, gave Ryan a wave. "Marco said you should put your ears on," she said and dashed back out into the night. She returned with an arm full of blankets and big duffel. She took a minute to organize the blankets atop an empty crate and used the duffel as a backrest.

Ryan checked wires and made notes. "What is Marco doing?"

"He is working on that armor suit he wears. He wanted me to help, but I didn't want to be in there, but I felt a little bad because I thought he would be lonely. He said he was fine. He locked the doors when I left. He told me to knock if I came back."

"Where are your radio and the headset?" Ryan asked. "You don't have to knock if you can just talk to him."

"I put it up on my bed. I don't like wearing that vest you guys wear, so the radio is hard to carry around, and besides," Hailey said, wrinkling her nose, "the headset pinches my head and gives me a headache if I wear it too long."

"But I gave you that earwig. You didn't like that one either?"

She shrugged. "The cord tickles my neck."

"Well, you need to put the vest on. That is how you carry the radio," Ryan said. "We need to be connected."

Hailey gave him a sly smile. "And you are not wearing your radio. That is why Marco said you need to put your ears on."

"Smarty pants, at least mine is close," Ryan said. It was true. The cord that ran down the neck on those earwigs that the Secret Service wore did tickle, and the constant chatter between Simone, Raphael and Marco was tedious. He looped it around his ear.

"Marco? Can you hear me?"

"I read you fine. How are you doing out there with the monsters?"

"Ha ha ha," Ryan said, but his stomach tipped. He'd not really thought of it like that. "And here I was thinking I should check on *you*."

"I'm the one in a room that is behind two locked doors and two very sturdy barricades. My father is in a war machine just outside. And I have lots of guns."

"Yeah. Well, with the wind and the rain, they can't possibly hear us. Maybe they have forgotten we are here."

"I wouldn't worry. You have a lot of wall between you and them, and you can see in the dark with the ORACLE. Whatever 2091s are, they are not supernatural. So the night is your friend. And you also have your M16. Marines can survive using that, so I'm confident you can."

"Good to know you have so much confidence in me."

"You know where I am if you need me."

"Okay, talk to you soon."

"No, say 'out here,'" Marco corrected.

"Ah, yeah, we are in the Army now. Out here."

"Out here."

Ryan finished making his legend and started applying tags to units and connections.

This is going to take forever.

He watched Hailey work through each headset, trying to wipe off zombie germs—real or imagined.

"Could I use your expertise?"

Hailey smiled. "You want me to tell you a joke?"

"Sure, but I want you to use your handwriting."

In ten minutes, Ryan explained his method. Five minutes after that, Hailey had finished documenting the first set of connections with hearts atop the I's. She moved on to the next item and Ryan started breaking everything down.

Hailey looked up from her handwriting and said, "So could I ask you a question?"

Ryan raised and eyebrow and smirked.

"What's funny?"

"I was trying to think of something smart to say, but couldn't."

"That is because you went to school on the short bus."

"Ha ha." Ryan motioned for the cable tag. "What is your question?"

"I was thinking about the . . . what is it you call them? The 2091s? That is what Marco said they were. It was like a disease they got or something. Do you think they are people still?"

"That's a tough question."

"I was kinda thinking that maybe if they were still people, that it wasn't all right to kill them."

"What made you think of that?" Ryan asked, as he made some notes and undid another cable.

Hailey handed him another label. "After we got done with the claymores I was thinking about what we had done. I was kinda cheering, but then I was thinking that those people were mothers and fathers and maybe now their kids wouldn't have parents."

"Is your mom in the camp? Is that why you are asking?"

"No, she's not in the camp. She's . . . someplace else."

"Is she a 2091?"

Hailey took great pains to write out the next two tags. Finally she said, "Yeah. She is a zombie."

"How about your father?"

Hailey shook her head. "My mom didn't know who my father was. She said it could have been one of a few men. She said she went to an orgy. Do you know what that is? I think it is where people have sex, like with each other. She said she wanted to have a baby girl so it didn't matter. So I've never known my father. There was this one guy, Andel that was with my mom for a while. He was fun and came to the football games to watch me cheer when my mom was working."

Ryan still hadn't recovered from the casual discussion of an orgy. It took him a full minute to realize Hailey had stopped talking. "So . . . uhhh . . . so how long have you been alone?"

"It's always just been my mom and me."

"No, I mean how long have you been trying to live by yourself, since your mom was infected?"

Hailey finished another tag and said, "I think it's been a month but I've lost track of time. I'm not even sure what day it is. It was before they closed my school but she sent me to live with one of her friends, Kristana, a few weeks before that. She got in a fight with some girl at work. The girl thought my mom was trying to take her boyfriend, but my mom wouldn't do that. Not deliberately, but it did happen on accident sometimes. My mom was really pretty, so men liked her a lot and sometimes she didn't know they had girlfriends. During the fight my mom got cut pretty bad. She lost a lot of blood and they had to give her a transfusion and then a few weeks later she started to get really mean and couldn't sleep and had headaches all the time. That is when she sent me to live with Kristana."

Ryan's mind keyed into the important factoid: the transfusion transmitted the RVJC 2091 virus?

Holy shit does that mean the blood bank is tainted?

"So do you think she is?"

Ryan said, "What? I'm sorry?"

"My mom, do you think she's a person? And how about your sister?"

"How did you know about my sister?"

"Marco told me."

"Of course he did," Ryan said, "The short answer is, yes I think they are still people but I don't think that changes that we have to kill them."

"I don't understand."

Ryan wanted to launch into a detailed discussion of infectious disease and individual liberty but he caught himself. "How to explain this to a twelve year old—"

Hailey rolled her eyes. "How come no one remembers that I'm almost thirteen?"

Ryan smiled. "Because almost thirteen is called twelve. When someone has a dog that attacks people what do you have to do?"

"You have to put it down. But the dog doesn't understand what it did."

"And that is the problem. The dog doesn't understand what it did, so it can't ever do anything but attack people. The infected can't do anything but hurt people, even though they don't understand what they are doing."

"What if someone had a cure and could make your sister better, would you still kill her?"

Ryan stopped working on the system and sat on a chair. "Many years ago, if a boat came into a harbor and the people on board were sick they sank the boat to keep the sick people from killing the healthy people. And then people figured out how to cure diseases and we stopped sinking boats. Until we have a cure we will have to keep sinking boats, and that includes my sister and your mom."

Hailey nodded and went back to writing labels.

Ryan worked through ten more connections.

Hailey said, "Can I ask you another question?"

"Yes," Ryan said placing a console into a case.

"Are you gay? I don't mean to offend, but do you like men instead of women? I mean it's cool if you do. My mom had a few girlfriends and Old Man Renfro was gay, I think, and he a friend of mine. And I had this other friend in school who was gay, well she liked other girls. You know what I mean?"

"Uhhhh . . . no, I'm not gay."

"You don't have any kids, right?"

"No I don't have any kids. Both of my sisters had kids. One of them had two girls about your age. I think you would have liked Georgia and Xyla."

"Xyla? That is a pretty name. So are they zombies?"

Ryan finished stacking units on a cart. "No they are . . . dead. My whole family is dead." It was the first time he'd let those words come out of his mouth.

"You are alone, like me then," Hailey said. "I don't have a family either. Well, not in the US. I have a grandmother in Europe but I haven't seen her in years. It is kinda good that we found each other, right?"

Ryan pushed against the tears but it was a futile effort. He looked away and wiped his face. "I need to get this loaded. I'll be back in a few minutes."

Hailey finished the last label. "Ryan?"

Ryan stopped at the threshold. "If this is another question, can it wait until I get back?"

"I just wanted to say it was kinda mean when I said you weren't my dad."

"I knew what you meant."

Hailey yawned and lay back on the duffle bag pile to play Galaga.

Ryan pushed the cart into the warehouse. The Pagueros had filled the Lenco, so he ran out of space on the first trip. Hailey was asleep when he returned so Ryan finished documenting and loading the remaining equipment, his laptop and his iGlass into the Humvee.

He made the last trip back to the command center, the rain slapping against the clear plastic sheet over his head sounding like BBs. He powered off the remaining lamps, slung the M16 over his shoulder, tucked Hailey's phone into her pocket, wrapped her in the blanket and scooped her into his arms. Ryan picked his way through the camp, into the warehouse and to the storage racks. He shed the plastic sheet and started the forklift and rode it like an elevator to their beds. Hailey didn't stir as he laid her onto the air mattress.

Ryan brushed a stray curl off of her cheek. "Yes, Hailey it is good. It is very good."

79

Global Infection: ≤ 33.8095%

What is good?" Marco said,

Ryan jumped at the voice coming through Ryan's earwig, but it sounded like he was behind Ryan's shoulder. "Marco? You were listening to our conversation?"

"No, I just turned the volume up and heard you. I was about to come out to the bunker and get you. I was getting worried."

"Yeah. Well, getting the system broken down took longer than I thought." He pulled off the fireman's coat and unzipped his tactical vest and laid it on top of the fertilizer. He took off his damp scrubs, to hang them over the storage rack edge stepped into dry scrubs. "Are you still safe in the breakroom?"

"Turn around," Marco said.

Ryan turned and the ORACLE showed Marco sitting on a mattress leaning against a crate. He waved an exoskeleton-clad hand.

"You decided to join the cool kids, huh?"

"I made the bed earlier, but I wanted to wait until the new Stark was fully charged."

"I can't believe you can sleep in those things," Ryan said.

"It takes some getting used to, but they were designed to be worn for days, maybe even a week at a time. It doesn't make any sense for guys on patrol to have to get in and out of these things every time they lie down."

"Well, I will be glad when I get back to the penthouse and can sleep wearing nothing at all."

"That was TMI," Marco said with a chuckle. "So ask me what I found."

"Uhhh . . . is this a Hailey joke that you are trying to steal?"

Marco laughed. "No, but I *am* going to steal the s'mores need ice cream line. I about peed my pants when she said that. If she fails as a Delta force operator, she has potential in standup," he said. "So you have to ask me what I found."

"I'm hoping the answer is a brunette with blue eyes or maybe an Asian with green eyes who stands about 5'8".

"You are the idiot that let Ahou Derakhshan go."

The mention of Ahou brought back the few seconds of video to Ryan's mind and he immediately sprouted wood. He arranged himself behind the scrubs. "Can you imagine adding a woman who didn't want to be here in the first place? I shudder to think."

"Who cares if she didn't want to be here if she wanted to be with you?"

"Anyway," Ryan said. "What did you find?"

"I found out you saved a princess."

Ryan chuckled. "There had to be a better use of your time. How did you manage to get to the Internet?"

"You're not the only computer hacker here."

"Yes, I am."

Marco laughed again. "I just went into one of the offices, looked under the keyboard for the password. The username was already there."

"So much for good network security."

"So, a princess? You gonna tell me about this?"

"She wasn't a princess. I really don't understand British peerage . . . uh . . . she was somehow connected to the Queen. But when I say connected, it is more like seven degrees of Kevin Bacon."

"Who?" Marco said. "What?"

"Never mind, bad simile. Her connection to the Queen was distant, but the Brits take that stuff seriously."

"But you saved her. *And* she was pregnant," Marco said.

"You couldn't tell she was pregnant. If she was, it was only maybe a couple weeks. She was just a mouthy woman who would *not* shut up. She liked the Drogheda United, and these Longford Town football hooligans came into the pub, and they started mouthing back and forth. Well, *she* started mouthing off. I don't know if she expected them to know who she was or if she just didn't care, but she would not shut up.

"I felt sorry for her boyfriend or fiancé . . . or whatever he was. He was part of the Navy or no, part of the Royal Marines, or maybe the Royal Marines are part of the British Navy. The Marine kept trying to get her to settle down, but there isn't a woman on the planet that will actually take good advice from her significant other, so of course she just got louder and this stupid woman decided she wanted a piece of the action. She hit one of the guys and then they said game on and hit her back. The Royal Marine went into combat mode, and then it was ten against one. My buddy and I didn't care for that, so we tried to make peace. But the football hooligans thought that Americans should mind their own business. Knives came out and barstools were broken for clubs, and the rest was what I told you."

"I saw one article that said one of them was crippled."

Ryan lay in the darkness saying nothing.

"Ryan?" Marco said.

Finally, Ryan said, "Then they got it wrong. It was two guys who got crippled."

"You did that?"

Ryan paused, shaking his head.

"If you are shaking your head, remember I can't see details in the ORACLE."

"Oh right," Ryan said. "Yes, I did that. But what probably saved me was that everyone had a cell phone. The whole fight was recorded from a dozen angles. So it was indisputable what happened. The Marines had three. My buddy, who was an okay street fighter, was keeping one guy tied up. And when I wrecked one of the remaining guys, five of them keyed on me. They were putting a hurting on me with bar stool legs, and the guy with the knife attacked, so I flipped him into the bar and it broke his back. The second guy got driven into something. Actually, I don't even know what happened to him. Most of the fight was a blur, but I did . . . do remember the guy on the bar." Ryan paused. "I remember hearing the bone break, and the way he started screaming. It wasn't from pain, it was from fear. He knew he couldn't move."

"Why did the cell phones save you?"

"From an international civil suit," Ryan said. "Once the British got wind that one of their royals, however distant, had been defended, and that I'd come to the aid of one of their Royal Marines, they pulled some serious political strings with the Irish authorities. And the Irish couldn't, in good conscience, keep me locked up. The videos hit the net like ten minutes after the fight. So, by the following morning, even the Irish couldn't defend those guys. But the big concern was that the guys I crippled would sue. I don't remember the details, but they didn't."

"I saw your picture and you were buff," Marco said.

"I'm not that kind of guy, Marco," Ryan said.

"You have me mistaken for a sailor. Besides, it's been 'don't ask, don't tell' for a billion years."

"I'm going to tell Hailey you are ripping off her jokes."

"What has me curious is what happened? You were so in shape."

"I got older," Ryan said. "I mean the gray hair makes me look older. But the gray is genetic. I've been gray since I was 28 but I'm not much older than your father. For all I know, we might be the same age. And you do remember that getting older is what used to happen to the human race, right? We used to age, right? And we are not all genetically predisposed to looking like bikini models in our seventies."

Marco snorted. "But age doesn't have to mean fat. And the EVMT has certainly had time to rejuvenate your endocrine system."

"You sound a lot like my sister. Well, it is simple. I detest BOHMeC edicts. I detest that the government is empowered to dictate my lifestyle. So I protested medical constraints by eating lots and lots of Italian subs?"

"So you got fat to spite the government?" Marco said. "That is stupid."

"Yeah, it was," Ryan said. "But you have to remember I was almost thirty before the Eternity Vaccine hit the market. So my telomeres were already starting to break down. And I deliberately put off starting the Maximov therapy because it was such a sports scandal it made the fuss over steroids look like a fuss over aspirin. I was trying to compete by the book and virtually no one else was complying. So, since I started the EVMT late, I didn't get some of the same benefits as those who have been receiving the treatment since they were children. That was the biggest reason I had to retire from professional track and field. My body couldn't outrun Father Time."

"So you were an Olympic champion?"

"Oh no, I was never that good. I was close, but close only counts in hand grenades."

"I guess that explains how you were able to run away from them," Marco said.

"Run away from who?"

"The 2091s. Hailey told me all about what happened the other night. She said you walked on their heads like Jesus walked on water. And then she said you ran like a billion miles to get away from them."

"It felt like a billion miles. And I wish that I had been in shape," Ryan said. "That would have made that night a lot less terrifying."

"She loves you."

"Who?"

"Who? Are you an owl? How many girls are here? Hailey, of course. She hangs on your side all the time. And she is always smiling and looking for you. She told me that you ran through the zombies so you could save her from the storm."

"Funny how perspectives change the same event. She saved me. Had she not been in that building, I don't know what I would have done."

"You are a good man, Ryan Sage," Marco said, his voice disembodied in the dark. "She is lucky to have found you. And tomorrow when she tries to give her food to this Timmy, we will follow her to make sure she is all right."

"Thank you," Ryan said, and after a few minutes he could barely hear Marco's even breathing.

She loves you . . .

He pulled the ORACLE off his face and laid it within reach. The warehouse was as black as the ocean on a starless night.

She loves you . . .

The words rolled over Ryan's mind as the rain started pounding the roof just a few feet above his head, like a billion 2091s trying to get inside.

80

Global Infection: ≤ 33.9895%

Ryan," Hailey whispered. "Are you awake?"

"Yes, Hailey," Ryan said. He'd heard her climb down from her nest ten minutes before, his sleeping mind attuned to her movements. She had climbed back up the storage shelves and was less than two feet from his head, but the morning light was still very dim beyond the skylights, barely cutting through the darkened rafters.

"There are guys standing on top of the wall," she said, her voice an excited whisper.

"What?"

"I just went to the Porta Potti, and there are all these people standing along the top of the wall. I think they are zombies."

Terror shot down Ryan's spine. "Are they in the pit?"

"I didn't see one on the ground. But it is still dark. I wasn't wearing an ORACLE, but the sun is coming up and I could see them along the wall."

"They didn't see you?"

"I don't think so."

"Okay, climb on up here."

"I wanna be with you."

"Hailey, I'm up here."

"Duh?! But you are gonna climb down."

"Okay, get your stuff on, the vest and the radio and the ORACLE."

"I told you it tickles my neck"

"Hailey, no arguing here. We need to be able to talk."

Hailey's dim form crawled onto the shelf and over the pallet of grass fertilizer to her bed.

Ryan reached above his head and felt the ORACLE exactly where he left it. A small groan escaped his throat as the electronics took over, and his eyes adjusted to the eerie green three dimensions of crates, cross beams and roof trusses. Ryan looked across the expanse to where Marco slept: the glow of his body heat imposed over a green background. Marco waved. He was on a knee, his carbine in his hand, looking back.

"Don't you ever sleep?" Ryan asked.

"I heard her climb down," Marco said. "What is going on?"

"Hailey saw zombies on the wall."

"What?"

"Yeah, that's what I said."

"One second," Marco said, and he started keying the coms unit to send a series of clicks.

Marco cycled through the signal twice and Raphael responded. *"Que?"*

"Hailey saw the 2091s on the wall."

"Que?"

"Yeah, that is what I said," Marco said.

"*Es* she sure?"

"I know what a zombie looks like," Hailey said, her voice indignant. The mic rustled as she fastened it. "They are just standing on the wall. They weren't moving. But they just looked like they were watching."

"How do they get there?" Raphael asked, somehow making it sound like an accusation.

"How would I know?" Hailey said, frustrated.

"Don't shoot the messenger," Marco said.

"Yes, *es* true," Raphael said. "One minute," he said. There was a space of silence and then his voice came back on. "The monitor show no movement. I will come with Simone."

"No, stay put," Ryan said. "They will hear the bay door open. We'll sneak out and take a look. If we need to retreat, we'll head to the Lenco. Get the Stryker ready to fight."

"Yes, *es* good."

Ryan shrugged into his tactical vest, slid his Beretta into its thigh holster, and grabbed his M16. He stepped onto the forklift that he'd been using as an elevator. He waved Hailey to step on.

"Can you climb down?" Marco asked. "They might hear the hydraulics."

"They might hear my fat ass falling," Ryan said. He followed Hailey down the shelf.

Marco met them beside the lift. He adjusted Hailey's earwig and radio, and then put her hand on his belt. He then signaled for Ryan to take point and put his hand on Ryan's shoulder. They walked quickly and quietly down the aisle, scanning the shadows. Ryan slowed at the hole in the wall. Beyond he heard a sound; it was like a thousand locomotives chuffing in a rail yard.

Chuff! Chuff! Chuff! Chuff!

Fog swirled at the threshold as if it knew not to cross uninvited. It ebbed and flowed through Fort Pitt, a filthy living thing turning the unholy ground beyond into a contaminated bog. The world was doused in darkness but backlit by a forlorn distant glow from the eastern horizon.

Chuff! Chuff! Chuff! Chuff!

The sound grew and multiplied like an echo chamber.

Ryan leaned around the edge. “Fuck me.”

Marco tilted his head around Ryan’s shoulder. “Oh, fuck me,” he said his voice quaking.

Hailey peeked around their hips and mewled low and tremulous.

Chuff! Chuff! Chuff! Chuff!

The 2091s were lined along the HESCO wall, their numbers seeming to fade into the murk like tilted tombstones in an abandoned graveyard. The fog twisted and coiled and swirled around their legs as if to caress their bodies from toes to nose.

Chuff! Chuff! Chuff! Chuff!

The fog swallowed the sound and spewed it back out, greasy and malevolent. The infected were poised at the wall’s edge looking into the pit, projecting menace and aggression and harm, huffing deep like they were trying to suck the liquid air into their souls.

Chuff! Chuff! Chuff! Chuff!

“Back up,” Marco whispered, his voice barely more than a thought. He pulled Ryan and Hailey deep into the warehouse, deep to where the blackness swallowed them. “I estimate a thousand 2091s along the walls,” he said.

“Are they in the fort?” Raphael asked.

“Yes,” Ryan said. “I saw a pile tangled at the bottom of the wall. I think they are pretty busted up.”

“We need to know how they are getting over the wall,” Marco said. “Someone needs to take a look.”

“No,” Ryan said. “We leave. We go to the Lenco, open the bay door, and drive out.”

“But the communications gear,” Raphael said. “*Es* it ready.”

“Are you kidding?” Ryan rasped. “If more of those things spill into the pit, we are in a world of hurt. We leave, regroup, and figure out how to come back later.”

“Copy that,” Marco said. “Let’s move.”

Ryan took point and Marco followed, sweeping their way toward the only large bay door that allowed trucks to pull in and out of the warehouse. Three vehicles were lined up facing the door: the Lenco, the Humvee, and the military transport.

“Get in,” Marco said. “I’ll open the door, but don’t start the engine until I get it up.”

“I had to break up the coms gear,” Ryan said. “The other half is in the Humvee.”

“Copy that,” Marco said. “I’ll drive the Humvee. Poppa. Poppa? Are we clear to exit?”

“Clear,” Simone said. “Nothing on the monitors.”

“Copy that,” Marco said. “Mount up.”

“Hailey,” Ryan said. “Get in the passenger seat.”

Silence . . .

Ryan turned looking through the darkened warehouse. "Hailey?" he said, pressing the earwig deeper into his ear. "Hailey!" he rasped. The world froze as panic clawed through Ryan's belly.

"Hailey?" Marco said, his weapon drawn to his shoulder sweeping the floor for threats.

"I'll just be a minute," Hailey's voice came back quiet in the headset.

"What?" Ryan said. "We don't have a minute."

"I gotta get my food," Hailey said. "I've got to make sure that Timmy has some sandwiches."

"Oh God," Marco breathed.

"Hailey, leave it," Ryan said. "I have more food."

"I can't leave my food." The sounds of Hailey's movement filtered through the head set.

"Go get her," Marco said. "I'll check on our friends."

Marco moved his weapon ready toward the hole in the wall. Ryan held his carbine against his shoulder, muzzle toward the floor. He moved past the barrel filled with cold ashes, the faint smell of cooked beef clinging to the air. He moved down one aisle and then went left.

"What *es* taking so long," Raphael demanded.

"We hit a snag," Marco said. "Hold please."

"Hailey's missing," Simone said.

"I'm not missing. I had to get my stuff—"

No one knew what made them fall, but the posts to the shelves that had been disassembled days ago—the same metal used to create a pen to hold 2091s, that had leaned against the wall without incident for days while forklifts shuttled past—shifted one into another like a long line of dominos; the ringing spread out through the warehouse like church bells tolling during a funeral.

Chuff! Chuff! Chuff! Chuff!

Chuff! Chuff! Chuff!

Chuff! Chuff!

The roar sounded like Steelers fans turned rabid: high-screeching gibbering madness. The infected started pouring down the HESCO wall like blood draining down a sacrificial altar.

ACT 5

81

Global Infection: ≤ 33.9896%

The 2091s tumbled down the wall, breaking bones and snapping limbs in waves. The last in line fell on soft flesh, scrambled to their feet, and dashed toward the hole in the wall like blood gushing from a severed artery splattering against anything in their path.

Ryan ducked against a crate as the horde streamed by . . . their ragged, dirty bodies doused with the amplified green light, the heat imaging making their bodies glow like a white-hot iron.

"Remember, they can't see in the dark," Marco whispered into the coms. "Just hide!"

"What *es* happening?" Raphael demanded.

"They are coming over the wall and into the warehouse," Marco said, his voice calm like he was ordering lunch. "Get fire support on the back side of that wall. Hit them with the .50. Gotta stop the flood."

The Stryker roared to life, and its eight-wheeled drive train sped around the warehouse.

Ryan dashed between the infected. The door to the stairwell was a hundred feet away. Hailey swung the door wide.

"Stop!" Ryan whispered. "Stop! Pull the door shut!"

Hailey clutched the backpack to her chest and stepped into the warehouse darkness but still backlit from the stairwell light.

"Hailey, shut the door! Shut the door before they see you."

The door swung shut suddenly, seeming to scream on its hinges. It wasn't loud or overbearing, but in a building filled with creatures homing like bats, it sounded like a colicky baby. The infected surged, their feet slapping concrete like a machine gun.

Ryan dropped to a knee and sited down the aisle. Suddenly the refrain from *Superbeast* rolled through his mind:

The ragged they come and
The ragged they kill!

You pray so hard on bloody knees.
The ragged they come and
The ragged they kill!
Down in the cool air I can see

They moved too fast; the leading edge slamming into a forklift and those trailing behind piling over like a river over a rock. He couldn't take them all. Ryan's lungs seized and his trigger finger froze. He rolled hard toward the shelving, squeezing into a space between a crate and a shrink-wrapped pallet as the infected howled past. "Run, Hailey," he rasped into the coms. "Run to the Lenco!"

Hailey screamed and ran back through the door.

"No!" Ryan snapped.

"There is a door up here," Hailey said, her breath coming in gasps as she ran back up the stairs. "It goes to the catwalk."

The infected banged and clawed and beat through the door and up the stairs.

"Alamode. Alamode. Blow it! Blow it!" Ryan said.

"I can't move!" Marco whispered. "They are all around me. I'm hidden in a shelf."

Ryan ducked out of his hiding space, slamming the butt of his rifle into the face of a straggling 2091. He sprinted to the intersection and then toward the hole in the wall. "Jesus God," he said as he saw the opening glutted with human flesh. He ran to the Alamode—two forklifts pulled into a V in front of a metal box. He grabbed the M57 firing device, moved the safety ball, and shouted, "Clear! Clear! Clear!" Ryan paused for two beats and crushed the handle, smartly sending a three-volt electrical pulse through the firing wire.

Wwhooommp!

Seven hundred steel balls in a horizontal 60° fan-shaped arc slammed into a wall of flesh, cutting it in half.

The back blast slammed over the forklifts like a hand pounding against Ryan's temple.

"Hit 'em again!" Marco said. "Hit them again!"

Ryan grabbed the second firing device, moved the safety ball. "Clear!" He crushed the lever. Nothing happened. He crushed the lever twice. Nothing. A third time. Nothing. He grabbed another firing device and smashed the lever over and over. Nothing.

"They are not working," Ryan shouted. He grabbed the last firing device and smashed down the lever. "Nothing is happening!"

"What?" Marco said. "I—"

Ryaaaaannn!" Hailey shouted. "Ryyyyannn! Help!"

Ryan stood and looked to the rafters. Almost sixty feet above, Hailey was pushing against the door that let office employees get to the catwalk. The infected clawed through the smashed-out the window grabbing for her head.

"Just run!"

"I can't!" Hailey shouted.

Ryan scanned the catwalk bathed in green light. The infected had climbed the stairs on the warehouse far side; the heat signatures of feral human beings running toward Hailey.

Ryan ran.

"Oh, *Madre Dios*!" Raphael said into the coms. "There *es* so many!"

"They are gonna die!" Simone said, his voice shrill and piercing. "They are gonna die!"

"We need that fire support!" Marco said, his voice even. "They are pouring over the wall. Fire now. Fire for effect."

"Fire," Raphael commanded.

The Stryker's M151 Protector Remote Weapon Station started spitting .50 caliber lead in a chugging, ripping roar.

A .50 caliber bullet in its casing is about as long as a dollar bill, the slug about the size of a man's index finger from nail to knuckle and travels at 3,044 feet per second. It hits its target with 13,310 foot pounds of force. Its combat purpose is to chew through armor and vehicles and battlements. The Stryker's M151 swept a line of lead through the warehouse walls like they were made of cardboard. The ordinance vaporized human flesh along the catwalk.

Ryan dropped and clung to the metal, the air suddenly filled with a storm of concrete. "Point that gun down! Point that weapon *down!*" he screamed.

"Down!" Raphael ordered, "Shoot the top of the HESCO!"

Ryan scrambled to his feet, jumping over legs and arms and gore. "Marco! Marco! I need you to make a path to the door."

"I'm a little busy here!" Marco snapped.

"Damn it. If you froze . . ."

"I didn't!" Marco said, and then his weapon started barking in three-round bursts. "You want some of this!" *Crack! Crack! Crack!* "Oh, you want some of this too." *Crack! Crack! Crack!* "You too? Fuck you!" *Crack! Crack! Crack!* "Fuck you! Fuck you!" *Crack! Crack! Crack!*

Ryan turned the catwalk corner just in time to see Hailey lose the battle against the horde pushing through the door from the office space to the catwalk: The door slammed open wide and the 2091s poured forth like pus from a wound. The first twenty pitched headlong over the rail, but they kept coming and coming, dozens filling the walkway between Ryan and Hailey.

"Run!" Ryan shouted.

Hailey sprinted away.

Ryan started shooting and shooting and shooting, trying to clog the door way with bodies.

Hailey dashed down along the catwalk's far side, the backpack still clutched to her chest. She reached the dead end. The infected closed. Hailey looked over the catwalk at the shelving below. She dropped the food and crawled over the railing.

"Oh, God. No!" Ryan said.

Hailey jumped. She landed like a cat atop a wooden crate, scrambled to the bag and clutched it to her chest. And just like she said, the zombies were stupid. They followed her over the edge. The bodies hit the warehouse floor sounding like water balloons. Two zombies landed on the shelf and scrambled toward their prey.

"Get down!" Ryan shouted.

Hailey dropped to a knee behind the crate. Ryan fired four times, and the bullets slammed the zombies over the edge. He dropped the magazine, slapped a new one home, and spun toward the infected descending on him like a swarm of ants. He kicked the first one—a pimply boy wearing a Patriots coat and bloodstains around his mouth.

"Ryan! Look out!" Hailey called.

He turned to see the infected blitzing across the catwalk from behind. "Need some help here!" Ryan shouted.

Marco's weapon thundered below. "Be there in a minute!"

"I don't have a minute."

"Jump, Ryan! Jump!" Hailey shouted.

The Stryker's weapon fell silent. "They're attacking us!" Simone shouted. "They're attacking us. Drive! Drive! We are going to be buried."

"*Mierda! Meirda!*" Raphael swore.

Ryan shot and pivoted, shot and pivoted, measuring the distance. "Marco?"

"One minute!"

"Damn!" Ryan swore. He saw his bed ten feet below. He unsnapped his rifle and dropped to the shelf. He crawled over the railing and leaped for Hailey's mattress. There was no tuck and roll; there was barely enough room to land. He hit the pile of blankets and felt the mattress rupture under his weight, his momentum carried his head into fertilizer. He eyes filled with stars.

"Ryan! Ryan?!" Hailey cried.

"I'm . . . I'm . . . all right," Ryan mumbled. "Get to the Lenco and lock yourself in!"

Infected started hitting around him like hail. He kicked one over the edge, then a second, and a third, he swept its leg. He scrambled to his bed and grabbed his weapon. He came up firing as the infected poured over the railing. Ryan dropped a magazine and reloaded. He fired into the 2091s along the catwalk until was empty, scrambled for the bag of magazines stashed by his bed, and reloaded his pouches. The last 2091 flew past his head as he stepped onto the forklift. He looked down into a mosh pit of carnivores' mouths.

"Marco?"

"Stay put," Marco said and pulled the trigger on the SAW. He was standing at the aisle's far end. Tracer rounds flew in a line looking like Roman candles on the Fourth of July.

Ryan scrambled back to the shelf as Marco mowed a path. Ryan looked for Hailey and found her sneaking from hiding place to hiding place exactly like she described. She dodged into the space just before the large open area. A glut of infected dashed back and forth, distracted by the roar beating against their ears.

"I'm almost there," Hailey whispered back. "Hurry!"

"Ryan?!" Marco said. "Jump."

Ryan saw the scoop on the forklift dropping. The SAW had ruptured the hydraulics. He jumped and rode it down into carnage. The hot smell of bowel and bladder and the musty flavor of copper hung in the air like liquid.

"Follow me!" Marco said, stepping through the mush and mess. They climbed through the groping bodies, ignoring the 2091s' babbling, moaning, keening madness. They turned toward the exit and sprinted.

"Hailey?" Ryan said.

Hailey screamed.

Marco and Ryan saw Hailey sprinting toward the large double doors that led to the long section of the warehouse, the ragged throng on her heels. A 2091 leaped—a man in a frayed business suit and Florsheim shoes—and tackled her by the ankles. The backpack slid toward the double doors. Hailey screamed and screamed and fought and fought. The business man grabbed the vest with his left hand and swung at her ribs with the right. His fist bounced off the magazines. He sat up tall, straddling Hailey and raised his fist high.

Ryan pressed the trigger. The businessman's head exploded.

Hailey twisted and grunted under his weight, unzipping the vest scrambling away from the dead man's clutch.

The horde surged around her.

Ryan heard the rustling in his ear, heard Hailey's breathing, heard her struggling and then she went blank—like a hole in the universe.

82

Global Infection: ≤ 33.9897%

Marco triggered the SAW and the tracer rounds lanced through the darkness showing the line of destruction.

Ryan ran forward, guns blazing into the infected, leaping toward Hailey, slamming them out of the air with a barrage of lead. "Hailey! Hailey!"

The 2091s smashed against the large double doors like a wave breaking against a cliff. Ryan let out a primal scream and sprayed the mound of human menace on full automatic. He dropped the spent magazine and slapped another home. His perception drew down to the size of a straw as the M16's bolt cycled like a tap dancer on concrete.

And then there was a new sound. It was like the roar of Steelers fans after a touchdown, starting low with anticipation and rising to a roar.

"Oh Jesus God!" Marco shouted. "We've got to go! We've got to go now!"

Ryan dropped the spent magazine and slapped a new one into the weapon and racked the charging handle, continuing his destruction, brass spitting from the weapon clattering to the ground ringing like a thousand pennies. "Haileeeyyyy!"

"Ryan! Ryan! *Ryan!*" Marco said and grabbed him by the shoulder.

The M16 ran dry, the smell of cordite thick and choking. And suddenly the world rushed into his mind like a thunder clap as his perception expanded.

"The next wave!" Marco shouted. "They've breached the wall!" He pointed.

The infected squeezed through the hole in the wall like a python twisting between tree roots.

"But Hailey—"

"They are coming!" Marco shouted as he grabbed Ryan's tactical vest drag handle, the Stark's servos lifted him off his feet and pulled Ryan to the Lenco. He dropped the SAW and opened the door to push Ryan into the driver seat.

Ryan fought. "Hailey!" he shouted. "We can't leav—"

Marco grabbed Ryan by the throat. "We are going to die if we don't leave now. Start this goddamned car and drive. Do it now, soldier! Do it now or so help me, I will shoot you. Drive!" He sprinted bay door and pulled the chain.

The Lenco roared to life and Ryan hit the gas, rolling a hundred feet through the warehouse and then down the ramp to the street. He braked, waiting for Marco to get into the passenger side. But Marco ran back into the warehouse and snatched up the SAW. The infected closed on him like a wolf pack and were cut in half by a wall of bullets.

"Get out of there!" Ryan said.

The machine gun ran dry, and Marco started swinging it like a club sweeping infected left and right like he was scything through wheat. "Drive, soldier! Drive! That is an order!"

Ryan drove slow toward the northeast, waiting, waiting, waiting to see if Marco exited the warehouse. He could hear Marco in the earwig, grunting and fighting and cussing. And then the Humvee engine turned over, and the tires squealed on concrete. "Fuck you! Fuck you!" Marco shouted as his handgun blasted ten times, killing the infected trying to crawl into the cab through the .50 cal turret.

The Humvee shot down the ramp.

"Drive!" he shouted. "I told you to drive, Greg! I fucking told you to drive. Get your ass moving, Greg!"

Greg?!

Ryan hit the gas and saw the horde pour out of the loading bay door like vomit.

Crack! Crack! Crack! "Got you, motherfucker!" Marco shouted. "Got you, sick crazy fuck!" he laughed hysterically.

They sped through the fog, dodging cars and driving through parking lots heedless of streets and throughways.

"Goddamn, they run fast. Move, soldier, or we are gonna die!" Marco cackled like a psych ward patient.

Ryan turned right and then an immediate left, unaware of what street he was on. And then he felt the engine miss and then miss again. He pushed the gas pedal and felt the engine miss again.

"Greg?! Do not slow down! Do you hear me, soldier? Do not slow down!"

"I'm out of gas!"

"What the hell?" Marco raged. "Simone, I'm gonna kick your ass!"

"What did I do?" Simone said into the coms.

"You didn't put diesel in the Lenco," Marco snapped.

"But Poppa was goin—"

"Shoot! Shoot!" Raphael ordered. "We can no get buried under them!" The Stryker's weapons system belched lead, the sound coming from downtown Pittsburgh.

The Lenco rolled to a stop, and Ryan scrambled out as the Humvee skidded. Six legs flopped around in the .50 cal turret where the infected tried to crawl through the roof like snakes. Ryan yanked the gore-splattered passenger door open and a river of blood poured down the side. The stench of unwashed body hit him across the nose. He pulled the first infected to the ground and then the second. Ryan reached deep into the vehicle to wrestle a third body though the door, but its legs were tangled in the turret sling.

Suddenly a forth infected—a man in a New York Giants coat—scrambled around the back of the vehicle and bellowed. Giants Fan lunged and thrashed and fought without heed, without restraint, without mercy. Ryan blocked the blows to his head, both arms held up like a prizefighter pushed into the turn buckle. He kicked at Giants Fan's knees until he heard the bone snap. Giants Fan stumbled. Ryan drew his sidearm and slapped the trigger: Bullets hit Giants Fan from belly button to nose.

Ryan slumped against the door, sliding the gun back into its holster as the horde emerged out of the fog like chupacabras come to drink the blood of the livestock.

"Get in! Get in now!" Marco shouted.

Ryan pushed the body inside and sat on the remains of its head. He slammed the door as the horde mobbed the Humvee. Marco hit the gas, but the vehicle was swamped with extra weight as the 2091s pawed at the bumper. "Fuck! They are gonna bury us!"

Ryan crawled over the body toward the .50 caliber turret. He scraped the 2091 and the smell of blood, feces, urine and rot made him puke.

Marco floored the throttle: the engine whined under the load. "Shoot them off, soldier! Shoot those motherfuckers, Greg!"

Vomit dripped down his vest as Ryan squeezed into the turret and swung the .50 towards the rear, but it caught as the body slammed into Marco's shoulder. The Humvee swerved.

"Spin the other way!"

Ryan reversed and brought the weapon around, the body catching against the passenger seat, but it was close enough. He pulled the trigger, and the .50 caliber bullet turned human bodies into puree: blood and burning flesh and rubber and exhaust mixed into a heady tonic.

The infected made a long chain like a barrel of monkeys, each clinging to the next and then the second layer using them to claw toward to the Humvee.

"Greg!! Greg!"

Ryan pushed the muzzle hard to bring it fully around, holding the lead hose into the face of the undying, turning the fog into a flesh and bone soup.

The 2091s kept coming and coming and coming.

The .50 ran dry, its bolt snapping open, hot and smoking.

The infected surged.

The tires chirped and the engine whined.

Ryan pulled his sidearm and shot and shot and shot.

"We gotta run!" Marco yelled.

"Run where?"

And then, like a whale breaching out of the deep blue sea, the Stryker emerged from the fog, slamming over a car and splashing down into the long line of infected snaking through the streets, severing the head from the body. It turned hard into the endless tide, its eight wheels grinding forward, the IDE blade plowing bodies like a snow truck.

"Go!" Raphael shouted. "Go!"

The Humvee's tires caught on the asphalt and it surged forward.

Ryan shot at the clingers, bitterly hanging onto the government vehicle until the last one fell off.

83

Global Infection: ≤ 33.9899%

Ryan slumped on his knees in the high grass, his cheeks soaked, his body trembling, his world shrunk down to a fine point of grief and anguish. He looked down into the valley at the warehouse, and the image of Hailey buried under mounds of bloodthirsty flesh made him wretch. He pitched forward and heaved and heaved, but he was empty.

"Take a right," Marco said quietly into the coms. "Turn toward downtown. Okay, now stop. I'll tell you when to go."

Marco and Ryan raced from the horde, picking their way through back-streets until they were sure nothing had followed. Then Marco drove to Bedford Hill Overlook, which was exactly what the name implied: a park on the edge of a cliff that over looked the Allegheny Valley. From the overlook, they could see everything from the farthest western part of the camp to well past the 31st Street Bridge. They had a panoramic view of the carnage.

"Okay, go!" Marco said and the Stryker pulled down the street 50 yards ahead of the sprinting mob. "Drive two cross streets, then take a right. Stop at the second intersection behind that building on the right."

Ryan's stomach settled. He wiped his mouth with the back of the orange sweatshirt sleeve. He sat back onto his heels, exhausted. "Oh, Hailey," he whispered. "Oh, Hailey."

From the overlook, they saw how the 2091s got into Fort Pitt. The horde migrated to the wall, and the first to arrive were caught along the HESCO length like snow across a drift fence. But then the ones at the back pushed over the front like a stampede at a rock concert. They piled up, layer upon layer against the wall until the mass of humanity surged to the top. Builder Bob had been right. The African lunatics were just like army ants fording a river, using the bodies buried below like a staircase of flesh.

The first 2091s to crest the walls spilled into Fort Pitt, breaking limbs and shattering bones. Who knows why the next wave stopped, but they remained king of the hill until the sound of falling metal summoned them to violence. They spilled into the fort layer by layer as the teeming, writhing mass untangled itself until Simone pointed the Stryker's guns at the invasion and unleashed a barrage of destruction. The top half of the HESCO wall looked like it had been painted by a macabre monkey tossing red paint against a canvas and then nailed body parts without reason in a nihilistic impressionist orgy.

"No . . . they are still too close," Marco said. "I'm trying to get them a little more spread out. They are still coming. Let's do another lap around."

The infected poured into Fort Pitt like a human wave of North Korean peasants invading past the 38th parallel until they saw the new target. The 2091s untangled themselves by the thousands and rushed to smother the Stryker. They swarmed around the vehicle, piling on like a rugby scrum gone mad. Raphael engaged the eight-wheel drive and pushed the Caterpillar C7 engine to a red line and drove through the camp until he could get to the open street. Infected sprinted down Smallman Street pursuing the machine like beagles after a rabbit. Raphael drove through their mass, shredding flesh and rending bone; the gutters ran thick with blood and clotted with intestines.

"I'm trying to get you back there, little brother," Marco said. "Just trust me. We do not want these creatures following you back to the tower."

Ryan made himself breathe deep, once, twice, three times, trying to push the grief down an inch from the surface, trying to push the pain away far enough that he could stand. He breathed again, once, twice, three times. He pushed himself to his feet and wobbled. He breathed again, once, twice, and then a third time. He felt the earwig tickle along his neck, and the memory of Hailey complaining almost drove the line of despair back into his heart. He pulled the earwig back around his lobe and pressed the bud into the ear canal.

"Why will these devils no die?" Raphael said. "This *es* the work of Satan."

"I just want to go back to the tower," Simone said. "Can't we please go back?" He was crying.

"It will be okay, little brother," Marco said, his voice soothing. "You did great today. Your shooting saved us."

"But I shot at Ryan and . . . Hailey—"

"Friendly fire happens in combat, little brother. You had no way to know where he was. You had no way to know where any of us were. You didn't hurt Ryan. You saved our lives."

"That is right, Simone," Ryan said. "You saved . . . us."

"Where is Hailey?" Simone said, his voice watery with emotion. "I haven't heard her. Is she . . ."

Ryan choked. He rose to his feet and started walking.

"Ryan, where are you going?" Marco asked.

"I've got to go get reloaded."

"What? No. Wait," Marco said, "Poppa go. . . as soon as you hit Liberty, take a left and then drive toward downtown." He jogged to catch up. "Ryan, stop! Stop!"

"Marco, I can't leave her in there. I can't leave her body there." He spoke the words, and his throat and jaw hurt from the grief that seized his body.

"Ryan! Let us get—"

"The monitor shows clear," Raphael said.

Marco ran back to his vantage point. "Yes, go. They can't see you, but they can hear you. Go quiet."

And suddenly the rumble of the Stryker's engines faded from the background of their coms as Raphael engaged the stealth mode—the hybrid drive system that could travel for five miles—and headed toward downtown.

Marco ran to Ryan. He said, "I'll drive you."

As the Humvee rolled through the streets Ryan didn't care that he was sitting on a corpse with a head blown open like a watermelon or about the smell that came from just over his shoulder. He didn't care that he was sitting in a clotting pool of blood or the dozens of cuts across his arms, or that his clothes were crusted over with puke and stale sweat. He didn't care about the bruises across his face where the Giants Fan had brutalized him, or that Pagueros followed him into the tower, or that they rode with him to the penthouse, or that they refused to help him load dozens of magazines. He didn't care when the Pagueros looked at him with pity as he headed toward the elevators or that Marco came up to him, tears streaming down his face, and said, "I *am* your friend. I *am* so sorry." Marco wrapped his exoskeleton clad arms around Ryan in a bear hug.

Ryan knew he should return the affection, but he had nothing to give.

It wasn't until Ryan felt the needle prick in his neck and he saw Raphael's hand holding a syringe, that he cared.

84

Global Infection: ≤ 35.2499%

Ryan woke in his bed to sunlight streaming through the three narrow windows high on the wall. His eyes traced the light down to the oblong rectangles cut into the carpet. They reminded him of something, but he couldn't coax the memory into his mind.

Ryan's tongue felt thick and his head throbbed and his stomach growled. He pushed the blankets back and swung his feet to the floor trying to remember . . . anything. He raked his hand through his hair, suddenly noticing the bruises and cuts across his forearms and as if on cue, the rest of his body screamed a thousand protests from a thousand locations. He tried to remember how he got so beat up, but memory failed. He stood, suddenly realizing he was naked, but he couldn't remember getting into bed. He walked on feet as inflexible as stumps into the bathroom and sat on the commode trying to shake off the lethargy that seemed to hung on his body like a blanket.

He cleaned himself, flushed and then stood at the sink looking at the man staring back. The man's face was drawn. His beard was days past unruly. The left side of his face was in the later stages of bruising, the yellow gray tint starting to fade. There were more bruises across his chest and belly that were even fainter. He looked deep into his own eyes and saw the burst blood vessel on the right. He filled a glass with water and drank in gulps, filled a second glass and drank in gulps and then a third.

He looked at his face again, noticing that he was thinner. The rounded jaw line was being replaced by the square shape he'd had twenty-five years ago. He picked up a trimmer and started removing the wiry gray-brown mix until it was nothing but stubble. He wiped the sink and stepped into the shower turning the hot on as high as he could stand waiting for the heat to take the ache from his muscles and bones.

He washed, dried with three towels, combed his wet hair, and retrieved underwear from a drawer. He put on jeans, grabbed a pair of socks tossing one over his right shoulder as he put on his left sock. He'd done this move a thousand times when getting dressed, but today that sock tickled at his neck. He pawed the sock away and scrubbed at his skin. And then the memory began to rise like a shark from the deep, unwanted and terrifying: sunlight through skylights splashing pools of on concrete . . . and earwigs that tickled his neck . . .

The pain was like someone lit a fire in his soul.

Ryan rushed to the bathroom and heaved; only watery bile came out. His body bent in half against the searing emotion until, exhausted and panting, he lay on the marble floor and fell asleep.

Simone woke him with a tentative hand. "Mr. Sage? Mr. Sage?"

Ryan startled.

Simone flinched and backpedaled to the bathroom door.

"What?" Ryan said, his voice hoarse, as he tried to orient himself.

"I wanted to see if you were all right." He looked afraid.

"I'll be all right." He ran the water and rinsed his mouth. "Where are Marco and Raphael?"

"I'll go get them."

Ryan turned.

Simone stepped back, his face slack, fear touching the edge of his eyes. "I'll be right back."

"Simone?" Ryan said as he toweled his hands dry, but the boy was already out the door. The throbbing in his head seemed to have grown to drumming. He pinched the inside of his nose against the relentless beating. He hadn't been drunk in decades, but it felt as if he'd spent a year inside a bottle. His mind wandered back to the memory of the warehouse, but he forced himself to keep a safe distance from the open flame.

He put on a shirt and threaded a belt through the loops in his pants. He pulled and noticed that the belt was a notch tighter. He put on his shoes, stood, and stopped.

What am I forgetting?

But he couldn't remember.

Ryan walked to his office—through the Molitor minion outer sanctum, past the desks of those at the very edge of the Daniel Ryder orbit, to the inner offices where the luminaries that played an essential role in the Molitor Group echelons, through Mora the gatekeeper's office and finally to his desk. He dropped into his chair and leaned back, feeling as if there was something he should be doing, something that demanded his attention, something that should be driving him to action.

That was when he noticed the IT equipment organized on tables around the far office wall. Servers and monitors and laptops were plugged into surge protectors, and the cables collected into neat bundles. All the machines bore the Army's distinctive marks, and all were encased in protective green polymer. And then he saw the color-coded tags, and his mind took a step closer to the open flame.

Ryan fished a bottle of acetaminophen out of a drawer, dumped four pills into his hand, pulled some bottled water from a mini fridge, and popped them into his mouth. He was two swallows from emptying the bottle when the video chat chimed. He answered.

"Ryan?" Daniel Ryder said. "You are awake? Thank God."

"I'm not sure," Ryan said. "My head feels like it's full of bees and nothing makes sense."

Daniel leaned into the camera, his shaved face holding concern. "Maybe that is better for the moment," he said with a smile. "You are looking thinner."

"It's because we don't have any of those damned Italians making delicious sandwiches anymore," Ryan said. "Plus the pace has been rough and meals have been MREs . . . "

Ryan's mind took another half step toward the flame, but when he tried to touch the memory, it skittered off into a dark corner.

"Ryan?" Daniel said. "Ryan?"

"Sorry, just a stray thought that I can't seem to capture," Ryan said. "So to what do I owe this call?"

Daniel Ryder continued his warm smile. "I expected Simone to answer, but I called to see how you have been doing. I understand things have been rocky there."

"This is not for the faint of heart. But we knew that going in, right? So how are things there?"

"Like you said, it's not for the faint of heart. Actually, I called this morning to tell you something. But under the circumstances, I think it can wait."

"Earlier?" Ryan said. "When earlier?"

"You were sleeping," Daniel said. "Marco and I thought it best not to wake you. I only mention it because, well, I'm sure you will want to know."

"Well, if I'll want to know, then you might as well tell me now."

"Really, it can wait. Everyone is fine here."

Ryan breathed deep. "Since the only people we talk about is you, Raphael, and Ahou, and since you are here, and I doubt there is anything wrong with Raphael, that must mean something has happened with Ahou. Did she decide to get married to that Scandinavian god? What was his name? Thor or some such?" He remembered Ahou's e-mail and the video that he had started to watch . . .

Why didn't I finish that video???

Ryan shook his head again, but the bees in his mind would not settle down. And now in retrospect, he remembered that he and Ahou had been down that path before: declarations of affection and sweet nothings into video chat only to find out she was engaged. And the fact was, Ahou had never said that it was over with Thor.

"Sven? Is that who you are talking about?" Daniel asked. "Sven was his name, and no, he's a half an inch from useless. He'll be lucky if he ever has a woman. You have no worries there."

"I don't have any worries about who she ends up with," Ryan said. "That seems obvious. You guys are a billion miles away in the wilds of North America, and I'm in Pittsburgh, Pennsylvania, with a billion zombies—"

A billion zombies? A billion zombies?

Ryan's heart skipped and his mind danced close to the open flame again.

"Ryan?" Daniel said.

"Fucking memory," Ryan whispered as he rubbed the crease in his forehead above his eyebrows. "Anyway, you were saying? Or wait, no, I was saying we are miles apart in a world of hostility that defies description, with no ability to close the distance. The reality is that if it isn't Thor, it will be someone else. So there is no us, really."

"Ahou would be very sad to hear that I think," Daniel said.

"I don't mean to be cruel," Ryan said. "But the notion of love surviving in this madness . . ." He shrugged like the conclusion was obvious.

Daniel bit his lip. "It pains me to hear you say that. You are a good man, Ryan Sage. I know what you've tried to do. I hope someday you can be happy."

85

Global Infection: ≤ 35.2501%

Ryan felt his breath hitch and the constriction of grief in his throat. He breathed once, twice, three times. "So what is the big mystery? What happened—" he paused, his mind connecting the dots. "It's Richard, isn't it? What did he do to her?"

Daniel's face washed out white, and his mouth dropped open. Finally, he said, "Do you not know how disconcerting that is? Do you not understand how it seems like you are a mind reader?"

"It probably seems magical, but it really isn't," Ryan said. "I don't get the impression that she is dead. I don't see grief in your face."

"No, she isn't dead," Daniel said. "I think you would be proud of what she did. She found a long article on John Locke on your blog that inspired her to find a copy of the *Second Treaties of Government*. Two days ago, she went into the cafeteria after Richard got done speaking and began talking about the political primary of the individual. They came after her last night. She has about thirty stitches. Afterwards, she told me you warned her. How did you know that Richard would try to kill Ahou?"

"It's who he is," Ryan said. "I know he is your son, so it is probably painful for me to be so blunt. I don't mean to hurt you, but Richard is a committed socialist. Socialists try to tell themselves they are the pinnacle of benevolence, but at the root, they believe in enslaving some to the benefit of all. Their benevolence vanishes when they finally realize that the producers don't like being enslaved. So, it is no mystery that Richard will see no problem with killing to achieve his political ends.

"Progressives can never tolerate an intellectual pushback to take hold, because a free and confident people will never tolerate enslavement. This is why all progressive governments infringe on free political speech. And this is why universities suppress free intellectual inquiry. They can't win on ideas, because the outcome of progressive public policy is such an obvious disaster they must prevent everyone from pointing out the self-evident. They must destroy their opponents and indoctrinate followers. If public smearing doesn't work, then private violence is the next best thing. And since Richard couldn't control the cafeteria, he had to find a way to silence the one voice challenging his indoctrination."

Daniels eyes trailed off camera. "It is a tragedy that I have been this blind to people so close to me all these years." He shook his head. "I guess I should go ahead and tell you then that Richard's attack failed because Ahou took your advice. She is hurt pretty bad, but she had a gun. She killed the men who tried to kill her."

"That is how I thought he would do it," Ryan said. "I thought Richard would send henchmen. And she killed them? Good for her. Well, good that she lived. There is nothing fun about killing. I've done too much of it already." He pinched his eyes shut wishing the buzzing in his head would subside. "She actually listened to me? She's a rare woman."

"She is a rare woman, and resourceful," Daniel said. "She managed to find a gun when no one here but my security team is armed."

"And how do you know that Richard did it? I can't imagine that he is admitting anything."

"Richard is denying that he had anything to do with it," Daniel said, "But I know my son. I had him locked up."

Ryan nodded, impressed. "I didn't expect to hear that, since he remained free after trying to put bullets in me. But locking him up for a crime you can't prove he was part of only gives him fodder for illustrating how you are corrupt *bourgeoisie*."

"That is exactly what he said until I told everyone that he was jailed for your attempted murder. And since his mother is a key witness against him, his political subterfuge failed."

"Well, okay, good. That is a start, but he isn't going to quit. Now he just has to bide his time until he can reshape the narrative that he is a political prisoner on a trumped-up charge who isn't able to confront his accuser," Ryan said. "And if he tried once, he will go after Ahou again. She still isn't safe. And for that matter, I doubt the key witness against him is safe. The truth is none of you are as long as he is part of your summer home."

Daniel's face went slack. "It never occurred to me that my wife, his mother, might be in danger. Goddammit. I am such an idiot. I thought it was love, but all I did is let his poison into this place." He looked off-camera trying to collect his thoughts. Finally, he said, "Speaking of poison, I guess we should talk about you and Raphael."

"And why am I talking to you about Raphael? I'm pretty sure I made my disdain for his tattling to daddy clear."

"No, he didn't tattle to me. It was quite the opposite," Daniel said. "He has talked to me about the last few days. What do you remember about . . . those days?"

"I can't seem to remember a damned thing about the last few days, but I do remember that Raphael is a lying, deceitful bastard."

"You took him in on my recommendation. It seems that was the worst recommendation I ever made."

"Yeah, I don't understand how he ever worked for you," Ryan said. "Wait. I just saw Simone. I told them they were not welcome here . . ." He shook his head. "Why are they here? I told them they weren't supposed stay in the tow—"

"Ryan?" Daniel said. "Why don't we maybe wait a minute?"

"I remember the fight. I remember telling Marco . . . Why is everything so damned hazy?"

"Marco told me the whole story. He told me that you forbid them to come to the tower and that you took Raphael's access card."

"I did. I took it from him because . . ." Ryan paused. "What did I do with that card?" He shook his head again. "Oh, yeah they were going to bring stuff from the warehouse. I guess that is how Simone is here. I just saw Simone. Did I tell you that?

"Yes, you did," Daniel said.

"It was the strangest thing. I asked him where Marco and Raphael were and he ran away. It was like he was scared."

"He learned what you did to his father."

"Oh, I didn't think they were going to tell him."

"You know I've seen Raphael fight," Daniel said, "I've seen him in combat. So, if I hadn't seen the bruises, if I hadn't seen the damage, I'm not sure I would have believed it. You continue to amaze."

"Don't be too impressed," Ryan said. "The only reason I survived is because I shamed Raphael into dropping his guns. I could never have survived a gunfight."

"From all accounts, you've taken to guns very well."

"I don't have the Paguero skill by any measure. If Raphael had picked up a gun instead of a knife, he would have killed me. He is a murderer. Did you know who he was when you asked me to let him stay here?"

"Yes, and no," Daniel said. "The Raphael Paguero I've known for the last twenty years has been a loyal and virtuous man who has saved my life twice and has been an invaluable asset to my business. But I did know about his life in Paraguay. I knew he was part of some cartel as a kid. But most of the poor kids were in the gangs. It's a way of life for them. I knew he'd done some bad things. Of course, I knew about the teardrop tattoos. I insisted that they be removed when he came to work for me. And later, I found out what he did during the revolution . . ." Daniel shook his head with the memory. "Leona saved that boy from a short life of savagery. She is no virginal saint, but she saved him . . . mostly from himself."

"Well, he slides into old habits when she is not around," Ryan said. "Speaking of which, has there been any word from her?"

"No, and we are now officially worried," Daniel said. "So are you going to make them leave the tower?"

Ryan remembered the counterproposal. He remembered that they were to stock the tower with fuel and ammunition. He was to work on the computer system. His eyes trailed over the equipment set up in his office.

That stuff was packed into the Lenco. "We had to abandon the Lenco," he whispered to himself. "It ran out of gas . . ."

Ryan's mind stepped closer and closer to the open flame. "We left all those supplies. And we left that door open. We were so careful to close all the doors, and yet we left it open." His mind took another step closer. "How can the Pagueros stay there now?" he said as he rubbed his forehead.

"Ryan," Daniel said. "Ryan?"

"I'm sorry. What?"

"I'm hoping that you will maybe reconsider asking them to leave," Daniel said. "I can't in good conscience ask you to do it for me, but I'm asking you to maybe consider letting them stay because of Marco."

"Marco?" Ryan said, confused. "He's not much better than his father."

Daniel shook his head and said, "No, son. Marco may have some divided loyalties, but his actions are not his father's actions. Marco holds you in the highest regard. And whatever shortcomings his father might have, that young man is an amazing person, a first-class soldier, and one of the most virtuous men I've ever known. Would you consider letting them remain because Marco considers you a friend?"

Friend.

Ryan's mind took the last step toward the open flame.

I consider you my friend. I am so sorry.

Ryan turned in his chair and saw Marco and Raphael standing respectfully just inside the office door.

His mind reached out.

Hailey!

And Ryan Sage burned.

86

Global Infection: ≤ 35.2508%

Ryan Sage wept until he was dry as the memories of death and loss seared his soul. He cried for his sisters, Tess and Lenna, and their children, Georgia, Xyla, Steve Junior and Aaron. He cried for Hailey, the young girl who somehow tapped into his primal desire for fatherhood. And finally Ryan cried for himself: for the loss and isolation that seemed to plague his life. Then his grief turned to rage.

He hunted the Pagueros in the penthouse. He found them talking in low tones in the kitchen. Marco and Raphael sat wearing Starks at the island counter while Simone shrank away to the far corner and only spoke when grilled by Ryan, the grand inquisitor. Forty-eight hours had passed, give or take an hour; that was how much time Ryan had lost. Since Marco held him in the bear hug and Raphael dosed him with Ativan, he'd been asleep or delirious for two days and one of Ativan's side effects was memory loss. Certainly Hailey's body remained in the warehouse, because she had not shown up on the cameras. Unsatisfied, Ryan vented his fury. He raged about Hailey, and about the Paguero betrayal and about the injustice of the universe. He raged until he was spent, until his head hurt from the wicked energy pouring from within.

When silence fell, Raphael rose from his chair, uncovered a plate and set it down. "Here, eat."

Ryan feared he would bring it up until the first bite hit his mouth. He had to stop after one egg, one piece of bacon.

Finally Marco said, "I told you I would make good on the agreement. But if you've changed your mind, we can leave tonight. But before we leave we want to show you some things. When you are ready please meet us on the street."

Raphael produced a rifle from behind the counter, a Colt LE6920 AR-15 with a 16-inch barrel and a EOTech EXPS4-4 with magnification mounted on a rail. "You are a warrior. Warriors need excellent weapons. From now on you will carry this wherever you go."

It took a while before Ryan felt confident that the food would stay down and another while for him to dress and meet Marco and Raphael on First Avenue with a full load out: ORACLE on his head, rifleman radio connected to an ear wig and a tactical vest with 240 x 5.56, and 75 rounds of 9mm, two Gen6 Glock 17s.

"You have that look," Marco said.

Ryan squinted against the sun that suddenly blossomed from behind the clouds until the ORACLE transitioned to sun visor mode. "What look is that?"

"The look of a warrior," Raphael said.

"The look like you are going to kick my ass." Marco said.

Ryan scanned the length of First Avenue feeling the breeze, smelling the air carrying the hint of rain. He ran his hand across the Stryker M1132's armor. It returned from the Fort Pitt battle dripping blood and shedding bone-like scales, looking like it had been dragged through a slaughterhouse, but now the flat brown paint was smooth and clean.

"I figure that is why you both wore your Starks so I wouldn't think about violence."

"I told you he would know," Marco said to Raphael.

Raphael shrugged. "It worked."

"I wasn't thinking about that. I understand what you did and why you did it. It was a hard choice, but both probably saved my life. Right now I just have a massive headache."

Marco relaxed. "Sorry about the Ativan hangover. I couldn't think of a way to get you to take Ambien. Unfortunately I had no idea how much to give you because you are a big guy. After you were out for almost sixteen hours straight, I was afraid that I'd killed you. And then you woke up and talked and talked, and then you passed out again. After you lost two days, we were afraid of what would happen when you woke."

"The Pagueros afraid of me? That qualifies as irony."

And the Paguero fear had transformed into productivity. Except for the vehicles used to block tower vulnerabilities, First Avenue was empty of cars, leaving nowhere for anything to hide. Learning the lessons of Fort Pitt, they had stacked two additional shipping containers at the Smithfield intersection. They found another bus, covered its windows with metal sheets and used it to close off the Wood Street intersection. Then they shifted an Alaska barrier from the jobsite to Wood Street to seal off the cracks. Now First Avenue between bus and the shipping containers seemed like a safe haven, but Ryan knew that high walls were an illusion. "So what is this tour you want to give?"

Marco said, "We can start here. We recovered the last of the .50 caliber ammunition from the two M1126 in the sub-structure and loaded about 1000 rounds in this vehicle." He patted the hull.

Ryan nodded, hearing but not really caring. "So, let me understand something. It was safe enough to retrieve the Lenco, but it wasn't safe enough to get back into the warehouse and find her . . . her body?"

Marco sighed. "I told you, we went back to look for Hailey. We couldn't get close."

"There *es* many devils still alive," Raphael said, "I walk near the warehouse doors, but I could no go inside. We do no have the weapons to kill them all."

"And you say they just froze?" Ryan said, trying to picture the blitzing horde suddenly stopping like a spent spring on a windup toy. The Pagueros had struggled to explain what they saw, but they made it clear that one second the 2091s were a running mob pouring over everything like water and the next second they stopped. Simone called the dangerous ones Chia Pets: deadly when in full bloom.

Marco nodded. "We can take you to the overlook but they are slow and sluggish like the first day we were there."

"This is so screwed up," Ryan said. "How in the hell can we ever survive these creatures if they can suddenly turn into . . . into . . . Chia Pets?"

"We must kill these devils," Raphael said. "When I walk amongst them, many were still alive even though their bodies were broken. They crawl to me with hate in their eyes. This *es* no natural. This *es* the work of the devil, and we must fight."

"Fight, yes," Ryan said, wanting to engage his passion, wanting to feel the same spark of rage, but all he could muster was fatigue. "So you get to the warehouse and decide not to waste a trip? Is that how you got the Lenco?"

"Ryan," Marco said. "You say that like we would put that stuff over Hailey, but it wasn't—"

Raphael interrupted. "It *es* my fault that you think this about my family, but it *es* true. We went back at night to get in unseen, but it was still very dangerous."

"I'm struggling to believe you." Ryan said, "I want you to take me to the overlook."

"We will take you, but I want to show you one thing. It is important." Marco headed toward the stack of shipping containers and climbed to the top.

"More buses?" Ryan asked, looking at the purple Port Authority bus that had been pulled across Smithfield cutting off the street to the north.

"We know where all the buses are parked," Marco said. "And they were kind enough to leave the keys. We also blocked Wood Street to the north to keep the Chia Pets from mobbing the tower. Our plan is to retrieve more buses and block more northbound streets. That will be our outer perimeter."

Ryan said, "God, what a disaster. How in the hell did we ignore the signs? Didn't I say they looked more animated? Didn't I stand on that goddamned wall and say the person that built it knew something that no one else did? Didn't I warn about the Yonkers videos?"

Marco said, "What you are doing won't fix anything. You will go crazy playing why and what if. We worked hard to survive, and we still suffered a loss. It is a bitch, but that is how war goes."

He hated misplaced self-recrimination, but Ryan thought he'd earned this. "She trusted me. I told her I would always come back for her. And I didn't."

"No, you did go back for her. You fought thousands of infected trying to get to her and then you almost got killed and then you fought thousands more."

"I feel so . . ." Ryan's words failed.

"Guilty," Raphael said.

"Yes," Ryan said. "That is exactly how I feel."

"It *es* normal," Raphael said, "It *es* normal for warriors to feel this thing. I have feel this many times. There *es* no fix. There *es* only living."

Ryan climbed down to Smithfield, and Marco led the way over the cars parked in the Renaissance Tower terraces until they were near the front of the bus spanning the glass. Hidden by the tower's south wall, a support pillar and the bus was a small alcove. There was barely enough space to squeeze through, but there was the front door that led to the lobby security desk.

"This is what I want to show you." Marco pointed to a six-foot high platform piled with sandbags. Barely peeking over the burlap was a 7.62 caliber machine gun mounted on a motorized stand. "I think you are going to like this. Meet the Virgin Jinns, or officially known as the UHSP-T. And before you ask, that means, Unmanned Hostile Suppression Pacification-Tactical."

"I was actually going to ask about the first name," Ryan said. "The Virgin Jinns?"

"Jihad Johnny wants his seventy-two virgins. Their wish is his command. All they have to do is step into range. Alakazam! Poof! They get to see if there are virgins in the afterlife." He pulled a small computer from under a sandbag that was wrapped in green ballistic polymer. He tapped the screen to engage the system and then stepped across the sandbags and stood in front of the weapon.

"Halt, restricted area," the Virgin Jinn said in a soothing female voice. "You will be—identified. Paguero M. As you were."

"Is this what I think it is?" Ryan asked. "This is the AI system they deployed on the Mall in D.C. a few years ago?"

"This is the military version," Marco said. "We used these units extensively in Italy."

"Military version? The ones on the Mall were military enough. Ask the two thousand protestors that died. And I thought the AI failed recognition tests, and there were friendly fire casualties."

"Those were the old models," Marco said. "The early AI did have some recognition problems, but they fixed that. Now the AI is 99.817% accurate."

"That isn't too comforting, since that tiny percent of failure means I get shot," Ryan said. "Is this really a good idea? I mean, not having to guard this front entrance is fantastic. But if the AI fails, it kills me. That kinda defeats the purpose, and I can tell you I don't care about seventy-two virgins. I like my women a *lot* more experienced."

Marco rolled his eyes like he was talking to an old woman. "I've been using these for years. And I know that the failure ratio was exaggerated because it was connected to Special Operations units out in the field for long periods of time. The UHSP-T's AI was not updated with the Spec Ops recognition signatures, but they fixed that. For anyone garrisoned with Virgin Jinn, the recognition rate is 100%."

Ryan said, "So how did they fix the problem with the special forces guys?"

"That information is top secret," Marco said.

"Well, tell me the secret, because it is on the top of my list not to get shot."

Marco said, "That was part of my clearance. I can't."

"Uh, Marco, you're dead," Ryan said. "The Army buried you. They can't convict a dead man for treason."

Marco chewed on the inside of his cheek. "Good point," he said. "Let me think about it. Let me get you set up with a recognition signature," Marco said. "That at least gets you 99.817 protection as opposed to zero."

"Where did you find this?" Ryan asked.

"They were already deployed," Raphael said. "This *es* what I find in the nests along the wall. But they did no have the AI working."

"You know," Ryan said. "I saw these gun mounts in the nests, and I had no idea what I was looking at. You could have taken these, and I would never have been the wiser. Why set these up for me?"

"The agreement was to fortify this tower," Marco said, "and then you would do the communications system. I told you I would make good on the deal."

Where was this three days ago? What would have been different if you'd just fulfilled our contract? You wouldn't have needed to sleep. We wouldn't have been exhausted, so we would have had more people with eyes on the bad guys. And Hailey might be alive!

"Uh, Mr. Sage," Simone's voice boomed over the lobby PA system. "Team Bruptrick wants to talk to you. I don't know how to answer their question."

Ryan looked up trying to find a camera, but the tower security cameras were always so well-hidden from view. "I will be up in a few minutes."

"Mr. Sage," Simone said. "They say it can't wait."

Ryan rolled his eyes. "Coming now."

They rode the elevator to the eighth floor. On the promenade level, they took a quick turn to the right and stepped into the penthouse express elevator. Out of habit, Ryan waited for Raphael to press his hand against the bio reader to enable the car.

Raphael held up his right hand.

Marco looked at his feet.

"What am I missing?" Ryan said. "I know I took your card, but you have the bio scan." No matter how much the Pagueros were bending over to make up for the betrayal, Ryan wasn't ready to give in to heavy hints or even relent on letting them stay.

Raphael bent his lips into a frown and pressed his hand against the reader. Four seconds later, the screen backlit red: access denied. He held hand up, palm out.

Ryan looked at the angry scar across index finger and the subtle degree of twist. And then he understood. Raphael's biometric print was no longer good. "Well, isn't that cute?"

87

Global Infection: ≤ 35.2509%

"No, you idiot," said Bruce, his oily face looming large in the two-hundred-inch video conference display, his voice booming over the office AV system. "I said an RJ-45!"

"Bite me, faggot!" Simone snapped back. He held up the cable toward the screen. "This *is* an RJ-45 and it goes here."

"About time you got it right."

"About time you quit being a knob!" Simone said.

"About time you quit being a doob," Bruce said, and then he gave a big cheesy grin into the camera.

Simone flipped the bird toward the display, but he was smiling.

"Now connect that cable to the box that has serial number SN00001252," Bruce said.

Ryan stood at the threshold of his office, trying to decide which he found more disturbing, Simone putting together IT equipment, or the fact that Bruce and Simone seemed to be having fun. He looked at Marco and then at Raphael. They both shrugged.

"Oh hey, Mr. S," Bruce said. "IT guys rule, right? I heard you are a total badass." He looked off-camera. "Patrick! Patrick? Get your skinny ass in here. Mr. S. is here." Bruce looked back at the camera. He smiled, revealing Doritos-stained teeth. "We got some cables wrong because somebody . . . who shall remain nameless . . . didn't plug them into the right port."

"Not my fault you're blind," Simone said. "I told you the video showed it in this port."

"No, you didn't," Bruce said. "Sorry, Mr. S. It's hard to get good help."

"Yeah. Sorry, Mr. Sage," Patrick said, sitting down in front of his camera splitting the screen with Bruce. His eyes were bloodshot. "You know those Mexicans aren't good for anything but picking tomatoes."

Simone rolled his eyes. "All you white boys can do is pick your nose," he said as Bruce dug his finger in looking like he was scratching his sinuses.

"Bruce!" Patrick barked looking off-camera. "You are such a doob."

"Am not!" Bruce said, flicking something from his finger.

Ryan stepped into the middle of the room. "So, what was the emergency?"

"I wanted to hear how many zombies you killed," Bruce said. "The Mexican said you were like a super secret—"

"I told you not to *say* anything," Simone said.

"Oh right," Bruce said. "Never mind, but you have to tell me—"

"That is what couldn't wait? How many zombies I've killed?"

Bruce looked confused. "Yes."

"That's not what we have to talk to him about," Patrick said. "We have to talk to him about . . . you know . . ."

"Oh right," Bruce said. "We are not sure—"

"What Bruce is trying to say is, well, we weren't sure what to do about . . ."

"I mean we couldn't see you on any of the cameras," Bruce said. "And all we saw is . . ." he nodded toward the camera. "You know . . ."

"Guys, spit it out."

"Uh . . . well," Patrick said as his eyes darted to the threshold. "He's kind of a scary dude."

Ryan looked over his shoulder and saw Raphael's stoic, well-armed visage leaning against the wall. "Who? Raphael? Don't mind him. He's a sweetheart once you get to know him."

"That's easy for you to say," Bruce mumbled. "You're the assas—"

Simone's eyes went round and he shook his head. "I'm a what?"

"Nothing," Bruce said. "It's just that he said he would hunt us—"

". . . hunt us down if we didn't let them back into the penthouse," Patrick finished.

"And we didn't know what to do," Bruce said. "We hadn't seen you on the security system in days."

"And we had that e-mail you sent," Patrick said. "And we knew that you and the Mexicans had a fight."

"We come from Paraguay," Raphael said. "That *es South* America."

"Right. Right," Patrick said. "Whatever you say. We knew you had some trouble with them and we were trying to protect you."

Bruce said, "But then we saw the equipment they were bringing into the tower, and we were like . . ."

"We were like, oh my God!" Patrick said, "WIN-T communications."

Bruce's hand started tapping the desk in rhythm. "Military grade sat com! Oh, oh, oh!"

Patrick's eyes glowed. "We were like, if you set it up, we'll let you in."

"Military grade sat com!" Bruce said, his head tilting back, his hand still tapping the desk in rhythm.

"So, what do you want to ask me?" Ryan asked.

Bruce said, "Well, we were kinda wondering if we . . ."

"If we did the right thing by letting the Mexicans into the tower," Patrick finished. "I mean, we got it all set up. Simone was our hands, because of course, we couldn't do it ourselves."

"And your documentation was great," Bruce said. "I'd hire you."

"Even if your handwriting looks a little bit like a girl," Patrick said.

Ryan felt the color drain out of his face, and his stomach twist.

"Not that I'm saying that is a bad thing," Patrick said.

Ryan raised a pausing hand. "It's okay, guys. So do you have it working?"

"I just sent you an e-mail with some things we need done," Bruce said, "because Simone is probably better suited for picking tomatoes."

"Bite me," Simone said, as he flipped off the camera.

"I might let you if you keep offering," Bruce said with a wink.

Ryan said, "I tell you what. I'll look at the e-mail and get done whatever you need done."

"Military grade sat com! Oh, oh, oh!" Bruce said.

"On a different subject," Ryan said, "how are you coming with the bio scanner?"

Bruce's smile vanished. "Well, it's not that we haven't—"

"We still have some bugs to work out," Patrick interrupted, and his eyes cut hard off-camera.

Bruce frowned. "I'm not a bug."

"I'm just saying," Patrick said.

"You're just saying . . . what?" Bruce demanded. "I thought we weren't going to talk about that?"

Patrick shrugged with his palms up. "Well, we have to be honest, and we don't have it done—"

"I'm not the only one who—"

"Guys!" Ryan said, his voice firm. "I have one interest right now. Getting that scanner reset. So, I need you to focus on that."

"But we have military grade sat com!" Bruce said as his hand started tapping the desk again.

"Bruce, Patrick, this is important. So I need you to work on the scanner. You won't be able to do much on the communications system until I do my part here. So, in the meantime, work on the bio scanner."

Bruce's and Patrick's shoulders slumped. "Okay," they said at once.

"Guys," Ryan said. "You did good. Thanks for having my back."

"IT guys rule," Bruce said, "even if they are a secret agent—"

"God!" Simone said. "Shut up! I'm never going to tell you anything."

Patrick said. "We'll get this done, Mr. Sage."

"Thank you," Ryan said. "Now I need my office for a while. So let's sign off."

"Bye, guys," Simone said with a smile.

With waves all around, the video chat went dark.

Ryan walked to the coms system, finally realizing that the familiarity was because they set it up exactly as it had been in the command center. Bruce, Patrick and Simone had duplicated what they had seen on video here in his office. He reviewed the connections and the wire management and checked the displays. He looked at Simone. "You did this?"

Simone swallowed. "Yes . . . Yes, I . . . did this."

Ryan nodded approving. "It's good work. I thought you just worked on cars."

"When you work on cars, you have to work on computers too," Simone said. "And besides, my brother Lucas, he has a bunch of computers that we used to play with." His eyes darted toward the office door. "You want me to leave?"

Why is he scared of me? Ryan said, "I'll need more help later, but you can go do something else if you like."

Simone walked out of the office.

Raphael said, "These two are good at computers?" His tone made it clear he thought it more likely that all men could walk on water.

Ryan held up a finger and then went to the AV panel and turned the system off, pulled the security room door closed, and then he made sure the mic on his desk computer was off. He slumped into his chair and said, "I wanted to make sure we were alone. I'm pretty sure they like to listen to what is going on in the tower. It is hard to explain those two. They are good guys, but like many in their chosen profession, they struggle with some basic social skills. But they will probably make this system work." Ryan pointed to a monitor connected to the WIN-T system. "That is a login screen that I have no idea how to get past. And there are a dozen machines here that I have no idea what they do. But between the three of us, I am hopeful."

"So you will still do this thing for us?" Raphael asked.

Ryan sat back in his chair thinking. Finally he said, "No matter what I said in the kitchen a few hours ago, I did make an agreement with Marco. I will honor the spirit of the agreement even though we didn't get everything on the list out of Fort Pitt. You've done a lot here. I'll get to work seeing what I can do."

"Thank you," Marco said. "But you don't need to work on it today. You are still exhausted."

Ryan said, "I feel like I've got ants in my pants, and didn't I hear someone say that war stops for no one?"

Raphael nodded, approving.

"Well, as your doctor, I need to insist that you eat more food," Marco said. "It's been almost three days."

"A broken heart is a great way to lose weight," Ryan said, trying to smile, but the effort didn't reach his eyes. He pushed himself to his feet. "One more question. What *did* you guys tell Simone?"

88

Global Infection: ≤ 35.2519%

For the first time since buying the Renaissance Tower, managed IT services business owner Ryan Sage finally looked at the tower's network backbone, and he was almost as giddy as Bruce. The people who built the network knew what they were doing. The network organization was well thought out and thanks to Bruce's obsession with documentation, simple to understand. It took Ryan a few hours to complete Bruce's list of primary tasks and then Team Bruptrick had their tenth IT orgasm of the day when they confirmed they could finally touch the hardware from their end. Now the penetration testing—between insults to and from Simone—started in earnest.

Ryan let the boys play in his office and went to do more work. He had to work; he had to keep moving. But his effort on Bruce's list of secondary tasks halted at the MDF server room.

If only I'd cut off the finger from the left hand.

The combination of the subtle twist and the scar where the finger had been severed made Raphael's hand print unrecognizable. And now there was no way to get Ryan added to the biometric.

The ragged they come and
The ragged they kill!
You pray so hard on bloody knee . . .

The ringtone sent Ryan into a flashback—the ragged mob coming to kill, the smell of the blood, bowel and body odor washing past like a river, the feeling of terror that ripped down his spine. He pinched the bridge of his nose as if that would squeeze the nightmare out of his mind. It didn't work. Ryan stabbed at the phone. "Hello?"

"Those two idiots want to speak to you," Raphael said.

And Team Bruptrick did want to talk and talk and talk. They sounded like two girls having buyer's remorse after a one-night stand: hesitant, evasive, embarrassed and very defensive.

Ryan and Raphael leaned against the desk, arms folded, frowning at the video conference display. "So what you are telling me is," he said, pausing for effect, "you don't know how to hack the system."

"Well, uhmm . . . I'm saying that we can't get to most of the functionality," Bruce said.

Patrick amended, "*Can't most likely* get all of the functions. Like eighty percent—"

"Maybe seventy percent," Bruce mumbled.

Ryan said, "Patrick, what—"

"Bruptrick," they both said at once.

"So what are the options?" Ryan asked.

"You don't have to yell," Bruce whined.

"I'm *not* yelling," Ryan snapped. "I just need—"

"You've been angry since we started talking," Bruce said.

Ryan took a deep breath again. "Gentlemen, I have way too much going on to worry about hurt feelings. There is a whole shitload of 2091s two miles from where I'm sitting, and they will kill us if we are too stupid to live. So my goal is brilliance. My goal is to be able to communicate with little girls so they don't run into a pack of infected and get eaten. So, my questions are simple. I would *really* like simple answers."

"Little girls?" Bruce said.

Patrick looked confused. "What little girls?"

"I'm sorry. What?" Ryan said.

"You said little girls," Bruce said. "That they got eaten."

"I did? Look, whatever. The point is this is very important. What other options are there?"

"It's just that this is a 1024 AES encryption," Bruce said, "so we would have to—"

"Just tell him," Patrick said.

"Are you crazy?" Bruce said, "We don't want *him* in our network?"

"Guys! *Stop!*" Ryan pinched the bridge of his nose. "Pretend you are the dungeon master explaining a dungeon to a five-year-old."

"We know a guy that can probably do this. We've never met him personally, but communications and encryption are his expertise." Bruce paused. "And he's a little different."

Ryan frowned. "Okay . . . so different. Ax murderer different? Boy George different? Different how?"

"Boy George?" Patrick said, confused.

"Well, he goes by the name Blue Pill," Bruce said, as if that explained everything.

"Patrick told me about Blue Pill. He's the one who cracked the primary DNS servers, right?"

"You told him that?" Bruce asked.

Patrick looked confused. "Why wouldn't I? I got an IT hard on and so did Mr. Sage. I think Blue Pill should take out a billboard."

"Yeah, but no one was supposed to know who did it." Bruce whispered as if the gods were already listening.

"You are such a doob," Patrick said. "Blue Pill likes Mr. Sage."

"He does," Bruce said, sounding hurt. "Did he say he liked me?"

"Anyway . . ." Patrick said, "speaking of your blog, your stats are way up. Everyone is talking about you."

Ryan closed his eyes, desperate for a Zen moment. "Yeah, thanks for that info, Patrick. But let's focus. How do we get Blue Pill to do this for us?"

Patrick said, "He will pretty much own the whole network."

Now Ryan understood. "So if we ask him to crack the military communications, he will ultimately be inside every network security system we have in place."

"Basically, yes," Patrick said. "That is how he takes payment. He wants to be able to use resources connected to the network."

"And is this guy malicious?"

Patrick and Bruce exchanged looks. At the same time they said, "Maybe?"

"Talking to you guys should not be like pulling teeth," Ryan said.

"These two are idiots," Raphael said storming from the office.

"He is one scary dude," Bruce said.

"Yeah, he scares the shit out of me," Patrick said, "and I'm not sleeping down the hall from him."

Bruce smiled like a co-conspirator. "But he doesn't scare Mr. S. You probably have like ninja training and can smell him coming in your sleep. Or maybe you sleep upside down above the door so you can strike from above."

"That is Dracula, you doob," Patrick said.

"I'm just saying," Bruce said and then he winked at Ryan. "Your secret is safe with us."

Raphael decided that it was better to let Simone infer that Ryan was a highly-trained government agent to account for the beating he took. Raphael's logic was simple: if Simone thought Ryan was a professional killer Simone would be too afraid to seek revenge. The little white lie to Simone was spinning way out of control. "Okay, let's talk about secret agent and secret ninja sleeping tricks later. For right now, getting the bio scanner to work and figuring out how to get this coms system to work are the top two priorities."

Bruce looked at Patrick and whispered. "I'll bet he needs it for a mission."

"Well, he's not going to tell us now, will he?" Patrick said.

"You know, I just realized this doesn't matter," Ryan said. "If Blue Pill can hack the primary DNS, then this network must be child's play—"

"Hey!" Patrick said.

"Our network security is *not* child's play," Bruce said.

"I'm sorry," Ryan said. "What I meant to say is . . . that it is easier . . . uhh . . . than the primary DNS server's—"

Patrick snorted. "Not since net neutrality took over. How the idiots in Washington ever thought a bunch of European hacks could keep things running shows how much a bunch of idiots politicians are."

"It's not child's play," Bruce mumbled.

Ryan's phone chimed. He frowned. He pulled his phone out of his pocket and saw the screen.

The text read: CHILD'S PLAY 😉

Ryan looked at the originating number and saw a 902 area code. "What the hell?" he whispered. And then he understood. Ryan typed back: I HOPE YOU ARE THE BENEVOLENT HACKER TYPE.

Blue Pill: I'LL LET YOU BELIEVE WHATEVER YOU WANT TO BELIEVE.

89

Global Infection: ≤ 35.5217%

Ryan worked until he couldn't move. He fell into bed without undressing and woke with light coming through the narrow windows high along his bedroom walls. The light reminded him of her. He tried not to think of her name.

Hailey . . .

His stomach twisted and he knew that sleep was over. He showered and shaved, trying to avoid his own eyes. He dressed, took dirty clothes to the laundry, started a load and went to the kitchen hoping that he would be able to keep food down.

Simone sat at the island counter eating eggs, potatoes, bacon and toast. He paused mid-bite.

"Don't worry about me," Ryan said and went to the refrigerator.

Simone ate in silence.

Orange juice sounded too acid, bacon sounded too greasy and potatoes too heavy, so Ryan settled for an egg and a piece of toast. They didn't have many eggs left. He would have to check the restaurant and see what was down there. He ate slowly, fearing that every bite would be the one that made it all come back up. He washed it down with water and said, "So, you moved out of the master suite."

Simone swallowed and looked up, his face holding a trace of real fear. "I'm sorry I did that. My dad said I should apologize. I took a room down the hall from him, by where Marco is sleeping."

Fort Pitt had affected Simone deep into his core. The braggadocio and the *gung ho* Paguero warrior had faded so that the little kid was coming through. And Simone was a kid, with a touch of pimples on his cheeks, and peach fuzz, and big round brown eyes.

"Can I ask you a question?" Ryan asked.

"Sure," Simone said, pushing away his empty plate.

"Why did you want to sleep in the master suite?"

Simone shrugged.

"You didn't have a reason? You just wanted to sleep in the big bedroom?"

"It's stupid," Simone said.

"It doesn't matter. Just tell me."

"I like the smell."

"What do you mean?"

"I told you it was stupid," Simone said.

Ryan sipped on his water and waited.

"I know he's not really my grandpa and that Mrs. Ryder wasn't my real grandma, but they kinda were," Simone said. "I've known them since I was old enough to know anyone. I've been all over the world with them, and I liked sitting with Mrs. Ryder. She would always fix me food when I came to her house, and we would talk. I remember that she would tuck me into bed sometimes when I stayed with them, and I always thought their blankets smelled so good. Like I said, it's stupid, because I even got the same detergent for our house, but it didn't smell the same. When they were gone, you know, when they left for wherever they went, I just went into their room, and it smelled like I remembered. I fell asleep, so I stayed."

Ryan nodded.

Simone drank his orange juice slumped over in his chair, suddenly self-conscious. "I told you it was stupid."

Ryan rinsed out the glass and set it in the drying rack. Remembering how he wanted to hold Ahou's pillow. It was still in the bag he'd used to preserve the small when he ran to the tower. "Not at all," he said. "When I went to college, my mom sent a comforter with me. And I liked it because it smelled like their house. I'm not sure how that is possible, because I washed it many times. I used it until it was threadbare. And I put it in a plastic container and stored it in the closet."

Simone almost smiled. "Why did you pick that small bedroom? You could have told me to get the hell out the first night."

"It didn't seem like the right thing at the time. And then I went to the other big suites, they just weren't . . . I don't know . . . I didn't feel safe in them."

"*You* didn't feel safe?" Simone said. "With all you have done, with what you can do, you still felt scared?"

"No matter how old you are or how much you do in life, everyone needs someplace where they feel safe, at least for a little while. It isn't possible to be brave every second. I don't even want to live like that. I want to create a place where I and those who are with me can be safe."

Simone looked perplexed. "You just always look like you don't need anyone. You're like my dad."

Ryan crossed his arms over his chest, thinking. "I've been told that before. I think I understand what people see, but it's not true. I need people, and for all of Raphael's stoicism, he needs people too. I think we both look for certain kinds of people."

"But you are not looking for people like us?" Simone asked.

Ryan knitted his brow. "People like us?"

“Pagueros”

The tribal mind was so very hard to overcome. “Simone, I look for individuals. I look for people like your brother. I think Marco is a good man. I understand that he loves his father, but he knows there is a problem with how your father has acted.”

“How about me?” Simone asked. “Am I the kind of person you are looking for?”

Ryan raised his eyebrow. “You know what I thought the first time I saw you? I saw you on the cameras, and I was mesmerized by how good you were with a gun. And I told myself I needed that man to help me survive.”

Simone looked at Ryan sideways. “Really?”

“Yes, really. Didn’t your father tell you that I was the reason we got you off the street?”

Simone said, “I heard you say that you saved us, but I thought it was just bullshit.”

“Nope, no bullshit,” Ryan said. “I was in the security room. I don’t remember exactly what I was doing, but I happened to see you on the monitors. Raphael and Daniel were in the office plotting something.”

“And you liked the way I was shooting?” Simone said. “There were like twenty infected on the street, and I was about to shit my pants.”

“I was about ready to do it for you. I just couldn’t get over how fast you were.”

Simone looked confused again. “I’ve seen you operate. You’re fast.”

Ryan laughed. “It’s all relative I guess.”

“I guess I want to know if you will let me stay here. I don’t want to live on the street and we can’t go back to Fort Pitt. I’m sorry about what I said about Hailey. I know she didn’t cause everything, but don’t kick us out because of that.”

Ryan leaned back against the counter and crossed his arms. The obnoxious teenage retarded adolescent had transformed into a scared, cautious respectful young man. “Simone, first, my problem is not with what you said to Hailey. I thought it was mean, but I also understand you are sixteen. My problem with Pagueros staying here is with your father. And when he leaves I suppose your father will expect you to go with him. I would be surprised if he would let you stay.”

“How about if he would . . . let me stay? I could help around here. I promise I won’t be like I was before.”

“I tell you what; we don’t have to worry about this right now. Just . . .” Ryan paused, unsure what to say next. “I’m sure it will work out.” He started to leave.

“Would you mind if I took some blankets out of their room?” Simone asked.

“I think that is a great idea.”

“Can I ask you one more question?”

“Yes.”

"Are you going to kill my dad?"

Ryan raised an eyebrow. "Has your dad done something that warrants being killed?"

"No, he's a good father. He's just very scared for my mother."

"Well, as long as he doesn't make me pay the price for his fear, there is no reason for your father and I to ever fight." Ryan left the kitchen.

90

Global Infection: ≤ 35.6088%

Ryan had Richard Ryder to thank for hanging 40 feet above the Renaissance roof, clinging to the side of the cellular data tower. Whatever the disaster of Richard's Marxist ideological leanings, according to Raphael, he proved a master of political pull and crony socialism. He struck a deal with a national cellular carrier and the city government to have a node built on the tower's apex. Maybe Richard struck the deal to improve the notoriously poor cellular connections in high-rises for Renaissance Tower tenants. Or maybe Richard did it because he wanted to make sure he never dropped a call to his South American Marxist dictator friends. But whatever the reason, Blue Pill had very specific requirements for helping Ryan penetrate the WIN-T system. Connect everything as prescribed or no deal: not that Blue Pill actually said those words. The whole conversation happened between Patrick and Blue Pill via e-mail and text. Patrick forwarded detailed instructions on how to connect the WIN-T system to the cellular data node, the Molitor Group satellite uplink, and the military's satellite uplink. It seemed that Blue Pill's goal was to integrate the military system into the Renaissance Tower's backbone, which meant it was also integrated into the Pittsburgh data grid, which meant as long as there was power, the system was connected everywhere. Ryan applauded the objective but cursed the requirements: He had to run new fiberoptics and he hadn't done this work in a long time. And he had certainly never done it dangling hundreds of feet in the air.

Blue Pill wanted fiberoptic cable spliced into the cellular node's central system. And for reasons Ryan didn't understand, this specific task meant running the connection into to an interface near the top of the tower. While performing the work, Ryan had thought at least once that whoever designed a system that required climbing to the top of the node to access a central control panel should be shot. And then he thought that maybe Blue Pill was playing a rather elaborate practical joke, because certainly the tower manufacturers didn't expect this kind of technical enhancement. And then Ryan thought maybe he should be shot for agreeing to such a daredevil technical solution.

Ryan used rappelling gear to secure himself and then went overboard tying himself off at three separate places. He couldn't possibly fall, but hanging on the side of the node gave the illusion of dangling 30 stories above the ground; it was unnerving to look out into the vast expanse beyond of the Monongahela River and Mount Washington.

Ryan felt the warm breeze. The city's silence was so deep that he could hear the generator inside the nacelle of the nearest wind turbine as the blades spun in the early summer air. Thanks to Richard Ryder's dream of creating a totally green modern building, three such wind towers were installed on the roof of the Renaissance Tower. The math was clear: every wind turbine manufactured on the planet was an energy sinkhole, because it took more energy to produce and maintain a wind turbine than it could ever generate. The fact that a wind turbine burnt more coal to create its blades than the coal it replaced with a lifetime of spinning was a secret that the green energy tyrants were desperate to keep everyone from knowing. But when people got global warming fever, pesky things like physics and thermal dynamics never penetrated their minds.

However misguided Richard's vision had been, the wind turbines, the solar cells and most importantly, the Renaissance Tower's large bank of deep cycle batteries were going to be an enormous value when power failed.

And that is exactly what happened while Ryan was fastened to the tower. He saw the street lights across the Monongahela flicker once, twice, three times . . . and then they went off. Then the tower's massive cooling units cycled and fell silent. Soon every stray manmade noise throughout downtown Pittsburgh went mute.

This moment was inevitable: the end of mass energy production and the collapse of the power grid. The disintegration of civil society meant the failure of all services provided by the people living peacefully. It was foreseeable, but being witness to the moment, living at the collapse 21st century civilization sent fear through Ryan's soul.

Suddenly, hanging by two centimeters of nylon was more than he could take. Ryan loosened one tie off line, climbed down a few rungs, unloosened a second tie off line, and repeated the process for the third until he felt his legs relax standing on solid ground.

He unbuckled the harness and walked to the mechanical units and found them dead. He opened an outbuilding that housed the instrument panels and saw exactly what he'd feared: They were dark.

Ryan's stomach growled hard and angry so he went to his backpack, pulled out a sandwich. He'd taken one bite a few hours ago, but it felt like a brick in his stomach. He tried again. The first bite seemed to scrape down his throat, but his taste buds told him he wanted more. The second, third and fourth bite seemed to hold the promise that they would stay down.

Ryan's stomach lurched. He ran for the edge of the roof, gripping the half wall like it was the source of life, willing himself back to calm, forcing himself to not puke. Slowly, his body settled and just as slowly, he walked back to his water bottle. He drank and put the remaining sandwich in the baggie. Ryan climbed the stairs to the helipad looking at everything in general and nothing in particular letting his mind wander to any detail . . . any detail that was not . . . Hailey.

South Side Flats was little more than cold damp embers. Vultures circled just beyond Mount Washington. Three infected stumbled out of the Liberty Tunnel on the south side of the Monongahela. The wind brought the faint trace of wood smoke. There was a small fire burning on the western horizon, like a campfire, but it could have been a distant house set ablaze. And farther to the west were dark clouds, which reminded him of rain and rain reminded him of storms, and storms reminded him of . . .

"Dammit! Stop!" Ryan said, willing his mind away from the image of Hailey being buried.

Suddenly he noticed the landing lights. Gus had said he needed to turn them off. And then Ryan realized that every second he stood staring at the landing lights was a second that power was being drained from the tower's system. In the first few days of tower ownership, Ryan and Raphael worked diligently to turn off circuits, but over time, out of necessity, they had turned them back on.

He jogged off the helipad, down the stone path to the tower roof door. And for thirty seconds, he thought he was seeing a mirage. He touched the golden metal and ran his fingers over the double R, hammer and cycle crest. And rage exploded in Ryan's soul.

"Oh, come on! I fixed you," he shouted. "I fixed you! I Fucking! Fixed! You!"

Before Ryan dared step onto the roof, he looked through the tower's security interface for the system that controlled the rooftop door. If it closed, anyone caught outside was locked out. The door could be opened from the inside by logging into the security console beside the door, but without a biometric profile, there was no way to open the door from the outside. He tried propping it open with a 2x4, but the blasted door crushed the wood like a trash compactor.

Ryan almost reported back to team Bruptrick that the WIN-T project was a nonstarter until they fixed the bio scanner, but he found the solution buried deep in a sub-menu of a sub-menu: a setting that controlled the door time-out. If the door was left open, the system was set to close automatically after thirty minutes. Ryan set the timeout for 9999 minutes which meant it should never have closed.

Ryan Sage took out his pent-up rage on the intercom button. "Guys, I'm locked out on the roof." He paused. "Marco? Raphael? Simone? Can you hear me?"

Silence . . .

He waited for a minute then called again . . . and again.

Silence . . .

Simone was helping Team Bruptrick in the office. He should have heard the intercom in the security room.

"Come on, Simone," Ryan said. "I thought we had a good conversation." He pushed the intercom. "Simone, can you hear me? Hello?"

Raphael and Marco knew nothing about splicing fiber. Their usefulness ended when they got the cable pulled from the IDF through the wire chase to the roof. Determined to make good on Marco's new agreement, they left to work on other things.

They left hours ago. Where the hell were they?

Ryan dug out his phone. "What are the chances," he said as he dialed the pink nugget he'd given to Raphael. As the phone rang he the faint melody of a pop song. He ended the call and the song stopped. He dialed again, the tune floated across the roof, and he followed the sound until he found it under a grate covering a wire chase. Raphael left the phone inside when he was pulling cable.

Ryan walked back to the door and jabbed the intercom. "Hello? Anyone there?" He gazed over the stone face around the door looking for a security camera, but as usual, the designers chose to hide the camera lens and the speakers in the public spaces. Finally, he just spoke into the air.

"Bruce? Patrick? Are you watching the cameras like usual? I'm locked out. Can you do something? Can you send Simone up to open this door?"

Silence . . .

"Bruce? Patrick?"

Silence . . .

And suddenly his mind tripped down the rabbit hole . . . tumbling down, down, down until he could see Alice's shoes. The Pagueros got caught by the horde. The Pagueros took a Stryker and ammo and supplies and left. The Pagueros—

"Stop!"

Then he heard the tower air handlers cycle on.

Shit . . .

He could feel the tower's independent power system sucking the batteries dry.

Ryan's phone chimed. It was the same 902 phone number: Blue Pill.

The text read: I FIXED RAPHAEL'S PHONE. TEXTED THAT YOU WERE LOCKED ON THE ROOF. YOU'RE WELCOME!

Ryan typed a message back: THANK YOU, BUT I HAVE RAPHAEL'S PHONE.

The phone chimed.

Blue Pill: NO YOU HAVE SOMEONE ELSE'S PHONE. I UNLOCKED RAPHAEL PAGUERO'S PHONE.

Raphael still regularly used the tower systems app. The chances were high he was carrying his own phone. Ryan dialed.

"Hello?" Raphael answered, confused. "Who *es* this? How does this work?"

"This is Ryan and it's hard to explain. Did you get a text?"

"Yes. I do no recognize that number."

"It is a new friend . . . I think. And I am locked on the roof."

"We are on the penthouse level," Raphael said. "We will be to the roof in a minute."

Ryan's phone pinged.

Blue Pill: BTW, I CAN BE A GR8 FRIEND. ;)

These texts meant one thing. Blue Pill was in the tower system so deep that he was a cyber voyeur. Ryan said, "So, a friend, huh? Blue Pill. Glad to meet you. I'm Ryan Sage. I understand you are a hard person to talk to."

Blue Pill: BEING A GHOST HAS ITS ADVANTAGES.

"Being a ghost can be lonely, so since you can text me, you can call me?"

Blue Pill: MAYBE SOMEDAY.

"All right then. Good talk," Ryan said, "Would you mind explaining how you got the phones to work?"

Blue Pill: MAYBE SOMEDAY. FRIENDS ARE HERE.

A few moments later, the blast doors slid apart.

"I thought you fixed the door problem," Marco said.

"So did I," Ryan said stepping behind the security desk. He tapped through the security interface to the sub-submenu. And then he saw the setting for the door time out: fifteen minutes. "Unbelievable," he said. "The system reset when the power cycled. The door fails closed when the power drops."

"The power *es* draining the system," Raphael said. "I will start shutting off circuits and start the generator."

"Good, I'll finish up here. I think we are going to get some rain. And oh, I found this," he said, holding up the pink phone.

"I thought I lose this," Raphael said. "I did no tell you because you will make me go hunt girls again."

A phone chimed.

Ryan frowned and looked at his phone. No message. Then at the pink nugget. No message.

The phone chimed again. And again.

Raphael frowned and pulled his phone out of a pocket. "I have message?" he said. "Ahh. Yes, it *es* Leona telling me she *es* taking her time walking on the beach. That *es* why she take so long." He winked as he tapped into the voicemail interface and activated the speaker. The voicemail system gave the date and time of the last call. The message was five days old.

> *"This is Deputy Carol Weismann from the Meriwether County sheriff's office. I am calling on behalf of Leona Paguero, Timoteo Paguero, and Lucas Paguero. You have been listed as the primary contact. We are required to inform you that these people are being held in custody in the Meriwether County Jail for grand theft. A murder charge has been added to the charges against Leona Paguero. This is the fourth and last call on this matter. Please call us back at . . ."*

91

Global Infection: ≤ 35.6090%

Raphael called the sheriff's office immediately, but got no answer. They found other numbers for the municipal offices in Greenville, Georgia, everything from the DMV to the dog catcher, but no one was picking up.

It was all hands on deck in Ryan's office.

Ryan hung up the office phone and looked into the video conference feed. "Bruce . . . Patrick. Are you *sure* the VOIP system is still working?"

"I told you it was up," Bruce said. He chewed on the inside of his lip while he tapped at the keyboard. "External traffic is still getting to the phone circuit. But we keep telling you that the rest of the world has gone crazy."

"The sheriff left a message just a few days ago," Marco said, "The infection is centered in the big cities. It can't be that crazy in a little burg in the middle of Georgia."

Patrick said, "I keep telling you the CDC is ground zero, so it probably took a little longer for the infected to spread out from Atlanta."

Bruce said, "I'm looking at some forums. All major north and south interstates are blocked from Florida to Canada."

Marco bent over the iGlass beside Raphael. "It is 700 miles from here to Atlanta and another 60 to Greenville. And that is in normal travel conditions. We'll be taking back roads and off roads. I say we pack the Humvee and—"

"We can't lock the Humvee," Simone said. "The infected will crawl through the turret. Besides, there isn't enough room in the Humvee. "The three of us could squeeze in, but how would we drive back with Momma, Teo and Lucas?"

Raphael turned from studying a map. "We need the Stryker. Let me have it to save my Leona. We will come back with them and we will work for 60 days."

Ryan's mind flashed through the considerations.

Raphael took his hesitation for negotiation. "90 days."

"Sixty days is fine, Raphael. Take the Stryker. Go get your wife and kids. Maybe someone can be saved in this insanity."

Raphael walked to the desk and extended his hand. "Thank you. But now I will ask that you come with us."

"Me?" Ryan said shaking his hand.

"You are a warrior. You must come with us. We need men who face these devils when they are so much dangerous and have lived. I think that only a few men do this. Four of them are in this room."

"IT guys rule," Bruce said, looking at Patrick off-camera.

Patrick reached across the space offering a high five and then said, "We know you are a badass, Mr. Sage. But I'm telling you, you can't leave Pittsburgh. It is way too damned dangerous."

Ryan felt a wave of grief build at the edge of his throat. To leave Pittsburgh meant leaving Hailey. It made her death seem . . . final. Tears welled in his eyes.

"Why's he crying?" Bruce rasped.

"Shhh . . . It's about that girl Simone told us about," Patrick whispered.

"The hot one on the security camera?" Bruce whispered back.

"Shut up! You doob!"

Ryan wiped his eyes and said, "It never occurred to me that you would ask. Give me a minute to wrap my head around it."

"Mr. Sage," Marco said. "You are the one who says that we need people who have abilities. That is how we will survive. You, here, by yourself . . . that is a recipe for bad."

"Just give me a minute, please," Ryan said. He opened a drawer, pulled out a folio and walked into the security room. He closed and locked the door behind him, went to the far wall and pressed a button behind a bank of monitors. The wall swung wide, revealing a walk-in safe. He found a card in the folio, pressed his left hand against the palm reader and punched in the code. Fortunately, the palm reader on the safe had nothing to do with the tower security system.

The safe latch gave a soft click, and the door popped open revealing shelves with enough cash—foreign and domestic— and gold to start a bank. He cut out $400,000 and twenty Krugerrands. The last time he checked the value of his South African gold coins, they were worth close to $2,500. In the face of total financial collapse, the value of the coins was likely double. He'd probably never see his coins again, since they had been given to his lawyer to hold as a preemptive measure against the totally unconstitutional practice of civil forfeiture used by all levels of America's criminal government. But the stack of coins—among other treasures—in this vault took the sting out of the loss.

It must have been a common occurrence to pull large sums out of the safe because there was a stack of blue duffels on a bottom shelf. Ryan grabbed the top one, closed the safe door, listened for the lock to set and pressed the button. The monitor bank swung back into place and once again the safe was impossible to see.

Ryan packed the duffel with the money and the coins and grunted as he hefted it to his shoulder. He left the security room by the other door and walked through the penthouse and around to the office suites. The Pagueros might already know about the safe, but then it didn't make sense to tempt them if they didn't. Raphael might be making short strides toward honesty, but were they really indicative of a value overhaul? And that was the million dollar question: didn't going with Raphael violate the principles he'd been using to guide his actions? It was the pragmatic choice to go with the Pagueros. He was in a city full of infected, with at least 10,000 infected roaming its warrens and who knew how many more in the convention center and Heinz field.

A city full of zombies alone or face a tribe full of Pagueros, who believed they were morally right to sacrifice his life to their greater good?

An entire city of amoral carnivores or amoral collectivists who claimed the right to seize whatever they wanted whenever they wanted it in the name of God and family?

Ryan still didn't have an answer when he walked through Mora's office, through his office door and to his desk. He put the duffel down and sighed. Money and gold were heavy.

"Mr. Sage," Marco said. "Where did you go?"

Ryan opened the bag. "They might still be asking for bail," he said. "Or maybe someone with the jailhouse key will accept a very large bribe."

Patrick whistled.

"Oh my God!" Bruce said. "Mr. Sage, you are rich!"

"What the hell?" Marco said.

Raphael's mouth pulled down in a frown, and the lines in his forehead deepened to crevices. He looked at the money and then back at Ryan. "You would do this? You would give me all of this . . .?"

"Look, this is going to be toilet paper or maybe it already is toilet paper," Ryan said, holding up a stack of hundreds. "If you use this for bail, I will be able to pretend that I actually got some money out of the Richard Ryder deal."

Raphael let the coins shift through his fingers. "But these . . . these have much value. Why would you sacrifice this for my wife?"

Ryan shook his head. "You misunderstand. I don't live based on sacrifice. I live my life based on life, and in the last few months every member of my family has died: my two sisters, their husbands, and their children. And in the last week, we've seen four people . . ." the pain in Ryan's throat made his voice catch. "My threshold for death has been maxed out. I've lost family, and I know the pain that awaits you if . . . if they are gone. So this is my investment in life."

"Oh, *Madre de Dios*," Raphael said, his dark black eyes wet. "*Madre de Dios*."

Marco stood and pulled Ryan into a hug. "Thank you."

"You are welcome," Ryan said, hugging him back.

Simone stood up and said, "You have to come with us. I know you loved Hailey, but you can't die, too."

"Who's Hailey?" Bruce whispered.

Patrick rolled his eyes. "The girl, remember. The one that Simone told us about. You have got to quit smoking so much weed. It's making you stupid." Patrick looked into the camera. "I hate to be a big downer here," he said. "I know I look and act like an idiot, but I am really, really smart, and I am telling you that this is a suicide mission. The world is burning. The big cities have collapsed and the chaos is spreading."

"Pittsburgh hasn't been a picture of tranquility," Marco said. "We've almost died three times."

"However hard it is there," Patrick said, "I think it is worse every place else. We don't get out much, so all we do is listen to broadcasts. We got a guy here that is a ham radio operator. He spends all his time talking to people who are not filtered by the government censors. The government is writing off every state east of Ohio's border. The leaders who have survived pulled back to the Rockies. The President has been taken to a naval ship. Everyone is running as fast as they can toward the mountains or Canada. What I am trying to say is that . . . look, I hate to be the guy who tells you this, but my buddy on the radio said they were purging the prisons—"

"Oh God! Oh God!" Marco said, "Oh God! I did this. I swore on my mother's life. I did this."

"We must go find Leona!" Raphael said, a rare flash of worry and fear boiling to the surface. "You do not know my Leona. She has fought her way through 2000 miles of jungle to live. She *es* no dead."

"I'm just saying—"

"You are no just saying," Raphael shouted. "She *es* no dead. She *es* in jail. The jail protect her and my sons."

"Look, I get it," Patrick said. "You don't want her to be gone. But how long has it been since you talked to her? Over a week? If they left her in the cell, how long before . . ."

The thought of his wife starving to death in a cell put panic in Raphael's eyes. "There *es* no debate."

"It is crazy to leave that tower," Patrick said. "You have no idea the bubble you are in.

Bruce's inhale sounded like a vacuum stuck on carpet. He choked out smoke. "Oh, I know which girl you're talking about. The hot blond in the bubble." He started to laugh. "I said bubble. I said bubble. I mean the blond in the trouble." He leaned back in his chair laughing louder. "I said trouble. That was hilarious."

"Bruce, you doob," Patrick said. "You gotta stop doing that shit. It is rotting your brain."

"She's really pretty," Bruce said, pointing.

Ryan took a step toward the screen. "What did you say?" he said. "What did you say about a blond?"

Bruce inhaled and then choked out the smoke. "She was in the bubble."

"You are such a perv," Patrick said.

"I am not," Bruce said, his voice suddenly sounding like it was experiencing time dilatation, his words were long and slow and low. "I'm a doob." He started giggling.

"Sorry, Mr. Sage. He watches the tower cameras looking for women so he can . . ." Patrick nodded meaningfully. "You know."

"Oh gross," Simone said. "He's beating off to the female zombies."

"But the one in the bubble is really petty," Bruce said with a giggle. "I think she will be my wife. She's a little dirty though," he said pointing.

"Bruce?" Ryan said. "When did you see this blond? Where is this bubble?"

Bruce giggled. "It's right here."

Patrick looked off-camera. "Oh my God! Bruce, you idiot."

"What is it?" Ryan said. "What has Bruce done?"

Patrick looked back into his camera. "You are going to want to see this," he said, his fingers flying over his keyboard. "Look at your screen. I'll patch the building intercom into the office room."

Ryan, Raphael and Marco looked up at the screens showing the security cameras around the building.

Hailey's voice filled the room. "Ryan? Can you hear me? Ryan, I have a map. Could . . . uh . . . could I maybe get some more food, please?"

92

Global Infection: ≤ 35.6091%

The bubble turned out to be the landing at the loading dock door. Hailey looked relieved when Ryan told her he was coming down. But when he got to the street, Hailey had retreated to the top of the shipping containers. He found her sitting, cross-legged, playing with the ragged edge of her dirt-encrusted boots. Ryan envisioned scooping her into his arms and sobbing, but he was confronted with a face radiating the words "Don't touch me." There was a distance of a thousand miles in her eyes, and she inched close to the edge, leaning toward the ladder down to the street.

"Hailey?" Ryan said. "What is wrong?"

"I have a map. Could I just get some sandwiches, please?"

"Come on inside," Ryan said. "I'll get you as many sandwiches as you want." It didn't seem possible, but she looked dirtier and skinnier than the first time he'd seen her. Her cheekbones stood out underneath the grime. Her pink coat was back, as were all of her old clothes. She smelled terrible. "Hailey, what happened to your other coat?"

She sniffed and wiped her red, running nose on her coat sleeve. "That coat didn't have as good of a force field as this one," she said. "I don't want to come inside. I'm fine out here. I have a map. I just want to get some sandwiches."

"Would you like some hot food?" Ryan asked. "I could have Marco fix something."

Hailey fidgeted with the sleeves of her coat. Finally she said, "Could I maybe get some spaghetti?"

"Okay," Ryan said. "Marco could you please make some spaghetti?"

"I can get some ravioli made in a few minutes," Marco said, his voice strong and clear in Ryan's headset.

"Is ravioli okay?" Ryan asked.

Hailey nodded, still fidgeting with her sleeves.

They sat in silence until Ryan couldn't stand it anymore. "How did you get out of the warehouse? Did you get bit?"

"They bit me, but it was like through my pants and my army coat. Can I get sick from that?"

"If it didn't break the skin, I doubt it. Where have you been?"

Hailey shrugged, her eyes traveling down the street.

"Please, baby, tell me what happened."

"I've just been . . . busy," Hailey said.

"Busy? Doing what?"

Hailey kept staring out at nothing. Birds flew overhead as if they were trying to outrun the rain that threatened from beyond the western mountains. Finally she said, "You said you would come for me. You said you would always come."

"Oh, Hailey," Ryan said, his stomach rolling. "I tried. We tried. We killed thousands of them trying to get to you."

"Really?" she asked a faint glimmer of light in her eyes.

"Yes, really. And then I saw them . . . I saw them on you . . . I thought they were eating . . . I thought they killed you." He choked back a sob. "And then later, Raphael and Marco tried to sneak in to get your . . . body."

"How come *you* didn't try to get me . . . my body?"

Ryan's mouth fell open. "I . . . I—"

"Here you go," Marco said, climbing over the edge, holding out a bag. "I put a pop in there for her, too. Hey, Hailey, I'm so glad you are back. I heard what Ryan was saying. You should know we couldn't find you. Ryan here almost got himself killed trying to get to you."

"Really?" Hailey said.

Marco nodded. "Yes, he cried when he thought you were gone."

Hailey looked at Ryan as if she was studying a math book. "You cried for me?"

Ryan opened the plastic bowl, and the ravioli steamed into the cool evening air. "Here. Eat."

Hailey took the fork and buried her nose in the bowl.

Ryan and Marco exchanged looks.

She slurped down the last bite and handed the bowl back. She pulled the tab on the soda can and gulped it down.

"Would you like some more?" Ryan asked.

"I only have like one map," Hailey said.

"You know I will feed you as much as you like."

Hailey held her belly and nodded.

"I'll be right back," Marco said.

The silence dragged on, and the wind continued to pick up. Ryan couldn't hold back his emotions. His head slumped forward, and his body shook. Something bad had happened, and he couldn't tell what. She didn't seem to have a mark on her, but then she kept pulling her sleeves over her hands. He feared she'd been bitten.

"Why are you crying?" Hailey asked.

"I'm just glad you are back. But, Hailey, why didn't you call? Why didn't you come back?"

She gave a one-shoulder shrugged. "Moe said he wanted to beat my Galaga score. He took the phone. He said he was jealous and didn't want to share with anyone."

That made no sense. "He wanted to beat your Galaga score? Jealous? Of a score on a game? Who the hell is this Moe?"

Hailey fiddled with the frayed edge of her boot.

"Will you tell me what happened to your shoes?"

"Moe said he liked them too."

The sick feeling inside Ryan's stomach grew and grew as the details added up: The phone, the clothes, the shoes, the force field. "So you have been with Moe for the last few days?"

"Just one day. Well, not even that." Hailey's eyes cut hard to Ryan's face. "Why do you care? It's not like we are going together or anything, and besides I just didn't want to be a pest. You probably wouldn't want me anyway."

Going together? And then the twisted picture started to smooth out. Moe was *jealous*. Ryan breathed deep to keep the pressure from exploding out his ears. Finally he said, "Hailey, look at me. Look at me, please. We've already had this conversation. Have I ever treated you like a pest?"

"But you might think I am and you're just being nice because you want . . ."

"Want what?"

"Never mind." Suddenly she leaned over the edge of the shipping containers and puked. Ryan held her hair back and kept her from taking a nose dive. When she finished, she started crying. "I'm sorry to waste your food. I'm sorry to waste your food."

"It's okay, baby. It will be okay," Ryan crooned. On the coms, he said, "Marco could you bring some wet towels and another can of Sprite?"

They sat in silence until Marco arrived.

Hailey didn't touch the ravioli but sipped on the Sprite until the first ripple of thunder rolled across the sky. By the time the Sprite was three quarters gone, the sky was black and menacing, and lightning flashed in the distance. Hailey counted to ten between sips and slowly crept closer to Ryan's side. They continued in silence until a blast of thunder made the shipping container ring like a drum. She crawled under his arm and started shaking.

Ryan said. "Why don't you be a pest tonight? You don't have to sleep in the storm by yourself if you don't want to."

"But you will let me leave in the morning?"

"Yes, Hailey. I will never compel you to stay here."

She looked at him hard as if to search out the corners of his eyes and memorize his face. "Really?"

The knot in Ryan's stomach cinched tight. It was the way she said that single word that told him the story about Moe. "You don't have the key card anymore, do you? Did Moe take that too?"

Hailey's eyes were wet. She nodded.

"I will give you another key."

"Okay," she said, relief washing across her face like summer rain. That was the last thing she said all the way to the penthouse. Hailey took off her boots and set them neatly by the front door. She wandered around in one dirty sock, looking like she had just stumbled into a fantasy. Hailey ran her hands over chairs and couches and tables like they might not be real. She stopped at a window overlooking west. Simone walked through the foyer and into the room. Hailey pressed her back to the glass, clutching her coat at the throat, staring daggers.

"Well, excuse me for living," Simone snapped and walked out.

Hailey didn't turn back to the window until Simone was gone.

Marco met Ryan at the edge of the room. "You talked her into coming inside."

"The storm did the talking, but she is terrified of being in here with all men. You know what that means right?"

"I do," Marco said, "do you know this dead man's name?"

"I think that dead man's name is Moe."

"When we get back we will make it a priority to introduce this Moe to his maker," Marco said, "did she say how she got out of the warehouse?"

"No, and I can't guess how she got out from under that dog pile. She should have suffocated but she didn't, and she said they bit her but that it didn't break the skin. So the miracles keep piling up. But I think it took her two days to escape. She is obviously skinnier and her stomach isn't holding food."

"Holy shit!" Marco said, "She was alive all that time and we were right there."

"You couldn't have known."

Hailey walked past a couch and then to another window. She pressed her face into the glass looking down at the streets far below. "Is this really yours?" she asked.

"Yes," Ryan said.

"You are rich?" Hailey said. "Why didn't you buy your way out of the city?"

"It just didn't work out that way," Ryan said.

"It is good to see you again Hailey," Marco said, "You were my best student. I'm glad you are back. I hope you tell me how you got out of the warehouse."

Hailey shrugged. "Maybe."

"Okay, well, I've got some work to do," Marco said to Ryan, "But we need to talk some more. I'll be on coms." He tapped the ear bud and moved toward the penthouse front door.

Ryan said, "Would you like to sleep or do you feel up to trying to eat again?"

"Sleep."

Ryan showed Hailey to a where one of Daniel's granddaughters slept. "I think you will like this room."

Hailey checked the room from corner to corner scanning for threats, a habit already burned into her psyche.

"I hope you like the pink sheets," Ryan said.

"They're nice," she said, her voice flat. Finally, Hailey walked into the room. She traced a hand over the dresser and touched a row of stuffed animals resting on top. She stopped at a big purple hippopotamus, fingering its soft ears. Hailey grabbed the hippo and clutched it to her chest. "I used to have one of these. He's called Pedro, Pedro the Hippo."

"It is yours now."

"Where do you sleep?" Hailey said.

"I will be just the next door down. But I have some work to do."

Hailey pulled a bedside table until it was only a couple of feet from the wall. Then she tugged a chair in front, making a small fort. Last, Hailey grabbed pillows and blankets from the bed making a nest wedged behind the barricade and shut her eyes.

"Do you want the light on or off?"

There was a long pause and then Hailey said, "On."

"Okay, sleep well . . . and . . . uh . . . remember there is a bath right over there," Ryan said. If she heard him, Hailey gave no indication.

Ryan hustled to the foyer and put on his tactical vest, clicked on the radio, and put the audio buds into his years. "Test, test, test," he said. "Can you hear me?"

"I read you," Marco said.

"I'm headed to the roof," Ryan said as he exited the penthouse and went to the door behind the security desk that led to the floors above. "Don't forget me."

"Not likely," Marco said. "If you are not going to come with us, are you sure you want to part with the Stryker? It has all the ammo in it."

Ryan walked up the ramp to the 31st floor. "You told me that those tanks have thousands of rounds in them, right? We've seen five . . . six tanks? I figure I can get that ammo and resupply."

"Slow down there, Commando Sage. You forget that there are thousands of 2091s hanging around those tanks."

Ryan badged through one security gate and then another. "I haven't worked out the details. I'm just saying that I have options. You don't."

"I know you are thinking you can save this girl," Marco said. "But Hailey is not going to stay. The only thing keeping her here now is the storm."

Ryan froze at the last security gate. An idea niggled at his mind—rain, rain and more rain. The infected trying to catch rain in their mouths. The infected drinking out of the river. The infected breathing like a thousand yoga practitioners in the fog. "Fog is water," he said.

"What?" Marco said.

"It was a stray thought," he said as he set the time out to 9999 and went onto the roof. "I'm not sure why that went together. Anyway, I need to get this cell tower access panel closed."

"How long will that take?" Marco asked.

Ryan looked at the sun dropping closer to the top of the mountain and the storm clouds moving in from the east. "It is a race, but it should only take me say fifteen minutes." He started to climb.

Marco said, "Can you see the tanks over by the Convention Center?"

Ryan climbed to the panel, fastened his tie offs and looked north. "I have some buildings in the way, but I can sort of see one of them."

"How many infected do you seen around them?"

Lighting flashed in the distance, and Ryan started using the screw driver in earnest. "I can't see the ground around the tank to count. Wait, are you thinking what I'm thinking?"

Marco said, "Well, if you are thinking about a stealth mission at night, in the rain, with zero visibility for the bad guys and four of the baddest men in Pittsburgh armed to the teeth using ORACLES to see in the dark, then yes, I'm thinking what you are thinking."

Ryan tightened down the third screw on the panel. "What happened to all that caution about thousands of 2091s?"

"The infected are slow now," Marco said. "I figure we take advantage of that. We need a lot more ammunition than 1,000 rounds."

Ryan finished the last screw just in time to grab hard against the cell tower as the wind beat against his body. He swayed in the harness.

"Did I lose you?" Marco asked.

Ryan unfastened the tie off line and climbed down. "No, the wind is just kicking up hard." Lightning flashed across the sky, its fingers long and wicked. "The rain is coming."

"You are not afraid of a little rain, are you? That is our advantage."

Ryan was hustling past the hot tub rippling in the wind and he stopped. "What did you just say?"

"I'm really just thinking out loud. The more I think about a raid on those tanks in Indian territory, the worse I think this is."

"I just figured out how 2091s become Chia Pets. And if I'm right, the rain is not our friend."

93

Global Infection: ≤ 35.6099%

Marco rose from behind a car, grabbed the infected by the forehead and slipped the KA-bar blade into the base of the skull. He let the body drop and disappeared below the vehicle. When the glut of infected turned toward the noise, Raphael stepped from a shadow and buried his knife into two more RVJC 2091s. And so the two agents of death worked around the edge of 40 infected, striking silent and unseen as the rain pelted out of the black sky. Ryan sat behind the wheel of Toyota Tundra a hundred yards west on Penn Avenue watching the display of guerrilla warfare in the ORACLE's eerie green overtones, awed at the killing efficiency and terrified at its implications. They returned to the truck, Ryan put it in neutral and they pushed it toward the tanks while he steered. It was trivial work for three men wearing exoskeletons.

Ryan and Raphael took up lookout positions while Marco and Simone started the ammo raid.

Ryan's phone chimed. He patted himself down while trying to keep his eyes on the darkened streets. The wind blew the rain in sheets down Penn Avenue, the water cascading down a marble sign that said Liberty Center Parking rising out of the brick sidewalk like a boulder in a river. The Westin Hotel lobby was wrecked, and the ground floor windows were ravaged by bullet holes as were all the windows of the Small World Kids Care Center across 10th. Dead bodies lay in the street face down like they were swimming away from the David Lawrence Convention Center at the start of an IRONMAN race.

The phone chimed again.

"Silence that," Raphael said. "They will hear," his voice quiet in the audio buds in Ryan's ears. Raphael stood in the parking lot where 10th Street continued under the convention center, his weapon trained toward the north.

"Copy that," Ryan said, digging behind his tactical vest until he found the phone. He glanced at the front and saw the security system notification: something was moving past a camera on the 28th floor.

What the hell?

"Simone," Marco said. "Where are you?"

"I'm coming," Simone said as he jumped out of the truck bed, the Stark servos whisper quiet as it vaulted him a dozen feet down Penn Avenue and then over a car flattened by tank tracks.

"Hurry your ass up," Marco said.

"I thought you said the goal was quiet, not speed," Simone said as he took two more strides and leaped. The Stark powered him from the ground fifteen feet to the tank turret. The haul rang when he landed.

"How about for a little of both?" Marco said as he handed the ammo cans through the commander's hatch.

"Always complaining," Simone said, stacking them on the hull.

"It is a soldier's prerogative," Marco said, ducking back into the tank. "How are we looking out there?" he asked.

"Clear here," Ryan said. The darkness was near absolute, but the ORACLE revealed that nothing lurked in the deepest shadows.

The tanks flanking 10th Street were not the hoped-for gold mine. Both tanks had seen action, and their ammunition supply was depleted below a third each. And the .50 cals in the gunner's nests beside the tanks were bone dry. If the corpses strewn across the street were evidence, the rounds had been used to slaughter anyone that crossed their line of fire.

Raphael said, "ETA?"

"That depends on Simone," Marco said.

"Bite me," Simone said, hustling the ammo to the Toyota.

Ryan felt his phone vibrate and then a few minutes later vibrate again. He resisted the urge to look and continued scanning the darkened lobby and the skywalk running from the Westin Hotel into the convention center and the looted Jimmy Johns sub shop on the street level below. He was the first line of defense against anything coming from Fort Pitt. Thousands of 2091s still lurked a mere two streets to the east.

His phone vibrated again. Ryan couldn't take it anymore. He saw notifications from the 28th floor to the 20th floor. *Did a rat get into the building?* He desperately wanted to tap into the security feed and see what was moving around. "How much longer, guys?" he asked.

"This is the last," Marco said, handing four tank shells through the hatch. "Ryan, you are driving." He dropped to the street, the Stark servos giving a slight whine as he took two strides and jumped into the truck bed. Simone jumped in beside him, weapon ready, scanning the rainy street. Raphael slid into the passenger seat. "Let's roll," Marco said, thumping the top of the cab. Ryan hit the ignition, flipped on the lights, and rolled through the cluttered streets, rolling over curbs to get to an open patch of sidewalk. He scraped by abandoned taxicabs until he hit the ramp up to the Crosstown Boulevard.

Ryan's phone vibrated again. "My phone is pinging security messages," he said to Raphael as he drove. "Are you getting anything?"

Raphael dug into his vest, tapped through his phone and frowned. "What *es* moving around the building?"

Ryan made the turn onto Wood Street.

Marco banged the cab when Ryan drove past the bus. "Hold here," he said. "Simone, you are on blockade detail."

"On it," Simone said as he bounded out of the truck and ran to the bus. Moments later, the engine turned over and the bus rolled forward, closing off the street.

"So, are you sure that water is the key ingredient?" Marco asked. "The 2091s didn't act like Chia Pets. At least none of the ones we encountered tonight."

Ryan badged the security plate that opened the gate to substructure. He said, "I'm pretty sure. The 2091s are humans. They are not superhuman, so heat, hunger and dehydration make them sluggish. Water and food make them perk up."

"Come on, Simone," Marco said. "I'm getting wet out here."

"Bite me," Simone said as he locked the Port Authority bus door. He lay the bus battery in the truck bed and jumped in.

Ryan put the truck in drive and said, "Remember how hot it was before we went to Fort Pitt? Remember when we got there the 2091 were sluggish? We didn't think they were a threat, because they just kind of stood around smelling bad and making that awful sound.

"So my theory is that I start killing them, but killing some is the same as feeding the others. And then it rained nonstop for two days, so it's not like they run to the water cooler for a drink, so most of the 2091s soaked up water like sponges. The more water and food they have, the more they move like normal people. The faster ones are hydrated and have full bellies. The slower ones are basically starving and need water."

"I hate to tell you this, Mr. Sage," Simone said in the coms. "But you bought a tower surrounded by water."

"Oh shit," Marco said. "You know how fucking creepy it is to think about the 2091s breathing in the fog? They were trying to inhale the moisture."

"Yeah," Ryan said, "I'll never hear a yoga class the same way again."

Marco said. "Pull right up to the Stryker and we'll get this unloaded."

Ryan rolled to a stop and killed the ignition. Everyone dismounted. They stood in a circle, soaked to the bone and smiling—everyone except Raphael.

"Come on tough guy," Ryan said. "I think that was an unqualified success. No bad guys came after us. We killed bad guys and got ammunition."

"Yes, it *es* a good mission," Raphael said. "I frown because I know you will no want to see this." He handed Ryan his phone. The security app was open, and the camera feed showed Hailey standing at the eighth floor promenade exit. She stood in the threshold, a bag over her shoulder, looking into the rainy night. She took a step out and then caught the door before it closed. She hovered at the exit, one foot in, one foot out.

Ryan turned and started to run up the ramp.

"Mr. Sage," Marco said. "Wait, please."

"I have to—"

"If she is going to run, you can't stop her."

"She *es* no going to stay. She *es* going to leave, and then she will no come back," Raphael said. "You must come with us. It *es* a fool's errand to remain here alone. You need many peoples to survive. So we need you with us to help us survive. This *es importante* to have people's that we trust to help fight."

"Yeah, Mr. Sage," Simone said. "You have to come with us. We need your help, and you can't die too."

Ryan looked down at the phone. Hailey was gone.

94

Global Infection: ≤ 35.6104%

Ryan kicked off his sodden shoes into the pile of wet boots in the penthouse foyer. Hailey's ragged boots were still neatly placed off to the side sending a brief thrill of sadness through his heart. After drying off and getting changed he went to Hailey's room and found Pedro the Hippo sitting on the bed facing the door, Ryan's iGlass lay on Pedro's back. The remains of a PBJ and a drained glass of milk sat on the bed stand. The room smelled of Hailey even though she'd only been there for a few hours.

Ryan went to his room, stripped to his underwear, killed the lights and crawled into bed. The bedroom was lined by high, narrow windows that allowed the soft glow of moonlight to spill in, but tonight it let in the flashing and flickering storm.

She left too soon.

His thoughts swirled and jousted for ascendancy as he tried to make the balance sheet work out. He was flattered that Raphael had asked him to go, that the god of war considered him enough of an asset to warrant the mission to save his wife. But on further consideration Raphael had not revisited the request. The cynic in Ryan thought that meant the real motive behind asking him to travel was because it was the easiest way to get the Stryker; if Ryan went, taking the Stryker was a given. And no matter the ego stroking, the facts were that Ryan wasn't really that much of an asset, not by Paguero standards. The more insidious part was that the flattery made it easy to overlook that the underlying split in world view had never been resolved. In the last few days how many times had Ryan indicted Raphael's mystical collectivist world view? Ryan had lost count.

The realities before Ryan were harsh. Man needs, food, water and safety for the barest level of subsistence and not necessarily in that order. In fact, safety was a corollary to food and water because it was impossible to be vigilant every minute of every day. It was impossible to forage for food and water and focus on self-defense. It was impossible to create the rudiments of survival while standing guard. Consuming food and water required a fundamental expectation that no violence would come. As John Locke, the intellectual predecessor to the US constitution pointed out, individual men enter into social contracts for the sole purpose of securing their right to consume the fruits of their labors. Government's singular job was to protect the individual as he pursued life, liberty and property.

But how could man ever enter into a social contract that defended the individual when it was presumed the individual must subordinate to the tribe?

The answer was simple: the presumption was wrong.

The choice between the freedom of rugged individualism or the security of warrior ruling tribalism was a powerful conflict—one the founding fathers keenly understood and exactly why Benjamin Franklin penned the words:

"Those who would give up essential Liberty, to purchase a little temporary Safety, deserve neither Liberty nor Safety."

No matter how academics quibbled over the context of Ben's words, the quote summed up Ryan's conflict and gave the answer as to why it would never really work to go with the Pagueros. Raphael was a committed collectivist. Ryan was committed to the rational self-interest of rugged individualism. Ryan knew that if he took the safety of the tribe he would likely lose his individuality, if not his life. But of course, staying meant accepting the brutal world of individual survival. The ability to retreat 30 floors above the savage streets was his only hedge against the dystopia below. And with the work done and the supplies recovered from Fort Pitt, Ryan thought he had a chance. He had lots of guns and ammunition. He had food. He had power. City water was still coming into the tower, but when it failed—and it would—he was pretty sure he could find enough water to subsist until he could figure out a permanent solution. And finally, he knew what it took to survive a 2091 attack. He'd lived through one Chia Pet assault, and he would do everything to prevent the infected from growing into full bloom again.

He was committed to his principles and this declaration wasn't bravado, but a calculated choice, fully aware of the dangers and values required. Finally Ryan's mind settled and then his head relaxed into his pillow. He would live to achieve his highest goals and if he died, he would be content.

Done with one problem Ryan's mind shifted to another—Hailey. And so began the swirling and tossing of strategy and counterstrategy to persuade Hailey to remain in the tower. He was in the middle of a full-blown mental tornado. Lightning flashed and thunder rolled. The storm seemed directly over the tower.

Then he saw his bedroom door slowly open . . . .

A shadow slid into his room and the door closed.

Ryan's breath seized as he watched the shadow move to the closet, duck underneath the hanging clothes and into the back corner.

"Who's there?" Ryan rasped.

The silence made his heart beat faster.

He reached for his gun.

Then he heard her soft girl voice. "Good night."

"Good night," he said, his heart returning to normal. He fought the urge to get up and ask Hailey where she'd gone.

Ryan woke to the sounds of Hailey's crying. He adjusted the dimmer and slid the closet door wider. She was curled in a ball deep in the corner muttering, a sofa pillow under her cheek soaked. He stroked the hair from her face, and Hailey's hand shot out and grabbed Ryan's fingers like a vise. He tried to pull away.

"Maria! Maria!" Hailey mumbled. "Please play dolls with me. Come play with me. I'll let you have my Barbie mountain."

Ryan stopped pulling. Hailey quieted. He stayed still until his knees ached and his legs fell asleep. He tried to slip out of her grip.

"Maria! Please! Here! You can have the strawberry pencil," Hailey whimpered.

Ryan situated himself against the wall with her hand still crushing his.

He was wakened at dawn. Somehow there was a blanket over him and a pillow under his head.

Raphael's face was grim. "She came back?" he asked. "I think this one can walk through walls."

"I gave her a security card," Ryan said, trying to push the fog out of his mind. "The storm brought her back." He tried to message the kink in his neck. "She had a really rough night. She talked about Maria and Tim and Pogo and Nanna. I don't think she let go once all night.

Raphael crouched down. "You'd make a good father."

"Father? You have to have a woman and then you have to have . . ." Ryan checked to make sure she was still sleeping, "S-E-X to be a father." He tried to raise his hand, but it was asleep.

Raphael chuckled. "Spelling only works when they are four. A woman and sex are nice, but this have nothing to do with being a father." He sniffed. "And a good father gets his daughter to bathe."

"You didn't have to sleep by it."

Raphael nodded. "I have no girls. So, I have no knowledge in these matters. But I know fathers with girls, and they can no keep them out of the bathtub. Always cleaning."

This force field is better . . .

Ryan said, "I think it is man-deterrent."

"What *es* this man-deterrent?" Raphael said.

"You don't understand," Ryan said, "because it never occurred to you to have sex with a twelve . . . well, almost thirteen-year-old girl."

Outrage flashed behind Raphael's dark black South American eyes. "Who has done this to her?"

Ryan tried to shake out his legs. "I think his name is Moe. And I think she is trying to stink to keep men from wanting to be near her."

Raphael said, "We will take her with us. She will be safe. We can no leave her in this city with this man."

Ryan grabbed his pants and stepped into them. "She doesn't make a distinction between Moe and other men. My guess is that Moe is not the first, so I doubt that she will want to get in a small sealed machine with four men."

Realization dawned on Raphael's face. Finally he said, "You are staying then? Even though she will leave when there are no more storms."

"I don't think she left the tower. I think she hid in one of the lower floors thinking she was safer. She only came back to the penthouse when the storm started."

"It *es* suicide for you to stay here with her."

"You, of all people, shouldn't underestimate me. Go find your sons and your wife."

Raphael nodded. "Marco *es* fixing breakfast. Simone *es* loading the last supplies. Daniel's security team give us a detailed report and many photos. We will be going—"

Hailey bolted upright, eyes glazed, hair a mess, looking around underneath the hanging clothes, confused. "What happened to the horses?"

"The horses are fine. I'm sure they are in the barn," Ryan said. "Do you want to come out and eat?"

"Yes," she said, not moving. She yawned. "Can I have pancakes? I think they are my favorite."

"I think we can manage that."

She nodded and promptly put her head back down on her pillow, snoring softly.

95

Global Infection: ≤ 35.7904%

The Stryker M1132's diesel engine purred like a lion in on Boulevard of the Allies, its displacement blade shining in the early morning sun. Fastened to its haul were two 55-gallon drums filled with diesel fuel. The added fuel gave the vehicle an effective range of a thousand miles, but the Pagueros stowed a pump and a Solar Stik flex fuel generator to scavenge more.

Simone crawled through the double rear doors without a comment. Raphael jumped from the ground to the command hatch, slid into his command seat and put on a helmet wired into the Stryker weapons system. He saluted and started testing the Protector M151; it swiveled and tracked wherever Raphael pointed his nose.

Marco stood facing Ryan dressed like Simone and Raphael, arrayed in the dark black Molitor Group security BDUs, Dragon Skin body armor and the Stark. "We should have left one of these," he said, pointing at the exoskeleton. "It would be the difference between life and death in a fight."

"That is why you guys should have them," Ryan said. "I don't plan on getting that close."

Marco said, "I saw two infected trapped on Starks by Fort Pitt. They are near the refugee camp on the left side. The power cells are drained, so the 2091s were just wallowing and helpless."

"That kinda defeats the purpose, right? Take on the horde to get something that helps me take on the horde. Not really high on my priority list at the moment."

"Speaking of things to do, I hope you don't mind," Marco said, holding a credit card between two fingers. "I bought some things for you last night. Hailey was holding your hand like it was a lifeline, so I didn't want to wake you. And when I saw that she had come back, I knew you were not gonna come with us."

Ryan took back the card. "Are you the one who gave me a blanket and pillow?"

"Yeah, you didn't look too comfortable."

"And what did you buy me?" Ryan asked, taking the card, "A mail-order bride? A tropical island?"

"I would have bought us both a tropical island if they were on sale. I figure Richard Ryder's Platinum card could do it. But no, I bought you some training videos. I downloaded them to a folder called Shooting Videos for Ryan. You can't miss it."

"I think I can find that."

"Listen to me," Marco said. "I was part of a special force. . . ." His voice failed him, and his eyes drifted into the distance. Marco shook his head once, then twice, trying to get something out of his mind. "The details don't matter. Here is what you need to know. I've been thinking of Gus' formulas and what the numbers mean. This is an extinction level event, but I think his conclusion was wrong. The way to survive is to exterminate the 2091s. We must kill them until every single last one is dead. This means you can't stay bunkered in the tower."

"You want me to become a one-man army?"

"No, I want you to become a two-man army. You and Hailey and anyone else you can recruit to the cause. We have a very small window to wipe these things out or the human race dies."

"When I have the opportunity, I can try—"

"No, you're not hearing me. You must kill as many as you can, as often as you can. You must start by clearing Downtown Pittsburgh and then move across the river. If for no other reason, you cannot let them mass around the tower. If you do, eventually they will get in, or they will make it impossible for you to get out. Either event will kill you."

"Yes, true. But I am outnumbered a thousand to one."

"It is very likely a hundred thousand to one. The best thing you can do for *your* survival, for *her* survival . . . for *our* survival is to hunt constantly. And to do that, you must train. Do you understand what I'm telling you?"

"I have got to get better with guns."

"No, you have to become an expert with guns," Marco looked Ryan deep in the eyes. "You have to become better than me. You have to be as good as my brother Timoteo. I know you have never seen him, but that is how good you have to become. And Hailey, she has to be as good as you."

"Didn't you say I needed five years and maybe I would be goo—"

Marco clenched his fist. "No!" he said with too much heat. He paused, collected himself and then said, "I know what I said. I was treating you like a recruit. I was trying to motivate you like a stupid kid filled with delusions of grandeur who needs taken down a peg before he can learn anything. But you are not a kid, you are not stupid, and you do not suffer delusions. You need to get back into world-class shape and train like you are going to the Olympics. You have to drop eighty pounds and get your reflexes back. You cannot fail. Do you understand? You must set your goal that high if you are to have a hope to prevail."

"All right," Ryan said. "I get it."

"Good. You need to train with all weapons so you can do everything in your sleep. And remember, you must train like you will encounter enemies that shoot back. And it will happen. As you hunt, the sounds of gunfire will draw the bad guys to you, and you must be ready to answer with overwhelming force."

"Okay, I can do that," Ryan said.

"Most combat takes place inside a hundred meters, so train with short barrel rifles. And if the 2091s get into the tower, the shorter barrel will be an advantage. In CQB, you must get proficient with a handgun. You have lots of real targets, so practice, practice, practice." He sounded like a father trying to inject his every thought into a teenager before handing him the car keys. "Run the drills all the time. Train. Train. Train."

"Marco, you are worried about me."

Marco looked away. "I am. We, my whole family, owe you so much. I will be back. So you must live until we return."

"Marco, I appreciate what you are saying, but I have no illusions. I saw the recon photos covering the Adirondacks all the way to the north. Your father will make a beeline to the camps. I'm pretty sure this is goodbye."

"I won't let my father do that," Marco said. "We haven't paid for the Stryker, and you gave all that money and the gold. The least we can do is come back for the 60 days to make good on the deal."

"You and I both know what Raphael will do."

"No, he will have to come back north to get to the camps. It makes sense to come here, then proceed."

Ryan shook his head no. "The interstates north and south are impassable. We happen to be in the one city where getting across the Ohio and the Monongahela is less than a mile away. Once you get across, those rivers are a big obstacle. Daniel's security team already plotted the best way. Skirt Atlanta to the east and then use the routes available north through the Appalachian Mountains. He will have the Stryker and his family. Your mother and father are tacticians. That is the choice I expect them to make."

Marco reached toward the Rifleman radio on his left hip and turned the power off, killing the coms. Then he said, "That is why you are not coming with us isn't it? You know that to leave is to never come back. You don't trust my father to keep his word."

Ryan shrugged. "He is who he is."

"For a minute I thought you were doing the noble thing and staying for Hailey."

"Staying for Hailey, while it sounds very self-sacrificial and therefore very moral by American ethical standards, it would really mean I placed the moral responsibility of my adult choices on a twelve-year-old girl. That wouldn't be noble. That would be a contemptible a level of evil. But if that is what Raphael wants to think, then maybe it is for the best."

Marco looked west, his mouth pulled down into a frown, and in that moment he looked exactly like Raphael. He nodded. "Your weapons are what stand between you and an attack. You must learn to reload faster. You must learn a tactical reload. You must learn to clear a weapon after a double feed. Remember the acronym SPORTS. There is so much for you to learn, so much I want to teach." He pinched the inside of his eyes trying to squeeze back the emotions. "Just study the videos. Start with the basics. Keep doing the basics. Keep your finger off the trigger until you are ready to shoot. And make sure you keep a syrette of morphine and a syrette of Combat Medic on you all the time. You know what it does. You know it will save your life."

Ryan said, "I will make that part of my load out."

"I put two boxes of morphine and CM on your desk. Hang one of each around your neck and leave it there. Never go anywhere without them. You are all alone, and those syrettes are all that stand between you and death. If you get shot, inject yourself first with the green, then hit yourself with the red. Say it, green first then the red."

"Green first. Then the red," Ryan repeated.

"And then get one of those protein sticks. You saw my father sucking on those nasty things, but it's what your body will crave. There is a box of them on the skids down on the docs." Marco looked skyward, trying to think of something else to say. "If you pull the trigger and nothing happens, remember SPORTS. Wait, I said that already."

"Marco, I tell you what. I'll start fighting from here and you start fighting from Maine. We'll meet somewhere around Boston. And if Hailey stays with me, she will be your little protégé."

Marco smiled a dazzling South American smile and said, "I will hold you to that. If you get killed and fuck up our rendezvous in Boston, I'll kick your ass." He looked hard into Ryan's eyes. He snapped off a salute and then pulled him into a hug.

"You are not going to drug me again, are you?"

"I am your friend," Marco said, and then he turned to step into the vehicle.

"Before you go," Ryan said, "I do have one question."

Marco paused.

"Uh . . . the morning I woke up after you drugged me . . . uh . . . I was in bed . . . uh . . . naked. I'd obviously had a shower. Care to explain how all that happened?"

Marco suppressed a smile. "Sailor, what happens in Pittsburgh stays in Pittsburgh," he closed the hatch.

96

Global Infection: ≤ 35.7907%

Ryan watched the Stryker drive toward the 376 overpass and disappear into the Fort Pitt Tunnel. Then he moved east along the boulevard, his rifle tracking with his eyes until he turned the corner and stopped in front of the Renaissance Tower. He knew nothing had changed, but it made him feel secure seeing the triple stack of shipping containers, the cars parked tight on the terraces, and the port authority bus pulled across the bullet-riddled plate glass. Days ago the tower had as many holes as a basketball net, now it was sealed up like the bastille.

He looked south across the car-clogged Smithfield bridge, listening for the telltale sounds of humans, but the river valley was as silent as the days when the Iroquois contended with the Seneca, Delaware and the Shawnee for territorial dominance. The quiet pressed down on his mind, reinforcing the isolation to come.

Feeling his nerve start to fade Ryan worked his way through the parked cars, around a support column and into the barely visible alcove that gave access to the tower lobby.

"Halt, restricted area," the Virgin Jinn said in a soothing female voice.

Ryan froze, his heart thumping like an out of balance washing machine.

"You will be sho— Identified. Sage, R. As you were."

"Marco, that is some creepy shit," Ryan said, not sure he appreciated the sense humor that put a female voice in an AI weapon.

He made his way through the debris strewn lobby to the elevators. He lifted a small smooth faceplate, swiped his security badge over the reader, a motor engaged behind the marble walls and a titanium security gate slid to the floor separating the elevators from the world beyond.

Ryan stepped onto the penthouse landing and killed the elevator power. He walked past the marble South American dictators and the long line of ammunition-loaded pallets. He stopped at the security desk to review video feeds, but saw nothing of concern. He shut off the monitor and unplugged the desk clock.

When Ryan stepped into the foyer, he called Raphael's phone. He wandered the penthouse, shutting off lights and unplugging anything making a demand on the tower's deep cycle batteries as he listened to the description of the world beyond the three rivers valley—the devastation in Carnegie and Rosslyn Farms until the signal was lost somewhere south on Interstate 79.

He heard Hailey rattling around in the kitchen. "About time you got up, sleepyhead."

Hailey jumped like she'd been shot. "I'm sorry. I'm sorry. I'll get to work." She took steps toward the bedroom, holding her bottom with her right hand.

"Hey, slow down. We'll get to that," Ryan said. "Earlier you said that you wanted pancakes."

She stopped and backed against the wall, suddenly self-conscious that he'd seen her holding her butt. "But you need those maps. And if I don't get them, I won't get a sandwich."

Ryan shrugged. "I have other jobs and you can't work on an empty stomach."

Hailey's stomach growled. She bit her lip, her eyes filled with wariness. Then she seemed to come to a conclusion. "No, I like getting you maps, so I need to go back outside," she said. "And I have to check on Tim."

"We need to do something about you always needing to check on Tim. You can clearly see that I have plenty of space and enough food for you both."

"No, Moe would be mad. Really mad. He has a gun."

"Hailey, you also know I have lots of guns."

Hailey tugged at her shirt sleeves. "He said he'd kill me and Tim if I ever told where he was. He said he'd do it without thinking. He shot Pogo and then said, 'See, just like that. That is how I'll kill Tim.'"

Ryan sat on a kitchen stool. "Who is Pogo? You talked about Pogo while you slept last night."

"That was Kurt's dog," Hailey said, wincing as she took a few steps. "He was like my dog too. We slept together and he would point when the zombies were close. Kurt cried when he shot Pogo but Moe said we needed food so he should stop crying. I didn't cry until I had to eat Pogo. But I was hungry."

"When did you eat Pogo?"

"Like, yesterday?"

Ryan tried to remain stoic. "What happened to the food from Fort Pitt? The steaks and sandwich stuff?"

"I lost it in the warehouse."

"And you were in the warehouse for how long?"

"I don't know. I lost track. I slept a lot because I couldn't move."

Ryan took a deep breath, scared to hear the answer to his next question. "It's been three days since we ran from the warehouse. How long since you got out before you came here?"

Hailey bit her lip thinking. "I snuck out yesterday morning."

Holy Shit. She'd been in there for almost three days. "Oh Hailey, I am so sorry. How come you didn't come here?"

Hailey shrugged. "I thought you were . . . you know. Like my mom."

"You thought we were dead?"

A tear formed in the corner of Hailey's eye, and she looked away.

"How did you figure out we were alive?"

"When I snuck back to the warehouse to get some things I saw that the Lenco and the Humvee were gone. I figured the only people who could have taken them were you and the Pagueros." Her hand went between her legs, rubbing. She caught herself and blushed. "I just want to get the sandwiches for Tim."

Ryan said, "I think we can manage getting Tim. And I think I can persuade Moe to give you back your phone and those shoes."

Hailey's face went white, her eyes round. She grabbed her pink coat from the back of a chair and tried to run toward the front door, but could only manage a wide legged stride.

"Hailey, please stop. Please?"

Hailey leaned against the foyer wall trying to stuff her bare feet in her worn-out boots. When they wouldn't go in quickly, she tucked them under her arms and started to open the white door.

"Hailey! Please look at me."

"What!?"

"I know something happened, and I know you are afraid. I won't hurt you. And if you will let me, I will make sure that no one hurts you again." He paused, watching the defiance rise in her face.

"You said you wouldn't compel me to stay here," Hailey shouted. "You said you would let me go back outside."

"You left last night and I didn't stop you. I gave you the access card, and you left and then you came back.

"How did you know that?"

"I saw you on the cameras. You were on the 8th floor, where we were before. And you stood in the door trying to decide what you wanted to do, right?"

"Oh," Hailey said.

"So you know I won't try to stop you. I'll help you get back outside. And if you change your mind, you can come back in. And I will still give you food. You don't need to get me more maps. You have done great with the maps. I have plenty."

"You don't need any more?" Despair climbed on Hailey's chest and squeezed. "But I have a week's worth. Me and Tim, we need the sandwiches."

"All that work you did with the zombies, helping us with Fort Pitt, and then helping us load the trucks, that is yours too. That is quite a few MRE's."

"Oh."

"And I have other jobs."

"Like what?" She winced. She tried to rub her bottom but caught herself.

"I have plenty of work here, in the tower."

"But Tim might not have eaten today, and he will be hungry. He was in trouble with Moe. Moe wasn't letting him eat because he thought Tim was hiding me. That was when I was staying with you."

"What are you not telling me, Hailey?"

"Nothing!"

"Why did Moe let you leave?"

"I told him that I was looking around the city for more stuff to eat. I told him that it would be a while, because it was harder to find food in downtown. He took all my MRE's."

"So you paid Moe MREs from Fort Pitt to let you go?" Ryan asked. "How did you get them?"

"I snuck back to the barge. You didn't see me, but I stashed a few boxes out there when you and the Pagueros weren't looking. Moe was mad that I was gone for so long. He told me I had to give him a bunch of food before he would let Tim eat. I know I'm not supposed to steal, but that stuff isn't yours either."

"No, Hailey I wasn't accusing you. The problem is Moe, and I'm trying to understand.

Did Moe let Tim eat after you gave Moe the MREs?"

"He said he would, but he said I had to come back," said Hailey, "I need to keep paying to feed Tim."

"Keep paying to feed Tim?" Ryan asked, a picture forming in his mind. He was pretty sure he knew the real payment. But he couldn't get into that right now. He needed Hailey to stop feeling the need to save Tim.

"Hailey, do you know what extortion is?"

"I think so."

"Moe is using a threat against something you love to manipulate your actions. But here is the thing; there is no way to ever pay enough. It won't matter how much or what you give, because what he is really doing is manipulating your affection. You care for Tim, so Moe will always demand more. The only way to stop Moe from hurting Tim is to stop paying. But just because you stop paying doesn't mean you don't care for Tim."

"But he said—"

"Yes. Moe said whatever he can say to keep you doing what he wants. It will never be enough Hailey. Ever. It is important for you to understand. You can't save Tim. Tim will have to save himself."

"What?!" Hailey demanded, with her hands on her hips, her hair trigger for defensiveness going off with a bang. "No! Tim defended me. I need to help him."

And there was the root of the issue. And Ryan hazarded a guess that Tim tried to keep Moe or Kurt from having sex with her and he paid the price for his chivalry: Moe beat Tim for daring to stand up. "Hailey, tell me where Tim is and I will make sure Moe and Kurt never hurt him or you again."

"I can't!" Hailey shook her head, adamant. "Moe will kill Tim!" She opened the penthouse door and strode out like a queen. Her act worked until she got to the elevator bank. She punched the button, and when it didn't immediately come, she started to cry. "It hurts. It hurts so bad." She dropped to the floor holding herself between her legs, sobbing.

Ryan lifted her from the floor. When she'd slept in the closet, the smell was muted by distance. But the stench of feces and urine and unwashed sex hit Ryan in the nose like a fist. He carried her to the bathroom and laid her on the floor while he started a bath and poured in some bubbles. "Go ahead and get undressed and get in. I'll get you some clean clothes and set them outside the door."

Hailey lay on the floor in a ball, body shaking, tears dripping down her face. She struggled to sit up and then struggled with the coat's zipper. "I can't get it to work," she sobbed. "Can you help me, please?"

The despair in Hailey's voice broke Ryan's heart. He helped her out of her coat. "Can you handle it from here?"

She tried to pull her shirt off, but she was weak from exhaustion. "No," Hailey whimpered, barely able to hold herself up. "Help me please."

Ryan helped her undress. And as he lifted her into the tepid water, he saw the fading bruises from where the 2091's bit her legs. Thankfully, the bites had not broken the skin. But then he saw the swollen flesh between her legs, amidst the dirt and filth, and got very concerned.

"I'll be back in a minute. I am going to put these clothes in the trash," Ryan said, "When you are done, get dried off and come see me. I'll have clothes for you, but we have one more thing to do."

Hailey hugged her knees and cried softly as he left.

97

Global Infection: ≤ 35.7911%

One advantage of buying a billionaire's tower is that it acquires everything times five. If the dresser drawers were any indication, the Ryder granddaughters never wanted for fashion. Ryan found underwear, pants, socks and blushed when he found the drawer with bras.

Does she need one of these?

Hailey was so skinny it was hard to tell if she was filling out, and she hadn't been wearing one a moment ago. He put it back and went to wait for Hailey in his office. He checked his e-mail to kill time and saw two from Ahou.

Ryan,

I heard about your troubles. I am so sorry. I wish I could hold you. Don't give up on love, please. I am recovering. I hope you think scars are sexy. And oh, I am so excited. "Thor" has found another victim. Thank God!

Ahou
xoxoxo

The only way Ahou could have known about his Thor reference was if a little bird told her.

"Really? Daniel, did the apocalypse banish confidentiality?" He clicked to open the second email.

Ryan,

I am out of the infirmary, and it didn't come too soon. I was about to go stir crazy. My mind needed stimulated . . . If you know what I mean. But now I've got my mother hovering over me. She means well, but she is such a nattering somebody.

Anyway, I have hatched a plan, and I think it will make our lives better. If you don't hear from me for a while, please don't worry.

(Well, maybe worry a little bit.)

I will write you when I can. And maybe I'll get to do another video. ;) or maybe not. The Skinfuse helps, but they still had to put stitches in. I'm not sure you will like my scars. I hope they fade before you see me again.

Ahou
Xoxoxo

P.S. Please tell me if you liked my video.
P.P.S. I hope I didn't come on too strong.

Sven was out of the picture. Ryan didn't want to care, but he did. He missed Ahou, as absurd as it sounded since they had spent scant hours together and most of the time was via video conference. He shook the melancholy away. See him again? They were separated by hundreds of miles and untold hardships. In what fantasy world was that happening?

Ryan closed his eyes and squeezed the feelings down out of his chest. But the more he tried to push his heart aside, the more desire woke from slumber like a ravenous beast. He hadn't had a sexual thought about a woman in longer than he could remember, but the video suddenly beckoned like sirens to Odysseus. Ryan adjusted himself behind his zipper as Ahou's image came alive in his mind. He wanted to touch Ahou. He wanted to feed his hunger.

Ryan Sage clicked to the video and the cursor hung over the file for an eternity.

Hailey?!!

Ryan pressed his eyes shut hard and willed himself to stillness. He'd wait. Hailey would soon sleep, and then he could watch. He started and restarted an e-mail to Ahou, but couldn't seem to find the words. He felt absurd to feed into the delusion that they would ever be in the same city again and it was strange to reduce the conversation to female puberty and parenting techniques, even though Ahou would certainly know if Hailey needed a bra.

In the end, he settled on a simple missive:

Ahou,

I'm glad things are well with you. The apocalypse is the definition of insanity, so I guess it seems cliché to say that things have been crazy here, but I'm alive and there have been developments. I suspect that our very chatty mutual friend will give you all the gossip before I can. But when you get a chance, I need your opinion about something I'm embarrassed about, so maybe you will get another chance to see me blush.

Ryan

P.S. . . . your video . . . uh ... wow. And who is running the camera?

Ryan paced up and down his office walls, pausing at each monitor, concerned that any minute the horde from Fort Pitt would find its way to the tower, fearing that if he sat back down in his chair, he would not be able to refrain from watching Ahou's video . . . over and over.

Finally Hailey waddled into the office, hair combed and a big fluffy white towel wrapped around her chest, her blue eyes looking up at him with a combination of vulnerability and maybe a glimmer of hope.

"You . . . uh . . . look like you feel much better." Ryan smiled.

"I do, thank you," Hailey said.

But Ryan's smile was mostly façade; he fidgeted with the tube of cream on the desk.

How do I tell her that since she's been having sex and been less than hygienic there could be an infection?

He took a deep breath and said, "Okay . . . uh . . . I don't know how to do this. There are no girls here but . . . uh . . ." He spun the tube. "I'm concerned . . . uh . . . I don't mean to embarrass you . . ." While helping her bathe, Ryan saw just enough to be very concerned with what was going on down there. Ryan sighed. His face grew hot. "We need to see if . . . uh . . . I need to see if you have an infection . . . down there. Or if it is just a really bad rash," he said. "We got a lot of antibiotics from Fort Pitt so in case there is a problem . . ."

Hailey's smile vanished. "You want to look at me . . . down there."

"Hailey, I'm so sorry. I don't mean to embarrass you. I don't know what to say. And I'm sure you are . . . I'm just—"

She blushed furiously and the flash of hope died a quick death. Defiant, Hailey dropped the towel and walked to the desk. She sat on the desk and started to lean back, opening her knees.

Ryan looked away. "No, you don't have to do that. Just turn around and bend over a bit. I should be able to tell."

Exasperated, she turned and stuck out her butt.

Ryan was quick. "Mmm . . . I am not a doctor, but I don't think that its infected. But you do have a very serious rash." He grabbed the towel from the floor and handed it back. Then Ryan picked the tube off the desk. "I found this stuff used for diaper rash."

Hailey wrapped the towel tight around her chest again and said. "That is for babies."

“Hey, I put it on my butt when I get a rash, so . . .”

Hailey took the tube and looked at him warily. “So are we done?” she asked. “Should I put it on . . . or do you want to?”

“What? No . . . No! No, you’re the one who said you were not a baby. You can do that part yourself. Get dressed. And, uh . . . yeah . . . uh . . . get dressed.”

Ryan left the office.

98

Global Infection: ≤ 35.7913%

Hailey came to the kitchen dressed in jeans, a baggy sweatshirt and some New Balance running shoes. She asked for five pancakes, ate without talking and kept her eye on Ryan like he might devour her on the spot. He tried small talk, but Hailey could only grunt behind a full mouth. She ate two pancakes and leaned back in her chair as if she were puzzling through a quantum mechanics equation looking like someone let the air out of her body. "Would it be okay if I take a nap?"

"Of course," Ryan said. "I have the bed ready for you. I put the pillow you slept on last night in the wash. But there are plenty of fresh pillows on the bed."

Hailey gave a wan smile and waddled toward the bedroom. Ryan cleaned all the dishes from the last two days and ran a load of laundry in the double washer and dryer in the utility room. It had a flat panel television with a surround sound audio system, two gaming consoles with a broad selection of games and a play area for little kids, an ironing area, and a dry-cleaning machine with a mini clothes conveyer.

He wandered into his bedroom to get his iGlass, and found Hailey, deep in the closet snoring softly on a pile of blankets and pillows from his bed. She was dressed in blue PJs with purple elephants, clutching Pedro the Hippo like he might run away.

Tethered close, Ryan made another sweep through the penthouse to eliminate power drains, finding stray clocks and chargers and appliances plugged in and drawing the battery system down to zero. Afterwards, Ryan logged into the tower management system wanting to see a baseline on power consumption.

The interface opened.

Ryan's heart beat hard and his breath caught in his chest. The tower had drained over twenty percent since the grid failed. He did the math; his stomach dropped, his mouth suddenly tasting like cotton as panic rippled through his soul. He worked through the system trying to figure out how to stop the power carnage.

Understandably, the environment control system—the most energy efficient system available—was still leading in power consumption. The fourth, sixth and eighth commercial floors showed excessive usage as did the eleventh, fourteenth, 26th and 27th residential floors. The 26th floor was where the Blancos had lived. No one had been back to that condo since their deaths, so it was likely that every light inside was blazing away. *Mon Pierre's* on the 28th floor was a power hog: the likely culprits were the freezers and refrigerators.

And then he saw the problem. The flex fuel generator was not feeding power into the system. Ryan checked once and then twice to make sure he wasn't seeing things. His heart rate began to slow.

The generator wasn't even on.

Could the solution be this simple?

Ryan verified the generator was set to natural gas and hit the start button; in minutes the system surged, and the batteries started charging.

Ryan changed into shorts and a T-shirt and pulled an old exercise schedule from his data storage folder, modified it for his current physical condition, went into the gym and began a yoga practice, followed by a protein and vegetable lunch that he ate while watching the first shooting video. The how-to video inspired the idea that he needed to accumulate similar videos on a broad array of knowledge.

He found *Scientific American* and *Popular Mechanics* still available online and bought every electronic archived edition. Then he found videos on canning and long-term food preparation. After two hours of shopping and downloading, Ryan realized he needed help.

Team Bruptrick might have poor social skills, but they were far from stupid; they knew that survivalist knowledge would be very valuable in the days to come. Patrick suggested that Blue Pill could hack any server and rip down any content they wanted. And since time was the primary factor, Ryan agreed. If the content was public domain, he didn't care. But if it was intellectual property, he would pay. Ryan gave them a debit card attached to an account with more money than he could spend in an apocalyptic lifetime.

"Hey guys," Bruce said, "how about if I download all the porn in the world?"

"You are such a perv," Patrick said.

Ryan stared into the camera. "Bruce, only morons pay for porn, and if I see one charge I will hunt you down using my super secret ninja assassin skills."

Hailey woke three times throughout the afternoon to eat a few bites and drink some water. After each meal, she leaned back as if working out a sum and then asked if she could take a nap. Ryan always found her minutes later in the closet, fast asleep mumbling about Maria, Pogo and Nanna.

Ryan continued watching gun videos while field stripping weapons and putting them back together. He did a cardio workout, and for dinner ate fish, vegetables and vitamins. Then Ryan went to the restaurant to remove power drains and empty one walk-in, hauling the contents to the penthouse master kitchen. Before bed, Ryan checked on Bruptrick's progress. In twelve hours, they had set up SharePoint with content types and a full taxonomy for managed metadata to organize everything by subject matter and medium: audio, video, electronic book. But they had only spent about a thousand dollars. That seemed a little low, and the content a touch limited, but they might have had other things to do.

A hydroponics video caught Ryan's attention, so he practiced shotgun reloading drills with dummy rounds while watching. When the video ended, Ryan knew four things: hydroponics was a great idea, agriculture was magic, he was no magician, and he was going to starve unless he found some dirt. Overwhelm danced around his head as he tried to understand pH balance, water composition, and the price of bat guano.

His last thought before he fell asleep was: *Who in the hell pays twenty dollars a fluid ounce for bat shit?*

99

Global Infection: ≤ 35.9717%

Ryan woke at 6:30, checked the security monitors and found no problems, then logged into the power management system and checked the power. He was pleased that his effort in the restaurant had already registered. He did a yoga practice and had breakfast. Hailey woke at 9:00 dressed in the same jeans and sweatshirt outfit. She ate like a bird trying to consume three times her body weight. She finished the last bite, leaned back, and burped. "Excuse me," she said, her cheeks flushed. She asked if she could take a nap. Minutes later she was back in the closet, dressed in a new set of pink PJs covered in clowns, curled in a tight ball, Pedro the Hippo's face poking out of the closet door like a guard dog.

Ryan checked her for fever, but she wasn't hot. Something was wrong, but she didn't seem sick.

Ryan found a wireless baby monitor that he fastened in the closet and then integrated into the tower network. He took the AV receiver to the roof and finished splicing the fiberoptic cable into the cell node's interface. He cleaned up his tools and sent a text.

You should have connectivity . . . check my work.

An hour later the text came back:

Perfect! . . . Be in touch.

Ryan ran dry fire drills until he was itching to shoot live rounds. He donned a full load out and ran through a final gear check. He was sitting at his desk writing a note for Hailey to call him on his cell when the video conference notification trilled.

"Patrick?"

"Hey, Mr. Sage."

"You look terrible," Ryan said. "What is going on?"

Patrick shrugged into the camera. "The zombie apocalypse. That is what is going on. I kinda just wanted to talk to a friendly face."

"Where is Bruce?"

"That is part of the shit that is going on." Patrick looked off-camera. He lowered his voice and said. "I can't talk about it right now."

"How can I help?"

Patrick chewed the inside of his cheek. "Help me figure out how to get to Pittsburgh to stay with you."

Ryan laughed. "I think we'd all like to be somewhere else right now but I don't even know where you are so it is hard to help you get here."

"Oh right," Patrick said as if that factoid hadn't occurred to him. "It is an abandoned government installation in the San Juan National Forest, some miles from Durango. Don't bother looking for it. It isn't on any map."

"How did you find it?"

"Are you kidding? Who did we work for? The Molitor Group builds secret installations all over the world. I know we are geeks. For God's sake, I haven't been laid in longer than I can think, but we are not stupid. Some friends were tapped into the Internet scuttlebutt that only geeks care about. When we compared notes, we realized that some bad shit was happening. For about a month, it was just nerd conspiracy theory. But then we realized it wasn't conspiracy. A friend of mine found a copy of this document called *Tekhiya Narrative*. Honest to God, the Israelis were telling the world zombies existed over a year ago."

"That is interesting," Ryan said, wondering how a top secret document got into general circulation. He'd read that same report in this very office, and Daniel Ryder got it from a highly-placed government source.

"Eventually we figured out that we had to do something, or we were going to be zombie bait," Patrick said. "Bruce found the plans for this place tucked into the Share with Everyone Folder in Office 365. Some idiot didn't realize he'd misplaced a top secret set of plans where the world could see it. Once we figured out what and where it was, we realized the government facility was abandoned, but being electronically monitored. That is how we met Blue Pill. Somehow he hacked the security and made it disappear from the rest of the world. Blue Pill loves to fuck with governments." Patrick nodded like his stream of consciousness made perfect sense."

"Colorado to Pittsburgh?" Ryan asked. "That is a tall order in the middle of the zombie apocalypse."

Patrick looked crestfallen. "Stupid idea, right? Anyway, I found some really good stuff to download, but doing it through their interface will take forever, and we have no guarantee how long those servers will remain live. How about if we pay for the content but still have Blue Pill rip it down? Basically, we will mirror their site on our servers. It will be so much more comprehensive, and we won't have to spend so much time."

Ryan nodded. "That works. As long as we don't get stuff we didn't pay for, I'm good."

Patrick was exasperated. "Look, I get the do-gooder thing . . . well, no I don't. The information we need is important. If we do manage to survive, it will be a great asset. But what difference does it make? We don't have time to weed out the bullshit. It isn't like anyone is going to know. And the clock is ticking. The grid is failing."

Ryan nodded. "Here is a solution. Pay for everything. That will save time."

"That's dumb," Patrick said, "If you are not going to use the information, why does it matter if we pay for it?"

Ryan said, "Patrick, it might seem ridiculous, but let me explain. Until the network collapses and it is impossible to electronically pay for products, whoever organized that information into instructional form has asked to be compensated. It is my moral responsibility to give them what they have asked for even in the face of societal collapse. The right to property doesn't magically vanish just because social convention is going to hell."

Patrick frowned. "You realize this is the real world, not a college classroom."

"And that is exactly why what I'm saying matters," Ryan said. "The only way for man to live in social context requires two things: a specific respect of another human being's life and a peaceful means to exchange resources."

"That is fine in theory," Patrick said. "But this is the zombie apocalypse for God's sake."

"No, Patrick, the theory and the practice are the same," Ryan said. "There is no right to loot just because social conventions have gone to hell."

Patrick snorted, "So you are telling me that you are not going to take anything from anyone in the days ahead? And how can you say that? You already took the WIN-T system for God's sake."

"No, you misunderstand some crucial distinctions," Ryan said. "Government does not *create* anything. Things a government owns—and I use the term *ownership* loosely—it seized at the point of a gun from someone who created it. Taking stuff from a corrupt and immoral government is called reparations. But scavenging resources that have been abandoned is not stealing. Stealing is when you take stuff from people who are alive and using—"

Patrick said, "Are you off your meds? How in the hell are you going to survive without stealing stuff? It's not like you can run out to the store and grab some eggs. There isn't even a cashier. So how are you gonna pay for what's in Walmart?"

Ryan leaned back in his chair. "The irony here is rich. You smoke lots of weed and criticize me for being off his meds. And here is what I find more ironic. I'm *crazy* for condemning looting and murder? Do you really fail to see what you just said?" he asked. "You just called defending individual liberty . . . crazy."

"People have to do things to survive."

"Yeah, they do have to do *one* thing to live: have a *peaceful* way to exchange value. Crazy is believing that men are the natural prey of other men. We put human predators who can't understand that in psychiatric wards."

Patrick wouldn't make eye contact with the camera. "This isn't a perfect world."

"Patrick, the state of the world has nothing to do with the moral imperative. But I get the feeling that your reaction is because of something else. What really happened there? Where is Bruce?"

"Just don't worry about him," Patrick whispered.

Ryan matched his tone. "Has he been bit? Is he infected?"

"Nothing like that. Look, I don't want to talk about this anymore."

"Patrick, if you won't tell me what is really going on then we have a problem. If there is really nothing going on there . . . nothing that is affecting your judgment, then I can't overlook your challenge to my sanity. I won't pretend that accusing me of needing medication is a reasonable rebuttal to a moral standard. If you *really* believe what you said, then I would be a fool to continue our relationship. If you really think defending private property and individual liberty, condemning looting and pillaging, is crazy then you will steal from me or murder me whenever the whim strikes your fancy and you will blame your moral failing on the zombie apocalypse."

100

Global Infection: ≤ 35.9719%

Patrick rocked back in his chair emotions shifting over his face like leaves tumbling in a storm. "Look, I'm sorry. I didn't mean to be insulting. But what you are saying just sounds very convenient. It's okay to rob the government blind, but not okay to take stuff from a vacant grocery store—"

"Patrick, the *definition* of convenient is your vague hazy ethical standard which amounts to 'How dare you judge me for doing whatever the hell I want to survive?' I'm not offering justifications. I'm offering distinctions. There is a fundamental difference between scavenging and looting. There is a fundamental difference between a legitimate government that protects the individual and an illegitimate govern—"

"What's the difference?"

"My explanations are obviously useless, since you are unwilling to think about what I've already said."

"I don't need this shit," Patrick said. "You have no idea what is going on here. You have no idea what is going on in the rest of the world.

"Tell me what is going on."

"Why would you even give a fuck?" Patrick shouted. "You're in Pittsburgh!"

Ryan waited; the dam was about to burst.

"I've got a dozen stoners living here, and none of them work! And if it hadn't been for your god damned secret agent ninja skills, Bruce would be all right! All your high and mighty bullshit almost got Bruce killed!"

"What happened to Bruce?"

Patrick's chin slumped to his chest; his body started to shake and hitch. "Bruce tried to stop them from killing the old man and his wife. He thought IT guys should fight like you." He sobbed quietly for minutes, then he wiped his eyes and looked off-camera. When he looked back he lowered his voice. "We've got these three guys who are former infantry. I was a bubblehead in the navy, but that kind of training doesn't really translate to land warfare. The rest of them are a bunch of tech geeks, so we thought it was a good idea to have some people that could help fight. We asked them to join us here. Two nights ago we saw a man and a woman, an older couple on the security cameras, who were living in one of the outbuildings on ground level. They weren't hurting anything. They were just trying to hide from the chaos like we are. The soldiers could see they had weapons and supplies. Most of us said we should let them in. But we only have a few guns and the soldiers said we should take what they had. The people were trespassing." Patrick's voice hitched with emotion. "They made us beat them to death. When Bruce wouldn't do it and tried to fight back they made an example of him and then all of us had to hit the old couple with a baseball bat wrapped with barbed wire. They said it was a valuable lesson and it would toughen us up. I was the one who killed them. I hit them both hard enough to put them out of their misery. I couldn't stand to listen to the sound that woman made." Patrick looked to the ceiling, tears flowing, "It was supposed to work. We were going to hide in our hole and we were going to share everything."

"Well, there is the root of your problem. Socialism sounds like it should be a magical utopian commune with everyone pitching in where necessary, but it always ends in tyranny and death.

"It wasn't magic," Patrick said. "And I don't need a lecture."

"Actually, Patrick, you do need a lecture, because you keep trying to evade the outcomes of your actions and you refuse to judge the bankruptcy of your ideas. When has socialism ever worked? How many drugs do you have to take to deceive yourself that communism has *ever* raised the standard of living for anyone but those who control of the guns? It sounds wonderful when talking about sharing everything in the name of unity and the common good and brotherly love, but the practice is despotism, slavery and carnage. What you saw yesterday is just the beginning."

"God, you are such a dick."

"I know, you think I'm being insensitive. You think, I'm kicking you when you are down. Patrick if you want me to be your friend then you need to hear me. Your self-pity will get no compassion from me. I won't let you practice guilt-free looting."

"You've killed people. You are a super secret ninja assassin."

Damn you Raphael, Ryan thought. "Look, two things. I'm not an assassin. That was a lie Raphael told Simone because he didn't want to admit I beat the shit out of him."

"What? Why did he say that? Bruce got hurt—"

"Bruce got hurt because you all brought immoral men to your perpetual Dungeons and Dragons party. And second, don't drop the context of my actions to draw a moral equivalency to your behavior. Maybe you should get some credit for ending the old couple's misery, but Bruce is the one who demonstrated real character. You should have all done the same thing. You should have all fought back."

"They had guns."

"Yes, tyrants always have the guns and that is why you must destroy them at the first sign of despotism."

"How were we supposed to know it would go like this?"

"History," Ryan said, the answer obvious. "The same thing happens every time the weak sell their souls to the strong."

"That is deep," Patrick said, rolling his eyes, making it clear that he thought Ryan was full of shit.

"Patrick, I don't really care if you listen to a word I say. You are the one who is trying to live the collectivist utopian dream and complaining that it is a disaster. I'm pointing out that the disaster is rooted in your moral vacancy. Between the two of us, you are living the greater manifestation of intellectual bullshit."

Patrick rubbed his unshaved face. When he looked back into the camera, his eyes were haunted. "I thought this would be a video game. A bunch of friends would get together, smoke some weed and ride this thing out role-playing our favorite characters." Patrick looked off-screen and then looked back. He whispered, "So I know you are disappointed in me, but I don't have many friends, and no matter what I just said about you being crazy, you're the sanest person I get to talk to. Could we go back to the way it was before? Could you maybe forget about the old man and woman? I mean, I want to keep working with you. That way we can keep talking. Maybe, eventually I could find a way to get to Pittsburgh." He looked into the screen, hopeful.

Ryan could see that Patrick was lost and scared and living a nightmare "Okay, Patrick, let's work on your commitment to principles and then maybe we can talk about how to get you to my tower."

Patrick smiled. "Thanks, Mr. Sage. I'll get that stuff downloaded. We can chat again, maybe tonig—"

"Who are you talking to?" Hailey interrupted. She was standing in the office doorway clutching Pedro the Hippo. Her hair was tangled, and slumber pressed down on her eyelids.

"Hello, sleepyhead," Ryan said. "How are you doing?"

"I'm okay," Hailey said, shuffling to Ryan's chair. She dropped her head on his shoulder.

"Patrick, this is Hailey. Hailey, this is Patrick."

"Hi," Hailey said, but hid her face in the crook of Ryan's neck.

Patrick said, "Glad you came to the tower."

"Yes." Hailey said, unsure how to respond. "I'm really sleepy." Then she noticed that Ryan was fully loaded. "Are you going outside?"

"Yes, I need to take a look around the building."

"Don't leave me, please," she said, throwing her arms around his neck.

Ryan pulled her into his lap. Hailey clung to him like she was hanging on to life. "Patrick, we will talk this evening. Okay?"

Patrick waved and hung up.

Ryan brushed Hailey's unruly hair aside. "Marco taught you to shoot, so we have to train."

"I don't want to go back outside," Hailey said, her words muffled. "I don't want to be a pest, but I know I can't live out there alone. I think I might die. I want to stay here. I want to be with you."

Ryan hugged her tight, smiling through his tears. "Hailey, you are not a pest. You are safe here. You never have to be dead alone."

www.ingramcontent.com/pod-product-compliance
Lightning Source LLC
Chambersburg PA
CBHW030417310726
48979CB00002B/455

* 9 7 8 0 9 8 5 2 7 1 3 4 3 *